THE DEVIL'S PLAY BOOK

Also by Markus Heitz

THE DWARVES

The War of the Dwarves
The Revenge of the Dwarves
The Fate of the Dwarves
The Triumph of the Dwarves
The Return of the Dwarves Book 1
The Return of the Dwarves Book 2

LEGENDS OF THE ÄLFAR

Righteous Fury
Devastating Hate
Dark Paths
Raging Storm

DOORS

Doors: Twilight
Doors: Field of Blood
Doors: Colony

Oneiros
AERA: The Return of the Ancient Gods
The Dark Lands

CONSULTED LITERATURE

(where one can find even
more literature for self-study)

Erhard Gorys: *Das Buch der Spiele*. Über 500 Freizeitspiele für Erwachsene. Herrsching: Manfred Pawlak Verlagsgesellschaft 1975.

Claus D. Grupp: *Die Spielkarten und ihre Geschichte*. Historisches um des Teufels Gebetbuch. Leinfelden: ASS Verlag 1973.

Oscar von Hase: 'Breitkopf und Härtel', in: *Allgemeine Deutsche Biographie 3*. Leipzig: Duncker & Humblot 1876.

Detlef Hoffmann: *Spielkarten*. Inventarkatalog der Spielkartensammlung des Historischen Museums Frankfurt am Main. Frankfurt a. M. 1972.

Erwin Kohlmann, Hellmut Rosenfeld (ed.): Die schönsten deutschen Spielkarten. Leipzig: Insel 1964.

Wolfgang Mayr, Robert Sedlaczek: Die Strategie des Tarockspiels. Wien: Edition Atelier 2008.

Peter Weise: Rund um die Spielkarte. Ein Streifzug durch das Altenburger Spielkartenmuseum. Berlin: Tribüne Berlin 1986.

Manfred Wilde: Die Zauberei- und Hexenprozesse in Kursachsen, Köln/Weimar/Wien: Böhlau 2003.

Arcadia

MARKUS HEITZ

THE DEVIL'S PLAYBOOK

Translated by Sophia Nayakshin

Arcadia

First published in Great Britain in 2025 by

Arcadia
An imprint of
Quercus Editions Limited
Carmelite House
50 Victoria Embankment
London EC4Y 0DZ

An Hachette UK company

The authorised representative in the EEA is Hachette Ireland,
8 Castlecourt Centre, Dublin 15, D15 XTP3, Ireland (email: info@hbgi.ie)

Original title: Markus Heitz *Des Teufels Gebetbuch*

Copyright © 2017 by Verlagsgruppe Droemer Knaur GmbH & Co. KG, Munich, Germany
www.mahet.de
Translation: © 2025 by Sophia Nayakshin
The book has been negotiated through AVA international GmbH, Germany
(www.ava-international.de)

The quotation from the article 'Playing Cards in Late Medieval Bern'
was used with the kind permission of the author.

A CIP catalogue record for this book is available
from the British Library

PB ISBN 978-1-52942-496-6
EBOOK ISBN 978-1-52942-497-3

1

Typeset by Jouve (UK), Milton Keynes

Printed and bound in Great Britain by Clays Ltd, Elcograf S.p.A.

MIX
Paper | Supporting
responsible forestry
FSC® C104740

Papers used by Arcadia are from well-managed forests and other responsible sources.

This book is dedicated to card players and gamblers,
whose experiences and stories are real-life legends
that are still told to this day – full of laughter,
arguments, anger, joy, grand entrances and quiet exits.
Like in my first round of mau-mau:
one more damn seven and I would have won!
But it was as if the Devil had dug his claws into the game . . .

PROLOGUE

The Baltic Sea,
18 nautical miles northwest of Tallinn, Estonia

Whirring, the wet wire cable wrapped itself around the barrel as the power of the engine heaved the spoils from the depths of the sea. Dirty, grey droplets freed themselves from the oily rope and spilled back into the gentle waves. Metre by metre, the bounty rose out of the water.

Like dark balloons floating on the billowing sea, the black neoprene heads of the divers observed the laborious process from a distance. Though their work was done, they remained where they were. If the hook were to slip, they would have to rush to the rescue once again. That is, provided the worsening weather allowed them to.

Despite the twilight, the *Anatevka*'s navigation lights and headlights were off. The work on the converted trawler was to remain a secret; nobody had authorised their venture.

'Just in time,' Captain Lugaschin remarked laconically. He rested his arms on the railing and smoked an unfiltered Russian cigarette. The thick jumper paired with the skipper's hat on his short black hair made him look like a caricature from an advert for cigarettes or alcohol.

'Aye,' said a sailor, wearing a mariner's jacket and a well-worn forage cap. He operated the winch just two steps away from the captain and took turns glancing between the rope and the equipment in the dim light.

Anjelica Clark anxiously monitored the progress of the operation. She was only wearing her life vest as a precaution – it was her bright yellow raincoat that protected her from the wind and salt spray. Anjelica had her hands in her pockets, a Bluetooth set in her left ear for taking calls and a satellite phone safely stashed away in her trousers. 'We're almost there, sir,' she reported, updating her employer on the progress.

The hull of the *Anatevka* rose and fell noticeably. The waves crashed against the boat, as if warning the sailors that they had no more than half an hour before the oncoming storm would force them to abandon their position for the safety of the shore.

'The weather reports aren't looking too good for where you are,' said Anjelica's boss, who sat in a British club chair with tea, scones and sandwiches while she braved the forces of nature. 'Am I right, Clark?'

'Yes, sir. A storm is coming.' Anjelica gazed at the rectangular black shadow as it came into view from under the surface of the lead-grey water. A mere moment later, it broke through the waves. Little white bubbles remained on top of the dark-brown wood. Several wide straps tightened around the cargo and held it securely.

'Steady,' Lugaschin ordered calmly, refusing to budge.

'Aye,' the sailor replied and skilfully intercepted the swinging of the enormous chest with the load arm.

'We have it, sir,' Anjelica said loudly to drown out the increasing howl of the wind. 'No damage done. It's all in one piece.'

'Excellent!' Her employer's voice buzzed with excitement. 'Don't let my treasure slip away!'

'No, sir.'

The sailor carefully pulled the carved oak chest towards him and, with a swing of the metal hook, brought it over the railing, where it hovered within a hair's breadth of Lugaschin.

The captain had no intention of moving. 'Out you come!' he shouted to the divers and flicked his unfinished cigarette into the Baltic Sea.

The men responded with affirming hand signals and swam towards the ladder.

Anjelica approached the chest, which dropped down with a thud. Water seeped from the wide cracks and broken wooden slats, spreading mud and dirt everywhere. A musty smell wafted towards her; the old silt seemed determined to drive her away with its stench. The last rays of sunlight flooded the deck with a dark-golden hue, smudging the outlines of the boat.

'Turn on the light, Captain,' Anjelica urged.

The skipper pulled out a torch from his belt and shone it across in response. He continued to stand at the railing just as if he were leaning against a bar counter. 'You can see everything else for miles. The coastguard doesn't miss a trick and there's a naval drill happening nearby. They'll be wondering why we're still out here and haven't transmitted a signal.'

The sailor bent down to the box, undid the clasp of the loosely hanging straps and, on Anjelica's affirmative nod, snapped off the rusty, corroded lock with a bolt cutter.

After repeated prying and the use of a chisel, the lid burst open, revealing the contents inside.

'Tell me I'm right. Tell me my treasure's there,' Anjelica heard her employer mutter anxiously.

Curious, the sailor bent over the cargo and held his little cap in disbelief. Then he started to laugh and exchanged a few words in Russian with the captain.

'Is it true?' Lugaschin tucked another cigarette in his mouth and lit it. 'No gold?' He cursed, audible even over the noise of the wind. 'Then I may as well forget about my share . . .'

In the lamplight, Anjelica saw black and grey mud, the remains of decomposed organic matter and more silt, from which crabs and other creatures crawled out to escape the glare of the torch. Sighing, she removed her hands from her pockets and rummaged around the freezing cold sediment. She hadn't thought of wearing gloves and hoped she wouldn't come across anything sharp or pointy.

Then she felt some resistance.

Anjelica gently pulled out the object and held it in her hands – it was a bottle with a wire cage fitted over the cork. She cleaned it as best as she could with the seawater that had collected on the beams. The trawler bobbed up and down even more, making her feel sick to her stomach.

'There's no need to be so dramatic, Clark,' her boss whispered nervously in her ear.

'Sir, I have to be sure. It's definitely a bottle, and . . .' – Anjelica held the cork up to the light – 'I can see an anchor on it. We've got at least one hit, sir! As for the rest, once I get a look at the contents –'

'Go on, Clark! If you make me rich, I'll come over there myself,' he interrupted her, laughing and slurping his tea loudly. 'This really is the best entertainment!'

Anjelica looked up at the sailor. 'Do you have anything to clean it with? A water hose to rinse it down with, maybe?'

He nodded curtly, trudged across the deck and returned immediately with a hose. On her instructions, he gradually rinsed the chest of the silt, which ran from the wooden slats in broad streaks all over the metal panels of the *Anatevka*.

Lugaschin followed the events and shouted something to the divers without turning his head. Cursing, the divers hauled themselves aboard and helped each other remove their heavy oxygen tanks.

Determined, Lugaschin passed the torch. 'What is it?'

MARKUS HEITZ | 5

'Something to drink,' replied Anjelica. 'It's no good any more – it's gone off.'

'Who are you talking to, Clark?' her boss asked.

Gusts of wind howled violently in her ears and muffled her voice. 'The skipper.'

'Don't tell him what treasure he has on board,' he urged her. 'You should never have done this alone.'

'We ran out of time, sir. The storm and the naval drill could have made the recovery impossible. We were lucky to even find the wreckage before anyone else did.' The limited stream of water exposed bottle after bottle before her eyes. While some corks had an anchor on them, others did not; there was a chance that the find was even older and more profitable than hoped. Anjelica estimated the number of bottles. 'As far as I can tell, there are around sixty here, sir – double the first find,' she reported quietly, before raising her voice and adding: 'Oh no, it's all the same! How disappointing – still no sign of any treasure.'

'Don't overdo the acting, Clark,' her boss retorted quickly over the satellite phone. 'Otherwise he'll get suspicious. Reload the goods.'

'Yes, sir.' She asked the sailor to fill the plastic boxes on deck with seawater and loaded one bottle after another onto the padded Styrofoam racks. The liquid gold would now survive the rest of the journey. Her employer's experts had set off for Tallinn and would take care of the inspection on land, and, if necessary, preserve the ancient corks so that they remained leakproof.

'Is that wine?' Lugaschin asked. He stood impassively at the railing, shone his torch and waved up to the flybridge. With that, the helmsman turned on the engine of the *Anatevka* and lifted the anchor to prepare for the trip back to the harbour.

'Yes,' Anjelica lied.

'And you *knew* it would be here.' Lugaschin waved his torch back and forth, its bright beam swaying. 'You have the right transport boxes for it, too. This isn't a bloody coincidence.'

'That's true, but we should have found gold,' she replied calmly, giving nothing away. From the corner of her eye, she saw the sailor combing through the remaining silt, as if he still hoped to find treasure. 'The wine is just a little souvenir. According to our records, the sailor was supposed to deliver important dispatches and gifts to a Russian tsar from the French king, Louis XVI. I expected to find at least a small chest of diamonds, jewellery or something similar.' She pointed at the waves. 'The Baltic Sea stood in our way.'

Lugaschin laughed. 'Do you think I'm stupid?'

'What's going on?' Anjelica's employer asked. 'What's he been saying?'

'I'll explain later, sir,' she whispered. The *Anatevka* chugged away and made a huge arc turn, rocking side to side as she quickly cut across the waves, and then set off. Her headlights were still out. Although the sun had set in the meantime, the natural light that remained would be enough to cover the first portion of their journey without the glaring lamps.

'Let's talk shares again.' The captain lowered his torch and got out his smartphone. 'I read something here about a similar find between Sweden and Finland. Champagne, worth at least fifty-three thousand euros. Per bottle.'

'No, you're wrong.' Anjelica played down the find.

'Shall I read you the report? It says that this symbol was only used by one champagne producer, Veuve Clicquot – produced around 1772 and sold from 1782. From 1798, it had its own trademark – an anchor on the cork.' Lugaschin shone his torch at the bottles.

'What does the man want, Clark?' her employer chimed in.

'More money, sir.'

'We're looking at around three million here, and I want my agreed five per cent. And, since you tried to screw me over' – the captain took a long, indulgent drag on his fag – 'I'll add another five. Otherwise, you'll find yourself overboard. These kinds of things happen during a storm, and the life jacket won't save you.'

The divers stood next to their captain on the deck, silent and threatening in their black wetsuits even though they resembled little sea lions.

The bow of the trawler sliced through the waves, dividing and separating them. In the dying light, water and salt spray poured onto the boat.

Anjelica sighed again and snapped a plastic lid shut. She could taste the salt on her lips. 'Six per cent. And there's no guarantee that we'll get three million. If it's no longer drinkable, then –'

'Is this worth anything?' The sailor retrieved a clay pipe bowl from the chest, stood up and held it by its rounded chamber. Lugaschin immediately shone his torch at it. The pipe bowl had an illustration of a dark-haired woman's torso on it.

'I'm afraid not,' Anjelica said, irritated by the interruption. 'I'm not an expert on –'

'That's a shame.' The sailor carelessly threw the pipe bowl onto the deck, where it shattered to pieces. 'Back to the negotiations, then.'

One of the divers burst out laughing and trudged towards her.

'Seven per cent!' Anjelica quickly raised her offer. Lugaschin was right: the icy Baltic would be the end of her.

But the diver walked past her, grabbed one of the bottles and snapped off its neck, which broke evenly, leaving behind a perfectly smooth glass top. The champagne fizzed and escaped from the bottle. There were still enough bubbles left for the drink to foam. Grinning, the diver took a sip. 'Tastes good. Bit corky though,' he said and moved back to join the others, laughing. The 18th-century bottle was passed around the small group.

'The oldest champagne in the world.' Lugaschin put away his torch, drank and laughed. 'That's the most expensive thing I've ever tasted.'

'I'm deducting that from your share,' Anjelica snapped. 'And seven is my final offer.'

'Good work, Clark,' her boss praised her. 'Now bring me my treasure.'

'Certainly, sir.'

Stunned, the sailor who was bent over the chest let out a confused shout. He pushed back his forage cap with his forearm and held up a slim little notebook case. After a splash of water from the hose, the notebook was revealed to be made from tarnished silver. A sealed lock secured its contents.

The skipper pulled out his torch again and pointed it at the silver case.

Anjelica spotted an unusual coat of arms and an illustration of a scene, but, until it was cleaned and thoroughly analysed, no light could be shed on the find. 'Sir, did you happen to come across anything about a silver box in the records?'

'I only knew about the champagne,' came the reply. 'But it belongs to me just as much as the bottles. Bring it to me, Clark.'

'Of course, sir.'

The sailor washed the case with clean water and pointed to a layer of red sealing wax that protected its contents from moisture.

Underneath, Anjelica saw a line where the seam had been joined together. Someone had wanted to make sure that whatever was inside the notebook reached the tsar in one piece. She suspected that it contained a personal message to the ruler, but not from King Louis XVI, from the champagne manufacturer.

'Could I please take a look?' She reached her hand out.

The sailor turned to Lugaschin, who shook his head and adjusted his peaked cap.

'Is that impertinent bastard negotiating again?' her employer enquired, agitated.

'Ten per cent,' said the captain, who remained rooted to the spot. He tucked the lit torch under his armpit. The foaming waves rolled behind him, pitching the *Anatevka* towards the shore. Little by little, the darkness enveloped the sky and pushed the sun below the horizon, as though wanting to drown it in the sea.

'Sir? He wants ten per cent.'

'Because of that silver junk?'

'Yes, sir.'

'Then he can keep it for all I care, but it stays at seven.'

Anjelica passed on the offer. She felt that her boss was doing the right thing. Silver wasn't worth much, and, even given its importance historically, the flat case wouldn't fetch more than twenty thousand. Beyond being of interest to Veuve Clicquot as an addition to its in-house collection, the complimentary gift from a winery hoping to secure more orders from a tsar's court was dispensable.

Lugaschin frowned and lit another cigarette with the rest of his last one. 'All right. Just don't whinge about it later if that silver thing makes me a richer man than your swill.' He took the bottle that was handed back to him, where one last drop sloshed around inside. 'Want some?' He stretched out his arm, offering her the last of the champagne.

Before Anjelica could respond, the thick glass shattered in Lugaschin's coarse hands. The jagged green shards clinked on the deck in front of his shoes and the champagne mixed with the water from the Baltic.

'That was clumsy,' Anjelica said, annoyed. Since the bottle

was already open, she would have loved to taste it. It would have been a privilege.

Lugaschin stared at the cuts on his fingers, slid from the railing, and collapsed onto the wet floor without supporting himself. The cigarette remained stuck to his lips. Its sparks floated upwards and were carried away by the wind. After emitting a dry, choking noise, his body went limp. The hat fell from his hair and was blown into the sea by the gusts. The torch slid out from under his body and cast its bright beam across the deck.

'What's wrong with him?' Anjelica wondered aloud, but, just as she stepped towards him, the diver to her right toppled over, groaning. Seconds later, blood poured from a wound that had appeared on the forehead of the diver to her left, who also buckled and faceplanted onto the steel floor.

Anjelica ducked down and made herself small. 'Shit,' she whispered, frightened. She had never been in a gunfight before, but she knew that the men were dead. The silent shots had killed them. Where the bullets came from, however, she hadn't a clue. Anjelica looked around for the sailor who had been bent over the chest – and put a hand over her mouth to stop herself from screaming.

The man lay on his back, his body sprawled out on the deck as if he had fallen asleep while trying to do gymnastics. The torch beam fell on him. Blood spread around his torso and mingled with the alcohol and seawater; the fabric of his cap soaked it all up greedily.

'Sir, we're under attack!' she shouted, distressed, and hid behind the winch. Her heart thumped hard in her chest like the engine on the boat. Her face was white from fear. She quickly glanced up at the dimly lit flybridge and saw the fogged-up glass speckled with red blotches – the killer had taken out the helmsman too. With a haul worth three million at stake, killing was clearly of no consequence to the stranger.

'Under attack?' her boss repeated in horror. 'But my treasure!'

Flickering, the bright headlights of the pitching, swaying *Anatevka* went on and illuminated the entire deck.

'And my life, sir!' Anjelica cried. Blinded by the lights, she closed her eyes for a few seconds. 'Call the police, the coast-guard, anyone,' she whispered urgently, as if it would stop the murderer from finding her.

Suddenly, jumping into the Baltic Sea seemed like a tempting option, but the cold would kill her just the same, and it would be a slower death than one from a bullet.

'What about the crew, Clark?'

'Dead. Or at least, I can't see any survivors.'

She didn't care about the mission; she cared about her life. Maybe, if she negotiated with the phantom on board, it would let her live. 'Take the bottles!' Anjelica shouted. 'I don't know who you are or what you look like! Please, just let me live!'

She felt like a helpless child. Her begging wouldn't stop someone who murdered in cold blood, but what else was there left for her to do?

The engine of the trawler suddenly roared to life at full throttle. The exhaust pipes spewed out black smoke into the air and the *Anatevka* made a sharp turn to starboard.

The unexpected movement caused Anjelica to scream and slip from her hiding spot. Lugaschin and his men's dead bodies slid around and rolled across the wet deck like grotesque dolls. Their dull, lifeless eyes stared at and through her.

'Clark? Hang in there! I'll make some calls! I've got your location.'

Anjelica was a sitting duck, and she knew it. Desperately, she tried to jump backward, but before she could hide behind the winch again she felt a blow to her right shoulder. A sharp pain followed immediately; the blow had reached through her life vest and spread like hot lava to her arm and back. Instinctively, she placed her hand over the wound, and felt the warm blood gushing from it. The mysterious murderer had struck her.

The shock made her blood pressure plummet, instantly causing her blood circulation to slow.

'Hold on!' she heard her boss say softly.

Every nerve in Anjelica's body was determined to escape, to go somewhere the killer wouldn't follow her. She crawled towards the railing with the firm intention of throwing herself into the sea, deciding that her chance of survival would be better in the icy waters than at the mercy of a clip of lethal bullets. Everything spun and her surroundings blurred.

The arrival of the next wave caused the boxes containing the ancient, precious champagne to slide around. One of them turned over and the bottles rolled down the *Anatevka*.

Anjelica pushed through the pain, moving herself over to the side of the boat, the growing weakness obscuring her vision. The deck shot up and down like a seesaw, her view alternating between the white foam crests on top of the waves and the ash-grey sky with its midnight-blue clouds.

The silver case suddenly slipped past her and banged against the railing.

Then, a pair of yellow wellies stepped into Anjelica's field of view with the hem of a green raincoat flapping around them. The figure retained its disguise, its head shielded under the hood of the raincoat. It bent down slowly, picked up the little case and slipped it into its pocket.

She saw the stranger turn towards her in the reflection of the shiny welly toe caps.

'Take the shitty champagne,' Anjelica said, panting and powerless. 'Just let me live . . .'

'Clark! Clark! I've got hold of someone!' her boss yelled. 'The coastguard is on their way.'

One of the bottles bounced between her and the stranger and smashed against the side of the boat without the murderer making any effort to save it. As if in celebration of a belated boat christening for the *Anatevka*, the expensive alcohol foamed and poured. The man need only have been quick enough to put his foot out, and €53,000 would have been his.

'Please, I—' Anjelica suddenly saw something metallic tumble onto the wet deck in front of her with a *ping* and bounce and spin rapidly, followed by another identical object. Her waning consciousness made it difficult to see, but she was sure they weren't coins.

Then came the pain, a new pain. It slashed violently through the flesh and bones of her back, forcing her head to hang limply. Her heart pounded so hard in her chest that it pained her more than any of her injuries.

As the two empty bullet cartridges washed overboard, Anjelica Clark died without ever knowing the reason for her death.

On gamblers God has never smiled,
The gambler is the devil's child.

From *The Ship of Fools* (1494),
by Sebastian Brant (1457–1521),
translated by Edwin H. Zeydel (2003)

INTERMEDIUM

Leipzig, the Electorate of Saxony,
the Holy Roman Empire,
January 1768

'I have rarely – no – *never* come across such a talented man as yourself,' remarked Johan Gottlob Immanuel Breitkopf, who, together with his father, ran a publishing and printing company under the same name. He held up the copperplate engraving. 'Albrecht Dürer's *Knight, Death and the Devil*. And how long did it take you to engrave this, Kirchner?'

'Half a month, Mr Breitkopf.' Bastian held on to his cap with both hands and wrapped his fingers around it tightly as if he were about to wring it out. His excitement had got the better of him and he didn't know how to behave as he stood in front of the desk in Breitkopf's impressive study. The grandfather clock ticked away noisily in the corner and the rattling of carts could be heard from outside. 'But I only engraved it, I didn't design it.'

'Only half a month, he says, as if it were nothing.' Breitkopf was a little older and wore a white wig and fine clothes, as befitted a man of his station. He looked up at his workshop master, who stood diagonally behind Bastian. 'Did you hear that, Stock?'

'I did, Mr Breitkopf.' Stock was in charge of the printing business and had a great deal of experience with engravers.

'And you've also worked as . . .' – Breitkopf glanced at Bastian's papers – 'A woodcarver and card-maker. I see that you're originally from Altenburg.'

'Yes, sir.' Bastian nodded, feeling secretly ashamed of his overly plain clothes. He couldn't afford anything else. 'I taught myself how to engrave copper. It wasn't difficult – it's just like carving wood, only the other way around.'

'How old are you?'

'Twenty-three.'

'How long have you lived in Leipzig?'

'For four years, Mr Breitkopf. Before then I ran a small workshop in Altenburg.'

'And you have a wife and three children and find you're still able support them *all*?'

'As I said, sir, it comes naturally to me.'

'Three children, yes, that certainly appears to be the case.' Breitkopf smiled. 'Did your wife follow you to Leipzig?'

'No sir, she's from Leipzig. My beautiful Susanna can do almost everything that I can. She refuses to make cards, but her engraving skills are as good as my own.'

Breitkopf couldn't contain his laughter any longer. 'My dear Stock! Remind me how on earth you came across this maestro again!' He looked at the engraving. 'Unbelievable! Utterly un-be-liev-a-ble!'

'Master Kirchner approached me a while ago. He was looking for work and asked if there was anything he could engrave – little things here and there, book and novel illustrations, and so on,' Stock said, reaching back for something. His clothing made it clear that he earned a good living. Stock was about twice as old as Bastian. 'As soon as I saw for myself how quickly and finely he etches and carves, I hired the man. He's now so skilled that I would prefer him to work exclusively for you, Mr Breitkopf. If our competition were to employ him, we'd be in trouble.'

'Splendid! What a splendid idea!' Breitkopf leaned forward and steepled his ink-stained fingers together. 'Where do you live, Kirchner?'

'On Town Piper Alley with my wife and three children. We're subtenants of a bailiff, Mr Breitkopf.'

'That won't do! That's a hideous part of town.' Breitkopf slammed his fist on the table. 'You'll move into the converted attic of my Silver Bear publishing house, next to my dear friend Stock, so that you can develop your skills even further.'

'That is very kind of you.' Bastian could hardly believe his luck. 'Thank you!'

'And you can teach Goethe, too – two masters are better than one. As for the salary, it'll certainly be above what you earn per month at the moment. None of my workers should have to go hungry.'

'Mr Breitkopf, I don't know how I could ever re–'

'Nonsense! You'll thank me with your work, Kirchner. You are incredibly talented.' Breitkopf tapped the engraved copperplate. 'A skilled man like yourself should never have to settle for anything less.' He glanced at Stock, satisfied. 'Kirchner will make a fine addition to our workshop, Stock. My congratulations!'

'At your service, Mr Breitkopf!' replied Stock, who wore his long hair in a plait at the nape of his neck. 'But you know, I simply wanted to lighten my workload, and with an engraver like Bastian' – he slapped Bastian on the shoulder and gave him a friendly shake – 'I've accomplished my goal.'

The men chuckled.

'Then off you go and organise the move. We'll talk about the card-making business another time,' Breitkopf said. 'I have some scores to attend to. There are some lovely little songs from Italy that need copying.'

Bastian and Stock left Breitkopf junior's meeting room, which was located on Alter Neumarkt Street on Sparrow Hill, where the family had set up its publishing headquarters.

Bastian had already heard about the kinds of skilled merchants that the Breitkopfs dealt with. After the Golden Bear guesthouse was demolished, the Breitkopfs built a stately home next to the print shop on Sparrow Hill and assumed the bear emblem as their own trademark. Last year, when the front and back buildings became insufficient room, the Breitkopfs built a second house: the Silver Bear. If business continued as usual, especially if there was an increase in demand for printing music, the Breitkopfs would require a third house.

The corridors and stairwells smelled of printing ink. Workers harshly reprimanding apprentice boys for foolish mistakes, the occasional rumble of hand and high-speed presses and the natter and chit-chat of customers asking for books and comparing the contents of works could be heard from the ground floor, which was where the print and bookshop were located.

Bastian relished the hustle and bustle. He couldn't believe that he was going to live under the same roof as where all the magic happened. *Susanna will be over the moon!* he thought. He extended his hand to Stock. 'Sir, please accept my thanks.'

'Only if we drop the titles. You are my equal, or rather, even my superior. I should be the one to address you formally,' Stock said.

'I am honoured!'

The two men walked down the stairs of the three-storey building and removed their coats from the hook.

Bastian pulled his hat over his short, black hair. A biting wind and crisp snow ushered people into restaurants, wine cellars and homes – wherever they felt most comfortable.

'Shall we meet later in Auerbach's Keller?' Stock asked. 'If your Susanna can spare you?'

'Oh, she will. I'll have a quick celebration with her at home, and then I'll meet you and the others.' Bastian pantomimed himself playing cards. 'For a nice little game.'

Stock raised his eyebrows. 'Have you been making cards in Breitkopf's workshop again?'

'Shhh!' Bastian said, looking around.

'You know that it's illegal to make your own cards. The fine –'

'But I don't sell them, I . . . just play with them,' Bastian replied, laughing. 'I find other cards far too ugly. I don't even enjoy winning when I see the queens' harsh faces staring back at me, and it makes losing pure agony.'

Stock laughed. 'Well, that's fine by me.' He opened the door. 'See you later! The first round is on me.'

Bastian followed him outside and braced himself for the blustering gale, which either puffed up his bell-shaped coat, thereby releasing all of the warmth inside it, or transformed it into a sail, against which he was then forced to struggle and trudge through the snow with his head facing the ground. He had forgotten his scarf and gloves.

'Oi, Kirchner!' The call sliced through the howl of the wind. 'A word.'

Bastian stopped and saw young Goethe walking towards him. Although Goethe had been sent to Leipzig to study law, he was visibly becoming a poet, a philosopher and an artist. 'Ah, here comes our young poet! What is it? It's too cold to chat.'

'I've got a poem I'd like to read to you. I wrote it last year.' Goethe held on to his tricorn with one hand to stop it from falling off his head.

'Please don't.'

'Oh yes, here it comes:

I saw Doris by Damoetas' stand,
He plucked her tenderly her by the hand;
Long they held each other's eye,

Looking around, lest the parents wake,
And with no one there to pry,
With haste they made love, as lovers make.

Bastian grinned. 'It's too baroque for my taste.'

'And yet, it'll be printed one day. I bet it will.' Goethe, who had spent his time writing poetry and courting a certain Kate instead of burying his nose in legal clauses, appeared offended. 'Will I see you at Auerbach's? Whatever game we play, be it whist, German solo, thirty and forty, passe-dix, ombre or sheep's head, we need all hands on deck.' He looked at him innocently. 'There'll be wine, too.'

'What a fine student you are,' Bastian had just finished saying, when he spotted the large, dog-shaped shadow lurking in the snowstorm.

'Upon my word! What an accusation! I study my fellow men and their habits assiduously in order to apply it to my—' Goethe followed Bastian's gaze. 'Can you see that black dog roaming through the snow and storm?'

'I saw him a while ago. He seems harmless.' It was a lie. Bastian sensed that nothing good could come from this creature.

'Take a closer look! What breed do you think it is?'

Bastian strained his eyes. 'A poodle . . . A rather large one.'

Goethe backed away from the animal. He too felt that there was something sinister about it. 'Does the way it's behaving seem normal to you? Have you noticed how it's prowling in circles and seems to keep getting closer to us?'

Bastian turned to follow the twists and turns of the stray dog: it stalked them incessantly, skilfully avoiding the bright spots beneath the streetlamps. The creature moved with a threatening carelessness and kept its eyes fixed on the men, as if they were wild game that it would hunt down and bring back to its master.

Bastian could hardly believe what he saw next: the dog drew a blazing line around them! Its paw prints glowed yellow and red in the white snow.

'And, if I'm not mistaken, it also leaves behind a whirlpool of fire wherever it goes,' Goethe whispered next to him, terrified. 'I haven't had a drop to drink, I swear it, I swear it on my life!'

Bastian told himself it was impossible. 'I see nothing but a black poodle. It's probably just a trick of the light,' he replied and slowly carried on walking.

But Goethe panicked and clung on to Bastian and his hat. 'The way it's magically drawing those silent loops around our feet . . . They may as well be shackles!'

'My dear scholar, don't be so daft,' Bastian said, feigning a laugh to soothe his friend and himself. 'It's clear that it's afraid and nervous because it's in the presence of two strangers and has strayed away from its owner.'

Still, Goethe refused to settle down. 'The circle is getting narrower! It's so close to us already.' He pushed Bastian in front of him. 'Get away, beast! Go back to hell where you belong.'

The poodle kept still. It was unusually large for a dog of its breed. Its eyes reflected the faint light and its gaze alternated back and forth between the two of them, as if deciding who to attack first.

Then, taking them by complete surprise, the creature plopped itself down onto the snow, as though leaving what to do next up to Goethe and Bastian. As it suddenly began to wag its tail and bark, inviting them to play, the eeriness vanished as if it had been swept away by the icy wind.

Bastian peeled Goethe's hands away from his arm. 'You see? You coward, it's only a dog, not a ghost. He's wagging his tail, as dogs do.' He laughed at him. 'You'll never be a hero if you carry on like this.'

'I never wanted to be one. I just like writing about them.' Goethe couldn't bite down his grin. 'I'm behaving like a fool.'

'A big one, at that.' Bastian's teeth chattered. The wind had stolen that last shred of warmth from his clothes and he was eager to finally break the glorious news to Susanna. 'I'll see you later, Goethe. At Auerbach's.' He walked off quickly. 'And don't let the ghost-poodle bite you and drag you all the way to hell to throw you at his master Mephistopheles' feet!'

Goethe waved him off and walked away in the other direction, the snowflakes shrouding him from view.

The dog, however, remained rooted to the spot: a sinister shadow against the whirling white.

Bastian reached his lodgings at Town Piper Alley. Breit-kopf had called the alley hideous, and Bastian couldn't help but agree with his description. The gloomy, winding little alley and its predominantly council-owned, wooden buildings had seen better days. Writers, domestic servants and, last but not least, town pipers – after whom the alley was named – lived here.

Bastian, Susanna and their children lived in a hole of a home as subtenants, as the actual tenant, a bailiff with lots of children, found it too cold and draughty in the winter months. Water dripped through the roof and ceiling when it rained, which made Bastian thankful for the harsh winter as the rain turned to ice instead, even if they frequently felt cold. But the children never got tired of marvelling at the frost patterns.

Bastian opened the door of the sloping, crooked house and cheered loudly as he ran into the room, startling Susanna and the children. They sat around the dinner table in thick, coarse jackets. Steam rose from the broth in the cold room and it smelled of meat stew.

'Who's come storming in like a wild beast?' Susanna cried,

her voice filled with both joy and reproach. Her braided blonde hair shimmered in the candlelight.

Bastian threw his hat and then his coat onto the hook and stood by the wooden stove, stretching his frozen fingers in front of it to get warm. 'Glad tidings, I would have thought,' he said. He could see that the soup was mainly made up of beans thickened with flour. Only the children had meat in their bowls.

'Glad tidings are always welcome. Let's hear it.' Susanna filled his bowl. 'Has someone placed another order?'

'Keep guessing.' Bastian smiled at the children. 'You too, go on!'

'Two new orders!' Johann shouted.

'Gold!' Ilse cooed. Armin, too little to reply properly, babbled something to herself.

'We're moving out,' Bastian said, giving them a mysterious look as he sat down. 'I spoke to Breitkopf.'

Susanna laughed heartily. 'Which one?'

'With the big boss, I believe, Johann Gottlob Immanuel.' Bastian grabbed his wife's left hand and squeezed it. Her beautiful face lit up. 'I've got a job at The Bernhard Christoph Breitkopf and Sons Printing House.'

Susanna dropped the ladle and clapped a hand over her mouth in delight.

'And we're going to move out, too. We'll leave this hellhole and move into the publishing house!'

'I . . . God almighty!' Susanna cried and wrapped her arms around his neck. 'All of our hard work, all of our blood, sweat and tears. It's paid off.'

'We're rich!' Johann yelled.

'Gold!' Ilse shouted again, playing with the broth with her spoon and splashing it everywhere. Noticing that everyone was in good spirits, Armin clapped her hands together and laughed merrily.

Bastian got up, rummaged around the supplies cupboard and found a sealed bottle filled with cask wine. 'Let's have a toast,' he said and excitedly poured two mugfuls before joining his loved ones back at the table. 'Here's to a better life for our children.'

'And to us doing all right, too,' Susanna added with a cheeky smile, drinking with him.

'I wouldn't be opposed to that.'

'Gold and happiness will be ours!' Bastian exclaimed and kissed Susanna, who returned his affection. He then took a sip of the wine, which was rather bitter after being kept for so long.

'Oh dear!' Susanna coughed. 'It could do with some . . . Honey and spices, I think. Lots of honey.'

'I've got an even better idea,' Bastian replied, taking advantage of the opportunity. 'I can get us some more from Auerbach's Keller.' He stood up and tried to discretely get his self-made playing cards out of the drawer. 'If I come back late, it'll be because I had to sample all the wines first to find the best one for us.'

Susanna laughed. 'Do you think I haven't noticed?'

Bastian went red and turned to her. He tried to look innocent. 'What do you mean?'

She pointed to his pocket. 'You've taken the cards. That's why it'll take so long, and that's without you sampling all the wines.' She rose, told the children to go back to their meal and looked at him, putting her arms on his shoulders and stroking his neck. 'I know how much you love cards and making them, but I've already told you that I don't approve of it.'

'Susanna, the other cards are hideous, and—'

'My love, it's forbidden for one thing. If they catch you, you'll be fined, and on top of that you'll lose your job at Breitkopf's,' she interrupted him softly. 'Nothing good can come of these cards.'

'We're not causing any trouble.'

'And yet people say that cards are the Devil's prayer-book.'

'But even the clergy play with them.' Bastian cleared his throat. He wanted to tell her that Breitkopf was even thinking about setting up a card manufacturing department at his publishing house to expand beyond just printing books, publications and sheet music. Stock had secretly confided this fact to Bastian and made him promise not to tell a soul. Knowing Susanna could forbid him to work there altogether if he told her, however, Bastian remained silent.

'That doesn't mean you should be and doesn't make the game or the pastors and priests any better,' Susanna said, snuggling up to him. She smelled of lavender soap and spring. 'Leave the cards at home.'

'Just this one evening,' he protested, gently kissing the tip of her nose. Then he freed himself from her embrace and threw on his coat. 'See you later, my dear, my queen of hearts!' He turned to the children. 'And as for you: listen to your mother!'

Bastian headed out into the snowstorm while he could still be forgiven for not hearing Susanna's reply, which he might not like. He felt over the moon, as if he were walking on air, and he wouldn't let anything dampen his spirits.

Clutching his playing cards in his left hand, he sprinted along Town Piper Alley and reached the entrance of Auerbach's Keller. Auerbach's was one of Leipzig's oldest wine taverns and had been established over two hundred years ago by a local Leipzig city councillor, doctor and professor called Stromer. The fact that the tavern would still be welcoming customers after all this time, however, was something that its founder had never in a million years thought possible.

Bastian stumbled down the steep, well-trodden steps and

made his way into the underground wine tavern and past the old paintings on wooden canvases.

One painting depicted the magician and astrologer Faust, drinking with students, and the other one showed him rolling out of the door on a wine barrel. Bastian had once found Goethe staring at it, lost in thought and woozy from wine. When he had asked why he was gawking at Faust like that, Goethe had told him that he was fascinated by the painting's depiction of the idea of striving for something, searching for it, then being mistaken and still not finding it, and not losing your mind in the process.

'Kirchner! Over here!' Stock shouted over the buzz of conversations of the taverngoers; a wall of sound penetrated by shouts and laughter.

Councillors and craftsmen, journeymen and students, lovers and married couples alike all sat in the vaulted cellars, drunk on wine and clouded by tobacco smoke, playing games. Those with instruments played music, and Bastian could also hear singing from further away. Powerful voices had broken out into a song that echoed off the vaulted ceilings.

Stock had managed to grab a table with Goethe and a group of young people. Jugs and goblets were already on the table, and the cards had been handed out. Some of them had already been played, while others remained in people's hands.

Bastian recognised the German deck. It was of basic, tavern quality and no doubt often pressed together after many hours of play to keep the cards in shape. He saw the blotches on the backs of the cards. It would be far too easy for a player sitting in a corner to win, provided they had a good memory.

'There you are!' Bastian said, making his way down the benches and through the crowds, apologising politely as he pushed past and picking up hats he knocked on to the floor.

'Grab a seat,' Goethe replied. He elbowed the young lads sitting next to him. 'Allow me to introduce you to Frosch, Brandner, Siebel and Altmayer. They're all brave, and, as you can see, poor students who cannot afford fine threads.'

Bastian greeted the group and took a seat, setting down his coat and hat behind him.

The young men had met up a while ago and had spent the time playing cards with the stained deck. They spoke loudly and roughly and made crass jokes about their opponents and other guests in the tavern. The general consensus was to finish playing sheep's head and then move on to another game.

The thought of touching the stained cards revolted Bastian. Besides, he had never liked the German game and much preferred French colours, thinking them more elegant.

'What's the matter?' the chubby Frosch addressed the group, mischief twinkling in his eyes. 'Is no one laughing? No one drinking? I'll teach you how to grin, I'm thinking. Today you're like wet straw, so tame; and usually you're all aflame.'

'He's speaking in rhyme again,' Goethe muttered, shaking his head. 'He always does that when he's had something to drink.'

Bastian smirked.

'Oh, I can do that too. Now that's your fault; from you we nothing see,' Brandner, who wore a very large, curly wig, spoke up. 'No beastliness and no stupidity.'

'Oh, so it's my fault, is it?' Frosch took his goblet and poured the wine over Brandner. 'There's both together!'

The group laughed and Bastian couldn't help but grin.

'To hell with you, you're twice a swine!' Brander shouted, wiping the red from his eyes and throwing his cards on to the table. They immediately began to soak up the puddle of red wine. 'The game is ruined, and so is my wig.'

'As if you would have won with *that* hand,' Siebel retorted, laughing. He laid his cards on the table for all to see. 'Tough luck, my friend. But don't despair, red hair is rather popular with the ladies.'

'Enough already, enough,' Altmayer said and asked a waitress to bring him a cloth to clean up the wine with. There was a fresh scar on his left cheek. 'Let's play something else.'

Bastian saw that Goethe was vigorously scribbling away in his notebook, as if transcribing minutes in court. He had most likely been inspired by something and was noting down his ideas for a new story or poem. Suddenly, Goethe glanced at the table, which had been carelessly built and whose wood was damp from the spilt wine. Goethe knew that they were waiting to see the new cards, but Bastian's cards were too precious for them; they didn't deserve to be touched by greasy fingers or pick up other dirt.

Frosch leaned against the wall behind him. 'Ah, what a splendid evening.'

'Leipzig to me is dear,' Goethe mumbled. 'Paris in miniature. How it refines its people!'

'Or makes them *conceited*. That can be said of many in this cellar,' the uncouth Siebel responded. He glanced at Bastian. 'Well, what are you waiting for? Show us the cards!'

Bastian looked at Goethe, who tried to appear innocent and buried his nose in his little notebook. 'What makes you think I have cards?'

'Our old friend Goethe told us,' Altmayer said and leaned forward. 'But we'll keep this between us.'

'We only want to see them,' Brandner added and gestured for another glass of wine. 'Goethe boasted about them, said the cards were a masterpiece and that he wants to learn more about the intricacies of carving and engraving from you and Stock.'

Stock glanced at Bastian and shook his head suggestively.

But the students' expectant looks and the desire for his

work to be praised and admired, something Susanna hadn't done, made Bastian pull out the deck from his pocket with his left hand and show their French colours. He had left the designated tax stamp spot on the ace of hearts blank, so as to avoid being accused of deceiving the electorate or even forging the stamp.

'Here they are,' he said and handed out the cards one by one. 'Gentlemen, avoid leaving marks. It would be a pity to spoil such beautiful cards.' The first card was still making its way round as Bastian relished the astonishment on the young men's faces. Stock, whose appreciation meant far more to Bastian than the students', also widened his eyes and nodded approvingly. 'I know there are still some things I need to refine but, if Breitkopf decides to pursue card manufacturing, I'll make him the best cards.'

'I don't doubt it,' Brandner said, impressed.

'Not for one second,' Siebel added. 'I'd buy them on the spot!'

Bastian smiled happily and kept an eye on the cards as they were passed around, worried that something might happen to his precious paper children before they made their way back to him.

'I can't sell them to you, Siebel.'

'Oh, surely it's only a question of price,' Altmayer interjected. 'How many thalers will it take for you to change your mind?'

'It's forbidden,' Bastian maintained, feeling anxious.

The cards were now being passed back and forth between the students. They twisted and turned them in their hands, and even held them up to the light to test if they could see through them, which only drew attention from the other tables.

'All right, pass them back to me, quick!' Bastian demanded. Susanna had warned him that it wasn't a good idea, and she had been right.

'Now, now, why the rush?' Frosch asked, stroking the queen of clubs. 'I'd win with this one.'

Bastian turned around and inspected the vaulted cellar to check if a councillor or the authorities were making their way towards their table.

Sure enough, a man roughly in his sixties wearing a simple, elegant yet military-like frock coat came over, limping slightly. His eyes looked ancient, as if they had seen over a hundred years go by. He wore his long, salt-and-pepper hair in a braid, which was held in place by a dark velvet ribbon at the back of his head. Melted snow dripped from his adorned tricorn hat.

Bastian froze. The same, extraordinarily large, black poodle that had frightened Goethe and him in the snowstorm walked by the man's side. He looked down and examined the wine cellar floor to see if he could spot any glowing marks on its paws, but the magic from before didn't repeat itself.

'Give me the cards!' Bastian hissed at the group and held out his hands.

But the man had already reached them. The black dog sat down beside him, its eyes darting from the card-maker to Goethe, as if it wanted to be praised by its master for having tracked down the men again.

As if it were cornering its prey.

'Good evening,' the man greeted them in a sonorous voice. The students jumped, frightened. They hadn't seen him arrive until that very second. 'Forgive me, dear students, but I couldn't help but notice' – he extended a scrawny hand with long, filed nails and pointed at the deck with his index finger – 'these cards. They're *exquisite*. Who do they belong to, and where can I purchase such a deck?'

The men silently exchanged glances and tried to think of a way to evade the question. Goethe stared at the poodle and made himself small.

'I bought them in France,' Bastian said finally with all the courage he could muster. 'They're brand new. From Lyon.'

'Ah, Lyon. The famous city of card craftsmen,' the man said, and bowed. 'My name is Dietrich, and I'm from the beautiful city of Leipzig. But if these cards are from Lyon, why is the tax stamp missing from the jack of clubs?'

Bastian felt his heart pounding in his throat. 'Oh, I . . . I dropped the cards and they fell into the water, and—'

Dietrich laughed softly. 'You have nothing to be afraid of, sir. I am not a man of authority, just a friend and a lover of cards.' He leaned towards Bastian. 'It was *you*. You made them.'

'They're only samples,' Bastian said. 'To prove to a manufacturer that I can do it.'

'That you can, without a doubt. You are an even better craftsman than Stock.' He nodded a greeting to Stock, whose age set him apart from the young crowd. 'I mean no offence.'

'I know what you mean, and it's true,' Stock replied, suspicion written across his face. 'We'll get rid of the samples right away. Kirchner meant no harm.'

'I know, I know,' Dietrich said, smiling and flashing his set of immaculate, unstained and fresh, white teeth. Bastian had only seen their like on young children. 'Would you make me a pack, Master Kirchner? If I were to give you my specifications? I shall make it worth your while.' He held out in his clawed hand a clinking leather pouch, which had seemingly appeared out of thin air. 'How long would you need?'

'Hey, old man! I asked Kirchner first,' Siebel complained.

'And I have more money,' Altmayer added. Their looks at the seasoned gent now grew hostile.

The poodle growled threateningly and pulled back its lips. It evidently disapproved of the way its master had been spoken to.

Bastian backed away from the animal. If the group hadn't still had his cards, he would have got up and left.

'Now, now, gentlemen, dear students,' Dietrich reassured them with a mirthful laugh, and took a seat. 'Why fight over something we won't even get?' He looked at Bastian. 'Isn't that right?'

Bastian looked into the man's ancient eyes: blood flooded his pupils and flames danced in them, dyeing the whites of his eyes. There was something demonic about him. 'I don't have the right to make them yet,' Bastian stammered, on the verge of giving in to the stranger's request – out of fear; the money in the pouch, which sounded like gold when it jingled, meant nothing to him.

'You could do it in secret. No one would have to know,' Dietrich whispered enticingly. 'Do this as a favour to me. In return, I will grant you whatever it is you wish most.'

'Let it go, Dietrich,' Siebel shouted. 'Kircher's with us.'

'Listen to his promises! I'll grant you any wish, he says! Pha! Only God and the Devil have that kind of power, not you,' Altmayer reprimanded the old man, with a raised index finger, as if he were a priest. 'Not men.'

'Not if he had them by the neck, I vow, would e'er these people scent the Devil,' Dietrich replied, quoting *Faust*. He accepted a jug of wine from a waitress and paid for it. 'But now, let us forget our quarrel and drink to the secret card craftsman. May he soon be able to make his cards freely and delight us with them.' He rose to fill the students' cups and goblets.

Shortly before Dietrich poured the wine, Bastian was sure he saw the man sprinkle a pinch of whitish powder as fine as flour into the jug. But it was gone in the blink of an eye, and for all Bastian knew he might have imagined it.

Dietrich shared out the wine, which, strangely enough, ran out once Siebel's, Brandner's, Frosch's and Altmayer's goblets had been filled. He quickly ordered another carafe.

'Hurrah for freedom! Hurrah for wine!' Altmayer cried exuberantly after taking his first sip, laughing like mad. He clutched the glass at the edge of the table and pretended to draw himself more wine from the wood. 'Ha! Look, more grape juice! I can see it gurgling and spluttering from the table.'

Bastian watched in disbelief as, much to the amusement of the other customers, the four students played, pretending that the wine flowed straight out of the furniture. He seized the opportunity to swiftly grab and pocket his cards. Goethe continued to write in his little notebook as if he were possessed.

Dietrich stood up from the table. 'It's clear that you gentlemen are enjoying yourselves and entertaining others. I'll be on my way.' He leaned forward. 'As for the cards, Master Kircher, my offer still stands. Think about it – perhaps you'll take me up on it after all.' With that, he walked away, limping slightly.

Bastian shuddered as the giant black poodle shot him another look. The dog rose and yawned, as if wanting to bare its nasty teeth one last time at him, before it trotted after its master. *The beast from the pits of hell.*

He lost his train of thought to the loud clamouring at his table and the laughter from the wine cellar. The other guests in Auerbach's were enjoying the show as the drunken, enraptured students rose from their chairs and looked around as if they had been transported from the vault to another world.

'Where am I? What a lovely land! Altmayer shouted enthusiastically.

'Vines?' Frosch cried cheerfully. 'Can I trust my eyes?'

Siebel reached out and touched Brandner's nose. 'And there are grapes here – delicious and juicy ones,' he declared and drew his knife. Screams erupted from the crowd of onlookers. A fear that the fun and games could take an unpleasant and unexpected turn filled the room. 'We'll cut them right off the vines.'

The four students grabbed each other's noses and pulled out their pocketknives. But before they could do anything, Bastian, Goethe, Stock and a few brave strangers broke them apart and stopped them.

Dietrich and his sinister dog had long since vanished.

I

Enrico Pedro García Hermano wore a classic, exceptionally expensive dinner jacket paired with a narrow tie and felt out of place. The city's famous Buddha Bar was frequented by wealthy people like him, but most of them were dressed casually. Although nobody took any notice of him – evening attire was very common in Monaco – he grew increasingly eager to slip away.

Enrico stirred the drink on the bar in front of him with one hand. The taste appealed to him. The bartender had mumbled 'very sophisticated' when serving him the drink, which turned out to be a concoction made up of vodka and something else – most likely ginger and home-made syrup. The uplifting feeling that the alcohol had first stirred in him, however, had faded.

He'd already been waiting some time for his adventure to start. The 42-year-old composed himself; the bar's incredibly chic and dignified decor wasn't helping his restlessness. A roughly three-metre-tall Buddha statue was situated opposite the bar of the dark, wood-panelled dining room. While people on the ground floor were content with drinks and snacks, those on the terrace and in the adjoining rooms dined as if they were at a restaurant. A terribly popular DJ, whose name Enrico refused to remember, was playing pulsating club music. The lighting was pleasant, quiet conversations and music drifted through the building, and an occasional laugh pierced through the wall of noise.

A bodyguard and a very good-looking receptionist in a white dress, who was wearing a headset and holding a tablet in her hands, strutted through the venue at regular intervals to personally escort new guests to their seats, including celebrities, VIPs from Hollywood or the world's social scene. Monaco had retained its popularity.

'Un autre, monsieur? Peut-être un–' the bartender tried to tempt Enrico.

'No, merci,' Enrico replied, flashing him a friendly smile. After all, the bartender wasn't responsible for his bad mood. Enrico leaned against the counter and pulled out his smartphone. Perhaps a nice message would help soothe his agitation. Luckily, some pleasant news was waiting for him in his inbox.

Firstly, his stable manager had contacted him to let him know that, after some lengthy negotiations, the purchase of the Arabian stallion had been successful.

Secondly, the latest revenue figures indicated that he'd managed to boost his sales of cut roses to Russia by twenty-one per cent. His contacts and new business partners from Moscow, whom it was unwise to cross, were finally paying off. And, with the equivalent of two euro cents per rose sold being donated to a charitable foundation, it was also a win for those in need.

Last but not least, his fiancée had texted him to wish him a wonderful evening.

Enrico put away his smartphone with a smile and congratulated himself on having the most beautiful, loving and best girlfriend in the world. He fiddled with the platinum ring on his right hand, which was in the shape of a rose with a diamond-encrusted dewdrop. The ring was flashy and expensive and served a purpose. It fitted his nickname, Florecita – the little flower – as he was somewhat unflatteringly called in Ecuador, his homeland. He had earned the name on account of the millions he made from exporting long-stemmed roses.

Enrico smiled. He couldn't care less about what people called him or their attempts to insult him. He'd rather play along with the image, which only provoked their jealousy even further.

'Monsieur!' Enrico beckoned the bartender, brushing his curly brown hair out of his eyes. He decided to have one more drink before moving on to the casino. 'Vôtre meilleur vodka. Pure et sans des glaçons.'

'Bien sûr, monsieur.'

Enrico had come to appreciate the drink during his travels. The Russian flower market was fiercely competitive due to the popularity of flowers and the standards Russian ladies demanded from their husbands and suitors. Since his meeting with a couple of gentlemen from Moscow to conclude an agreement, however, business was running better than ever. While his parents took care of the roses, he took care of business.

The vast sums of money he earned went to charitable projects that he settled on together with his fiancée, and, provided there were no new horses to purchase, towards his general passion for collecting. The latter was Enrico's entire purpose in travelling to Monte Carlo. It was why he was sitting in the Buddha Bar and it was what he was most looking forward to.

Enrico shouldn't have to wait much longer, and he tried to tell himself that the waiting only helped to further whet his appetite for the main event.

He set down the polished glass of crystal-clear vodka. The alcohol sloshed against the rim and slowly trickled down in streaks.

He was about to reach for his drink again when his smartphone vibrated: a call.

In the hope that some positive news would put an end to him twiddling his thumbs, he accepted the call from the unknown number: 'Oui?'

'Forgive me for speaking English, señor García Hermano,' Enrico heard an older male voice say with a slight accent. 'My Spanish isn't very good, and, although French is the best language for getting around Monaco, it doesn't suit me either.'

'No problem, señor.'

'I have a business proposal for you.'

Enrico frowned. This was clearly not the adventure he had been waiting for.

'I'm sorry, but I—'

'You have something I want,' continued the man, who seemed accustomed to being listened to.

'That could be any number of things, señor. I wish you a . . .' Enrico removed the phone from his ear, wanting to end the call before the conversation stole the last of his good mood.

'If you *don't* sell it to me, there'll be trouble during your round of supérieur,' the man continued, his voice soft against the music of the club.

Enrico sighed. The only thing he liked less than waiting was threats. He quickly picked up his phone and held it to his ear again. 'Your name, señor? I didn't catch it.'

'That's irrelevant until you and I seal the deal. I know you're in Monte Carlo right now and are intending to recklessly gamble away the object of my desire.'

Enrico's anger transformed into unease. 'I'm not planning on selling it to you or anyone else.'

'I'm offering you—'

This time it was Enrico that interrupted the stranger. 'I'm not interested in the money, señor.'

'Very well. Then you should know that you'll meet one of my men later this evening. He's a great fellow. I'm warning you, selling me the item *now* would be a wise move.'

Enrico scanned the bar. 'Are you here?' he asked. Apart from himself, he couldn't see anyone else on the ground floor speaking on the phone.

'No, señor, but I can arrange that in a *snap*, if you'll allow me the pun.'

'Don't ever call me again.' Enrico hung up the phone and stuffed it into his pocket. Tomorrow morning he would ask his secretary whether there had been any more calls from the unknown person in Ecuador. It was no secret that Enrico was in Monaco, but the stranger knew more about his movements than Enrico was comfortable with.

'Señor García Hermano?' As if having appeared out of thin air, a brunette in a dark-grey dress stood next to him. She must have arrived at the bar without being escorted by the receptionist. She was of average height, and, as befitted a messenger, had a modest build and manner about her. Neither deodorant nor perfume enveloped her, only her lips revealed traces of minor cosmetic surgery, and the absence of wrinkles on her face hinted at Botox, all of which was typical of Monaco.

Enrico grabbed his drink and toasted her in response. The diamond dewdrop on his ring flashed fervently. He wondered if this was the start of his long-awaited adventure or if the unknown caller had sent her.

She pulled out a card from her dress and handed it to him, face up. 'A free seat has become available, señor.'

This made it clear where she had come from.

'You're very late,' he said, accepting the card and turning it over. It was the ten of diamonds, just as agreed.

'I regret that I couldn't welcome you sooner, señor.' She made a welcoming gesture. 'Besides, I wanted to make sure that you were alone and were not being followed.'

Enrico laughed and fixed his brown hair again. 'My security team is on standby, but I'm here alone.' He took the vodka with him and left a hundred-euro note on the counter for the glass. The bartender would be delighted with the generous tip.

Nobody called him back and he left the Buddha Bar with the mysterious woman.

'Does this often happen?' Enrico asked, sipping his vodka. His spirits had improved.

'What, señor?'

'That you're followed when it comes to supérieur?'

'Sometimes, señor.'

With that, Enrico stopped trying to initiate small talk. It was clear that the brunette wasn't in the mood for conversation. They went downstairs, then to the left, and up a little incline before reaching the casino. After a few metres, the woman stopped in front of a side entrance that led to the private gaming rooms and could only be accessed if you had a booking.

She pulled out a chip card and ran it through the discreetly fitted reader. The door opened with a buzz and she stepped inside.

Enrico had another drink of vodka, then followed her in. This was proving more exciting than he had expected.

They walked past the closed salon doors, which featured famous names and key figures in history and literature.

'Do you have everything you need, señor?'

'Of course.'

'Forgive me, I only ask because there was already an incident today when someone did not wish to pay their stake,' she explained kindly. 'You know the game that we'll be playing?'

'Yes. Supérieur.'

'With the complete set of rules?' She stood in front of the Dostoevsky Salon.

Enrico took another sip. The questions irritated him, but they also made his heart race and his anticipation grow. He just wanted to take his seat at the table. 'Shall we?'

She smiled sympathetically. 'At this point I'd like to mention that the casino only provides the premises and is not responsible for any winnings or losses. The maximum limit is entirely up to the players.'

'I have no limit.'

'Excellent, señor.' She opened the door with the chip card and allowed him to pass. 'Welcome to our round of supérieur.'

Enrico took a decisive step into the dark-green room, which reminded him of the salons from the Wilhelminian era. As a newcomer and a beginner, he couldn't afford to give the impression that he was an easy target. Green and white stripy wallpaper hung above the dark wood, waist-high panels that ran along the walls. A chandelier dangled from the ivory-coloured stucco ceiling and lit up the room.

Nine finely dressed players – four women and five men – sat at the green felt-covered table. A dealer in a shirt, bow tie and waistcoat let the cards rattle in the card shuffler machine and stacked tall towers of differently coloured playing chips in front of the participants. While some players preferred water, others had drinks and cocktails in special holders to prevent the glasses from accidentally tipping over and flooding the table cover.

The brunette escorted Enrico to the empty seat. 'Ladies and gentlemen, the ten of diamonds has joined us. Please, make him feel welcome.'

The players raised their glasses to him and Enrico nodded warmly to the group. He would have loved to text his fiancée to let her know how thrilling he found this curiously serious and solemn scene.

Then the woman removed a tray from a chest of drawers that, in addition to an array of alcoholic beverages, had various storage compartments. She turned to him. 'Your smartphone please, señor? You will get it back at the end of the round.'

The device landed in one of the pockets, where, upon closer

inspection, he also saw two semi-automatic pistols: one black and one chrome-coloured. Not everyone had arrived at the table unarmed.

Beside the usual smells of alcohol and exhaled air, Enrico caught a whiff of something pungent that stood out against the various colognes, perfumes and drinks in the room: cleaning agent. There were wet patches on the carpet next to his chair. The previous guest had presumably spilled their drink, and some employees had immediately cleaned it up.

'Please, monsieur,' said the dealer and pushed a stack of chips towards him. Enrico had bought them in advance via bank transfer for a million euros. This game wasn't called supérieur for nothing. With the name of the game meaning higher, more, or superior, only the rich could afford to play it.

'Merci,' Enrico replied, stealing glances at the other players as he emptied his vodka.

They were all of different ages, ranging from a woman of around sixty to a dark-haired young man of no more than eighteen, whom Enrico immediately identified as the son of an oligarch. He had seen a few of them around in Moscow, and the local youngster fitted the stereotype perfectly, from his haircut to the ostentatious clothes, arrogant facial expression, excessive jewellery and the luxury sunglasses that sat on his forehead. As for the other players, Enrico was in the dark about their origins and professions. Wealth and their thrill-seeking nature was what united them, especially when it came to gambling.

Not much talking took place. Any quiet conversation revolved around how the previous rounds had progressed. It was as if the game was all that existed. Discussing personal matters was considered taboo, and even names weren't mentioned.

'Your stakes, please,' the dealer announced. 'Ten thousand each.'

Enrico set down his vodka and slid across a chip, after which everyone received a card.

The rules of supérieur were simple. The game consisted of three rounds. The stakes were raised once per player bid, and players could swap a card up to three times by taking a new one from either the top or the bottom of the deck. The value of the exchanged card would then apply. The winner was the player with the highest-value card after the third round.

But there was a catch: if a player drew the ace of spades, they lost automatically. The player would then be ruled out of the game and the ace of spades would be returned to the pile. The deck would be reshuffled and the game would continue. None of the remaining players could be sure they were safe if they chose to take a new card.

Enrico had drawn the ten of clubs. He held on to it for the next round, only to fold later. The oligarch's son won with a queen of clubs. Enrico then picked up the two of diamonds. He exchanged it for an eight of clubs in the second round and went out. The older Asian woman won this time. She gambled and bid like the Devil's grandmother, quickly and recklessly.

There was a tension in the room that Enrico couldn't put his finger on. He studied the young and old faces that surrounded him, some filled with joy and others with disappointment. Still no conversation had transpired and any rejoicing was done discreetly. Nobody trusted their success and no one appeared interested in engaging with their opponents. Only the young Russian player confirmed every cliché of the super-rich by gloating at the losers and mocking the winners.

Enrico lost round after round. Sometimes he gave up, sometimes he went down in a showdown against his opponent. His cards failed him time and time again. The chip mountains melted away, and yet, despite his losses, he was enjoying himself immensely.

Five players were eliminated during the course of the eerily quiet evening. They gambled away all their money and were escorted outside by the brunette. The farewells were very pleasant and Enrico thought he saw relief on the dropouts' faces, as if they had just run a strenuous marathon and were thankful to have made it to the finish line, even if they couldn't expect to be awarded a medal for their efforts.

With such huge losses, Enrico had expected anger on the players' part, but no such feelings ensued.

Apart from him, there now remained the oligarch's son, the Devil's grandmother, an older gentleman in a three-piece suit with yacht club symbols on his breast pocket, and a young blonde in a slinky dress who, despite looking like an infantile it-girl, was well aware of what her feminine charms brought to the table.

The intangible tension among the four players left remained, even if the Russian tried to gloss over it by making grand gestures.

Enrico drew the queen of hearts, so far his best card of the evening. It seemed like the tide was finally turning for him.

He held on to the card as he raised the stakes in the first and second rounds, bringing the value of the pot up to two million.

'Fuck.' The elderly Asian woman uttered a series of curses, including many in a foreign language, and carefully placed the drawn card onto the green felt. Her immaculately painted, bright red fingernails drew even more attention to her card's abundance of white and lack of black. It was unmistakable.

The ace of spades.

The group let out a collective sigh of regret. Enrico stayed quiet. He couldn't quite understand the other participants' dismay and their murmurs of sympathy. It seemed unusual to pity losers, even if it did just come down to bad luck and not a mistake on their part.

'To your health, four of diamonds,' the hostess said and filled a small shot glass for the loser. The older woman emptied the glass in one go to the round of applause of the group and sat bolt upright.

'The game giveth, and the game taketh away. Supérieur,' uttered the woman and stoically accepted her defeat and the grave loss of funds.

'Supérieur,' repeated the other three solemnly as if they were at a church service.

Enrico was still trying to understand what was happening when the brunette approached the older woman from behind, abruptly placed her hands on her chin and the back of her head and snapped her neck in one swift, powerful motion.

The loud crack made the hair on Enrico's neck stand up. Stunned, he saw the loser topple forward and smash her head into a pile of chips. The discs clacked and clattered as they bounced off the table.

He suddenly felt a gentle blow to the left of his chest, as if his suit had given him an electric shock. But there was nothing electric in it with a battery that could have discharged like that, and he had been forced to hand in his phone. He massaged his aching chest.

'You've just—' Enrico began, unable to hide his distress. He had witnessed a murder right before his very eyes!

'It was the ace of spades, señor,' countered the brunette and straightened her dark-grey dress as if she had only done something mundane like wash her hands. 'The death card. You look surprised. I thought you knew the rules?'

Meanwhile, the dealer took the devastating card and put it into the shuffler machine again along with the remaining deck that the players drew from. Death was back in the game.

The machine indifferently fulfilled its duty, whirring as the cards emptied into the dispensing rack, bottom side up. Doom lurked somewhere in the pile.

The dealer used the chip rake to move the dead woman's chips into the pot and lifted her head to remove the pieces from her forehead and cheek, which he also placed into the centre.

Nobody spoke.

Then the dealer set down the smaller deck on to the table and clasped his hands together in anticipation. 'That brings the new pot total to eight million, four hundred and seventy thousand,' he announced. 'Your stakes, messieurs-dames. This is round three.'

Enrico's heart was beating so hard that he could feel it clanging against his ribcage. He had broken out into a sweat. Every fibre of his body felt like it was on fire as it dawned on him that the lunatics in this room were playing supérieur according to the historical rules. Instead of just losing your stake, you lost your life and all the money you had brought with you. After all, the dead had no use for a fortune. This variation of the game allegedly originated from Russia and had been invented around 1900 as an alternative to Russian roulette, which explained the tension experienced by the remaining players and the concealed relief of those who had already left.

No, he wouldn't play with his life.

'I want to leave the game,' Enrico said and made the move to reveal his own good card. He was tempted by the eight million, and his queen of hearts was by no means worthless, but he didn't want to sit at a table with some people who had lost their will to live and die just because he happened to pick up the ace of spades. He had too much to live for: a wedding with the woman he loved, new business in new countries, new charity projects . . .

'Coward!' The oligarch's son gave a nasty laugh and leaned forward, his Rolex dangling a little too loosely around his wrist. 'I'm raising the stakes.' He reached into his jacket with a grand gesture and retrieved a cigarette case, from which he carefully removed an old playing card wrapped in foil. He then deliberately unwrapped it as slowly as possible and dramatically placed it on top of the collective stack of stakes.

The card depicted a man in ancient dress and a cap, writing. He had one leg resting on a tree stump, his upper thigh serving as a desk for some paper, a quill and an inkwell. He was surrounded by nature; a branch sprawled out above him. It was a German card: the Laub-Ober.

Enrico had been distracted by the game and the horrific incident, but this was the real reason he had come. His passion as a collector stirred inside him.

The oligarch's son gestured to his extra stake. 'This is a hand-coloured, wood-cut Peter Floetner card, made around 1540 and signed by its master.' He pointed to his jacket pocket. 'I've got the certificate with me here,' he said and grinned invitingly. 'Surely you've brought something as well? I heard you had.'

Enrico immediately thought about the unknown caller who had threatened him. The man had said that one of his people would be at the table and would steal his card away from him. In-game.

As if it were magic, the Laub-Ober card captivated Enrico's gaze. It was a unique and centuries-old piece.

He had spent a year searching for it in museums, at auctions, and in private collections.

And now here it was, lying in front of him.

So close.

Within his grasp.

Within his power to win it . . .

The it-girl and the man in the yacht club suit also pulled out historical playing cards, which were added to the total stake of the game in addition to the money.

Enrico took a deep breath and ran his hands through his brown curls. His hair wrapped around his fingers, as if trying to hold him back, to stop him.

But something spurred him on. There wasn't a single herb, magic rose, or anything that grew in his fields in Ecuador that could save him from his gambling nature. He'd lost all reason.

To stay in the game, he reached into his inside pocket and placed his card on the table. 'The seven of clubs, from 1804. It's a hand-coloured, copper engraving using the drypoint method from the very first deck, published by Johann Friedrich Cotta in 1805 as part of an almanac,' Enrico explained, loosening his tie. 'The figures depicted on the card are from Friedrich Schiller's play, *The Maid of Orleans*.' Enrico was sure that the lines on the card were more prominent and distinct than before, as if they had been re-coloured and gone over again in his suit jacket pocket. Perhaps his body heat had affected the card somehow? He unconsciously massaged his aching chest. 'Count me in.'

'Excellent!' The oligarch's son snickered and revealed his card. 'Jack of clubs. That won't do.' He took a new card from the dealer, looked at it and put on a terrible act of being upset before laughing and placing it face down in front him. 'I've got an ace of clubs. That's got to be the highest card.' He threw it into the round and smirked. 'Does anyone fold?'

The provocation had worked: both the it-girl and the man in the yacht club suit stayed in the game for the chance to get their hands on the historical artefacts. No one called the young Russian's bluff and they continued playing without the death card making an appearance.

There were now lots of discarded cards on the table, both high and low in value.

The it-girl knew that her plunging neckline had lost its allure; she didn't even bother to smile any more. The man in the yacht club suit nervously fidgeted with his card between his fingers. The tension in the room grew. Enrico looked at his queen of hearts in his left hand, and then at the dead Asian woman still lying on the table, killed by the ace of spades. The smell of urine mingled with the air in the room.

He then glanced at the deck from which he had to draw if he didn't believe his card was a safe bet. Would the queen of hearts be enough to win? This was the adrenaline rush that he loved and needed.

Enrico felt clammy. The sweat burned in his eyes and he wiped it away with his shirt sleeve. The expensive cufflink scratched his skin and he felt something sting. He saw blood on the white fabric. Was this a sign?

With a flourish, he discarded his queen of hearts. The card landed face up on the felt table between the others.

'You're throwing away the queen of hearts?' The oligarch's son leaned forward, surprised. His light eyes darkened, turning wicked and furtive. 'Someone's feeling brave.'

Enrico couldn't think straight. His decision could do more than change his life; it could end it. His subconscious told him the ace of spades was near, which slowed the adrenaline rush. 'I . . .'

'A new card, monsieur? From the top or bottom?' the dealer asked, smiling. 'Or would you like to fold, monsieur?'

This was his opportunity to leave the game, but his gambling nature got the better of him. If he gave up now, he would stay alive, but he would lose the historical card.

'What's the matter? What's taking you so long? Are you shitting yourself, *Florecita*?' the oligarch's son tormented.

'How do you know . . .' Enrico began, but he knew the answer. The young Russian was the mysterious caller's minion. Throwing in the towel was no longer an option. He had to win. 'A new card please, from the bottom.'

But as soon as he said it, Enrico knew that he had made the wrong decision. The completely, utterly and irreversibly wrong decision.

The dealer drew the card from the bottom and pushed it towards him. The card quietly and covertly slid across the felt.

Enrico knew it was the ace of spades: the card practically oozed death. All that was left was seeing it with his own eyes. The thrill of the game faded, and his conscience scolded him for getting involved. He gently reached out, grasped the left corner of the card and closed his eyes, praying desperately that fate would deal him another card. Then he turned it over.

'Yes! Florecita has lost!' the oligarch's son cried out in delight. The it-girl and the man in the yacht club suit expressed their regret with sympathetic applause.

Enrico lifted his eyes and stared at the death card. His wish had not come true.

He suddenly felt his own lust for life fight against the absurdly lethal rules of the game. Unlike the Asian woman, he had no intention of having his neck snapped by the Botoxed brunette who was currently pouring out some schnapps.

His fiancée, his wedding, his parents, his charity projects and his business deals ... There were so many good reasons not to die, and losing a game of supérieur certainly didn't outweigh them.

'To your health, ten of diamonds,' said the hostess and approached him with the shot.

'No.' Enrico stopped her. He got up very slowly and pushed the chair back. 'I'm sorry, but I'm not going that far. You can keep the money and the card, but I'm not dying for a game. No one will ever find out about this. You have my word.'

The table was silent.

The brunette held out the tray to him invitingly. 'You knew the rules.'

'There was never any mention of *this* version of the game.'

'This is the *only* correct version,' she countered. 'Everyone who plays with us knows that.' This earned her a couple of nods from the it-girl and the man in the yacht club suit. 'You were informed of this in advance and could have left the game when you discarded your queen of hearts,' she said and pushed the tray towards him.

Enrico angrily shoved it out of the way. The glass clinked, landed on the table and shattered. The alcohol spilled over the chips, the old cards and the felt. 'Give me an additional fine,' he said, glancing at the tempting weapons in the tray and loosening his tie even more. He was finding it hard to breathe. 'Then it's settled, and I can go.'

'That's not how it works,' the it-girl interjected in a sickly-sweet voice. 'Otherwise, what would be the point? A death card is a death card.'

'The game giveth, and the game taketh away,' added the man in the yacht club suit.

'There, you see,' the brunette said. She picked up the empty tray with one hand and tucked it under her arm. 'You picked up the ace of spades, señor.'

'And oh did Florecita have it coming!' the oligarch's son shouted spitefully. 'We play by the rules, señor. I'd be in the same boat as you if I had picked up the death card. Supérieur!'

Enrico was revolted by the young man and his little speech in support of his death. 'You're all insane!' he cried out. There was only one way to save himself. His eyes darted between the brunette, the dead woman and the two pistols.

'And yet you stayed,' the hostess stated calmly.

He needed the chip card to get out of the room. He couldn't predict how the it-girl or the man would react, but he knew that the oligarch's son would definitely intervene if he tried to escape; that bully was desperate to see Florecita's head roll. Enrico could use the chair and throw it at the Russian, which would give him enough time to push the hostess out of the way and grab the guns.

'Señor, relax.' The brunette spoke in a soothing voice, smiling. She seemed to sense what was troubling him. 'We'll find a solution.' She rested her left hand on his upper arm. 'This happens sometimes when people are suddenly faced with the ace of spades. Don't blame yourself. You're not a failure.'

Enrico hadn't felt like a failure. He had felt like a sane, rational person among a group of insane, suicidal gamblers. The voice in his head berated him incessantly for the mess he had got himself into.

He accepted the implied offer for him to leave the game with a friendly smile. He wouldn't let another opportunity like the one he had had with the queen of hearts pass him by. 'As I said, you can keep my money and the card,' he reiterated. The loss of the Laub-Ober card pained him, but he would have given a hundred of them in exchange for his life. 'I won't tell anyone anything about what I saw.'

'Of course, señor. We'll discuss the fine outside.' The brunette turned to the side slightly to make way for him. 'Come with me. I'll escort you out.'

Enrico took one last look at the dead Asian woman as he was leaving. The it-girl and the man in the yacht club suit didn't spare him another glance. 'How will you explain the body?'

'We have our ways, and good connections. People often fall downstairs and break their spine,' she replied casually, 'or the occasional larynx.'

There was no way Enrico could have anticipated her attack. The thin edge of the tray slammed into his neck, followed by a gristly crack.

Enrico immediately couldn't breathe. He managed two or three steps before collapsing onto the table, gasping. The historical cards swam before his clouding eyes, as if the colours had deepened again. The card's contours, details, everything was crystal clear. Every drop of life that he lost, the card seemed to absorb.

'The game giveth, and the game taketh away. Supérieur,' he heard the brunette say.

'Supérieur,' the trio repeated as Enrico choked and slid from the table onto the floor, writhing. Chips clattered around him. Desperate for help, he thrust his fingers into a trouser leg and clung on to a high heel.

No one came to his rescue.

* * *

Baden-Baden, Baden-Württemberg,
the Federal Republic of Germany

Tadeus jogged down from the small slope onto the cobbled street at a gentle pace before veering into the quiet pedestrian zone, just as he had done every morning for the last four years. Neither rain nor darkness, heat nor ice stopped him from sticking to his routine. His feet had been rising and falling for almost an hour, despite the pain in his right knee; a sign of old age he knew all too well.

He had been running up and down, through Baden-Baden, through parks, streets, alleyways and across squares since nine o'clock. Tadeus felt comfortable during the uphill stretches, where other fifty-year-olds would have slowed down or given up. In between the jogging, he did sprints and push-ups, undeterred by his arthritis.

Sweat trickled through his finger-length, dark-brown hair, which was streaked with silver. He was beginning to develop a white patch at the back of his head. Tadeus needed the exercise, the endorphins and the sweet pain that came with it, to kick-start his day – as well as the distraction.

There was a time when he had almost become a decathlete, but his abilities only served him for a few years in the German Federal Armed Forces before life had other plans for him.

Apart from the wear and tear of his joints and the occasional back pain, he was still in great shape. Behind the glass of the hotel windows, people were having breakfast, some of them staring after him. They would most likely have described him as an inconspicuous type, not exactly tall or slim. There was nothing in particular that set him apart from the crowd – not his face, his height or his build. They would forget about him in a second if Tadeus wanted them to, but, should a situation arise at his work, he could also establish a presence that commanded respect.

Tadeus ran past the still-closed luxury shops in his cheap running clothes. Behind the barred windows lay jewellery and watches that he hadn't been able to afford for a long time. When he wasn't exercising, he wore a chunky silver chain around his neck: a memory of his first big win at a card tournament and a small reminder of a time when he could still afford luxury. Back then he had been one of the super-rich, and then one of the super-in-debt, followed by divorce, bankruptcy and rehab. Now he was clean and poor.

He took another turn, ignoring the stab of pain in his left ankle. He ran past more hotels and over a bridge with slippery wooden planks, welcoming the balance exercise.

Apart from him, there were only a few people out in the cold, wet weather. Drops of sweat ran down his three-day stubble and got caught in the short, trimmed beard that ran around his chin and lower jaw.

Baden-Baden's city centre was no place for the poor, but Tadeus' employer was kind and provided him with a small, one-bedroom apartment, which he now approached.

His breathing steadied and he returned to a light jog.

Soon he was standing on Schiller Street in front of the entrance to his little residence, which consisted of one main room, a kitchen and a bathroom. The good thing about the old building was its high ceilings: they were almost four metres high in his sixty-square-metre room, which gave the impression that he was not entirely destitute.

Tadeus started doing his stretches, realising once again that he was no longer a young man. At that moment, his phone rang. He pulled it out from his jacket to take the call from his daughter, a beautiful, German-Japanese young woman.

She must have got her blood test results back. His anxiety for her wellbeing caused his heart to leap into his mouth, but he wouldn't let it show. 'Konnichiwa, Michiko.'

'Hi Dad,' she replied. She refused to speak Japanese with him, because even as a *gaikokujin* – a foreigner – he knew the language better than her, despite her having been raised by a Japanese woman. 'Is this a good time?'

'Of course, give me ten seconds.' Tadeus unlocked the front door and took three steps at a time until he reached the third floor. He then walked through the door of (what he liked to call) his temporary home. His knee burned from the strain. 'Fire away.'

It still smelled of drying laundry and the goulash he had cooked himself yesterday. Although he wasn't allowed to hang up laundry in his flat, Tadeus was sure keeping his windows open would keep the damp out of the room.

'I've just come back from my doctor's appointment,' Michiko began. She sounded calm and collected. 'Everything's come back fine so far, you don't need to worry.'

'That's great!' he said, feeling immense relief. He kissed his middle and index finger before pressing them to the picture of a fishing ship hanging in the hallway next to the corridor leading to the bathroom: his ship. He'd managed to save it from the bailiffs by signing it over to a friend, just as he'd done with a cottage.

For Tadeus, it wasn't about cheating his creditors out of their money; it was about keeping the things that mattered, even if he hadn't seen them for years. He gave every other cent that he earned, and didn't spend on making ends meet, to the banks.

'You can never be too careful. The sooner they find signs –' Tadeus broke off. 'No, I never want them to find any signs. Ever.'

He stood in front of his debt calendar and crossed off another day on it: there were seven hundred and one days left, along with the two and a half million euros that he still had to pay back to various people and banks. This knowledge and the fact that life had given him a second chance made him feel grateful.

Tadeus cleared his throat. 'How's the job? I heard that Christian quit. Are you guys going to be okay? I mean, with the house and all . . .'

'It'll be tight, but we'll figure it out.' He heard someone call her name in the background. 'We have to go, it's our friends' first baby shower. Bye!'

'Bye, Michiko, and –'

She hung up.

Tadeus studied the photo of the cutter in the harbour. The ship symbolised his perseverance and was his antidote for when he wanted to give up, for the despair and darkness that often crept into his soul. He would get back on his feet, shed the self-imposed burden that he had acquired due to his own irrational behaviour, and sail away in his ship. He'd see the Baltic, the North Sea, coasts and countries; he would travel in peace and see the world with a clear head.

His resolution to do so was no accident. He had spent many years in a drug-induced haze and his time had blurred together as if it were no longer his own. Sometimes the only way of knowing where he'd been was by the colourful stamps in his passport, his visas, tickets or old hotel bills.

'But I snapped out of it,' Tadeus murmured pensively, then

stripped down and got into the shower. *Only I should have done so sooner.*

The warm water washed away the sweat from his skin as his mind drifted to the past.

He always anticipated surprises from his other life. Tattoos adorned his body, the origins of which he couldn't remember: a black Pac-Man on his left shoulder, which he had then had turned into a skull; the abbreviation 'NIN' on his right chest for the band Nine Inch Nails, despite him never having particularly liked them; a small Buddha on his right butt cheek, and, for whatever reason, an unknown Indian god on his left calf. He had kept the tattoos as a reminder. Tadeus had also learned different languages during those strange, dark times, but he couldn't remember which courses he had taken.

Sometimes this buried knowledge jumped out at him like a jack-in-the-box and got him into bizarre, funny and embarrassing situations, like the time when he had inadvertently overheard two female casino guests from Abu Dhabi discussing in Arabic the length of their husbands' penises. Until that moment, he hadn't even known that he understood Arabic.

And Tadeus had a feeling that he knew other languages, too.

He turned off the water and stepped out of the shower. Once he popped two painkillers and wrapped an orthopaedic bandage over his worn-out knee, his day could start. Tadeus was technically supposed to wear it while jogging, but he hated the thing.

He spent the next few hours food shopping and building a shoe shelf, which he had treated with wood stain and designed to look old to better match the flat. He still had eight pairs of handmade shoes from his wealthier days that nobody had wanted to take from him. Although the shoes were worth a great deal, they were made to measure, and therefore useless to anybody else.

Tadeus looked after the shoes and polished them regularly so that the leather remained smooth. The cobbler had given him a lifetime guarantee, but not on the soles of the shoes, just on the upper material. When the day came, he would have them put in his coffin. Every pair. Until then, the masterpieces would live on his new shelf.

Then Tadeus decided to do some online research about the latest card cheating tricks, on who the high rollers were and who in particular were known for spending their money like water. This kind of information was all very useful in his job.

He also happened to come across some news about two deaths in Monaco. After suffering substantial losses, a player named Marstella Suarez had apparently thrown herself off a hotel roof. The other player had died in a shower accident after a long night. *Unlucky in cards and in life*, Tadeus thought.

The names of the victims meant nothing to Tadeus, but according to the tabloids Enrico Pedro García Hermano, the man who had died in the shower accident, was a rich businessman who had made a fortune from selling stem roses and had intended to marry soon. There were photos of his fiancée, who worked as a doctor in London. She was of Asian descent and oddly reminded him of his own daughter. A few water stains, a slippery bathmat, a drop of shower oil . . . Something had pulled the plug on the man's life, leaving his fiancée behind. The unpredictability of life was something Tadeus could also relate to. At least, as far as he could remember.

At around half past nine he put on his dark suit, some subtle aftershave and his pair of understated, black reindeer-leather shoes. He then made his way to his workplace. The painkillers had worked and the bandage sat perfectly.

As always, the tingling sensation intensified the closer he got to the striking building.

Tadeus looked forward to the atmosphere, the sound of the

bouncing roulette balls, the rattling of the card shuffler machines, the smoke of cigarettes in the separate gaming areas, the clinking of ice cubes in people's drinks, the regretful groans and the cheerful laughter of the players, and the click-clack of the playing chips: everything that makes a casino a casino.

He'd been standing on the other side of the table for four years now.

Hypnosis, therapy, discipline and excessive exercise had not completely freed him of his gambling addiction, but it had at least stopped him from gambling away thousands upon thousands of euros.

Tadeus saw his job as an incessant test, as a way of becoming inured to what had ruined him, his life, his love and his marriage. Just as allergy sufferers could become desensitised, he wanted to become immune to the lure of happiness. He had managed to resist so far.

His therapist had warned him and pointed out the risks, which were significantly higher with him working close to the card tables. After all, a recovered alcoholic wouldn't work in a distillery.

But Tadeus took the risk anyway. He trusted himself and his willpower. If he could resist temptation until the end of his insolvency period, he could do anything.

If he failed to resist, he would gamble away his dream of a round trip on his boat in the flip of a card.

Tadeus went upstairs, turned right, walked through the entrance and waved to his colleagues in the registration area, who returned his greeting. He then marched through the two long salons and entered the security area through a discreet panel door, which unlocked after a buzz. The cameras had already recognised him, and announced his arrival.

Numerous devices located in corners and on ceilings surveilled the rooms and corridors of the casino. Only the toilets remained private. Images were gathered at the head office to provide video evidence in the case of betting disputes. They were also used to keep an eye on cheating players in poker, card counters in blackjack and skilled pickpockets who fished out chips from inattentive guests' pockets.

'Ah, Mr Boch,' Alexa said in front of the monitor wall. The blonde in her mid-forties had her hair up and wore a dark suit like the rest of the staff. 'Our best security guard has arrived.'

'Don't exaggerate or there's bound to be trouble,' Tadeus replied and made a shushing gesture. The rest of the security guards grinned. He was handed his equipment, which he put on. Like everyone else, he kept in touch with the head office via an earpiece and a hidden radio transmitter on his wrist.

Alexa stood up and Fred, another staff member, took her place. She gave Tadeus a tablet, nervously fiddling with her pearl earring. 'This is the VIP guest list for tonight.'

He skimmed the names and the planned groups. 'Don't play with it or we'll be in for a messy evening,' Tadeus teased.

There was a hen do and a stag party of around twenty people each, plus half a dozen high rollers, a registered delegation from Japan that had been invited by their business partners, and four Hollywood bigwigs who were shooting their latest blockbuster nearby and had decided to take a short detour. They blended in with the usual weekend customers.

'It'll be tight, but we'll manage,' Tadeus said, turning to look at his boss. 'Was there anything else?'

'My earring oracle reckons there could be. A hotel owner reported the arrival of some people from the US who have attracted some attention by repeatedly winning poker tournaments in Las Vegas. Big winnings. I reckon they work as a team. They'll either try to target our VIP guests, or there's a private round happening elsewhere in the city. I hope it's the latter.' Alexa swiped her finger across the tablet screen. The faces of a young couple captured by a security camera appeared. 'These two are currently sat in the bar. Security say they're both skilled pickpockets. We haven't been able to prove anything yet. Keep an eye on them. If we catch them, we'll have something to celebrate.'

'Got it.' Tadeus memorised the couple's faces. 'Should I ask them to leave after the first incident?'

'No. Let's see how far they go.'

'Boss. Trouble at AR4,' Fred reported from the monitors. 'There's a stake dispute. An old housewife is arguing with a young housewife.' He ran the footage from American roulette table four backward and zoomed in on the hands. It was clear from the rings and the wrinkles who had placed the deciding chip. 'The older one is entitled to the winnings.'

'Will you go?' Alexa asked Tadeus. 'You can take care of the couple afterwards.'

Tadeus nodded, left the head office through the panel door and took a detour to the American roulette table so that the pickpockets at the bar wouldn't see him and suspect anything. He kept a low profile as he walked through the casino. His average stature played to his advantage. Nothing was to interfere or distract the uninvolved guests from having a nice evening.

As a former professional gambler, he knew all the tricks, especially when it came to blackjack and poker, which proved very valuable to casino operators. No training could compare to the experience that people like him possessed. Tadeus had exposed a few cheats before. Subtly and discreetly.

He reached table four and positioned himself next to the ladies, who were dressed in evening attire, as was appropriate even if they weren't wearing luxury brands.

'Excuse me, please,' he said and calmly asked them to step aside. He was polite but firm as he explained what the cameras had seen.

The younger woman appeared baffled but didn't go against Tadeus' word and left her opponent the eight chips worth two euros each.

Tadeus looked at the green plastic discs that the older lady proudly threw into her handbag. She left with a triumphant expression on her face as if she had just won a war and headed towards the next table. To soothe her frustration, the younger one turned to the bar to order a drink.

The two players had fought over sixteen euros, most probably more out of principle than money.

Sixteen euros.

That had been the price of one glass of vodka at a tournament somewhere in Russia. Twenty millilitres of it. He had forgotten the exact location thanks to the drugs.

'Crisis averted,' Tadeus reported and remained with his back to the wall in the hall. He merged into the surroundings and soaked up the atmosphere.

The casino rooms gradually filled up with eager players and curious guests. As Tadeus had predicted, it would be crowded, but not overwhelmingly so. The suspected thieving couple hadn't gone on the prowl yet and were still at the bar, emptying cocktail after cocktail as if they were glued to their seats. Either they suspected that they were being watched, or they were still sounding things out.

'Tadeus, please go to poker table two,' came the instruction from Alexa. 'We've got a young oligarch who doesn't want to accept our limit.'

'Copy that,' Tadeus replied. He set off, gliding through the crowd without brushing past a single guest. 'What should I do?'

'Explain the rules to him again, and, if he doesn't cooperate, get him out of here,' she said. 'But do it nicely. That's Vladimir Mikhaïlovich Lazarev, the son of Mikhail Alexandrovich

Lazarev. Mikhail's wife comes here often and if she attends the festival . . .'

'Understood.' Tadeus approached the crowded poker tables, which were separated from the adjacent roulette playing area by a rope in the middle of the room and several glass windows. The initial buy-in – the so-called entrance fee – was 250 euros. Judging by the stack of chips, the blinds were already fairly high.

Tadeus immediately recognised who was causing trouble out of the four players at table two. The dark-haired young man sat in his chair with his arms folded behind his head and insulted the helpless, overwhelmed dealer in Russian. Due to the young man's clever intonation, it sounded like an argument. The Russian's designer sunglasses rested on his hairline; his extravagant, high-end suit must have cost him several thousand euros, but money by no means granted people good manners.

'*Dobryĭ vecher,*' – 'good evening' – Tadeus said in an overly friendly manner. He shifted his posture to better present himself. Occasionally it was important to make his presence known.

Lazarev spun his head around and glared at him with his pale grey eyes. '*Danunakh! Der'movshchik!*'

Roughly translated, Lazarev had greeted Tadeus by saying, 'You've got to be kidding me! You bloody toilet cleaner!'

Tadeus had a feeling that this time a friendly escort out wouldn't be possible, no matter whose rebellious offspring the troublemaker was.

Fate shuffles the cards and we play.
                    Arthur Schopenhauer (1788–1860)

II

'That's a Beretta 21A Bobcat, Miss Poe,' the man explained in an experienced manner, the pistol lying in front of him on the glass table of the hotel room. The white polo shirt paired with his chequered trousers made him look like a golfer; a small moustache the same colour as his light blond hair sat on his nondescript face. 'It's only the size of a palm, discreet and holds seven shots in the clip, plus an extra one in the barrel if you load it beforehand. You cock the pistol, release the safety, aim, and pull the trigger. The Beretta reloads automatically.' His strong finger pointed at the compact, ugly weapon. The oily black Beretta gleamed. 'Be careful, the empty cartridges are ejected up and backward. They're meant to fly over whoever is operating it, but you could get hit in the face or the neck. The metal is quite hot.'

Hyun was wearing a hotel bathrobe and sitting in an armchair opposite him. She had forgotten when Andreotti was supposed to be coming over to deliver the gun and his findings, and when she'd heard the doorbell go she'd been forced to step out of her suite's shower and quickly grab a bathrobe.

Hyun leaned forward and reached for the Bobcat. The serious expression on her face reflected by the table startled her. Her shoulder-length black hair felt heavy and was glossy like a shadow, her cheeks had sunk and made her Asian features look somewhat skull-like. The stimulants and mood-enhancing tablets she had taken kept her hunger at bay. She'd have to cover up her scrawniness and the countless freckles to avoid drawing attention to herself. Her grief had left clear traces behind.

Yet her plan consumed her. It was the only thing keeping her going and the only thing she could think about.

Her full name and the one she'd assumed after being adopted by her British stepfather was Florence Hyun-Gi Poe. Her tall and extremely thin figure meant that she was no stranger to attention and had started getting looks as a teenager. Despite her wealthy parents, she had worked as a hostess at events and taken up some small modelling jobs to fund her studies. After a few years, she stopped doing both, escaped the circus of superficiality and graduated from medicine with top marks. She began working as a doctor to help others, which was what she had wanted to do since she was a child. She chose the name Florence, after her big role model, Florence Nightingale, but also because it was easier for Europeans to pronounce than her Korean name. Her personal preference was the abbreviated version of her actual name, Hyun.

This evening, however, the thirty-year-old wasn't concerned about helping others or doing good in the world.

For her, there was only the plan.

Hyun weighed the semi-automatic pistol in her hand and found it to be surprisingly light. She could easily conceal it in the side compartment of her handbag or tape it to the inside of her thigh. Her legs were thin and there was enough space for her to hide the weapon without it getting in the way of her walking. No one would notice a thing.

'Thank you,' she said and placed the Beretta back onto the small table. 'Shall we talk through your findings again, Signor Andreotti?'

'Of course, Miss Poe.' The detective she had hired to shed light on the case handed her some printouts, which included a police report, an autopsy report and witness statements. 'As I mentioned in my last email, the police in Monaco believe it was an accident. These are all the documents and copies that I could acquire.' He rubbed his moustache several times, as if the fair hairs recharged his batteries. 'At first glance, it seems plausible: your fiancé slipped on the wet floor after getting out of the shower in his suite. He then hit his neck on the edge of the bathtub, fractured his larynx and suffocated.'

Hyun followed his words, transfixed.

It sounded absurd. Surreal. One moment she had wished Enrico a nice evening while pouring over her books and patient files because she knew how much he had been looking forward to Monaco, and the next . . .

He was gone for ever.

'Housekeeping found him the next day,' Andreotti went on. 'There were no signs of violence, struggle, or a break-in.' He flicked through the pages and pointed to the relevant records. 'On the same evening, 61-year-old Marstella Suarez threw herself off the roof of one of the high-rise buildings on the lower promenade. She was known to be an ambitious gambler and the employees at the casino described her looking devastated that evening. She had lost a large sum playing blackjack. Hence, the police suspected that it was suicide.'

'But?' Hyun asked hollowly.

'It's not a real *but*; my research established that your fiancé was at the Buddha Bar, where he was escorted out by a young lady.' Andreotti picked out a photo. 'That's her: Ekaterina Solov'ëva. She's the daughter of Maksima Dimitrivna Solov'ëva. They organise private events, the theme of which is decided by their wealthy clients. Previously, they only operated in Russia, but now it appears they follow rich Russians wherever they go.

The events include rounds of card games with exceptionally high stakes. When I did a bit more digging, I found out that Marstella Suarez had also been accompanied by Solov'ëva. Now both of them are dead. That's a pretty extraordinary coincidence, but nothing further can be done without any supporting evidence.'

Hyun took the printout from the detective and stared at Solov'ëva and her mother, who had clearly undergone some very good plastic surgery. 'She has to tell me what happened that night,' she said quietly.

'One of the Solov'ëvas does. I'm afraid I don't know yet who else took part in the round, otherwise I would have done more research.' Andreotti gathered the documents into a respectable pile. 'What makes you so sure that your fiancé's death wasn't an accident, Miss Poe?'

'We had an understanding that he would always call me as soon as he got home from a game,' Hyun explained in almost a whisper. Her eyes stung and tears welled up in them, blurring her vision. 'He never forgot that, no matter how ecstatic, drunk or devastated he was afterwards.' She picked up the Beretta. 'This was the first time I heard nothing. The first time he didn't call. It's never happened before, and that's why' – she looked directly at him – 'I don't believe it was an accident. Something happened in that card game that cost him his life. Maybe it was another player, or maybe it was the two women who organised it.' She cocked the pistol. 'Whatever or whoever it was, I'm going to find out.'

'I've written down the address of where the private tournament in Baden-Baden is due to take place on the last page of the document. I wouldn't rule out the possibility of you meeting people there who were at the same table as your fiancé in Monte Carlo.' Andreotti stood up and took the brown envelope that had his name on it from the table. 'Thank you, Miss Poe.'

'Thank *you*, Signor Andreotti,' Hyun countered and slowly

slid the hammer forward. She didn't look at the detective. 'I trust you'll find your own way out.'

From the corner of her eye, she saw him bow briefly and leave the suite.

Hyun put the Bobcat on the table and paused for a few minutes, going over her plan; it was the only thing on her mind. Then she left her chair and slipped out of her bathrobe.

As she walked through the bathroom, she saw how much weight she'd lost in the reflection of the mirrors and tiles. She had never been a particularly skinny woman before, but now her ribs, joints and bones jutted out. Sadness had replaced her appetite, but she forced herself to eat small snacks, drink lots of water, and take her pills to stop herself collapsing altogether.

She no longer felt at home in her own body.

Hyun had learned a lot from her grandmother, who, like many Koreans, followed the old beliefs. Her grandmother had helped people as a mudang, a shaman and a medium between the spirits and the living.

Hyun had also tried turning to traditional methods, but nothing came of her praying, meditating and summoning of the spirits. She helped people in hospital to lead a better life every day, but failed when it came to alleviating her own pain.

During her childhood in South Korea, she'd taken lessons in tae kwon do – the country's national sport. But even hours of training, exercise and pain didn't help her. All that remained was medication, which as a doctor she had easy access to. And her plan. Her plan would cure her.

She put on the underwear she had laid out and attempted to attach the Beretta to her inner thigh, managing it after a few goes

Suddenly, a new wave of fatigue overwhelmed her. Hyun lowered herself into a chair and stared at her glass of water.

She'd take the stimulants just before she set off, when she knew she'd have to keep her wits about her.

The soft cushions tempted her to close her eyes for a moment, to mentally decompress and gather her strength. She leaned back, breathed deeply and tried to relax.

Small white dots swirled and expanded in the darkness behind her eyelids. A flurry of trickling, dancing cards surrounded her, the motifs of which appeared old, despite Hyun not being able to recognise them very clearly. She could hear a man's voice, soft yet urgent. She recognised the language as German, and his tone was threatening and dangerous.

Hyun's breathing quickened. She wanted to open her eyes, but they remained glued together. The nightmare had dragged her into its world.

Whispers encircled her, and suddenly all but one of the swirling cards disappeared. It floated around in the darkness with its back to her, and she saw her own hand reach for it and turn it over: it was that hateful seven of clubs that her fiancé had brought back from an auction.

She quickly flipped the card over again so it was face down, and heard Enrico call out her name.

'Where are you?' she asked, spinning around in every direction, searching for him in the dark, but there was nothing except the seven of clubs.

'Turn the card over again,' she heard him say in a muffled voice.

'Why?'

'If you manage to turn it over again two times, I'll be free. I'll come back to you,' he promised. 'Save me, Hyun! Please!'

Her fingers reached for the seven of clubs again. She grabbed the card by its bottom right corner and turned it over, but a flash of molten silver stopped her from seeing its motif. What was that?

She moved closer to the card. The liquid silver flickered and faded to black, making the card almost invisible. 'Enrico? What do I do?'

'Hyun, run! Run!' he shouted from nowhere. 'Or else he'll kill you! He'll kill you!'

'Enrico!' she cried out, furious. She sensed the presence of something evil in the darkness. 'Enrico, you need to—'

Hyun heard a shrill scream. A death cry. At that very instant the card flared up in front of her, sending countless arms of liquid mercury flying towards her. Clawed fingers grasped at her and loud, inhuman howls and moans broke out. The hands seized her, nails sliced her open and blood trickled onto the card, which only made the terrible sounds grow louder.

'Run!' Enrico yelled. 'Save yourself! Run!'

Hyun's eyes flew open. She sat bolt upright in the hotel arm-chair, panting and sweating. The glass of water was still in front of her, and she was still in the suite. The silence felt almost unbearable compared to the howls and moans in her subconscious.

She had had such nightmares before; they'd haunted her for several weeks. Enrico had laughed and said it was childish to be afraid of a playing card, but even after his death the horrifying images continued to torture her.

The plan, she forced herself to think, and managed to push the last memories of the nightmare to the back of her mind and calm her breathing. *The plan. Today. Pull yourself together.*

Hyun got up, showered again and began her preparations to forget the nightmare.

She chose a knee-length, black dress with a slit and match-ing gloves that went up to her elbows, put on some understated earrings and a necklace, and slipped on a pair of flat shoes. She might have to move quickly, and that would prove difficult in high heels.

Her make-up served as a mask for her face. Hyun painted on a healthy complexion; the large sunglasses concealed most of her striking features. She swallowed two pills to stay awake and tucked her hair under a short, black wig. The Bobcat was loaded and strapped to her body.

Before heading out the door, she took a good look at the photos of Solov'ëva, Solov'ëva's mother, and of the hosts of this secret, private, VIP tournament. She looked up the address in the documents.

An online map of the street claimed that a former private hotel, the Belle Époque, used to be located at the address Andreotti had given her. A further search revealed that it was now closed for renovation. It was the perfect spot for a tournament – slap-bang in the middle of beautiful Baden-Baden, but away from prying eyes.

She kissed her engagement ring, picked up her handbag and walked through the suite. Her heart began to race, but she felt numb. Determined. She left the nightmare behind in the suite and hoped it would all end after this evening.

Fuelled by stimulants, she stepped out into the hallway and headed for the lift. Personal invitation or not, Hyun would find a way into the Belle Époque and ask the Solov'ëva family about her fiancé's death. At gunpoint if necessary.

As was her plan.

* * *

Tadeus bent down to the young oligarch's son. 'I'm sure you real-ise you're not dealing with a toilet cleaner,' he replied in Russian, smiling. It was another language that he must have learned at some point. 'Unfortunately, I must inform you that the limit cannot be raised if you're the only party that wishes to do so, Mr Lazarev.'

'The rest of them are pussies,' the young man remarked snidely, looking at the stack of chips. His head was clean-shaven except for the very back, where his black hair was tied into a ponytail at the nape of his neck. 'They don't understand the game. They don't get what poker's all about. It's about pushing boundaries. Taking risks.' He put on his sunglasses defiantly.

Tadeus knew exactly what he meant. He had been no different back then, only he had pushed his boundaries too far and hit rock bottom. Too much risk and too much arrogance. 'I'm pleased you see it that way, but the rest of the table do not.' He turned to the other players apologetically. 'Forgive me, ladies and gentlemen, the round will resume shortly.'

'No, it won't. Not until the limit is raised,' Lazarev interjected, grinning from ear to ear at the others. He tapped his golden Rolex with his finger, as if to show the others that they needed to hurry up. 'What's the matter with you all? I'll lend you pussies the money.'

'Okay, that's enough,' Tadeus heard his boss's voice say in his ear. 'It's time to kindly escort him out.' Alexa had realised that a peaceful solution wouldn't be possible. Moreover, the cocky Russian was spoiling the atmosphere of the round for everyone else. 'Be nice.'

Tadeus pointed at the chips. 'Mr. Lazarev, would you be so kind as to bring your stake with you and come with me?'

'Why?'

'We've prepared another table for you. A separate one, where there won't be a limit.'

Lazarev stared at him. His boyish face suddenly twisted into an expression of anger, his sunglasses only adding to the effect. The Russian leapt to his feet.

Tadeus didn't bat an eyelid. He slowly stood up to his full height, no more than a hand shorter than the oligarch. 'Thank you very much for agreeing to accompany me.'

'I know what's going on,' Lazarev hissed and stuffed the

plastic chips into the pockets of his expensive suit. 'You want to throw me out.'

'Not at all, there's only been a misunderstanding,' Tadeus countered and looked at him with a smile. The relief on the remaining players' faces was unmistakable. 'You'll see.'

'I'll call your boss over,' Lazarev said threateningly. He moved away from the poker area and proceeded to walk towards the blackjack table. 'I'll play here.' He pushed his sunglasses back onto his forehead and untied his ponytail. His shoulder-length black hair fell over his undercut.

Tadeus took a deep breath. 'Alexa?' he asked the central office discreetly through his microphone. 'Are we letting the kid play?'

'No. Get him out,' came the order. 'If he keeps acting like this, he'll cause another fight. It's too crowded. We can't have him causing havoc with so many guests around.'

'Roger that.' Tadeus drew closer to the oligarch's son. 'Come this way please,' he said and used his body to gently push him into the gold-leafed hall with its four American roulette tables and steer him towards the exit.

'I'm not going anywhere!' Lazarev snapped at him and, in a helpless attempt to appear threatening, towered over Tadeus with his muscular physique. 'I have a right to play here!'

'No, you don't,' Tadeus responded casually and discreetly to the outraged young man. He lowered his voice to a murmur to avoid attracting the attention of the other guests. 'I can get your father on the phone, if you like. I'm sure he'll be delighted to hear how much fun you're having here.'

Lazarev's gaze flickered as his arrogance turned to anger. The daddy threat was working; there was nothing he could do.

To save face, the Russian quickly glanced at his polished, luxury watch. 'I'd better be on my way. Besides, I'm bored. There're no risk-takers here.' He turned towards the exit and pushed through the crowd.

'Shall I follow him?' Tadeus asked when he suddenly saw the pair of pickpockets rob Lazarev. They were skilfully pulling out chips from his pockets. He watched with a grin on his face and didn't intervene. The spoilt asshole wouldn't notice anyway. 'Did you see that, Alexa?'

'Yes, I got it on zoom. I'll send Oscar and Ben to grab those two. The police will handle it. Get the boy outside. I still have faith that he'll change his ways.'

Tadeus closed in inconspicuously on the oligarch's son once again. 'You're welcome back any time, Mr Lazarev,' he said. Together they reached the cash register, where Lazarev exchanged his chips for euros. Just as Tadeus had suspected, he hadn't noticed that the thieves had cleaned him out. 'But please respect our limit.'

'*Da, da*,' replied Lazarev. He swore quietly in Russian as he walked through the entrance.

Tadeus stayed close, pausing at the first big door to let the unpleasant guest leave. 'Have a nice evening and bonne chance.'

As soon as Lazarev was outside, he patted his pockets and fumbled around in them frantically. He turned on his heel and walked up to Tadeus, holding his smartphone, hotel card and wallet in his hands. 'I've been robbed!' he cried.

'What are you missing?' Tadeus responded calmly.

'A playing card.'

'You didn't steal it playing poker, did you?' Tadeus asked, amused. 'That would be cheating, and theft.'

'It's not one of yours. It's a historical one. Really old and worth a shit-tonne of money,' Lazarev snarled. 'It's gone. I had it a moment ago.'

'Just a moment,' Tadeus said and turned away. 'Alexa, did the two magpies steal a playing card by any chance?' he checked, quietly enough for the Russian not to catch it.

'No, only the chips.'

Tadeus turned to Lazarev. 'Nothing's been found, but if you give me your number then I'll let you know if the card turns up.'

The young man recited it to him. 'It's not just some old piece of cardboard. It's ... Never mind, I need it back! Today! In exactly *two* hours!'

'We'll keep our eyes peeled for it, but we're busy today. It could have stuck to someone's shoe or got pierced by a high heel ...' Tadeus grinned. 'You should have been more careful.'

Lazarev didn't find this funny. 'I'll wait for two hours in the Equipage dance club over there for your call.' He took a wad of five hundreds from the inside pocket of his suit, counted out five and thrust them into Tadeus' hand. 'Don't forget to ring me! I'll give you ten times that if you find the card.' Then he turned to the right and disappeared around the corner.

Tadeus looked at the money and pocketed it. The creditors would be pleased. He went back into the casino to get back to his actual job, but his gaze instinctively shifted to the floor.

As he walked past the front French roulette table, he saw something flat lying on the ground. It clearly stood out against the carpet pattern. He couldn't say why, but it immediately caught his eye despite everyone else carelessly walking past it. Many players noted down numbers on slips of paper and threw the memory aid away when it disappointed them. It could just be a note.

Then again, it could be the missing card.

Tadeus cautiously made his way through the crowd placing bets around the table. 'Excuse me,' he apologised pre-emptively and bent down. He picked up the small piece of cardboard, which was protected by a thin plastic cover: a card, an old, historical playing card. Its motif showed several people gathered around a dancing bear and playing music. The symbols scattered around the people resembled crosses, of which he counted seven.

He didn't recognise the card's significance, but who would have lost a playing card that evening except for Lazarev?

He smiled and stowed it away. He would get a tidy finder's fee for it, even if he liked the card so much that he was almost tempted to keep it.

'I saw that,' Alexa commented in his ear.

'Don't worry, I'll give it back to that annoying kid in . . .' – Tadeus glanced at his watch and felt very old for doing so – 'exactly one hour and . . . fifty-seven minutes. That oligarch boy will be shitting his pants by then.'

Content, he walked towards the secret panel door.

He had successfully, and, most importantly, silently resolved the situation. The Big Game went on merrily in the rooms: the clacking of balls, shuffling of cards, laughter and groans, and that very particular sound of heaps of jetons being pushed together by dealers because the bank had won, could be heard. There was the clink of glasses, the scent of perfume and traces of cigarette smoke – this was a place of fortune and misfortune.

Tadeus sighed happily, intoxicated by it.

'A coffee would be nice,' he said into his mic.

'Go for it,' his boss replied. 'When you're done, head to the blackjack game at table two. The two Americans I mentioned previously are there. I think they're counting. Will you take care of it?'

Of course he would.

The evening passed smoothly. The pickpockets were taken into custody by the police and the stolen chips had already been exchanged for euros. After the security team had allowed the thieves to rob the young Russian, it was rather disappointing that he would get his money back. Tadeus dialled Lazarev's number after almost two hours.

It took some time for Lazarev to pick up.

'*Da?*'

'Good news: we found your card, Mr Lazarev.'

Lazarev's cry of joy surprised him. 'I can't come right now, but I'll stop by later and pick it up,' the young man spluttered and hung up.

Tadeus glanced at the time. It was almost one in the morning, and his shift was coming to an end. Apart from some Asian visitors who were still stubbornly playing roulette and rejoicing over small victories, most of the customers had left. It didn't look as if Alexa needed him any more, so he headed for the bar.

Tadeus took off his name tag and ordered himself a beer.

'Is this all right?' he asked the head office.

'Of course, you're free to go. Good work as always.'

'I'll stick around for a few more minutes. Just in case anything comes up.' He got a small pilsner and guzzled it down before ordering another. Being vigilant was thirsty work. 'Games and gamblers like to keep people on their toes.'

'Words of wisdom spoken by a man of experience,' Alexa said.

Tadeus refrained from commenting. He pulled the Russian's card from his suit and took a photo of it with his phone. Curious, he scoured the internet for information about its motif, and had to stop himself from taking the card out of its case and touching it.

The search results turned out to be more extensive than he had expected.

It was an old German seven of clubs made in 1804 and issued in 1805 by a publisher named Cotta as part of an almanack. Back then, there had been a little booklet dedicated to card games.

The design was engraved out of copper using the drypoint method and hand-coloured, which made it unique. The various figures on the card represented characters from Friedrich Schiller's play, *The Maid of Orleans*. According to the internet, the idea of filling previously blank counting cards with motifs and incorporating suits in the design was later used by illustrators of satirical card games.

'Well, what do you know,' he said aloud. He was fascinated as he read that the first ever original hand-coloured card sold was supposedly kept in a museum. Tadeus examined and turned over his find. Lazarev junior had evidently acquired this historic, one-of-a-kind piece for a large sum. *But what is he carrying it around for, and why does he need it today? Was it some sort of lucky charm? Something for an illegal tournament?*

He found nothing about the value of the seven of clubs. Besides, as opposed to stamps or coins, there was generally a lack of accurate information about individual cards.

But it definitely wasn't just some ordinary playing card that had become badly worn and had simply been thrown away, used to make fires or its remains repurposed as ointment scrapers in a pharmacy as was mentioned in some online encyclopaedia entries. He kept scrolling and marvelled at what he learned. Despite having been an incessant poker player, he had never bothered with the history of cards before.

Hand-coloured, signed. This card must have been specially made for someone wealthy so that they could amuse others and show the piece off. Perhaps it had been made for the owner of the publishing house or as a gift for a statesman or a nobleman.

'I just got a call from reception,' Alexa's voice sounded in his ear. 'Lazarev's here and wants his card back.'

'Okay,' Tadeus said and got up from the stool. 'I'll go home then.' He smiled at the nearest camera and blew her a kiss.

'See you tomorrow,' she replied.

Tadeus removed his communication pack, which was immediately collected by the man behind the counter, took his beer and wandered off.

The young Russian stood in front of the casino entrance. His hair looked messier than it had a few hours ago, a dark patch adorned his neck and his shirt had been sloppily tucked into the waistband of his trousers. Sex. In whatever place. That was probably why he had sounded so rushed on the phone.

Tadeus took another sip of his beer and held up the historical playing card. There was a part of him that felt sad about giving it up.

'Here you are, Mr Lazarev,' he said in Russian. 'We found it on the floor. There are no signs of any damage.'

Lazarev junior snatched the seven of clubs from him and inspected it hastily. He turned it over several times before sighing in relief. 'Excellent! You've just made my evening.'

'This also belongs to you.' Tadeus pulled out a stack of 500-euro notes amounting to ten thousand from his suit. 'We caught some thieves who robbed you earlier.'

'Keep it,' Lazarev said absent-mindedly as he typed away on his phone. 'You're drinking on the job?'

'I'm off the clock.'

'Perfect.' Lazarev smiled. 'I did a bit of research on you.'

'Oh, so now you're my fan?' Tadeus permitted himself to slip into a more casual tone now that he wasn't wearing his name tag.

'I guess you could say that. You had a remarkable career as a gambler until things got ugly. I think it was the drugs.' He flashed a winning salesman's smile, something he must have learned from his father. 'I have a suggestion: accompany me tonight as my bodyguard.' He pulled out a wad of purple notes from his pocket. 'I'll give you this for your trouble. You have my word.'

'Mr Lazarev, I'm tired and my bed is waiting for me.' Tadeus hadn't the slightest interest in playing chaperone to the spoilt oligarch's son. Still, he pocketed his reward: it was something to feed to the creditors, who never questioned where it came from. 'That's very generous of you.'

Suddenly he was consumed by the thought of risking the sum he had received by chance. He could raise it at the table and buy his way out of his debts two years before the deadline. This was his addiction's shoddy attempt to lure him back into gambling with its feeble excuses. But it would be away from the casino ... 'No one would know,' his addiction purred.

As if that made it any better. He had a feeling that he wouldn't be able to hold himself back. The rush of sitting at the felt table, placing bets, watching and sizing up his opponents, playing game after game, making small talk about strategy ... All until he could make his move and win. Then the feelings of happiness would follow, and the vicious cycle would start all over again.

Tadeus shuddered at the thought. He couldn't let that happen. He finished his beer and turned away to return the glass to the bar.

'Did you know that there are illegal rounds in Baden-Baden?' Lazarev asked suddenly, as if Tadeus' addiction had prompted him to do so. 'They play poker there with no limits. And supérieur.'

Tadeus didn't know what supérieur was. A popular new game or some sort of variation of poker perhaps?

'With historical cards?' Tadeus asked. He paused and turned halfway to face Lazarev. 'I doubt it.'

'No, *for* them. For the historical cards. At least, that's what's happening today in the grand final.' Lazarev fanned himself with the seven of clubs. 'This is my ticket.'

His addiction wheedled. It reminded him how much he could win with the money he had been gifted that no one knew about.

At illegal rounds, nobody cared about existing or self-imposed bans to avoid people from ending up at a casino or a gaming table. No one would ask him a thing. He could simply take a seat, place a bet, and gamble like the Devil himself. And if something went wrong, he had nothing to lose.

But if he won, and won a lot, he could buy his way out. He could say that he had got a private loan, and neither the insolvency administrator nor the creditors would suspect anything . . .

An unexpected internal battle unleashed itself within Tadeus, and he didn't feel prepared for the fight. The addiction leapt at him, enveloping him and teasing him like never before during his years of abstinence. He prepared to open his mouth to say no to the Russian.

'I'll feel much better if you come with me. You'll keep an eye out for anyone who tries to screw me over. With your knowledge and expertise . . .' Lazarev went on, feeding Tadeus' addiction. 'We're talking big sums here.' He glanced at him quickly. '*Really* big sums.'

But Tadeus saw right through him. 'Your father doesn't know what you're up to, does he?'

'What? How—'

'Otherwise you would've had an armada of bodyguards around you. But I think' – Tadeus looked past the Russian and at the street where no one was waiting and no limousine was parked – 'you've got something to prove.'

Lazarev grinned: he'd been caught red-handed. 'You'll get another twenty thousand and ten per cent of whatever I win tonight.' He stretched out his arm. The diamonds on the dial of his Rolex sparkled. 'That way it's entirely in your interest that I do well.'

Tadeus watched himself lift his arm and close his fingers

around the Russian's. *I'm only acting as a chaperone*, he told himself. *Just so he doesn't lose the card again.*

At the same time, he knew that this would be an extreme test for him. It was an illegal round with a wad of cash in his pocket and no questions asked.

His conscience cried out, but his addiction pleaded innocent.

The two men who couldn't be more different from one another shook hands and sealed the deal.

III

Tadeus knew the place he and Lazarev were going. It was very close to his home-away-from-home.

The former Belle Époque was one of the most beautiful private hotels from the Art Nouveau period. It was a chic villa with historic furnishings in the rooms of the main building.

When it was first rumoured that it would be sold to the Arabs, the Russians or an Asian consortium that wanted to demolish the building and rebuild it in Beijing, it had caused quite a stir in Baden-Baden, but it had all turned out to be just that: a rumour. According to the latest gossip, it now belonged to a rich American and would soon be reopened under the name The Villa, but nobody could say for certain. The building was allegedly currently undergoing extensive renovation. Substantial considerations were also being made to the protection of historical monuments.

'Are you sure we're in the right place?' Tadeus asked the young Russian.

'I'm very sure. This is the perfect spot for a private game,' Lazarev confirmed. The young man oscillated between euphoria and anxiety, which didn't exactly inspire confidence. If Lazarev sat down at the poker table in this state, he would lose his chips within two or three rounds. Card sharks ate players like him for breakfast.

They walked down Maria-Viktoria Street and reached the wrought-iron gate. Tadeus' knee ached and he discreetly bent down to adjust the fit of his bandage.

'Do you know the game supérieur?' Lazarev asked as he rang the bell and held the seven of clubs in front of the camera of the control panel. He then tied his hair into a ponytail. His undercut looked both pretentious and rebellious at the same time. A few seconds later, the electric gate swung open. 'Did people play it back in your day? The nineteen-hundred version?'

'No.' Tadeus recognised the entrance hall, the adjoining fireplace room and the breakfast room from inside the villa. He had once picked up a rich Russian from the Belle Époque on behalf of the casino – a high roller who received special treatment. That was when he had noticed the beautiful garden behind the villa, which had a small fountain, a lawn and a narrow gravel path surrounding it. The handsome tree had been cut down after taking a battering in a storm. 'Is supérieur a card game?'

As they walked up the well-maintained path to the steps leading into the building, Lazarev stared at him, astonished. Two men in suits and earpieces stood guard, watching the newcomers with friendly, vague smiles. It didn't look like they let just anyone through. You needed to say the magic word first.

'That surprises me,' Lazarev said.

'My game was poker,' Tadeus replied. This wasn't strictly true. He had also played blackjack when he'd been desperate to satisfy his addiction, and hearing about a new game only sparked curiosity and caused his addiction to rear. Tadeus instantly decided that he wanted nothing to do with supérieur.

But what if it's fun? More fun than poker, the addiction whispered. *The money isn't yours anyway. Just once. It'll be our little secret.*

Tadeus clenched his teeth together tightly.

He couldn't give in. He had a feeling that he wouldn't be able to recover from a setback like this. No, he *knew* he wouldn't be able to. This test was a thousand times harder than walking between the tables at the casino. This time there was no control and no work to be done; this wasn't a protected area where he felt he could control the danger.

'I don't know what I'll play yet,' Lazarev said. 'I was quite lucky with supérieur in Monaco. I wonder if I'll get lucky a second time?'

The large door swung open and a young woman in a dark-grey dress with an enchanting smile emerged between the two guards. Tadeus guessed that she was in her mid-twenties. Her lips looked just as unnatural as her wrinkle-free forehead and her red, pinned-up curls.

'A very good evening to you,' she greeted Lazarev in Russian. 'I'm delighted to see you again.' She then turned to Tadeus and asked in English: 'And you are?'

'This is my escort,' Lazarev replied. 'He's here to support me tonight.'

'At poker by all means, but if you choose to play supérieur again admission is strictly on a one-party-per-card basis,' she explained firmly. 'Those are the rules. No exceptions. Now, if you could please hand over your phones.' She held out her hand. 'And make sure they're switched off, gentlemen.'

Lazarev complied, but Tadeus hesitated.

'You'll get them back as soon as you leave the villa,' the young woman said with a confident smile. 'That's our custom.'

After a second of deliberation, Tadeus turned off his phone and handed it over.

'Thank you,' she said and gestured invitingly to the hall. 'Please come inside and help yourselves to the refreshments in the fireplace room. Unfortunately, all the rounds are currently full. I'm afraid you'll have to wait a little, gentlemen.' She went ahead and they followed her through the entrance. There was no sign of any renovation work taking place.

Both of the adjoining rooms were beautifully and authentically furnished in the Art Nouveau style that at times almost bordered on kitsch. Around a dozen elegantly dressed guests, more men than women, were deep in conversation in soft, hushed tones. English, Russian, French and even Spanish could be heard.

Tadeus poured himself a drink. To be on the safe side, he switched to mineral water after the two small beers he'd had at the casino. He didn't want to lose his inhibitions and be tempted into playing a round. He had to pass this test so that he could show his addiction who was in charge and be able to look at himself in the mirror tomorrow morning as a winner without having touched any cards or chips.

Lazarev picked up a large glass and scanned the vodkas available. All of them were ice-cold. He filled his glass and raised it to Tadeus. *'Den' granënogo stakana!'*

'I'm sorry?' Tadeus asked, unfamiliar with the toast. 'Day of the glass?'

'Day of the faceted glass,' Lazarev corrected him and waved around his own. 'It's actually celebrated in mid-September, but it always makes for a great toast.'

He took a few caviar canapés, which comprised various types of generously spread roe that differed from black, to light and dark red, to grey and pale yellow in colour.

'I'm not sure,' Lazarev said, drinking.

'About what?'

'About what I should play. I'd be happy with poker, but I'm always rather tempted by supérieur. My father would be furious if he knew that.' Lazarev downed the rest of his vodka and spooned a mouthful of caviar from a tin that had been placed on a bed of ice. Then he helped himself to another vodka. 'I think I'll start with supérieur, and if my luck runs out I'll switch to poker. You don't mind waiting, do you?' He looked at Tadeus. 'Do you think you'll play at one of the other tables in the meantime?'

Tadeus' addiction stirred his thoughts like a spark of electricity flashing through his mind. It filled his stomach with butterflies and made his fingertips itch desperately for the cards. Cards, chips, betting, sizing up other players, raising the stakes, winning . . .

'We'll see,' he said evasively. 'It's been a while.'

'You won't have forgotten how. I was very impressed by what I read about you.' As if by magic, Lazarev pulled out another 500-euro note from his seemingly bottomless pocket and thrust it into Tadeus' hand. 'That's for waiting. Just like I'd give a cab driver.'

'Thank you. Oh, I forgot to ask: can I see your card again?'

'Why?'

'I just want to make sure that you haven't lost it again,' Tadeus explained. 'It's such a unique piece.'

Lazarev grinned. 'I'm not losing anything tonight.' He removed it from his suit and handed it to Tadeus. 'But yes, I'm rather fond of it too.'

Tadeus held it in his right hand and marvelled at it one more time. 'Such a shame,' he murmured and reluctantly gave it back to the Russian.

'Cross your fingers for me so that I hold on to it. If you prove yourself valuable at poker, I might gift it to you,' Lazarev said. He then approached the receptionist and quietly asked when a seat might become available at supérieur and if he could speed things up, but she only shook her head. The game's simple rules meant that Lazarev's endless reserves of cash would get him nowhere.

Tadeus found this reassuring.

He wandered around with his glass and studied all the people who had gathered in the centre of Baden-Baden to gamble away enormous sums of money. Millions. Illegally. Unbeknownst to and without the permission of the proper authorities. Tadeus found this both brave and brash in equal measure. Passers-by would just think it was an ordinary party. A VIP demolition party.

Tadeus dimly remembered such evenings and nights. The loss of note after note, until even the players' or their escorts' jewellery was on the table. Car keys, house keys, promissory notes for the overwriting of a yacht . . . Everything and anything was staked to stay in the game.

Tonight's guests were dressed in exclusive and expensive clothes. Some, like Lazarev, had a tendency to show off, whereas others opted for an understated look. None of them would bat an eyelid if they lost a few hundred thousand, or a million or two. It was all about the thrill, the competition, the desire to win and beat your opponents. There was no feeling in the world like casually revealing a full house or four aces.

His own memories of victory stirred something inside him.

The money in his pocket whispered to him longingly, wanting him to place a bet at the table. The venue, the atmosphere, the forbidden aspect and the knowledge that no one could prevent him from raising the stakes too high provoked his addiction further with every heartbeat.

The laughter of players who were busy in various rooms upstairs echoed down the stairwell. Swearing, then applause, and the frequent clink of the chips could be heard. The smell of tobacco wafted through the air. Someone was smoking a cigar.

Tadeus closed his eyes and fought the rising feeling of bliss. *This is just like in the casino*, he told himself again and again.

In moments like this he would have pulled out his phone and looked at photos of his son and daughter, whose lives he had hardly been present for. Their faces grounded him. But since he had been forced to hand in his phone, he had nothing to distract him.

'Well, fancy seeing *you* here,' Tadeus suddenly heard an older man's voice say. 'Good evening, Mr Boch.'

Tadeus looked up in surprise.

He didn't recognise the man in his mid-sixties, who was dressed in fine tweed and looked like a British aristocrat. His features didn't ring any bells, and he definitely would have remembered his bushy, salt-and-pepper whiskers. 'I'm sorry, where do I know you from again?' Tadeus asked.

'Macao.'

'Macao,' Tadeus repeated to give himself a few extra seconds. According to his old plane tickets and bills, he had spent a lot of time there, all under the influence of alcohol and hard drugs. What little he did remember of his time there were blurry snapshots of tournaments, drunken parties and sex. It was how people in a state of hubris celebrated their victories.

'The tournament at Chinese New Year. At the Magnolia,' the man reminded him, astonished. He held out his hand. 'I'm Morgan. Arthur Patrick Morgan. You knocked me out of the tournament with a dead man's hand.'

Tadeus waited for something to click.

'At the VIP tournament. We were the only Europeans there,' Morgan went on. 'Don't you remember? Everyone stared at us like we were aliens. They were all CCP leaders.'

Nothing happened. Nothing clicked. 'Ah, yes,' Tadeus nonetheless replied. The memory lapse was like an ice-cold shower for his flaring gambling addiction. This was what happened when he let his addiction get the better of him: blackouts and strangers who he didn't remember meeting.

'I wondered if you'd be up for a rematch?' Morgan continued. 'Back then you promised we'd have one one day, Mr Boch. We could play at the same poker table. I'm sure Miss Solov'ëva could arrange it.'

It was as if Morgan now poured kerosene over his addiction; his greed ignited as quickly as it had dwindled to a smoulder. It whispered into his ear, telling him that it would be an honour, the proper and the right thing to do. A duel between gentlemen.

'I'm sorry, but I no longer play,' Tadeus said, biting out the words as if they caused him physical pain.

'My goodness! A daredevil like you?' Morgan laughed in disbelief. 'I'll never forget how you outbluffed Huan with just a pair of jacks. He threw away his hand – a full house! Nobody could read their opponents better than you,' he said, smirking. 'But I've learned a lot since then, even if we can't show our faces in Macao anymore. That raid nearly landed us in jail. Hopefully that won't happen here. Miss Solov'ëva is careful.'

Tadeus felt like he was eavesdropping on stories from someone else's life who just happened to share the same name as him again. Nothing the man had said meant anything to him. *Dead man's hand* . . . Vague scraps of memories swam through his mind like fleeting clouds that floated past and dissipated in the sun. He couldn't get a hold on them.

'As I said, I don't play any more,' Tadeus said more firmly this time, saving himself. He nodded towards Lazarev. 'I'm here as a poker advisor.'

'Ah, the little oligarch hired a professional.' Morgan lowered his voice. 'Nothing's sacred to him. Take his money, but don't take him at his word. If there's an opportunity to win, he'll leap at the chance. In supérieur he usually draws three times, as if he's desperate to pick up the ace of spades.'

Tadeus wished he had his phone with him. 'Well, I hope you have a lovely evening.'

Morgan clapped him on the shoulder in a fatherly manner.

'That's a big shame. I was looking forward to our rematch. Another time, perhaps?'

The corners of Tadeus' mouth twisted into a faint smile. His addiction raged inside him, berated and tormented him as his mind anxiously praised him and held its breath. There were too many temptations at the villa. He had to keep his guard up. 'Have a good game.'

'Thank you, I learned from the best – from you.' Morgan bowed briefly and went back to the bar to pour himself a glass of sherry.

Suddenly, something from the back of his mind came flooding back to him, travelling past the layer of drug debris and remains of alcohol.

There were thirty-five casinos in Macao. And he had been to all of them. He remembered the official areas and the VIP rooms where the rich Chinese guests sat; gambling was banned in China. Macao's casinos generated seven times the amount brought in from slot machines and other gambling in Las Vegas, despite the desert city being home to ten times more gaming venues. Two-thirds of Macao's gambling revenue was accrued from backrooms. Organised gangs made good money off them. They laundered money, tricking those who weren't careful, or shook them down afterwards on the streets. It was best not to mess with the Triads – the Chinese organised crime syndicate. They operated in Macao and Hong Kong, and had contacts almost everywhere.

Tadeus vaguely remembered a long conversation that he'd had in Chinese with a man covered in tattoos. It had been about the raid that Morgan had mentioned. He'd been drunk and most likely had all sorts of drugs on him. He should have ended up in jail.

But Tadeus had no memory of what happened afterwards. Another blackout.

Suddenly his eyes fell on an extremely slender Asian woman who was standing at the stairwell door and discussing something in English with Solov'ëva. A loud and heated argument ensued. One of the security guards turned from the door to face the inside of the villa.

Tadeus recognised her face from somewhere. *Where had he seen her? At the casino?*

The tall Asian woman eventually shoved Solov'ëva out of her way and they both went into the fireplace room. 'Who played with Enrico Pedro García Hermano in Monte Carlo?' she shouted, furious.

Hermano's fiancée. The doctor from London. Her name was something . . . Poe.

A faint sheen of sweat glistened on her upper lip. A pair of sunglasses covered her eyes. 'Solov'ëva organised the tournament, and Enrico died soon after it. Just like Marstella Suarez, she took part in it too!'

Tadeus saw Lazarev flinch suspiciously. The young Russian had mentioned Monaco. And supérieur.

'You'll leave this building at once!' Solov'ëva said in a voice icier than a Siberian winter, beckoning one of the watching guards. 'If you do as I say, I won't—'

Poe abruptly reached under the slit of her dress, which rustled. In the next instant, she was holding a burnished gun in her left hand. 'Nobody move!'

Most of the guests froze. Some hid under the tables or took cover behind the doorframe. Escaping wasn't an option; she blocked the only exit. Anyone considering slipping away through the garden door would have to get past the gun first.

Judging by the gun's dimensions, Tadeus guessed it had a small calibre, but it would be enough to severely injure or even take someone's life. It all depended on how she handled the weapon.

Poe cocked the pistol and released the safety in a way that revealed her lack of experience. She looked nervous and wound up, as if she'd taken some kind of stimulant. The compact barrel pointed at Lazarev as she walked towards him.

'You know something,' Poe said decisively and removed her sunglasses. 'Go on, spit it out!'

* * *

Hyun aimed the Beretta Bobcat at the young player. She could see right through him. 'Tell me the truth!' she shouted.

There was nothing left of her composure. The drugs pumped hysteria through her body. Her blood rushed through her veins and she felt her heart pounding in her chest like a drum. He had been there, in Monte Carlo. It was undeniable.

A shorter man old enough to be her father stood next to Lazarev. Some well-maintained stubble covered his face and he was wearing a visibly less expensive suit than the rest of the guests.

'Miss Poe, please,' he addressed her. She might have fooled the guards at the door, but she wasn't fooling anyone here. Monaco and Enrico's death was common knowledge in gambling circles, and her face was all over the tabloids.

'I want to know what happened in the room where my fiancé was playing,' she said. She remained standing and listened nervously to what was happening behind her.

Nobody appeared to have any intention of attacking her. The semi-automatic pistol worked like a charm. Although she didn't have the capacity to shoot everyone, it was clear that no one wanted to make the first move. But Solov'ëva wasn't prepared to put up with Poe's dramatic performance for much longer.

'Why was he killed and why was his death made out to be an accident? Was there a fight? Something about money?' Adrenaline mixed with stimulants coursed through her body. 'What was it?' she screamed at the young player, who looked like he'd been caught red-handed. 'I'd hurt you without a second thought,' she said hastily, pressuring him further. 'I'd k–'

'I don't know your fiancé!' he yelled back at her. It was a pathetic attempt at a lie, and everyone knew it. 'I have no idea what you're talking about, you're crazy!'

Hyun lifted her arm and fired once at the ceiling. She was startled by the fairly powerful recoil; she'd only shot at cans a few times in Ecuador and was by no means an expert. It had been an impulse, not a carefully considered action.

The guests screamed. Stucco floated down from the ceiling and landed on the floor. The carpet swallowed up the crumbs.

She pointed the barrel of the gun at Lazarev again. The used bullet cartridge rolled down the marble hallway outside with a clink. 'You were at the same table as my fiancé. Tell me what happened!'

The young man turned as white as the stucco. 'I–'

'Put the gun's safety on,' calmly ordered the older man standing beside the Russian. His behaviour was too passive for him to be a bodyguard. 'Trust me, you don't want to kill him,' he said before adding quietly: 'That's Lazarev junior. If you do so much as touch a hair on his head, his father would destroy you, Miss Poe. Nobody could stop him.' He slowly offered her his open hand. 'If you give the gun to me, I'm sure that it'll be much easier to get him to talk in the other room.'

'Yes! Of course I'll talk,' agreed the young gambler. 'Put away the gun and I'll tell you everything I know,' he promised, avoiding Solov'ëva's eye. 'Listen, I don't want to die just because you're paranoid or you've taken some kind of drugs.'

Hyun could hear footsteps behind her. Since tonight's event was an illegal gathering, a police raid was unlikely. No, these were Solov'ëva's security guards.

She forced herself to remain calm. Her grandmother had always said that doing things in haste was always a bad idea.

Hyun looked at Lazarev and slowly lowered the weapon. She slid the safety lock back on. 'I'll hold you to your word.'

She glanced at the door and saw two guards standing with tasers in their hands. They didn't plan on shooting her, only knocking her unconscious. Hyun struggled to think. She had to come up with something if she wanted to avoid being kicked out. 'I left a letter with a friend,' she said to Solov'ëva. 'If something happens to me, he'll meet with my lawyer and present all the allegations and evidence that I've gathered against you and your mother to them.'

'Of course,' the Russian replied with a masterful smile. It was as if she knew that Hyun had neither evidence nor protection, but she played along anyway to defuse the situation. 'Come with me to the other room.' She turned to the crowd. 'My dear guests, I can assure you all that the event can now continue as if nothing has happened. Please don't let this little incident spoil your evening.'

Lazarev slowly walked away. The older man followed him and flashed Hyun a warning look. Solov'ëva and her men formed a barrier as whispers in the comfortable rooms instantly broke out about the incident, the woman and her fiancé.

The group walked down the hallway and entered a room where the furniture had been covered in tarpaulin. One of the walls lay on the floor. It had been stripped of wallpaper, knocked down, and had visible gaps for new cabling. The window shutters had been closed to avoid any prying eyes.

Hyun chose the chair facing away from the wall. Her hand trembled as she put down the Bobcat on the table as a sign of her goodwill.

Now that she was in a different environment, she felt the tension leave her body. The effect from the stimulants had faded, leaving a sort of vacuum behind that threatened to swallow her up. Hyun bit her bottom lip, hoping the pain would steady her. She couldn't afford to break down.

Lazarev remained standing. The older man lurked in the background and kept a low profile. He watched her so intently that it was as if he was trying to read her mind and predict her reactions.

Solov'ëva stood by the entrance. The security guards spread out to the right and left of the room.

'Before Mr Lazarev speaks, I'd like to say something,' Solov'ëva spoke up. 'I've lost many people that I loved in my life, and every time it was a shock. I was standing on a cliff' – she walked into the room, sat down, and fixed her grey dress before continuing to speak. The dress accentuated her perfect face and unnatural, red curls – 'when my brother died in a car accident shortly after he'd had an argument with an adversary. I was convinced that his brake lines had been cut.'

Hyun listened to Solov'ëva calmly deliver her story. It was clear that the Russian woman was used to soothing people in distress, but she was one of the guilty parties responsible for Enrico's death.

'The fact that I didn't want to believe it didn't make it any less true: it was an accident. The same is true for your fiancé, Miss Poe. He died in a shower accident, just like the media says. I know it's awful. It's terrible, but lying to yourself won't help,' Solov'ëva went on in a lulling tone that resembled a hypnotist. 'Searching for something to prove it was otherwise is a burden you shouldn't have to carry. It's only a distraction from the grieving.'

There was a part of Hyun that agreed with her. The adrenaline wore off. Uncertainty and despair gradually took over and the vacuum inside her expanded, its pull becoming harder and harder to resist.

Hyun lowered her gaze to the covered tabletop. It was clear that her mind had given in. A collection of thoughts and theories swirled around in her mind in a tangled, hopeless mess. Enrico's face and laugh jumped out at her from the confused pile. He was lost for ever.

A tear welled up in the corner of her right eye, drooped over her eyelid and rolled down her cheek.

'Your fiancé was sitting at the table with us. We were playing,' she heard Lazarev say as if he were speaking from an abyss. Hyun's mind drifted through memories of Enrico, one after another, causing her pain and sparking joy in equal measure.

Somehow, she still felt numb inside.

The young Lazarev's voice turned into a sort of rising and falling sound. Hyun had imagined her entrance differently, had expected people to scream and confess, terrified. She'd pictured clues, the culprits, someone who could be held accountable and responsible for Enrico's death.

None of that had happened.

She felt like a fool. Like an overexcited, hysterical fool who had let herself cling on to the fact that there must have been a better reason for his death than a wet bathroom floor. Something more than just bad luck. Something other than an accident.

'. . .then Florecita left,' Lazarev stressed, rousing Hyun from her memories and thoughts. 'I have no idea what he did next. Showered, probably.' He laughed wickedly.

Hyun began to sob with one hand clutching her forehead. She leaned forward and shook; a crying fit like she hadn't experienced in years came over her. Her tears trickled onto the plastic, her vision blurred, and her sunglasses fell from her wig and landed onto the table. She flinched when someone quietly set down a clinking cup of coffee in front of her.

She pulled herself out of her crying fit, got out a tissue,

dabbed her face with it and did everything in her power to remain calm. She imagined that she was standing in the operating theatre and that everything depended on her and her nimble fingers. That someone's life depended on her composure.

This and the smell of coffee helped her, and she stopped crying.

Hyun looked up. 'I'm sorry,' she said in a strained voice.

Solov'ëva and a security guard were the only ones left in the room. Lazarev and his escort had left. The matter was settled.

The coffee aroma tried to entice her, but she had no appetite for it. She felt miserable and empty like a deflated balloon. Hyun wanted to hole up in bed and wallow in her misery. To lie still, ignore any calls, and wait. Wait until something happened that negated her fiancé's death.

'You have my sympathy, Miss Poe,' Solov'ëva said empathetically. 'I think I would have done the same in your position. And your heroic efforts to investigate do you credit.'

Hyun sighed and wiped the tears from her cheeks. Her makeup was ruined and her eyes were puffy, but her tinted sunglasses would help disguise that.

'It's needless to say that you're our guest for this evening. The room is yours,' Solov'ëva kindly explained. 'You'll have everything you need. Food and drink will be provided. In the meantime, please remain calm and refrain from using your phone, Miss Poe.' She pointed to the stocky man. 'Molotov will keep you company. He's a brilliant chess player. The evening will fly by.' With a nod, she got up and left.

There was a click as Solov'ëva locked the door from the outside.

The man set up the pieces on the chessboard, which must have been brought with the coffee, and pushed the white side of the board towards her.

She had been called a *guest*, but she knew she was a hostage and she understood why. Millions were at stake at these illegal rounds in the villa, meaning Solov'ëva couldn't afford to risk releasing her until everything was over.

Hyun composed herself and stirred some sugar into her coffee. She sipped it gradually, focused on her breathing and her pulse, and tried to close her eyes and meditate like her grandmother had taught her to.

After half an hour or so, she felt better. With her inner peace restored, her mind felt sharper. The stimulants had worn off. Hyun opened her eyes and saw the man still sitting opposite her in the same place.

'You have to start,' Molotov told her. There was something boyish about his weak, clean-shaven chin. 'You're white.'

'I don't know how to play chess,' she lied. 'Have you ever played go?'

'No. I'll teach you chess.' He grinned. He pointed at the pawns, explained each piece one by one, which squares it could move to and attack.

Hyun pretended to pay attention, taking the opportunity to secretly look around. Her first thought was to contact the authorities in Baden-Baden and put an end to the event.

But the window shutters were secured with small padlocks to prevent break-ins and breakouts. Escaping was impossible unless she got the key.

Her inner sense of calm enabled her to think clearly again.

Hyun resented the fact that she had let her emotions take over and thwart her plans. She would have really liked to question the young Lazarev about Marstella Suarez, the woman who had allegedly committed suicide, and she was also still in the dark about Solov'ëva. The longer she sat there, staring at Molotov and not listening to his words, the more confusing Enrico's behaviour and the fact that he hadn't called her became. All of her preparation, all of the detective's work and her obtaining the weapon had been in vain. All because she had let a crying fit get the better of her.

In her distraught and hysterical state, she had let the Russian have her way.

She wouldn't let that happen again.

If she managed to escape and lead the police back to the villa, there might be a second opportunity to question Solov'ëva. She could make sure that the Baden-Baden authorities carried out a full-blown investigation into what happened in Monaco. A dismantled ring that organised illegal games around the world would be a real feast for the media and leverage for the police to investigate further.

Then it dawned on her: her Beretta Bobcat was missing.

'It's your turn,' Molotov barked.

'I think I'd rather lie down,' Hyun replied and stood up, taking the empty cup and the saucer with her. 'Is it all right if I rest on the sofa?'

Molotov looked frustrated. He had gone out of his way to explain the entire game to her for nothing. 'Fine by me. Sleep if you want.' He decided to play against himself and moved a white piece on the board.

Hyun dropped the cup and saucer. They shattered on the chessboard, toppling both of the kings at once. 'Oh, I'm so sorry!'

Molotov jumped up and instinctively tried to catch the rolling wooden pieces.

Hyun followed up with a swift kick to the man's chest and an upward snap kick to his head. She had mastered the attack sequence from countless tae kwon do training lessons.

The stunned Molotov didn't stand a chance. Never in his wildest dreams did he imagine such a brutal attack from a tear-stained, skinny woman. The blows swept him off his feet, and he collapsed onto the parquet, motionless. He hadn't even had time to cry out.

'Checkmate,' Hyun breathed. She quickly searched him, finding a set of keys and her phone, from which the battery had been removed. Solov'ëva had taken precautions. Hyun immediately unlocked the door and slipped out.

Nobody was looking for her. The poker evening carried on as usual. Her surprise appearance certainly hadn't been forgotten, but it hadn't spoiled anyone's fun either.

The police would soon change that. Hyun closed the door behind her to avoid anyone instantly noticing her escape. Molotov would sleep for a little while and wake up with an aching head. She just had to inform the authorities and round up the players, Solov'ëva and Solov'ëva's mother.

Then she had to slip out of the estate unnoticed.

Hyun darted around the corner, where she came across a small, abandoned kitchen with ingredients for canapés lying around. The narrow window was open, and the entrance gate was only a few metres away. If anything was going to give her away, it would be the crunchy white gravel.

But for a featherweight like Hyun, that shouldn't be a problem.

* * *

Together with Lazarev, Tadeus left the little room and the resolved situation with Poe. The young woman reminded him of his daughter, Michiko, and he felt sorry for her. The news that he'd read this morning about the death in Monaco had even reached Baden-Baden.

It was none of Tadeus' business what had happened at the gambling round in Monaco in which Lazarev had also taken part, but something didn't add up. It was unlikely that Monaco's investigators would take the matter further in order to preserve the principality's reputation. Hapless players did take their own lives sometimes, although it was more common in Las Vegas, Shanghai or Macao than in tranquil Monaco. Dead bodies were discreetly retrieved from all kinds of hotels all over the world, whether they were dirt-cheap or fancy establishments, but two corpses after one private tournament was out of the ordinary.

Tadeus pondered on the matter. He pitied Poe. She was a picture of misery. A broken-hearted fiancée searching for the culprit, who was likely right in her accusations about something having been covered up.

But it's none of my business.

An expensively dressed, older lady approached Lazarev. She was a curvaceous woman with traces of cosmetic surgery on her face. Jewellery sparkled and adorned every inch of her body, even her pinned-up hair. There was something about her hairstyle and features that bore a slight resemblance to the much younger Solov'ëva. *I guess they share hairdressers and surgeons.*

'I'm going to go play a round of supérieur,' Lazarev murmured to Tadeus. 'Just a quick one or two. Don't go anywhere, I'll need your help later for poker.' With that, he hurried up the stairs to the upper floors of the villa.

'*Dobryĭ vecher,*' the older lady greeted Tadeus and linked arms with him. She wore a brightly coloured dress with sleeves that came down to her wrists. 'My name is Maksima Dimitrivna Solov'ëva. I'm Katia's mother, who I believe you've already met. I'm the organiser of this wonderful evening that you helped save.'

'I had my reasons,' Tadeus responded in Russian.

'My, your Russian is excellent. Not a single trace of an accent. I gather you know Mr Lazarev well?'

'Only from throwing him out.' He grinned. 'But that's not important. He hired me as his advisor for the poker tournament.'

They reached the small bar.

Tadeus helped himself to another glass and filled it with blackcurrant juice. He hadn't drunk it since he'd been a child. It was thick, sweet, and yet slightly bitter. 'May I ask what supérieur entails?'

'It's a card game that very few people know about. There's a theory that it emerged at the same time as poque, the precursor to poker,' Solov'ëva explained. 'It's a simple and quick game, but it's very fun.' It was clear that she didn't want to go into any more detail about how the game worked. 'Most people like playing it with us because of the thrill it incites.'

Tadeus caught himself wanting to try out this new pastime, and his addiction stirred. He felt a powerful tingling sensation in his fingers. 'And the cards?'

'You mean the historical element?'

He nodded.

'I am a service provider, Mr . . .'

'Boch.'

'. . .and I was asked by a good customer of mine, a passionate card collector, if I wouldn't like to use these historical artefacts as the oldest examples of a passion for gambling and as a special kind of stake.'

'I see. Clearly there are plenty of them.'

'There's still more. And before you ask: you can't play without having one of these cards.' Solov'ëva pulled away from him and squeezed his upper arm like a grandmother would squeeze a grandchild's. 'I'm much obliged to you, Mr Boch. You prevented the worst from happening tonight. Not only did you save your own life, but the lives of the other guests too.' She pulled out a business card from her sleeve and handed it to him. 'Don't lose it. If I can ever return the favour, you can call me on this number.' She squeezed his arm again before turning away. He watched her walk towards another guest, welcoming them with open arms.

Tadeus grabbed his glass. The smell of Solov'ëva's sweet, heavy perfume lingered on his suit. He hurried past the fireplace, walked through the garden door and reached the villa's terrace.

Outside it smelled of wet grass and fresh morning. The former Belle Époque was silent, and no light filtered through its windows. The only source of light was the open door, which illuminated the garden and the fountain.

In the fresh air, Tadeus' addiction loosened its grasp. The juice was delicious and brought back memories from his childhood.

Tadeus relaxed a little and adjusted the fit of his knee bandage again, feeling a stab of pain in his lower back. *I'm an old man who needs to go to bed.* He stifled a yawn and took a sip of the blackcurrant juice. Savouring it, he sighed quietly and glanced at his wristwatch: it was just after two in the morning.

Tadeus knew that the wicked tingling feeling in his body, hands and fingertips would return as soon as he took his place behind Lazarev at the poker table and watched the round unfold. But the tranquillity of the garden gave him the confidence to face the challenge. *I can do it.*

He climbed the well-trodden steps, marched up the white gravel path to the little fountain, which had been turned off, and sat down on a bench.

Tadeus looked at the magnificent villa and thought about the kind of people who might have lived here, and how such a large house wouldn't suit him. He could easily stay there for a weekend, but he'd long for his cutter, for the salty air of the sea and the fresh breeze, the thud of the engine, the hull that threw itself against the waves and sliced through the water, the glittering clouds of salt spray and the cries of the seagulls.

Just two more years. Tadeus patted his suit jacket. The young Russian's cash rustled inside it. The money would considerably reduce his debt and save him time. *Or why not take a gamble at a round and pay it all off in one fell swoop?*

He quickly tried to push away the thought and hastily gulped down the juice as if it were a remedy against the temptation of the game. But his addiction held on, coaxing him and whispering to him about the prospect of winning a huge sum: how he'd pay off all his debts, write off another twenty-four months of struggle in a single day and be out of the red. Free to start a new life. Free to sail away in his ship and live at sea.

But Tadeus knew the price he'd pay. Regardless of how the one round went, he wouldn't be free any longer.

He got up and determinedly walked towards the villa. He couldn't let his addiction sabotage his plans; he decided that now was a good time to leave and call off the test.

Tadeus had already proved himself by not playing poker without the surveillance of the cameras or Alexa's voice in his ear. He could wait another two years for his freedom.

If Lazarev complained, so be it. The oligarch's son had lied to the distraught Miss Poe without blushing and made fun of her dead fiancé. Assholes didn't deserve his loyalty.

He went upstairs and reached the terrace. A thought occurred to him. *I could cash in Solov'ëva's favour and check on Poe. She'd benefit from—*

Two window shutters suddenly flew open, clinking.

Tadeus looked up and simultaneously dodged a falling piece of wood from the window.

A figure came crashing down onto the marble terrace in the shimmering shower of glass shards. Pieces of glass shattered and flew everywhere. The next shutter that fell narrowly missed the body on the floor and smashed.

'What the . . .?' Tadeus gasped, recognising Morgan, who had sustained several injuries from his crash through the closed window. His left arm lay bent unnaturally to one side.

He had broken it in at least one place. In his right hand he held a playing card, a historical one. A single glimmer of light revealed it as the seven of clubs – the same card that the oligarch's son had used to gain entry to the tournament.

Tadeus' heart gleefully skipped a beat without him knowing why.

'Shit!' Morgan panted and used the railing to pull himself up. He spotted Tadeus. The tiniest shards of glass glistened in his whiskers. His suit jacket and trousers were ruined and had visibly ripped in several places. 'Boch, help me,' he begged in pain. 'Get me out of here.'

Cries could be heard from the fireplace room. The crash hadn't gone unnoticed. Faces that looked like bright, round blurs peered out at the fallen man from the shattered window above them.

'You fucking cheat!' somebody shouted. Tadeus identified the voice as Lazarev's. 'You had the ace of spades! You won't get away with it!'

Morgan tried to take a step forward, suppressing a groan. 'Boch, help me! I'm begging you! I helped you in Macao, now it's your turn.'

'Did you jump out the window?' Tadeus didn't know how much he owed him for Macao. 'Did you–?'

'I'll explain when we get out of here. My car's around the corner.' Morgan wrapped his uninjured arm around Tadeus' neck. The front of the card glowed, as if it was delighted to be next to Tadeus. 'Let's go! Go through the garden, and then we'll get over the fence at the back by the tree house.'

Someone by the window shoved the players aside. The man drew a weapon, his arm outstretched, and aimed just as a torch lit up and blinded Tadeus.

A soft *plop* sound was followed by the clatter of crashing

marble. The bullet had blasted off a piece of the railing. Fragments struck his face.

Tadeus stopped asking questions, grabbed Morgan and threw himself over the railing. They landed in a bed of gnarly rhododendrons. A stab of pain ran down Tadeus' lower back from the collision, but he ignored it.

A couple of muffled gunshots sounded behind them. One and then two beams of light flared up, searching for them in the darkness.

'This is about the seven of clubs, isn't it?' Tadeus asked, hunched over and hurrying with Morgan through the bushes that grew along a villa wall. No one had found them yet. 'Give them the—'

'No! Never!' the injured man wheezed.

'It's not worth dying over,' Tadeus said urgently. 'Give me the card and I'll take it to Solov'ëva. Nothing will happen to me – she still owes me a favour.'

'This has nothing to do with Solov'ëva,' Morgan replied, groaning. 'It's so much more than that. This card is one of a kind. It's part of the Devil's Playbook! It's—'

The bullets ripped past him, hacking through the bushes and destroying branches.

Tadeus ducked, avoiding the searching, blueish glare of the torch.

'Give them the seven of clubs!' Tadeus pleaded with Morgan, who shook his head stubbornly.

They managed to make their way through the dense plants to the path leading to the villa's guesthouse. Next to it there was a tree with a little wooden hut built on top of it, where they'd be able to jump over the high, pointy fence and flee to safety. At least for the time being.

Tadeus looked at the roughly made rungs of the ladder.

Getting a severely injured man up it without being spotted by their pursuers would be impossible.

Morgan had realised it too. He shoved the seven of clubs into Tadeus' hand. 'Take it, Boch. Keep it safe. See that it never falls into the hands of—'

A torch beam shone close by. The henchmen were on their tail. 'There are footprints here!' one of them cried and fired randomly in their direction.

Tadeus ducked, escaping the bullets, and thought he saw a slender figure climbing over the fence on the other side of the garden.

Morgan gave a phlegmy cough. His breathing became raspy and shallow, and warm drops fell onto Tadeus' face. 'Boch, get out of here,' Morgan managed. 'They'll think we're working together.'

'There they are!' one of the men shouted.

'Get up!' Tadeus seized Morgan and felt blood running from the man's torso where he'd been shot.

'No, you have to go. The card! It's important,' Morgan urged. 'Whatever happens, whoever wants it, don't give it away. You'll soon find out what I mean.' Morgan went on, slack-jawed, but Tadeus could barely follow his stammering. He tried to remember his every word. He would ponder over it all later when there were no bullets whistling past his ears.

After a long sigh, Morgan's body went limp. In the same instant, Tadeus felt a violent blow hit his hand, the one holding the seven of clubs.

At first he was sure he'd been shot, but then he saw a bright glow spread across the entire card. Tadeus couldn't help but stare. He stood rooted to the spot, fascinated.

One by one, the contours of the depicted musicians, the dancing bear, as well as the cross-shaped symbols, glinted with a shimmering silver glow, each line changing colour. An unmistakable warmth transferred from the printed paper to Tadeus' fingers. An unknown pandemonium, consisting of a mixture of deafening singing and deranged laughter, rang in his ears. In a heartbeat, everything became clear: the card had to remain in his possession. Giving it up was out of the question.

A surge of sinister power coursed from his fingertips to his body. It prompted him to leap to his feet and climb the rungs of the tree house despite the hail of bullets. The blades of light illuminated him, the bullets ripping into the wood from the left and right. Solov'ëva's people had no regard for his life.

He vigorously pushed himself off, jumped over the fence's deadly spikes and landed on the adjoining property. He ran like the wind and tried to get as far away as possible from the villa.

Tadeus' legs didn't stop for one moment as he made his way back to his flat. He needed to think in peace, with a coffee containing a splash of rum.

He whirled into Schiller Street and stopped, realising that going back to his apartment wasn't a good idea. Lazarev knew who he was and most likely where he lived, too.

What am I going to do?

He held the seven of clubs in his hand and examined it.

He couldn't help but laugh grimly: one card had got him into trouble. Without him having played a single game.

There are no friends
at cards or world politics.

Finley Peter Dunne (1867–1936)

INTERMEDIUM

Leipzig, the Electorate of Saxony,
the Holy Roman Empire,
January 1768

Bastian walked through the frosty streets with a sinking feeling in his stomach. He'd wanted to stretch his legs during his short lunch break and couldn't put his finger on the reason for his now low mood.

There was a smell of coal and wood fires as the burning furnaces inside the houses tried to fight off the cold within the walls. The chimneys on the roofs spewed out dark clouds into the clear, blue sky. Although the sun was shining, it wasn't enough to drive away the winter chill. Icicles hung from the roofs like lurking daggers made of diamonds and glass, glistening beautifully and perilously.

Bastian came to a stop and turned around, as he so often did these days.

His instincts hadn't betrayed him. The large, black poodle crept up behind him, sniffed a street corner, left its mark and cast Bastian a glance with its demonic eyes before disappearing down a small alleyway, as if to assure him that they'd meet again.

'Bloody hound,' Bastian muttered and continued walking along Alter Neumarkt Street towards the property of the Breitkopf family.

Since their first encounter, the dog's path seemed to constantly cross with his, but its trail no longer glowed as it had that evening when he and Goethe had met the beast for the first time. Perhaps he had imagined it, just like the students in Auerbach's Keller had imagined the grapes in their hands. If the bystanders hadn't intervened, their wine mania would have cost them their noses.

People hurried past Bastian. Some greeted him.

Did Dietrich put something in their drinks? Bastian touched his hat absent-mindedly without taking it off – it was far too cold without it, and his scarf and gloves were once again lying in the room under the roof. *But why would he do that? Out of pure malice? To play a trick on them?*

Bastian pushed the memory of the strange incident to the back of his mind.

Susanna's, his and their children's lives had turned a corner. Their new lodgings were warm, spacious and had thick walls; neither rain nor snow blew in.

Having Stock and his family as neighbours meant he could continuously work on motifs that he liked. It was easy for him to get to the workshop late at night to make sample prints of the cards, and to touch up the printing plates when he didn't like the results. Breitkopf gave Bastian free rein, only reminding him to show him the motifs and designs of his work soon.

Shortly before reaching the publishing house, he realised what had been subliminally bothering him. It had been a note in the *Leipzig Zeitung*, a subtle dig at book publishers and printers like Breitkopf.

The writer criticised the common practice of artists' famous works being simply copied and used as templates for copperplate and wooden engravings for the illustrations of fairytales, novels and poetry collections.

In addition, the writer questioned if it wasn't brazen and impertinent to reproduce these works without actually celebrating their original creators, or, at the very least, citing them beneath the copied works. Such cases were becoming more and more common. The stealing of printing plates was the only practice considered even more despicable, which, as the *Leipzig Zeitung* pointed out, was exactly what two card-makers in Altenburg were doing.

Although the author of the article didn't name any names, Bastian knew that it was about him. His old competitor, Voigt, hadn't been able to refrain from dragging his name through the dirt. Voigt's mudslinging had spread all the way to Leipzig, where the papers had picked it up, rolled it in printing ink, liquified and printed it for all to read.

The news would get around.

Bastian cursed Voigt, who was incapable of delivering good work, but was too stubborn to admit it. He envied the success of talented people and had driven Bastian out of Altenburg with his smearing.

'I can't let that happen ever again,' Bastian mumbled and entered the publishing house via the side entrance, which led directly into the printing room.

He threw off his hat and coat and marched through the room where the printers and typesetters were busy at work printing booklets and sheet music, crafting copies of the finest quality for customers. Ignoring them, Bastian went to his printing press.

The new card forms were prepared, the copper plates had been treated with aqua fortis and were ready for use to make another sample print. He'd impress Breitkopf with this. Bastian laid down the various plates so that the designs would all be on one sheet. He swiftly applied the paint and operated the handle. As he turned it, the printing blocks pressed down onto the paper and came up again.

Bastian thoroughly inspected the end result and breathed a sigh of relief. It had worked!

With the damp sheet in his hands, he proudly, albeit anxiously, made his way to Johann Gottlob Immanuel Breitkopf's study.

After a knock and a curt invitation, he entered and saw the publisher poring over a stack of sheet music. Breitkopf had annotated them and added corrections where something hadn't been printed as required. His pencil bobbed back and forth between his fingers.

'Ah, Kirchner my man. Come here, come here!' Breitkopf said plainly. 'You promised to show me something.' He went back to his corrections.

'Yes, Mr Breitkopf,' Bastian replied and drew closer. He scanned the room for a suitable place to put the sheet of paper without bending it. 'Where should I . . .?'

Without saying a word, the publisher pointed to the chest in the right corner. 'I'll only be a moment,' he muttered, fervently scribbling on the paper. 'This movable type of printing still has its challenges. It needs sorting out, or else nobody will buy my sheet music.' Breitkopf grumpily threw the pencil onto the mountain of papers, shot to his feet, stretched and supported his lower back with his hands. 'Oh, my back, my back! All this sitting isn't doing me any good.' With a serious look on his face, he approached the chest. 'Well, let's see what cards you want to print at my publishing house then, Kirchner.'

As a sign of respect, Bastian stepped to one side. 'I've used the French suits, Mr Breitkopf, as you can play more games with them than with the German or the Italian ones,' he said, explaining his thought process. 'There are also a few lines to refresh the players' memories and teach them a few things. The card numbers appear on—'

'Before we proceed, Kirchner . . .' the publisher interrupted him. 'You've done a fine job here, with the vines, the curlicues and the queen of hearts' angular face, which, or so I've heard, resembles your wife, but . . .' He rubbed his chin, which made a soft scraping sound.

This wasn't good. 'Is something the matter, Mr Breitkopf?'

'Have you read the *Leipzig Zeitung* today, Kirchner?'

Bastian desperately tried to push down his fear, which burned like hot coals in the pit of his stomach, making his mouth drier than sand. 'I have.'

'Did you read the note about the copying of designs and the two card-makers from Altenburg?' Breitkopf looked up and scrutinised him with his bright eyes.

'Yes,' Bastian said, mustering every drop of his courage. 'And since you ask, I assume you know who the newspapers are referring to. But please, allow me to reassure you that what you've read is all a pack of lies.'

'Michael Voigt himself was standing in front of my very desk this morning, Kirchner, and he swore blind to me that you'd stolen from him. Both back then' – Breitkopf ruefully ran his hand over the print sample – 'and now. He said that the printing plates for the cards had been stolen from him at the time, and that he later recognised them in your designs.'

'You let him into the workshop? To inspect my things?' Bastian was furious.

'Settle down, Kirchner, settle down.' Breitkopf looked equally displeased but remained calm. 'What was I supposed to do? He threatened to go to the authorities, to write to the council and the guild.'

'But it's all lies!'

'Kirchner, I believe you, but do you have the proof that they are definitely your designs?'

'But you saw me engrave them.'

'That I did, but who's to say that the drawings are yours?' Breitkopf seemed to have adopted the neutral stance of a businessman, something Bastian could understand. The reputation and integrity of his publishing house, which Breitkopf's father had spent an age building, was in danger. Even the best of reputations could be destroyed in seconds. 'The fact of the matter is, Kirchner, if you can get me the supporting evidence, the proof that these designs are yours, business can resume as usual. In the meantime, you and your family can continue to live under my roof. But if a month passes and nothing changes, I'm afraid we'll have to go our separate ways.' His expression softened. 'You'll receive a settlement, of course. I wouldn't leave any man and his family in the lurch. But you understand my request, Kirchner?'

'I understand, Mr Breitkopf.'

Bastian left the print where it was, sleepwalked out of the room, stumbled down the stairs and through the workshop, grabbed his coat and hat and stepped out into the street.

His mind was spinning. Only a moment ago it seemed his life had changed for the better, and now: Voigt. *It is always Voigt, that jealous bastard!*

Bastian aimlessly wandered the streets and the alleyways of Little Paris, as Leipzig had been named during the card round in Auerbach's Keller. He continued walking in the cold sunshine, passing through squares and markets, his gaze fixed on nothing in particular, and fuelled by the fear of losing everything again. Only this time he had a family to support; it wasn't just his own life that was at stake.

He didn't know how he'd able to provide the evidence that Breitkopf needed – there wasn't any. Then again, Voigt also didn't have any proof to support his claim, but his hypocritical ways of acting like the victim had carried him through life before. He had a talent for pitting people against each other in order to get what he wanted.

Bastian lost track of time. He barely felt the biting cold.

Behind a passage between the houses, he reached a gloomy

merchant's house. Not a single ray of sunshine filtered through the building. A chill from beyond the grave prevailed from within the high walls, swallowing up any sound that wanted to seep through from within.

The eerie atmosphere woke Bastian from his brooding. He didn't wish to linger here, and quickly crossed the cobblestones to the footpath opposite the house.

Suddenly he heard a soft, delicate patter.

The black poodle trotted towards him from the entrance gate. The large animal looked at him and sat down in the middle of the empty alleyway as if it were guarding it.

Bastian stood still.

'You stupid fucking mutt. You're the last thing I need right now,' he snapped, looking around for a loose stone to throw at it. He would have preferred a stick, but he found neither, so he carefully moved backward instead, his eyes still fixed on the animal.

'Master Kirchner,' he heard a sonorous voice say behind him. 'Do not be afraid of him. He only bites people who deserve it – you do not.'

Bastian turned around and saw Dietrich standing before him, his hands casually stuffed into the pockets of his breeches. He was wearing a black coat, the kind a schoolmaster would wear. A red beret with a long pheasant feather perched on his hair. 'Your competitor Voigt, on the other hand, does.'

'That . . . would be too good to be true,' Bastian stuttered, realising in the same moment that he must know what had happened in Altenburg.

'The man is an ape, a blusterer and a slacker,' Dietrich continued. 'Or so people say who knew him in the old days.'

'That's true, too.' Bastian allowed Dietrich to saunter towards him and put his arm around his shoulder as if they were old friends. The gesture comforted him and brought him warmth as they stood in the alleyway. He sighed involuntarily. 'If only there were more sensible people in this world like yourself, Mr Dietrich.'

'Indeed, then we would live in a better place.' Dietrich patted him on the back. 'Chin up, Kirchner. In a year, it'll all be forgotten.'

'We'll be out on the street by then,' Bastian uttered bitterly. 'Breitkopf believes Voigt. He threatened me.'

'He actually threatened you? A good man like Breitkopf?' Dietrich asked, astonished.

'No. He didn't threaten me, but . . .' Bastian couldn't hold back any more and poured his heart out to Dietrich. He told him what had happened and was glad to spare his Susanna of the details, just for a moment. She would worry about it all soon enough.

'I understand, I understand,' Dietrich said thoughtfully after listening to Bastian's story. He rubbed his chin. 'Voigt has spoiled things for me too.'

'How so?'

'Ah, who will make me my cards if you're no longer in Leipzig—' Dietrich snapped his fingers. 'I've just had an idea. How about a business deal, my good Kirchner?'

'What sort of deal?'

'A deal that would benefit us both.' He tapped his long, pointy nail on Bastian's chest. 'You make me a deck of cards, French ones and to my specifications, and after that you can use the press plates for as long and as much as you like. But the first set shall be *mine*.'

'And how will that benefit me?'

Dietrich laughed. 'Of course, of course. In return, I will do you a favour, Kirchner. Anything you like, just like I promised.'

'You'll get rid of Voigt for me!' Bastian couldn't stop himself from laughing wickedly. 'Why what a fine thought! That swine lying dead in a ditch somewhere!'

'That can be arranged,' Dietrich whispered enticingly. 'I have my ways and my methods. I wasn't a soldier for nothing. And his lies would die with him.'

'But . . . That would be murder!' Bastian hesitated, even if he did wish for Voigt's demise from the bottom of his heart. As long as it was in his best interests, Voigt was a man who would ruin other people's lives without a care in the world.

'I see myself as part of that power not understood, which always wills the bad and always works the good,' Dietrich replied with a smile, quoting Mephistopheles. 'The world is better off without Voigt.' He extended his claw-like left hand, dark-purple veins glowing through his parchment skin. 'Do we have a deal, my dear Kirchner?'

'I . . .'

'All I want is a deck of cards. What could be the harm in that?'

'But . . .'

'Voigt and his lies will all be forgotten,' Dietrich promised him in a whisper, his gaze luring Bastian as if by magic. His voice bounced off the walls, building into a haunting chorus that eliminated any shadow of doubt as it trickled into Bastian's ears and his mind. 'Breitkopf will keep you on, you'll become his master card-maker, and your family will be safe until the end of time. All I ask in return is a deck of cards. I'm not asking for your soul, Kirchner.'

Bastian shook the man's hand. As he did so, he cut himself on Dietrich's nail and his hand burned as if liquid fire had seeped into the wound. 'There, you see? We've sealed our pact with blood.'

'As is custom.' Dietrich shook Bastian's hand. 'Not a word to anyone, or else our deal will collapse like a house of cards.'

'My lips are sealed.'

Dietrich let go of Bastian, stepped away from him and

brought his right hand to his red beret in salute. By the time he'd taken his second step, he'd already melted into the shadow of the entrance gate. The pheasant feather swayed one more time before vanishing.

'Prepare yourself for some good news, Master Kircher.' His voice echoed in the alleyway from a thousand corners.

With that, the sinister man and his dog were gone.

Lost in thought, Bastian looked at the cut on his palm. A red drop oozed out of it and fell onto the white snow.

'A deal,' he said quietly and gave himself a little shake.

He rushed out of the creepy road and soon found himself standing in Leipzig's pleasant evening sunshine, sighing in relief. Several hours had flown by; time must have passed twice as quickly where he'd been.

Bastian hurried towards the Silver Lion to meet Susanna and the children with a renewed sense of calm about his future.

As he walked, it occurred to him that he knew nothing about his new ally: not what he did for a living, nor where he lived.

Never mind, he thought. *His dog will find me.*

The notion of it made Bastian feel uneasy.

And when he really thought about it, there was nothing about Dietrich that didn't make him feel uneasy.

* * *

Michael Voigt lay on his bed in an inn on the southern outskirts of Leipzig where he had taken up quarters. The sheet barely covered him and the embers of passion burned in his veins, warming his body.

The drunk innkeeper's daughter, one of five sisters who had very willingly been at his service for a little money, lay snoring next to him. She slept on her back, her heavy breasts remaining upright thanks to her youth. Her strands of long, dark blonde hair were scattered all over the pillow. For a girl borne by a coarse woman and fathered by a stupid man, she could be considered beautiful.

Michael presumed that he wasn't her first and wouldn't be the last suitor in her life. She had earned herself a few extra thalers from him, and he had also had to pay for the wine.

He grinned and took a sip from the water jug, folded his arms behind his head and looked at the low beams on the ceiling.

His plan had worked. He had spread the false news, leaked it to the *Leipzig Zeitung*, and had taken up the matter with Breitkopf. *Just a little more blathering and complaining, and my work will be done.* Michael's grin widened.

One earned practically nothing as a card-maker in Altenburg; there were too many of them. As soon as he had heard that Breitkopf's publishing house was considering printing cards, he had travelled to Leipzig, and had been delighted to discover who he would have to drive out of the workshop: Bastian Kirchner, that good-natured fool. His Altenburg tricks should work just as well in Leipzig.

Michael closed his eyes and laughed to himself quietly. People would believe every lie if you told it well.

The innkeeper's daughter gave a wet cough and couldn't settle back down.

Michael turned to her, puzzled, but she only threw herself on him and fell silent. Something warm and damp ran down Michael's chest. At first he thought that she had played some sort of nasty joke on him and had emptied the chamber pot over him, but then he recognised the smell, before he saw the red that had spilled over his chest and the bed. *Blood!*

He quickly pushed her away from him. She lay next to him with her throat slit open, her lower legs severed and her arms neatly chopped off. Warm loops of intestines and other organs twisted and curled up above Michael as if they were still alive.

Michael began to vomit, terrified, his nausea triggered by the pungent stench of copper that filled every nook and cranny of his chamber.

This has to be a nightmare! Michael closed his eyes, opened them again, and repeated the same process a few times.

The scene, however, remained the same: guts, organs, blood and a mutilated woman's corpse lay next to him.

Before a horrified scream could escape his throat, he noticed a male figure sitting in the corner on top of the chest where he kept his things. The elderly man regarded him in a calm and expectant manner, his seemingly ancient eyes glowing wickedly. A magnificent beret with a long pheasant feather sat on his long, mottled grey hair.

'Good evening, Master Voigt. You've made quite the mess. Poor Gretchen . . . She was still a virgin, curious about love and lust, and you slit her open, you beast.' The stranger spoke reproachfully, exaggerating his words as if he were acting in a play. 'That's how you thank her for being her first?'

'No!' Michael cried and sat up. The entrails slid off his body, and as he got up from the gory bed he slipped and fell. 'I . . . No! *You* did this!'

'And who will believe you when you say that?' The man pointed to Michael's right hand. 'It was your knife. You murdered her.'

Terrified, Michael looked down; sure enough, he was clutching his pocketknife, its blade razor-sharp.

'And the axe is from the dining room,' the stranger continued, drawing attention to the tool that was lodged in the bedposts, glistening with blood. 'Drunk on wine and lust, you didn't show poor Gretchen any mercy.' He crossed his arms in front of his chest and flashed his dazzling white teeth. 'It won't take long for the judge to sentence you.'

'But this can't . . . I must be in a dream.' Michael dropped the knife and rattled the doorknob. 'There! I knew it! It won't open. The nightmare's coming to an—'

'Because you locked it from the inside and destroyed the key so the girl couldn't escape.' The man gestured to the floor. 'See?'

Now Michael was sure that he was hallucinating. He was dozing and had succumbed to his own mind's tricks. 'This isn't real.' He slowly walked towards the stranger. 'It's only a nightmare, nothing more, and I'm going to prove it to myself.'

'I wouldn't rush, if I were you.' The older man laughed and pointed to the mangled Gretchen. 'Or else the same thing will happen to *you*.' He leaned forward, propped up an elbow on his leg and beckoned enticingly with his index finger. 'Listen, Master Voigt. I am only a messenger, sent by both God and the Devil as part of an amicable agreement.'

'Hah! Oh, but of course you are.'

'You can be *absolutely certain* of it.' The man bowed briefly. 'Should you need a name, you can call me Lucifuge Rofocale.' He made a semicircular movement with his outstretched hand, his palm facing upwards. 'Heaven and hell have placed their bets: the Devil says that, even in your current position, you would never repent of the sins you've committed. God, on the other hand, believes that you would confess and repent your sins so that your soul may go to heaven.'

Michael blinked, looked at his naked, blood-smeared body, then at the bed and at the dismembered girl. Dream or not, this wasn't right, and he didn't want to be trapped here a moment longer. 'That doesn't sound like the Almighty to me.'

'But alas, it is, because your wretched soul, Michael Voigt, already belongs to the Devil.' Lucifuge laughed. 'Thanks to all those lies you told to hurt others, you're going straight to the hottest pit in hell that the demons can poke up for you.'

'What?' Michael gasped.

'Well, naturally. What did you think your reward would be

for the life you've led so far? There's no heaven for liars and crooks.' The man adjusted the collar of his schoolmaster-like coat, then his beret, blithely flicking the feather. 'Here's what's going to happen: they'll find you and drag you before the court once there can be no doubt about your guilt. After the interrogation, which, knowing the Leipzig authorities, will be painful, you'll dangle from the gallows. And then you'll go to hell.'

'Hell,' Michael repeated. He felt the fear creep into his limbs.

'I could describe it to you, but that would take too long. Just picture what you've heard before, only much worse,' Lucifuge said. 'You'll be taken from one cauldron to the next, then to nail boards with red-hot irons. Pinching pliers will dig into your rotten, ugly soul and torture you for eternity.'

'No!'

'Oh yes, Master Voigt. But only if the Devil wins the bet.'

'How do I keep my soul from being tortured?' Voigt asked desperately.

'That's simple.' The man pointed to the small table under the fogged-up window. 'Take a piece of paper and write down what you regret. All your misdeeds, the wrong you've done to innocent people, all your slander, and forget no one and nothing.'

'I'll do it.' Michael breathed a sigh of relief. 'Anything else?'

'Then you will need to beg for forgiveness in writing and sign your name.'

'Is that all?'

'Yes.'

'But ... What happens then?' Michael looked around the chamber. 'Will this nightmare end?'

Lucifuge laughed softly. 'As I said, they will find you and drag you before the court once the evidence against you is clear. After the interrogation, which, knowing the Leipzig authorities, will be painful, you'll dangle from the gallows. But then you won't go to hell, as you'll have repented of your sins.'

'What?' Michael screamed. 'In that case I'd rather flee to the other side of the world!'

'You won't be able to. The bet doesn't allow for it. But don't be angry with me, I'm only the messenger'. He went on thoughtfully, 'There might be one way to save yourself from the entire interrogation, the gallows, the pain, and the weeks of excruciating torment to come.'

'What is it? I'll do anything!'

Lucifuge pointed to the beam on the ceiling, from which a rope that seemed to have appeared out of thin air swung. The hangman's knot with thirteen loops had already been tied. 'I'll help you by clinging on to your feet too, so that your neck breaks and you don't suffocate so miserably.'

Michael looked at the thick rope and began to tremble. 'But . . . I would go to hell for taking my own life! That would be playing a trick on the Devil.'

'Not quite. If you repent, it's agreed that your soul will go to heaven.' He gestured to the noose with his clawed hand. 'God is merciful, you know.'

'I don't care for this bet,' Michael breathed, shaking. 'It's cruel.'

Lucifuge bellowed with laughter. '*You* were cruel, Master Voigt. You caused your fellow men nothing but misfortune and bad luck and grew rich off their misery. What you are being offered is nothing shy of the greatest act of kindness, which no living person could give you. Not even the Devil. Only a god.'

Michael didn't know what to think any more. The stench in the chamber made him retch, dizziness overcame him and the drying blood on his skin was already pulling it taut. Nightmare or not, it had to end before he woke up and lost his mind.

Besides, Lucifuge was right. His life consisted of betraying others to the best of his ability.

Michael went to the little table, picked up the quill and scribbled down everything he could remember. It didn't surprise him how long the list became. He apologised for each of his wrongdoings individually, begged for forgiveness from the aggrieved parties and admitted that it had been nothing but his lies that had plunged them into ruin. Finally, he signed his name at the bottom, his signature more erratic than usual.

'Very good,' Lucifuge praised him and folded his hands together to give Michael a leg-up. 'Now you just need to stick your neck through the noose and you'll wake up in heaven. May God have mercy on your repented sinner's soul.'

Michael walked over to the rope barefoot and placed his right foot on the man's overlapping fingers. The old man effortlessly lifted him as if he weighed no more than one of the girl's severed arms.

'Is this certain?' he asked.

'A bet is a bet. Even God and the Devil have to keep their word. They're both men of honour, after all.' Lucifuge tilted his head promptingly. 'Have faith.'

'You'll hang on to my legs and break my neck?'

'As sure as my name is Lucifuge Rofocale.'

Michael grabbed the noose with both hands and pulled it open to fit his head through. The coarse rope felt heavy. Its knot would snap his vertebrae when the messenger clung on to him.

His eyes did a last farewell sweep of the chamber.

Michael looked at Gretchen, torn to pieces and rotting. The floorboards were soaked in puddles of blood, the red drops trickling below into the guest room, determined to tell the world about the murder he hadn't committed. Some of the girl's guts and entrails lay on the bed, while other parts drooped down like swollen garlands. Lucifuge was right. Dream or not, he wouldn't have a leg to stand on.

Michael stuck his head through the loop and tightened it. The rough hemp of the rope scratched and chafed his skin – it would leave a bloody mark. But what did he care about his body, when either his soul would go to heaven or he would finally wake from this nightmare?

'Are you ready, Master Voigt?'

'Yes.'

'Then I wish you a safe journey, and please give my regards to my master.'

'Your master? But then surely I'll wake up in–' But before the horrified Michael could finish, Lucifuge slowly let him go.

The noose tightened around his throat, constricting his breathing without fully cutting it off.

Gasping and wheezing, Michael hung from the rope. His own weight wasn't enough to immediately strangle him or break his neck.

Michael had never been more afraid in his entire life.

He tried to widen the noose again and wriggled in an attempt to fall from the beam along with the rope, but it was no use. The pressure in his head grew, his vision blurred, and he felt his tongue loll from his mouth pathetically like an animal trying to force extra air into its lungs.

Lucifuge watched him perish miserably, laughing with his arms by his sides. He even pushed him so that he swung and swayed from side to side. 'You thought you'd have a quick death?' he said, delighted. 'I am neither Lucifuge nor Rofocale. My name is Martin Dietrich. Your soul may well end up in hell, Michael Voigt, and I don't care if it does. Your confession, however, makes up for a lot of your wrongdoings.'

Michael wanted to scream loudly, but nothing more than a

high-pitched, shrill and barely audible croak escaped from his straw-thin throat.

'Now be gone, you good-for-nothing dawdler,' Dietrich said, laughing again. 'Your head is already red as a beet's. I think I'll take my leave before it bursts and splatters all over me. The sounds you're making aren't very pleasant either. I'm afraid you'll have to sing your way to your grave alone.'

Michael's senses faded.

Dietrich darted out the window, the tip of the pheasant feather on his beret bobbing mockingly in salute.

* * *

When Gretchen awoke in the guest's bed the next morning, the room spun around her like a merry-go-round at a fun fair, and she quickly shut her eyes to wait out the dizziness.

She reached out and found the other side of the bed to be cold and empty. The guest must have already left, which she by no means minded. It meant that she could slip away and act as if nothing had happened.

Her mouth felt dry and she could taste sulphur, salt and ink on her tongue. That hadn't happened when she had drunk her parents' wine.

The drink had also produced some other, unusual effects: hallucinations, living shadows and all sorts of things that frightened her. However, since her guest had promised her a tidy sum, she hadn't tried to protest and had closed off her mind when he took her. She'd fallen asleep as soon as their bodies had parted.

The pulling at her temples finally subsided.

Gretchen sat up, and there he was: the guest had hanged himself naked from the beam. A suicide note hung from his neck.

'Lord in heaven, help me!' she cried and jumped into her underwear and dress. Just as she was about to flee the chamber, however, she paused and took the stranger's wallet. The dead man had no more use for his thalers, and a wage was still a wage.

Then Gretchen called for help.

* * *

Bastian sat over the copper plate with a light heart and a nimble tool in his hand. Every flick of his wrist, every scratch of the etching needle, every crosshatch and every vine that he engraved into the soft metal brought him the greatest joy. It was as if each embellishment wanted to reward him with a pleasant sensation.

He used every spare minute that he had and when he wasn't busy with his children to work on Dietrich's plates. Business was business.

For Bastian, this was the best deal that he had ever agreed to.

He didn't know how the strange man had done it, but Michael Voigt had been found hanging from the beams of an inn, naked and with a very long letter of apology and confession around his neck. In the letter Voigt begged God for mercy and for the injured parties' forgiveness.

Goethe had told him that Voigt had been found by one of the innkeeper's daughters, a pretty little thing called Gretchen, who the student incidentally had his eye on, just as he also had his eye on Kate, another of the innkeeper's daughters. The young man knew how to get hold of wine and pleasure cheaply.

Bastian completed the next few engravings and crosshatched according to the little pictures that Dietrich's dog had brought him, along with a short note saying he would come back in five months at the latest to pick up the deck.

Bastian knew that time was of the essence, but he'd felt energised as soon as he'd sat down to work on the copper plates.

The *Leipzig Zeitung* had written about the suicide in great detail, exposing Voigt's shameful web of lies in its entirety. On the same day Breitkopf had apologised to Bastian, and, out of embarrassment, paid him double his monthly salary.

'You're working again?' Susanna asked, approaching the back end of the attic where Bastian always retired to work under the hatch. It was the spot with the best light. He had placed several mirrors around him so that he could engrave and etch late into the night under the mirrors' artificial, reflected light.

'Well yes, I want Breitkopf to see how special my cards will be,' Bastian said. He honoured the agreement and didn't breathe a word of the pact between Dietrich and himself. His ally had also allowed him to use the card forms for his own purposes. Bastian sat up straight and arched his back, feeling proud of himself. 'Look what I've forged: the queen of spades.'

Susanna came closer and set down a pot of tea beside him that smelled of herbs. 'Oh.'

'*Oh?*' Bastian looked up at the sound. She didn't seem impressed, but rather startled. 'You don't like them?' Susanna's opinion meant a lot to him; she was skilled and had an exceptional flair for form patterns when it came to engraving. 'What can I improve?'

'No, no, I like them very much.' Susanna traced the lines and rubbed the crests' fine copper edges. 'I'm just surprised.'

'By what exactly?'

'The delicacy and the ornamentation.' She studied the papers with the preliminary sketches for the cards he was yet to engrave. 'Where did you find these?'

'I collected them. From lots of old books that I found in the Paulina library,' he said vaguely. 'There really is so much to discover there. It's a treasure trove of inspiration, my one and only queen of hearts.'

She smiled at him and ran a hand through his dark hair, caressing the nape of his neck, where she planted a kiss. 'I see you still found a way to make your cards after all, even though I don't like it.'

'Don't be angry with me. Breitkopf really wants me to, and how could I refuse him?' Bastian savoured her affection and encouragement. 'But you still like them?'

'They're far too beautiful to be thrown around shabby tables and be surrounded by drunken laughter,' Susanna replied, laughing, and kissed him tenderly. She tasted of herbs and passion. 'They're wonderful, my husband.' She pulled away from him. 'Don't work too hard. The little ones want to see their father again before they go to bed.'

'Tell them I'll be there and that I'll read them a lovely fairy-tale,' he called after her and picked up the burin in his other hand to get started on the next ornamentation. He really wanted to finish it before he checked in on the children.

By the time Bastian got up it was pitch black in the attic apart from his workspace, where he had lit lamps. He hadn't noticed how the time had flown by. There was now one more detail on the plate, and he was sure it would make the queen of spades a collector's item.

He blew out the paraffin lamps and fumbled his way through the dark flat. Bastian washed his hands, face and neck, slipped on his night robe and climbed under the covers to join Susanna.

He snuggled up to her and felt like the happiest man in the world. And, thanks to his new ally Dietrich, that wouldn't change.

The sloth enjoys playing cards with the villain.

Proverb

IV

Ekaterina Petrovna Solov'ëva moved through the rooms at lightning speed, checking to see if anyone had forgotten or lost anything that might give the German police a clue about their gambling ring. Nothing could be left behind. She hadn't had any time to change yet, only managing to switch her pumps for some comfortable trainers.

'How's it all looking?' her mother's voice drifted from the staircase, speaking in Russian. She had asked the guests to leave after the second major incident, without any rush or panic, offering them kindness and gifts instead.

'Everything's fine up here so far,' her daughter replied.

Ekaterina was furious.

First there had been that madwoman who had hurled a Molotov into the building and slipped out, and then Morgan, who had drawn the ace of spades in supérieur and had tried to cheat in order to run off with the card that Lazarev had previously staked. There was no leeway when it came to dealing with such cases. Whoever broke the rules had to bear the consequences. All the guests knew that, and that was what made supérieur so appealing. And then there had been Boch, who had made everything worse with his intervention.

Ekaterina hurried up another floor and looked around, fixing her dyed-red curls into a bun.

Within less than fifteen minutes, everything had been loaded up and packed away. She only had to make sure that the clean-up team hadn't missed anything, including the empty bullet cartridges and Morgan's body.

Ekaterina checked room after room, searching every nook and cranny. She wasn't afraid of getting down on her knees in her grey dress and expensive tights.

She found nothing.

Her phone rang – it was her mother. 'We have to be out of here in five minutes,' she told her.

'The police would have been here by now,' Ekaterina replied, reassuring her. 'Poe didn't go running to the cops.'

'She definitely did. They could already be watching us. Let's go, my little dove. We got what we came for.'

Ekaterina continued to scour the villa. 'Do you think that this is the last of our tournaments? Today's players won't exactly be singing our praises.'

'Well . . .'Her mother laughed bitterly, 'Nobody could say that it wasn't exciting. I gave every guest a hundred thousand by way of apology. Though perhaps we should host our future tournaments elsewhere, little dove.'

Ekaterina entered the last room that required her close attention. 'Not a bad idea. Palm trees, beaches, glorious weather and a round of poker.'

'And traditional supérieur.'

'Are you sure about that? It was why we –'

'I know what you think of the traditional version of the game, but that's what our guests find so exciting. With us, they get to play it the way it *used* to be played. No amount of money can save you from the power of the ace of spades; that's what the super-rich love about it,' her mother said, sounding convinced. 'Let's go and find a quiet place to talk about where we want to host the next round. I think the Black Sea is a lovely place. With our connections, Mother Russia will welcome us with open arms.' She hung up.

Ekaterina did a final sweep and returned to the basement, where, to her surprise, she ran into Lazarev. 'Oh. You?'

'That's right – oh, me.' He loosened his black hair, which fell over his undercut, and lifted his smartphone in the air. 'This isn't mine. You gave me Boch's.'

Ekaterina mumbled an apology and went into the kitchen, which looked perfectly innocent. There was nothing left to suggest that there had been a party. Cutlery, caviar, champagne, everything had been cleared and stowed away. Poe's Beretta, a forgotten knife and the casino security guard's phone – which turned out to be Lazarev's – were the only things left in the small cupboard.

'Yes, that's the one,' the oligarch's son confirmed. He had followed her in. She threw it to him, and he caught it deftly. 'Has anyone ever told you that you've got a great rack, pretty Katia?' He took off his jacket, folded it in half and set it down on the countertop.

Ekaterina didn't like his tone or his demeanour. He was ten years younger than her, but that didn't seem to stop him trying his chances with her, or rather he was the type that would have the audacity to demand sex from her as compensation for his loss. 'We've already apologised, and in future you will—'

'*In future?*' Lazarev placed his phone on his jacket and unbuttoned the sleeves of his designer shirt. The cufflinks landed next to his smartphone. 'What future? Boch already knows everything. He knows you and your mother. He'll rat you out to the casinos, and that'll be the end of it.' He came closer. 'They've got a network all over the world. As soon as you want to rent anything out, everyone will know and call the cops. Nobody wants rounds of supérieur being hosted near legal casinos.'

Ekaterina didn't agree with him, but she let him talk. As long as he felt superior, he was more or less tolerable. Besides, he was the one who had brought Boch with him and had got them into trouble in the first place, and now he was acting as if he had nothing to do with it. The spoilt boy would pay for that. But not now. 'We'll find a solution, Mr Lazarev.' With a little charm, she would get him off her back. 'If you—'

'You will,' he interrupted her, reaching into his discarded jacket. He showed her four historical cards. 'But that's not all. I've got another question for you: do you notice anything?'

She knew what he was getting at. 'You're missing a card.'

'Exactly. Morgan doesn't have it any more, so it must be in the garden. Or Boch took it.' He stepped towards her, pushing her further into the cramped kitchen. 'That's a serious loss for me. No amount of money can make up for it.' He widened his stance and played with one of the red curls that had come loose from her bun. 'And you know that I have plenty more where that came from anyway.'

Ekaterina wouldn't humiliate herself so much as to touch the man. 'Mr Lazarev, I must ask you to leave. The police will probably be here soon, and you definitely wouldn't want to get arrested. Your father wouldn't like that.'

'I know what I would really like . . .' Lazarev suddenly made a few clumsy movements and flung himself against her.

Ekaterina slammed into the wall, her back crashing against the window. 'Stop it!' She quickly pushed away the Russian, who looked equally as stunned as she was.

'I . . .' Furious, he turned around and looked over his shoulder. 'What the hell was that? I'll punch you right in the mouth, you—'

Ekaterina looked past Lazarev and spotted a man of average

build wearing street clothes and a black balaclava over his head. The man had punched Lazarev before pulling back.

'Shut up and give me the cards,' came the harsh demand. His gloved fingers held the Beretta Bobcat that they had taken from Poe.

'What?' Lazarev laughed dismissively. 'You motherfucker! You're standing in front of a man who—'

The masked man pulled the trigger twice.

Despite the gun's small calibre, the gunshots echoed loudly around the kitchen as flashes of fire blazed brightly out of the barrel.

The victim's neck burst open as if a firework had exploded in his veins. The second bullet ripped through the young man's upper body, his blood spraying over Ekaterina.

Lazarev collapsed. The ancient cards fell onto the kitchen countertop. He writhed and convulsed, choking as his blood flooded the floor. After a few seconds, he went still.

Ekaterina didn't dare move. The man's icy brown eyes and self-assured composure were ample warning for her to stay still. This wasn't his first kill. He knew what he was doing.

'Little dove?' She heard her worried mother's voice. 'Little dove, what are you doing?'

'What do you want?' Ekaterina asked the masked man, stammering.

'I'll tell you that in just a moment,' he replied. He leaned back with his upper body and glanced out through the door-frame into the hallway. 'Well, here we are, Ms Solov'ëva.'

She could hear footsteps approaching, then her mother's voice. 'What's . . . Who are you?'

'I'll tell you that soon.' He swung his arm around, took aim and pulled the trigger twice.

The bang reverberated so powerfully through the entrance and the stairwell that it could've been mistaken for a church bell. Ekaterina and her mother screamed and her mother fell to the floor.

The stranger immediately pointed the gun at Ekaterina again. 'Four bullets, plus a spare one in the model. There's still another three rounds left for you, Ms Solov'ëva.' His dark eyes remained fixed on her. 'I'll let you go if you give me the list of players who signed up with you to play supérieur.' As if in passing, he pocketed the four historical cards that had belonged to Lazarev.

Now Ekaterina knew what the man was after: the incredibly valuable, one-of-a-kind cards, without having to play the game. He had killed the oligarch's son for them, was prepared to risk going to war with Lazarev senior for them and had shot her mother in cold blood in the process. Ekaterina knew full well that he wouldn't let her live.

That meant she could refuse to help him.

That it was her duty to fight for her life and avenge the death of her mamochka. Ekaterina glanced at the knife on the countertop.

The masked man laughed softly. 'You really think you're capable of that?'

'Da,' Ekaterina retorted. She pretended to jump and then ducked, the soles of her sneakers squeaking and sliding about in the pools of blood.

The first bullet ripped past her and drove into Boch's smartphone, which smashed to pieces and went flying across the kitchen. A pungent smell immediately filled the room – the battery had exploded.

Ekaterina grabbed the knife. She swung it around and stabbed the masked man, a scream escaping her throat as she channelled all her strength into the thrust.

Her blade met with resistance, which travelled up to her arm and all the way to her shoulder. She had caught the knife in the doorframe.

The masked man was standing in the hallway behind her. He tilted his head slightly. He'd dodged her attack with a small step back. Laugh lines appeared around his eyes. 'I'm sure I'll find the list in your house. With your level of organisation, you'll have kept records.' His finger curled around the trigger. 'Don't worry, I'll see myself out.'

Ekaterina tried to escape the bullets, but the narrow kitchen provided little shelter.

She heard the first gunshot. A bright flash travelled through her nose and into her skull, blinding and deafening her.

Ekaterina's legs buckled. Her mind went blank.

* * *

Tadeus sat in a room of the Atlantic Hotel, which he'd checked into after making a quick detour via his flat, his mind racing. He'd laid a bag of ice on his battered knee, and the cold water helped to suppress the tiredness.

He hadn't wanted to sleep within his own four walls after what had happened. Solov'ëva and her mother had probably sent the same killing squad after him that had shot Morgan, and, with a few clues from Lazarev, finding out where he lived would be easy enough.

On the table in front of him lay the seven of clubs that Morgan had forced him to take and a piece of paper, onto which Tadeus had jotted down the cryptic syllables that the man had spoken to him shortly before his death.

He couldn't make sense of it, most likely due to his utter exhaustion and everything he had experienced in the last hour.

Cheats and frauds didn't get shot in the civilised world. Beaten up, sure. Tadeus had seen that happen at backroom parties. Sometimes, people had their fingers or hands broken. But Morgan had been hunted down like an animal.

The gurgling coffee machine poured him a triple espresso to sharpen his mind. Sleep would probably have been the healthier and more sensible alternative.

No time for that. Tadeus rubbed his eyes and looked at the card.

Thanks to the internet, he had found exactly what Morgan had fought tooth and nail for. It was the seven of clubs, a card from 1804. Tadeus didn't like its motif. It looked like an illustration from an old children's book onto which the seven cross signs had been forcefully added. The fact that it had been hand-painted didn't help either. It may be a special, historic and valuable card, but Tadeus didn't think it was worth murdering someone over.

Yet, despite the card's ugly motif, Tadeus felt drawn to it, as if there was more to it than met the eye.

He had heard several sirens pass by and stop very close to his hotel. The Solov'ëvas' party had come to an end. The neighbours would have heard the gunshots and called the police.

It then suddenly occurred to Tadeus that his phone was still at the villa, but, if he reported it as stolen now, it would raise more suspicion than if he pretended to only notice it missing later. He debated going back to the former Belle Époque to check if it was still there. But what good would that do? The authorities definitely wouldn't let him look around or take his phone home even if he found it.

Tadeus forced himself to be pragmatic and write down everything that he knew from the night at the villa to try to solve the mystery of the card that Morgan had jumped out of a window and died for.

Clearly, the seven of clubs couldn't fall into the hands of a certain person – but why?

Tadeus grabbed a pencil and scribbled down on the hotel's notepad:

- *Look up Morgan (travel destinations, connections)*
- *Research 'The Devil's Playbook'*
- *Ask about Solov'ëva in casinos*
- *Find out more about the card: is it valuable? Any other owners involved?*
- *Look up the deaths in Monaco → are they connected?*

He then drew a box around it and crossed it out with a sweeping motion. *It's none of my business.*

Tadeus looked at the seven of clubs. The card had given him an electric shock and left him with the strangest impression, which had made him wonder if he had just imagined it all. There had been the singing, the words in an alien language and the pleasant shiver up his spine.

But none of it was his concern, and, with his personal financial issues, the last thing he needed was to get into more trouble. He had nothing to hide and didn't want to hide anything. He didn't owe Morgan anything and had nothing to do with Solov'ëva or their little gambling rounds. So he would go to the police and hand in the card and his report. Tadeus could justify his visit to the Belle Époque by saying he had been investigating on the casino's behalf in an attempt to crack down on illegal gambling. His escape during the gunfight would pass as a panic response to the events in any court of law, and the matter would be settled.

And that's what I'll do. Tadeus finished his espresso.

To maintain credibility, he couldn't wait too long before he showed up at the police station. The authorities were most likely at the former Belle Époque now, so he would make a little detour past the villa before continuing onwards to the station and handing in his report.

Tadeus glanced at the seven of clubs again; the card kept drawing his attention. He touched it gently and waited for tonight's phenomenon to repeat itself.

But nothing coursed through his fingertips, there were no sounds, and he didn't feel any kind of energy flowing through him. He would have liked to experience those extraordinary sensations again. The part of his brain vulnerable to addiction had remembered the blissful feeling and demanded more, but now that was a thing of the past too.

Tadeus impulsively lifted the card up and held it against the light.

Sure enough, something shimmered through the seven of clubs' motif.

Tadeus became curious.

He gently flicked the card and listened, carefully rubbing the old paper to see if anything poked out from under the motif.

Suddenly, he heard a corner crackle from the friction and burst open a few millimetres, which separated the layers that had been glued together. This revealed another cover, a stiff middle layer and the back of the card.

'I must be going crazy,' he murmured in surprise. He went into the bathroom and fetched his little sewing kit. With a needle from it he separated the card further and exposed the protected layer on the inside.

A second card in the French style appeared. It was the nine of spades, with lustrous details and colours, ranging from dark blue to gold, black and grey lines. You could even make out the tiny details on people's faces and clothing, but Tadeus was unable to decipher the writing, likely an epigram of some kind. It looked like the card-maker might even have used gold leaf.

Tadeus slumped back in the hotel armchair. He felt deeply moved and inexplicably drawn to the card, just like the first time he had seen it. He knew that what lay in front of him was the real masterpiece. Morgan hadn't been after the seven of clubs; he'd wanted the nine of spades.

The paper was old, but it hadn't yellowed and hardly looked

worn. The card lay before him as fresh as the day it was made, reflecting the light. It was far more valuable than any ordinary playing card. It was a work of art that belonged in a museum, and undoubtedly ridiculously expensive.

Tadeus turned it over, fascinated.

The back of the card was a dark red that resembled the colour of fresh liver and looked moist, despite being dry to the touch. There was a fine check pattern drawn on in grey and black, and in the four corners silver fleurs-de-lis glistened faintly.

Even Tadeus, who knew nothing about antiques, knew that this had to be a precious, irreplaceable and one-of-a-kind piece.

It was so unique that someone had killed for it.

And so unique that someone from another time had hidden it.

Despite spending months and years playing with the modern cards that had succeeded this masterpiece, Tadeus knew little about the history of playing cards. He couldn't even begin to try to narrow down the period of this treasure, let alone estimate how long people had been playing cards for.

Tadeus was gripped by a new fever, a new obsession: he wouldn't give up the card again. He had stumbled across it for the first time in the casino, had been given it a second time, and the card had revealed and shown itself to him – so it would stay with him. Morgan and the nine of spades itself had chosen him as their protector.

More questions arose in Tadeus' mind: were there other cards like it? Perhaps an entire deck? Or was this card just an individual, decorative piece? Who had made it? For whom? Had Lazarev known about the secret, hidden card? He doubted it. And from whom or what did the card need protecting, just as Morgan had instilled in him?

Tadeus looked at the dismantled seven of clubs that served as the other card's hiding place. The police would need some supporting evidence to go with his statement when he told them about Morgan and the card. He had to give them something.

Tadeus plucked the fruit drop from his unused pillow and poured himself a glass of water. He carefully wetted his index finger and ran it over the sweet so that it formed a sticky film on the tip of his finger. He then spread it over the edges of the card, and quickly repeated the same process until the seven of clubs was covered in the substance all the way around. For his next step, he firmly pressed the front and back of the card together and laid the card on the floor, then grabbed the hotel Bible and placed it on top of the card for a few minutes to increase the pressure.

To his relief, the fake card held. He could now hand in the seven of clubs to the police with ease. The real card wouldn't be lost.

The extraordinary nine of spades would go into the safe. There was no other place in the room that Tadeus felt was secure enough to hide the card. He would have even preferred to lock the safe in a larger vault and build a wall around it.

He then went into the bathroom to take a look at himself in the mirror. His suit revealed that he'd been forced to trudge through mud and shrubbery, which made the story he was about to tell all the more believable. He'd also acquired scratches on his face, which stung when he washed them briefly.

Old. Old and tired. Tadeus rubbed his stubble and the salt-and-pepper beard on his lower jaw, and then combed back his dark brown hair, the mottled patches glistening under the glow of the bathroom lamp. *Very tired.* He would shower when he got back – he couldn't show up at the police station looking overly neat and tidy. Refraining from another espresso, he brushed off the worst of the dirt from his clothes and left the Atlantic.

Tadeus walked to the former Belle Époque with the seven of clubs hidden in his inner jacket pocket. The pain in his right knee was worse than before, and the bandage didn't help. Every now and again he felt a stab of it in his lower back as if he hadn't taken any painkillers. *You have to expect less of your body when you turn fifty.*

As Tadeus came up Maria-Viktoria Street, the brilliance of numerous circling and flashing blue lights immediately jumped out at him. There were several police cars parked outside the villa, as well as three hearses and a white van with the letters CSI written on it – forensics.

The closer he got, the more clearly he could hear the beeping of the radios of the officers who were in front of the villa securing the entrance. Camera teams, members of the press and other onlookers lingered by the wrought-iron gate of the villa, gawking and snapping photos and videos. Social media was most likely blowing up with the groundbreaking news from Baden-Baden.

Two long, black limousines with crosses on the rear windows drove off, pursued by a flurry of flashing cameras.

Why are there so many hearses? Was there more than one dead body? The drama must have all unfolded after his disappearance.

He slowly approached the scene and listened to the conversations between the spectators and the camera teams filming the first reports.

'. . .according to witnesses from the street, there was a shooting at the abandoned hotel, which is currently closed for renovations,' a reporter from a private channel said behind the glare of a small handheld camera. 'Several gunshots were reportedly heard. We saw the second coffin ourselves earlier, which was loaded and is now being taken to forensics.' The man looked into the lens with a sorrowful expression. 'The police have since confirmed that the bodies of a mother, her daughter and a young man have been found. Unofficial reports claim the young man was the son of the Russian businessman Mikhail Alexandrovich

Lazarev, who is believed to be a friend of the Russian president. Meanwhile, rumours are circulating about what happened in this beautiful building, which was sold to an American investor just a few weeks ago.'

Lazarev. Dead. Tadeus took a deep breath. Dealing with the German police would be the least of the murderer's problems.

Suddenly, a commotion broke out at the railings. A frenzy of flashing cameras followed the proceedings opposite the entrance, from which two men in dark undertaker suits carrying a simple zinc coffin emerged. While the onlookers watched the third body being loaded into the car, Tadeus saw a man in a white full-body suit hand a gun in a plastic bag to his colleague, who put it into a safety case. The gun was small and burnished. Its tip-up barrel was open.

Poe. Tadeus remembered the woman's Beretta Bobcat. She must have used the weapon after all and killed the alleged culprits for her fiancé's death. *I should have made her come with me. Then there wouldn't be so many coffins.* Morgan's leap from the window had scuppered his plan.

But why had she left the murder weapon behind? Out of haste? Had she panicked?

Tadeus turned away from the villa.

He slowly walked along the street and pondered it all. Three deaths: a mother, daughter and Lazarev – but what about Morgan? He didn't believe that his body was still lying in the bushes somewhere, undiscovered.

His sortie into the illegal gambling world had turned into a fiasco: several murders, a very wealthy oligarch who had lost his son, and Tadeus caught in the crossfire as a witness.

And then there was his card, the nine of spades, which was so unique and beautiful that he didn't want to give it up. Ever. The thought of the exhilarating experience in the garden repeating itself, the evocative singing, the captivating voices, that blissful feeling that had coursed through him practically made him tingle with anticipation. Nobody knew that he had the card.

Tadeus changed his plan.

He went back to the hotel and disappeared into his room. He was too tired and overwhelmed by events to think clearly or be interviewed by the police, and decided he would formally hand over the fake card to the authorities tomorrow morning. Besides, the police already had their work cut out for them at the villa. He'd approach them away from the cameras and reporters, and, most importantly, when he was well rested.

Tadeus stripped down to his underwear, jumped into bed and closed his eyes. His first task after breakfast tomorrow would be to go to the police station. Case closed.

Except for the card.

His card.

As soon as he thought about the nine of spades, Tadeus felt compelled to get up and take the card out of the vault.

He gazed at it pensively and found himself gently stroking the card before returning it to the ironclad box. He imagined that the card glowed for him again as if it were pleased to see him. Just like last time.

* * *

London, England,
United Kingdom

'And now let us move on to lot 42, ladies and gentlemen,' the auctioneer from Sotheby's announced from a stand that resembled a pulpit. The rows of chairs at the auction house on New Bond Street were packed to the rafters. 'To the uninitiated eye, this may look like an incomplete set of playing cards,' he explained condescendingly, a hint of benevolence nevertheless audible in his nasal voice.

Dorian Blessington found this amusing and wiped a couple of sandwich crumbs from his understated green jacket, which he had paired with black trousers and a light-grey shirt. Instead of a neck- or bow tie, he had pinned a brooch onto his collar. This was one of his finds and part of the collection from which he had grown rich thanks to the shopping channels.

He enjoyed the charm of eloquently worded impertinence, with which one could insult customers without them even noticing. The man in his mid-fifties had used the same kind of language in the past while working at the sales counter of a jewellery shop. Everyone had found it delightful and thought they were being treated with the utmost respect, when, in actual fact, every 'of course' meant *douchebag*, and every 'sir' or 'madam' meant nothing other than *fuck you, fucker*.

A low murmur went through the unadorned white room. People grew curious.

Dorian scanned the room for any loud colours. Nothing was to distract from the items on display that were up for sale to the highest bidder. A row of spotlights on the ceiling illuminated the stand and the low stage so that everyone could see what was on offer.

Diagonally behind the auctioneer, two Sotheby's employees were waiting and helping at a counter where a hidden computer was located for handling any issues. Several gentlemen sat directly next to them, manning the telephones to keep the connected bidders up to date. Hushed conversations were taking place.

An auction house employee wearing the obligatory apron pushed the presentation trolley in.

On a screen above the auctioneers' heads, the current status of lot 24 was shown. The first bid was 10,000 British pounds, with the equivalent sum in other currencies flickering below.

Dorian looked at the auction prospectus and marked a tick next to the set he desperately wanted. He collected all kinds of curious items connected with death, such as a chopstick that had been the cause of the accidental death of a tourist in Tokyo in 1963; the lighter that had started the 16 February 1983 forest fire in Australia and caused seventy-five deaths; various murder weapons, and a swivel chair on which a man had accidentally smashed through his window while replacing a lamp bulb and fallen to his death.

Lot 42 would make a perfect addition.

A camera captured the objects and projected magnified images of them onto the wall behind them.

There were five stained playing cards under the glass of the display case. An expert would know that the cards' rusty brown colour was in fact dried blood, and there was a fair amount of it.

Dorian compared the photo in the catalogue with the per-fectly illuminated originals on the rotating stands, which gave the bidders a chance to view the pieces from every angle. It was a perfect match.

'As you can see, ladies and gentlemen, here we have the queen of spades, the ace of spades, the ace of clubs, the eight of spades and the eight of clubs,' the auctioneer explained. 'Those of you who play poker will be familiar with this as the well-known dead man's hand. Here' – he gestured to the box with his little ebony hammer – 'you can see the original and namesake, which was in the hands of a Wild Bill Hickok on 2 August 1876 in No. 10 Saloon when he was shot in the back of the head by Jack McCall. Mr Hickok died holding these cards, which have since become known as the dead man's hand. Sotheby's is selling this set of deadly historical playing cards' – the people in the hall laughed politely as the telephone operators repeated the auctioneer's words – 'on behalf of an anonymous seller. Certificates proving the age and origin of the cards are enclosed with lot 42. Lab results have confirmed that the stains are human blood, which we believe to be Mr Hickok's.' The auctioneer paused dramatically. 'I'll open the bidding at ten thousand pounds sterling.'

In order to avoid appearing too eager or cause a bidding avalanche, Dorian waited a few seconds before raising his card.

'And there we have it – ten thousand. Thank you very much, sir,' the auctioneer began the show, trying to drive in a higher bid.

To Dorian's delight, the offers went up in modest amounts, the monitor displaying the updated price each time. The sum increased in increments of fifty, with the auctioneer being the one generating the most pressure.

Dorian joined in when someone threatened to outbid him at the last second. He firmly believed that no one had studied the history of cards as thoroughly as he had.

The dead man's hand had actually caused two deaths, not only having killed Wild Bill Hickok, but also his murderer, McCall, who had been executed in March 1877.

Hickok himself had also shot at least eight people in eight gunfights until April 1871, when he first shot the gambler Phil Coe and then accidentally shot a deputy. In the subsequent trial he was able to prove that this had been unintentional and a mistake. Legend had it that Hickok never shot another man after this incident.

His mistake. He should have got rid of McCall first. Dorian lifted his bidding card and raised his offer to £21,500. There were two other competitors sitting in the hall, and a third occasionally joined in over the phone. No one seemed particularly interested in the strange cards.

This was ideal for Dorian, who considered himself to be a typical British eccentric and had consequently placed a bet that the price wouldn't exceed £100,000.

He firmly pinned his hopes on nobody knowing what he did: if he had got his sources right, the dead man's hand held a secret.

Before Hickok had got shot in the back, in 1872 he had taken part in a buffalo hunt that had been organised for the grand duke Alexeï Alexandrovich Romanov, son of the Russian tsar Alexander II. Even General Custer had joined in the hunt. To this day, the hunt was remembered in the USA as the Great Royal Buffalo Hunt.

Hickok, who proved himself to be an exceptional hunter and assistant, was then personally presented with a pack of cards by Alexeï Alexandrovitch himself. The former gunman later toured the USA with Buffalo Bill's Wild West Show. He always carried the Russian grand duke's pack of cards with him on his journeys, until he arrived in the gold mining settlement of Deadwood in the Dakota Territory. Hickok kept his head above water in Deadwood as a gambler until McCall shot him.

Dorian lifted his card again. The latest offer had just come in at £30,000. It was just him and the telephone bidder left. 'Thirty-five thousand,' Dorian said clearly, raising the bid by a tidy £5,000 to make it plain that he wouldn't let his treasure escape his clutches.

'Of course, sir,' the auctioneer said and glanced at the operator. 'Going once, going—'

'Forty thousand!' the man at the receiver cried.

A murmur went through the hall. The anonymous bidder had picked up the gauntlet and made it just as obvious that he wouldn't let the dead man's hand go without a fight.

Dorian smiled. He noticed that nobody was sitting behind him, and this reassured him – a corner provided cover. According to the legend, Hickok on this occasion had chosen not to sit with his back against the wall, despite this being against his usual preference. The decision to do so had cost him his life.

Why McCall had shot him, however, remained a mystery. He hadn't even been part of their round.

'Fifty thousand,' Dorian countered firmly. He wanted the cards.

In truth, it was only one of them that he wanted: the queen of spades. Women often had secrets, and so did this one. Without knowing it, the Russian grand duke had given away something special, hidden away inside the card: a second card of extraordinary sentimental and financial value.

The ace of spades was considered a peculiarity, a unique and legendary card associated with spectres and the supernatural. It inspired Alexander Pushkin to write his story 'The Queen of Spades', which then inspired Tchaikovsky to write an opera with the same name.

But it wasn't the actual card that was so mysterious, but rather its well-hidden inner workings.

'Sixty thousand,' the man at the receiver stated calmly.

The bidding war suddenly resembled a stock market boom. The visitors whispered their estimations to each other.

Dorian suspected he wasn't the only one who knew about the queen of spades' secret.

'Eighty thousand,' he said.

'One hundred thousand.'

That was the end of his bet. Dorian was frustrated, but losing lot 42 would be even worse. Just as he was about to raise his card again, his smartphone rang with the melody to the River Kwai March. Although it was frowned upon during an auction, he answered the call – there was a chance it was business. He gestured apologetically.

'If you keep raising the bid, sir, you might find yourself cursed,' he heard the stranger's voice on the line tell him. 'Three, seven, ace. Three, seven, queen.'

Click.

'Sir, going twice. Do I hear a counterbid?'

Dorian raised his eyebrows. The anonymous caller had quoted the words of the deranged Hermann from Pushkin's 'The Queen of Spades' and was actually trying to intimidate him. 'One hundred and fifty thousand.'

The murmurs turned into suppressed exclamations. No one had expected this. Never in a thousand years.

The telephone operator shook his head.

Applause broke out in the auction room. Dorian's aggressive counterbid had paid off.

'. . .And gone! Sold to bidder number twenty-three,' the auctioneer proclaimed in a relaxed, professional and matter-of-fact tone, nonetheless failing to contain his smile. The old cards had fetched more than expected. The hammer slammed down loudly like the crack of a whip. 'Congratulations, sir.'

Dorian stood up and walked towards the counter at the side where the formalities were completed and where he would be presented with the cards. He insisted on receiving them immediately and was a little irritated that he'd underestimated how much they'd sell for.

As Dorian only had £50,000 with him, he paid by instant bank transfer; after a short phone call with his bank the matter was settled. He was handed the cards in a neatly packaged, water-resistant box with the name of the auction house printed on it.

With a smile strapped across his face, he made his way home.

Dorian could hardly wait to have the queen of spades all to himself, to examine it in private.

And yet he forced himself to hold off for a while longer.

To savour it.

He had stumbled across the queen of spades ten years ago and had spent eight years meticulously researching the card, the card-maker, the events connected with it and its whereabouts.

Dorian headed for the nearest café. He wanted to drink tea,

eat scones and stare at the box to build his anticipation. He knew that soon he would be holding the reward in his hands and that it would have all been worth his time and money.

He walked into TeaTeaTwister, a relatively hip café where primarily young people hung out and 'partied hard' with their tea instead of savouring it. The place was full of hipsters and young people who looked like they'd walked straight out of a fashion magazine. Some of the customers occasionally looked a little shabby, but they could still afford and feel superior drinking the tea even though its image had taken a hit in recent years. Dorian liked it when conventions were broken. It was the only way anything new ever evolved.

He ordered himself a Spiced Teatea and a Full Britbrit Scones Feast and ate in peace, enjoying every mouthful of the sweet and spicy flavours. He gazed adoringly at the Sotheby's box as he ate, as if this was the best date he'd ever been on.

Suddenly, a man over sixty plopped into the seat next to him. Dorian immediately noticed the stranger's bushy eyebrows, which had been combed upwards, his cunning, flashing, hazel eyes and his eccentric Dalí moustache.

'Oh, I'm glad I caught you,' the stranger said hastily. He had a slight accent.

'That you did. To what do I owe the pleasure?' Dorian asked.

'The auction.' He tapped the box, pulled out a pair of loud red glasses from his tweed jacket and put them on. The man certainly liked to stand out: he looked like he'd just escaped from a play. 'I wanted to bid.'

'Well I'm afraid you're too late, sir. And no, you can't buy them off me.' Dorian was pleased to have beaten another bidder. 'What's your name, *sir*?' *Fuck you, fucker.* He protectively moved the box away from him.

'Henry Pierre Gillot. I'm a patron and collector.' He reached into his inside pocket and pulled out several historical playing cards carefully wrapped in foil. It took only one glance for Dorian to recognise their worth, and he almost choked on a piece of scone that he had shoved into his mouth. 'May I suggest a trade? These for your dead man's hand.'

Dorian laughed. 'I'm afraid not, sir. Besides, your cards are worth a lot more than mine.'

'I don't think so.' Gillot watched him furtively from under his bushy eyebrows. The long black hairs stood up over his eyes like little flicks of fire.

Dorian realised that this man knew just as much about the secret inner workings of the ace of spades as he did.

And *that* fascinated him.

He dipped another plain scone into his SpicedTeatea. 'How long have you been looking for the dead man's hand?'

'Three years.'

'It's taken me eight.'

'And you beat me to it. It appears luck was on your side. Congratulations, sir.' Gillot gathered his treasure collection of cards and carelessly stuffed them back into his pocket. 'If what they say about the card proves to be true, would you be so kind as to invite me to your house? So that I could at least take a look at it?' He extended his arm and placed a business card on top of the box. 'That's a genuine request, sir.'

'Of course, Monsieur Gillot.'

'Thank you very much.' With that, the man rose, bowed briefly and left the TeaTeaTwister café, dragging his feet slightly. Dorian guessed it had to do with a hip replacement that hadn't been fitted properly; he recognised the limp from his mother.

After finishing his tea and four scones with clotted cream, and gazing tirelessly and adoringly at the box, Dorian got up and wandered through the city centre with his new acquisition to draw out his anticipation even further.

He made himself stroll through the streets for the rest of the afternoon, until he couldn't hold himself back any longer and hurried to the underground car park where he'd left his white Mini Cooper Countryman. The car was modest in size, understated yet expensive, making it perfect for central London.

Dorian jumped into the driver's seat and placed the Sotheby's box next to him. The machine to pay for his parking ticket was by the exit.

At the back of the car, a shadow stirred suddenly and darted behind a pillar.

Dorian immediately started the engine and stepped on the gas. He wasn't going to let some random garage thief steal his treasure on his last stretch home.

The Mini flew up the short ramp until it reached the lowered barrier. The machine demanded payment. Thankfully, there was a card payment option for those who had forgotten to bring cash.

Dorian wasn't a worrier, but he found himself looking into his rear-view mirror and checking the dark tunnel behind him as he rummaged around for the card in his wallet. His pursuer could appear out of nowhere – some drug addict who needed money, perhaps. Dorian didn't judge desperate people who had fallen into a vicious circle, but he didn't think that gave them the right to attack him. Especially not today.

His fingers fumbled with the ticket and his credit card as he inserted it into the machine. Once he entered his pin, the transaction was processed automatically.

It felt like decades before the green light flashed and the machine spat his card out. Dorian fished it out of the slot and waited for the barrier to go up.

He could hear footsteps coming from the darkness. They sped up. It appeared that the invisible pursuer had decided to attack.

The red and white aluminium bar finally snapped into a vertical position.

Dorian put his foot on the gas, cursing. The Mini Cooper's smoking tyres raced out of the car park with a screech before weaving recklessly through the London traffic, which, despite the congestion charge, hadn't noticeably improved.

Dorian took a deep breath. He'd lost the thief.

He drove leisurely through the city, fighting his way through traffic jams to his house in Bloomsbury. He'd bought the house twenty years ago at an obscenely cheap price and had the dump built into a mansion with a garden, which was nothing other than a decadent waste of space in London. In the meantime, its value had increased tenfold. Bloomsbury had plenty of sights and cultural attractions to offer and was considered a desirable neighbourhood.

Dorian was looking forward to the champagne he would soon open to celebrate the occasion. The queen of spades. His lady. Carrying the fabled child in her perfectly flat stomach.

He was turning in to Argyle Street when a violent blow smashed into the side of his Mini. The bang and metallic screech of bending material sounded simultaneously. Despite having his seatbelt on, Dorian flew up from the seat and slammed against the roof of the car. He heard the back of his neck crack loudly.

His car had been knocked several metres to the side, and his engine had died. The other car must have hit him at full speed.

Dizzy, Dorian collapsed onto the steering wheel, from which the burst remains of the airbag dangled like a limp, grey tongue. It reeked of talcum powder, his neck felt like it was on fire and his headache made him groan. Blood poured from his nose and down his throat. He could taste it clearly.

Dorian vaguely made out a man's face next to the destroyed passenger window. A pair of hands covered in black latex opened the Sotheby's box, rummaged through the cards, snatched the queen of spades and replaced it with an identical version.

'What are you doing?' Dorian protested weakly, unbuckling his seatbelt to stop the man. *This was no accident.*

'Carrying out my threat,' the man said. He reached for the light-headed Dorian's chin and jerked his head back violently. 'The owner of the card must suffer the curse. You knew that.'

His injured neck cracked once again, and this time Dorian Blessington lost his senses for good.

The man tucked the queen of spades into a case he had brought with him.

He didn't see how the lines of the card hidden inside the queen of spades flared up and burned through the bloodstained cover. The queen's face faded in the dancing black flames and transformed into a skull, before the paper disappeared and fell away altogether as grey flakes of ash.

A vague heart appeared beneath it.

Dorian Blessington would have been delighted. After eight years of searching, his theory had proven true.

* * *

Baden-Baden, Baden-Württemberg,
the Federal Republic of Germany

Tadeus stood in the non-smoking area near the blackjack table in his signature, discreet manner and observed the young, dark blonde in the simple trouser suit who had been winning alarmingly often for the past hour. The jewellery on her fingers was cheap – not even real silver. He guessed that she must have had to save up to go to the casino and was likely a saleswoman, a beautician or a hairdresser; a woman with a modest basic salary who was fulfilling her casino dream.

Since the woman didn't have any accomplices, Tadeus hadn't yet been able to determine how she kept on winning.

Sometimes, a guest's winning streak was down to pure luck.

Against all odds, it happened occasionally, sometimes even several times in a row. Tadeus himself had been at a roulette table when a player placed a bet on the same number twice and won three times in a row – a James Bond moment.

He hoped this was the case for this woman, who rejoiced like a child every time she beat the dealer with exactly twenty-one and shouted 'Blackjack!'

His mind drifted back to the last few days' events.

He had got away with much more than he thought he would. The police had taken his statement, questioned him several times and taken the seven of clubs he had handed in as evidence. Inspector Klim from the Baden-Württemberg Criminal Police Office didn't say a word about what had happened at the villa or comment on the three deaths. He advised Tadeus to leave Baden-Baden, but only once he'd unregistered from the state. According to the current state of the investigation, he was not a suspect, but rather an important witness.

This reassured Tadeus immensely. He also hadn't received a phone call asking him where the hidden contents of the card had gone. His nine of spades.

The media had reported that Morgan's body had been found in a little wood. Solov'ëva's men had disappeared as fast as they could and had presumably carelessly disposed of the body.

Tadeus couldn't help thinking about the fiancée who had turned up at the villa.

He had searched for Poe on social media, but she hardly used it. She worked as a trauma surgeon in London, and her last posts were from a long time ago and revolved around her voluntary medical work in Nepal and some poorer regions of Asia that he'd never heard of. Her name often came up in gossip magazine archives due to her relationship with Enrico Pedro García Hermano, the godfather of roses, who had ended his first marriage for the 'gorgeous doctor', or even the 'beautiful angel from

Korea'. It had taken over four years for the talk on the streets to settle down.

Poe reminded Tadeus of his daughter; he decided he would call Michiko in the evening. It had been too long since they'd last seen each other. *I'll visit her, and—*

'What's the latest on the young woman?' he heard Alexa say over his earpiece.

Tadeus flinched. 'She just keeps on winning so far. It seems she's been blessed by Lady Luck,' he reported quietly and stepped back into the shadows. 'She's playing alone.'

'Okay. That's bad news for us and the tax office, then. Head to the bar, please. There's somebody waiting for you in the sitting area on the right.'

'On official business?'

'Yes. He wants you to teach him how to play poker and is prepared to pay a thousand euros for it. He said he's a fan of yours. I thought you could use the extra money.'

Tadeus sighed. He couldn't seem to escape his past as a gambler. 'All right.'

As he walked towards the bar, Tadeus continued to ponder his situation.

The press suspected the existence of an illegal gambling operation in Baden-Baden. The police were withholding his name, and Klim had assured him that they wouldn't give it out.

Tadeus, however, remained unconvinced. Someone from the media was bound to get wind of it all, and then they would be on to him. The guest who had asked for him could be a reporter in disguise, hoping to use the opportunity to get more information.

In the meantime, Tadeus had moved back into his flat and carefully hidden the mysterious card so that it wouldn't be stolen from him. He hadn't yet had the chance to find out more about the nine of spades, but he felt as if he were in love with it.

Every time he looked at the card, he discovered something new, like a painting in which the artist had hidden little details. It was an enigma that Tadeus was unable to resist. And why should he? It made him happy.

He didn't feel as excited any more when he walked into the casino, as if his addiction had fixated on the nine of spades. His nine of spades, which he would cherish and protect so that it would sing to him again; but the card left him stewing.

Tadeus turned right in front of the bar and walked into the club-like lounge.

A man sat in the corner with his back to the wall. He was around ten, fifteen years older than Tadeus and had a Dalí-like moustache, the ends of which stuck out like long antennae. His red and white glasses made him stand out even more, and his red tweed suit and white shoes made him impossible to miss. If there was a competition in the casino for who could attract the most attention without moving or performing a silly dance, the stranger would have won by a landslide.

He waved enthusiastically at Tadeus and nodded to the empty chair. 'Please tell me that's not him,' he said to Alexa. This stranger didn't look like a reporter.

'That's him,' she replied, amused. 'Doesn't he look sweet?'

Tadeus approached the guest and reached out his hand. The man already had a pack of cards in front of him and looked eager to start the lesson.

'Good evening. My name is Boch. I've been told you wish to learn the mysteries of poker?' Tadeus said, suspicious.

The man's grip was surprisingly tight. 'I'm so pleased to finally meet you! I've heard a lot about you, and to think that one card came between us meeting at a tournament,' he said.

Tadeus thought of Morgan and Macao. He hated the blackouts from his wilder times. Having heard a slight French accent, he switched into the stranger's language. 'Then you must already know how to play poker, monsieur.'

'I do, but I'm usually the poor loser who leaves the table with his head hanging low'. The man laughed. 'I'm Henry Pierre Gillot. And please could we switch back to German, even though your French is perfect, Mr Boch?'

The man's name rang no bells for Tadeus. Besides, even if he had been as drunk as a skunk, he would have remembered such a striking character. *Or maybe I mistook him for a hallucination.*

'Of course, Mr Gillot.' He took a seat and had the waiter bring him a mineral water. 'Since you're already familiar with poker, to what exactly do I owe this pleasure? You won't learn any cheating tricks from me.'

'Oh, no! Nothing illegal! It's all perfectly simple and will come as a surprise.'

Gillot removed the top card from the deck and held it up so that Tadeus could see its motif.

The following words were written on the joker in felt-tip pen:

I.

WANT.

MY!

NINE OF SPADES.

Life is not always a matter of holding good cards,
but sometimes, playing a poor hand well.

Jack London (1876–1916)

V

Mikhail Alexandrovich Lazarev, whose friends and family called him Oprichnik due to his loyalty to the president, leaned against the doorway of the huge bathroom and watched the proceedings happening inside.

The luxuriously furnished, tiled room was located on the top floor of the luxury Tsar hotel in Lazarev's penthouse, which overlooked the rooftops of the metropolis. This was where the blond in his mid-fifties made decisions regarding future projects and strategies, where he received guests, and where some people had met their deaths. The penthouse was soundproofed, which blocked out party noise just as well as it did screams and pleas.

Curly, chin-length locks framed his round face, which contrasted with the strong physique that he'd earned thanks to many hours of wrestling and judo training. A thick, gold signet ring with the Russian coat of arms adorned his middle finger. His hands were as coarse and strong as a bricklayer's. They were feared. They could inflict pain. And they could kill. Today, however, he'd let the others do the dirty work. With a cup of coffee in his hand, he stood barefoot in a pair of light-grey trousers and an open white shirt and mercilessly watched his people work.

They had put a black fabric bag over the naked woman's face and poured water over it, making her fear for her life and feel like she would suffocate. Over and over again.

Then she was lifted up and plunked onto the bath stool for a break. Every inch of her scrawny body shook; she gasped loudly and snorted. Her chest rose and fell frantically – she was on the verge of hyperventilating.

She hadn't been asked any questions yet. The preparation came first.

Lazarev could clearly see her ribs. She was wiry like an athlete, but far too thin. There was almost nothing to her bust, and countless bruises adorned her arms. Cable ties held her hands behind her back. But the tragic sight didn't evoke the slightest pity in him.

In the little rest between the pouring of icy water, she received electric shocks from the wires that were attached to her toes with clamps. Although these shocks didn't cause burns and were comparatively harmless, they still coursed through her entire body, making her wince. His people reconnected the ends of the wires to the transformer, which could be turned all the way up.

Lazarev picked up the biscuit from his saucer and ate it mechanically. The biscuits had been made by his wife: ginger and dark chocolate-flavoured and just the right level of sweetness.

'Can you hear me?' he asked her in English. He gestured to the tormentors to stop.

The prisoner panted hastily and sputtered water into the bag, choking audibly. 'Yes,' she managed. She couldn't stop trembling, as if she was still twitching from the electric shocks despite the fact that no one was operating the switch. 'What do you—'

'Why did you murder my son?'

The prisoner gasped and swayed from side to side, struggling to maintain her balance on the tiny seat. 'I don't understand what you mean,' she said quietly.

'His name was Vladimir Mikhaïlovich Lazarev.'

'I should—'

'He was twenty-one and touring Europe to celebrate his coming of age.' Lazarev spoke coldly and pointed to the transformer.

One of his men turned the control knob and the electricity surged through the prisoner's body.

She thrashed about and fell sideways from the stool, unable to support herself. The electricity continued to flow through her.

'You shot him in Baden-Baden,' Lazarev said, watching her suffer without feeling the least bit compensated for his own pain. 'Before I decide what to do with you, I want to hear what made you pull the trigger.'

He lifted his cup as a signal for the switch to be turned back to zero. Lazarev took a long sip. The coffee was an Arabic blend, heavily roasted and made exclusively for him – a gift from the president.

The woman panted as if she were about to give birth, rolled to one side and assumed the foetal position. 'It wasn't me,' she sobbed softly.

'The preliminary investigation findings suggest otherwise.' Lazarev's mind raced. After her confession, he would tear her apart. Alive. He would do it little by little, inject her with drugs so that she would stay awake for a long time and so he could feast on her agonising screams. He wanted her to experience at least a fraction of his suffering before he disposed of her and wiped her from the face of the earth. No one knew where she was and no one would ever find out. 'It was your Beretta that killed my son. You threatened him with it.'

'I didn't do it,' she repeated, making herself even smaller.

'If you give me a good enough reason, I might understand,' Lazarev lied. That wouldn't help her.

'I didn't do it!' she screamed.

He walked into the bathroom and yanked the bag off her head. She blinked in the light and looked at him. The expression on her face was of pure fear.

'Did Vladimir threaten you?'

She closed her eyes and spoke softly in a language he didn't understand. Korean, probably.

He seized her by the neck and her eyes flew open. A stifled cry escaped her throat. 'Did he rape you?' he demanded. Lazarev watched for any reaction on her once beautiful face, which had twisted into a terrified grimace. The make-up from her face had washed away long ago and her black, shoulder-length hair dangled like dark, torn seaweed. 'Did he hurt you?'

'It wasn't me,' she whimpered, tears rolling down her cheeks.

He thrust his cup and saucer into one of his men's hands and dragged the woman by her neck, making her gag and gasp. Lazarev pulled her over the edge of the bathtub, grabbed the shower head, turned on the water and aimed the fine jets at her face.

She gave a suffocating cough, droplets flying everywhere.

'Why the fuck did you shoot my son?!' he shouted at her and turned up the water temperature.

She flailed around with her legs and tried to escape, but she was no match for his strength. What he did gather from in between the gurgling and gagging were more proclamations of innocence.

Gradually, he became more sceptical. Lazarev turned the water off before it became too hot and burned her.

Even the most experienced spies, professional criminals and police informers were not entirely insusceptible to torture and confessed sooner or later. His prisoner, however, didn't spare a single thought about what she could tell him. He had given her various prompts for talking her way out of it, and she hadn't seized any of the opportunities. *Because she was telling the truth.* Lazarev relied on his unfailing, trained intuition more than he did on torture.

He exchanged a brief glance with his men and loosened his

grasp. The woman collapsed on to the tiled floor, half conscious. 'Dry her off, get her in a dressing gown and bring her into the living room.'

He got up and, on his way to the room, threw off his shirt, which had got wet during the interrogation; it landed on the white suede sofa.

Lazarev used the automatic espresso machine to make himself another coffee. He stood pensively in front of the bulletproof panorama window, pushed his blond curls back and stared out at the view of Moscow at night, the swamp of lights flickering below him.

He had been convinced that he had caught his son's murderer, but it obviously wasn't her. This put him in the awkward position of having to apologise.

His men led the woman into the living room. She was wrapped in a bathrobe, and, as he saw in the reflection of the window, was offered something to drink: coffee and water. They had removed her restraints; the cable ties had left behind welts and grazes on her skin. To prevent her from escaping, the men discreetly stood in front of the exits.

Lazarev doubted she would try. She was too weak, dazed, and too much of a realist. The woman knew that she would only get as far as the lift.

'Miss Poe,' he began. He slowly turned to face her, shirtless and with one hand casually resting in his trouser pocket. 'Let's start again.' He nodded to her as if this was their first meeting. 'My name is Mikhail Alexandrovich Lazarev. I am the grieving father of Vladimir Mikhaïlovich, who you—'

'I didn't shoot him,' she interjected immediately and rubbed her pretty face, which had lost its lustre. She sat in front of him, pale and trembling. The young woman was utterly exhausted. Lying was impossible in this state.

'—met,' Lazarev finished. 'Allow me to explain the present

situation: I pulled a few strings. The German police have the murder weapon and a witness statement that claims you threatened my son with it.'

'You'll also find my fingerprints on it.' Poe spoke slowly and drank her coffee, the liquid spilling slightly around the brim of the cup. 'I didn't shoot anyone. Those crazy people ... The Solov'ëvas ... The mother and daughter locked me in a room. They took the gun away from me and left it at the villa when I escaped. Then everything got out of control in the garden, but I was already a long way from the scene.' She placed the cup down and leaned back, sinking into the cushions. The trembling subsided.

Lazarev brushed several fair strands of hair from his face. 'I believe you.'

She laughed once, mirthlessly, and glanced reproachfully at her bruised wrists. Her fingers were gradually losing their blueish tinge and regaining their normal colour.

'Still, the police won't bother looking for other culprits.' Lazarev pointed at the printouts on the table. 'They already have their killer, the murder weapon, a witness statement and fingerprints. Case closed.'

'But I—'

'Circumstantial evidence is enough.' Lazarev gently pulled her to his side with the caution of a fisherman who didn't want to lose his catch. He first needed her to understand his actions. 'You have been betrayed and wrongly accused, Miss Poe. And I have lost my son.' He moved away from the window and approached her in the seating area. 'As I'm sure you've noticed, I have no intention of leaving the murder of my child in the hands of the gentle German justice system.'

Poe recoiled from him.

'I'm not going to hurt you any more,' Lazarev reassured her, keeping his distance. 'I just want to know what happened in the villa and who killed my Vladimir.' He set down his cup. 'Here's what I propose: you go back to Baden-Baden and try to find out more about what happened, and in the meantime I'll make the evidence against you disappear.' He smiled encouragingly. 'The murder weapon, for example, will be easy to get rid of.'

Poe stared at him, then lowered her gaze and glanced at the black surface of her coffee. Steam rose up from it.

Lazarev took this as a good sign that she didn't immediately reject his suggestion. 'The next step of my plan involves the witness who testified against you: Carl Heinrich Tadeus Boch. You know him.'

Poe nodded.

'He knows more than what he told the police,' Lazarev explained. 'I believe that because I received some information suggesting that someone else is also interested in him.' He pointed to her. 'Miss Poe, you might be able to get more out of him than my friends here.' He motioned to his people, who grinned in response.

'Your son and my fiancé were at the same round of cards in Monte Carlo. Now both of them are dead, as if the round was cursed somehow,' Poe replied. 'Do you know what happened in Monaco?'

'No. My son preferred not to tell me everything, otherwise I would have sent someone to keep an eye on him. He played supérieur, just like your fiancé, according to the historical rules.' He recognised the expression of surprise on her face. 'You're not familiar with it?'

'No.'

'You risk your own life in the game. If you draw the ace of spades, you're dead. Stone cold dead.'

Poe looked absolutely horrified. 'That . . . Enrico would never have played such a game! We had plans, plans that−' She broke off mid-sentence and seemed to consider this for a moment. 'They murdered him – those crazy Solov'ëvas,' she whispered. 'He was a daredevil, but something like this . . .' She looked petrified. 'Supérieur, you say?'

The bait had worked; Lazarev had caught her on his hook. Now all he had to do was reel her in and get her to work for him. 'I did some research on Arthur Patrick Morgan, the man who, according to witness statements, stole a historical playing card from my son at the table and took off with it.'

'A historical one? Was it the seven of clubs? Yes! He– My fiancé said it was seven! The seven of clubs!'

'Why do you ask?'

'Enrico took it with him to Monaco as his stake, and I . . . I hated the card. It had a bad aura, and I wish he had lost it. It gave me nightmares and still does.' She waved her hand dismissively and wrapped the dressing gown tighter around herself. 'It's hard to explain what I mean to people like you.'

'Boch will be able to tell you about that. Speaking of, they found Morgan's body in the woods.' It was time for another bait, to really lure Poe in. 'I don't want to rule out the possibility of greed having played a role in the death of your fiancé and my son. It may not have been one of the Solov'ëvas. Perhaps the murderer wanted the card for themselves.'

'Do you think it was Boch?'

'No, I first thought it was you,' Lazarev said. He leaned back in his armchair. 'Go to Baden-Baden. Get Boch to talk, find out what he knows and how involved he is in all of this. If you need my Oprichnik's help, call me. In return, I'll take care of the circumstantial evidence against you and you can resume your medical career as if nothing happened. You have my word.'

Poe glanced at the printouts, pulled out Boch's photo from the pile and studied it. As she did so, she unconsciously kissed her ring, which looked like an engagement gift.

Lazarev permitted himself to smile broadly. He had secured Poe, and without having to explicitly threaten her life in the process.

* * *

Avignon, Vaucluse,
Provence-Alpes-Côte d'Azur,
France

Frédéric Roux smelled the ice-cold rosé he was drinking in the shade of some large, sprawling sycamore trees.

A discreet briefcase rested beside him, the contents of which were protected with special security equipment. Frédéric himself looked equally inconspicuous in his slacks, a polo shirt and flat, fabric shoes.

No more than twenty metres from him, in the park next to the 14th-century Temple Saint-Martial d'Avignon church, a group of retirees were playing the popular game of pétanque, or boules as it was called in other regions of France. Occasionally he would hear the metallic clinking of the heavy balls bouncing off each other after a throw, followed by applause and the elderly citizens' discussions of the outcome.

The first mild days of spring had arrived in Avignon, but it was still too early for the usual crowds of tourists from abroad and other parts of France. Early birds and solo travellers wandered the alleyways and squares that Frédéric still found beautiful.

He knew the medieval, magnificent city of popes inside out. Avignon's old town had earned world heritage site status thanks to its still-intact, impressive fortress walls, the Gothic Palace of the Popes and several stone statues dedicated to clerical power from past centuries. The city's narrow and winding streets were a nightmare for drivers; its facades were bright and its roofs crimson, and everything lined up perfectly, dappled with little patches of green or tiny squares in between.

Frédéric liked the flair of Avignon and had often visited its old town as a child. The River Rhône meant the city had something Mediterranean about it even though it didn't border the sea. Needless to say, he had also stood on the half-destroyed bridge, the Pont Saint-Bénézet, whose image endured in countless paintings, books and songs.

It was always quieter here, and the atmosphere more dignified than in his hectic, dirty hometown of Marseille, where people called him Fennec – Desert Fox – because he had fled Tunisia with his parents over thirty years ago and because of his keen, entrepreneurial mindset.

His father was French and his mother North African. His darker skin tone and facial features made it clear where his roots lay, which occasionally made things difficult. Not every compatriot acknowledged him as one of their own. The man in his mid-thirties had acquired the name Roux through marriage. His wife had left him, but he had kept the French surname; that was something, at least.

He adjusted the cap sitting on his frizzy, short, black hair and lifted his camera.

Frédéric watched the group of elderly citizens through an eyepiece. To avoid bending down to pick up the heavy balls, the pétanque enthusiasts had magnets attached to cords with which they grabbed them and pulled them up.

He was particularly interested in one of the older ladies. Making eye contact while she was surrounded by countless senior peers, however, would be impossible. He would have to wait until she made her way home.

The madame didn't live far from here. Her home was in the

centre of town: a former vineyard with a barn where she lived with her two grandsons, Charles and Renard.

He lowered his camera, pulled out his smartphone and used the opportunity to check his emails.

His inbox was empty. It appeared that no one dared bother him via email or any other electronic means in the lovely, ancient city of Avignon. A messenger on horseback would have been more appropriate here; the sight of it wouldn't even have taken many people by surprise.

Frédéric selected a photo album that he'd called *Les triomphes*, scrolled through each photo and reminisced. He swiped through the years and the victims: Clark, Lugaschin and the crew on board the cutter, Dorian Blessington and that annoying, young Russian boy. They weren't the first and wouldn't be the last victims to end up in his album.

The killing itself didn't concern him in the slightest. He only cared about the cards. And yet, every time, he felt that the cards compelled him to eliminate their former owners. Frédéric wasn't interested in why they deserved to die. Young, old, rich, poor, smart or stupid – none of it mattered to him. If that was what the cards wanted, he obeyed.

There had been the fortune teller in Milan, whose predictions had been astonishingly accurate thanks to a little help from the queen of hearts. La Voce – the voice – had been her stage name. When Frédéric had visited her on the premise of a consultation, La Voce had been taken aback. Her queen of hearts told her that death was sitting at the table, but she was still too slow to react. He had grabbed La Voce, strangled her unconscious in the crook of his arm, and then hanged her in the attic to make it look like suicide.

Then there had been the professional card player in Las Vegas, Magic Magnus, whose lucky card at tournaments had been the three of diamonds. Frédéric had got him drunk and dumped him in the sewers after a heavy rainfall in autumn. Nobody ever asked after him. People disappeared all the time in the gambling capital.

As he scrolled, Frédéric reached the triumphs that left a bitter aftertaste.

One was from the Cards bar, in an Irish hamlet in Connemara, where the ace of clubs had been prominently displayed behind some glass on a wall next to the toilets. Frédéric had thought the matter would be simple, but it had rained terribly on the evening of his visit and there were no other guests, meaning he unfortunately had no other choice than to press the card onto a lovely employee – Annabell Douglas. She was a pretty, somewhat naive girl who had spoken to him for a long time. Although she technically hadn't been the owner of the card, the ace of clubs had wanted her. Frédéric had disguised the affair as a raid and murdered her as quickly as possible so she wouldn't suffer.

The next part of his collection was called *chercher & trouver*: it contained the cards he still had to look for and find.

Out of all the cards, Frédéric was mostly concerned about the jack of clubs. According to his sources, the card was inside the luggage of two individuals who liked to travel between Brazil, Colombia and Venezuela in their private jet. That made it difficult to catch them.

The bells of the Saint-Martial d'Avignon church close by announced that it was six o'clock. It was time for Frédéric to leave.

The people in the park didn't stir. They sat on benches on the edge of the paths or wandered into the small open-air café to have some food.

Frédéric picked up his glass, twirled it between his fingers and let the rosé swirl around before he finished it. In addition to the pair of jetsetters, there was another person who had been missing for over a year along with their card. They were all giving Frédéric a headache. The matter of the shipwreck off the coast near Tallinn, on the other hand, had been a piece of cake.

A loud clap of thunder forced him to look up. Some passers-by cried out, startled.

The sky over Avignon darkened rapidly as a summer thunderstorm rolled down from the Haute-Provence mountains.

The group of retirees collected the boules. They embraced one another, bid each other heartfelt goodbyes and disappeared from the park in different directions.

Frédéric left a tenner on the table, stowed away his camera and picked up his briefcase.

He followed Madame Darlan. She was a small woman of eighty-two – shrunken by old age – and incredibly tanned and wrinkled, as if she had spent her whole life working in the fields. Her long white hair was tied in a chignon at the back and centimetre-thick glasses sat on her nose.

Everyone in Avignon knew her. She was famous for her dedication and precision.

Frédéric put away his camera in the dirty, rented Renault that he had arrived in, still keeping pace with her. He had no problem with paying for the parking ticket attached to his windscreen.

Madame Darlan's patterned apron dress was her trademark. She carried lots of different objects inside it, from a knife to a magnifying glass for when her glasses weren't strong enough. As if she'd been marooned in a foreign country and had to fend for herself.

After moving from Vichy, Madam Darlan had opened a small stationery shop. Her passion for ancient texts led her to restore old parchments and documents. Following further training, she'd made a name for herself as a restorer and soon began travelling all over the world, visiting museums and private collections. She had even been permitted to work in the Vatican.

Madame Darlan moved slowly. She placed one dainty shoe on the pavement and hesitated for a moment before taking another step. The apron of her dress flapped around her decrepit body in the rising wind, the thunderstorm rumbling as it approached.

Frédéric suspected that the fragile Madame Darlan could be knocked over by a gust of wind, and, under the pretence of rescuing her, he caught up with her.

At that moment two children appeared, dancing around and accompanying her. It was obvious that they knew each other. They must have been about eight or nine. They received sweets for their kindness from Madame Darlan's inexhaustible apron dress pockets. The boy and the girl only left the old woman's side at the entrance to the barn on Nicolas Lescuyer Street, where Madam Darlan immediately stepped over the threshold and disappeared.

The door, which had once been painted blue and was now weathered, clattered into the old lock and sprang back slightly in the draught without locking.

The wind gently played with the door. Softly clicking, the bolt banged against the latch again and again, as if tempting Frédéric to sneak into the building.

He decided to make the most of the opportunity.

The first flash of lightning struck, bright and hissing; the clap of thunder followed within a matter of seconds. The storm wasted no time. The first heavy drops of rain landed on Avignon and stained the streets with dark spots, which soon turned into black patches.

Frédéric pushed open the door, slipped inside and closed it properly this time.

There was a jumble of old farming equipment inside the barn. Harrows, ploughs, tools he didn't recognise, containers for harvesting grapes, sieves, and plenty of other instruments hung from the walls and the ceiling. A scythe swung back and forth above the passage into the main house, as if to symbolise that there could be danger up ahead.

Frédéric approached it quietly.

He heard the old beams creak and crack, as though they were reminiscing over their time as swaying trees. He listened for any movement from the house nearby, for footsteps and muffled conversations between the grandchildren and their grandmother.

Suddenly, he heard someone walking towards the barn through the rickety connecting door. A man's footsteps.

Frédéric stood beside the doorframe and lifted his briefcase, ready to strike. A blow to the neck should do the trick.

The door to the passage swung open.

'Are you sure you locked the barn, Grandmère?' one of the grandchildren called. 'I told you to use the front door.'

'But I'm so used to going through the barn, Renard,' came the reply. 'I've been doing it since before you were even born.'

Renard had barely taken half a step before the edge of Frédéric's briefcase slammed into him. The bold man wearing sweatpants and a shirt collapsed onto the dusty floor, right under the swinging scythe.

Frédéric grinned and went into the main house.

From the kitchen came the clatter of dishes and the smell of coffee and freshly baked cake. Charles hummed a Breton song, which made for an odd choice in Avignon.

Frédéric turned left and crept down the corridor, which smelled of damp stone. The steps below led to the cellar, whereas those straight on led to Charles. It would only take a few seconds to knock him out if he was as careless as his brother.

Frédéric set down his briefcase next to the door, loosened his muscles, rolled his shoulders and stretched his neck like a boxer preparing for a fight. He was ready.

Charles carried on humming, then swore softly. 'Merde, merde, merde, chaude, chaude, chaude!'

Frédéric used the distraction to storm into the kitchen, and saw Charles, wearing an apron far too small for him as he set the pound cake on the table. He had burned his fingers, despite the tea towels in his hands.

Just as Charles turned to face Frédéric, he tackled him like a rugby player.

Both of them fell onto the black and white kitchen tiles. Before Charles could reach for the poker lying next to the old oven, Frédéric drove his elbow into the right side of his face, causing him to slump to the ground.

Frédéric stood up and cut himself a slice of the warm, dark cake. He only had to take one bite before the flavours unfolded in his mouth. Charles must have added some spices.

'Merci,' he said and nodded appreciatively at the unconscious baker. He then picked up his briefcase and set off to find Madame Darlan. Taking down the two grandsons had been far too easy; they hadn't been of much help to their grandmother.

Frédéric climbed the stairs, finishing his cake. He was impressed by Charles' baking skills. The grandson had even added some chocolate sprinkles and red wine to enrich the otherwise plain cake.

He reached the front of a large door. It had been painted with piano lacquer and had the words Where the magic happens written on it in curved letters.

Frédéric shoved the last of the cake into his mouth, wiped his fingers on his trousers and laid one hand on the brightly polished door handle.

He managed the feat of pushing it down silently and stepped

into the room. The wooden floorboards didn't creak, as if they were on his side.

What sounded like soft, classical choral music filled the room. It was very different to the jazz he listened to on the car radio.

Madame Darlan sat in front of the elongated window at her metre-long desk, on which magnifying glasses and lamps were attached to various long-armed mounts: a forest of glass and light that could be moved back and forth.

Papers, documents, pieces of parchment and letters, many of them stored in glass boxes that had certain humidity and temperature conditions, lay scattered around the room on the other tables. The ceiling-high cabinets contained sheets of papers, brushes, drawers with inscriptions that Frédéric couldn't decipher, jars with copal varnish, mastic varnish, ammonium carbonate, ox gall, potash, sodium bicarbonate, pure ether, alcohol and dozens of other chemicals, as well as laboratory equipment to tackle centuries-old dirt, impurities and forgery attempts or to touch up any imperfections.

The restorer hadn't heard him. She was bent over an old playing card – the seven of diamonds – drawn in a style that had only existed in the past. Madame Darlan inspected it through an enormous magnifying glass and turned a small dial that changed one of the lamp's lights to a greenish glow. Satisfied, she uttered a sound of approval and dipped a tiny brush into a jar labelled *cinnabar gold*.

Frédéric held his breath.

'My advantage,' Madame Darlan said, her hand completely steady as she applied the tip of the brush to a spot at the bottom of the diamond suit, leaving behind a reddish-gold fleck of colour that could only be spotted under a microscope, 'is that my hearing improves the more my eyesight deteriorates. And since your footsteps don't match Charles' or Renard's, I presume it's you, Monsieur Roux.'

He laughed and set his briefcase down to clap. 'Bravo, madame. You've caught me.'

'Not that that's worth anything. I'm an old woman. What could I possibly do to stop you if you were some villain?' She laid down the brush and turned around on the stool to face him. 'Bonjour et bienvenue en Avignon. Encore une fois,' she said, spreading her arms out.

He took off his cap, walked towards her and hugged the petite woman. There was something motherly about her, particularly when she pushed back her thick glasses onto the delicate bridge of her nose. 'I've said before that your grandchildren should pay more attention to you. After all, you are irreplaceable, madame!'

'As are the cards, mon petit fennec.' Madame Darlan smiled craftily. 'Are Charles and Renard still alive and well?'

'Of course! It was only to teach them a lesson. Even if you're the one to blame, Renard and Charles still deserved a beating. I threatened them with one last time I saw them.'

'The barn?' She looked at him, frightened.

'Yes, the barn,' Frédéric said and stroked her narrow, fragile shoulders reassuringly. 'I'm sure it won't ever happen again.' He put his cap back on, picked up the briefcase and laid it on an empty table. He first unlocked the snap locks and then turned the number combination padlock to 666 – a classic combination.

After ten seconds, the soft click from the inside of the case revealed to him that he had unlocked the time lock. You were in for a nasty surprise if you tried to force open the case any earlier.

Frédéric lifted the lid and removed the two new cards he had collected. To avoid incriminating her, he wouldn't tell her where he had found them. His heart leapt with joy as he handed them over to her one by one. 'Here are your new patients,' he said.

Madame Darlan reverently accepted them and placed them beside the completed card. 'Merci, I look forward to treating them,' she replied. She picked up the freshly restored seven of diamonds with her gloved fingers and held it as closely as humanly possible to her eyes to check if the paint had dried. Then she transferred the card into a plastic sleeve and placed the finished product into a cardboard envelope. 'And here's your other patient back.'

Frédéric was delighted and savoured the feeling of the card in his hands. Despite the two protective layers, he could still feel its power and strength. 'Thank you ever so much. As always, here is your payment for your work.' He felt for the envelope in his briefcase, pulled it out from the second compartment and handed it to her. 'Fifty thousand.'

'Merci.'

'De rien.' With that, Frédéric stood up and closed the briefcase. 'It was a short reunion, Madame Darlan, but I'll stay for coffee and cake next time – I promise. What I managed to sample today was formidable.'

'It would be my absolute pleasure. I'm sure Charles would be happy to bake his famous red wine and chocolate cake for you again, mon petit fennec. As long as you weren't too rude to him, anyway.'

Frédéric suspected that next time he would be served a cake with laxative or rat poison. 'You'll have to put in a good word for me, madame.'

'I'll check on those two and patch them up,' she said and smiled at him as if he were another one of her grandsons who seldom showed his face. 'Where are you off to this time? Where else are the cards hiding?'

Frédéric warned her playfully with his finger. 'Oh, là, là, madame! You know that's a secret.'

She winked at him. 'I'm only curious.'

Frédéric couldn't resist. He stepped towards her and kissed her on the forehead. She placed one of her wrinkled hands on his forearm. 'À bientôt, madame.'

'Adieu, mon cher.'

He left Madame Dorlan's restoration room and walked back the same way he had come, breaking off another piece of the cake in the kitchen as he did. It was too delicious not to, and it was unlikely that he would ever get to taste Charles' baking again.

Frédéric poured half a bucket of cold water on both of the grandchildren so that they would wake up and take better care of their grandmother. Then he left the house through the barn door.

The rain pelted down on Avignon and the fierce wind swept through the streets and alleyways and over the roofs like a cloak. The locals and tourists had all disappeared; the cafés and pubs would be looking forward to the guests seeking refuge from the weather.

Frédéric looked up at the raindrops and smiled. He had new cards to find.

* * *

Odette Corinne Martine Darlan watched her little fennec leave from her window. She had grown very fond of him over the years. He brought her these unique, magnificent cards.

Throughout her professional life she had seen many documents, paintings, codices, almanacs and works to do with mysticism and the supernatural without a demon, god or spirit ever making an appearance.

But these cards.

These cards!

Odette was delighted every time Frédéric Roux presented her with a new one. This time, he had brought her two. She examined them meticulously over the next few hours with various magnifying glasses and under different lights to establish the condition they were in, whether they were forgeries and what her next steps should be. The ace of hearts and the two of clubs. Hundreds of years old.

She turned her attention to her beloved work and lost herself in a series of hand movements, in her precision and reflections regarding her patients.

She quickly realised that there was lots to be done.

At first glance, the cards appeared to be in a more or less passable condition. They had recently received a small surge of strength, which made the paper resilient and had brought some of their colour back, but they still looked drained, hungry and angry; they were starving and suffering from the undeserving condition they were in. Both their motifs and their numbers had been damaged. It would require a cure for the cards to be nursed back to health.

The raging thunderstorm outside had turned the sky black. The wind howled and shook the tiles of the old building; somewhere in the house the woodwork rattled and groaned.

Odette turned on the lamps and lights and marvelled at the fascinating pieces again. The loud pelting of the rain against the window didn't bother her.

In the meantime, Charles walked in with an ice pack pressed against his face. He complained about Fennec's violent entry and that she should finally stop using the barn entrance. She ignored him and he disappeared, swearing under his breath. Fennec had taught them a lesson, and they had to live with it.

Odette blamed herself nonetheless. She promised to take better care of herself in the future. If someone else had followed her home after her game of pétanque and found the cards . . . No, she couldn't bear to think about it!

The restorer inspected her patients and decided that the

cards would need intensive treatment before she could focus on the little details. A basecoat, so to speak.

She reached for the silver bell and rang it twice. Renard and Charles immediately appeared at her door. They knew the signal.

'Is the cellar well stocked?'

Both of the men nodded. Odette got to her feet. She decided to start with the ace of hearts. The three of them headed down into the cellar.

Some well-trodden steps led to a large, stone vault, which had once been used to store wine barrels. But those days had long gone; no wine had been stored here since Odette's parents had bought the property. Back then, there had been too many people in Vichy who had hated her father, which, in hindsight, did not surprise her. As a girl, she had failed to understand the crimes that he had been guilty of in the forties.

Her father had taken his mistrust to the grave. He'd turned the cellar into a bunker and a shelter. For one thing, he was afraid that the Germans would recover just as quickly after the Second World War as they had done after the First, and that they would strike back. For another, he wanted a place of refuge from angry mobs. After his death, Odette had disposed of all the expired supplies and removed all the weapon and ammunition boxes from the cellar.

But she had still found a use for the place.

She let Charles unlock the enormous, heavy door.

Renard went ahead. As he passed, he picked up a staff with a long, hand-forged iron blade attached to the end of it. Odette's father had made it to use in close combat against intruders. In the end, he had only used it for slaughtering and beheading chickens – until Odette had found a better use for it. Long hairs and dried blood hung from the edge of the blade.

Charles picked up the no less gruesome axe that hung on the mount next to the door.

They entered the several-metre-high cellar, where a pungent smell, like that of a stable that hadn't been mucked out in a long time, lingered inside. Odette used the rotary switch to turn the light bulbs on. They had been in their sockets for as long as she could remember and were as indestructible as herself.

There was a loud rattling of chains as half a dozen figures crawled away from the swaying, sepia light; they knew it meant disaster.

Odette's eyes wandered over the people as if they were treasure.

There were no beggars, no homeless people, and no paupers in Avignon. At least, never for long. Renard and Charles picked them up at night, either by tricking them or by force, and brought them to the cellar.

Odette held the ace of hearts in front of her and, without taking her eyes off it, gently moved the card from left to right over the crawling people. Individual lines and numbers glowed occasionally, but this was by no means a final decision.

The bedraggled people backed away from the ace of hearts, pressing their backs against the walls, whimpering and cursing. Most of them were familiar with the ritual.

There were scratches and messages carved into the bricks above their heads. Some of the prisoners had tried to dig their way out, but Odette's father had made sure the brickwork was solid. Odette had also fitted some chains, the cuffs of which were attached to the prisoners' ankles and limited their movement to a set radius. The men, women and children couldn't touch or help each other, only talk.

Suddenly, Odette heard a rising, gentle chorus that was only audible to her. The cards had accepted her. They loved her and were becoming increasingly assertive. The first time and with the first card, it had taken days, but now it took no more than twenty minutes for the card to reveal its wishes to her.

Her eyes remained transfixed on the ace of hearts through her glasses as she eagerly moved her arm back and forth as if she were scanning the figures. The card had found a true, knowledgeable and loyal ally in the restorer. It would show her what it wanted.

The glowing beams from the central motif flared abruptly: the sign!

Odette lowered the card slightly and looked across the edge to see who it had chosen.

She recognised the dark-haired man with brown skin; she presumed now that he had no permanent address and wandered around begging. When they had put him in chains a few months ago, the man had sworn at them in an unknown language. He didn't have any shoes and his simple clothes were dirty and stained.

Odette didn't even know his name, nor did she care.

'Him,' she said, pointing.

Renard smiled and struck the wall twice with the flat edge of the blade, and a clear clang echoed through the vault as a sort of announcement. At some point this had become a habit of his, and it had been a part of the ritual ever since.

He then gripped the staff with both hands and held it with the blade pointing forward, ready to thrust. Renard walked towards the chosen prisoner, who sprang to his feet and prepared to block the attack with the chain.

Odette frowned. The man's resistance changed nothing, but it still irritated her. She would give the prisoners even less to eat or administer them more sedatives. She didn't want any rebellion.

The man struck with the chain and tried to grab and snatch away the staff, which Renard parried skilfully.

The other figures silently watched with their backs pressed against the wall. Occasionally one of the teenagers would whine or shout a torrent of insults.

Odette couldn't care less. She was responsible for restoring the cards to their best possible condition and making them look as good as new. She would do whatever it took.

Renard quickly caught the man's upper arm. Blood oozed from the prisoner's gaping cut, and the injured man failed to defend himself with the chain against the second attack, distracted by the pain.

Odette watched with a smile as Renard drove the spear forged by her father deep into the man's stomach. He stabbed him before quickly pulling the blade back out.

The bleeding man screamed and collapsed, clutching at his wound, but he couldn't stop the red from gushing out. He gasped and stared at his injury.

Odette approached the dying man, lifted the ace of hearts and turned it face up, as if opening the cards' eyes. A glow and the rays of light spread across the back of the card; all of its symbols, lines and embellishments sparkled and glimmered. The card feasted on the dying.

The choir in Odette's mind grew louder and sang with joy, praising her with sounds and syllables that one didn't need to understand to register their blissful content. A shudder went down her spine, her fingers tingled and she felt the energy from the card seep into her. Odette never wanted to live without this feeling. It triggered a kind of euphoria, a rush for more. Her old heart beat gleefully, as if she were a young girl receiving her passionate first kiss.

Renard stabbed incessantly. He struck the defenceless man's lower and upper thighs, pierced his hands and arms and then solely focused on his chest. Hole after hole, gash after gash appeared. The blood spilled onto the floor and flowed towards the drain, which then trickled into the Rhône.

The other prisoners whimpered and crouched, frightened. No one wanted to attract the butcher's attention or be the next victim.

The prisoner only twitched when the tip of Renard's spear pierced his skin. After a final, merciful stab to his neck, the man moaned softly and let out his last breath.

Odette felt the tingling sensation in her fingertips instantly dwindle and fade away. She turned the card face up and inspected it.

The little mould spots had disappeared, and the lines and details were clearly visible, as if the card had only been printed and finished by hand yesterday. Nevertheless, she still spotted some small imperfections that the first treatment, or cure, as she liked to call it, hadn't erased. At least one more prisoner would have to suffer and give their life for the ace of hearts.

Odette turned on her heel and walked back to the stairs with the card between her thumb and forefinger. The basecoat had been applied.

'Dispose of him,' she ordered Renard and Charles. 'Then we'll have coffee. I'm looking forward to trying the cake.'

She heard the blows of the heavy axe and spear behind her as she climbed the stairs. Renard and Charles smashed the dead man's bones and hacked his flesh, breaking up his corpse into small pieces.

The Rhone would wash away his body parts, just like countless times before.

One should always play fairly
When one has the winning cards.

Oscar Wilde (1876–1916)

VI

Tadeus knew that only he could see the labelled card that Gillot held up in front of him. There were no CCTV cameras in this area of the casino.

He carefully turned off the transmit function on his radio. This conversation was not for the ears of head office. If Alexa asked, he would blame it on connection problems.

'I don't know what you mean, Monsieur Gillot.'

The man twirled his Dalí moustache in clockwise, then anti-clockwise circles and looked at him through his red and white glasses. He lowered the arm holding the card.

'I'll buy the nine of spades off you,' he said, brushing off Tadeus' objection. Gillot raised and wiggled his bushy eyebrows. 'Where is it?'

Over the last few days, Tadeus had expected the police to ask him this very question; the fact that it was coming from a stranger caught him off guard. 'Monsieur, I—' he began.

'I'll give you twenty thousand euros for it. Without tax.'

Tadeus propped his elbows on his knees and looked up at him. 'I have no idea what you're talking about,' he said, but he realised too late that his body language didn't match his words. *I should have got up and left.*

'Tadeus? Can you hear me?' Alexa asked in his ear. She was checking in on him sooner than he'd expected.

Gillot showed him the joker with the writing on it again:

I.

WANT.

MY!

NINE OF SPADES.

'Monsieur, I'm at a loss here. I keep an eye on the players in this casino, not the cards.' Tadeus pointed at the scribbled nonsense. 'The nine of spades means nothing to me.' He made a move to leave the sitting area. *It's too late.*

'You were there, at the former Belle Époque. You accompanied Lazarev junior before he was shot,' Gillot began to explain calmly. He sounded annoyingly cheerful, as if he were making some sort of joke. 'You tried to help Mr Morgan escape after he jumped out of the window and chose to ignore the ace of spades, which is a no-go in supérieur.' He waved the card and chuckled. 'But the seven of clubs that Morgan stole in the round is mine. I bought it a long time ago, with the hidden contents.' He leaned back in his seat, pressing his back against the chair. 'Which means, Mr Boch, that *you* are the thief.'

'Hidden contents?' Tadeus asked, listening attentively. He decided to fight back. 'If that's true, why don't you turn me in? This is a strange way of doing things.' He wanted to hold on to the nine of spades with every fibre of his being. The card fascinated him far too much, and its secret was for him to discover, not Gillot. How the sacred paper made him feel when he touched it, and its otherworldly singing, belonged to him and him alone. Morgan and the card must have had a reason for choosing him.

'Tadeus, are you still in the bar? Report back,' Alexa called, sounding amused. That was about to change.

'Monsieur Gillot. In no uncertain terms, and with all due respect, this is what happened: Morgan handed me a seven of clubs, and that same seven of clubs I handed in as evidence to the police.' Tadeus did his best to sound sincere and convincing.

'The seven of clubs was only the sleeve, Mr Boch, and you know it. People say that, once the card draws you in and you fall for its charms, it's practically impossible to resist.'

'Well, if there was another card inside the seven of clubs, it might have fallen out. Maybe somewhere at the villa, or on my way to the police station, or even earlier than that. But I' – Tadeus held up his hands – 'don't have it. End of conversation.' He stood up and gestured invitingly to the bar. 'I'm assuming you don't want a poker lesson from me after all. How about a drink on the house before you go, Monsieur?'

'How about a supérieur lesson, Mr Boch?' Gillot countered, still glued to his chair. 'I know you're denying it, and I can understand why. Some people can touch the cards without feeling anything. And then there are the chosen ones, the exceptionally weak or the exceptionally powerful ones, who fall under their spell.' He smirked. 'You being a gambling addict who thinks he's immune to old temptations, I'm not sure which group I'd assign you to.'

'May I escort you to the door, Monsieur Gillot? Or would you like to stay in the casino?' Tadeus reverted to his workplace persona. 'You'll find everything you need at your disposal.'

'Apart from very few exceptions, most of the former card owners are dead, Mr Boch,' Gillot continued without stirring. He made eye contact with a waiter to order them a bottle of the most expensive champagne. The waiter disappeared after giving a questioning look at Tadeus, who nodded to the bar for him to fetch the bottle. 'Oh, but please don't take that as a threat! It's only a warning. Think of Morgan.'

'Okay, it seems you can't hear me,' Alexa said into his ear. 'I'll send Oscar to check your radio.'

'I hope you have a pleasant evening in our casino, Mr Gillot,' Tadeus said, pulling away, trying to flee the increasingly overwhelming scene.

'Oh, I will. As long as there's enough champagne, the evening is saved. Even if I would have loved to buy my own card off you tonight.' Gillot nodded to Tadeus and sank into his chair. He squinted with his right eye and stared at him with his left over one of his spiky moustache hairs. 'We'll meet again, Mr Boch. Perhaps in the casino, perhaps over a chat and a Danish pastry in your daughter's house. Or maybe on your cutter.' He rubbed his hands together as the bottle was served in an ice bucket and with a glass. 'Oh, perfect, thank you.'

Tadeus clenched his jaw, gritting his teeth. His escape would have to wait. Threats against his children and the things he loved were not something he could ignore, even if Gillot had made them so casually.

The cork was removed with a *plop*, the champagne foamed into the glass and the waiter withdrew.

'Monsieur Gillot, you will kindly abandon such insinuations,' Tadeus said.

'What insinuations?' the extrovert asked, sampling the alcohol and rolling his eyes in delight. He could move each eye independently from the other, like a clown or a pantomime. 'Absolutely divine!'

'The insinuations regarding my daughter. And my boat.'

'Fine. Then we'll see each other in your son's student halls.' Gillot looked at the ceiling thoughtfully. 'Ah, no, that's right, he's currently on holiday in Porto.' As he smiled, his whiskers almost pricked the lenses of his glasses. 'Mr Boch, I'm not threatening you. All I wanted to say is that our next meeting should be more casual. Less formal.' He raised a glass to Tadeus. 'Take good care of my card while I take care of . . . other matters.' Gillot graciously bade Tadeus farewell as if he were a prince who had grown tired of his subjects. 'As I said, we'll meet again, Mr Boch. And when we do, you should have located my possession and have no qualms about handing it over. I will make it worth your while.'

'I don't have the card,' Tadeus said, sticking to his line.

'That's a shame. I suggest you look into its whereabouts.' Gillot took a sip of champagne. He had an air of delusional cheerfulness to him, as though he were high or had inhaled too much laughing gas. 'Because in my book, you're the one who has my nine of spades.' He swirled the alcohol in his glass and greeted someone behind Tadeus. 'Your colleagues, Mr Boch?'

Tadeus turned around and acted surprised, secretly switching his transmitter back on. 'Oscar? What's up? Is there trouble?'

'Forgive the intrusion,' the stocky man said to Gillot and then turned to Tadeus. 'Head office want you. Is something wrong with your equipment?'

He tapped his transmitter unit, spoke into it and received an immediate response from Alexa. 'It's working again. Must have been a problem with the connection,' she said.

'Well, at least I did a sweep of the area.' Oskar shrugged his shoulders and returned to the tables.

'Are you finished with the lesson?' his boss asked. 'That young girl has won in blackjack again. She's cleaning up.'

'She's so lucky it's getting suspicious. Understood.' Tadeus turned away from Gillot and left without looking at him again. He had nothing left to say.

And he still had no intention of giving up the nine of spades. He had to send Gillot on a wild goose chase. It wouldn't be easy. His plan would have to be sound. Watertight.

Tadeus walked over to the blackjack table and watched the young blonde in the cheap trouser suit and costume jewellery from afar. A pile of exclusively fifty-euro chips was stacked up in front of her.

Tadeus studied the woman and her surroundings. No companions, no furtive looks and no eye contact with the dealer. The probabilities of chance were on her side.

Since there was nothing Tadeus could do, his mind drifted back to Gillot. The man was the most bizarre character he had ever met, as far as he could remember. He was mad and yet completely himself, as well as presumptuous and confident enough to carelessly make threats.

Tadeus urgently needed to find out more about Gillot. He had to know what sort of man his adversary was, what he was known and notorious for. He might even learn something new about his nine of spades in the process.

The Devil's Playbook. Morgan had used that term, and Gillot had mentioned a deathly curse that wiped out the card owners. Therefore, there must be more of these cards: some in the possession of the madman, others scattered around the world.

Tadeus was gripped by an abstruse desire to find the cards before Gillot did, to collect them and cherish their song. *I belong to the powerful ones*, he told himself. *It cannot be otherwise. Why would the nine of spades pick a weakling?*

The thought cemented in his mind.

The card had already chosen him in the casino when it had caught his eye, and Morgan had entrusted him with a clear task, which Tadeus had accepted the moment he had been struck by the card's power, by that electrifying sensation. He hadn't realised it at first, but now he was fully aware and conscious of his mission: *Gillot will come away empty-handed.*

He needed a plan.

The easiest course of action would be to have a forgery made. Tadeus knew a few regulars from the casino who collected art, including paintings. Someone from that circle would be able to put him in touch with a skilled individual who could legally copy classics. There was a market for convincing copies of major works of art. A historical playing card would be a piece of cake in comparison, and, thanks to Lazarev, he now had some cash to spare.

I'll palm off the duplicate to Gillot and get him off my back. Tadeus thought this was an excellent idea. At the same time, he would do so some research around the cards and on the Devil's Playbook.

'And?' he heard Alexa ask. 'How does she do it?'

'No tricks,' he reported. 'She's just a lucky devil.'

The young blonde had eight pairs of eyes watching her – too few to stop playing, but too many to win. If she went over twenty-one, she would lose.

'I find that hard to believe.'

'Shall I search her? At the table?' Tadeus asked with a broad grin. 'That wouldn't go down so well.' He crossed his arms in front of his chest, the fabric of his suit gently rubbing against his skin. 'She's winning, Alexa, there's nothing else to it. I don't miss a trick.'

'All right, take a break. There's some fresh coffee here for you.'

Tadeus withdrew from the corner and walked close by past the blackjack table and the young woman.

'Hit me,' was her determined instruction to the dealer.

'Jack of diamonds,' the casino employee announced and elegantly cleared her chips from the table. 'You're bust, madame.'

Tadeus smiled and turned to look up at the CCTV cameras. 'Did you see that, Alexa?'

'I saw. Your charisma broke her streak. Good work!'

For a heartbeat, Tadeus felt that it was the nine of spades' doing and that it had wanted to please him, but then he immediately dismissed the notion. He didn't have the card with him.

A yearning for it swept over him.

* * *

Three hours later, Tadeus was on his way home. As he marched through the light drizzle with a beer for the road to help numb the nagging pain in his back and knees, he thought about Henry Pierre Gillot, the man he had enquired about to his casino contacts.

According to the internet, he was quite the character.

Tadeus wouldn't make the mistake of simply dismissing Gillot as an oddball who, according to various reports, had sometimes been spotted wearing a frock coat, sometimes a pith helmet, sometimes performing as a jazz clarinettist, and sometimes strumming an electric guitar while playing with the metal band, The Graves. To say the man had a flamboyant personality was an understatement, him being eccentric was closer to the truth, and a frenzied maniac was spot on.

Gillot enjoyed a globetrotting lifestyle. He was a Walloon who lived in Bruges and supported the unity of Belgium, but split his time between London, Paris, Hamburg and St Petersburg. Gillot was always on the lookout for new pieces for his large private collection, which knew no bounds and included ancient treasures from all over the world, ranging from the size of a coin to the colossal remains of statues and buildings.

And playing cards. He lent quite a few pieces to museums, so that, as per one of his quotes in an article, mankind could see them and they didn't disappear into secret chambers.

The 63-year-old Gillot made no secret of his life. He had started out as a salesman, and had then studied archaeology and thrown himself into excavation work. Some people described him as a plunderer who had grown rich off illegal art dealings. He was accused of having dubious contacts in the Emirates and working with criminal organisations in the Middle East to organise excavations in areas where foreigners were occasionally shot or kidnapped. His teams, however, remained untouchable.

And yet Gillot was also seen as a generous patron, art dealer and businessman. Anonymous posters on internet forums referred to him as a dude with money, a very dangerous man, or an unscrupulous art dealer and exploiter who enjoyed his role.

This was the man at Tadeus' heels – his and his children's. He had to act as soon as possible, before Gillot's false serenity and kindness turned into concrete action. Tadeus might have not been the best father in the years that he'd lost to his addiction, but he couldn't let anything happen to his son and daughter.

He turned into Schiller Street and looked forward to his card. He simply had to touch, hold and look at it again before falling asleep with his head swimming with thoughts. The empty beer bottle landed in a bin.

The Devil's Playbook. The deaths surrounding this special deck. Tadeus thought about what the crazy patron had said: 'While I take care of . . . other matters'. *Matters.* What he really meant was acquiring the other cards, which could mean more deaths, just like at the villa. *How long had he been doing this?*

Tadeus was very eager to find and secure more of the cards from the pack before the Walloon did. And yet the thought of it seemed childish. His rival possessed an infinite amount of money and a degree of knowledge and influence he couldn't match. Nevertheless, he wouldn't part with the nine of spades. Instead, he would have a forgery made to get himself and his children out of Gillot's line of fire.

Tadeus had reached the entrance to his house. Lost in thought, he fished for the key in his pocket and was about to unlock the door.

Suddenly, he heard a car door slam on the street and quick, heavy-heeled steps approach his back.

Tadeus turned around. To his great surprise, he saw Poe walking towards him.

She was wearing dark clothes and a baseball cap that cast a shadow over her features.

'You owe me answers,' she said. She stood before him in a short, black leather jacket with her hands in her pockets. She was tall, well over six foot, and thin, looming over him like the shadow of death.

'Me?' Tadeus couldn't help but laugh in disbelief.

'You told the police that I was the killer,' Poe said, glaring at him angrily. 'Do you know what that means for me and my career as a doctor? Why the hell would you do that?'

Tadeus didn't remember making such a claim. 'I told the investigators that you brought the murder weapon with you and that you threatened Lazarev,' he said thoughtfully. 'I'm not responsible for their conclusions.' He secretly wondered why she was roaming the streets if she was a suspect.

'It wasn't me. That Solov'ëva woman locked me up because she thought I would rat her out, but I escaped from the villa before the shooting even started.' Poe stood with her feet slightly apart, as if she were trying to find a stable position on solid ground. 'When you left the room with that Russian, the Beretta disappeared too, Boch. It could easily have been you.'

'It definitely wasn't.' Tadeus remembered that night and the slender shadow that had swung over the fence. Lazarev had still been alive then. Nevertheless, he hadn't testified to that observation. But how could he have known that the figure had been Poe?

They stood facing each other in the cold drizzle, waiting. Neither of them spoke.

'What do you expect me to do?' Tadeus asked finally and wiped the rain from his eyes.

'To go to the police and clear things up, tell them that you were wrong.'

'Did you have the Beretta or not?'

'It was gone when you left the room,' Poe countered.

'If my fingerprints had been on it—'

'You could have been wearing gloves. I'm just the only one who left fingerprints,' she interrupted him, frustrated. 'That was stupid of me.'

Tadeus noticed the tremor in Poe's voice and her trembling body. She was freezing cold and struggled to maintain her composure. 'Let's go inside and talk. I'll make you some tea.'

'Coffee would be better,' she said, following him inside after he unlocked the door. They climbed up the stairs and went into his apartment.

Tadeus mentally congratulated himself on keeping his home tidy as he offered Poe a seat in his studio flat. He threw his jacket onto a hanger and hung it on the door, went into the kitchen and turned on the coffee machine. The machine came to life and, with a series of electronic beeps, prepared their coffees. 'How did you manage to avoid getting arrested, Miss Poe?'

She appeared in the doorway. She had removed her coat and he saw that she wore a simple black blouse, and a chunky gold chain around her neck. She shivered, looking scrawny and bony in her jeans. She grabbed her cap and pulled it off, revealing shoulder-length black hair.

'Didn't you have short hair at the villa?' Tadeus asked. He was reminded again of his daughter, who was a little younger than the doctor. His heart filled with parental love. He decided to help her; he would change the statement he'd given to the police.

'It was a wig. It matches the photo in my old Korean passport, which I'm currently using,' Poe explained and accepted a cup of steaming-hot coffee. 'Thank you for listening to me.' The words escaped more quietly this time from her curved mouth. Her blue eyes looked tired. 'I've lost my fiancé and now I'm suspected of murdering multiple people.'

Tadeus leaned against the countertop as the machine poured him a double espresso. 'If I were the police, I'd go for the obvious suspect too. What does your lawyer think?'

'That he'll have to pull out all the stops.' Poe gave him a piercing stare. 'When I climbed out of the window, you and your friend had just crawled out of the bushes to run from Solov'ëva's men. Did the investigators not find that suspicious?'

'They did. And I would too.'

'Why were they chasing you? Did you cheat?'

'Morgan wasn't my friend, just someone I knew.' Tadeus could understand that she wanted to find out what had happened that night at the former Belle Époque on her own.

According to what he already knew, Gillot had hired a hitman to carry out the murders. Perhaps more cards had been brought to the round, perhaps by the young Russian, hidden just like the nine of spades. That would explain why Lazarev junior had met his death: he had wanted to protect the cards.

'So?' Poe snapped Tadeus out of his musings.

'So what? He'd been shot, and I didn't think that was ... right. Even if he cheated, this isn't the Wild West.'

'Wasn't it something to do with a card that he'd stolen?' she asked him as casually as if they were discussing the matter on the street. 'The seven of clubs?'

Tadeus stirred sweetener into his espresso, followed by a shot of milk. It was sacrilege, but that was how he liked it best. 'So you do know more.'

'It shouldn't surprise you that I've done some research of my own. This concerns my life and my career as a doctor. But most importantly' – Poe looked him dead in the eye, her blue ones glowing – 'this is about the truth, Mr Boch. The truth is better than any lawyer. It would clear us both of everything.'

The truth. That part was a little inconvenient for him. Tadeus nodded ever so slightly to avoid rousing suspicion.

'I didn't do it, you didn't do it, and yet it can be pinned on both of us,' she summarised. 'Who else could it be? Do you have any ideas? What has your research shown?'

'What do I think?'

'You spent more time in the villa than I did,' Poe considered and blew on her coffee. 'Was it another player? Someone seeking revenge? Or was it out of greed? Money?'

'I'm sure there are many reasons, but I didn't notice anything out of the ordinary,' Tadeus said. He kept his meeting with Gillot and the likely reason for the murders – the one-of-a-kind, historical playing cards – to himself.

'Have there been any new developments in the death of your fiancé?' he asked to distract her.

'He took part in a round of supérieur alongside Lazarev and a few others in Monte Carlo. I found out that it was a lethal version of the game, where if a player draws the ace of spades they die.'

'Just like Morgan. Lazarev called after him, saying that he'd picked up the ace of spades.'

'I'm a hundred per cent sure that Enrico didn't know about the rule, but they killed him and disguised it as an accident,' Poe concluded. 'The Solov'ëvas were behind it. Or someone who desperately wanted Enrico's seven of clubs, which then turned up in Baden-Baden.'

Tadeus finished his small, incredibly potent coffee in one go. The distraction hadn't worked.

Despite her contacts, it appeared she hadn't deduced the fact that Lazarev junior had brought the seven of clubs to the round at the villa. This meant that the oligarch's son could be the murderer or the instigator of the murder of Poe's fiancé, something she hadn't considered thus far.

'I didn't know that the seven of clubs was your fiancé's.' Tadeus sidestepped her suspicions. This lead would mean danger for both Poe and the nine of spades. 'But I presume the death of the two women doesn't resolve the issue?'

Poe sighed. 'I'm afraid not. I have to know what happened,

Mr Boch, I *have* to!' Tadeus saw the sudden fear in her eyes. 'So much depends on it.'

Who is she afraid of? He was torn between his growing suspicion and his willingness to help. Had Gillot sent her to quietly steal the nine of spades from him? Or was she acting in the interests of the police because the investigators considered him a suspect after all?

'The police will get to the bottom of it, Miss Poe. Don't fret. With my amended statement, your lawyer should have a good chance of removing you from the list of suspects, or at least putting up a good fight in court.' He pointed to her coffee. 'Would you like another one? I can walk you back to your hotel afterwards.'

Poe nodded and handed him her empty cup. Tadeus placed it under the spout of the coffee machine, inserted a new pod and pressed the start button. 'I'll be right back, Miss Poe. Help yourself to milk and coffee.'

He disappeared into the bathroom.

* * *

Hyun watched the man close the bathroom door behind him and then looked at the hot, black brew pouring into her coffee cup. The conversation with the older man was dragging, and she'd managed to avoid getting kicked out by accepting another drink. She felt uneasy and unsure.

At least Boch would amend his statement, which, even if it didn't vindicate her entirely, might strengthen her lawyer's defence strategy. But it still didn't help her solve the mystery behind the murders.

He's hiding something. Hyun picked up the coffee from the machine and took a sip as she wandered through the large studio flat. Boch might not be the killer, but he knew more, and she had to find out what it was. For herself and for Lazarev senior.

She began to feel worse, and it wasn't the coffee.

Hyun set her cup down on the sideboard and leaned against it. She closed her eyes for a few seconds to focus, and the floating cards appeared in the darkness. She gasped, tried and failed to stop the oncoming nightmare.

An ominous rumbling sounded from the darkness, and the seven of clubs hovered in front of her, poster-sized and with the face of her dead fiancé painted on it. Enrico's face had been slashed with claws and blades, and blood gushed from his gaping wounds.

'Hyun,' he pleaded. 'Hyun, save yourself!' The red poured from his mouth, trickling down his chin and neck. 'Run and save yourself!' He lifted his arm and reached out to her from the card.

She tentatively held her hand out, but the seven of clubs moved away before their fingers could touch, spinning faster and faster on its own axis. The wind that blew from the card reeked of decay and infected wounds. The old card suits transformed into new ones, and the seven of clubs became the nine of spades.

Hyun ran after it. The shapeshifting didn't fool her. *I'd recognise you anywhere!* 'Enrico! Stay! What do I need to do to save you?'

'Run!' she heard him shout from the card. The rumbling and howling swelled to an infernal chorus. 'Run and save yourself!'

Hyun didn't want to save herself; she wanted to save him. She picked up the pace, chasing the nine of spades in the darkness. The card shrank and tried to escape her grasp. Enrico's voice faded and reduced to a feeble echo.

An invisible pair of hands reached out and yanked Hyun's hair, holding her down by her arms and hips to slow her down, but she wrenched free and ran after the nine of spades, the card that had robbed her of her fiancé. 'No, I won't let you steal him from me again!' she cried.

She jumped and stretched out her arm, her fingers grasping one of the corners of the card. At the same time, she could feel malice and evil radiating from the card, which almost overpowered her.

She opened her eyes abruptly.

She was standing in Boch's living room.

Hyun squinted at the card in her right hand. She'd pulled the nine of spades out of her nightmare and into her hand. The unpleasant feeling still emanated from the printed paper. She realised that this was the same card that Enrico had brought into their home and into their lives, which had subsequently fallen apart.

White flecks of wall paint clung to her fingertips. Hyun quickly scanned the room. Boch had hidden the card, but she couldn't remember where she'd found it.

The card was the reason. Enrico had died because of the card. Boch wouldn't be able to talk his way out of this one. The evidence was in her hand, and she was curious to see how he would react to her discovery.

* * *

Tadeus washed his hands and looked at his wrinkled, weary face in the mirror. He scratched the beard on his lower jaw. Back in his gambling days, he'd been clean-shaven, and, thanks to the drugs, always lively and alert. He'd had the hunger of a wolf and the charisma of James Bond. Now he looked like a washed-up agent who'd been rightfully reassigned to office duty until his retirement.

Gillot, my children, the card, Poe. How am I going to figure this all out? He longed to touch the nine of spades; it gave him strength and comfort in equal measure. The ritual of looking and feeling the card between his fingertips when he first woke up and before he went to bed had become an addiction. *No, a nice habit,* he corrected himself immediately, not wanting to use the negative word. The nine of spades couldn't be an addiction. It wasn't a game. It was just a card from a deck.

Tadeus rinsed his face with cold water and patted it dry. 'Pull yourself together,' he said to his reflection. 'You're the only one who can sort this out.'

When he returned to the high-ceilinged, large room, he found Poe standing in the middle of it holding his card between her spider-like fingers.

She turned around to face him, an expression of horror and realisation on her face. 'This is the card!' she cried out.

Tadeus' pulse went through the roof. In defence of his nine of spades, his muscles tensed as if before a fight. 'Where did you—'

'It's Enrico's card!' Poe shouted, furious. 'I can feel it. I hated this thing. It' – she turned and twisted the card around in her fingers as if she were looking for something – 'It had a different pattern before, a different motif, but . . . But I recognise it! This energy that it's radiating! Ruin, malice, a sort of bewitching evil.' Poe lifted the card reproachfully. '*This* is why Enrico died! Not because of the seven of clubs, but because of *this card* here! Am I right, Boch?'

Tadeus resisted the urge to throw himself at the fragile woman and snatch back the nine of spades. She held his treasure in her hands, his precious possession that he wanted to hide from Gillot and the world. Worst of all, she'd now discovered his secret.

He composed himself. If she had wanted the card, she would no longer be stood in his apartment. No, she'd be running for the hills with her spoils.

'Who gave you permission to snoop around my apartment?' Tadeus asked slowly.

'I didn't snoop. You . . .' The doctor pointed to the card. 'You might laugh, but I . . . My grandmother was a mudang, a Korean shaman, and she taught me her ways when I was a child. I never got to finish my training, but I find certain things . . . easier to grasp, and to understand, than others.' She raised the nine of spades. '*This* is the card that my fiancé took with him to Monaco. It looks different now, but it carries the same evil.'

'You should tell me more about what it means to be a mudang some time. I thought you were a surgeon? How do conventional medicine and shamanism go hand in hand?'

'As I said, I didn't receive proper training from my grand-mother. In the operating theatre, I only rely on my instruments.' She put the card down on the side table in disgust. 'But what I learned was enough to make me see that there's more to this world than meets the eye.'

Within a few seconds, a plan formed in Tadeus' mind. Now that it was clear that Poe hadn't been sent to him by anyone, he could enlist her help and her abilities to acquire more cards. She would be his key; his dowsing rod and finder that he would look after and protect. Poe would be able to tell the difference between a forgery and an original. She'd be able to see through the cards' disguise, identify them, and quite literally unveil them. How else could she have found where he'd hidden the nine of spades?

The cards she found would be Tadeus' arsenal against Gillot. In exchange for the cards, he could demand anything from the collector, including staying away from him and his children. The nine of spades would be the only one he'd forge. *He'll never get it off me.*

But how would he get the doctor on his side?

The answer was simple: Tadeus would have to tell her about Gillot and make him out to be the mastermind behind the mur-ders at the former Belle Époque. Based on Poe's actions at the illegal gambling round, she was someone who faced the things that mattered in her life head on. Together they would go after the Walloon and investigate his activities in order to lay the blame on Gillot and convince Poe that he was involved in her fiancé's murder – there was a good chance that he was.

Tadeus thought this was an excellent plan. His amended statement to the police in her favour would also take the pressure off and make her feel grateful.

'I'll call the police first thing tomorrow and tell them that I saw you leave the villa before the murders took place, Miss Poe,' he said.

'Thank you,' she replied, relieved.

'There's something else I should tell you, but I don't want to give you any false hope. There's a man who I at least suspect of being behind the death of your fiancé in Monte Carlo and the events in Baden-Baden,' he began. 'And he said something about a curse, that—'

There was a soft scratching at the front door. Tadeus paused. Poe turned to face the door.

The iron scraping was followed by a sharp, dangerous click.

'Get down!' Tadeus shouted and threw himself at her.

The door exploded with a bang. Splinters flew into the apartment, shattering his TV, the windows and picture frames. A shimmering, perilous rain of glass came crashing down on top of them.

Through the chaos of falling debris and dust, Tadeus saw two masked men dressed in black and holding long-barrelled shotguns storm into his flat.

'See if anyone else is here!' the one on the left ordered. 'I'll take care of these two. Ah, yes, there's the card!'

This was exactly what Tadeus had been afraid of. His treasure, the nine of spades, was in grave danger. It was clear that Gillot had no intention of wrangling over the card for long. Tadeus' beautiful plan had been thwarted.

No. He won't take it from me. Not yet. Tadeus stared down the enormous, smoking barrel of the gun and felt no fear.

* * *

The Amazon,
ca. 240 kilometres west of Manaus,
Brazil

'Another two miles to the southwest,' shouted the native guide over the waves in the first, thick-walled canoe, and steered the narrow boat into a densely overgrown tributary. 'The pilot said there was a fresh trail there.'

They slowed down.

Frédéric Roux, who was at the helm of the outboard motor in the second canoe, reduced the speed of the propeller. He didn't want to risk damaging the motor and having to paddle along with the rest of the search team. He was already sweating from the sweltering heat and the humidity, which had reached over ninety per cent. The headwind barely helped; drops of sweat trickled down from his curly hair onto his dark skin and into his eyes.

Frédéric was sitting in the canoe because of the Sparks couple: Pedro Armando and Valerie. They had managed to crash their private jet in the Amazon jungle behind Manaus. The small aircraft had still not been found and the two passengers, as well as their luggage and the jack of clubs, were missing. A lost aeroplane in the Brazilian rainforest was his greatest challenge to date. As soon as Frédéric had read online that some volunteers were forming a search party, he had set off for Brazil to join the group.

A dozen people spread over two boats had set out for the Amazon with supplies, equipment and a statement from a pilot claiming to have seen a fresh trail. Two-thirds of the volunteers were friends of the missing couple. The others, such as Frédéric and the guide named Oritz, their local guide, had joined them for safety reasons.

Frédéric avoided speaking to the others. He only made small talk when he had to and otherwise played the part of a grumpy, lone wolf.

To his dismay, Silvy, the brunette who thought she was some jungle version of Lara Croft, kept herself close to him and introduced herself as Valerie Sparks' sister. Judging by Silvy's looks, smiles and attempts to speak to him, she fancied him. This made Frédéric feel uncomfortable. If he found the jack of clubs, the card would demand sacrifices, and friendly people were harder to shoot.

The group had prepared themselves for the trip and half expected to come across illegal loggers, who could also be responsible for the trail. Military-style automatic rifles, disused M16s and some licensed G3 rifles lay with the rest of the ammunition in what looked like waterproof bags. There hadn't been a reason to remove them from their covers yet.

Frédéric secretly carried a Russian PSM pistol attached to a leg holster – a semi-automatic gun with eight rounds that was easy to conceal, and, like most Russian weapons, was practically indestructible. In addition to the other two magazines that he carried, it was enough to kill a snake ... or a few people.

The canoes glided through the thicket of foliage, lianas and branches. Orchids bloomed and exuded a beguiling scent. The temperature had dropped slightly, but Frédéric was still dripping with sweat, which attracted mosquitoes. The emerald-green water lapped softly against the hull of the boat.

Silvy reached out and plucked a low-hanging flower. She tucked it behind her ear and smiled at him.

Frédéric nodded to her as a sort of frivolous compliment. He was no friend of the jungle. He was Fennec, the desert fox. Not a panther or an anaconda.

Occasionally, he heard a snapping noise coming from the dense undergrowth that obscured his view. Birds cried and monkeys whooped threats from the treetops high above the expedition group. Then a shadow appeared underneath the hull, a silhouette just beneath the surface, and disappeared again, as if the predator had realised that the intruders were not easy prey.

Frédéric looked at the ubiquitous jungle. In half a kilometre, they wouldn't be able to get any further in the boats. They would have to continue their journey to the trail on foot, carrying their supplies. And the weapons.

All because of Pedro Armando and Valerie, the couple who had crashed in their single-engine Noorduyn Norseman. Officially, the pair were known for being private suppliers to camps in the rainforest as their hydroplane was able to land in the Amazon, but Frédéric had recently discovered that the Sparkses made very good money smuggling drugs and foreign currency, which, when they had the opportunity, they brought across the border.

'This is my first time in the Amazon,' Silvy announced to the volunteers in the boat. 'I like it here.'

Frédéric didn't like it, but he smiled nonetheless. He had been plotting for some time now how he could take out the dozen people if necessary. So far, he hadn't spared any witnesses. The cards had always wanted it to be that way, and this time would be no different. Twelve human lives would please the jack of clubs very much. It would make the card sing and give it strength. Frédéric was especially looking forward to the death of Silvy, who was undressing him in her mind with supposedly inconspicuous glances.

'We're here!' Oritz shouted from the first canoe, its prow cutting through the silt. 'Everyone takes something with them, and then we'll keep going.' He picked up his machete and took the lead.

Frédéric quickly reached for the duffle bag with the weapons. Nobody threw him a suspicious look. His compact stature meant he was predestined to carry heavy things. Besides, his role was to protect the group.

The search group disembarked from the boats, their boots sinking into the mud up to their ankles. They marched ahead one after the other, their camouflage blending in with the jungle.

Frédéric was fourth behind Oritz in case the weapons were needed. There were only three women in the group: the irritating Silvy, Penelope, a close friend of the missing couple, and a reporter, a stranger named Calderon who was filming the participants with her tiny action camera and an LED strip of lights. The proceeds from the coverage were to be used to fund the expedition.

The camera made Frédéric nervous.

He couldn't afford to have his face and his involvement in the expedition circulating online. He would burn the reporter, along with all her content, and then blame the illegal loggers for her death. Those things often happened in the Amazon. Just like the poachers who killed jaguars and panthers to sell the individual animal parts to China.

Calderon filmed the group. Silvy spoke gladly and often into the small camera as if they were on a tour, blabbing on about the colours of the Amazon. The only thing missing was make-up tips. She seemed to have forgotten that their entire purpose in coming here was to find her missing sister and brother-in-law. Oritz urged her several times to keep her voice down, but the woman seemed to find it difficult to follow his instructions.

'She's insufferable,' said Penelope, next to Frédéric now, and held out her hip flask to him. 'I can hear what you're thinking.'

It smelled of rum. He declined it, thanking her. 'Sorry,' he said.

'Don't be. Her sister feels the same way about her.' Penelope took a sip and handed the flask to someone else in the group. 'Do you think we'll find the pair?'

'You should ask Oritz,' Frédéric said. He didn't want anyone talking to him. 'We should keep quiet.'

'I get the message.' She reclaimed her flask and fell back to her old position.

After two hours, their leader signalled them to stop. There wasn't a single dry spot left on his shirt, as was the case for everyone in the group.

'We've got another three hundred metres left,' Oritz announced, wiping the sweat from his face. 'We should hand out the weapons.'

'There's no need,' Frédéric said casually. 'Unless someone can hear any chainsaws or loggers making noise?' He heaved the duffle bag onto his shoulder. 'It's just a suggestion, but we're all carrying enough as it is. The guns are heavy.'

'All right,' Oritz agreed and resumed hacking through the flora of the Amazon, trying his best to be quiet. The group tiptoed down the last few steps of the trail without slashing any plants.

Through the dwindling greenery, they eventually recognised and reached their desired location.

Frédéric could see from a glance that it was a crash site: the trees were either damaged or had been hacked off at various heights, and debris lay scattered on the ground or had got tangled up in the branches. There was also the resultant smell of kerosene, which filled the air. He spotted several destroyed canisters labelled FUEL and DIESEL on the ground. The Sparks couple had been carrying them.

As long as the card was safe, that suited him perfectly. Frédéric prayed that the jack of clubs had survived the crash, which could have seriously damaged its hand-finished markings.

The volunteers' faces only relaxed for a moment. They didn't have to go up against illegal loggers, but the realisation that the clearing was most likely soaked in fuel was not a comforting one.

'Nobody light a cigarette!' Oritz yelled.

'Or fire a gun,' Frédéric added and dropped the bag of weapons. 'We won't be needing them. Thankfully.'

The group left the safety of the undergrowth and stepped into the open area, which was ten by four metres in size. This was the area that the fallen Noorduyn Norseman had demolished, tearing down entire trees and leaving behind a hole in the jungle. Pieces of branches and tree trunks, twigs and leaves lay in a confused, tangled heap, which they had to dig their way through.

'Everything is covered in diesel,' Silvy said and looked around anxiously. 'What if it catches fire by itself?' She looked into the camera. 'This is so dangerous. I hope we find my sister soon.'

Frédéric wondered if the woman really was that naive and stupid. Penelope sighed audibly.

'Listen up!' Oritz said loudly. 'Let's form a chain and start searching from this end. Follow the trail and make several passes. If we don't find anything, we'll have to look beyond the clearing and in the jungle. If you find something, shout.' He gave the military signal to move out. 'Right, let's go.'

Frédéric looked up sceptically at the overcast, grey sky. It looked like the heavens were about to open on them, and night was approaching.

A high-pitched buzzing in his left ear warned him that a mosquito was close by and he quickly swatted it on his neck. He'd sweated off all the insect repellent.

'Get me out of this shitty, green hell,' he muttered under his breath. He imagined sitting in a hotel room in just a few hours, drinking a cold beer and marvelling at his new card. It was the best possible motivation.

Frédéric waited for the chain to form. Unsurprisingly, Silvy positioned herself next to him. It was time for the first step of his plan. 'I've got to go. I'll be right back. Go ahead, I'll catch up.'

He moved aside, made his way back through the undergrowth to their pile of equipment and opened the bag of weapons.

He hastily got out all the magazines and stuffed them into a hollow tree trunk, then grabbed a G3 rifle and ten magazines, placed them under a blooming, pungent bush and covered them with some leaves. This was to avoid his rescue of the jack of clubs backfiring.

Before he left the shelter of the dense thicket, he flicked on the silencer of his PSM and stuffed it under his shirt for easy access. The attachment not only absorbed the blast from a gunshot, but also the muzzle flash, which reduced the risk of starting a fire. Apart from their guide, nobody else carried a weapon, and as long as Frédéric had magazines and bullets he wasn't afraid of knives or machetes.

'I'm back,' he shouted and emerged from the branches. The group had been waiting for him. Naturally, Silvy flashed him a smile. 'Sorry, stomach trouble. I must have caught some bug. We can start now.'

The search party got moving.

Step by step, they made their way through the jumble of destroyed flora and the stench of diesel. The danger that they faced even silenced Silvy. They kept coming across small fragments of the Noorduyn Norseman, which had crashed into the mighty trees and shattered into the tiniest pieces. It occurred to Frédéric that Glenn Miller had gone missing in the same model in the English Channel in 1944.

After another half an hour, Frédéric began to worry that he wouldn't find the card during their first search. The volunteers were looking for two survivors, for a sign of hope, not some object measuring roughly ten by six centimetres. But unlike the missing couple, the card was irreplaceable. A one-of-a-kind piece. It had to be recovered, even if it meant him shooting the group first to conduct a more thorough search of the crash site. That would be a first for him, even after all these years.

Frédéric trudged through the scraps of trees, plant remains and leaves with a sinking feeling in his stomach. What would he do if it became apparent that the jack of clubs hadn't even been on board the plane in the first place?

For the first time, a sense of unease crept over him and he wondered if he would succeed. But losing the card to the Amazon was out of the question, even if it meant spending weeks in this green hell. And yet this was no place for a fennec.

Frédéric forced himself to stay calm.

They had covered half the trail when Penelope, who was somewhere in the middle of the chain they'd formed, stuck her hand in the air. 'I found something!' she shouted.

The team rushed past the tree debris towards her.

Frédéric saw a wrecked part of the cabin of the Noorduyn Norseman, which had turned green from plant sap and was speckled with dirt. A man's severed arm and shoulder lay inside it. Flies had already laid their eggs on the flesh and there were marks from where small predators had fed.

Silvy vomited and Calderon filmed her. She probably thought it made the footage more authentic, and Frédéric smiled at her with malicious delight, which he disguised as encouragement.

'Oh my God!' Penelope cried out. The woman clearly had a thick skin, or perhaps her senses had simply been dulled by the rum: she bent down, dug through the branches and pulled out the severed limb. 'This is ... belonged ... was ...' she said, searching for the right words, 'Pedro.'

Frédéric doubted that the missing man would have survived

the wound. The upper arm could be bound with a ligature, but there were huge veins under the armpit. Wherever the rest of Pedro Armando was, he had bled to death. Predators had most likely feasted on him.

A horrified gasp sounded from the group and Silvy began to cry hysterically. The horror and realisation that she had lost her brother-in-law had hit her. The jungle trip no longer felt like a romantic adventure.

Oritz took the severed arm from Penelope and gently placed it on a large leaf. 'Okay,' he said hoarsely and carefully stepped past Silvy's vomit. 'Let's look for Miss Valerie. We can't give up on her. She might have survived.'

The group murmured in agreement, but the mood had changed. Disillusion and shock had replaced the relief of having found the wreckage without having to fight off heavily armed loggers.

Frédéric was bewildered by the group's behaviour. During a search operation after a plane crash, you'd expect to uncover bodies and mangled corpses. There were far too many naive people in this world. He smiled to himself – far too many naive people who trusted him and were happy to accept his help.

One of the missing couple's friends ventured on, but made it no more than two metres before stopping. The group all gathered around again.

Half buried under the wreckage of the Noorduyn Norseman they found some luggage. Parts of it had been ripped open and its contents scattered, while the rest remained in the metal suitcases. There were banknotes, too – counted-out and sealed, bound bundles of American dollars and euros – but the plastic was wet on the inside from condensation. Moisture and diesel had seeped in. It was worth millions. The couple had either wanted to leave the country or had been transporting drug money. Officially, it had been a supply flight.

No one said anything. Calderon continued filming.

Frédéric couldn't resist and knelt down to take a closer look. Would the card be with their belongings, or would Pedro or Valerie have carried it with them?

'Rick, what is it?' he heard Silvy ask.

'I thought I saw a body underneath,' Frédéric explained. As she'd addressed him by his fake name, he had almost ignored her. This wasn't the right time to look for the jack of clubs, even if he didn't want to admit it. He got up. A pungent smell of diesel wafted from the miscellaneous pile. There was a puddle of fuel underneath. 'I was wrong.'

'That's a lot of money,' Calderon said.

'My sister's money,' Silvy added. 'Or mine, if—' She stopped herself, but it was too late – her blatant greed had slipped out.

Frédéric congratulated himself on having left the bag of weapons behind. People killed each other for far smaller sums. The money was an unexpected turn of events; he could already see the greed in some people's eyes.

'We knew the Sparkses were rich,' Penelope said, looking around, 'but—'

'So we found some dollars, so what?' Oritz remarked and returned to his original position. 'We've got to find Miss Sparks first. Let's go!'

The search team hesitantly split up and started walking.

After an hour of intense searching, they reached the end of the worst of the wreckage without having located the remains of Armando and Valerie. Either the missing couple were on the periphery of the crash site, or the team hadn't been thorough enough with their search. Oritz discussed with the group how best to proceed.

Frédéric scowled. While he hadn't expected things to go smoothly, his mood continued to deteriorate.

He moved away from the crowd, sat on a fallen trunk and

put a cigarette in his mouth without lighting it. The taste of the tobacco soothed him.

He urged himself to be patient for another two days before he took them out. Even if they were idiots, they were useful ones. The discovery of the treasure, however, could provoke someone in the group to choose greed over the noble purpose of the expedition. People forgot their morals when there were millions at stake.

Suddenly, he heard a muffled moan.

He quickly glanced at the group behind him to make sure it hadn't come from their direction. Silvy was being held by a man and crying, Calderon was swapping out a memory card and Oritz was bent over a map, talking to the volunteers. Nobody was missing.

Frédéric stood up and fumbled with the zip of his trousers to make it look like he was about to go and relieve himself again. 'I'll be right back!' he shouted.

Penelope waved to signal that she had understood, and he made his way through the bushes.

The moan turned into a strangled cry for help, which he quickly hurried towards.

He pushed through a thicket of large, fleshy leaves and saw a brunette leaning against a trunk: Valerie Sparks. She was covered in dirt, injured and exhausted.

She had bandaged a serious wound in her thigh; blue marks, scratches and bruises adorned her face. Empty water bottles and wrappers from chocolate bars lay scattered around her.

'Miss Sparks,' Frédéric said kindly. 'Thank goodness we found you.' He came closer and crouched down in front of her. 'I'm part of a search party organised by your friends. Apart from the wounds, how are you feeling? Any other injuries?'

'I think my right rib is broken,' she wheezed, looking relieved.

Tears rolled down her cheeks. Despite herself, she laughed. 'Walking will be difficult.'

'Yes. You're right about that. But we'll make it.' He put his hand on her shoulder reassuringly. 'Your husband is with us. We found him.'

'Oh, God,' she sobbed with new-found joy. 'He's alive!'

'Yes. He's badly injured, but alive.' He flashed her a disarming smile. 'He wanted me to ask you about the old playing card right away. I assume you know what he's referring to?'

'The card?' Valerie snorted. 'That fucking piece of cardboard! That's what's so important to him?'

'It is, Miss Sparks. In his condition, anything that gives him hope is a big help.'

'It was in the bag with the money.'

'Great. We found the bag.' Frédéric's panic grew as he thought about the diesel and kerosene puddle that the bags, as well as the card inside them, were lying in. One spark would be all it took. One spark and the masterpiece would be destroyed. He had to salvage it as soon as possible. 'That makes it easy for us to return it to your husband.'

'It should be in the front pocket of the blue one,' she said and lifted her arm with a groan, trying to push herself up from the ground. 'Help me stand up, please.'

'Of course, Miss Sparks.' Frédéric picked up a thick branch. Now that he knew the jack of clubs wasn't far, things were looking up. 'This will make an excellent crutch,' he said and seamlessly smashed the wood against her neck with all his might. Once, and then a second time to make sure.

Her larynx cracked and broke after the first blow. The second blow made it worse. No more oxygen reached her windpipe and her lungs ran out of air.

Valerie croaked, fell backward onto the jungle soil and toppled sideways. Her head turned red and then dark blue. 'I lied,

Miss Sparks,' Frédéric said, standing up. He looked at the dying woman and dropped the branch. 'Your husband is dead. And so are you.'

Thanks to him, there were no survivors left from the plane crash. Now he just had to take care of the rescue mission. It saddened him that the card hadn't received any of the radiating energy from the woman. She was too far away.

Frédéric turned to the side and found himself staring at Silvy's petrified face and one of the volunteers. They had followed him to check on him.

He drew the PSM and instantly shot Silvy in her gaping mouth. Blood and pieces of skull splattered against the green jungle leaves before the scream could escape her throat.

The barrel of the gun jerked towards the second target as his finger squeezed once, twice, three times.

The 5.45-millimetre calibre bullets caught the man in the chest and threw him backward into the thicket, where he vanished.

The beginning was complete. Frédéric would kill the rest of the group as soon as possible to avoid any trouble. The card was in the clearing – close enough to absorb the emanating energy of the dying.

Two people down, nine to go. And, most importantly, that annoying journalist's footage.

Frédéric trotted back and switched out his magazine on his way just in case, leaving one bullet in the barrel.

He emerged from the bushes, hiding the slim semi-automatic in his long arm.

'Did you see that too?' he asked with a nervous look on his face and pointed to the right, away from himself. There were no fuel vapours at the edge of the clearing that could catch fire. 'Over there! There was a panther!'

They turned to look in the direction he had pointed. Oritz reached for his pistol.

Frédéric exhaled, held his breath and then raised his weapon. He fired in rapid succession as if he were at a shooting range, knocking volunteers in the head and through the temple, the back of the head and the ear. Oritz was the first one to be eliminated. The others didn't pose a threat. His targets didn't move; they hadn't expected the ambush. The silencer of his PSM provided ample muffling.

He had managed to take out six of them before the group realised what was happening and who was after their lives: a fennec, not a panther.

The remaining people dived for cover like frightened rats between the fallen trees and the surrounding foliage. Two bullets went flying after one man and struck him. He fell to the ground and landed in a puddle of fuel. Frédéric was then forced to reload his PSM.

Satisfied, he was about to go after the two women when he saw a little flame flickering brightly. A hot bullet shell must have set the kerosene and diesel mixture on fire as it burned out.

'Shit!' Frédéric cursed and ran to the bags with the cash and the card. This had to come first. He would take care of the other two unarmed survivors afterwards.

The blazing fire crackled and spread haphazardly across the trail. The raging flames kept finding new patches of fuel, and rose several metres high into the gloomy sky. Canisters exploded, hurling fireballs and burning droplets that caused the fire to spread even further. Elsewhere, the flames furtively crept forward and crawled under tree trunks, prowling the jungle. The wrinkling, curling leaves were the only way of telling where the fire was stealthily spreading to next.

Frédéric ran, stumbled and reached the dismembered arm and the buried luggage. Ignoring the pain in his fingers, he quickly and forcefully dragged the wreckage from the Noorduyn Norseman to one side.

The blue bag lay face down, meaning he couldn't open it with his hand and rummage around for the card.

So Frédéric grabbed the bag by the handles and began tearing at them; flames swarmed around him from both sides, as if wanting to pre-empt him and destroy the card.

One of the battered handles broke off with a rattle.

Frédéric gave a howl of rage and fell back onto the branches and the dead man's arm, rolled over and scrambled back on all fours.

The flames rippled towards him, dipped down and set the pool of fuel alight.

He ignored the flash fire that threatened to engulf him, grabbed the remaining handle and jumped back, pushing off with all his might.

Hissing, the cloud of flames rolled over him. It billowed out in shades of orange and flung its radiating heat towards him as if it were about to melt gold.

Frédéric fell and wrapped his body around the bag to protect the jack of clubs. He rolled away, followed by the fire.

Out of reach of the flames, he rose with a triumphant cry that turned into a loud laugh. The card was his!

He bent down, carefully fumbled around in the front pocket of the bag and found the card.

Frédéric pulled it out very slowly. He could feel its presence through the Italo-Spanish card, an old ten of denari from 1863 that it was encased in to mislead him.

That Sparks fool hadn't even bothered to put the card inside a cellophane bag, and, to top it off, had let someone sign it. With permanent marker. Thick permanent marker. The scribble was all over the card and had probably permeated to the valuable contents inside; a crime that Madame Darlan would have to rectify.

Suddenly, a piercing scream rang out.

Through the raging flames, Frédéric spotted a burning woman. She dropped to her knees, shrieking, and frantically tried to pat out the flames on her body and smoking hair with her bare hands. He couldn't tell whether it was the reporter or Penelope. The burns and the flickering heat made that impossible.

Frédéric lifted the PSM pistol, aimed it at the woman's forehead, and pulled the trigger. Not because he pitied her, but because he wanted to be the one to gift the card her life.

The jack of clubs in his hand glimmered gratefully from underneath the ten of denari and thanked him with a faint, dark, otherworldly singing. It had grown extremely weak.

'Soon you'll be beautiful again,' Frédéric promised the card and heaved the heavy bag with the cash onto his shoulder. Dollars were always useful, even if they reeked of diesel.

He recognised the banging that suddenly resounded near him. The rapid succession of single shots was being fired from a G3 rifle.

Frédéric felt all at once the blows to his body, which started at his navel and then travelled up to his stomach, chest and neck, followed by a 7.62-millimetre bullet that tore his right ear off.

He instinctively held the card away from him to prevent it being pierced by a bullet. His muscles gave out, and the physical shock made him freeze and collapse. Frédéric wheezed and gasped for air, which barely entered his lungs any longer.

A boot sole turned him onto his back.

Calderon looked down at him without any hatred or anger, which surprised him. She only smiled gratefully.

The woman pointed the hot muzzle of the G3 at his face as she bent down and snatched the card from his trembling fingers. 'It would have taken me longer if it wasn't for you.'

Another flash fire made her intuitively duck her head and

look at the flames, the edges of which were gradually getting closer.

With a tremendous effort, Frédéric twisted his arm with the PSM from under his body. In her euphoria of victory, his astonished opponent had forgotten all about the semi-automatic.

Frédéric Roux fired. As many rounds as he could.

The gambling known as business looks with austere
disfavor upon the business known as gambling.

From *The Devil's Dictionary (1911)*
by Ambrose Gwinnett Bierce

VII

Baden-Baden, Baden-Württemberg,
the Federal Republic of Germany

Tadeus played the part without really knowing what he was doing. It had been a long time since his last self-defence course, so he improvised.

He knocked the gaping muzzle of the pump action shotgun away from him with a heavy blow to the barrel and then simultaneously kicked the kneecap of the masked man in front of him, which gave way with a crack. The man's joint buckled. A gunshot shredded the parquet floor.

His opponent cried out and limped away from him, but Tadeus immediately swept him off his feet. The man's broken knee made him unstable and he collapsed to the floor.

Tadeus threw himself at the stranger, rammed his elbows into his torso and tried to wrestle the shotgun away from him. The man groaned and stopped resisting; his limbs dropped powerlessly by his sides.

'You stupid fuck!' the second attacker shouted as he returned from the kitchen. 'You should've stayed down!'

Tadeus dived behind his worn chesterfield armchair just as another gunshot sounded. Several small bullets tore off pieces of furniture, causing scraps of leather and padding to go flying.

Poe sat behind the bed with her head down and looked at

him with her big eyes. He couldn't understand her rushed hand signals.

Tadeus motioned for her to stay where she was. His fear for the nine of spades gave him the courage he needed. From this distance, cartridges would turn the card into a piece of perforated pulp. It would destroy it. Damage it beyond repair. Rip it to shreds. *I have to be quick.*

Through the flying fragments, he heard footsteps. The crunching and clinking revealed his enemy's movements to him.

He reloaded his gun to make sure there was a new cartridge in the barrel. After the roar of gunshots, the mechanical noise and spilling out of the ejected cartridges seemed quiet to him.

'Whoever you are, you can fuck off through the window,' he shouted. 'Take your mate with you and we can forget the whole thing.'

Pure adrenaline surged through his veins. He looked at the tilted, broken picture frame on the opposite wall and saw the attacker's reflection in the cracked glass. The stranger stopped for a moment and then silently did a run-up in order to jump onto the armchair behind which Tadeus was hiding.

The moment the man pulled the trigger, Tadeus raised the barrel over the curved backrest and fired.

The firearm discharged and a cry of pain rang out. The attacker's jump caused him to collapse uncontrollably in the chesterfield armchair. His shotgun clattered onto the floor.

Tadeus stood up in what felt like slow motion, reloaded his gun again and pointed the muzzle at the injured intruder.

The masked man lay face down on the backrest, his back arched and his legs hovering above the floor. Blood poured onto the scraped off leather in wide streaks and seeped into the bullet holes. The shot had knocked him out completely. It smelled of raw flesh and burst intestines.

'He's dead,' he said to Poe without taking his eyes off their opponents. A wave of nausea came over him. 'Don't move yet.' Doctor or not, Tadeus wanted to spare her the sight.

The other attacker lay unconscious on the floor. His friend's blood snaked towards him, trickling past the glittering shards of glass and filling the gaps between the fragments.

Tadeus heard approaching police sirens through the shattered windows. The gunshots hadn't gone unnoticed. After the recent events in Baden-Baden, the city's residents were on high alert.

'Look out!' Poe shouted in alarm.

The supposedly unconscious man pulled a long knife from his sleeve and rose up high enough to stab Tadeus in the stomach.

Tadeus quickly jumped back and threw himself at the masked man. 'Stop!' he yelled.

Undeterred, his opponent swung around, squatted and reached for Tadeus' weapon. His fingers gripped around his gun and the trigger.

In his panic, Tadeus pulled the trigger, and felt the shotgun recoil.

The bullet struck the attacker in the chest and knocked him backward with his legs still bent beneath him like a puppet. The blood rose and gushed out from several of the little bullet holes, soaked his jumper and spilled onto the carpet.

'Miss Poe,' Tadeus said hoarsely, realising that he was breathing too quickly. Vast quantities of adrenaline pumped through his veins, making him feel dizzy. 'I don't want the police to see you here with me. Go now and quietly walk down the street, just as if you're taking an evening walk. And leave me your phone number, please.' He had to tear himself away from the sight of the streaming blood, and looked at her. 'I'll call you; you have my word. And then we'll talk things over. I . . . I have an idea who we have to thank for all of this.'

'I knew you were on to something!' Poe said. She got up and left the shelter of the bed.

Tadeus listened at the stairwell. 'There's someone there,' he said. He still kept his shotgun raised in case more enemies showed up. 'There's a fire escape at the end of the hall. Go. Quickly.'

The lanky Poe hurried into the corridor, opened a window, climbed out and disappeared.

The card! Tadeus dropped his weapon onto the floor and picked up the nine of spades, which lay under a large piece of blood-splattered glass.

A sense of relief overcame him, followed by a warm, blissful feeling that travelled through his body through the tips of his fingers and toes, like water seeping into the roots of a plant to nourish it with vital nutrients.

He closed his eyes and relished the card's energy, its power, and the soft, unintelligible voices that filled his mind with their soothing and enticing singing. Finally, the card was rewarding him again with its magic after that night in the villa!

The blue lights and sirens lingered outside. Several doors were slammed shut.

Tadeus pocketed the nine of spades, slowly walked up to the smashed window and clearly raised his arms in the air. The light-headedness subsided. He desperately needed to drink something. As the adrenaline faded, he realised how much danger he and Poe had been in and how close they had come to losing their lives.

'It's all over,' he shouted to the officers on the street, who were wearing bulletproof vests and carrying MP5s. 'They're dead.'

'Stay by the window,' one of them advised in a loud voice. The bluish LED light of a bright searchlight hurt Tadeus' eyes. 'How many are there?'

'Two men, in masks and with pump action shotguns. They attacked me,' he replied dutifully and squinted at the glare of the torch. 'I'm Boch. I live here.'

'As I said, stay where you are, Mr Boch. We're coming to you now,' he heard the man shout from the street. 'Access granted,' someone said softly. Several footsteps rushed towards the entrance.

It didn't take long for the officers to reach his floor.

'Some guys from the Russian gambling mafia broke in,' he told the police officers and carefully turned around to face them. They would buy that explanation. 'They told me to keep my mouth shut and to not say another word about what happened at the villa. Please call Inspector Klim from the State Criminal Police Office. He's the one leading the investigation into the murders.'

The officers held their MP5s in firing position for a few seconds before lowering them at the sight of the two dead men and the unarmed Tadeus. They certainly didn't see a crime scene like this every day.

'Can I get something to drink?' Tadeus asked. 'I'm not feeling very well.'

The police officers stood around indecisively and then radioed the head of operations in Stuttgart to notify them of the events.

Tadeus was permitted to fetch himself a glass of water from the kitchen, which he gulped down to settle his nausea. Then he quickly made some coffee for the officers to counteract the stench of blood in his apartment. It would be a while until all the questions were answered and the crime scene was secured: they were in for a long night.

Inspector Klim phoned Tadeus to let him know that he had set off in his car from Stuttgart, which wouldn't take him very long at this time of night.

He didn't mind the wait – on the contrary, it bought him more time to draft and flesh out his story. Klim and his squad would believe his account about the Russian gambling mafia. He could use the opportunity to clear Poe's name with his statement on the night of the murders by saying he had seen her disappear halfway through the night.

Then his hunt for Gillot and the cards would begin. He needed some leverage against that dangerous, reckless man. The two killers who had broken into his flat were probably only just the beginning.

Four hours later and after copious amounts of coffee, Tadeus turned up at the *Atlantic* Hotel, where Poe was staying. It was early morning.

He had given his landlord notice and temporarily covered the broken window with some tarpaulin. For the time being, living there was out of the question. Tadeus showered, packed his clothes and his most expensive shoes into two large suitcases, and loaded them into his rickety Skoda. He expected to lead a rather nomadic lifestyle in the coming days.

The casino gave him some time off to deal with the police, his insurance claims and flat repairs, but he decided to dedicate his free time to looking for Gillot and the cards instead.

He spotted Poe eating a rather ascetic breakfast consisting of muesli and buttermilk, along with some black coffee in a porcelain pot that was being kept warm on top of a small stove. Her grey sweatpants and hoodie made her look younger than the thirty-year-old doctor that she was.

Tadeus helped himself to a big breakfast from the buffet: chorizo, scrambled eggs, cheese, olives and bread. He needed something to soak up all the coffee with.

'Forgive the intrusion, Miss Poe,' he said and slowly sat down. Last night's stunts in his flat had left him with severe back pain and an incessant burning sensation in his left knee, which he was reminded of with every movement. 'But Inspector Klim from the State Criminal Police Office asked a lot of questions.'

'And what did you tell him?' she asked.

'The truth,' Tadeus said, pricking some egg, cheese and an olive onto his fork. 'It's now official: the illegal gambling organisers sent their men after me to intimidate me.'

'And their visit got out of hand,' Poe added, eating with a refined elegance.

Tadeus gestured in agreement with his empty fork. 'I refused protection from the police, but the inspector thinks that I might get another visit.' He skewered a piece of chorizo on his fork. 'You're not in the report of course, Miss Poe. I've also expanded on my statement on the night of the murders. Under oath. That means you were officially no longer present at the crime scene before the deadly shooting took place. Though that still might not be enough to stop the police from launching an investigation against you.'

'My lawyer already called and told me that. He thinks it's a good development, but that evidence is better than statements. I think so too.' She bowed her head in a manner that would have suited an empress. 'So, I'm really curious to hear what you've got to tell me, Mr Boch. You mentioned a mastermind who you think could be behind the death of my fiancé and the murders in the old hotel. And a curse.'

'Yes. His name is Henry Pierre Gillot.' Tadeus recounted his meeting with the Walloon and the clear threat that he'd made. 'It was about the card that Morgan gave me,' he went on, telling her about their escape. Ignoring the voice in his head, he pulled the nine of spades from his inside jacket pocket and placed it in front of Poe. The plastic cover protected it from dirt. 'This card, hidden inside the seven of clubs.'

'That's my fiancé's card,' she said and looked at Tadeus' find with disgust. 'Judging by what you've told me, there's more to the story. There's a whole pack of cards. And, if you take it further, the owners of these cards are in danger. Gillot seems mad enough to take that risk.' She laid her right middle and index finger on the card and a shadow spread across her features. 'It's hideous. So cruel and malicious,' she said softly. 'If only I'd listened to my intuition and destroyed it. Then Enrico might still be alive.'

Tadeus became afraid that Poe would try to destroy it on another occasion. He quickly picked up the nine of spades and pocketed it again, immediately overcome with relief and joy. 'We can save other people if we find where the other cards are and get a hold of them before Gillot does. We could lure him into a trap.'

'The Devil's Playbook.' Poe repeated Morgan's words.

'That's the historical and derogatory term for the card game in Christian circles,' he said. 'I did a bit of research on the fly.'

'How did Morgan know about Gillot's collecting mania? Didn't he tell you to stop him from getting the nine of spades?' Poe lifted her cup with both hands to her lips and took a sip.

'Morgan didn't mention Gillot specifically.'

'Where does he live? Maybe we could find some clues there.'

'No idea.' Tadeus liked her approach and kicked himself for not having thought of it first. He'd spent too much time marvelling at the nine of spades and often found himself sitting in his chesterfield armchair, doing nothing but staring at the card's lines, lettering and fine touches, waiting for the voices and chorus to bewitch him. 'It's been over a week since that night at the villa. If Morgan had been hiding something, Gillot would have already found it.' He massaged his aching knee and his spine cracked softly as he leaned to the side.

Poe agreed. 'That's true. Then we have to follow Gillot and hope that his movements lead us to the collectors that he's after.' She set her cup down. 'He'll definitely have notes about the cards and their history at home. And his plans. We need evidence of his involvement in the murders at the villa. Only then can I clear my name.'

There was one thing that troubled Tadeus to no end. 'Can you really feel that the nine of spades is evil?'

Poe gave him a weak smile. 'Now I sound crazy, don't I?'

'Just a bit. But given what's happened . . .' He implied that he wanted to believe her every word. 'There was talk of a curse.'

'My grandmother was a mudang, Mr Boch. She was a mediator between our world and the spirit world. When I still lived in Korea, she was entirely convinced that I was destined to follow the same path. I loved listening to her as a child.' She sat bolt upright, her blue eyes fixed on Tadeus like a lurking cat. 'The older I got, though, and having grown up in London, the more I distanced myself from it. But my desire to do good remained, and becoming a doctor felt like a good choice. It somehow fitted with my mudang calling. It's all about helping other people.'

'The spirit world?' he repeated.

'You don't know what to make of that, do you?' Poe asked, looking amused. 'I'll go back a little. Back home, we still practise old customs to please the spirits. It's not as strange as it sounds. Christians consecrate new buildings and pray to God for help; we make offerings to the spirits to appease them.' She poured herself another coffee. 'I would describe the shamanism approach as holistic: mudangs resolve issues by bringing the people and spirits who cause harm and problems together. They are a bit like healers or psychologists, and some studies have shown that mudangs are particularly good at treating psychosomatic and mental disorders.' Poe made a swaying movement with her hands. 'It's all about harmony. Between the body and the soul and between people and spirits, which are capable of both good and bad. As a surgeon, I see myself more as an artisan. My profession has less to do with spirits.'

Tadeus couldn't stop thinking about what she'd said. 'Spirits,' he uttered. Until a week ago, he would have at least described her as someone who was lost. Thanks to the nine of spades, however, he was now ready to believe in many things. 'Spirits that torment people. So that means that shamans' – he searched for the right word – 'are a kind of medium.'

'Something like that, yes. I've never forced it. During my occasional trips to Daegu in South Korea, which is where I grew up, my grandmother always made me go to some mudang lessons. She felt that I was wasting my talents as a doctor in the West. I had the feeling for it.' She pointed to Tadeus' jacket pocket, where the nine of spades was hiding under the fabric. 'Speaking of, I could feel it. I sensed the card's evil from the moment Enrico came back to London from an auction and proudly showed me the seven of clubs. That could be the curse you were talking about.'

'And what was your reaction?'

'I wanted to flush the thing down the toilet. Burn it. Anyway, it's hard to describe. The . . . air around it was charged. I'm sure my grandmother would have said that the spirits were throwing a fit and screaming around the card.' Poe propped her elbows on the table. 'I think there's a story behind this nine of spades and the deck that it belongs to that we don't know about. The card-maker must have had the darkest intentions when they made it. Whatever forces were at work when it was crafted, they want the worst for whoever holds the cards.' She fixed her gaze on him. 'You do know that you're in danger, Mr Boch?'

Tadeus didn't believe her for a second. The nine of spades didn't mean him any harm; it only wanted to be held and protected by him. It longed to be reunited with its siblings, and calmly told him that the voices would sound even sweeter by their side. Together. In unison. A celestial, mystical and rewarding chorus. He would grant the nine of spades' wish.

'The danger that I believe in,' Tadeus answered in a guttural voice, clearing his throat, 'is called Gillot. In my eyes, he's the real threat here and the owner of the remaining cards. There've been two killers so far, and more could show up.'

Poe remained unconvinced. He could see it on her pretty face. In the end, she would still go against his wishes and try to destroy the nine of spades and its siblings. Tadeus couldn't let that happen. He had to keep the card safe. 'You're right, Miss Poe,' he lied. 'I trust your expertise. As soon as we have all the cards, we'll destroy them.'

'Why not now?' she interjected. 'This thing, and the terrible power that dwells within it, it killed Enrico and is giving me the worst nightmares. It has to be—'

'Because we might still need it. To lure Gillot. We can use it as bait,' he said, dismissing her suggestion. 'It's still valuable.'

Poe looked at him, lifted the pot off the little stove and refilled her cup. 'That's true. Let's keep it then.' She held out her thin, wiry hand. 'Can I see it again?'

So as not to rouse any suspicion, he reluctantly gave it to her. He anxiously watched as she removed the card from its case, grabbed it by its edges with her middle and index finger, and suddenly held it over the small tea light at the base of the small stove.

Tadeus clenched his fists to stop himself from hitting the Korean woman. He could feel the blood rushing in his ears, but the card whispered reassuringly in his mind that he shouldn't worry. It told him that she couldn't hurt it and that he should stay calm. Tadeus hated to watch her toying with it, but the nine of spades put his fears at ease.

Poe and Tadeus watched as the little flame danced around the card without setting the foxed paper on fire. The multilayered cardboard didn't even bend under the heat. Instead, the card's illustrations shimmered in a murky, dark purple colour. They then turned dark red until the tea light simply went out.

Tadeus' heartbeat gradually slowed. *It was indestructible!*

She handed him back the card with a look of fearful admiration on her face. 'I can understand why you're sceptical about what I said about being a mudang and shamanism,' she said, alarmed. 'But you have to admit, that isn't normal behaviour for an old card. This has just confirmed what I thought. If this card can't be destroyed by fire, then it's even more dangerous than I feared.'

He put away the nine of spades. 'No it isn't,' he choked, covering up his fear with feigned surprise.

'You disagree? After seeing that?'

'But that shouldn't change our plan or hold us back right now.'

She scrutinised him with her blue eyes. 'Fine. We'll follow Gillot and see what he does next,' she said in her calm, albeit firm voice. 'I'll call a few people who might be helpful to us.'

'You have those kinds of contacts?'

'As a doctor, you sometimes have to show your face at social events.' She pulled out her smartphone. 'Let's see what I can find out from my art dealer friends.' She dialled a number and retrieved a pen from the pocket of her hoodie to note down any new information on her napkin.

Tadeus was impressed by Poe, but he needed to find out more about her. She could be his divining rod and his strongest rival all wrapped into one. Her rough handling of the nine of spades left no doubt in his mind. In the end, she would find a way to destroy the card – something he couldn't bear to think about.

I know too little about the subject myself. Tadeus got out his own new smartphone and looked up the history of playing cards in Europe and their origin on the internet.

He found plenty of information about when people first began to gamble away their homes, farms, money and lives with cards. Tadeus wasn't surprised by the fact that historians weren't entirely in agreement about where cards had originally come from.

Playing cards most likely first appeared between the 12th and 13th centuries. The earliest playing cards can be traced back to Korea and China in the 12th century, a popular online information platform claimed.

Korea. Tadeus lifted his head in surprise and looked at Poe, who was speaking on the phone in her mother tongue. After listening more carefully, he was stunned to discover that he could understand her.

There's no such thing as a coincidence.

* * *

Avignon, Vaucluse,
Provence-Alpes-Côte d'Azur,
France

Odette sat at her long desk and examined the two of clubs and the ace of hearts through her magnifying glass. The paper of the cards looked fresh, smooth, white, and as if its powers had been restored. The cure, the life force from the human sacrifices in the cellar, had had a positive impact on the cards' condition. Finally, she could make a start on the finer details.

Sunlight flooded through the tilted windows, as if there had never been a storm in the city in the first place, and the chirping of cheeky sparrows drifted into the room. The birds bounced on the branches of the outer wall's climbing ivy and hunted for insects, which Odette only recognised as excited, thumb-sized shadows that fluttered and scurried around. Despite her poor eyesight, she was still delighted with the little creatures.

Charles and Renard were busy fixing things in the medieval house that they knew nothing about. Odette had given up lecturing the men about her home. The building had a mind of its own that had evolved over the centuries. Certain parts of Avignon had changed considerably, but her small winery's beams and walls had remained.

She stroked the cards with her cotton-gloved fingers, then carefully clamped them into some padded holders and slid one illuminated magnifying glass on top of another. Then she played with the lighting to reveal the hidden details on the paper that were otherwise invisible to a casual observer.

Odette removed her thick glasses and looked through the polished, large, square lens made from mountain crystal, which unveiled the cards' mystical peculiarities. If she found that certain features were missing from the ace of hearts and the two of clubs during her inspection, such as a signature, any supplementary lettering or messages, it meant that Roux had brought her some brilliant forgeries.

This had already happened twice before. Duplicates of extraordinary quality. The copies had been in such good condition that a cellar treatment had not been necessary, and only the mountain crystal lens had brought the mistake to light. Unfortunately, Odette was unable to attribute the forgeries to an artist. She would have been very interested to know if the imitations had been produced out of admiration or as a distraction.

Her right ankle itched and she bent down to pull her greywhite stocking down a little.

A thin, black plastic band with a transmitter the size of a matchbox rubbed against an insect bite. Odette had skinny legs, meaning there was lots of room between the band and the awkward spot where the mosquito had bitten her. A bit of ointment and a plaster would relieve the pain before it became infected.

The itching disturbed her work, so she decided to get up, put on her glasses and leave the restoration room. Like the prisoners in the cellar, she also had a cuff on her foot, only without the iron chain. Her every movement was monitored, even when she wasn't in Renard's or Charles' presence.

She went down into the kitchen, where it smelled of Charles' new cake. The man was always baking and successfully trying out new recipes. Thanks to his high-calorie creations, Odette had already gained a few kilos. She suspected that it was his concern for her wellbeing that provoked him to constantly offer her something home-made to nibble on. She spotted a large cake on the table, which was unusually laid out for three and decorated with candles.

Odette felt that Charles had gone overboard. She pulled open the drawer with the mishmash of blister packs, ointments and plasters inside. They needed the countless tranquillisers to make the people in the cellar apathetic. Although the cellar was soundproof, life was simpler when the prisoners didn't pull on chains or injure themselves in pointless escape or suicide attempts. Following the incident with that rebellious man earlier, she had increased the dose of sedatives in the prisoners' food.

'I really ought to organise it better,' she muttered disapprovingly, and finally found the ointment she was looking for.

The doorbell rang.

She slipped the tube into her apron dress pocket, checked the position of her bun and walked towards the front door, but quickly realised that Renard had beat her to it.

She heard voices. Something was being discussed.

Ongoing disputes made Odette feel restless, and she wondered what the reason for the visit could be. It couldn't be Monsieur Libeau – the pétanque game didn't start for another two hours. She hadn't ordered anything, and neither a chimney sweep nor anyone from the municipal utilities had announced their arrival.

An uneasy feeling came over her. She moved somewhat stiffly

along the corridor and towards the door. She couldn't stand surprises.

'. . . want to see my grandmother,' she heard a woman say angrily.

'She's not feeling very well at the moment. Why don't you ring her later?' Renard said pleasantly.

Odette felt her body run hot and cold. It was Denise! Her granddaughter! What was she doing here in Avignon?

Every one of her children and grandchildren knew that Odette hated surprise visits. It was rude to turn up at the door unannounced, regardless of what was happening in the house and the cellar.

It had been three years since Odette had actually seen Denise. She had met her and the children in a café in town. Since then, Denise, just like the rest of the family, had settled for phone calls, emails, letters and large gifts for the children. Odette's family saw her as old and eccentric, but nice and generous. They had accepted her wish for peace and quiet.

'Grandmère!' Two little shadows – Jean and Hermine – pushed past Renard and hopped around Odette, clearly delighted to see their great-grandmother again. 'Happy birthday!' they cried in unison.

The cake. The laid-out kitchen table. She had missed the signs. She always shut herself off from the outside world when she was working on restoring the cards. No calls. No emails. As a result, she'd forgotten her own birthday.

Renard, dressed in dirty overalls, turned his shiny head towards her and tried to communicate with her with glances. There was no room for mistakes now, or else disaster was inevitable.

'Thank you,' Odette said and tried to remember whether she had pulled her stocking over the transmitter band. She hoped her apron would conceal it. 'Oh, my loves!' she marvelled at how tall her great-grandchildren were. She had forgotten how old they were. Ten? Twelve?

'It smells of cake,' squealed Hermine, who looked like a smaller version of her mother. She was dressed in smart, youthful clothes and her light hair was woven into plaits.

'Yummy!' added Jean, whose bookish outfit made him look like a mini country club member, complete with a gelled side parting.

'Well, welcome!' Renard said and finally moved aside. There was no putting them off any longer.

Denise and her terrible bore of a husband, Robert, came inside. Robert owned a wallpaper business with four branches in Paris and was ripping off the rich with hugely inflated prices. Odette dimly remembered a single roll genuinely costing four hundred euros.

She saw for the first time that both of them were wearing holiday clothes: matching shorts and polo shirts adorned with the company's logo. Advertising even on holiday, that suited Robert. It was a miracle that his children hadn't been pressured into doing the same.

'Well, what brings you to Avignon?' she asked cheerfully, feigning joy at their visit to avoid making things worse. 'Surely not just because of my birthday?'

'We were actually on our way to Marseille, but it's been so long since we've seen each other, Grandmère, and we thought you'd be happy if we celebrated together. I called from the road, but there was no answer,' Denise said and came towards Odette and hugged her. 'Mon Dieu, you're so thin! You don't eat enough.'

'Ah, you don't need much at my age.'

Renard pointed outside. 'Monsieur, your car!' he said to Robert, who would have easily won every Clark Kent lookalike competition. 'You can't leave it there. The street is too narrow.'

He grabbed a key from the shelf. 'I'll open up the barn for you. You can park it there, monsieur.'

Odette closed her eyes for a moment. She hoped that whatever Renard was planning could be stopped.

'Of course, thank you,' Robert said. He handed his wife the bag of biscuits he had bought and followed Renard outside. The rattling of the heavy gates sounded a few seconds later.

'Who is that man?' Denise asked quietly. 'I thought we'd turned up at the wrong house at first.'

'My . . . helper around the house. Both him and his brother,' Odette explained. She ushered the family into the kitchen for cake. Sweetness made for the perfect distraction; any fairytale would tell you that. She tried to regain her composure after the surprise. The visit could still end well.

As if on cue, Charles appeared at the table, laid down the cutlery and plates in a flash, and cut the fragrant cake into slices. It didn't bother him that he was wearing a woman's apron that was too small for him. 'Bonjour,' he said merrily, holding the long knife with the straight blade. 'Oh là, là, we have guests! I thought we might. This is lemon, cardamom and chocolate cake.' He winked at the children. 'You must be Jean and Hermine. Your grandmère talks about you all the time,' he said, and then looked at Denise. 'Madame Leroy, it's so great to meet you.' He pointed to the gurgling coffee machine. 'It's almost ready.'

'Grandmère! You never wrote to me or told me about your newly acquired wealth!' Denise exclaimed, taking a seat at the table. Her children followed suit. The astonishment on her face was plain to see. 'House staff?'

'You know that I live comfortably.' Odette brushed off her granddaughter's exuberance and slumped into an empty chair. 'What else am I supposed to do with it all?'

'Leave it to us!' Jean cried cheekily.

'Buy presents!' Hermine suggested, grinning.

Odette couldn't hold back her laughter. 'I already do both of those things. But as for my everyday life, two pairs of helping hands allow me to keep this old shack in good shape.'

'Well, what a surprise!' Denise thanked Charles with a nod as he handed out the large slices of the lemon, cardamom and chocolate cake. 'Good idea, Grandmère.'

'I thought so too,' she said and accepted some coffee. 'So, tell me, what's new in Paris?' Odette wanted to distract her, and feigned normality.

Her granddaughter prattled away. New furniture, their move to a fancier neighbourhood and collaboration with designers abroad to add an element of foreign chic to Robert's wallpaper designs. She then seamlessly steered the conversation to the children, what Jean could do, the things Hermine was particularly good at, hobbies, friends and acquaintances. Denise rattled on like a German machine gun, Odette's father would have said.

Renard and Robert joined them in the meantime. No one except Denise got a word in, which Odette found to be no bad thing. It meant that she didn't have to make anything up.

At some stage, the children grew restless and wanted to stretch their legs.

Charles immediately agreed to go and play with them in the barn. As he left the kitchen, he gave Renard a barely perceptible nod. Renard innocuously raised his cake fork to signal his approval and tapped the table twice, just as he did in the cellar with the victims. The men were ready.

Odette's heart pounded painfully under her ribcage.

'It sounds like you've been keeping busy. And thank you for thinking of me, but you'd best be going soon.' She had to try to get her family out. 'A storm is coming, I can feel it in my bones. And I'm rather tired, too.'

Denise served herself a second piece of cake. 'We were just thinking that, weren't we Robert?'

'Yes,' Robert agreed. He glanced at his expensive wristwatch, which sparkled in the light: a status symbol for the wealthy. 'Grandmère, would I be able to steal a bottle of wine from your cellar? I promised a business partner that I'd bring him back some of the wine that you always send us.'

Odette's heart beat even faster. Robert couldn't know that the wine she claimed came from her family's reserves was in fact delivered to her. She forged the labels on the bottles herself for fun. 'Sadly, I've run out.'

'Oh, that's a shame.' Robert presumptuously held his cup in front of Renard for a top-up. Renard complied reluctantly. Neither Denise nor her husband noticed.

'The wine was excellent.' Robert set his cup down in front of him and then pointed at the bald man. 'Don't you two know each other?'

Denise frowned. 'No. Where from?'

'You're family after all, aren't you?' Robert laughed. 'And not a very big one either. Haven't you bumped into each other before?'

'I don't understand what you mean.' Denise shoved another piece of cake into her mouth.

Renard looked at Odette, who was rooted to her chair with fear. Her mouth was dry and the kitchen swayed around her slightly. She was angry at Denise for putting her in this position. There was a reason why Odette didn't want any visitors.

'Well, you, Renard and Charles – you're related,' Robert went on, peering through his Clark Kent glasses. He then smacked his forehead with his palm and pushed the shop-bought biscuits towards Odette. 'Happy birthday from us too. We've added a bit of money as well.'

Odette looked at the packet. It was the most stupid gift she could have received, but it suited Robert, whose idea it had doubtless been.

'Oh. I don't think so,' Denise replied and turned to look at Odette, stunned.

'I . . .' Feeling overwhelmed, Odette struggled to breathe.

'You can tell her now,' Renard said, supporting her. 'The time is right. No one is going to judge you for it.' He laid his hand on her skinny fingers. 'Tell her that our father was from an affair.'

'No!' Denise cried out and clapped her hand over her mouth to stop bits of cake from falling out. Baffled, Robert set down the cup he had just raised to his lips.

Odette felt a weight lift from her shoulders. The simplest of lies would never have occurred to her. 'Well, it's out now,' she said. The relief was genuine and palpable, which supported the lie. 'It happened after my divorce. I had to hide my pregnancy from everyone and secretly gave birth to a son. I gave him away to a children's home. I couldn't afford for there to be a scandal.'

Renard patted her wrinkled, old hand. 'She took us in after we came to see her and told her about our father's death. We're very grateful to her for that.'

'Oh my goodness!' exclaimed Denise after she had swallowed the cake in her mouth. 'Two cousins!' She stared at Renard. 'You don't look very alike.'

'I take more after my mother,' he said with a faint smile and offered her his hand, which she shook.

'Welcome to the family,' Denise said, laughing. 'Robert, I told you that something special would happen on Grandmère's birthday.'

Her husband, however, didn't seem so pleased. 'Well, thank goodness Grandmère is rich, am I right?'

'Robert, please!' Denise looked around the room, embarrassed. 'You and your business mindset!'

'It's quite all right,' Odette intervened, trying not to look so tense. 'I should have told you about it sooner.' She could feel the house of cards beginning to collapse.

'Where are Charles, Hermine and Jean hiding, anyway?' Denise asked as she scraped up the cake crumbs with her fork, clearly trying to divert the conversation.

'Oh, the barn is one big adventure playground,' Odette reassured her, taking the hint. 'There's always something new to discover.'

Robert appeared dissatisfied. 'Forgive me for speaking so openly, but Odette is a wealthy woman and – long may she live – has a considerable inheritance to leave behind.' He glanced at Renard. 'I can imagine that there might be some unscrupulous people who might want to take advantage of her and secure a mention in the will, despite not having cared for her for years.'

'They're taking very good care of me,' Odette interjected. 'I've already told you that everything is fine.'

'I don't think so.' Robert, who had acquired a thick skin from all his negotiations and contracts, bit down like a shark. Finally, he had been presented with the opportunity to show off and be seen as more than just a despicable businessman selling overpriced wall decorations. 'It hasn't even been proven that they're your *actual* grandchildren. There's nothing to say that they're not just pretending and that they haven't simply made up this entire story.'

'Robert, let it go,' Denise snarled. Her eyes darted between her grandmother and Renard as she read their expressions. 'I'm sure it's true.'

'And I'm not senile,' Odette added, vehemently cursing Robert in her head. 'I appreciate your concern, grandson-in-law, but believe me: Renard and Charles are mine. I've done the DNA tests.' She could tell from the look on his face that her argument had worked. 'Without them knowing about it.' She tapped her forehead. 'I'm not stupid, my dear.'

Denise laughed in relief. The growing doubts about their relationship, which had been clearly visible on her face just a moment ago, dissipated. 'Why didn't you say that right away?'

'I didn't know that my grandson-in-law would be so stubborn about my naivety.' Odette took a deep breath and sighed. 'Are you satisfied now, Robert?'

The wallpaper salesman had gone bright red. He turned to face Renard. 'I owe you an apology. I'm sorry, I didn't mean to offend you.'

'It's water under the bridge now,' Renard said calmly. 'It does you credit that you're worried for your grandmother.' He waved to the group with his cake knife, which could easily have been interpreted as a threat. 'Long live Odette.'

Everyone laughed and partook in the blessing, which Odette answered with a gracious wave. They all drank their coffee in unison and hoped to have put the awkward situation behind them.

'But, seriously, I'm still in shock. An affair,' Denise said and pulled out her smartphone, grinning. 'I'll have to tell Maman.'

'Wouldn't it be better for me to tell her?' Odette suggested.

'Definitely,' Robert agreed and glanced at his flashy watch. He had lost face and now was suddenly in a great hurry to leave. 'It's time we set off, my dear. Marseille awaits.'

Odette felt herself relax a little. Things were taking a turn for the better.

Suddenly Jean came racing into the kitchen and crawled under the table. 'Don't tell anyone,' he whispered. 'We're playing hide and seek.'

Renard and Odette exchanged worried looks. The chosen children's entertainment programme could prove to be a bad idea on Charles' part.

It occurred to her that she had left the ace of hearts and the two of clubs in the restoration room, clamped and out on display, not to be missed by the children's curious eyes and fingers. The cards were in danger of being carelessly played with and damaged. While some of the cards were fragile as they didn't possess their full power, others were stronger than concrete or steel.

'No, that's enough running around now. It's time for us to go,' Denise said. She bent down, lifted the tablecloth and looked at her son. 'Will you please go get your sister so that we can say adieu?'

'Just this round, Maman,' he begged her and giggled. 'But it could take a while.'

'You could have picked a better hiding place,' Clark-Kent-Robert remarked and stroked his miniature lookalike's parted mop of hair. 'Charles will find you in a minute.'

'Where is Hermine?' Odette asked sternly. Everyone heard the concern in her voice.

'Not in your workroom, Grandmère,' Jean whispered from his hiding place. 'We know that you don't like that. Charles told us.'

'Then where?' Renard interrupted.

'She's in the cellar,' the boy revealed, snickering. 'It's dark in there and you can hide in the corners really well.'

'Ah, the cellar,' Odette said, her voice hoarse with worry. The worst-case scenario was feasible. If Hermine opened the door to the dungeon and found the people in chains, there was no going back. 'That's . . . not good. There are some loose bricks in the wall. I should go and look for her.' She stood up.

'Absolutely not! You'll fall down the steps,' Denise intervened. 'Renard, could you—'

'I know the place better than anyone,' Odette insisted.

'Then we'll *all* go,' Robert decided, unsolicited. He got up. 'We'll find her faster that way.'

'Oh, that's no fair!' Jean complained and crawled out from under the table. 'I would have won.'

A continuous, metallic grinding noise could be heard from the corridor adjacent to the kitchen. The sound was like something out of a horror film, its hollow echo menacingly wandering across the walls and into the kitchen.

Odette and the others froze. The door creaked open.

Hermine emerged from the twilight, her clothes covered in dirt and speckled with blood. She dragged the bloodstained spear with the sword-like blade behind her. 'I found this at the top of the stairs, in the cellar,' she said excitedly, slightly out of breath. 'And I heard voices behind the door and the rattling of chains! Are they ghosts?'

Charles appeared behind her. His small apron was covered in cobwebs and his face was blank.

Odette closed her eyes. She didn't want to see anything.

Tock, tock, Renard knocked twice with the fork on the table next to her.

Hermine screamed first. Then Denise.

By gaming we lost both our time and treasure –
two things most precious to the life of man.

Owen Feltham (1602–1668)

VIII

'This card,' Frieder Honett said solemnly and held up the small sheet of cardboard featuring an illustration of a fool into the spotlight, 'was once used by the legendary Doctor Faustus, the wandering miracle healer, alchemist, magician, astrologist and fortune teller who has fascinated so many writers and people since the sixteenth century.' The tall, blond man in his early twenties stepped to the edge of the stage and showed the Fool card to the people in the first row. 'The rest of the deck was destroyed in the tragic explosion in which Faustus met his death. This is the only card that survived.'

Frieder wore black trousers and a frock coat with a high-standing, white-collared shirt underneath. To enable him to move freely, his sleeves were casually pushed up, and there was no jewellery on his manicured fingers. He had deliberately chosen an outfit in the style of a vaudeville performer in the 1900s.

'In just a moment I'll show you why it's so special.' He jumped down and slowly walked past the audience in the Friedrichstadt-Palast theatre, who had paid a lot of money for a premium ticket.

Two spotlights followed him. The remaining lights illuminated his twin sister, who sat on a high-backed chair on stage: Frieda Honett, the medium who could guess any object that he held in his hands. She was wearing an innocent-looking white dress, which, at second glance, proved to be subtly see-through. The lingerie she was wearing underneath could definitely be described as erotic. It was all part of the show; distraction made every trick more convincing. She had a thick, black, leather blindfold on, which contrasted with her long, platinum-blonde hair.

'Il matto, the sküs or the Fool is a trump card with a higher value than any other tarot card.' Frieder let the crowd inspect it and invited two ladies to touch and smell the card. It had a drawing of a man in a bright costume and an eye mask, around which different-coloured stains, scratches and burn holes had partially eaten their way through the paper. 'Can you see the traces of sulphur?'

The women nodded, entranced.

'Legend has it that the Devil himself came to collect the doctor's life. These' – he held up the tarot card – 'are the traces he left behind. Blood and alchemy. This is what gives the card its special, magical influence that my charming sister can work with.'

Frieder leapt up onto the stage and walked towards her with measured steps. 'Frieda, are you ready?'

'Yes, my brother,' she replied.

'Then place your hands in front of you and take Doctor Faustus' card with all ten fingers.'

Frieda had mastered the art. Her movements were as graceful as a dancer's. Grand deception required grand gestures to entertain the almost two thousand spectators. Her actual name was Sandra, and his was Klaus Ehrlich, but, since a pair of illusionists were already travelling under that name, they had decided on an even better-sounding synonym.

The prop card wasn't from the 15th century either, and it certainly wasn't Doctor Faustus' card. Klaus had paid a boy one euro for it at a Berlin flea market because he liked its colouring and the illustration of the fool. Upon examining it, his acquaintance had estimated that the card was from around 1825, but the public wished to be deceived.

The tiny, glued-on rhinestones on Frieda's black-painted fingernails made them sparkle under the light. 'You may begin, brother.'

Frieder descended the steps. 'Ladies and gentlemen, I'll now come to you and ask someone to hand me an object of their choice. It can be whatever you wish. I'll hold and examine it.' A spotlight followed him as he passed by the first rows and walked up to the arena-like upper level of the theatre. The audience there also deserved a show. 'Thanks to the powers of Doctor Faustus' card, my sister will be able to feel what I feel and see what I see, down to the very last detail.'

A murmur of disbelief passed through the crowd. In the days of TV and the internet, people had access to the latest technology and were difficult to surprise.

This was nothing new.

Modern illusionists worked incredibly hard and put in a great deal of effort. They had their own shows, in which they outdid themselves with tricks. Some of these performances were inspired by Houdini or the great Harry Kellar, while others were based on new ideas that cost unbelievable amounts of money. And then there were the frustrated colleagues who revealed every trick on the internet and called themselves 'The Unveilers'.

Frieder had chosen to go down a different path – one that didn't require making elephants, aeroplanes or people disappear. People were much more afraid of having their own secrets exposed.

And that was exactly what he did.

'Good evening,' Frieder said, approaching a woman

wearing thrifted clothes. She was in her mid-thirties and had an excessive amount of make-up on to give her a false sense of confidence. 'What's your name?'

Before the woman could open her mouth, Frieda spoke from the stage: 'Her name is Jessica.'

'That's . . . right,' Jessica admitted, taken aback. She fidgeted with her tight shirt as she slowly stood up. The spotlight pulled her out of the cover of the darkness.

'It's very nice to meet you, Jessica. Do you have anything you'd like to give me?'

The woman rummaged around in her trouser pocket and handed him her phone.

'Pay attention, sister,' Frieder called to the stage. The code phrase *pay attention* meant *smartphone*.

'The doctor's card tells me that it's a phone,' Frieda promptly announced.

'That's too easy. So, card, the card in my slender sister's powerful fingers: what is Jessica's phone's serial number?'

'I see it.' Frieda named the sequence of digits, thanks to their designated code words for the corresponding numbers.

Until this moment, the sceptics in the audience would think they knew how it worked; a very old trick that was often performed at fun fairs in the past.

Frieder, however, had taken precautions and deployed his electronic spies – a technique also known as hot reading. The bistro and the waiting area were fitted with secret microphones and cameras, which he and his sister used to select their victims and spy on them. Every snippet of information from a conversation was recorded and memorised by the pair of illusionists.

'Jessica, may I touch your neck?' Frieder asked, smiling shyly as he laid his hand on her. 'Sister, what does the Fool card reveal about our guest?'

'That she has a little brother,' Frieda said. Her voice was wickedly neutral, the kind one might expect from a medium in a trance.

Jessica was genuinely baffled. 'How . . .'

'The card tells me that he fell off a horse today,' Frieda continued. 'But it wasn't his own horse. The horse is brown. Brown with a white blaze. Her brother is called Philip, and the horse's name is . . . Iggy.'

Jessica's heavily painted mouth hung wide open. The first round of applause broke out.

'Oh, we're only getting started, ladies and gentlemen. Now, is there anything personal that the card can tell us?' Frieder intervened.

'Jessica, your dark green underwear has a small label,' Frieda's words flew out of her mouth like a shot from a pistol. 'There's yellow, white lettering. The manufacturer is—'

'Okay, that's enough!' Jessica quickly sat down and shoved Frieder's arm away from her. He let out a loud 'Well!', which was the signal for his sister to stop talking. The zoom and detail magnifying feature of the secret cameras was what had given away the brand of Jessica's underwear when she had leaned forward at the bistro. Magic was truly that simple.

'That's scary,' the spied-on woman stammered. 'Really scary.'

'Ladies and gentlemen, let's hear it for Jessica!' Frieder bathed in the applause and picked out a new, seemingly random victim from the audience, combining code word tactics with hot reading.

It was a spectacular performance that nobody in the Friedrichstadt-Palast theatre would ever forget. Information, secrets and knowledge that couldn't be extracted from social media were revealed. Nevertheless, Frieder and his team still remained discreet – affairs and other such intimate secrets were kept under lock and key.

And now it was time for the crowning glory of the Honett siblings.

'Now I'd like to ask someone to come up on stage with me to take a good look at my sister to ensure that we're dealing with mystical matters, not earpieces or other technical equipment. To confirm that all that was needed for our trick is Doctor Faustus' card, and nothing else.' Frieder straightened his tall, white collar and winked at a group of young men. 'And I know that the *men* here would be more than happy to do so.' The audience laughed. 'So, do I have a volunteer?'

A great number of arms flew up, most of them male.

Frieder always chose someone who didn't volunteer. Their timid nature and precision made the whole act more believable.

'We have an unwilling volunteer,' he announced loudly and walked towards the man cowering in the third row. His dishevelled beard dangled down to his chest, his nose was a smidge too big, and his jacket looked like it belonged to a time when he'd been thinner. The man's hesitation was overwhelmed by applause. He pulled up his baggy trousers and followed the magician up the steps towards Frieda. 'What's your name?'

'Doesn't the card know that?' a guy with mid-length hair that reeked of oil cried out. Some laughter erupted from his side.

Frieder was used to such loudmouths and dealt with the situation with ease. 'The card does, but my sister is now exhausted. You won't be able to hide anything from her at the next performance, I can promise you that. Not even your browsing history.'

This time the crowd laughed for Frieder.

'Karsten,' the man mumbled and blushed under his fuzzy beard. 'My name is Karsten.'

They had now reached the stage and Frieda. She was still holding the Fool card in front of her with both hands. It was a tour de force that she practised daily.

'Very good, Karsten. Now, run your fingers through her hair, inspect my sister's delightfully symmetrical ears, and feel around wherever it is you want to check,' Frieder prompted him. 'And then tell the audience if you've found any cables, transmitters, or any other equipment. Be thorough and take your time. I'm sure many people in the audience would love to swap places with you right now.'

Once again, almost two thousand Berlin spectators laughed. Cheers and shouts from envious young men rang out as Karsten first searched Frieda's outstretched arms and then wandered upwards.

Frieder relaxed; the adrenaline wore off. It had all worked like a charm and it was now time to end the show with a perfect landing. He turned to face the crowd, smiling. 'You see, ladies and gentlemen, I—'

'There! There's something there,' Karsten announced suddenly. He stood diagonally next to Frieda, pulled out his hand from her platinum-blonde curls and lifted an electronic device into the air.

Frieder turned around, annoyed, knowing that that wasn't possible. He looked at Karsten, who stepped to the edge of the stage without being asked and pointed out his find to the first row.

Another murmur swept through the hall. A wave of disappointment and anger swelled. The public wanted to be deceived, not disenchanted. The first nasty laughs and 'Boo' cries broke out.

Frieda quickly removed her blindfold, stood up angrily and threw it onto the chair, along with the card.

'That's so rude,' she said firmly, all sex appeal having disappeared from her voice. She now spoke like a punitive dominatrix. 'That's not ours!'

'What a load of rubbish!' one of the overly determined young men shouted, still upset that he hadn't been chosen to do the strip search.

'You're nothing but a pair of fraudsters,' someone else from another corner chimed in under the glaring spotlight.

'Please, calm down,' Frieder said, raising his arms. The commotion settled down. 'Ladies and gentlemen, I can prove that this has nothing to do with us.' He glanced at the small device, which was a transmitter at the very most and did nothing more than annoy the audience and make them doubt the performance. That had been precisely the plan of whoever had planted it. 'Frieda, please remove your clothes. Everyone needs to see that you're not wearing anything that shouldn't be there on your beautiful body.'

He heard a wave of relieved laughter spread through the hall.

Frieda began to playfully strip with such ease and frivolity that one would think this was a planned part of the show. His sister was a professional. The stage director, too, had the presence of mind to play a popular song from the Roaring Twenties.

Frieder turned off his headset and waved to Karsten to come closer. 'Sit in the chair,' he ordered. 'And wait.'

'What have I done?' Karsten asked, bewildered.

'I'm yet to find that out,' Frieder snarled and snatched the device he had found from him. 'Sit down and wait. Got it? If you try to run, my men will beat you up at the door.'

Karsten nodded, frightened, and took a seat.

While his sister took off her clothes and bought him time, Frieder frantically thought about who could have planted the transmitter: the hairstylist, a stage technician or Karsten. Their competition played dirty tricks to try to discredit their show. The Honetts' leap across the pond to Las Vegas was in danger.

Frieda had stripped down to her lace bra and panties. Her dress, stockings and high heels lay on the stage. Neither cables nor any telltale equipment were attached to her underwear.

'Ladies and gentlemen, please, enjoy the sight! I'd now like to welcome the entire front row to come up on stage.' Frieder beckoned them to join him. 'Come, you'll all be my witnesses to prove that there was nothing dishonest about our perform-ance,' he reiterated and held up the transmitter. 'What Karsten found doesn't belong to us. You won't find anything that matches this device.'

People made their way up to the stage and searched Frieda. She lifted her arms and turned on her tiptoes, holding still as they examined her ears and ran their hands through her loose blonde hair. Then the clothes that she had removed were inspected.

Frieder proceeded to ask every individual what they had found. He received the same answer thirty times: nothing.

'You see, Frieda didn't wear a hidden headset or a speaker, meaning it was impossible to pick anything up through this device,' he confirmed, satisfied. 'This thing was utterly point-less, just hanging there in my sister's hair, wouldn't you agree?' The random witnesses nodded. They were released from their duties and returned to their seats.

An encouraging round of applause broke out. The Honett pair had won back the crowd.

'Ladies and gentlemen, you have my word,' Frieder announced as his sister put her dress back on. 'We'll find out who tried to set us up and make us look like fraudsters, and we'll cast the curse of Doctor Faustus' card on them. We're the Honett sib-lings. We know every secret. And soon, we'll know this one too!' He lifted the device into the air. 'Have a wonderful even-ing, and get home safe. We'll now take care of Karsten and his attempt to discredit us.'

This earned him another round of applause from the audience.

He took Frieda by the hand and they bowed together. The curtain fell and stayed down at Frieder's signal. Furious, he turned to face Karsten.

But the man had disappeared.

His jacket, a fake beard with light-coloured make-up stuck to it, a wig and a silicone nose – the kind make-up artists used to create masks – lay on the chair.

Frieder had been played for a fool by a professional who had known exactly how to appear to be chosen by the illusionists.

'That little bastard,' Frieder muttered. It all became clear who had planted the transmitter.

'Cellini must have sent him,' Frieda guessed and put her hands on her hips angrily.

But Frieder had realised it wasn't just the man who had vanished. Doctor Faustus' card had vanished with him.

* * *

Rome, Italy

Under the cover of the crowd, Tadeus followed Henry Pierre Gillot through the basilica. Tadeus' casual sports clothing and baseball cap served as an inconspicuous disguise, his large silver chain hung around his neck underneath his clothes.

Finding where the eccentric patron had fled to after leaving Baden-Baden had been a breeze for him and Poe: it was all in the media.

The over-a-century-old church of the Camillian order, the Basilica of San Camillo de Lellis, stood on the corner of Piemonte and Sallustiana Street in the Sallustiano district. The lively throng of visitors confirmed that there was cause for celebration: a famous painting had moved into the basilica.

Tadeus had done some quick research on his flight to Rome. The patron saint of the building was Camillus de Lellis, one of the greatest charity saints of the church and the founder of the religious order, to whom some pope had given the neo-Gothic, Roman Catholic church.

Gillot was neither a saint nor a Camillian, but, as an art connoisseur and collector who had donated a generous amount of money to acquire the painting he had discovered by chance, he had been invited to attend the unveiling.

Poe was also in the basilica and was dressed like a tourist to attract as little attention as possible; she wore a long, brown wig and a classic round hat, and had a camera hanging from her neck. He could see her on the opposite side of the central aisle between the pews. She was looking at a wooden statue of a saint with apparent interest, trying to avoid standing out despite her well above average height, purposefully standing in the shadows or next to other tall visitors. Poe had had two violent nightmares during their journey, the contents of which she kept to herself. She needn't mention that the nine of spades had played a part in it.

Tadeus carefully watched Gillot, who made his way towards the group of clergymen dressed in black clerical garb and cassocks adorned with red crosses. As always, Gillot had a striking outfit on and his Dalí moustache was tidily bent upwards. He looked as if he were attending an Elton John-themed party rather than a church event; his loud, electric-blue glasses demanded attention from whoever laid eyes on the extroverted collector.

Tadeus kept his distance and hid behind a pillar so that Gillot wouldn't spot him.

The level of security at the basilica was not insignificant. Local Roman politicians, representatives of the Ministry of Culture and of the prime minister used the event as a publicity opportunity. These events were a great way of promoting a good image if you were otherwise at risk of ending up in the papers thanks to testimonies made in court for embezzlement or Mafia contacts.

Poe and Tadeus had no intention of attacking the millionaire. They only hoped to find out more information about his next targets, the other cards and his henchmen in order to follow his movements. They needed evidence for Gillot's involvement in the Baden-Baden and Monaco murders.

At the same time, they were searching for historical cards that were connected with tragedy, the manufacturers of such decks and their whereabouts. It looked like they would have to pay a visit to the Playing Card Museum in Leinfelden-Echterdingen outside Stuttgart, or take a trip to Altenburg. Both towns were strongholds of knowledge on the history of playing cards and had an extensive collection of literature and countless exhibits on the topic. Someone would definitely be able to help them there.

We'll see what Rome brings. Tadeus' eyes wandered around the church.

Since every corner of the basilica was already covered with paintings, statues and small altars of Saint Camillus or the Blessed Virgin, the clergy had decided to put up the new painting on the front right pillar so that it was visible to all the believers during prayer.

He watched Gillot shake the row of outstretched hands. A moment later the guests of honour began to hastily utter their words of welcome, which rolled off their tongues as they had a hundred times before. The security team stood around, relaxed, some of them looking at their phones instead of at the crowd; they didn't expect any trouble at this event.

And Tadeus wanted to take advantage of that opportunity.

He stepped out of the pillar's shadow when his phone buzzed. A glance at his screen revealed a call he couldn't ignore: it was his ex – the woman to whom, as the registry office would confirm, he had been married. Michiko's mother.

He retreated behind the pillar again and accepted the call in Japanese without thinking. 'Hi, Haruka. It's a bit of a bad time right–'

'I spoke with Elisa.' She cut him off, her words as sharp as a samurai sword.

Tadeus' ears pricked up. *Elisa?* She had been the second woman in his life. He'd been with her for years and they'd had a son – Georg – together. Haruka and Elisa knew each other from chance encounters, but generally avoided each other. The fact that they'd spoken on the phone was not a good sign. 'About what?'

'You told me to keep an eye on Michiko,' Haruka said. 'And I found that rather odd, so I wanted to know if you told Elisa to keep an eye on Georg, too.'

Tadeus sighed. 'Yes.'

'As I've found out for myself.' Haruka spoke politely in Japanese. Though she didn't raise her voice, she sounded as cold as the ice on Mount Fuji. 'What have you got yourself into? And now you're dragging your children into it as well?'

'It's not my fault, but I—'

'I don't care whose fault it is. *Nobody* has the right to do that.' Haruka lowered her voice by another ten decibels. 'Tadeus, if something happens to Michiko because of you, you'll see that our divorce was a peaceful tea ceremony in comparison to what happens next.'

'I'll do everything I can to keep her out of danger,' he said quietly. A few visitors threw him reproachful looks. An older woman pointed to the **no mobile phones** sign with narrowed eyes.

'Are you gambling again? Are you in debt?'

'No! This . . . This has nothing to do—'

'How long is this going to go on for?'

'Not long.' He remained vague. 'I'll handle it. Speak to you later, Haruka.'

He hung up, because there was nothing else to say, wandered down the side aisle and headed for where the event was taking place. The soles of his reindeer-leather shoes didn't make a sound against the stone floor. The echoing words of the speakers drifted through the middle aisle.

What else was I supposed to say to Haruka? Tadeus wished that his ex had some contacts in the Yakuza. That would definitely get Gillot and his threats off his back. Then again, Haruka would have had him eliminated a long time ago if that had been the case.

Suddenly, he noticed in the crowd a man with dark blond hair who was behaving rather strangely. He was around thirty, wearing a white sports jacket and grey stonewashed jeans, and holding a tablet in one hand and typing away with the other without looking at the screen. The man's eyes were firmly fixed on Gillot right until he stowed away the device and took out a notepad. As he did so, Tadeus spotted the grip of a gun in a shoulder holster for just a few seconds.

Was he a security guard? Assassin? Henchman? Tadeus would keep an eye on the dark blond.

'. . .I give the floor to Signor Gillot, who will lend his expertise and enlighten us as to why this painting is so special,' someone announced into the speakers attached to the pillars. Instead of being filled with the sound of psalms and prayer, today the church was playing host to secular art history.

The introduction was followed by soft applause.

'Buongiorno,' Gillot greeted the guests in his thick French accent. Thanks to his wide eyes, blue glasses and moustache, he had everyone's attention. 'Let's begin with the unveiling. Please join me in witnessing the debut of the previously unknown painting by Pierre Subleyras.' He pulled the cord and the fabric fell from the window-sized painting. The dramatic movement matched Gillot's appearance.

The painting depicted a man carrying another man over his shoulder. Various objects were swimming in the water at their feet, including playing cards.

Tadeus stood up straight. *So that's why he's here!*

Applause broke out, people murmured quietly and snapped photos with their phones without flash, as was polite.

Tadeus was standing too far away to see if the cards were painted or real. The artist or someone else could have hidden one of the special pieces in the painting. A disguise like the seven of clubs.

We'll find that out. Tadeus glanced over at Poe. If she could get close enough to the painting after the ceremony, she could use her intuition to discreetly determine if the cards were real or not.

'You're all familiar with the original, *San Camillo de Lellis saves the sick in the hospital of the Holy Spirit Sassia during the flooding of the Tiber*,' Gillot began. Someone handed him a short pointing stick. 'Here we have a life-sized painting, discovered in the attic of the Museo di Roma. Subleyras himself has even signed it.' He pointed to the signature and then at the saint without touching the painting with the pointer. 'Camillus, clearly recognisable, follows in the footsteps of Saint Christopher as the bearer of Christ, and is depicted as a virtuous hero. As far as symbolism is concerned, by portraying him as a hero of compassion and as a Christ-bearer, Subleyras paints Saint Camillus as the epitome of beneficence. Subleyras used this painting to test the dimensions for his actual work.' He was then given a longer pointing stick. 'Grazie,' he said and carelessly dropped the shorter one. 'Unlike the original painting, we can see a pack of cards. This is new. As I'm sure you know, ladies and gentlemen, Camillus de Lellis was an avid gambler in his former life and as a result soon became penniless. This is our reference: Camillus renounced gambling, leaving the cards in the water and thereby destroying them.' Gillot raised the stick, the tip coming dangerously close to the oil painting. 'Still, I'd go as far as to call him the patron saint of gamblers. *Someone*'s got to say it.'

The crowd laughed.

Gillot chuckled to himself and stepped to the side, then stumbled and regained his balance with his hand. The wooden top of the pointing stick drew a long line across the canvas, which left a visible scratch across the painting.

The church instantly fell silent. Everyone froze.

'Oops,' Tadeus heard Gillot say casually amidst the horrified silence.

He didn't believe for one second that it had been an accident. *He'll apologise for it in a minute and offer to have it restored.*

'I sincerely apologise for the mishap,' Gillot said in dismay. Needless to say, I will cover the restoration costs. I'll have my best people take care of it, and you have my word: Camillus will be returned to his home in a month's time.'

The applause that followed was far more muted than at the beginning. The media would rub their hands together with glee; the scorn that the extroverted Walloon would receive would be considerable.

But Tadeus had seen through his plan. Gillot would easily get his hands on the painting, examine it in peace and, if there really was a card in the painting, take it for himself.

Unless I . . . save it first. Tadeus avoided using the word steal. That wasn't what he was doing. He was only trying to protect the cards from the man to bring them back together, just as they deserved.

The party after the Walloon's faux pas was quiet. The guests quickly gulped down their wine to recover from the horror they had witnessed. Someone fetched a ladder and covered up the desecrated painting again with some fabric. It was shameful to display Camillus with a scratch.

But it's still in the basilica. Tadeus wanted to forestall Gillot. He would get Poe, disguised as a tourist, to move closer to the painting while the party was still happening. Provided she got up really close, she could examine it with her shamanistic powers. If there was a valuable card hidden in the painting, he would discuss how to acquire it with her before their rival got his hands on it.

Tadeus looked around.

Gillot was heading outside, playing with the tips of his Dalí moustache. Unlike the rest of the people in the basilica, he was in a great mood.

From halfway to the exit the dark-blond man with the tablet approached Gillot and they shook hands. After they had exchanged a few words, Gillot's mood turned sour and his features darkened.

Tadeus quickly tried to reach the pair, rushing through the rows of chairs and stopping behind a nearby pillar. On the other side of the dark aisle he spotted Poe. He quickly gestured for her to make a move towards the painting, and she nodded in response.

Tadeus listened very carefully, trying to catch snippets of the conversation between the two men. The impressive acoustics in the basilica worked in his favour.

'. . .lost contact with Manaus,' the armed man said in muffled English. 'All I know is that the majority of the volunteers are dead.'

'What do you mean, the *majority*?' Gillot grumbled.

'The rescue mission isn't over yet. Several people have been killed. All the bodies have gunshot and burn wounds, allegedly from small-calibre weapons. Half were flown over to Manaus, but the helicopter had to turn back before it could make its second trip due to bad weather.'

Tadeus pulled out his phone and made notes. Maybe this was about other cards.

'What do the authorities say?' the Walloon enquired. 'And why were there burn wounds?'

'People assume that there were some illegal loggers or foxes who were startled,' the man explained. 'Like with the earlier

THE DEVIL'S PLAYBOOK | 286

plane crash, the Brazilian police don't seem to care. They've got bigger fish to fry. And there was talk of a fire.'

Gillot groaned. 'A fire? When will we know more?'

'As soon as the weather improves.'

'For fuck's sake!' he exclaimed and immediately crossed himself. The people around him clearly thought that he was fretting over the painting. He lowered his voice. 'That means my card could be lying in the dirt somewhere, soaked!'

A card. Tadeus grinned grimly. *He'd been right.*

'That might be, Monsieur Gillot.' The armed man handed him a piece of paper on which he'd previously scribbled something down. 'Or someone might find it. I don't want to rule out the possibility that—'

'Get on the next flight to Manaus. Now. Make sure that this unique piece doesn't become a part of the Amazon.' Gillot cut him off. He read the note, then scrunched up the piece of paper and adjusted his glasses. 'What on earth am I going to do if it gets washed up by the river? I'd never find it, not in a hundred years from now.'

'I'll be on my way,' the man said. He reached into his pocket and gave Gillot a box that resembled a cigarette case. 'This is to calm your nerves in the meantime.'

A smile suddenly spread across Gillot's face. 'Doctor Faustus' card?'

'The very same. I had a lot of fun securing it,' the man told the Walloon as he snapped open the box. A horrified cry escaped Gillot's throat. 'I know, it's in poor condition.'

'*Poor* is an understatement.' Gillot retrieved the card from the box. 'A burn hole? It's almost burned all the way through!' He put it away. 'Change of plan: take the card to Darlan and have it restored. It's millimetres away from being ruined.'

A burn hole? How is that possible? The hidden card being potentially damaged pained Tadeus, but there appeared to be someone named Darlan who attended to such matters. Who could heal cards. *Perhaps this person could work their magic on my nine of spades, too?*

'As you please. I hear Avignon is rather beautiful. Who will take care of the matter in Manaus?'

'Me if necessary. I've travelled to and dealt with all sorts in my time. Sometimes you have to do things yourself.' Gillot lightly patted his chest and walked ahead. The armed man followed him and stowed the case with the damaged card in his inner jacket pocket. Gillot ripped the note he'd received once, twice, and then a third time before throwing it into a nondescript ash bin containing the remnants of memorial candles. Then the pair disappeared outside.

Tadeus' phone vibrated. It was Poe. 'Did you catch anything?' she asked.

'Yes. I'll go after Gillot. You fish the note out of the rubbish,' Tadeus told her, hurrying through the basilica.

'What's your plan?'

'I'll see if I can get us Doctor Faustus' card.' He stopped at the exit and looked in both directions. 'What about you? Did you manage to check out the card in the painting?'

'I need a hand. It's too high up.'

I should've thought of that. Tadeus watched Gillot walk across the zebra crossing to the parking spaces opposite the church. He was accompanied by a bodyguard who must've been waiting for him outside the door. The Walloon approached a brand new Bentley Mulsanne limousine where a chauffeur and two other security guards were waiting.

The dark blond with the card in his pocket swung into a taxi, which quickly drove off.

Tadeus swore. He could do without the car chase, and he didn't want to leave Poe behind. Plus he still had to check the card in the painting.

Poe appeared next to him and shoved the scraps of paper into his hand. 'Got it. It'll be easy to put back together.'

Her hands smelled like she'd just applied moisturiser, and he liked the subtle, unfamiliar scent.

'Great.'

'What did you hear?'

'The other man has a new card that apparently belonged to Doctor Faustus. He's travelling to Avignon with it to meet someone called Darlan, who I suspect is a restorer.'

'The same restorer who will fix the painting,' Poe added and lifted her camera. She took some photos of the Walloon, who walked towards the Bentley with his usual stiff gait. 'Let's take a look at the card on the painting.'

They turned around and walked through the remaining crowd of guests in the basilica to Subleyras' covered painting. Quiet conversations about politics, football and the quality of the wine filled the church. Nobody paid any attention to the sacred painting.

'It seems that another card was lost in the Amazon, south of Manaus,' Tadeus told Poe. He used his phone to google Doctor Faustus' card without expecting to find anything.

To his surprise, he immediately came across an article that reported that a cunning trickster had stolen the Honett illusionists' historic card on stage during a show. According to legend, the card was used by the alchemist Faustus, and it was the only one in the deck to have survived the explosion that ended the scholar's life. In a brief statement, Frieder Honett said that he regretted the loss of the old card, but that it had more sentimental value than financial. He had already found a replacement: Mephistopheles' card, which had been discovered lying next to the dead Doctor Faustus.

'Sentimental my arse,' Tadeus said and showed Poe what he'd

found. 'There's another card hidden inside the one he had stolen. It's part of the deck.'

'Gillot's got his people on the case.' She snapped another photo. 'Look – the painting is too high up. I need a ladder to get close enough to the cards to be able to tell if there's one hidden in it like your nine of spades.' She pointed to the back of the basilica. 'I can see a ladder over there.'

They reached the pillar and looked at the fabric covering the damaged saint.

'Let me try something.' Tadeus walked up to a clergyman dressed in Carmelite robes. 'Scusi,' he said. 'Would you be so kind as to do my friend and me a favour, Reverend?' His Italian was perfect. It was another language that he had collected. He pointed to the painting. 'She's travelled all the way from China to capture the Holy City and this particular work for her community. She's an art student and a Catholic.'

'Catholic?' The Carmelite stared back in surprise. Naturally, people in Rome didn't immediately think of Christianity when they saw someone of Asian descent.

'Si, si. Her entire community is looking forward to her impressions from Rome. She's already been to see the Holy Father.' Tadeus gestured to the painting again. 'Would it be possible for her to photograph the painting?'

'Oh, I'm sorry about that. It's damaged.' He shook hands with a few people distractedly. The church grew empty and visitors disappeared.

Tadeus waved his words aside. 'Oh, that's all right. She only wishes to capture it. It would mean the world to her if you could help, Reverend. She'll touch it up too. Nobody will notice a thing when she gives her talk to the congregation.'

Caught off guard, the Carmelite agreed. He even had someone bring the ladder since the student from China was so keen to take photos up close and without any flash for the purposes of her studies.

'Thank you very much, Padre,' Tadeus said and tapped the top of his baseball cap.

'Well, up you go,' he instructed Poe, holding the ladder in place.

'You did a great job, I'll give you that,' she said and climbed up the rungs. The fabric still hung over the painting protectively. Two altar boys reached for the cord.

Suddenly, a series of explosions erupted outside and the basilica trembled from the shock. Tall windows shattered and others cracked, causing a hail of brightly coloured fragments to fall inside the church. The candles near the entrance were extinguished. Rattling and banging noises could be heard from the street a second later as various weapons were fired.

The last few guests froze by the exit, while the first ones ran back inside, waving their arms. Panic spread as the staccato of automatic rifles filled the church.

'I think I can feel something,' Poe said. She clung on to the ladder, determined, and glanced at Tadeus. 'What—'

He turned towards the entrance and recognised the Bentley Mulsanne through the billowing smoke. The windscreen was covered in cracks and there were bullet dents in the bodywork. The armoured car shot up the steps and burst through the doors of the church. The limousine, which weighed several tonnes, crashed into a wall and zoomed up the central aisle. Dust and chunks of stone flew into the air; pews and chairs were hurled out of the way from the hood of the car. People escaped the all-crushing Bentley by a hair's breadth.

The Mulsanne swerved and lurched forward, then slammed into a pillar, causing wide cracks to spread across the stone. The car began to jackknife, and counter-steering was of no use.

'Get down!' Tadeus shouted to Poe, who jumped off the ladder. They both dived to the side.

The brakes screeched and the Bentley drifted. Seconds later, it crashed into the side of a pillar, next to which the painting hung.

Tadeus, having half landed on top of the doctor to protect her, propped himself up. 'Stay down,' he told Poe. He stood up and felt the familiar twinge of pain in his back, knee, and now in his left elbow, too. It was his body reminding him that he was getting too old for such athleticism.

Amidst all the chaos, three gunmen in masks appeared at the entrance of the basilica and fired volleys into the air from their assault rifles. The bullets obliterated the fresco on the ceiling; lamps, glass and stucco came crashing down onto the floor.

People ran for cover or for the side exits. Nobody stood in the way of the strangers.

Then the gunmen sprinted to the Bentley with weapons at the ready like professional assassins.

Tadeus ducked and watched Gillot force his way out the car and crouch behind it. He was immediately sprayed with bullets. *What was happening?*

In the shelter of the needlessly long limousine, the Walloon seized the cord attached to the curtain in front of the painting. He pulled it with such force that the entire painting fell forwards. Gillot kept his head down and moved the piece into the back of the car. Bullets ricocheted off the side and the roof of the car, sending sparks flying.

The armed trio aimed for the tyres, which deflated from the blast. Gillot tried to drive off, but the engine stalled.

Fuck! Tadeus ducked his head as bullets whizzed through the church, missing him by a whisker. *Were the three men after Gillot, the painting or the cards?*

'Poe!' he cried through the deafening gunfire. 'Are you—'

'I'm all right.' He heard her voice from a cloud of dust. 'They didn't get me.'

The trio had reached the car. They were armed with modern

Kalashnikovs with foldable shoulder rests and extra-large magazines. They quickly surrounded the Bentley.

Gillot hadn't been able to get the car going. The ignition whined, but the engine wouldn't start.

Intervening wasn't an option. Even if Tadeus had a weapon, he wouldn't stand a chance against the trained enemies. He attended a self-defence class once a year so that he could block and fend off blows from drunk, angry guests, but that was no match for automatic rifles. Yet the thought of losing the card to strangers infuriated him.

One of the masked men used silver-grey tape to attach two grenades to the significant crack in the limousine's bulletproof windscreen from where it had crashed into the huge pillar. Then the attackers took cover.

Those lunatics! Tadeus lay flat on the ground behind a pew with his hands over his head. *I hope Poe is safe.*

There was a snapping and splintering noise as a heavy blow hit the pew in front of Tadeus, which protected him from the debris.

As he looked up to inspect the damage, he saw the three attackers standing by the vehicle and using every bullet in their magazines to shoot through the hole in the sooty car window.

The card!

Loud, continuous honking noises and wailing police sirens could be heard from outside. The troops were running out of time.

'*Davaĭ, davaĭ!*' one of the masked attackers shouted and swapped out his magazine. 'That should do it,' he added in Russian and made a run for it. One by one, the men hurried out of the basilica, covering each other.

This wasn't about the card. Tadeus lifted himself off the ground and rushed over to the Bentley, still staying low. Thick, billowing smoke spilled out of the car. Flames danced over the seats and he could smell the corrosive fumes of burning plastic. The driver's door was ajar.

Tadeus wrenched it open to look inside the smoky car.

Gillot lay crouched in the footwell. He'd suffered several blows and it was impossible to say for certain whether he was dead or alive.

'Poe?' he called out. Tadeus didn't waste a single second thinking about saving the man who had threatened him and his loved ones. He looked around the basilica for the doctor, but he couldn't see her anywhere. There was nobody left in the building. Nobody would be watching them. 'Poe, we —'

The rear car door swung open.

The Korean woman rolled out from the wrecked vehicle, coughing and holding a cut-out piece of canvas with a playing card painted on it in her right hand. She couldn't speak; only strangled gasps escaped her throat as she staggered through the smoke towards him.

Tadeus caught her in his arms. 'Nice work! Let's leave through the back exit.' He helped her up, and she almost vomited from all the coughing.

'Is Gillot . . . dead?' she managed.

'Looks like it, yes,' Tadeus lied. He didn't want the doctor feeling compelled by her Hippocratic Oath to help Gillot, of all people.

They limped together past the chancel and then through the sacristy, where they found an open door. The clergy and some visitors had fled from the attackers the same way.

Poe and Tadeus were met outside by rescue workers and heavily armed police in bulletproof vests. Just like the other escapees, they were wrapped in gold foil blankets, as if in recognition for their outstanding achievements. A paramedic examined them for any external injuries and then instructed them to take a seat on the chairs near a restaurant. He told them that the police would want to take their personal details and ask them a few questions.

But as soon as the paramedic turned away from them, Poe and Tadeus continued their escape. They moved slowly and discreetly at first, then left behind the foil blankets and sprinted down the district's winding streets. The officers were too busy dealing with the witnesses waiting in the restaurant to notice.

'Now what?' Poe asked, coughing and spluttering. 'Avignon?'

'Avignon,' Tadeus said. The trip to Rome hadn't gone as planned, but they now had another card. 'That was very brave of you.'

'It was stupid.' She wiped a layer of sweat and dirt from her forehead. 'I didn't want Gillot to have the card. We got there first. And if he survives, who knows, we might need it for our research. It's in good hands now.'

'It is.' Tadeus laid a hand on her shoulder. 'That was brave. Really brave.'

He wondered who the attackers might have been. In Italy, a country where the Cosa Nostra, the 'Ndrangheta and other Mafia organisations operated, who turned up with Russian weapons and shouted orders in Russian?

Gillot had plenty of enemies thanks to his illegal trade of archaeological finds, his excavation methods and his contacts in the demi-monde. Nevertheless, even if there were lots of people who wanted to see the Walloon dead, the first person that came to mind was Lazarev, the father of the murdered oligarch boy. He would have been capable of such radical retaliation. And despite the attack, Gillot hadn't wanted to leave without the valuable card, which had cost him a hell of a ride through the basilica.

But how would Lazarev know that Gillot was the potential mastermind behind the three murders in Baden-Baden? Officially, behind it was the gambling mafia, which Solov'ëva and her daughter had established.

He glanced at Poe. 'Who do you think those guys were?'

'I don't . . . know,' she replied, between coughs.

'Did you understand anything they said?'

'They barely said . . . Anything. I don't . . . Speak Russian,' Poe gasped, then coughed again and had to lean against a lamppost to support herself. 'You think. The police. After Gillot's death. Were after evidence for what happened in Baden-Baden? Or should we. Give Klim. A clue? So he intervenes?'

'I'm not sure if Gillot's actually dead.'

'What? But you said—'

'I said it looks like it.' Tadeus smiled apologetically.

Poe wheezed and gave him a reproachful look. It took her a minute to gather her strength and resume walking. She was so pale even her freckles looked ashen. She groaned, struggling to breathe. 'Do you happen to know. What smoke poisoning. Feels like?'

'No, you're the doctor.'

'I'm a surgeon. Not a pulmonologist.' She grabbed his arm. 'In any case. I think. I've got it.'

'And we've done far too much running.' Tadeus slowed down and hailed a taxi to take them back to their hotel. 'You're injured, and I'm old.'

Poe grinned.

As soon as he climbed into the car, he got an even better idea of what to do next. 'Avignon isn't going anywhere,' he said and pulled out his phone.

Opportunities were made for seizing.

INTERMEDIUM

Leipzig, the Electorate of Saxony,
the Holy Roman Empire,
April 1768

Susanna happily walked along the Brühl, as always enjoying the usual hustle and bustle of the countless traders who had settled here. The street was especially lively in preparation for the fast-approaching Easter Trade Fair.

She had already tended to the children today, and the fun reading, writing and counting games were starting to bear fruit. She used the little pictures from failed prints to explain letters to the little ones and let them come up with and paint their own stories. If her children wanted to make something of their lives, they had to start early. To her delight, even their youngest was taking a keen interest.

Stock's wife was looking after the little Kirchner unit for the next hour, which gave Susanna time to run her secret errand.

Every street in the city was overflowing with horses, carriages and carts. There was a cacophony of clattering, rattling and snorting wherever you went; the cracking of whips and the shouting of coachmen at horses and pedestrians when they didn't get out of their way.

The trading houses were keen to do business, both big and small. The inns were overcrowded as always, and the students had vacated their rooms and gone away to the countryside to offer their beds to guests and merchants from far and wide. Leipzig was teeming with life during the fairs.

Susanna walked along the long street in her pale red dress and white apron with a smile on her face, embracing the comings and goings. She carried some cheese and a cheap bottle of wine in a covered basket. Her blonde plait was tucked under an embroidered bonnet.

She strolled past the Red Ox and the Golden Owl, where you could eat and drink well. Not far from here was the opera house, where the Grosses Concert Orchestra was rehearsing with the windows open, but their instruments still failed to drown out the commotion on the street. The fair had an incredible variety of attractions on offer, from upper-class entertainment to travelling showmen and puppeteers, which were very popular with the common folk.

Before Susanna's time, Caroline Neuber and her theatre group had performed plays at the Grosser Blumenberg House in partnership with Johann Christoph Gottsched, whose work Breitkopf still printed. Neuber must have been a brilliant actress, and Susanna would have loved to see one of her performances.

She dodged a rumbling carriage with fox pelts poking out from under its tarp. Primarily Jewish traders worked on the Brühl, most often selling smoked goods. But it wasn't just fine furs that were sold; rabbit fur, hog bristles and horsehair were also traded. The carts rolled in from London, Koppigen, the lands around Brody, Galicia, and Shklow, Hamburg, Königsberg and Breslau. There was a confused jumble of languages beyond compare, and yet, amidst the chaos, the sellers would still manage to come to an agreement on trades and money, often without speaking a word. In the squares, people celebrated and danced along to the music in the stalls.

Susanna continued along the Brühl. She walked past the

Crane and the Green Pine, where the carters liked to stop for a while. The diamond and gemstone traders, on the other hand, often got together at the Golden Apple coffee house opposite the Romanus House.

Then she turned and headed for the east side of the Brühl, which had become a dead end due to the city wall that had been built. The further Susanna walked, the fewer traders and cheerful fairgoers she met, which meant she was getting closer to her desired destination, the atmosphere of which was the complete opposite of Leipzig's lively fair.

The almshouse, penitentiary and orphanage, or the Georg House, as it was called by some, could be found on this side of the Brühl. The house provided lodgings and a small income to those who had become outcasts, often against their own will. Beggars, prostitutes, former soldiers, unemployed and impoverished craftsmen, delinquents and orphans lived here. Some of them were locked up for violating the laws and regulations of the council. There were a few lunatics in the mix, too.

Susanna knew that the warden made both the young and old work at the behest of the council in order to fill the coffers. She'd heard on the grapevine that it was a rough place. The workhouse was also seen as a deterrent for anyone toying with the idea of leading a lazy or dishonest life.

She was visiting the Georg House for one simple reason: Martin Dietrich lived here.

She was privy to this information not from some file or record, but thanks to Goethe. During his visits to the Stocks' and while she'd been working on the woodcuts and copper plates, he had told her what had happened in Auerbach's Keller and about the dog, which he called the Devil's oversized poodle or Mephistopheles' bloodhound.

The student hadn't been able to get the thought of where the master and his dog lived out of his mind and, in a fit of courage at an unexpected sighting, had decided to turn the tables on the beast and follow it. Goethe had ascribed his behaviour to liquid courage.

The dog had led him to the workhouse, where Dietrich had greeted and reprimanded him like a misbehaving schoolboy.

Since then, Susanna knew where Bastian had got the inspiration for his cards.

She didn't know why he had lied to her, and it was still too early to confront him. She'd get the best answers from the commissioner of the deck, and she suspected that Dietrich had asked her husband to make the cards in Auerbach's Keller.

Susanna walked up to the baroque portal in front of the building, which looked like it had been glued on to opulently conceal the misery inside. Saint George had been added to the portal as a guardian, as well as two female figures who she didn't recognise. Just a few years ago, during the war, the Georg House had served as a military hospital. Its walls were familiar with death, suffering and hardship in all its forms.

With a sinking feeling in her stomach, she stepped through the unlocked gate, and found herself in a kind of reception area. A broad man wearing a black leather apron was sitting behind a tall desk reading a newspaper. A pair of gloves lay in front of him.

'There's no one here at the moment. And there aren't any alms,' the man said. As he raised his eyes, his patronising rejection turned into curiosity. 'Oh, forgive me. I thought—'

'I'd like to visit someone.' Susanna flashed him a charming smile. 'His name is Martin Dietrich.'

'We haven't got a Martin Dietrich.'

Susanna didn't believe him – he'd answered too quickly.

'He's a former soldier of around sixty.'

'There's no Dietrich here, good woman. I swear to you.'

'Then perhaps I've got his name wrong,' Susanna replied

politely. 'But if I could just see his face, then I'm sure I'd recognise him. Would you be so kind as to take me to the people who live here?'

'What do you want with him?' The man tried to guess what gifts she was carrying in her basket.

'To bring him joy.'

'And how is it that you know him without remembering his name?'

'I met him at Auerbach's,' Susanna lied without blushing. This was a very important matter that could end in disaster for her entire family. 'Or was his name Dietrich Martin?' she deliberated. 'No matter, just show me to him. I promised him something in return for a favour.'

'Hm.' The warden put down the newspaper and reached for a small bell. After a short, bright ring, a boy of about eight wearing shabby clothes came running through one of the doors. 'Thomas, take this lady to our soldiers, but keep an eye on them. Tell them we'll break their fingers if they touch her,' he said.

The boy saluted the warden and took Susanna by the hand. They went through a heavy, metal door with several locks.

'I'm looking for Martin Dietrich,' Susanna told him.

But her little guide remained silent, only gently pulling her forward. It appeared that he'd been instructed not to speak to visitors.

It smelled of wood and sawdust because the inmates and residents of the workhouse made coloured wooden chips, which were needed to produce paint. The Georg House had the Saxonian privilege of engaging in coloured wood-rasping work, which gave it a certain economic significance, even if the occupants profited little from it. At least the smell masked any possible stench.

'Did you hear what I said?' Susanna asked. She was being led through corridors and past closed cell doors, from which the occasional sound of howls, abstruse singing and loud crying could be heard. The madmen, lunatics and the senseless were locked up and didn't seem to be allowed out of their cells today, most likely on the council's order to stop anyone escaping and disrupting the fair.

Then the boy silently led her down some steps into a vaulted brick cellar and to a door at the end of a long corridor that led to storage rooms on the right and left. Barrels of wine, potatoes, cabbages, apples and all sorts of perishables that couldn't be left in the sunlight were stored here.

In front of the oak door, the boy let go of Susanna's hand, turned around and disappeared back the same way they had come. Unlike the warden, he had known exactly who she was looking for.

Before she could knock, the door swung open.

At the threshold stood the man whom Goethe had described to her in very impressive terms: old in stature, a face full of wrinkles and yet with eyes that seemed to burn with an inner fire and reflect centuries of knowledge.

'I take it you're Kirchner's wife?' Dietrich asked. A crimson robe draped his body and his silver-streaked black hair fell loosely over his shoulders.

Susanna nodded. It was as if all words had dried up in her mouth. His presence crashed against her like a wave, gently enveloping her and washing her away.

'To what do I owe the pleasure?'

'The playing cards.'

'Ah, so he's broken his promise to me and told you.'

'No, I only joined the dots. I heard about you and your request in Auerbach's Keller, and I followed your dog to find you, Mr Dietrich,' Susanna lied. 'Your poodle is rather striking. There isn't a larger or stranger one in the entire city.'

'Yes, my dog. He's a loyal soul.' Dietrich looked at her, sizing her up. He was clearly undressing her with his eyes. 'What do you dislike about my request? Did I not give your husband some remarkable motifs? I told him he can keep them. Breitkopf will love them. All I want is one deck of cards. The first one he makes.'

'I disapprove of such cards. I've come to beg you to release him from the task.'

'Why? He owes me this favour, and it'll raise him in the eyes of his superior. The deck might soon make him an accomplished man.' Dietrich smiled at her with his immaculate, white teeth. 'That would only benefit both you and the children.'

'And yet I beg you: release him. Release him from whatever it is you've done to force this favour onto him.'

'But he enjoys it. I know he does. Tell me he doesn't spend every spare moment with his nose to the grindstone, engraving copper?'

'He does. And that's what worries me.' Susanna could hear her own fright, and lowered her voice so it wouldn't betray her feelings. It robbed the words of their effect. 'Release him.'

The man stepped to one side. 'I can see that this conversation is going to take a while. Come in, Mrs Kirchner, so that we may discuss the matter properly inside.'

To show him she wasn't afraid, Susanna bravely stepped over the threshold, but she was unable to conceal her surprise when she saw the spacious, well-furnished vault. There was an ornately carved, four-poster bed, bookshelves that reached up to the ceiling stocked with thick and thin works, almanacs and tomes and an alchemy laboratory with its own hearth and flue, as well as comfortable settees and chairs scattered in between.

The vault was partially lit by chandeliers and simple lamps, some of which were contemporary while others looked ancient.

Decorative paintings hung on the walls and there were free-standing statues adorned with jewellery. Real jewellery. For a retired soldier, Dietrich lived a life of unexpected opulence.

'Take a seat, Mrs Kirchner.' Dietrich pointed to a comfortable armchair. He opted for a throne-like chair opposite her, which elevated him slightly.

He poured her some wine, which Susanna politely refused. The scene in the cellar that Goethe had described to her was still fresh in her mind. 'What needs to happen for you to release my husband?'

Dietrich laughed darkly. The sound echoed through the vault, as if his laughter came straight from the pits of hell. 'It wasn't just the cards that brought you here. It was what you saw in them. *That's* what displeases you. And it frightens you, too.'

Susanna flushed. She put down her basket. 'What do you mean?'

'Do you think I don't know who I'm talking to?' Dietrich leaned back. He rested his old hands and his long, filed nails on the chair's arms like a king. 'You're Susanna Margarete, née Schöne, a descendant of Sibylle Schöne, who was married to Hans Georg Schöne. Sibylle was forty when she was accused of sorcery and witchcraft. This was in the year of our lord, 1699, when she was first imprisoned, and then later released.' He smiled and relished the look of horror on her face. 'I'd like to think we knew each other very well.'

Susanna crossed herself. 'Then . . . Then it's true!' she cried out. It hadn't escaped her notice that Dietrich had adopted a more informal tone with her.

'What's true?'

'What my mother told me. About you.' She forced herself to look at him now, whether she wanted to or not. 'You really are the Martin Dietrich who was accused of sorcery and quackery in Leipzig almost forty years ago.' She swallowed to help moisten her dry throat. 'You were already sixty back then.'

'That speaks to my methods,' Dietrich said, gesturing to the laboratory. 'I wouldn't exactly call it quackery.' He drank from his wine with an air of superiority. His crimson robe rubbed together as softly and smoothly as silk. 'The fellow who denounced me, Doctor Balthasar Friedrich Jacobi, was jealous. He reported me for trading boxes of rarities and herbs. I had to endure an admonition from the priest and swear an oath of purgation before they released me.' He set down his chalice. The inscriptions on it revealed that it had once been locked inside a tabernacle. 'But I haven't forgotten anything. I remember how my customers left me in the lurch, even though I always provided them with the best product so that they wouldn't grow old and die.' He took another sip. 'And you, Susanna, carry the legacy within you. Your ancestor's legacy. And mine.'

'What? No! That's impossible!'

'I told you. I knew Sibylle very well,' Dietrich said smugly. 'Her husband never knew that the sorceress and sorcerer came together in both body and spirit. In the search of so much – wisdom, wealth, youth – we brought ideas and spells into the world together.' He sighed. 'Not all of her children were fathered by her husband. You're my blood. I can feel it.'

'No!'

'You immediately picked up on the power dwelling within the cards. That is a fact. Nobody else can do this.'

Susanna felt dizzy. The vault and the man on his throne spun in front of her.

Her restless mind drifted back to her childhood. Her mother had taught her the wise women's ways in secret, so that if she ever found herself in the face of evil she could stand against it. And Martin Dietrich was one of the world's many corrupters, wreaking havoc wherever he went.

Susanna had almost forgotten her training and the warnings

she'd been taught. Had her mother suspected that she would have to go against her ancestors to protect her family?

She made herself look at him. 'Who are you really?'

Dietrich flashed a smile, his teeth sharp and menacing like those of a monster. 'As your friend Goethe would probably say, part of the part am I, once all, in primal might. Part of the darkness which brought forth the light. The haughty light, which now disputes the space, and claims of Mother Night her ancient place.' He swirled his wine around. 'I am the spirit that denies! And justly so: for all things, from the void called forth, deserve to be destroyed.'

'So that's the purpose of the cards,' Susanna said, realising 'You want to use them to corrupt humanity!'

'Oh yes, precisely,' he praised her. 'People will shuffle, deal and gamble with their lives. Whoever holds the cards will experience their harmful effects. The Devil's Playbook will exploit the vulnerabilities of the players and spread evil into the world, just as humanity deserves. It won't be war or the plague that consumes them, oh no! It'll be the things that bring them *joy*. From their children to their grandparents.' Dietrich laughed, satisfied, and the vault rumbled in response. 'And your Bastian is helping me because I killed his rival, whom I brought into the mix myself.'

'I—'

But Dietrich's mood changed in the blink of an eye. 'Don't you dare,' he threatened in a piercing voice. 'Don't you dare stop him or tell anyone about this. I'm incredibly powerful, and the misery I could inflict upon you and your loved ones would destroy you. I've made sure of that. It would be all too easy for Voigt's death to be traced back to your husband.'

Susanna was on the brink of despair. She had hoped that their conversation would go differently, to beg Dietrich and offer him money. If she'd remembered her mother's words sooner, she would have run to the council and reported him for practising sorcery.

But she could still try.

Then again, that would make her look suspicious, especially given her own heritage. Bastian could also be accused of helping her practise harmful magic, not to mention Dietrich's threat of framing him as Voigt's murderer.

So kill Dietrich? She rejected the dark thought as soon as it came to her. There had to be a better way of thwarting his plan and beating him at his own game.

Susanna decided she would go through her mother's notes. She kept the handwritten notebook in a secret place as a memento. She needed to consult the knowledge of the wise women.

'But why quarrel and argue? Since you're my blood,' Dietrich said patronisingly, 'here's my offer: work for me and I will teach you all the arts of sorcery and witchcraft, from the simplest of curses to how to summon the nether spirits.'

She stood up. 'I'd be happy to serve you, Mr Dietrich.'

'You've already decided?' He also rose. 'Have we come to an agreement on how best to proceed?'

'Yes.' She looked him straight in the eye. 'I'll keep quiet to protect my family. Let those damned card players ruin their lives with your deck, I couldn't care less.'

Dietrich put his chalice down and applauded her. 'I couldn't agree more.' He took her right hand. 'Let us shake on it.'

Susanna tried to pull away, but his grip was firm and he wouldn't let go. She felt a warm, pleasant feeling course through her veins and enter her mind.

'Are you sure you don't want me to teach you?' she suddenly heard Bastian's voice ask. Dietrich had vanished. 'Look at the things you can make people believe.'

'How . . . How is this possible?'

'Just a little mist in the air that tricks your senses into

thinking I'm your lover – in voice and form,' Bastian said with a strange smile on his face. He moved closer to her and kissed her. 'The illusion is so perfidious and persuasive that you fall for it. You and your body.'

She felt dizzy and returned her husband's kiss, which tasted strange, but she couldn't resist.

He removed her bonnet. Her blonde plait fell against her back and unravelled.

'Let us seal our pact more intimately,' she heard him coax as he placed his hands on her hips. 'I can't think of a better way to do it. Just like with Sibylle, once. You *really* remind me of her.'

Susanna melted into the curious, familiar arms. She closed her eyes and savoured the moment as her feelings of protest faded further and further away.

Suddenly, she felt someone jump on her, and awoke from her daze.

She flinched and saw Ilse clinging to her, waving a little picture made from print scraps. 'Mama, look! I made this for you.'

Susanna blinked and looked around her as if she'd just woken from a dream. She was standing in their attic, but she didn't know how she'd got there or when she'd picked up her little one from Mrs Stock's care. She held the basket in her arms. It was empty, but she didn't know if she'd lost the wine and cheese or given it away.

She glanced down. Her dress and apron sat perfectly. Nothing was torn, ripped or ruined. She rummaged around for her purse – it was there, and full. Her plait was tucked under her white bonnet.

'It's beautiful,' Susanna praised Ilse instinctively, and bent down. She could clearly feel that someone had left their mark inside her. The memory of it came flooding back: Dietrich, the madhouse, the cellar, the cards, her feigned promise to keep quiet and the sealing of the pact. With more than just a handshake.

She remembered nothing of the act itself, but she was still disgusted with Dietrich and herself. She wanted to take a bath at once, but it wasn't Sunday evening and her family would wonder why she was so eager to wash herself even though it wasn't her turn.

She bore the shame, which turned to anger and hatred with every moment that passed. Dietrich had no idea what an enemy he had created.

Susanna turned her attention to the small work area with the copper plates. 'Go play together,' she said absently to Ilse and approached the work corner to inspect the drawings that Dietrich had given her husband. She then looked at the already finished printing plates.

A plan formed in her mind.

She went to the secret place where she'd hidden her mother's little book. After hastily retrieving it from its hiding spot, she unwrapped it from its waterproof wax cloths.

Susanna opened the book. She was filled with an icy, deadly rage. She had to destroy the pack of cards, protect Bastian and kill Dietrich. No tincture, powder or essence would save him from death.

It took some time for her to get used to the handwriting, but once she did she immersed herself in the ancient teachings of the witches. It was as if a door had opened in her mind, unleashing a stream of ancient knowledge implanted by her mother during many hours of instruction.

She carefully studied the symbols, spells, conditions and provisions for a curse that she wanted to master until she finally read through the darkest chapters of the magical arts, her eyes lighting up in delight.

What Susanna learned soothed the pain under her skirts.

Then she heard Bastian come marching up the stairs.

She managed to hide the little book in her skirt pocket just in time and put on a smile that felt as fabricated to her as sunshine in the dead of night.

The door swung open.

Bastian came in waving a bag of roasted almonds. 'The fairs are the best time of year!' he cried out like a young boy, and shared the sweet treats with the two older children, who were delighted with their crunchy gift.

'Then why don't you go to Auerbach's today?' Susanna suggested. 'Play cards with Goethe and the others. There'll be opponents from out of town to play against.'

Bastian hesitated. 'Did those words really just come out your mouth?'

'Well, the fair's on.' She smiled.

He came up to her, kissed her and pulled her close. 'You're the best woman in the entire city,' he said quietly and brushed a golden lock of hair from her face. 'Ah, what am I saying? You're the best woman in the entire world!' He kissed the tip of her nose, grabbed their three children and started to dance around the room with them in his arms. 'This is the way we dance to the wild hunt!' he shouted and put his lips together to imitate a trumpet. The loud laughter echoed throughout the whole house.

'Mama, you're bleeding!' Ilse cried suddenly, frightened. She pointed to the floorboards.

There were streaks of fresh blood running down Susanna's thigh and onto her right foot. Her smile disappeared.

'I cut my leg with the freshly sharpened burin when I was cleaning up,' she lied. 'It'll heal soon. I've already put a bandage on it.'

'Let's see,' Bastian said, worried.

'Oh I'll be fine.' Susanna shooed him away playfully, laughing through the searing pain in her core. 'Go on, off you go! Wine and cards are waiting.'

Only once her husband had left and the children were tucked into their beds did Susanna break down in tears.

She made a promise to herself to end Martin Dietrich's life and swore to it with the blood that she had shed thanks to him.

You can discover more about a person in an hour of play than in a year of conversation.

Plato (427–348 or 347 BCE)

IX

European airspace

Yet again, Hyun was surrounded by darkness and the faint rustling of falling cards. The nine of spades. All the cards were the nine of spades. They spun around her in a new nightmare and feigned peace. Then a soft scream suddenly escaped Enrico's throat, growing louder and louder. The falling cards scattered and fled in terror.

Hyun's breathing became frantic; she was at the mercy of her dream, a horrified observer. The rustling of paper was accompanied by a soft pattering sound, as if it had started raining. Blood trickled onto the cards in thick drops from the darkness until a shower of red soaked the paper to the sound of her fiancé's piercing screams.

I've got to open my eyes! The nine of spades is trying to drive me mad! Terrified, Hyun tried to fight against it, but failed.

'Hyun, run! It'll kill you!' Enrico cried. 'It'll kill you! Run before it's too late! Hyun, promise me you'll save yourself!' Then she heard a sinister rumbling over the rustling and rain. Her fiancé fell silent. A monster was coming for her.

Hyun tore open her eyelids and found herself panting again.

She glanced at the time on the tablet lying in her lap: she hadn't even managed to drift off for five minutes. Boch was sitting next to her and appeared to be sleeping. He hadn't noticed that she'd been having what felt like her hundredth nightmare.

She took a deep breath. At first, she had thought that Enrico's ghost wanted to protect her from the cards' curse, but now she felt that this was the nine of spades' doing. It was trying to scare her off. *Because it's afraid of me. Because it knows I'll destroy it as soon as I find out how.* This gave her a grim sort of confidence that she was doing the right thing, even if, and, perhaps even why, her nightmares had become more frequent.

Hyun rubbed her face once with her hand and returned to the real world. The roaring of the plane's engine had a certain calming effect. One advantage of having a wealthy stepfather was being able to call him and have two first-class plane tickets booked. He never even asked her why she used her old name to check in.

She hated that it came to that, but it was the easiest option. Hyun had promised to tell her father everything at a later date, from her disappearance to her request and mysterious behaviour. Her mother and father knew nothing about what had happened in Baden-Baden either; the lawyer was handling the talks with the German police.

The flight to Brussels from Rome was a short one. They were due to land in half an hour. From there they planned to hire a car and travel to Bruges.

Hyun turned on her tablet and connected to the plane's Wi-Fi to scour the internet for news about the incident in the basilica.

She liked Boch's idea of making the most of the opportunity to break into Gillot's house while, according to the media, the millionaire lay in an induced coma in a hospital in Rome. Nobody dared comment on whether the man would recover from his wounds. Gillot allegedly lived alone, and the tabloids didn't know anything about there being a special someone in his life, which was good news for their plan.

Boch stretched his legs and wriggled his feet around to pump blood into his calves. 'I wasn't planning on sleeping,' he said and opened his eyes. 'You're working?'

'One of us has to. According to the media, Gillot won't be getting in our way any time soon.' Hyun spoke quietly so that none of the few other first-class passengers would overhear. She had a feeling Boch suspected her of having something to do with the attack. Apart from Lazarev, there weren't many other potential suspects; he could count on his fingers who might have sent the Russian killers to the Eternal City.

Boch glanced at Hyun's display and used his phone to search the internet and check his emails. 'Either way, he's not dead. That means sooner or later he'll make things difficult for us.'

'You knew that he was still alive.'

'No I didn't. I wasn't sure.'

'You stopped me from looking after him.'

Boch raised his eyebrows. 'With all due respect to your skills as a surgeon, in the state you were in you could have made his injuries worse.'

A stewardess wearing a smart navy uniform and a scarf brought them some drinks and snacks. 'Can I tempt you with anything?' she asked politely.

Hyun took a slice of salmon and a glass of white wine. Boch chose a cheese and salami sandwich and a double espresso. He went back to his reading in silence and the stewardess moved on.

Hyun looked out of the small window and watched the clouds, gathering her thoughts.

The sudden appearance of the commandos at the basilica had shocked her. She had agreed with Lazarev that she would keep him informed about Gillot and find out if there was any evidence against the man, but clearly the oligarch didn't like to be kept waiting and had decided to send four killers to strike with a force that Hyun had only seen in action films. The news reported that several people had been shot, most of them body-guards; a few passers-by and guests had been hit by stray bullets and suffered minor injuries. Two of the attackers had been killed, but the Russians had carried off their people with them. Apart from empty bullet cartridges and pools of blood, nothing was left of the deadly greetings from Russia with love.

But that wasn't all.

The basilica had sustained serious damage after Gillot's breakneck drive, which was a subject of speculation in the press and on the internet. Some believed that the Walloon had lost control of the car during his escape, while others thought that his art obsession was what had motivated him to prevent the painting from being stolen without sparing a single thought for anyone present. Subleyras' painting had been reportedly severely damaged in the process.

Hyun looked at Boch. 'Would you have been able to use an assault rifle?'

'In the basilica?' Boch asked. He stirred sweetener and milk into his strong coffee. 'Why do you ask?'

'The pump shotgun. You handled it well.'

'That was a fluke. I haven't held a gun in a long time.' He placed his smartphone face down on the table. 'I used to want to be a military police officer, but that didn't work out.'

'Why not?'

'It wasn't the right choice for me in the end. Before that I wanted to be a decathlete,' Boch told her, massaging his knee and then his left elbow. The stubble and weariness on his face made him look older. 'My father didn't like that.'

'Who was he?'

'A professional soldier. A military policeman.'

'Ah, a family tradition. I get it.'

'Which finally ended with me.' Boch slid back into his seat and sat upright. 'I'm sure you've read about it on the internet already. I don't exactly have a glorious past.'

'I have.' The small talk was helping Hyun better understand and find out more about her travel companion. She would have adopted a more informal tone with him a long time ago, but the older man showed no desire to do so. He clearly wanted to keep his distance from her. 'But I thought that there might be more to it.'

'Why should I tell you more?'

'Because . . .' Hyun hesitated. She understood his mistrust too well after the gunfight in Rome. 'Just because.'

Boch smiled. 'You remind me of my daughter. That's probably why my guard is up.'

'You were with an Asian woman?'

'Japanese. The marriage didn't last because of my too-much syndrome.'

'I've never heard of such an illness.'

'Too many casinos, too many parties and too much of everything that follows when you have too much money and take too many drugs,' Boch listed. 'I would have left if I was her too. Gambling addicts are deranged lunatics. My consistent winnings were what made it worse. It cost me my second relationship as well.' He poured himself some water. 'And what about you? You've had two very different careers, Miss Poe. Both sound pretty perfect. Which one is the right one?'

'I'm not perfect.'

'Says a former model and an exemplary doctor.'

'I snore. And I have a weakness for dirty jokes when I'm drunk. Really dirty jokes. I only modelled for two years, and I was very young then.' Hyun smiled back. 'Which career do you think suits me best?'

'I haven't decided yet, but I don't think you're the gold-digger who hooked the dashing rose merchant and ruined his marriage that the media say you are.' Boch smirked teasingly and pointed to the plane's high-end interior. 'You had cash to spare before you met him.'

'You can thank my stepfather for the tickets, not me. And even so, there was a time when you were richer than him,' Hyun said calmly. 'Have you ever been to Korea?'

'No, neither to the north or south.'

'You should. I recommend South Korea. For starters. You'll get around just fine with English.' Hyun thought about the last time she visited her grandmother, who never accepted any money or large gifts from her granddaughter. She had wanted a simple life. To be a mudang. Until the day of her grandmother's death, Hyun had never been able to tell if her refusals stemmed from a stubborn anger at her for renouncing the shaman way and becoming a conventional doctor.

'I'd speak Korean,' to her great surprise Boch replied in her native tongue.

'You . . . You can speak Korean?' She could hear his German accent in the way he pronounced his syllables, but any local would still be able to understand him. 'And Japanese too?'

Boch nodded. 'I learned both during the time I lost, but I can't remember how. Too many drugs, I guess.'

Hyun beamed. 'Have you ever seen the film *Demolition Man*?'

'No, which means maybe.'

She laughed. 'Watch it. It's an old action film. The hero and anti-hero are just like you. They're cryogenically frozen with their knowledge programmed in.' She took a sip of her wine, which was rather good. 'I had to learn everything from scratch. At first, I worked as a seamstress in a factory. That was until my mother remarried and I moved to London. You know the rest.'

Boch laughed. 'That sounds like a scandal-free life. Except for your relationship with Hermano.'

'That was love.' Hyun smiled sadly. 'I know it sounds cheesy, but he was the one.' She took a deep breath, pushing down the rising the sorrow. '*The* one. Otherwise I wouldn't have burst in on an illegal gambling round with a gun in my hand and threatened people, or be sitting on a plane with you to –' The deep breath hadn't helped. She looked down at her engagement ring. Her mask cracked. The grief brought on tears that welled up in her eyes and her chest felt tight. The loss of her fiancé and the realisation that she would never see, hold or feel him again consumed her. She quickly pulled out a handkerchief from her bag and wiped away the salty, liquid pearls from her cheeks. 'Sorry.'

'I'm familiar with Japanese customs,' she heard Boch say. 'How do they compare to Korean customs?'

She knew that he was trying to distract her and gratefully went along with it. 'The simplest ones are similar. There's the bowing when you greet someone, the marvelling at business cards, no blowing your nose at the table, no ramming your chopsticks into your rice bowl, various levels of politeness when addressing people, and so on. But the younger generation are no longer so dogmatic and stuck on tradition, as otherwise it makes things terribly complicated for people who didn't grow up with them.' Hyun tried to feign a smile. 'And then there's the singing. You have to sing.'

'Oh, I was afraid of that. Karaoke! I've always hated it.'

'*Noraebang*, that's what we call the Korean karaoke rooms. Everyone has to try it.' She wondered how he could know Korean without knowing anything about Korean customs and practices. 'When in doubt, I would always make an effort to be very, very polite. That'll win over people's hearts.'

'That sounds simple.'

'Giving you a hundred-page list of dos and don'ts would be pointless. It's the little things that could get you into trouble.'

'Such as?'

'Never wave at someone with your index finger raised. That's an insult. Only with your palm facing the ground and with a downward waving gesture.' She demonstrated.

'Hm. In Europe that could be interpreted as shooing someone away.' Boch tried to replicate the gesture. 'Thanks for the warning. I'll do some research before my first trip.' Then, as if in passing, he placed his hand on the right side of his chest.

She often caught him doing this, and she knew why. Since they were sitting close together, she could clearly feel the nine of spades' aura emanating from the inner, upper right pocket of his jacket. *The source of my nightmares.* Her grandmother would have said that the card had been possessed, or at the very least had been touched by evil spirits that could have a negative impact on certain people. A mudang could perform a ritual to release Boch from the card's influence before the spirits gained more power over him.

But I'm not a mudang. Hyun was torn. She had made a conscious decision to go down the surgical route. A cut was a cut and a severed finger was a severed finger. That left little room for ghosts. It was her knowledge of arteries, tissue, nerve pathways and surgical dexterity that was required of her.

And yet she couldn't ignore the spiritual world. Hyun could feel the evil, cursed cards' aura. That nine of spades, the card that had cost her beloved fiancé his life, wouldn't stop wreaking havoc and inducing nightmares, and neither would its siblings. And the unknown card they had run off with, which was still hidden inside the cut-out piece of Subleyras' painting, had a similar effect, although not nearly as powerful and wicked.

Hyun felt compelled to do something about it as a tribute to her grandmother. The fact that fire couldn't touch the nine of spades proved just how dangerous the cards were.

'Let's see what we managed to steal from Gillot.' She picked up her handbag and pulled out the scrap of canvas she had cut out from the painting. She put it down onto the table, examined it and felt a raised bump under where the cards had been painted. She then gently ran a cutlery knife between the canvas and the layer of oil.

'Be careful,' Boch urged her hurriedly.

'I am,' Hyun said. She could feel some resistance. 'I'm a surgeon, remember?' She was especially cautious with her incisions until she flipped the painted-on cards onto their front, which exposed a second layer of wax paper that had prevented the paint from seeping through.

She found a card – the eight of hearts – wrapped inside. It was clear that it had been made by the same artist as the nine of spades. It had the same make-up, the same hand-painted and hand-finished, delicate lines, was adorned with liquid gold and silver and featured the suit and card value as well as an aphorism in German that she didn't understand. But the card had visibly aged. The paper had soaked up the wax from the wrapping and turned yellowish in colour.

'The eight of hearts,' Boch whispered in her ear and leaned so far towards her that she thought he was about to climb into her seat.

She turned over the card. The back of it looked immaculate, just as with the nine of spades. It was crimson with a fine, grey and black chequered pattern. There were four, silver-shaded Bourbon lilies in each corner.

'We saved it from Gillot,' Boch said, and then added far too late: 'that's one more bargaining chip against him. Can I see?'

When Hyun had inspected the card, she had noticed a shimmering halo around the eight of hearts. It was white and pure, but then turned to grey and black around the edges. While the card pretended to mean no harm and portrayed itself as the epitome of innocence and kindness, it couldn't hide its true nature. Not from a granddaughter of a mudang. In truth, it was malicious at its very core.

In that moment, she deeply regretted not having received a proper shaman education. It was her own fault. Her grandmother would have loved to have passed down all her knowledge to her so that she could have learned how to talk to spirits and appease them. *Or how to fight against the evil of the cards.* Instead, Hyun had spent her last few years in lecture theatres and operating rooms in England and relief camp hospital wards. There hadn't been any time for the spiritual world, but now this knowledge would have been invaluable.

'It looks so fragile,' Boch said with concern and pity in his voice, as if the card was a living, breathing being. 'It'll get the care it needs in Avignon.' Before Hyun could react, he snatched it away and shoved it back into the case together with the nine of spades. 'The card will be safer with me than with you, Miss Poe, don't you think?'

Hyun refrained from protesting on the plane. She'd let him have the cards to lull him into a sense of security and give him no reason to attack her. Now that the two evil cards were close together, she could feel their influence swell. The nine of spades and the eight of hearts recognised one another and appeared to be sharing their powers and combining forces. The auras fused together, writhing and sparkling.

This confirmed her plan: from this day forward, she was no longer just concerned about her career as a doctor and solving the murders in the villa. She had to destroy the cursed cards. She would no longer broach the sensitive subject with Boch. He could think what he liked about her motives, as long as he stayed close.

An announcement informed them that they would be landing soon. The seatbelt signs lit up, the seats were adjusted to an upright position and the tables were folded away.

Hyun turned to look at Boch. 'Can't we stop hunting down the other cards?' she asked, watching his eyes to see how he'd react.

'No.'

'Why not?'

'Because we can use them as leverage against Gillot.'

'But Gillot's no longer a threat. And we'll definitely find another way to obtain some evidence against him.'

'Have you forgotten already? The news says he's alive.' Boch rubbed the right side of his chest again. 'The more cards the better. We need his confession to clear your name. And mine. That's why we're going to all this trouble with Bruges and Avignon.'

She saw the lie in his pupils. The card had him wrapped around its finger and made him believe, even, that this was truly the reason why they were hunting for its siblings. 'But what if it wasn't Gillot?'

'Then we'll cross that bridge when we get to it,' he replied evasively. 'This is more about your life than mine.'

Hyun couldn't hide the impact of his words. Though Boch hadn't meant it like that, it made her think of Lazarev senior. Oprichnik. The man who had had mercilessly tortured her without a care in the world, who had planned to do far worse things to her. She had struck a deal with him, and that could be equated to a threat.

'What happened to your wrists?' Boch looked at her arms. 'They look like cable tie marks.'

'Oh, that? That was from the basilica,' Hyun said, unable to

think of a better explanation. 'The cord from the fabric covering the painting got tangled around me in the car.'

Boch fell silent.

* * *

Bruges, West Flanders,
Belgium

Hyun found Bruges more kitsch than on any postcard she'd
ever seen and wondered why there were so few Asian tourists here. It appeared that the sightseers from the Far East
preferred the sunnier, summer season. Nevertheless, she
still felt confident in her outfit and that her disguise was discreet enough, though she'd had to replace her hat with a new
one – her old hat was lying somewhere among the Roman
rubble.

Boch walked by her side wearing the same clothes he had
worn in Rome. They had left their suitcases in the rental car.
'We'll need to turn right at the top,' he said.

Bruges old town with its old houses looked like a complete
film set. When the smell of Belgian frites wasn't in the air,
there was the constant, lingering smell of chocolate. The abundant grey of the huge, medieval buildings was the only feature
of the town that could appear oppressive to sensitive souls if
the weather insisted on heavy rainfall and clouds, as was the
case on the day of their arrival.

They crossed a small bridge and reached a secluded quarter
of Bruges where the town's residents kept to themselves. The
few passers-by they encountered weren't dressed in the outdoor
and multifunctional jackets typically worn by tourists.

Boch and Hyun had found clues about all of Gillot's houses
around the world, but his home in Bruges was referenced the
most, and was therefore likely to be his favourite residence.

Boch had suggested they try to break into the house during the day; to use the element of surprise to their advantage.

'I wonder what we'll find,' Hyun said, snapping random photos of the neighbourhood. She was taller than Boch, causing her to stand out when she stood next to him, but there was no better disguise than that of a tourist.

'Best-case scenario, we'll find the cards.' He studied the folding map to check where they were. 'And hopefully find out more about the murders.'

It didn't surprise her that he mentioned the cards first.

'This is it.' Hyun pointed to the three-storey, half-timbered house, the back of which faced a canal. 'This is where Monsieur Gillot lives.'

From the outside, there was nothing to suggest that the owner was immensely wealthy. There was an antique shop on the ground floor, where the collector sold tourists his cheaper items that he had brought back from excavations and markets. Above the shop there were two rows of windows, whose dark red and white striped shutters were closed; the unmistakable sign that no one was at home to get in their way.

'There'll be alarm systems,' Boch said. He again held up the map, which they occasionally looked at to maintain their disguise. 'Gillot won't have left his house without some form of security. Motion detectors and the like. Probably ones connected to the internet.' He folded the paper, which made a rustling noise. 'We'll have to be quick.'

'I expect there's some security guard, too.' Hyun nodded and lifted the camera again to take a photo of the front of the house. 'Wouldn't it be easier from the water?'

'I don't think it makes a difference,' Boch said, taciturn. Though he tried to hide his doubt, she could clearly tell that he suspected her of having had something to do with the Russian raiding party. It was true, of course, but she couldn't admit it or he would run a mile. She had to prevent that from happening. Now more than ever.

The cards glowed in Boch's jacket pocket; they seemed to be searching for their siblings. Hyun had discovered that she had to be within half an arm's length of a card to detect its aura, and even closer to the eight of hearts, as she'd noticed in the basilica. It most likely depended on how charged the card was. On the way to Bruges from Brussels, she'd wondered if there was a mudang trick to help her detect a card's presence from further away, but it had been too long since she'd practised her own, limited shamanistic powers. And there was no one left she could ask for guidance.

'Let's get closer,' Boch suggested. He marched up to the antique shop and looked into the display window, where statuettes, signets, jewellery and other items from various Eastern countries were presented under subtle lighting.

Hyun followed him. *We're both playing a game.* Since the man's reactions were unpredictable under the influence of the eight of hearts and the nine of spades, she would be on her guard. At the same time, she needed him to find all the cards and destroy them. She couldn't let anyone else die because of them like her fiancé had. Her grandmother would demand that of her.

They stood side by side in front of the window, their faces reflected in the glass.

Boch changed his mind. 'Maybe we should strike when it gets dark. The street is too obvious. And it'll be better from the water.'

Hyun smirked and clapped him on the shoulder.

A sudden clattering noise made both of them jump. A door in the wooden fence had opened between Gillot's house and the house next door. The neighbour dragged two grey plastic bags outside, plopped them onto the street and closed the door. The lock clicked shut and the man immediately disappeared into the maze of alleyways.

Hyun got an idea. 'Wait here,' she said, still casually taking photos as she wandered over to the little door with knotholes in it. She looked through it.

Behind the door she saw a tiny, sheltered storage space that was too small to be called a garden. It was bricked up from the canal side, completely cluttered and filled with rubbish bins that could be used as climbing aids. There were two small windows of different heights on Gillot's side.

'There could be toilets up there.' Hyun inspected the small padlock and beckoned Boch to come closer. 'Can you get it open?'

He retrieved a grey, patterned handkerchief from his coat, wrapped it around the lighter-sized cylinder and yanked down hard. The locking mechanism came undone with a clink and the shackle snapped open. He opened the door. 'These toy-sized locks can't take much,' he said and looked around to see if anyone was coming down the street.

Hyun darted inside, and Boch followed her. She pushed the larger bin into position and climbed up to check the little window.

'Watch out for wires or little, black dots,' he called to her from below. 'They could be sensors.'

She didn't see anything of the sort, but used her phone torch to inspect the window frame to make certain. 'Looks all clear to me,' she told him.

Boch handed her a rake that the residents used to scrape up leaves from the street. 'Use this to smash the window. Just be careful of the shards when you climb through.'

Hyun found his instructions unnecessary. She wasn't a child, and above all not his daughter.

One attempt was all she needed to destroy the window with the rake handle. The broken glass fell inside the house without shattering everywhere or making loud clinking noises, which suggested that the floor of the dark room was covered in carpet.

Hyun used the light from her phone to look around and spotted a storage room stacked with boxes and chests. *Good. No cameras.* She reached through the hole she'd created, opened the window from the inside and carefully climbed into the Walloon's house.

It smelled musty and of dry wood, varnish, paint and metal. Gillot stored objects here that probably fell short of his display window standards or were waiting to be shipped or collected.

Hyun heard some shuffling noises behind her.

Boch squeezed through the window, first cursing his knee and then his back. 'That's the reason why it wasn't secured.' He pointed to the huge steel door that stopped them from getting any further. The antiques dealer had anticipated a break-in, but from the other side, and no thief would be able to get those wide boxes out of the tiny window.

Hyun was bitterly disappointed. 'Now what? Do we wait until tonight and try again from the canal side?'

Boch shook his head. 'The broken padlock will look suspicious. We have to go through with it.' He gestured to the boxes, crates and chests. 'Let's find something solid that we can use to break through.'

'That will make a lot of noise, and what about the sensors and—?'

'I'm telling you, we have to do it now and be quick about it. Do you have a better idea?'

Hyun shrugged. 'Let's do it.'

They dug around the storeroom and found a Roman ruler's bronze bust, which Boch just about managed to lift. 'This could work.' He held it in his hands, sizing it up.

A deep rumble filled Gillot's home upon first impact, but the steel door held – as did the bust.

Boch continued to slam the bust into the door half a dozen times until a piece of the metal frame gave away. He bent down and tore it off, which then allowed him to push the door open.

Behind it was a long, dark corridor lined with thick carpet and many doors. There was a staircase that led below and above the storeroom.

Boch and Hyun listened carefully.

There was no sound of any police sirens on the street, nor were they staring into the eyes of a security guard or down the barrel of a gun.

Hyun lit up the ceiling with her phone torch. There were no cameras hiding in the corners. 'We're in luck,' she whispered, relieved.

'I'll hold my tongue until we're out of here.'

Boch walked past her without crouching or creeping around, which would have been superfluous after all that banging and crashing. He grabbed a cut-off piece of a ladies' stocking from his pocket, pulled it over his head and handed Hyun another one. 'Let's hurry before the neighbour comes back.' He pointed to all the doors in the corridor. 'I'll go right, you go left. I'll meet you at the top of the stairs.'

Hyun slid the nylon over her face and pocketed her hat. She fearlessly began searching through the five rooms: going in, flicking the light on and poking around. In doing so, she discovered a whole range of decor. It was as if Gillot liked to match his mood on any given day to an era to travel to. Although she couldn't place the various periods, she clearly recognised their differences.

She swiftly made her way through room after room, including a study with no folders or paperwork, a drawing room with books and lace doilies adorning almost every piece of furniture, a small library containing valuable works stored in humidors, as well as a billiard room, but she didn't find or feel anything. No cards. No spirits at play.

What struck her was the non-existent traces of the Walloon. There were no cigar butts in the ashtrays, no used tableware, no open books, printouts or notes. *Looks like Gillot hasn't been here for a long time.*

But when she opened the last door, she froze on the threshold.

A powerful wave of energy swept towards her and collided with her, as if it were trying to push her out of the room and wash her down the corridor. It was neither a good nor an evil spirit, but rather a place that possessed its own power, fuelled by an unshakeable, firm faith in a person. Hyun had experienced something like this before when visiting churches or holy places around the world where people celebrated their gods and religions, but nothing quite as palpable as this. Emotionally perceptive people would call it inexplicable reverence.

She braced herself against the wave and waited for it to die down. Only then did she turn on the light.

What she saw in front of her was what she'd already suspected: an altar room. But she'd never seen one like this before. Large and small paintings, as well as icons of a woman, hung all over the walls. The inscriptions read *Sarah the Black, Sarah the Servant, Holy Sarah, Sarah the Beggar* or *Sarah the Gypsy* and *Sara-la-Kâli.* Some of the colours were so bright that they couldn't be described as charming, and there was something off about the depictions, with people surrounding Sarah the Black and hanging on to her every word as if she were giving a sermon. There was Sarah in a photograph imitating a black and white one from the 19th century, alongside authentic photos of a cave showing people kneeling in front of a life-sized doll in colourful robes.

Hyun peered around the rest of the room.

On the right wall there was an altar with a picture of the saint. It had been richly decorated with gold lead and surrounded by candles and incense burners. A kneeling bench stood in front of the altar with an armrest and side handles.

Fascinated, she gingerly took a step into the room and took in all of the little details through her makeshift nylon mask. She would never have presumed Gillot to be a deeply religious man. This conglomeration was not a collection, but a shrine. *A private prayer room.*

The inscriptions and gifts bore the caption *Saintes-Maries-de-la-Mer*, where Black Sarah's crypt was apparently located and worshipped.

On the altar and in front of the picture, she saw a rectangular glass container the size of a harmonica box, which, upon closer inspection, contained a mummified finger.

Boch appeared behind her with an older-looking laptop in his hand. 'I found this. What about you?' he asked.

'A relic.' Hyun pointed to the glass case. 'But nothing else, unfortunately.'

He looked around in amazement. 'Gillot should have prayed harder before he left for Rome.'

'I think he hasn't been here for a long time.'

'I think so too. It's pretty slim pickings so far. Not a trace of the cards.' After another look around, he added: 'I don't think we'll find anything in this room.'

She stepped back and pulled the door shut. 'Then let's go upstairs.'

On their way up, Hyun checked the time on her phone. It had already been fifteen minutes since they'd forced their way into Gillot's house. She prayed that his neighbour would be gone for a long time.

There were fewer rooms upstairs, as well as a wheelchair-accessible bathroom. She'd read about the Walloon's limp in the papers and noticed it in Rome. His hip seemed to be bothering him, which also explained the stairlift.

Next to the bathroom was an opulently furnished guest room, which Boch immediately searched through while she went into the room opposite.

She stopped in her tracks once again.

In contrast to the other rooms, the light was on. A lamp hanging above an electrically adjustable bed illuminated the room, and a woman, who Hyun guessed to be around seventy, lay under a thick blanket. Her eyes were closed and an open book lay on her chest, which rose and fell beneath her white nightgown. Her features bore a resemblance to Gillot's.

Hyun guessed that this was a relative of his, probably his sister, but there had never been any mention of her in the press.

Vials filled with medication and tablet dispensers were lined up on the small, wheelable bedside table. Saline solutions and sterile-wrapped infusion equipment were stored below. Whatever condition the bedridden, sleeping woman was suffering from, her treatment was demanding. The fact that she hadn't woken up from the racket they had caused suggested that she had taken a strong sleeping pill.

Hyun read the title of the woman's book: *The Miracles of Black Sara. Healing, salvation, prophecies.*

Now it was clear whose shrine it was. The stranger put all her hopes in the saint because she didn't believe in medicine or had given up. The room smelled of a mixture of disinfectant and fresh laundry. Either the woman was fit enough to look after the house in her waking hours, or a carer visited regularly. Hyun spotted a bracelet with an unmistakable red button under a protective cover sitting on the slumbering woman's wrist.

A house alarm! If she saw them, she would sound the distress call. Hyun silently left the sleeping woman's room and intercepted Boch. Apart from the laptop, he hadn't taken anything. 'Someone's there. She's sleeping,' Hyun whispered.

'What?' he murmured back in surprise.

'An older woman, a relative of Gillot's. I think she lives here, not him. And she has an emergency call button on her wrist.'

'Shit.' Boch looked to the door as if it were about to open. 'How did our break-in not wake her?'

'Sleeping pills. Her bedroom looks like a private hospital.' Hyun looked past him and down the corridor. 'Did you find anything else?'

'No. There's one more room left, but I'm worried . . .' Boch looked irritated underneath his nylon mask. 'I have a bad feeling that we're in the wrong house.'

Hyun could hear the genuine disappointment in his voice. He wasn't hiding anything from her, and she could still feel the cards sitting in his pocket as always.

Boch seemed to be reading her mind. 'What about your mudang powers? Can you sense anything that would help us? It worked in the basilica!'

'No.' Apart from the flood of energy in the altar room, she hadn't noticed anything. If an evil energy like that of the cards had been hiding in the shelves or somewhere else, she would have felt it. 'Or maybe I just need more time to have a better—'

A distant crash sounded from the lower floor, followed by a clinking noise and muffled voices.

Hyun listened carefully, counting the number of people who climbed through the window and jumped from the ledge into the house. There were at least five. The strangers didn't bother keeping their voices down.

She immediately thought of Lazarev's men. The Russian had had her followed to find out her next move. Since their last phone call and the attack in Rome, there'd been no contact. *What was he up to?*

Boch took the laptop in one hand and signalled Hyun to follow him.

They crouched and quietly crept halfway down the stairs when they saw two men and a woman wearing balaclavas, carrying empty bags and jingling burglary tools.

Hyun and Boch held their breath on the dark stairs. Nobody noticed them.

Determined, the three burglars walked around the first floor and disappeared into the billiard room. Their entrance was immediately followed by the sound of blows. Before long, the steady sound of hammering filled the air.

'We clearly missed something,' Boch said quietly and walked down the steps and up to the door through which the trio had vanished.

Hyun shadowed him and listened at the stairs several times to see if anyone else was following them, but it was dead quiet. Either she had miscounted, or there were others standing guard downstairs. She wasn't so sure that this was Lazarev's minions any longer.

As she peered around the corner into the billiard room, she saw men with hammers and crowbars knocking down a wall. The woman sat on the table, spinning two balls in her hand. She held an electronic device in her other hand and wore a stethoscope around her neck. Her turn would come.

The brutal blows proved that the wall was fake. Painted plaster crumbled and fell to the floor in large chunks. The burglars hadn't gone to the trouble of searching for the opening mechanism; they'd known exactly where to strike to break through.

Behind the plaster was a modern safe with a lock and keypad. It looked so out of place in the beaten-up billiard room, like an object from a different era.

'We should go,' Hyun whispered. 'While they're busy. We'll have more luck in Avignon than here.'

But Boch wouldn't move, staring into the room.

The woman slipped off the pool table, walked up to the wall

safe and removed the front panel of the keypad to connect the cables from her electronic device to the controls. Then she retrieved lots of different lock picks, including an electrically operated one, from her pocket and turned her attention to the mechanism.

The men, on a break, were quietly playing a round of billiards.

'Quit fooling around,' the woman ordered in French. 'Go downstairs and help pack up the antiques. Stick to the list I gave you. We'll find buyers for what's on there, but not for the rest of the crap.'

Boch moved out from behind the door and pointed to the stairs. 'Go up,' he told her.

These aren't Lazarev's thugs. Hyun stood up and turned around. Disappearing upstairs seemed to her the best way to elude the gang of thieves.

She didn't see what happened next coming, but she felt it: a burglar dressed in black crept up behind her and attacked her with a long object, which Hyun instinctively ducked under.

The man struck Boch. The iron bar slammed into his chest and threw him against the doorframe of the billiard room. A pair of hands immediately grabbed him and dragged him inside. More noise and struggle followed.

Hyun focused on her opponent, who was waving around the bar.

'Who the hell are you?' he asked in French. 'Are you nuts? This belongs to us! We had a deal!'

He didn't appear particularly competent in the way he handled his improvised weapon. 'A deal? With who?' she shot back.

The masked man laughed. 'Hang on, I'll tell you,' he said, and pounced.

Hyun anticipated the attack. She blocked the blow with a counter-jab to his elbow joint, then kneed the groaning man in the stomach and followed up with a double kick to his chest and head, causing the attacker to collapse and lose consciousness. Her tae kwon do training from an early age gave her an edge; technique beat numbers. Plus, her height gave her a longer attack reach.

She heard an astonished shout behind her. 'There's another one!'

Hyun kicked backward without turning around, but the second opponent dodged the blow. She spun around and used the momentum to perform a vertical top-to-bottom kick, just as she'd been taught.

Her heel missed the attacker's head and slammed into his shoulder. The man dropped to his knees.

Just as she was about to move her feet again and follow up with a kick to the chin, someone's arm reached around the doorframe and zapped her collarbone with a taser.

A hot, searing pain coursed through her thin body, causing her to spasm. She clenched her teeth together and instantly collapsed from the electric shock.

'We've caught a flyweight,' one of the masked men remarked and dragged her by one arm into the billiard room, where Boch was lying on the felt table. His hands and feet were tied together with cables.

The dazed Hyun suffered the same fate and was plonked down next to her companion, who was recovering from the effects of the taser. Their nylon masks were pulled off.

One of the attackers patted both of them down and pinched their wallets and other belongings – including the cards. The eight of hearts and the nine of spades had changed hands.

'Hey! Give that back!' Boch demanded and crawled forward, as if he could do anything to threaten and stun the burglars.

Hyun shook off the electric shock and saw that the safe was open.

The masked woman was shoving bundles of mixed currency

banknotes into a bag: euros, pounds and dollars. There had been at least half a million dollars in the safe, if not more.

She then pulled out an envelope, opened it and looked inside. 'We've got them,' she said. The woman gently shook out the contents: little cards wrapped in foil, adorned with gleaming gold leaf and shimmering suits. The men sighed in relief. The unique treasure was returned to the envelope.

Hyun had only managed to catch a glimpse of it, but her powers revealed to her what the burglars had recovered from the safe: historical playing cards in perfect, restored condition. And although they emitted the same, malicious energy as the cards that had been in Boch's jacket just a moment ago, they were far more powerful and dangerous. Their energy had been replenished somewhere.

The masked woman inspected her hostages' personal possessions and was stunned when she found the eight of hearts and the nine of spades. She paid no attention to the old laptop. 'Well, would you look at that? So *that's* why you're here.' She put their cards into the envelope together with the other stolen cards. 'What a shame. Instead of stealing Gillot's cards, you've lost your own.'

The men laughed.

'No!' Boch roared so loudly that Hyun felt her eardrums might burst. He pulled at the cable ties, which scraped softly and cut into his flesh. 'They're mine! Leave them! Put them down!'

'Now that's what I call a passionate collector.' One of the masked men punched him in the jaw. 'Shut your damn mouth! You're getting on my nerves.'

Boch's head flew to the side, blood gushed from his burst lip, but his protests only became even more frantic until he fell headfirst off the table, which caused the burglars to burst into yet another fit of laughter.

'Let's go. We got everything we were after.' The leader winked at Hyun and the furious Boch. 'And you can stay there having a nice lie down. Then you can explain to Gillot or the police what you were doing here. Good luck with them believing your story. Better think up something good.'

One of the thieves kicked Boch in the head, which knocked the raving man unconscious. 'Leave him,' the woman ordered. She was the last to leave the room. 'Let's go, we need to deliver the cards.'

'Boch?' Hyun cried and slid to the edge of the billiard table, where the German's blood had stained the felt black. 'Boch, wake up! We have to get out of here!'

Groaning, the man lying on his stomach stirred. He threaded the plastic loop around a chair leg to use as a lever, which he pushed against with his body. The makeshift lever rattled and the latching hook of the bloody cable tie snapped, no longer able to resist against his strength born of desperation.

Boch pushed himself up. Watching him move was like watching a movie in slow motion; the blows and kicks had taken their toll. 'I'm coming,' he moaned, clearly struggling.

'There's a sabre hanging on the wall, you can use it to—' Hyun broke off and listened to the sound coming from the corridor: the persistent hum of the stairlift.

* * *

Avignon, Vaucluse,
Provence-Alpes-Côte d'Azur,
France

'My Fennec . . . is dead?' Odette stared at the stranger, who had introduced himself as Daan Mulder and looked no older than thirty. Charles and Renard knew him, which meant his visit wasn't a problem like her granddaughter and her family's had been. She wiped her cold, clammy hands on her apron dress and adjusted the fit of her thick glasses. 'My poor little Fennec!'

'That's not what I said, Madame Darlan. Please don't be so quick to lose hope,' Mulder tried to reassure her. 'I was only told that there'd been a loss of contact with Manaus. He was there on a mission.'

Odette nodded and looked at the Faustus card he had brought her, which was nothing more than a prison for the real treasure trapped within. She sighed. 'What's to be done about my Fennec now?'

Mulder, a man with a forgettable sort of face and light hair, shrugged his shoulders and leaned back; the kitchen chair creaked in warning. He had Renard top up his coffee and accepted a slice of chocolate truffle cake with freshly whipped cream. His eyes flitted over the large bloodstains on the floorboards without comment; they had proved difficult to remove entirely.

'To be honest, things are a little up in the air for me at the moment.' Mulder's eyes darted between Renard and Odette. He took care to ensure that not a single brown cake crumb ended up on his white sports jacket. 'I haven't received any instructions about where to travel to next.'

Odette's eyes lit up. 'Are you at a loose end, monsieur?'

'Yes. Unless' – he checked his phone – 'No. No orders. And I'd be surprised if there were.'

'Why?'

Mulder glanced again at Renard, who very slowly shook his bald head. 'Let's just say that it's likely that my employer will be indisposed for a long time, and without him, madame, there's nothing for me to do.'

'Your employer is also my employer.' Odette inspected the fake card, which had once been a very fine piece. It was certainly not from Doctor Faustus' time; it dated back to the 19th century. Nevertheless, the hidden card within glowed with its power, studying and examining the woman to determine whether she could be an ally. 'Then there's no need for me to restore it.'

'No,' Renard said abruptly. 'It must be restored. Things can change in the blink of an eye.'

Odette didn't expect to be dismissed from her services after all these years, but she would have wanted to know what her fake grandson's reaction would be if she had objected. 'Mr Mulder, how would you feel if *I* paid for you to fly to Manaus and find out what's happening with my Fennec?'

He raised his light-haired eyebrows. 'Do you have the money to fund such a venture, Madame Darlan?'

'What do you think? I've been paid for my restoration services for years.' Odette sampled the cake, which had a delightful flavour. She felt that Charles' talents were wasted and often thought that he should be managing his own patisserie on one of those expensive, wide shopping streets in Paris instead of sitting in Avignon, primarily twiddling his thumbs and making her life difficult when he wasn't helping in the cellar. 'I'll give you twenty thousand euros. And I'll cover your flight and all expenses.'

Renard coughed. 'That's very generous of you, but I'd like to remind you that Roux knew what he was getting himself into. He's a professional and a mercenary. He would have killed you had it been his mission to do so.'

'As would you and Charles,' she replied unflinchingly. 'I know that. But we had a bond. And he brought me back souvenirs from his travels. Besides, what am I supposed to do with the money that I've accumulated?' She looked at Mulder and laid her right hand on his. 'Would you do me the favour, monsieur?'

'For thirty thousand, certainly.' He took a bite of the cake and wiped a dark crumb from his grey stonewashed jeans, cursing under his breath. 'I'll bring back the missing card soon as well, madame. It's included in the price.'

'That's very kind of you,' Odette said, pleased. 'I'll pay you in cash. Do we have an agreement?'

'You have that kind of money in the house?'

'She has two good guards, a fat safe and an alarm system,' Renard interrupted coldly. 'Nothing gets out.'

Mulder pursed his lips, which had traces of chocolate on them. 'As if I'd dare rob the living legend. I have too much respect for you and your work to do such a thing, madame.' He finished the rest of his cake slice and drank his coffee. Perhaps he was already on his way to Manaus and the Amazon in his mind, or was silently wondering about her concerns for Fennec's welfare.

Charles came in humming through the hall door. He wiped his wet, red fingers on a cloth, bringing with him the metallic odour of fresh blood.

When he saw the visitor, he went to the sink, washed his hands with soap and scrubbed them vigorously.

'Those headless chickens,' he said casually. 'Running around the place like crazy.'

'Did another one get away?' Renard laughed.

'You would have done a better job, of course.' Charles cleaned the blood from under his fingernails with a little brush, scratching past his fingertips. 'You can be in charge next time. You're better suited to it.'

'Are the other chickens behaving?' Renard went on.

'They are. What other option do they have?' Charles laughed darkly. 'It's all under control in the barn. I would have clipped their wings if they dared kick up a fuss.'

Odette took Faustus' card and held it up to the light. The cover concealing the real card had endured plenty: there was a burn hole, stains and blood splatters. It looked as if it had been damaged on purpose to make the card look old and tattered.

She would free the precious treasure from its prison and take loving care of it. Odette didn't know for certain what card was hidden inside and was looking forward to the surprise reveal. She now had three special cards laid out on her restoration tables that were being treated. Replenished. Healed. Just like in a hospital.

Her only worry was whether there would be enough supplies in the wine cellar. Judging by the fragile Faustus outer casing, she suspected the card slumbering beneath it had suffered and seen a great deal; one or two lives wouldn't be enough to repair its foundation before she could get to work on the finer details. She tried to evaluate the scope of the restoration and estimated that she would need at least half a dozen lives to bring the card back to life. *Maybe even more.* Avignon appeared to lack beggars, homeless people and Travellers as of late. Word had got around that people should avoid the city, which the police attributed to their own good work.

She would send Renard or Charles to fetch her 'supplies' outside of Avignon. There were still plenty of provisions in other cities and towns, though her father would have phrased that differently using terms he had adopted from the Nazis.

Odette got to her feet. 'I'll go and fetch the money, Monsieur Mulder.'

She took the card with her and made her way with slow, sure-footed steps to her restoration room, where she placed the Faustus card on the long table in front of the window.

She then reached for a canister with a skull and crossbones sign on it from a shelf on the right. Acid sloshed inside, but the bottom of the can could be pulled out, and this was where she stored her money.

Odette counted out thirty thousand euros in five-hundred-euro notes and returned to the kitchen, where the three men were discussing what to do next. As soon as she walked in, they changed to the innocent subject of cake recipes.

'Here, Monsieur Mulder.' Odette calmly handed him his entire pay cheque. 'I trust that you'll do your job. This is a huge leap of faith on my part.'

'Of course, Madame Darlan,' he said. At first he just held the stack of purple euros, unsure what to do with them. Then he quickly divided the bundle and stuffed the cash into the pockets of his jeans. 'You can count on me. When it comes to tracking down what's gone missing, you won't find a better man for the job.'

'Except for my Fennec,' she corrected him with a smile.

Mulder stood up and finished the last of his coffee. 'Messieurs,' he said and took turns to shake hands with both men. 'I'll see you again soon. Take care of Madame Darlan.'

'How about a piece of cake to go?' Charles suggested, pulling out some aluminium foil from a drawer.

'I won't say no to that,' Mulder said and waited for his little food parcel to be wrapped up.

Renard excused himself and disappeared into the barn. He wanted to check on the car, a Peugeot 807, which they were going to repaint and fit with new number plates. The van was perfect for transporting new supplies to revive the cards. They'd cover the interior with tarpaulin and tint the windows, which would stop anyone from looking inside the vehicle.

'Good luck, Monsieur Mulder. Find me my Fennec!' Odette waved him goodbye and pushed her heavy glasses up the narrow bridge of her nose. She was eager to return to the cards. The new Faustus card was in desperate need of her attention and she was aching to find out what was hiding inside its case.

Suddenly, a loud beep sounded from the Belgian's direction.

'That's . . .' Mulder fumbled for his phone in his jacket pocket, bewildered. 'Madame, I ... I've received some orders,' he announced and showed his phone screen to Charles, who was licking chocolate off his fingers and nodded. 'My employer is feeling well enough to send me on another mission.' He started to unload the notes from his pockets and place them on the table. 'I'm sorry, Madame Darlan.'

Odette feared that her Fennec would be left without any help. 'Where are they sending you?'

'Usually I'm not permitted to say, but since it's a special case: Manaus, madame. I've been hired for the same job that you asked me to do.' Mulder pointed to the purple wad of cash. 'So there's no need to pay me.'

'Keep the money,' Odette said with a warm smile. 'I know that your employer is sending you to look for a card in the jungle. Take my thirty thousand and look for my Fennec, too. Agreed?' She held out her spindle-fingered right hand. 'Bring him back.'

'Yes, madame.' And with that, Mulder dutifully kissed the back of her hand.

If you must play, decide on three things
at the start: the rules,
the stakes, and the quitting time.

Chinese proverb

X

Tadeus took in the limestone house from their rented Citroën C-Élysée. He had parked some distance from the barn door in the only free space on the street. The dust and rust stains made their car look suitably inconspicuous.

'That should be where she lives,' he said. The pain in his wrists subsided. He had thin bandages wrapped around his healing wounds that the cable ties had left behind.

Their escape from Bruges had gone better than expected. The burglars had activated the empty stairlift as a joke and Boch and Poe had got away undetected. The sleeping woman upstairs had never woken up.

They had taken the high-speed train, the TGV, to Avignon and hired the Citroën locally, once again posing as a couple on holiday. Since the charges from Tadeus' account would have put him in debt and raised questions that he didn't want to answer, Poe financed their expenses.

Neither of them had read or heard anything about a robbery of the antique shop in the Belgian news, which raised their suspicions. The fact that the burglars had also talked about delivering the cards brought even more questions to mind. Tadeus expected that there was at least one other collector who had seized the moment to steal the cards while Gillot lay incapacitated in hospital. *Contract theft* – something the Walloon hadn't been opposed to himself, and now he was getting a taste of his own medicine.

He watched the house and hoped to find out from Odette Darlan where his nine of spades had gone. The very notion of no longer being able to hold the card made him feel anxious. His hands tightened around the steering wheel and squeezed hard.

'Well? Anything useful?' he asked Poe, who had Gillot's stolen laptop open in her lap. She scrolled and clicked through files.

The laptop's operating system was ancient. There hadn't even been a password prompt or a trace of any security settings. The computer was clearly not being used by the antiques dealer, but rather by the bedridden woman to write about Saint Sarah. According to the device's registration information, it belonged to a certain Magdalena de Graaf. An internet search revealed that she was the owner of the antique shop in Bruges, despite the name *Gillot* being written in large lettering above it.

De Graaf's fixation on the saint bordered on obsession. She wrote little stories set in assumed historical contexts. Fan fiction. Poe had read some of them and they sounded more like the adventures of a superheroine than a saint.

Tadeus spotted occasional movements from behind the curtains. 'There are at least two people inside. Looks like men. Could be the grandchildren who live with her.' He looked around, marvelling at Avignon's medieval town centre, which he had assumed would be full of timber-framed houses like those in Quedlinburg or Rothenburg ob der Tauber in Germany. Instead, there were plenty of smooth, sparsely plastered, beige stone walls and roofs covered with pale reddish shingles and tiles.

The name Darlan had come up in the basilica between Gillot and his henchman. After doing some research, Tadeus and Poe had discovered that there was a very famous restorer in Avignon named Odette Darlan who had made a name for herself in the production of historical documents, parchments, papyri and other works. That made it perfectly obvious who they had to visit to find out more about the cards.

The restorer was now well over eighty and led a quiet life. After popping into a baker's and passing himself off as a muse-ologist from Germany, Tadeus had learned that everyone in the town knew Madame Darlan, but he was advised not to turn up unannounced at her house. She didn't like visitors.

He suspected that this had something to do with the cards. *She's protecting them, like me.* Once Odette Darlan had attended to the nine of spades, however, it should return into his care.

'I found something!' Poe cried, showing him a folder she had discovered from the plethora of data. 'It was created by Gillot, not de Graaf.'

'TDG,' Tadeus read. *The Devil's Playbook* – the derogatory medi-eval term for the card game used by the devoutly religious.

Poe opened a file.

Together they skimmed through the document, which con-tained a conglomerate of internet links, literature references and selected scanned passages. Naturally, it was all about his-torical playing cards.

Tadeus recognised his nine of spades among the many illus-trations and markings.

'Stop,' he said and zoomed in.

There was an article that had been scanned from a book on the production of cards. The nine of spades was referenced as a prime example of cards that had been made during the second half of the 18th century, using copper plates instead of the woodcut technique, which allowed card-makers to create excep-tionally detailed pieces.

'The card is attributed to an unknown artist, who is only

known to have worked in Leipzig for the Breitkopf family of printers, publishers and sheet music traders for a time. The Breitkopf family later managed a card factory,' Tadeus read aloud softly. 'So there *was* an entire deck.' He glanced at Odette Darlan's house. 'No, there still is. She must know more!' This news made his skin prickle with goosebumps. He grew excited and imagined the nine of spades calling to him, yearning to be held and protected, then him looking for the other cards and bringing the entire deck back together.

Poe continued to scroll through the file. 'Gillot copied several 18th-century birth records from Leipzig.' She pointed to the barely legible old manuscripts. 'He was probably searching for the unknown engraver in question.'

'Why?'

She shot him a loaded look. 'Are you really asking me that? Given the terrible influence that these cards have? I told you, I might not have completed my mudang training, but I can still feel that these cards are possessed by evil, by a spirit or . . .' She tried to find the right words. 'They've come into contact with a very powerful, dark force or were created under the influence of a cruel spirit.' The fine hairs on her arms stood up. 'My nightmares are not a coincidence.'

Tadeus ignored her words. He wouldn't let her spoil his bliss. 'But what good would that knowledge about the engraver do Gillot?'

Poe scrolled faster through the document, but she was nowhere near the end. 'Looking through this will take at least a day.' She slammed the laptop shut. 'Minimum. With no distractions.'

'You haven't answered my question.'

'I think Gillot wanted to know who the engraver was to learn about the circumstances of the cards' origin.' She tucked her black hair behind her ears and glanced at the property. 'But before we rack our brains over it, let's see what this Odette Darlan has to say.'

'You're right.' Tadeus didn't know what the restorer's role was in all this, but he hoped that she was only doing her job. That she returned the cards and didn't cause any trouble.

He grabbed the telescopic baton he had bought at the petrol station from the car's footwell and stuffed it into his left sleeve. This and the tricks he had learned at his self-defence course would hopefully be enough to deal with the two grandchildren if necessary. *I'm better prepared this time.* He had even remembered to take his painkillers.

'So, what's our plan? Ring the doorbell and ask nicely?' Poe asked, hiding the laptop behind the driver's seat and under the foot mat to avoid tempting any thieves to break in. 'Or ring the doorbell and storm inside?' She had meant her second suggestion as a joke.

'Not a bad idea.' Tadeus pointed at the roughly timbered barn door inside the giant gate. 'We'll do both. You ring the doorbell and distract them, and I'll go around the back and take care of the grandchildren. Then nothing can get in our way.'

'Seriously, what's wrong with just asking?'

'Think about what we just went through. I doubt it'll be straightforward.'

'Odette Darlan is over eighty years old. What's she going to do?' Poe was clearly worried. 'We might give the old woman a heart attack. It's not unlikely at her age.'

'We'll handle this with no casualties. Besides, you're a doctor.'

'I'm a surgeon. Not a cardiologist.'

'But you can still do CPR,' he said and grabbed the crowbar. He would use it to open the side entrance, unless there was a flimsy yet effective deadbolt holding the door from the inside, as there sometimes were on old doors, in which case he would have to improvise. 'It's the two grandchildren I'm worried about, not the old lady. Do you know anyone who lives with their grandchildren instead of their children?'

Poe shook her head.

'I'll go first. You set off ten minutes later,' Tadeus told her and swung out of the Citroën. He turned right, took a little detour and prepared to approach the house from the right-hand side.

As he strolled along the little street, he glanced at the display window of the only shop in sight, which sold devotional objects. After so many centuries, Avignon still marketed itself as the city of the antipopes, and it did it well. Odette Darlan lived in a quiet neighbourhood. Most of the shops, cafés and restaurants were to the east of Nicolas Lescuyer Street, where the tourists crowded around the sights.

Poe left the car and rang the restorer's doorbell, her round hat sitting over her hair and her camera hanging around her neck. Tadeus didn't see who opened the door, but he could hear the smile on Poe's face as she spoke and saw her pointing to their car.

The nice tourist in distress. Tadeus nimbly used the crowbar on the door to exert a little pressure until a wider gap opened up. He couldn't see a bolt behind it. If there wasn't a supporting beam from the inside, he was in luck.

The lock burst open with a louder clanging noise than he had expected.

Tadeus quickly looked over to Poe, who was laughing with the invisible person at the door. Suddenly, she disappeared into the house.

'What the hell . . .?' he blurted out in surprise. That hadn't been part of their plan. Of course she would just walk in and ask for the cards . . .

He hurried into the barn, where he saw a brand new, green Peugeot van with Lorraine licence plates. It reeked of fresh paint. The two child seats in the back suggested that it wasn't

Odette Darlan's car. The tall building was otherwise filled with agricultural machinery from the last millennium as well as an old winepress and huge wooden barrels filled with grape juice to make wine. Scythes, rakes and other old tools that were once used to work in the fields hung from the beams.

As Tadeus crept further into the barn, he could smell centuries-old wood, dust and grease. There were only two doors leading out of the building: one that likely led into the former stables and the other into the main house.

He could hear Poe's and another man's voice, probably one of the grandsons', drifting through the door. She apologised profusely for her disturbance and thanked him for his willingness to help, while he praised his home-made cake.

Tadeus pushed down the door handle. He couldn't get into the hallway, but he didn't want to use the crowbar. That would trigger a loud, audible crash and the element of surprise would be lost.

Instead he decided to take a detour through the second door and found himself in another long corridor with a turn-off at the end. The smell of stone, the kind you'd expect in a cellar, and . . . blood filled Tadeus' nostrils. The scent wafted towards him from the end of the corridor, where he spotted a downward passage, presumably leading into a vault, as befitted a winery.

But blood? His chest tightened. Tadeus quietly walked towards the turn-off. He saw a door that looked like it led into the kitchen. The conversation between Poe and the stranger was relaxed and he could hear the clattering of plates. Whatever story she had told the grandson, she had clearly received a warm welcome.

Tadeus looked over his shoulder.

Behind him was another staircase, but this one would take him a floor up. Perhaps Darlan was sitting upstairs, working on the cards. What if he were to sneak upstairs and question her alone, without Poe disturbing him?

Then again, Poe was his divining rod, even if she hadn't been able to sense the presence of the cards in Gillot's safe. But she had been right about the eight of hearts in the basilica, and she was also financing their quest to find the cards. If Poe got into any trouble, he wouldn't be able to hear, and that wasn't something he was willing to risk.

He carefully placed the crowbar on the floor and pulled out the telescopic baton from his sleeve with his free hand. He prepared himself for the attack: go inside, surprise the man and take him out.

Take a deep breath. He tensed – there was a scraping noise behind him.

He instinctively dodged to the side.

Four clean prongs of a pitchfork bored into the wooden door with a clang. The conversation on the other side instantly ceased.

Tadeus swung around and struck, aiming not for the bald head but for the fingers wrapped around the handle of the pitchfork. The baton smashed into the back of a broad hand with a dry crack; there was the sound of bones breaking.

The attacker cried out and tried to kick Tadeus in the crotch.

Tadeus brought the baton down again and hit the bald man's knee, followed by a blow to his chest with the flat of his hand that sent him flying backward. The man collapsed.

But before Tadeus could knock him unconscious, the door behind him flew open along with the lodged handle of the pitchfork. It swung around and caught his arm, causing him to miss the man and knock a chunk of stone off the tiles.

Someone threw themselves at him from behind and he felt a blade graze his neck. 'Whoever you are, stop,' a voice warned, as the smell of chocolate and coffee enveloped Tadeus. The sharp edge cut into his skin painfully. 'Or it'll be your blood on that wall.'

The other man got to his feet, pulled out the fork from the door with his left hand and pointed it at Tadeus' stomach. 'You son of a bitch, you broke my hand!' the bald man roared with rage. His right hand looked crooked and fragments of bone protruded from the exposed, small fractures. Blood streamed down his skin and trickled onto the floor. Furious, the man trembled all over with treacherous anger.

Tadeus saw the attack coming. He grabbed the man's hand holding the weapon, bent down on one knee and threw the attacker over his shoulder at his second opponent.

Both of the men screamed, one out of shock, the other from pain. The abandoned knife clattered to the floor.

Tadeus wrapped his hand around the pitchfork handle and stopped it from being pulled from him for yet another strike. He then slammed the baton against the head of the fallen man, who immediately fell silent.

The bald attacker's kick missed Tadeus and he instantly kneed the man in the crotch in response.

Gasping, the bald man slumped over his friend and reached for his belt. He clearly had no intention of giving up.

Tadeus intuitively picked up the kitchen knife and hurled it at him while the other man drew a semi-automatic.

The adrenaline-fuelled throw turned out remarkably well: the tip of the knife sank into the target's chest, only stopping at the hilt. The bold man fell back against the wall, wheezing as he raised his pistol with his arm to load it, but his strength failed him. He slid to the floor.

Tadeus approached the dead man and grabbed his pistol, which had the acronym *MAB* embossed on it. The stamped label *WaA251* and the eagle on the barrel of the gun caught his eye. He felt briefly guilty for the fact that he'd killed a man who would never have managed to load the weapon with his injured hand in the first place. *But how was he supposed to have known that?*

'Poe?' he shouted into the kitchen.

'I'm all right,' she said and switched the light on in the hallway.

There were bloodstains on the walls; pools of red appeared on the tiles. The fresh smell of copper hung in the air and the stabbed man's chest remained sunken and still – he was no longer breathing.

'Shit, Boch! This is a massacre!'

'They started it. There was no other way.' Tadeus gestured for her to be quiet. 'Is there anyone else here? I saw a van in the barn.'

'Not in the kitchen. If there is, they'll be upstairs.' Poe held a stake hammer in her hand.

'Let's find out.' Tadeus tried not to think about how he would explain the bodies to the French police. Self-defence in the event of a break-in didn't sound so convincing if he was the intruder. They would have to act fast to avoid Odette Darlan alerting the authorities.

He carefully walked ahead with the MAB in his outstretched arm, which he supported with his other hand. The sight of the pistol would hopefully be intimidating enough to ward off any other enemies. He didn't think he was a particularly good shot.

They ignored the passage leading to the wine cellar and climbed up the stairs to the first floor. A chemical odour, like a developing solution in a photography lab, wafted down from the steps.

Tadeus couldn't hear any conversation, excited voices or shouts.

'That's the one,' he told Poe and pointed to the first door, which had a clear no entry warning sign emblazoned on it.

Poe nodded. He pushed down the door handle and stepped inside, swinging the barrel of the MAB around in case of any danger.

A woman with white hair tucked into a bun and wearing a bright, patterned apron dress sat by the window at a long table. She was surrounded by various magnifying glasses and lamps. The earphones she wore had blocked out the noise from downstairs. The sound of classical music floated gently towards to them.

Tadeus sighed in relief. They had found the restorer. The two of them cautiously approached her.

Odette Darlan was calmly toiling away. Her hands didn't slip and her bony fingers didn't tremble. A pair of glasses with thick lenses that she had removed to work and replaced with magnifying glasses lay beside her. She didn't appear to have noticed the unwelcome visitors.

She's working on cards! Are they from the same deck as my nine of spades? Tadeus put away his weapon. *Could it be here?*

'What are we going to do now?' Poe asked softly. 'Didn't you say there were other people in the house?'

'Maybe.' Tadeus got closer to the table.

As he looked over the restorer's bun, he finally saw what cards she was working on: the eight of hearts, the two of clubs and the seven of clubs. It was evident that they belonged to the same deck as his nine of spades. The style and precision of each piece made it perfectly clear that the same engraver had designed and brought them to life. Tadeus' card, however, was nowhere to be seen. That disappointed him.

Multicoloured bottles and jars containing liquids and brushes made from different materials and of various thicknesses surrounded Odette Darlan. The fumes escaping from the vases made him feel slightly dizzy when he breathed in – or was that from the aura emanating from the cards?

'Boch,' he heard Poe say excitedly. 'Can you feel that? The cards are –'

Tadeus had forgotten about his shadow, which now fell onto the restorer as he took his next step. She paused while reaching for the lancet with her wrinkled hand.

'I don't smell coffee,' Darlan said, removing her earphones. The classical music played a little louder. 'I asked you for some an hour ago, Charles.'

Tadeus didn't know what to do. He had a desperate urge to snatch the cards from the table.

Then, out of nowhere, without Darlan or Tadeus having done anything, the eight of hearts, the seven of clubs and the two of clubs began to glow. It was as if the cards wanted to send a message to the world, like a sonar waiting to hear back an echo from a great, big void.

The invisible wave of energy made the vials, jars, lamps and magnifying glasses vibrate. It rushed through the room and caused the papers to rustle and crinkle; the light flickered for two, three seconds.

Poe let out a stifled groan behind him. A shudder of irresistible pleasure coursed through Tadeus. He was sure that the other cards from the deck would hear this call.

Then Odette Darlan turned around.

* * *

Cotonou, Benin,
West Africa

Sowande Aristide Gondjia hurtled along the 880 on his rattling Honda motorcycle. The knobbly tyres of the vehicle tore up the bumpy road, leaving behind a trail of dust as he drove to his destination in the southernmost foothills of the city. The dark blues of Lake Nokoué lay to the right, as if wanting to blend with the gathering night and make people wonder what was sky and what was water.

The evening would be a profitable one for the voodoo priest. His client would have to dig deep in her pockets before he could fulfil her wish: to unleash evil spirits on her ex-husband. As he was a bokor who only summoned vicious, wicked spirits, desperate and unscrupulous people relied on his destructive powers to solve their problems when they saw no other way out.

Sowande turned off the 880 and swerved towards the lake. His loose-fitting white robe and braided hair flapped behind him in the wind. A painted, half-metre-long bamboo stick and a worn rucksack that no street thief would ever suspect was valuable sat on his back. He would use the contents of the backpack and the bamboo staff for his upcoming conjuring.

Years ago, when he was in his mid-fifties, he had been forced to leave his native Haiti as a result of his success. Influential people who worked with white magic sorcerers at the time had resented him for his voodoo powers, and he hadn't been able to beat them.

But he felt at home in Benin, especially in Cotonou. In the language of the Fon people, Cotonou meant *the mouth of the river of death*, and as a bokor that suited him.

Sowande took his foot off the gas and the Honda Africa Twin motorcycle slowed down. He sat upright in his seat to get a better view.

His client's home was somewhere between all the dilapidated houses. He felt suspicious of the poorer neighbourhood and would ask to see the money before he shook hands or began conjuring the Maître Carrefour, the spirit capable of unleashing evil and paving the way for other spirits. As soon as he received payment, the summoning would symbolically take place at a crossroads.

No one cared whether voodoo was practised on the streets or not in this neighbourhood. Sowande had not chosen Benin as his place of refuge for nothing. Voodoo was recognised here as the official religion, with its own annual public holiday on the tenth of January, which had now become a popular tourist attraction. Sowande didn't like the sell-out of voodoo to tourists; they'd already ruined the Día de los Muertos in Mexico. Though Benin needed the money, he wasn't obliged to sympathise.

Suddenly a woman jumped out onto the road and waved at him.

'Bokor! Over here!' she shouted over the rumble of the motorcycle. Her hair was braided into dreadlocks and she wore a shirt, shorts and sunglasses. She must have married very young – she looked no older than twenty-five.

Sowande drove towards her and shut off the engine. 'Julienne Ehezu?' he asked.

'Yes, that's me, bokor.'

'Show me the signal we agreed on.'

Ehezu looked puzzled and Sowande laughed. 'It's a joke. I know it's you.' He pointed to the crossroads, around thirty metres away from them on the bank of the lake. 'Over there?'

'That's right, bokor.'

'Have you got the money?' He held out his hand. Various chains made from shells and metal dangled from his wrist. 'Hand it over.'

'I . . .' She didn't seem sure whether to pay him in advance or demand a result first.

Sowande shrugged and fired up the Honda.

'Wait!' Ehuzu reached into the bag she had brought with her and pressed an envelope into his hand.

Sowande looked inside and counted out the cash in US dollars that he had asked for. It added up. 'Your ex-husband's luck will soon run out,' he said. He turned off the engine again, got off and pushed the motorcycle to the crossroads. The woman walked beside him. 'Do you have any questions about what's going to happen?'

'Thousands, but . . .' Ehuzu looked nervous. 'I've never tried voodoo before and . . . I'm a Christian, but I've heard that it works and—'

'There's not a huge difference between le bon Dieu and the other gods. At least, that's how I see it.' Sowande grinned. 'Le bon Dieu and his spirits are powerful – it doesn't matter if you believe in them or not. I'm the bokor – leave it to me.'

'Do I have to do anything?'

'Just a picture of your ex-husband.'

She handed it to him and Sowande stuffed it into his kaftan bag.

'I've heard that you need a temple for this.' Ehuzu spoke hesitantly, unable to hide her curiosity about the foreign religion that over fifteen per cent of the Beninese followed. A cross hung around her neck.

'I don't.' He pointed to his painted staff. 'This is from my temple and that's enough. One part of the whole. You'll see how powerful I am when I summon Kalfu.' Sowande spotted that some people had gathered at the crossroads. Most of them were women. 'Did you ask them to come here?'

'Yes. They hate my ex-husband just as much as I do and have come to support me. And they've brought gifts for the spirits.' Ehuzu smiled shyly. 'I've heard that they can be generous in return. Can you turn my ex into a zombie?'

Sowande nodded. 'I could, but not for the money you're paying me. What I'll do is hurt him. Make him suffer.'

They'd reached the crossroads. The people bowed deeply before the bokor; they couldn't conceal their respect and fear from the voodoo priest. There were too many stories, too many sayings and legends about the spirits' powers, and Sowande was known in Cotonou as an exceptionally gifted priest.

Sowande returned their bows with gestures of blessing and pulled his rucksack and the painted staff off his back.

Without offering an explanation, he rammed the staff into the centre of the crossroads, then grabbed a few tiny wooden stools from his bag and positioned them around it. He laid a velvet blanket over them, followed by small bones and pictures of Kalfu and a kind of slit-shaped holder on the very top.

Then Sowande reached under his clothes and retrieved something. At first glance, it looked like a business card in a plastic sleeve.

But it was something far more special.

He removed the playing card from its case. It was ancient and European. He'd stolen it from a dead Frenchman in Haiti who had died in a gutter with numerous stab wounds, choking on his own vomit. The card was a hand-painted, beautifully decorated ace of spades with ornate writing and lots of fine detailing on the front and back.

The day the card had come into his possession had changed his life. He used to be part of the Oungan voodoo priesthood that exclusively practised white magic and limited themselves to the worship of peaceful spirits. But Kalfu, or the Maître Carrefour, lived in this card.

Sowande had remained faithful to Kalfu ever since. He didn't need any other spirits; one was more than enough. The destructive spirit helped him with his witchcraft, his curses and black magic. For Sowande, Kalfu was a demon and a ruler who commanded the spirits of the night.

Thanks to him and the ace of spades, which was like a burning glass for Kalfu's powers, Sowande was capable of bringing great misfortune upon his victims. This ranged from persistent failure, the loss of desire in men and women, hallucinations and annoying illnesses, to fatal suffering and accidents that resulted in serious injuries or even death. He could ruin people's lives physically, mentally and financially.

'Kalfu!' Sowande cried out loudly, and reverently placed the ace of spades into the slit of the holder so that it stood upright. One by one the people around him handed him offerings, which he deposited onto the ground. 'Kalfu, arise and behold! Bless us with your presence. We seek your favour.' Sowande finally set down the picture of the ex-husband. 'This man, Josep Ehuzu, must face your wrath. Kalfu! Oh, great, mighty Kalfu!'

Sowande drank the rum mixed with gunpowder and poured it in front of the improvised altar and then over the playing card and the photograph. As always, the ace of spades remained unharmed. The alcohol rolled off the card and the dust didn't stick to it.

He kept calling the demon, repeating the request and dancing around the staff. Sowande spoke faster and faster, repeating his incantations, and the beloved trance began.

He saw how the card's aura changed, how its lines first glowed in silver and then turned a bloody red. A muffled, unintelligible chorus sounded in his mind, mixing with his own intonations and transporting him further and further away. The spirit of Kalfu was about to fill his mind and announce whether he would grant the woman's wish.

Sowande sensed the spirit enter him and felt like Kalfu himself: strong full of energy and thirsty for destruction. Until Kalfu left the bokor's body and fulfilled his duty, it wasn't always easy for those present at the rituals to appease him with gifts.

The red veil over his eyes confirmed that the demon had seized control. Sowande suddenly stood still, rolled back his eyes and stared at the crowd, who recognised the presence of the spirit and threw themselves back into the dust of the crossroads. One or two humble, shy cries of 'Kalfu!' could be heard.

'Silence, all of you! Do you not know that no one is to make a sound when I appear? Only those who I call upon may speak.' He raised his arm and pointed to Ehuzu with his index finger. The amulets around Sowande's wrist tinkled softly. 'You demanded my services. You wish for me to curse this man?'

'Yes! Yes, I seek your help. He was a bad husband. He beat me and abused me,' she explained, taken aback.

'What offerings have you brought me?'

Ehuzu looked at the backpack Sowande had set down. 'I . . . I gave you money. To the bokor. I gave the bokor money.'

'You gave him money to summon me,' he roared. 'But what is *my* reward?' There wasn't a trace of Sowande left; the spirit had possessed every bone of his body. The man gestured to the empty bottle of rum. 'Is that all?'

Ehuzu backed away from him. 'He said that three bottles would be enough.'

'Bring me more!' he shouted, furious. Kalfu's possession felt different today, unusual and unruly. Sowande felt very tempted to give in. 'Bring more!' He looked at the card. Its singing changed and swelled, growing more passionate than ever before. It was as if a new door had opened in his mind. His vision became clearer and sharper and he could look into every mind of every person around him and read their thoughts. He felt their fear, their fear and their reverence for him – the demon spirit in human form.

In the same second, a single ray the colour of blood emanated from the card and a blazing magenta aureole pierced the dark night sky for what looked like kilometres. Its trail reached out and touched him, energising him all the more.

'I am Kalfu!' Enraptured, he gazed at his hands, which could easily split a tank in half and squash steel bullets. Divine power throbbed inside him. 'Where are my offerings?'

Ehuzu threw herself onto the crossroads before him, dug

all her money out of her bag, removed her jewellery and offered it to the spirit. She trembled with fear. 'Mighty one, please, take this.'

'That is of no interest to me. It won't quench my thirst.' Sowande glared at the people who wouldn't give him what he desired. 'And if I cannot quench my thirst, then my anger towards you will only grow. *At all of you*, who dared come unprepared and still seek my favour!'

'Spare us!' Ehuzu stretched out her arm to him pleadingly. 'The bokor is to blame. He said—'

Sowande yanked the woman by her fingers and her wrist, stepped onto her neck with his right foot and pulled her arm with all his might. The joint snapped with a crunch, the tendons and muscles tore and the skin finally gave way.

Ehuzu only cried out once before fainting. The possessed Sowande swung her arm around and drank the blood spilling out from it.

'More!' he shouted and threw the limb aside. He grabbed the next person by the throat and ripped it out of their neck. The warm blood sprayed over him and he opened his mouth to laugh. 'More!'

The horrified screams and shouts of the crowd sounded like screeching rats and mice. Sowande saw the pale faces of the neighbourhood's inhabitants appear at the windows. They watched the massacre, unable to look away, taking photos and speaking into their phones. He could hear the thoughts of the people around him, who were torn between their deep veneration for Kalfu and running for their lives.

Sowande roared and pursued those who ran from him. The time had come to separate the wheat from the chaff and reward those who honoured him. He struck them down with blows to their necks, dug his fingers into their skin, ripped out their flesh and drank the red that trickled into his mouth.

He continued to hunt down his victims until the street was empty. Dead and wounded bodies lay scattered around the dusty earth, his laughter echoing around them.

The ace of spades sent a sinister, unwavering signal into the night. The card's singing and its stimulating glow spurred him on, his strength and powers incessantly growing. People had to sacrifice everything to a dark god and a demon like Kalfu.

'I am Kalfu!' Sowande bared his teeth and looked around him, searching for more victims. He could taste blood in his mouth, and he wanted more of it. More blood, more flesh. And since there was no one else left outside for him to feast on, he ran to the nearest house.

The people behind the windows backed away from him. A woman darted out of the door and ran past him with a child in her arms.

Sowande wouldn't let her escape. He shoved her impulsively. 'You wanted to make me a sacrifice!'

The woman stumbled, crashed into a wall and dropped the baby. The child rolled back onto the doorstep, crying, and crawled back to its mother, who pushed herself up against the wooden wall with a burst forehead.

'Your child!' Sowande ordered. 'Give me your child, mortal, and I shall give you the mercy of Kalfu.'

Wide and narrow beams of light suddenly fell on him. He turned around.

Several men came running down the street with weapons at the ready. They blinded him with their torches. The first few bullets struck him, but they felt as harmless as a few pokes and pricks. The men shot from the hip, hitting him in the legs, stomach, hands and arms.

Sowande bellowed into the darkness and charged towards the attackers firing their pistols and shotguns at him. He didn't care, as befitted a demon god. 'Prepare to die! Sacrifice yourself to Kalfu!'

He threw himself into the throng, lashing out and tearing off entire faces with his claw-like, crooked fingers, ripping out eyes and lips. Blood splattered over him, spurring him on. The ace of spades' sinister chants fuelled his defiance, his holy wrath.

Sowande lost himself in the red orgy of death. The screams of the wounded and dying mingled with the cards' singing in a sort of ecstasy, complementing and completing them. He never wanted this harmony, this symphony, this synaesthesia to end.

* * *

Leila Fignolé was carefully watching the movements of the recently arrived police officers after Sowande Aristide Gondjia appeared to have lost his mind. The flickering, bright lights of the patrol cars danced over her dark-skinned face as she stood on the veranda. The people in the neighbourhood had barricaded themselves in their homes in fear of the killing spree, some of them quickly leaving gifts outside their doors before locking them.

For emergencies, Leila had a sawn-off shotgun hidden in her spacious handbag.

The first wave of locals who had turned on Gondjia had badly wounded the bokor with blades and bullets. Blood oozed from his gaping wounds and his face was disfigured by cuts and bullet grazes. When he walked, he left red footprints behind him.

But the voodoo priest wouldn't stop. He continued to shout, declaring again and again that he was Kalfu, that he wanted more victims and that he would bring death and destruction to all those who didn't honour him. He refused all the gifts offered to him, except for the alcohol.

Leila estimated there to be over forty people dead and injured. The victims lay in the streets, on verandas or outside doorways. The man had cruelly ravaged them.

She turned her attention to the small altar that the bokor had erected at the crossroads. She could clearly see that something was happening with the ace of spades and that a mighty demon had left its mark, which explained Gondjias' powers. She couldn't let the card fall into the wrong hands.

Leila was a mambo, a voodoo priestess who purposefully only practised white magic to resist and stop men like Gondjia. She had been searching for the priest for ten years and had followed him from her home in Haiti to Benin in order to confront and annihilate him.

Since her own spells weren't effective against the powerful bokor, who could rely on Kalfu's protection, she had decided to end his life by more conventional means. There were fewer ways of resisting bullets and knives, even if some voodoo priests claimed otherwise. But now Gondjia was in charge of his own execution. He fervently pushed against the heavily armed approaching policemen and threatened them as if he were oblivious to the weapons in their hands.

'Stop! Get on the ground, you arsehole!' The policemen aimed their assault rifles at the raging man and hollered their final warnings at him.

'How dare you!' Gondjia ran towards them with a machete and a fresh bottle of rum in his hands, covered in his own and his victims' blood, his once white kaftan red and wet. He tore at his robe and continued to trudge towards them in his pants, which were no less covered in sacrificial blood. 'I'll hack you to pieces and drink you dry. Your blood and your souls shall be mine! You'll sacrifice yourselves to Kalfu, you pathetic little humans!'

A volley of bullets was fired.

Leila watched with satisfaction as holes opened up in the voodoo priest's body and his head was blown to smithereens by the hail of cartridges. The armed men didn't stop at his legs.

She smiled as Gondjia's bullet-pierced, headless body took his final few steps, toppled forward and dropped dead. She watched the execution with malicious joy and relief.

'Stop! Hold fire,' came the command. The policemen lowered their automatic rifles and slowly approached the body of the voodoo priest.

The first few curious witnesses ventured out of their houses and clapped. They whooped and celebrated the victory over the bloodthirsty madman who had clearly lost his mind during the delirious ritual. The bravest stormed up to the altar, crushing the little stools and breaking the painted staff in two, as if that would help defeat Kalfu.

The officials initially left them to it and stood around the corpse in deliberation.

They don't know anything about voodoo. The mambo looked at the ace of spades, which had been trampled under the rum-soaked earth. *They're clueless.*

The card was too dangerous to entertain the idea that the crowd would simply destroy it by accident. Leila knew how much this artefact could withstand and that it had been produced in Europe with the help of a dark demon. It had to be destroyed. Now that Gondjia had been eliminated as a willing helper of the card, it was her mambo duty to seize the opportunity and destroy it.

Leila clutched her handbag and mingled with the revellers, dancing and laughing. She moved through the swirling clouds of dust, her eyes fixed on the ground and searching for the ace of spades. Finding the card wouldn't be easy. Perhaps it sensed her presence and was hiding from her to try to save itself.

She heard a gunshot. A policeman pointed his weapon at the

bokor's ribcage to the sound of the cheering crowd, and emptied his magazine into the corpse until the bullets had beaten the voodoo priest's heart to a pulp.

Leila had no objection to this.

Then she saw the card amidst the sea of shards from the smashed rum bottles. Just as she'd expected, the sharp glass had done nothing to the painted paper.

She wasn't afraid. Her white magic powers and the good spirits gave her the strength she needed not to fall prey to Kalfu and become as corrupted, merciless and cruel as Gondjia.

She bent down and reached for the ace of spades. Just a few more seconds and she would have it.

Leila wondered how one destroyed the work of an evil demon when knives, fire and water had proved futile. She would try using acid after appealing to the good spirits and asking for their help. All that suffering, misery and atrocities that the card had brought upon the world had to end.

Suddenly, one of the revellers bumped into her before she could grab the card and almost collapsed on top of her. Leila's grip failed her and she cut herself on a piece of broken glass. Her handbag slipped off her shoulder and the contents of it spilled out onto the street. The alcohol burned as it came into contact with her wound and a drop or two of her blood, along with the rum infused with gunpowder, trickled from her finger onto the card. The red rolled over it without sticking to the paper.

Leila stopped and inspected the lines and patterns on the card. She crouched down and ignored the lively crowd, which gradually settled down. She hadn't noticed the singing emanating from the ace of spades before.

That couldn't be the work of a spirit.

She licked her finger, tasting the rum and copper on her tongue. Her plans had changed. She would stay in Cotonou for a while longer to investigate Gondjias' voodoo temple.

'Go on, it's time for you to go!' she heard someone order from a distance. The commotion had died down even further. 'Go back to your homes! This is a crime scene.'

Leila picked up the card, threw all the belongings she could find back into her bag and got up. She suddenly found herself standing alone in the empty street. A policeman shooed her away.

She walked away, holding the ace of spades between her left thumb and index finger, but then a sudden urge to take a closer look at the card consumed her; only to discover the secret behind its power, of course.

Slowly, she returned the card to her bag.

True luck consists not in holding the best of the cards at the table; luckiest is he who knows just when to rise and go home.

John Ray (1627–1705)

XI

Avignon, Vaucluse,
Provence-Alpes-Côte d'Azur,
France

Odette Darlan didn't appear frightened, and that irritated Tadeus. Two complete strangers had worked their way past her two grandchildren and now stood in front of her in her own house, and the old lady looked surprised at most.

'This is about the cards, isn't it, monsieur et madame?' Her awfully skinny hand reached for her thick glasses and propped them on her thin face. The frame balanced on the slender bridge of her noise.

Tadeus found the restorer remarkable. 'You were expecting us?'

'Not you specifically, but I was expecting a visit.' Darlan spun 180 degrees in her swivel chair. 'Where are Charles and Renard?' she asked, looking at the MAB in Tadeus' hand.

Poe approached her. 'Madame Darlan, we have some questions about the cards, and I don't just mean about what we all just experienced.'

'I know, otherwise you wouldn't be here.' She pointed to the two of clubs, the ace of hearts and the seven of clubs. 'Aren't they beautiful?'

Tadeus didn't know what to make of her behaviour. Perhaps she expected the two men to appear, or could she have pressed a secret alarm button under the table? The cavalry could already be on their way. 'They are, madame. We–'

'And what are your names?'

Poe and Tadeus exchanged glances, trying to communicate with looks. 'That doesn't matter,' Poe said.

'You want to ask me things. It would be impolite of you not to introduce yourselves.' She eyed Tadeus. 'That's blood. On your hand and on your clothes. The MAB isn't yours, either. Are Renard and Charles dead?' There wasn't a trace of worry or fear in her voice or on her aged face.

This only provoked Tadeus further. 'It couldn't be helped,' he said. *What the hell was going on in this house?*

Darlan's mouth twisted into a smile. There was relief in her eyes, magnified by the lenses of her glasses. 'If you think those were my two grandsons, as you may have been told: it's not true. They were my minders. My protectors. My jailers. And they weren't good people. They got what they deserved,' she murmured, feeling liberated. 'By God they did!' She lifted the hem of her apron dress to reveal a plastic band with a transmitter sitting on her ankle. 'It's an electronic ankle monitor. It reports where I am.'

'Who's holding you captive in your own house?' Poe looked at her pitifully. 'How long have you been living like this? Should we call the pol–'

'*That* wouldn't be a good idea,' Tadeus intervened. 'Maybe later.' He had to clean up their mess first.

'I agree with you, monsieur.' Darlan stood up. 'We should discuss this and all your questions over some coffee. There might even be some cake left. Let's go into the kitchen, and then I'd like to know who I'm dealing with.'

'There . . . I should go first and tidy up. Your two minders are still lying in the corridor.' Tadeus pointed downstairs. 'It's not a pretty sight, madame, and it might spoil your appetite.' He cautiously glanced at the open door. 'Is there anyone else in the house?'

The old woman shook her head. 'We live alone,' she said and began to walk with careful, tiny steps. Poe and Tadeus followed her. 'You can start explaining now. It'll take me some time to reach the kitchen.'

Tadeus peeked at the three restored cards. They fascinated him, but he didn't feel drawn to them or responsible for them as he did for his nine of spades. He could leave the room without them calling after him or tempting him to take them with him. If anything, the sight of the three cards only made him more desperate to reclaim his nine of spades. As soon as possible. The card would tell him what it wanted the moment he held it again.

'Madame Darlan, we've found ourselves in the middle of something we barely understand,' Poe began. 'Your name came up in this whole mess, and we need your help.'

Tadeus snapped out of his thoughts. They wanted answers from her, not the other way around. 'You're right, madame, we should be more open with you. I'm Müller,' he began, 'and this is Miss Tanaka. We stumbled across the cards, and now we've run into you.' He went on to explain what had happened over the last few weeks, how many people had died, what he had found hidden inside the seven of clubs and how it had been taken from him in Bruges. 'This whole adventure has led us to Avignon,' he concluded and raised his arms slightly. 'And now we're here, madame.'

Darlan moved slowly. 'The man who detained me is the Gillot you met. Charles and Renard took charge on his behalf. He doesn't just rely on my ankle monitor and the threats against my family.' They walked downstairs together. 'Gillot has people hunting down the cards everywhere. Like the blond man you saw in the basilica. They're all searching, tracking and doing everything they can to find them.'

'Do you know how many card hunters Gillot has working for him?' Tadeus intervened.

'No. His people only drop off the cards and I restore them.' After another few metres, they walked past the two bodies.

Darlan didn't flinch at the sight. 'I've seen worse, especially when I could still see well from a distance. Put the bodies into an empty barrel and take them to the barn for now,' she told Tadeus. 'We can get rid of them as soon as it's dark.' She linked arms with Poe and walked with her into the kitchen.

In the scarlet-stained corridor, Tadeus wondered when and where the old woman might have seen worse that the sight hadn't upset her. *Ah, of course! During the Second World War.*

He looked in the barn for an old wine barrel and wheeled it into the corridor using a sack barrow. Before loading the dead men into the barrel, he removed their wallets and phones. It wasn't the easiest task moving Renard and Charles into the container. He rolled the barrel back into the barn with the barrow and covered it with a lid. When Tadeus walked into the kitchen, coffee and cake were on the table, as if the dead in the corridor were nothing but forgotten dirt.

'As soon as I restored a card, Renard called Gillot and it would be picked up by a messenger,' Darlan explained upon his arrival. 'Though they thought I didn't know that Gillot was behind it, they still tried to keep it secret. I may be old, but I'm not deaf.'

The blood on the tiles in the corridor still needed to be cleaned. Poe and Darlan's shoes were resting on a rag so that they didn't spread the fresh red into the kitchen.

Tadeus also removed his expensive, custom-made shoes and placed them next to the women's smaller pairs.

'And it was these restored cards that were stolen from his house in Bruges,' he added. 'Intentionally and on order. That was what we heard the burglars say.'

Poe had taken off her hat and put it on the table next to her camera. She looked pale and more shaken by the events than Darlan. He assumed that she'd seen dead people before in hospitals and refugee camps, but the circumstances they were faced with now made all the difference.

'So there has to be someone who wants the cards as badly as Gillot,' Darlan inferred.

'Do you have any idea who that might be?' Tadeus asked. He washed his hands thoroughly, dried them on a towel and joined them at the table. He couldn't quite believe how they'd arrived at this point, especially since it felt so natural to speak about the cards and the events for which there was no rational explanation. Not to mention the two corpses; he wouldn't be able to get the red stains out of his clothes.

'No. Renard and Charles never talked about that.' Darlan took a big sip of her coffee. 'This isn't over yet for me, though.' She pointed to her ankle again. 'Gillot isn't dead. He'll soon send me new cards that I'll need to restore. New cards and new jailers. And when he finds out that he's been robbed of his treasures in Bruges, he won't waste any time in hunting down the thieves.'

'No, madame. Your martyrdom is over. Gillot is lying in a coma,' Poe chimed in. 'As soon as we leave you can go to the police.'

'That's what the media say, and that suits him perfectly. But Gillot is already giving orders over the phone again. I was there when it happened.' Darlan set her cup down. 'I still have to do what he says, or . . .' She struggled to keep calm. 'If I don't restore the cards or go to the police, Gillot will do worse than kill my family. That's what he told me when all this madness first started.'

'He threatened me and my family too,' Tadeus said. *My nine of spades is out there somewhere. In the hands of a stranger.* He could hardly stand the suspense any longer. He certainly felt sorry for Odette Darlan, but he was desperate to finally find out more about the deck of cards. It was a real shame that she didn't know who had sent the burglars. His nine of spades was lost for the time being, and that filled him with worry. 'We'll find a solution, Madame Darlan.'

'We?' She looked up in surprise. 'You want to help me?'

He nodded reassuringly. 'If anything, Gillot is a danger to us all. As for these cards,' he began, 'we discovered that they were made in Leipzig. One source said that they were made by an engraver in the late 18th century, but that doesn't explain why . . . they . . .' Tadeus paused, unsure how to explain it.

'Are you talking about the effect they have on you, monsieur?'

'From what I understand, the cards were created under certain conditions that gave them power,' Poe interjected. 'A dark energy that has a negative influence on people. A curse. I'm sure you felt it in the study earlier, too?'

'A curse,' Darlan repeated quietly, looking down at her cup. 'Of course I've felt it. This deck has unspeakably powerful, mysterious powers. Gillot sent me the cards and thought that I would only focus on restoring them, but how could I? With such beautiful pieces? And so I started to do some research, and I discovered the truth about the deck and its creator.' She lifted her gaze, her eyes twinkling. 'Thanks to my reputation as a restorer, I was able to gain access to historical works for my research. I read about the effects, the tragedies and disasters that could be traced back to the cards, about the voices and the singing that some claim to hear. Then Gillot restrained me, put this shackle on my ankle and brought in the guards. He said it was for my own protection.'

'What did he mean by that?' Tadeus hoped that neither Poe nor Darlan could tell that he was one of the few, that he belonged to the chosen ones who the card sang for. Just the thought of it made him miss his nine of spades even more.

'Now that I think about it, maybe he had other reasons for attaching the monitor,' Darlan said contemplatively, drinking her coffee. 'After what happened in Bruges, maybe he knew that there was a second collector, a competitor, and he was worried that they would poach me.'

'Where did the deck come from?' Poe asked, pouring herself a glass of water. Her blue eyes sparkled with curiosity. She'd temporarily forgotten about the bodies. 'And why is it so evil?'

'There are lots of different legends about the creator and the cards' origin. I can't say which of them is true,' Darlan began to explain. 'The engraver who made them was a simple man from Altenburg called Bastian Kirchner. He was initially a painter of holy icons and a card-maker. He came to Leipzig in search for work and was hired by the Breitkopf publishing family, who later established the Leipzig card-making factory. Kirchner taught himself copper plate engraving and etching, and he soon became one of the best.' She asked Poe for a glass of water and pushed her heavy glasses further up the bridge of her nose. 'Legend has it that Kirchner fell out with Breitkopf after he refused to pay him for designing the deck. So Kirchner put a curse on the cards.' Her voice didn't falter once when she spoke, which proved how well she knew the legends. 'Another legend claims that Kirchner had been a satanist who allied with dark forces to bring suffering upon the world.' She smiled. 'And then there's the version that he was a very devout man who deliberately put a curse on the pack to teach people that no good could come of playing cards. But I'll spare you the other ten – they're irrelevant.'

'That could all be true,' Poe said thoughtfully and pulled out a piece of paper and a pen to make notes.

'But *who* separated the deck?' Tadeus found it strange that the cards were all scattered around the world.

Darlan rubbed her wrinkled forehead. 'There are legends about that too, but they're not very helpful for tracking down the cards. Some people believe that the deck separated itself and the cards spread around the world to extend their dark influence.'

'I knew something was wrong with one of the cards as soon as I saw it. That it was deceitful, wicked, and that it wants to destroy people,' Poe said, scribbling hastily. 'The nightmares that I've been having: they're supposed to scare me away. As if the cards are defending themselves.'

The restorer looked surprised, even more surprised than when they had broken into her home. 'You . . . You can feel it?'

'Yes. And I don't just mean that . . . that signal that the cards sent out in your study. I come from a long line of shaman ancestors, Madame Darlan. I can feel when the cards are near.'

'I've never read anything about that before. It must be to do with your background. Tanaka . . . Are you from Japan?' Darlan asked. Poe hesitated for a moment before nodding. She had almost blown her cover.

Tadeus paused to think. 'Is this why Gillot collects them? Because he can feel their power?' The fact that the man stored them in a house in Bruges and didn't always carry them with him suggested otherwise.

Darlan shook her head. 'I don't think so. He's only concerned about the cards being special pieces and hunting them down. He's already paid me enormous sums of money to restore them and parted with even more to find the missing cards scattered around the world. He's a passionate collector, but he doesn't have any esoteric or spiritual motivations. He lacks the intuition for that.'

'That's good. But if someone knew that Gillot was hiding the cards in Bruges, then they might know where he finds them in the first place, Madame Darlan.' Poe looked out of the window and saw some people walking by, laughing loudly.

The restorer sighed. 'Knowing Gillot, he's already sent the

cards my way. He would have arrived at the same conclusion as you, Mr Müller.'

Then the cards will be here soon. Suddenly, Tadeus was struck by an idea born more out of desperation than reason. He was running out of options. Gillot was alive and they still had no proof of his involvement in the murders in Baden-Baden. The Walloon could also have kidnapped Michiko or Georg to blackmail him and demand the nine of spades from him again. How was he supposed to explain to Gillot that it had been taken from him during the burglary in Bruges? *We need some leverage against him.* 'Madame, since you'll know better than any of us: how many cards did Gillot have before he was robbed in Bruges? How many was he missing from a complete deck?'

'Why do you ask?'

'I said we could help free you and protect your loved ones from Gillot. He's no less of a threat to Miss Tanaka's and my family.' Tadeus glanced at Poe, who shot him a puzzled look. 'Gillot has been sending his people to look for the cards, but what if we' – he pointed to himself and the doctor – 'got there first, found the cards and used them to blackmail Gillot into leaving us all alone?'

Darlan's hand around the water glass shook gently. 'That . . . That could work!'

Poe looked at Tadeus, stunned. 'That's not a bad idea,' she said, clearly not having expected him to be so committed to the search. 'But it's not the best idea, either. There's a lot that could go wrong.'

'Until we come up with a better plan, it's a start. We can't go to the police. Currently Gillot still has a clear advantage. And who knows what else we'll discover along the way? What if we find a clue that leads us to the thieves from Bruges?' Tadeus continued. He understood their concern, but sitting around and doing nothing was not an option. 'But this plan will only work, madame, if you know how many cards there are left to find and where to look.' Tadeus hoped that the restorer had done her research. His divining rod wouldn't be able to do it alone; Poe either had to get very close to the cards to feel them or get stronger mudang powers.

'I know,' Darlan said in a firm voice. 'Renard and Charles underestimated me. Sometimes I went through their phones when they weren't looking. There are still four more cards left scattered around the world.' She took a sip of water. 'One is near Manaus, another one in Benin. The queen of hearts is in Arras, and the ace of diamonds is in a museum in Altenburg. That was what the latest messages said, anyway.' She stood up. 'I'll make some notes for you. Oh, and we don't need to worry about the card in Manaus. One of Gillot's hunters is already on the case and will bring it to me when he finds it.' Her gaze fell on Tadeus. 'I'll think of something to stall him, but you have to find and secure the other three cards by then.'

'You should call Gillot later and say that the three cards we saw lying on your desk upstairs were stolen during a break-in, and that Renard and Charles sacrificed themselves for them,' Tadeus said with a wicked smile on his face.

'Of course. I'll hide them right away. My new minders can take care of disposing of the two bodies. You two got your hands dirty enough as it is,' Darlan said and left the kitchen.

Poe fixed her gaze on him, watching him over the rim of her coffee mug as she drank. She didn't ask him any questions.

Tadeus smiled at her. He tried his best to hide his true intentions and hoped she couldn't read his thoughts or feelings.

He first had to get hold of the four cards in exchange for his nine of spades by tracking down the mastermind behind the thieves who had raided Gillot's house. Whoever had been responsible for the whole operation now had Tadeus' card. At the same time, he either needed to secure evidence against Gillot to prosecute him for the murders or frame him.

This would be a challenge. He would have to outwit Poe, ensure Henry Gillot was convicted, protect Odette Darlan and find the stranger responsible for the robbery.

One step at a time. Tadeus beamed at the doctor and poured himself some more coffee. This was just like a complex game of poker. 'I'm glad you're on board,' he told her.

'I'm in because I want to destroy this deck,' Poe said and set down her cup on the saucer. She lifted her eyes to look at Darlan, who had returned with a folder.

'Forgive me for taking so long. I was looking for what information I had about the cards. This is some reading for the road.' The restorer dropped the bound documents on the table.

'Tell me, madame.' Poe turned to her. 'Do you know anything about how to destroy these cursed cards?'

'How to destroy them? Oh là là! There have to be at least as many legends about that,' she said. 'People have died trying.' Her eyes flitted between them. 'That's what you want to do?'

'Yes,' Tadeus said quickly. 'As soon as our families are safe and Gillot is rotting in prison. How we get there doesn't matter.'

'Exactly,' Poe agreed and threw him a grateful look. His bluff had worked.

'Good, then leave that to me.' Darlan opened the folder, which mostly contained photocopied and scanned pages from various books, as well as a few original documents. 'I can put the ripped-out pages back together again,' she said, affectionately running her hand over the paper. 'It was too much of a nuisance for me to lug encyclopaedias around the house every time I wanted to look something up.'

Poe switched chairs and sat next to Tadeus so that they could read and look through the files together. 'How could you be so calm when you found us standing in your room?' she asked.

'Most of the legends say that the cards attract people. Certain kinds of people.' Darlan laid her spindly fingers over Poe's hand as if they were having a contest to see whose hands had less flesh on them. 'You said you have shaman blood, and who knows what ancestors Monsieur Müller has? Maybe there's a witch or a priest in his family tree somewhere? Someone who can sense things that most people can't hear, see or feel.'

'Yes, who knows?' Tadeus nodded. He wouldn't let himself be tempted into revealing the chants that he had heard or that his nine of spades had sung for him. He had already said too much. He was strong. The card had chosen him as its owner, protector and companion.

'So you often have intruders?' Poe asked, curious.

'Yes. My guards have had to dispose of a few visitors before.'

'Did the van in the barn belong to a visitor?' Tadeus pictured the child seats he'd seen.

'No. My so-called grandchildren randomly bought it without telling me.' Darlan drew her fingers back and furrowed her brows. 'You can have the car if you want. And my records on the cards. I've organised the file so that the information about the missing ones is at the top. Don't be fooled by the cards' exteriors, though. Some of them are hidden inside others by whoever and for whatever reason.'

'We know,' Poe said, already skimming the first page. 'I can sense the presence of the special ones.'

I hope so. We can't let what happened in Bruges happen again. Tadeus was pleased with himself. If this was a round of poker, he had the best hand. Just a little more passing, bidding, then playing his trumps, and the nine of spades would be his again.

'So, where do we start?' Tadeus asked.

Poe pointed to the notes on the queen of hearts.

* * *

Arras, Pas-de-Calais,
Hauts-de-France,
France

'First Baden-Baden, then you vanished from the face of the Earth, then you wanted to fly from Rome to Brussels, and now you're in Arras? I don't even know where that is! What are you doing there?'

'It's in France, Dad.' Hyun could hear from her stepfather's voice on the phone that his patience for her stonewalling had run out. There was no way she could tell him and her mother the truth, even if she'd considered it for a moment. Her grandmother, on the other hand, she would have confessed everything to. *I desperately need her advice.* 'I'm taking some time off.'

'In case you've forgotten, your work at the hospital is waiting for you. As a doctor,' he said, concerned, the poor reception breaking up his voice. 'I know that you're really torn up after Enrico's horrible death, but you have to remember that *your* life goes on. You're risking your own career right now!' He breathed. 'I can speak to the hospital board if you want me to.'

'No, you don't need to. I've already emailed the clinic to ask them to put me on unpaid leave until I recover. I won't need more than a few weeks.' Hyun was touched by how much he cared, but she was thirty years old and perfectly capable of handling things alone. She looked at the rough stone walls that surrounded them. There was a tiny bit of mobile reception where she was standing at the end of the shaft. Another metre and she could lose signal, which was why she'd had to run back and take the phone call here. 'I feel better already, really.'

He sighed. 'Don't leave me and your mother in the dark about where you're going to hide next. We're very worried about you. Please call us and keep us updated.'

Hyun felt her throat tighten. She couldn't afford to break

down, not now. She had to stay strong. 'I'm okay, you really don't have to worry. I just need to . . . find myself again. The travelling will do me some good.'

'You're a doctor. I don't need to tell you that there are people you can see to help you deal with grief. And medication,' he couldn't resist advising her. 'In case the travelling and finding yourself doesn't help.'

She didn't blame him for interfering. 'I'll find my own way. And tell Mum that I love you both very much. Talk soon, Dad.' She hung up and turned to the group, who had already moved away from the lift.

Just like the other visitors, Hyun was wearing an old British infantry helmet to protect her from small falling stones in case of any careless movements underground.

She quickly caught up with the tourists. 'Sorry, I had to take that,' she explained.

'I'm glad to see that we're all together again,' said their guide, Antoine, who was showing the relatively small group of seventeen people around the underground complex. Antoine beckoned Hyun and pointed to a small room that the workers had carved out of the limestone. He had red hair and wore an old, grey, true-to-style Royal Army uniform, and carried the equipment of one of His Majesty's infantry officers from the start of the 20th century, including a holster with an original Webley revolver. He had introduced himself as a history student who earned a little extra working as a tour guide around the underworld. 'Alors, this is where the officers lived. You can see the soldiers' bunk-beds at the back. There were always three beds per bunk.'

'Well?' Boch asked Hyun quietly.

'I managed to calm them down,' Hyun mumbled laconically. She didn't feel like talking. You didn't have to be a mudang to feel that the place had a certain energy about it. In the amber light of the likely century-old lamps, it unraveled before them like a sinister labyrinth. She couldn't stop shivering, despite her thick clothes and short leather jacket.

The group walked through the small publicly accessible area of the Wellington Quarry, which the British Army had dug out during the First World War as an assembly point for soldiers. It was located beneath the small town of Arras, eighty per cent of which had been destroyed by bombs and which by the end of the war had turned into a sort of ghost town. Only a fraction of Arras' citizens had survived as over 24,000 Commonwealth soldiers crowded into the tunnel system to lead a diversionary attack against the Germans.

They had taken the modern lift twenty metres below ground level and could now look at around 350 metres of the over twenty-kilometre long, convoluted complex. The British Army had transformed an old medieval quarry into the largest British underground tunnel system on the island to secretly dig their way to the German lines and launch a surprise attack.

The reason Hyun and Boch had travelled to Arras was Thomas Adams, a 21-year-old hotelier's son from Bath who had volunteered to fight in 1915 and had been sent to 'Bone Mill' Verdun. From there he'd been transferred to Arras and, together with a small army, had waited underground to pounce on the Germans. He'd mentioned in his letters to his parents that a certain 'queen of his heart' travelled with him.

But there was no mention of Adams in any records after he'd arrived in Arras, and so it was assumed that he'd died in the attack. Madame Darlan, however, had found some evidence of a tunnel collapse that had happened before the attack and left several dead. Now Hyun and Boch hoped to find the remains of Thomas Adams and his queen of hearts.

Adams and the queen of hearts – united in death. Hyun wasn't sure if it had been the powerful burst of energy from the three cards in Madame Darlan's study that had awakened her shamanistic powers, but she had felt different ever since. More perceptive. As if her mind and senses were prepared to fight against the cards' influence. The feeling that had overwhelmed her for a few seconds in the study had been one of disgust and malice, just like in her nightmares. The cards were trying to scare Hyun away, which only made her more sure of her goal and her view.

'There are records confirming that champagne and other alcoholic beverages were drunk by the troops who lived and waited here,' Antoine explained, guiding them towards the lodgings. 'But who can blame the young men for partying away the time?' He then pressed a small button on the control unit he was wearing.

Suddenly, English voices could be heard from the loudspeakers, the sound of laughter and lively conversation bouncing off the walls. The voices were accompanied by the clinking of glasses and the shuffling of cards. The acoustics in this part of the tunnel created an eerie echo.

'Hopefully that gives you an idea of what it might have sounded like,' Antoine said. He pointed to a wall and illuminated it with an old-fashioned torch, revealing a charcoal painting of a young woman. 'Some men drew portraits of their wives and girlfriends on the walls – sometimes well, and sometimes badly.' He gestured in front of him. 'This way.'

The group followed his lead, Boch and Hyun keeping to the back of the crowd. Nobody spoke. The atmosphere inside the complex was rather bleak. Hyun could feel the old energies of the soldiers who had once lived here, how they had projected their thoughts, fears and joys into the stone walls.

She tried to tune in to her senses, probing and searching to see if she felt anything that suggested the presence of the queen of hearts. *Nothing*. That didn't surprise her. They were far from the parts of the complex that were closest to the former front line.

There were ashtrays, small figurines of men, animals and various car models made from bullet casings on the tables in the recreated quarters: a distraction from life underground and the madness that had raged above them.

'The hospital had the capacity to care for seven hundred wounded. As strange as it sounds,' Antoine said as he walked, 'there was hardly a safer front-line location during the First World War than the Arras tunnel complex. To help soldiers find their way around the labyrinth, the corridors were labelled and named after New Zealand and British hometowns. Wellington was the name of the main tunnel.'

Hyun walked past the old pipelines and cables and saw the word *latrine* inscribed on one of the passage walls. She kept coming across graffiti, reliefs carved out of rock, as well as obscene insults and filth.

'Any progress with the queen of hearts?' Boch asked, whispering. He was wearing thick trousers and a jumper to beat the cold of the tunnels. He had to stretch ever so slightly to get closer to her ear. 'Are your senses telling you anything?'

'We're not in the right place.' Hyun brushed a strand of hair from her eyes and glanced at the time on her phone. The tour was almost over. They had studied and walked past ten illustrated sequences and light shows on the walls that had told them more about the tunnels. 'We need to stop and look around.'

'That won't be easy.' Boch looked at Antoine, who continually checked on the group. 'As soon he notices we're gone, they'll send a search party after us. We'd only have one shot.' He gave her an urgent look. 'Only *one*. Can you do it?'

'Yes,' Hyun said, though she wasn't sure.

There was something hostile in Antoine's eyes whenever he looked in her direction.

Although she had never met him before or done anything to upset him, she felt a wave of displeasure and resentment wash over her, as if there was some deep, existing enmity between them. *If he can sense the real reason I'm here, then he has some kind of connection with the card.*

Hyun's impulse was to grab the tour guide and question him. But would Antoine talk to her and tell the truth, if he felt it was his duty to protect the card? It would be far too easy for him to lead them astray in this maze of corridors and desert them.

Then again, there was no way they would be able to search all twenty kilometres of the tunnel system so quickly, especially in the dark and with only torches to hand. How Gillot's henchmen planned on finding Thomas Adams' card in these tunnels remained a mystery to her.

'Then we should drop off soon,' Boch said. He clearly trusted her to run around the labyrinth like a bloodhound and find her target within minutes. 'Tell me when you're ready.'

Hyun refused to let her gnawing anxiety get the better of her. She waited until the tour guide had disappeared into a passage and the group's helmets shielded her from view.

'Now.' She ducked and approached an iron door with the inscription *Staff Only* on it. 'Through here,' she said as confidently as she could and slipped inside. She had seen Antoine come out of here before the start of the tour, and he hadn't locked the door. Her hope was that the door wasn't just a changing room and that it would lead them further into the tunnels.

They darted into an anteroom, where several battery-powered lamps stood on charging stations. Large, general maps of the tunnel system hung on the walls with handwritten notes indicating finds, flooding and danger zones. There were breadcrumbs on the table and left-over ring marks from coffee mugs or Thermos flasks. Boch and Hyun had found an office from which Second World War archaeologists had set off to explore the tunnels.

'Ideal. That couldn't have gone any better,' Boch said. He tore off a map, hung several lamps around his neck and opened the door opposite. He then flicked the light on and went ahead. 'Just say where.'

The cone of light illuminating a passage was so narrow that they had to move sideways in order to push their way through. The soldiers had presumably built it as a temporary structure to hold off a potential enemy infiltration.

'Straight ahead,' Hyun said, pushing down her fear. She was a mudang. She was the granddaughter of a shaman. This was her time to shine. She silently prayed to her ancestor and asked her for spiritual guidance.

She followed Boch and pulled the door shut behind them.

The darkness that ensued was different from what they'd experienced in the main tunnel. The whitish light of their lamps reflected off the limestone, scattering uncontrollably and blinding them. There were old cables with sockets and a few light bulbs, but no light switch.

They moved quickly, their lamps like spears that stabbed through the dark. It smelled of damp, wet stone. Now and again, they felt the drip of water as it landed on their helmets or their clothes.

Hyun instructed him to keep walking straight ahead. She aimed for the front line without sensing the presence of the queen of hearts.

Boch, on the other hand, seemed to believe that she had picked up the scent. Not once did he question her orders.

The soles of their shoes scraped against the stone. They walked through puddles and rubble and sometimes had to squeeze through narrow cavities. Other areas, however, were as tall as cathedrals, and they slowed down in amazement to marvel at them.

Now and again they discovered rusty tin cans, corroded scraps of weapons, splintered helmets and the remains of equipment and reserves, as well as medical supplies such as syringes and broken glass vials. The remains spookily appeared under the glow of their lights and disappeared again immediately as they walked past. The Second World War archaeologists had left them lying around; they had no use for artefacts they already had hundreds of.

Hyun desperately felt her way around the corridors, falling back on what little she had learned from her grandmother. They now approached the front line. *How can I—*

'I'm coming to get you!' a voice suddenly echoed loudly through the hollow passage. 'I know you're here. And that's exactly where you'll stay!' The threat was followed by something metallic, ominous and dangerous grinding against stone: a blade. 'You can't hide!'

'Antoine's realised we're missing,' Boch said and removed the semi-automatic MAB pistol from his belt. 'And why we're in Arras.'

He had taken the weapon with him against Hyun's will, but now she was relieved to see him readying it. Antoine was clearly confident enough to deliberately draw attention to himself. He wanted to frighten them. *And it was working.*

'Keep going,' she choked out and wiped the sweat from her forehead. The tunnels didn't feel so cool any more.

She glanced at her phone: they'd been wandering around and searching the labyrinth for over two hours. According to the map, they were close to the exit that the soldiers had blown up in 1917 to storm the Germans and launch a diversionary attack.

Then, as if out of thin air, Hyun was struck by a wave of hatred.

The feeling was so powerful that the hairs on her arms stood up. This was far worse than what she'd experienced in Madame Darlan's study. Some invisible, evil force loathed her with such a vengeance that her nightmares seemed harmless in comparison. And though it wanted to drive her away and paralyse her with fear, she had finally found the trail she needed to follow, if only she could get a hold of herself and dare. It felt like walking towards a sharp, naked blade aimed directly at her heart. Nobody did such a thing voluntarily.

It's coming from . . . Hyun turned to the right and raised the lamp with her arm, trembling.

The quivering beam of light hit a board with a welded note that said the tunnel had been fully reconstructed and examined over ten years ago. Several official stamps were emblazoned on it. That made it uninteresting for any potential world war archaeologists.

'Behind here,' Hyun whispered and braced her feet against the limestone, preparing to face the wave of hatred. 'Do you not feel that, Boch?'

'No, I can't feel anything,' Boch admitted. He put away his weapon, pulled out the telescopic baton from his coat and used it as a lever to loosen the board, which came off easily at the side. The thick nails and screws were just for show. Someone had created a barrier that could be opened and closed. 'What can you feel?'

'The worst. The card wants us dead.'

'It'll get Antoine to try to kill us.' Boch shone his lamp into the darkness.

A path appeared out of the gloom with a sharp turning to the right after a few metres. There was no way of telling what was beyond it. The walls were carved the same as all the others, with the limestone flat at the bottom and sharp close to the top. There were several traces of soot from lamps and explosions. The smell that wafted towards them from the passage was stale and thick with . . . spices.

'Incense,' Hyun said, surprised.

Boch looked at the map. 'This passage isn't marked on the map.' He folded it up and stuffed it into his trouser pocket.

'Let's have a look,' Hyun said and took a determined step towards the path.

The hatred instantly grew more powerful and pained her, squeezing her heart together. Fear crept into the corners of her mind. The card didn't want her to go any further.

Groaning, Hyun took a big step back.

'What's wrong?' Boch shone his lamp at the corridor behind them to check if Antoine had followed them, but the tour guide was nowhere to be seen; only his deranged laughter and howls echoed in the darkness. 'Are you all right?'

'It's the queen of hearts,' she gasped, and patted her upper body to check for knife wounds. 'She's trying to fight me. This . . . This is worse than in my nightmares. It feels different.'

'I can't go down the passage without you.' Boch frowned. 'The card could be buried somewhere. You have to come with me.'

'But I don't want to . . .' Hyun struggled to fight off the oncoming nausea. Her muscles trembled as if she had a severe case of hypothermia, her heart pounded frantically and her head throbbed. This was worse than when she had had to spend two days in hospital as a result of a nasty case of food poisoning in Beijing. 'I . . . I can't do this.'

'Remember the tricks your grandmother taught you. We need the card, Miss Poe, and I won't leave you alone in this corridor. Antoine will find you and knock you out.' Boch seized her by the arm and pulled her into the side passage. 'Come on.'

Hyun reluctantly followed him as the wave of hatred continued to swell and made her choke. Her legs gave way and buckled, but Boch caught her, lamps slamming into her ribs and against her helmet.

'I can't,' she groaned. 'The card . . . It's . . . it's suffocating me!'

'We have to keep going! I'm sorry to put you through this, but I have to ask: where now?' Boch prompted her relentlessly.

He quickly lifted her into his arms and carried her around the corner, moving her further into the hatred step by step.

Hyun's vision blurred and she had just begun to lose consciousness when it dawned on her: her mind was shifting to another state. A kind of mudang protection trance. Something like that.

The hatred became more pervasive and evolved into a crimson aura that filled the corridor like a transparent layer of lava through which Boch carried her like a dependable, indestructible robot.

She turned around to get a closer look at the phenomenon.

The source of this negative feeling, which she wanted to defeat and destroy, was hidden beneath some stones that lay at the end of the passage as if by chance, but had in fact been purposefully arranged. *By Antoine.*

'There.' Hyun shone a lamp at the pile. 'Under there.'

'I'm on it.' Boch approached the spot she'd pointed to, gently set her down and leaned her against the wall. He pressed the MAB pistol into her hand and placed two of the lamps next to her, aiming the beams of light at the turning. 'I'll take a look. If Antoine comes around the corner, shoot.'

Hyun could no longer think. Her mind was caught in a rip current of brutal disgust, threats and death wishes, which she fought against with all her might, trying not to sink and drown. Her breathing was shallow and the pistol felt like it weighed ten tonnes. She couldn't hold it.

Boch dragged the stones aside one by one.

A small altar built from bones and five human skulls revealed itself beneath the pile. There was an incense bowl in front of the altar; the remains of resin lumps gave off an aromatic scent. The queen of hearts lay on top of the skeleton heads, which had been arranged in a circle. The card screamed in Hyun's mind – it was furious, shrieking for its life and crying out to Antoine for help.

'Wherever he got these skulls from for the card, they aren't old,' Boch observed as he picked up the card. He rummaged around the rubble with his foot. 'Ah. I've found the rest of the victims. There are some fresh bodies over here!'

Hyun couldn't hold on any longer. She vomited onto the weapon, choking, and slumped to one side. The entire tunnel was filled with the transparent lava now. It swept towards her and engulfed her.

'Shit,' Boch cursed and rushed over to her. He had hidden the card in the zip-up breast pocket of his jumper. Hyun felt scorching hatred burning her like the sun. 'Are you all right?'

She could barely speak, and tapped his chest instead. 'The card . . . it wants to . . . kill me.'

'It's the narrow cave. It's making you feel claustrophobic.' He glanced reproachfully at the semi-automatic, which was covered in her vomit. 'Take a deep breath. You're a doctor, you know—'

'I found you!' Antoine shouted close by. You could hear his footsteps coming towards them in the small passage leading to the shrine. 'Your skulls will be the next ones I sacrifice! *Your* skulls!'

'Let's hope the gun still works,' Boch said and picked up the dirty MAB.

Antoine materialised from the shadows, carrying a First World War-era carabine. He raised the weapon and fired. The muzzle flash illuminated the bayonet attached to the weapon and flickered like a lightning bolt under the barrel.

Boch fired at the same time, the ear-splitting banging and cracking erupting in the narrow tunnel.

Hyun clearly saw that Antoine had suffered several hits from Boch's MAB in the double glare of the two lamps, but the guide continued to advance towards them, undeterred. Bullet holes appeared in Antoine's historic uniform as his blood splattered over the tunnel wall behind him and covered it in flecks and droplets like a Jackson Pollock. Boch tirelessly paused to reload again, the empty bullet shells whistling past the blinking lamps. The projectiles flew around them. A lamp smashed and went out.

'He won't fall!' Boch shouted and positioned himself in front of Hyun to protect her. His magazine was empty.

'Stay where you are!' Antoine cried. He was also out of bullets. The guide dropped his carabine, drew a Webley revolver from its holder and cocked it with both hands. 'You belong to the queen of hearts! My queen of hearts!'

Boch picked up a stone the size of a child's head and hurled it at the man.

Hyun watched the boulder fly and strike Antoine in the chest. The blow threw him against the wall, but he didn't collapse. The Webley revolver spewed out its first bullet at them.

The last lamp shattered, clinking. Everything went pitch black.

Every time Antoine fired, Hyun caught a glimpse of something. It was like watching a strobe light flash in slow motion or lightning strike in the dead of the night: elaborate, crystal-clear, frozen images that vanished within milliseconds.

She recognised Boch as he advanced. Blood poured from his shoulder. Suddenly he was right in front of the Frenchman; he dived under the barrel of the revolver and reached for the ground with one hand. Antoine screamed as the bayonet rammed into his stomach. Another shot and the decapitated Frenchman toppled forward, the weapon that had stabbed his neck still in Boch's hands. The long blade scraped across the stone, throwing out sparks in the dark, until it broke off with a clang.

Silence. Darkness.

In the same instant, the hatred Hyun had felt vanished.

Hence, in all countries the chief occupation of society is card-playing . . . Because people have no thoughts to deal in, they deal cards, and try and win one another's money. Idiots!

But I do not wish to be unjust; so let me remark that it may certainly be said in defence of card-playing that it is a preparation for the world and for business life, because one learns thereby how to make a clever use of fortuitous but unalterable circumstances (cards, in this case), and to get as much out of them as one can; and to do this a man must learn a little dissimulation, and how to put a good face upon a bad business.

But, on the other hand, it is exactly for this reason that card-playing is so demoralizing, since the whole object of it is to employ every kind of trick and machination in order to win what belongs to another.

And a habit of this sort, learned at the card table, strikes root and pushes its way into practical life; and in the affairs of every day a man gradually comes to regard 'my play' and 'your play' in much the same light as cards, and to consider that he may use the utmost whatever advantages he possesses, so long as he does not come within the arm of the law. Examples of what I mean are of daily occurrence in mercantile life.

From *The Wisdom of Life* (1851)
by Arthur Schopenhauer (1788–1860),
translated by Thomas Bailey Saunders in 1901

XII

The Amazon,
ca. 240 kilometres west of Manaus,
Brazil

Daan Mulder had purposefully chosen to wear a baseball cap with a long brim, under which he now smoked a cigarette. The heavy rain, like a grey curtain over the Amazon, fell around him, the fumes curling up into a blue cloud beneath his cap, as if also seeking refuge from the downpour. The drops pelted against his camouflage-print cape, which protected him from the wet weather.

Daan spoke loudly in English to drown out the omnipresent pitter-patter without once removing the cigarette from his mouth; a trick he'd learned from a French wine merchant. 'Just give me one hour!' he said, waving a wad of dollars at the sergeant who was intermittently patrolling the clearing with ten other men who the small plane had left behind in the rainforest. His name badge read *Sanchez*. 'I only need to take a few photos for evidence before the rain washes it all away. It's for the plane's insurance company. If the pilot fucked up, we won't have to pay anything.'

The dark-skinned man, who was wearing a green poncho over his equipment, finally accepted the cash. 'Fine. One hour. But we never saw you here, señor.'

Daan breathed a sigh of relief. 'Yes, sir.' He grinned, then saluted the sergeant and set off.

On the off chance that he would find out something about the massacre, Daan had travelled to the crash site, which was officially a restricted area. And thanks to the heavy rain, he had had to use a boat to reach the clearing.

He knew nothing about forensics, but any rational person would realise that all the evidence must have been washed away by the persistent, fast-slowing stream created by the rain.

Daan also suspected something else about the blocked-off zone: the cargo on board the plane most likely consisted of drugs, money or smuggled goods.

He walked across the damaged area where the Noorduyn Norseman had crashed, balancing on fallen tree trunks that revealed traces of burning. There had likely been a fire following the accident. Jet fuel could have leaked from the plane and ignited, causing a brief inferno.

Bodies had been recovered; they lay in black plastic bags and would be taken back on the next supply boat. Sanchez had told him that a doctor had examined them on site and identified gunshot wounds to several victims. Therefore, the widespread suspicion was that the rescue party had come across poachers or illegal loggers, who were known to mercilessly eliminate any unwelcome witnesses.

Daan trudged through the debris. His alibi was his camera, which he raised to photograph the remains of the hydroplane. In the process he discovered some small-calibre bullet casings that no one had bothered to collect. He presumed that they were from Roux's weapon. But where was he hiding?

His body hadn't been recovered. Sanchez had shown him the passports and ID cards he had found. Roux was either lying somewhere far away from the crash site, rotting and being devoured by jungle predators, or wandering through the Amazon, or had fled to another country. With or without the playing card.

Daan had now reached the end of the small path. He snapped another photo and looked around the dense rainforest, listening to the rustling and cracking noises. The sergeant on the other side tapped his wrist, clearly gesturing that his time was coming to an end.

Daan gave him a thumbs-up and walked towards a spot where he had seen some broken branches in the undergrowth. It could be nothing, but a clue was still a clue.

Diving into the jungle unarmed admittedly wasn't one of his best ideas, but he hadn't been able to acquire a weapon in Manaus, and the military would have been suspicious if he had asked for a pistol.

After a few metres he arrived at a patch with several broken branches and empty cartridges, but he found nothing of Roux.

Gillot won't like that. And neither will Darlan. Daan had no idea how he was supposed to find the card and Roux in this environment. He looked around attentively and spotted a wet US-dollar note in a bush. Due to its green colour, he had initially thought it was just another leaf.

Daan got closer to the bush, pulled off the note and held it against the faint light. It appeared to be genuine. Brazilian soldiers definitely wouldn't throw away cash in the Amazon, so it must have come from the plane cargo.

He searched around him and found another note roughly two metres to his right. Someone had left a trail, using dollar bills instead of breadcrumbs.

Roux! He set off looking for the rest of the notes, which had-been dropped at random intervals, and came across some empty plastic film, and then a bank wrapper, the kind used to wrap bundles of notes. The money must have been shrink-wrapped. It was packaged and fresh.

Wherever they had been travelling to, the Sparks couple had

clearly taken plenty of money with them. The bundles had been found and taken after the crash. *From Roux?*

Bent branches on the ground and the path told him that someone had made their way through the jungle. The one hour that Sanchez had promised him must have been up by now, but he had no intention of turning back. He trudged through the greenery and the torrential rain, picking up notes and bank wrappers as he went.

The smell of fire fuelled by damp wood suddenly hit him.

Daan crouched down and crept forward. He followed the scent and found himself in a circular, ten-metre clearing. The surrounding trees were cleverly cut at a height and tied together with vines to create an enclosed canopy of leaves that couldn't be spotted from above.

He noticed a round hut that took up half the clearing, and a small boathouse on the left on a hidden, fast-flowing stream of the river. Camouflaged boats were resting inside, their outboard motors removed and dismantled for cleaning.

Countless newly stripped furs and skins from caimans, reptiles and spotted wild cats hung from the beams. Cleaned and oiled metal traps lay in a pile in a corner of the house and it reeked of tannery chemicals from the huge tubs and pots that stood around, which were probably used to treat the skins.

Daan didn't see or hear any people. The poachers were most likely out hunting or had withdrawn further into the jungle. For all he knew, they could have taken the money and Roux.

Some smoke billowed upwards from the hut, but a filthy blanket obscured the view into the only window. Daan had to find out whether Roux, his remains or the card were inside.

If the poachers caught him, they would skin him alive and hang him next to the other animal furs and hides.

He slipped out from his hiding spot and ran, never losing

sight of the entrance to the man-made shelter. As he crept around one of the large containers, he suddenly found himself staring at a dark-skinned man's mangled face, which was no more than a finger's length away from his own. The blood had clotted, the man's nose, cheeks and eyes were missing, his skin was torn and bite marks adorned his skull.

Daan gasped and crawled away from the corpse. The poacher had been ripped to shreds from top to bottom by a jungle cat; his intestines dangled and his lungs and heart were missing, clearly eaten. A nondescript pistol lay in the man's mutilated hand, the hammer locked into place at the back. The poacher had fired his entire magazine before his death. The weapon was worthless.

He reached the outer wall of the hut and paused, listening anxiously.

The crackling of poorly burning wood could be heard from inside. The smoke had an acrid smell, as if chemicals were burning in the flames.

He carefully poked his head around the corner and peered through the open door into the dark hut.

The smell of blood wafted towards him, most likely from the poached animals and their stripped skins. A weak fire burned in the centre. Thick smoke filled the hut and an over-turned tub lay on the coals. More hides and pelts hung from the high ceiling, as well as leghold traps, wire fishing lines and mounting chains. Judging by the shape of the cooked pieces of meat on the sideboard, the poachers hunted monkeys, too. All sorts of fangs had been hung up and organised by size and appearance.

Daan vaguely remembered reading in his in-flight magazine that illegal hunters were a huge problem in South America. They poached rare mammals, reptiles and birds – from ocelots to jag-uars and howler monkeys. He had found such an illegal camp.

The dark and the smoke inside the hut made it impossible to see the ground. If he was going to find anyone and determine whether they were still alive, he would have to go inside.

He picked up a club and crawled into the hut. The chains and traps clinked quietly above him and the pieces of wire rubbed against each other as if in greeting.

It took a moment for his eyes to adjust to the lack of light, but as soon as they did he was gripped with terror.

Daan stared at the bloodbath. The five indigenous corpses, two dark-skinned women and three men, were barely identifiable as human. The victims' bodies had also been brutally mauled by wild animals. Their faces had been bitten, their heads torn off or their throats ripped out. The hut's floor was covered in pools of red, which now stuck to Daan's shoes.

An open gym bag soaked in blood and filled to the brim with dollar notes sat against the back wall. A body was slung over it: a man had thrown himself onto the bag, as though the wildcats were more interested in eating money than people.

He then spotted a body still dressed in new camouflage clothes and with several bullet wounds, but no bite marks. They must have been part of the search team and had likely been kidnapped and dragged to the shelter along with the money.

'Holy shit,' Daan said, retching. There was another body under a disfigured carcass, and it had just raised a white, red-stained hand to signal that it was still alive. Lumpy, scarlet blood ran down the hand in thick streaks.

'Roux!' Daan cried. He dragged the human remains off the man and immediately saw that he wouldn't survive his gunshot wounds, despite him not having any bite injuries. The beasts had spared him.

Roux's face was a single expression of fear. His dilated pupils expressed no pain – only fear and delirium. 'Run!' he whispered, his voice laced with pain. 'Run before they come back.'

'Darlan sent me,' Daan said, trying to understand what had happened. Maybe the poachers had lured a particularly aggressive jungle cat, or released one by mistake. 'I'll take you to the assembly point. The soldiers have a doctor there.'

'Run!' the fatally wounded man repeated. 'Before . . . leave. And avoid . . . avoid . . .' He coughed up blood and shuddered, a seizure taking hold of him. His time was running out.

Daan saw the playing card in the dying man's other hand – a ten of denari. It was covered in Roux's blood, which had absorbed into and soaked through the paper. Madame Darlan would have a lot of work to do. 'I promised your friend in Avignon that I'd bring you and the card back.' He slipped an arm underneath Roux's neck to take the ten of denari from his hand. He pocketed it. 'She calls you her *little Fennec*.'

'Run,' the man whimpered, panting. His muscles spasmed. 'Don't . . . Not . . . not the card. They . . . they want . . .' Roux's body suddenly felt twice as heavy, his eyes rolled to the back of his head and became unfocused.

Daan laid him back down onto the muddy, bloodstained floor and checked his pulse. *Nothing.* 'Merde!' he cried out, and tried to perform CPR on the man, but the chest compressions only squeezed more blood out of the wounds. After several attempts, Daan gave up. Roux was dead.

But Daan wouldn't leave Fennec the desert fox in the jungle. He had received 30,000 euros for that promise. The soldiers could carry Roux's body and take care of relocating it.

He tucked the stained card under his raincoat and picked up the bag of cash. It weighed a tonne, both due to the weight of the money and because it was soaked with blood and rain , but there was no way he would let the millions go to waste. His cover as an insurance agent meant that he had every right to confiscate assets on behalf of his clients. He would give the understanding Sanchez a receipt and a little extra for his trouble.

Daan lifted the bag with its two hand straps onto his back like a rucksack, struggling with the hefty load; Roux himself couldn't have been much heavier to carry. He rummaged around between the carcasses for weapons and magazines in case he came across a wild cat on his way back. Thanks to his own blood-drenched stench, he was practically walking bait.

He found two Colt M1911 Government pistols and six magazines, readied the guns, got to his feet, turned around and ... turned to stone.

A panther crouched by the entrance. It must have been watching him this entire time. Its ears were pointed upwards and its yellow eyes followed his every move. The predator's black tail twitched to the right and left.

Daan held his breath. The beast had returned, enticed by the voices and noises. There was fresh prey for it to claim.

'Good kitty,' he said quietly and stole a quick glance out of the window.

He didn't think for one second that he could outrun the panther in the thicket. The panther lived here; he was just visiting.

But Daan had a semi-automatic pistol and six magazines. He could make it to the boats. Just five metres, and a few seconds to push one of the boats into the water.

The panther growled softly as he dared take a careful step towards the window. 'I might smell tasty, but you don't want to eat me,' he said softly as he moved closer to the window, slipping a leg over the frame and out of the hut. 'I'm all gristle, and I ate something funny.'

The big cat watched him, its tail swaying. It was as if it wanted to play with the man and give him a head start. For fun.

He didn't take his eyes off the panther as he moved the blanket covering the window aside and climbed out of the hut. The wild cat didn't move, only cocked its head to one side curiously. 'Stay ... Stay, good kitty.'

He stepped backward and quickly looked over his shoulder at the boathouse.

Two deadly jaguars with long teeth and sharp claws lay on the ground in front of it. One of them was gnawing on a human torso and licking the bones that protruded from the ribcage with its wide, shiny tongue. The other one was sizing up Daan.

'Merde!' the Belgian cried. How was he supposed to keep calm in a situation like this? *'Run before they come back,'* Roux had stammered. *They* – plural.

Daan raised one of the Colt pistols and fired over his head once, twice and a third time. 'Get!' he shouted. He had decided to change tactics. Noise was supposed to scare away big cats. 'Go on, beat it!' He also hoped the soldiers would hear the shots and rush to investigate.

As if to mock him, the idle jaguar yawned, exposing its finger-length fangs. Then it rose to its full height and gracefully walked towards the man, its muscles bunching as it moved.

Daan turned back and ran into the jungle the same way that he had come. He kept firing behind him to ward off the animals and attract the attention of the soldiers.

Leaves slapped his face, cobwebs brushed past him and insects fell on him, but he kept running. A click-clack next to his foot told him he'd narrowly missed the bracket of a leghold trap. He fell twice but still managed to heave himself up again despite the heavy bag on his back. He reloaded his pistol and looked around for his hunters.

He heard a snarl above him and spotted a jaguar perching on a branch. It poised itself, ready to pounce. A crunching noise to his left revealed the panther elegantly balancing on a fallen tree, stalking him. They were continuing to play with him.

He stubbornly held both Colts in his fists and fired at the jungle cats while sprinting. It felt like he had been running for an hour already. His thighs burned and he desperately needed a break, but the fear and adrenaline in his veins spurred him on.

There was a loud rustling in front of him as the first soldier appeared, holding an M16 rifle at a diagonal in front of his body. He jumped at the sight of Daan. 'What happened . . .? Is that blood? Was that you shooting?'

Daan pushed past the man without an answer. He didn't have any breath left to explain.

'Hey! Stop! What's—'

Daan hadn't run three metres when he heard a startled cry behind him and the rattling of an assault rifle. It was all over in a flash, followed by a triumphant growl.

The undergrowth rustled once again.

More soldiers appeared but Daan rushed past them too. He felt like he was running a marathon for his life. His body moved on autopilot and only limited parts of his field of vision were in focus.

He finally reached the clearing, but still couldn't bring himself to slow down, even though his lungs were on fire.

Sanchez stood in the middle of the path with a transmitter in his hand. The other men had spread out over the area, their weapons in firing position. 'Hey! Stop or I'll shoot! What the hell's happening in the jungle?' Sanchez demanded.

Daan's reason prevailed when he realised that the rifles were pointed at him. He stopped and put his hands in the air to show that he wasn't a threat. His heart thumped painfully in his chest and a burning heat overcame him, as if his body was ready to burst into flames. He gasped for breath and fought back the nausea. The cool rain hit his cap and trickled down his neck.

'You're covered in blood!' Sanchez cried, alarmed. 'Where are my men?' He lifted his large-calibre Desert Eagle pistol and aimed it at the Belgian. 'What have you done to them? What's in the bag?'

Daan saw where the soldiers had moored their powerful, military motorboats. That was how he would escape the claws of the vengeful beasts.

'Put the pistols ... Where did you get them?' Sanchez couldn't hide his surprise.

'Back there,' Daan panted. 'Over there. Poachers. Two. Rescue team. Attacked ... your men.' He lowered his hands and dropped the pistols. 'From there. Stolen and ... escaped.'

The sergeant lifted the radio to his lips again and spoke to the head office in Portuguese, which Daan couldn't follow. The wild cats didn't show up; they probably realised that they had little chance going up against assault rifles in the open.

'Get to HQ!' Sanchez ordered and took the two semi-automatic pistols from Daan. He then gave instructions to his men, who ran to the other side of the clearing to find out where the rest of the team had disappeared to.

Daan accompanied Sanchez into the camouflage tent, which was used for briefings. The exit of the tent was positioned so that they could still see the clearing. The soldiers had just vanished into the thicket.

'I was trying to photograph a piece of debris when two poachers grabbed me and dragged me into their hut,' Daan told Sanchez frantically. His heart still burned painfully. *So this is what an imminent heart attack feels like.* 'There were two bodies from the rescue team in the hut and the bag. I got away and the poachers went after me.'

'What's in the bag?' Sanchez slowly sat down onto the army stool, opened a notebook and retrieved a pen.

'It belongs to my client,' Daan said. The bag was still on his back.

'Then we should check' – Sanchez gestured promptingly with his hand – 'to make sure there's nothing illegal inside.'

Suddenly, the sound of gunshots and screams filled their

ears, echoing through the pelting rain. A soldier abruptly jumped out of the undergrowth, shouting hysterically, only to be grabbed by his leg and yanked backward.

'*Mierda!*' Sanchez cursed. He seized an M16 from an olive-green chest, locked in a magazine and stuffed a couple more under his belt. 'Grab one and come with me,' he ordered and ran towards the stream.

'I'm right behind you,' Daan lied. Instead, he picked up his own pistols and pulled the trigger three times, hitting the sergeant in the back and the head. He didn't need any witnesses knowing about the bag.

The fire in his chest immediately grew hotter.

That's not my heart . . . It's . . . it's the card! Daan pulled it out of his breast pocket. It was glowing and its lines shimmered under the paper as if there was another motif underneath the besmirched ten of denari. The card flared and the blood evaporated as its upper layer gleamed and tore in two places. It was just as Daan had suspected: a second card lay underneath. The motif revealed a jack of clubs flanked by four stylised cats.

Angry growls brought his attention back to the outside world. Two jaguars and three panthers were sprinting across the small clearing. The rain washed the blood of their victims from their fur, which glistened majestically. Drops of red dribbled from their chins and around their teeth.

They were guarding the card! Daan whirled around, ran to the mooring nearby and pushed the motorboat into the small tributary of the river. He pushed the button to start the powerful diesel engine and hit the gas.

The water foamed and swirling silt flew into the bushes as the bow swung around and propelled the Belgian down the river.

He watched the wild cats follow him in the undergrowth by the riverbank until they could no longer keep up with the motorboat and fell back. When he reached the wider arm of the Amazon, he revved up the speed and tore through the storm.

The lightning, thunder and torrential rain didn't bother him.

He wouldn't be surprised if the big cats chased him all the way to Manaus through the entire city to protect the card. They were predators and had picked up on his scent.

Daan glanced at his Colt pistols.

* * *

Rome, Italy

Henry Pierre Gillot laboriously opened his eyes and saw his sister's worried face next to him. She looked up from her book and tried to smile, but instead her face twisted into a single expression of reproach made up of hundreds of accusations.

Magdalena de Graaf sat next to his hospital bed with medical equipment piled up all around him. Tubes and cables poked out from his body, a white blanket concealing where exactly they ran from.

A cacophony of beeps and buzzes surrounded him, but Gillot found the electronic concert soothing. He was alive. And that meant he could take revenge.

'Does my moustache look okay?' he croaked. His vocal cords had suffered from the tubes. 'I'd hate it if it wasn't. I'm not even wearing proper clothes or glasses.' The Walloon attempted to laugh but was forced to cough instead.

'You could have told me that there was a safe,' his sister said. The next accusation. She was wearing a comfortable, salmon-coloured dress with a black shawl adorned with embroidery and tassels, which, paired with her topknot and oodles of jewellery, made her look like an aged gitana. 'And yes, I fixed your precious moustache.'

'I didn't want you to worry.'

'I was attacked and robbed because of the safe,' she replied in a pleasant yet reprimanding manner like her mother. 'My worries would have been justified, *n'est-ce pas*?'

'But *until now* you weren't worried. Not for a second,' he insisted with a smug smile, the twisted tips of his moustache creeping into his field of vision. 'My strategy worked.'

'What was in the safe?'

'Why?'

'The fact that you're even asking me means that it wasn't insured.' Samira, as she called herself, punished him with her hazel eyes by throwing him an irritated look. 'I promised myself to be kind and sweet to you when you woke up, Henry, but you're making me angry.'

'That's what I do best, isn't it?'

'So whatever was inside it was from your illegal excavations?'

Gillot wished he could go back to sleep. Waking up suddenly felt like more effort than it was worth. 'It doesn't matter. It's gone.' He was very fond of his sister. He took care of her and paid for everything so that, despite her struggles with polio, and her failed marriage, she could lead a good life in Bruges, the nucleus of his current empire. But some days she was a real pain in his *moustache*. 'And anyway, the thieves didn't *just* come for the safe. They *also* came . . .' Gillot paused and longingly looked at the pill dispenser. 'Is everything gone?'

'From the safe? No idea. I didn't even know that there was one, remember?' she snapped.

'Samira, please.'

She sighed, slowly leaned forward and stroked his hair. 'I'm sorry. I've been really worried and afraid for my little brother, and that makes me . . .'

'Unbearable,' he finished her sentence for her with a faint grin.

'Oh stop it!' she warned him immediately, narrowing her eyes. 'Black Sara, give me the strength to put up with this man without killing him.' She pointed to the equipment. 'Actually, that would be too easy for me to do be right now.'

Henry smiled, gratefully this time. 'How long have you been here?'

'Since I found out about the whole mess on the news.' Samira cleared her throat and picked up her handbag with her left arm. She could barely move her other arm. After some digging around, she fished out a printout. 'This is the list.'

'What list?'

'The list of things stolen from the shop.' She held it in front of Gillot so he could see. 'They've chosen very well. Turkish antiques, ancient Egyptian jewellery, two gold-plated busts . . .' She waited for him to add something.

Gillot tried to make an excuse. 'The safe only had money inside.'

Samira ignored him. She knew he was lying. 'I've emailed the list to the insurance company. They'll send someone to take a look at our alarm system before covering the costs.'

'It's irreplaceable,' he said weakly and closed his eyes. The thieves wouldn't know how valuable the cards were and would either throw them away or sell them for pennies. He would notify his contacts to keep their eyes open and their ears to the ground. 'Did the cameras get any footage of the robbers?'

'They wore masks in the shop and there were no cameras in the billiard room,' she told him. 'The alarm went off as it should have and the police arrived, but it was too late. They said they were stuck in a traffic jam.' Samira pulled a face. 'A traffic jam! *Mon dieu*! They knew that we have hundreds of thousands worth of goods in the house!'

'A traffic jam is a traffic jam – there's nothing they could have done.'

'Maybe they got paid off to get stuck in traffic?'

Gillot groaned loudly. 'I doubt it.'

His sister always assumed the worst, which he attributed to her lack of satisfaction in life. Some people found a way to live with their illnesses, but Samira grew more bitter every year. She spent her days reading and immersed herself in the magical world of Sara the Black, hoping for a miracle. Even after ten pilgrimages, her condition hadn't improved, but she still didn't give up. Naturally, the saint wasn't to blame.

'Who knew about the safe?' she asked.

The same thought had already crossed Gillot's mind, and he only had one answer to the question: 'The workers who installed it. And the company I paid to do it.'

Samira looked at him with a satisfied expression on her face not unlike her brother's. 'Give me their address.'

'For what?'

'I'll find out who paid them off or coaxed the information out of them.'

Gillot didn't want her interfering in his affairs. 'I'll sort it.'

'You can barely breathe right now,' she protested. 'How are you going to sort anything?'

He gestured to his phone. 'I have my contacts, Samira.'

'Who are useless.' She pointedly looked at his bandages and the equipment. 'Are you interested in who's behind this or not?'

His wounds throbbed painfully. 'You ask funny questions.'

'And you do funny things, Henry.' Samira pointed to the door, the list of stolen goods flapping in her hand. 'Two police officers are waiting outside. I'm going to tell them that you're not fit for questioning yet. The doctors will confirm it. There's also a group of journalists by the hospital entrance who are covering the story and your little drive through the basilica.' She laid her hand on his. The infusion needle gently stabbed his skin; her subtle way of punishing him. 'Through the basilica, Henry! What on earth were you thinking?'

Gillot opened his mouth to speak.

'And don't give me any nonsense about your foot slipping on the gas!' She stopped him before he could lie again. 'Even the dumbest police officer wouldn't believe that. You got out of the car in the hail of bullets, took down the painting and loaded it into the back.'

'I wanted to save the Subleyras,' he explained gently.

'It's only a painting! That's what you risked people's lives, vandalised the basilica and almost got yourself killed for?'

'Yes, the painting!' Gillot hated that his mind was working so slowly under the influence of the drugs. This must be what it felt like to be stupid. 'Where is it?'

'It's safe, as is your Bentley. But you ruined it.'

Gillot thought very hard. He admittedly hadn't exactly been gentle with the Subleyras painting when he had thrown it into the back of the car. It had been a knee-jerk, certainly questionable and exaggerated reaction on his part. 'Is there a large tear? It can be repaired.'

'Who said anything about a tear?' Samira drew a hole the size of a hand in the air. 'There's a whole chunk missing. That big.'

Gillot broke out into a hot sweat and his pulse and blood pressure immediately shot up.

'Oh, so it clearly wasn't your doing!' His sister was surprised by his response, which she could read from the beeping monitors. 'But . . .'

Explaining things to Samira would mean lying again, and Gillot wanted to avoid that at all costs. She could make up her own mind about what had happened. He wouldn't comment on any of it. In the meantime, he would have to come up with a backstory for his questioning with the police, perhaps something involving a threat from the art mafia, and that they had been after the painting. He needed a narrative that matched his background and his reputation.

But it was the truth that deeply concerned him.

For decades, he had been searching for the real, one-of-a-kind Devil's Playbook – the only deck of cards worthy of its name. He had spent and invested millions on its restoration and acquisition.

Just four more cards.

Another four more cards and he would complete the deck.

But now an unknown rival, one equally hungry for the playbook, had appeared out of thin air. Gillot would have accepted the break-in at his shop as just another inconvenience, but the card had been cut out of the Subleyras painting, and that gave the theft a whole new meaning, which he didn't like in the slightest. Someone had deliberately stolen his collection. This news meant that Darlan was also in danger. He would send backup to Renard and Charles to help them better keep an eye on the restorer. If his memory served him well, she was currently working on three of his cards.

No, that was a lie. She was restoring his *only* three cards.

The readings on the monitor instantly spiked. Nobody beat Henry Pierre Gillot when he wanted something. Nobody!

Someone had declared war on him for the playbook, but he was not prepared to lose unless it was to the Devil himself. Gillot had to find out who had sent the killers and card thieves after him in Rome. It was most likely the same gang that had robbed him in Bruges, and he had no doubt that they were now on their way to Avignon.

He picked up his smartphone, positioning it so that it blocked the needle marks on his bruised, blue arm and the attached tubes from view.

'What are you doing?' Samira reached out with her left hand to snatch the phone away from him. 'You'll get yourself worked up.'

'If I don't do this, I'll get even more worked up.' Gillot pushed her hand away harder than he had intended to. 'I'm sorry.' He typed out a message to some people who had put him in touch with a few good contacts with security staff in the Middle East. The kind of security staff who operated illegally, moved surreptitiously in public, were happy to occupy the whole damn Gaza Strip and every fought-over Libyan city as long as the money was good.

And money was the least of Gillot's worries. The artefacts stolen by the fools in Bruges hadn't sold for years, and the insured sum alone totalled a few million euros, which he didn't need.

While Gillot was finishing up his email, a new message came in. Daan Mulder had some bitter news from the Amazon: Frédéric Roux was dead, killed by poachers – but Mulder had found the playing card. A photo followed as proof.

'My ten of denari with the jack of clubs!' he breathed happily, and would have loved to kiss the photo on his display.

The dependable Belgian was on his way back, but was stuck in Bogotá, where he had a stopover on his way from Manaus. He attributed the detour to the bad weather and his connection to Amsterdam.

That suited Gillot just fine. He now had four cards and was back in the race for the remaining ones from the deck. And he would win. He would make sure of it.

A sudden wave of fatigue washed over him and he put the phone down on the little table. The medication healed and weakened him in equal measure, and he only caught a glimpse of Samira catching his phone as it slipped from his grasp.

Then Henry Pierre Gillot peacefully sank back into a deep sleep.

Quand vous entrez dans un maison de jeu,
la loi commence par vous dépouiller de votre chapeau . . .
Mais, sachez-le bien, à peine avez-vous fait un pas vers
le tapis vert, déjà votre chapeau ne vous appartient pas
plus que vous ne vous appartenez a vous-même.

When you enter a gambling house, the first thing the law does is to deprive you of your hat . . . But, know this: even though you have barely taken a step towards the tables, your hat no longer belongs to you any more than you belong to yourself.

From *La peau de chagrin* (1831),
Honoré de Balzac (1799–1850)

XIII

Odette Darlan held the seven of clubs in her right hand and walked down the steps into the wine cellar. The card had hidden long enough underneath the tattered, 1825 Fool tarot card made by Christian Theodor Sutor in Naumburg, Germany. It had a steel-engraved, stencil-coloured jester depicted on the front. The real Doctor Faustus could never have played with it.

Odette liked knowing such details about the cards as it gave her an idea of her patients' pasts.

She wasn't used to going into the cellar without Charles and Renard, who were lying dead in the airtight barrel in the barn. She had talked Boch out of disposing of the bodies since she needed the evidence to back up the robbery story she would tell Gillot. Now the two men who had brought an end to so many people's lives were decomposing hour by hour, day by day.

Odette had bigger fish to fry. She unlocked the door and grabbed the spear leaning against the side of the door. Its blade was brown from old blood.

She stepped into the cellar, which was filled with fear and whimpering, the clinking of chains, the scuffling of feet and the stench of excrement and decay. She didn't go to the effort of chopping up the bodies and pushing them down the storm-drain. It was too much work for a woman over eighty. The others could take care of that later should it be necessary.

She turned on the ancient light and walked ahead, letting her eyes wander through the lenses of her thick glasses. The reserves had dwindled; the cards had demanded many sacrifices tonight. There were only five people left.

'Grandmère,' she heard her granddaughter plead. 'Please, Grandmère. You've gone mad. Let us go!'

Odette turned around to face Denise. She had gathered her children, Hermine and Jean, who were also tied up, around her and pressed them close to her. The little ones' faces looked lifeless. The wine cellar wasn't good for their psyche. 'Shut up,' Odette snapped and briefly waved the tip of the blade encrusted with blood in her direction. Denise fell silent. 'If anything happens to you and your loved ones, then you only have yourself to blame.'

'But I—'

'I said: Shut! Your! Mouth!' Odette felt the anger rise inside her. 'I didn't ask you to come visit me. You put me in this position. You and your invasion of my privacy.' She stepped over the decaying, swollen Robert and waved the card around so that it could choose another victim to feed on. The rotting was bloating the dead man's intestines – soon his abdomen would burst. 'The cards don't need *you* yet. Pray that it stays that way.'

Odette had enjoyed Robert's death. Maybe the cards had sensed the presence of its benefactor's kin and had granted her the wish to spare her own flesh and blood. But she couldn't just let Denise, Hermine and Jean go. They were a threat to the cards.

As if confirming Odette's thinking, the seven of clubs flared and picked one of the beggars, who in desperation had dug a hole in the ground and piled the excavated sand knee-high in an attempt to protect himself. It reminded Odette more of a grave than a shelter.

She kissed the softly singing seven of clubs, tucked it into her apron dress and gripped the handle of the short spear with both hands. 'Hold still,' she told the fragile man, whose arms were covered in infected scratches and wounds. 'It'll be over soon.'

'No, I don't want to die!' he bellowed, flinging sand at her. Denise and her children immediately started screaming, but their resistance wouldn't do anything except annoy Odette further.

She lunged at the beggar. He dodged the spear and tried to grab it below the blade, but she stopped him. Sand hit her glasses, the thick lenses protecting her eyes from the damp, piss-stained grains. The game of life and death dragged on.

Odette grew weary after only a few minutes and without having fulfilled the card's wish. She panted and leaned on the spear, giving the man a hostile look. Torturing and stabbing victims had been easy for burly men like Charles and Renard. Odette, on the other hand, was an old woman and needed to find a solution.

She turned her head and looked at her great-grandchildren. Hermine and Jean would be easier targets and were full of life. The power of youth.

'No, Grandmère!' pleaded Denise, who knew what her hungry looks meant. 'Let them be!'

'Shut up,' she said in the same tone that her father had used to reprimand her. The seven of clubs only wanted the beggar, and it would get him. It was a shame that Boch had taken Renard's MAB with him.

Then she remembered her father's small firearm collection.

She dropped the spear and returned upstairs without locking the cellar door, went into the barn and up into the laundry room, which smelled of clean clothes. She inhaled and welcomed the fresh scent before approaching the black oak chest with the Vichy regime emblem on it.

She lifted her father's old SS uniform. Underneath, she found the old sniper carabine version of the 98K rifle, the MP 40 submachine gun and the old 712 model of the Mauser pistol, as well as several rounds of ammunition and matching magazines.

Odette had kept the weapons from the extensive, abolished collection for two reasons: as a sentimental memento, and so that she had the means to take her own life should she ever be diagnosed with an incurable illness. Since she couldn't have known which weapon would prove useful decades later, she had kept several.

She made her way back to the cellar with the well-maintained Mauser M712 in her hand and two twenty-round magazines in her apron pockets. The pistol had a rapid-fire function, but she wouldn't need to use it against the chained homeless man. What she did need was enough bullets to torture him and make him suffer, so that he would gather all of his energy for the benefit of the card.

She slowly returned to the cellar and descended the steps. Her knees ached and the strain made her heart race.

As soon as she stepped into the vault, she saw that the spear was gone.

'Die, you fucking she-devil!' the threat boomed through the cellar. The beggar held the short spear in his hand and raised his arm to throw it.

Odette abruptly lifted the pistol, took aim as her father had taught her, and, despite the target being nothing more to her than a blurry shadow in the distance, fired once. There was a distinct, powerful bang followed by the sound reverberating off of the walls.

Her old arm and shoulder joints twinged from the recoil. The children screamed and covered their ears. Denise pressed their faces against her body.

The beggar fell backward, gasping and holding his chest. The spear landed next to him in the sand.

Odette kept her arm outstretched and the smoking Mauser pointed at him. She moved closer to the man. She hadn't forgotten anything her father had taught her, but her aim was not what it used to be – she'd missed the heart. Blood gushed from the bullet hole in the upper right of the beggar's torso. Her poor eyesight and the dim light were a disadvantage.

The man lay in the hole that he had dug to protect himself and fumbled desperately for the spear to try to initiate another attack. 'You crazy witch!' he spat, his fingers closing around the handle. 'I'll kill–'

She fired again and hit him in the shoulder. Deliberately. Then she pulled the seven of clubs from her pocket and held it in front of the man so that he could admire the motif, which began to glow. 'Look. Your life finally has value,' she said and fired the next 7.63-millimetre bullet into his stomach. The louder he screamed, the more the card feasted on his suffering and replenished itself.

Odette fired bullet after bullet at the beggar, covering his entire body in wounds. Bangs and flashes filled the vault, as if a small thundercloud had strayed inside. After the eleventh blow, all the man could do was howl in agony like a wild animal. The last bullet pierced his skull and his yelping stopped.

She turned over the card and kissed it. The condition of the seven of clubs had noticeably improved. A further cure wouldn't be necessary.

The only people left were Denise, Hermine, Jean and the careless vagrant who Charles had found under a bridge. She had run away from home and was no older than eighteen. Full of life.

'You're insane, Grandmère,' her granddaughter whispered in a shrill voice. 'You've lost your–'

'You said that the first time,' Odette replied coldly and raised the spear. She glanced at the lifeless eyes of the bleeding corpse lying in the hole and kicked some of the piled-up sand over him. The dead man's arms and legs stuck out from under the mound, as if he was trying to dig himself out.

She approached the exit, pocketing the Mauser and the seven of clubs. Before leaving, she stared intently at her kin and suddenly lunged the spear towards them.

The blade scored just above Hermine's head and left a deep gash in Denise's upper arm. The wound began to bleed immediately. Her granddaughter cried out and pressed her fingers over the cut. 'You psychopath!' she screamed. The blood gushed out of her arm, the drops trickling onto Hermine's hair. Hermine didn't even realise what had happened at first.

'That's for not warning me about the beggar and his attack. I see you would have accepted my death happily,' Odette said as she walked towards the exit. 'You might still be alive, but I'll never forget your betrayal, Denise.'

She closed the door behind her, leaned the spear against the wall and climbed up the stairs to her workshop with leaden steps. Then she laid the seven of clubs next to the ace of hearts and the two of clubs and finally shuffled into the kitchen.

A colossal wave of fatigue swept over her. She turned on the coffee machine and, while it gurgled and hissed, pulled out the Mauser from her pocket. Odette skilfully dismantled the automatic pistol and cleaned the dark traces of gunpowder that the bullets had left in the barrel and other parts of the weapon with oil and an old tea towel. She could still do it all.

As the smell of coffee filled her nostrils, she missed the cake to go with it. Charles had been an exceptional baker, she had to give him that. She leisurely drank her coffee and savoured its stimulating effect. Then she put the cleaned and oiled Mauser back together and loaded it with a full, twenty-round magazine in the front slot.

Renard's phone buzzed.

Odette picked up the device, opened the message, turned up the brightness and enlarged the font so that she could read it.

Some news had arrived from Gillot. The man who could barely begin to understand the true value of what he had collected over the years informed Renard that he was concerned for Madame Darlan's welfare and was sending a large troop of armed men disguised as a tour group to Avignon. Their leader would introduce themselves as Ulrich. No effort was to be spared in preventing the cards from being stolen or protecting Madame Darlan.

Odette leaned back and sipped her sweet coffee. Her wrinkled, hard mouth twisted into a smile and her blue-grey eyes sparkled.

Thank you, she wrote back. Gillot mustn't suspect a thing. Her protectors would soon be here, and that brought her comfort.

* * *

Berlin, the Federal Republic of Germany

Tadeus got off the high-speed train and held out his hand to Poe despite every movement making him want to cry out in pain. They had travelled to Berlin Central Station by train, and planned to hire a car for ease of movement. The car rental office was one floor above the station. Altenburg was their next destination.

Poe jumped onto the platform and heaved their luggage out of the train. 'Leave it to me. And don't argue. You know why.'

Tadeus knew perfectly well why. In Belgium a doctor had disinfected and treated the bullet wound. A liquid bandage and steristrips held the flesh together, while a supporting bandage did the rest. Nothing would tear or burst under usual, daily strain, but every movement still hurt and sent a stringing sensation through his shoulder and to his head. Painkillers didn't help. If the going got tough, as it had done in the tunnels in Arras, it would be a great disadvantage.

Before boarding the train, Tadeus had stocked up on some useful supplies from an outdoor and military equipment store, including a glass cutter, a multi-functional tool and two coloured smoke grenades used by the military to mark certain points or locations. Poe didn't ask any questions.

'We need to go one floor up.' Tadeus pointed to the lift. 'The rental office is upstairs.' He carried the queen of hearts in his inner jacket pocket. It didn't sing, praise or say anything to him. Instead, the card played dead and pretended to be ordinary and irrelevant; a silent protest against its theft from Antoine's care. That was new.

'Okay,' Poe said and began to push their suitcases along. She had been silent the entire journey, processing the events in Arras. Shaken by new nightmares, she had tried to explain to him what she had felt, how the cards had attacked her, and what hatred had chased after her in the tunnels, but she had kept breaking down, shedding silent tears. He had comforted her as best as he could, even though he felt helpless and also couldn't forget the fact that she wanted to destroy the cards.

They walked side by side along the platform and stepped into the lift.

Escaping the bunker in Arras had been hard work. Tadeus had deliberately positioned the mad Antoine's body in a way that would make it easy for detectives to draw conclusions about who had erected the altar made up of human skulls. Then he had used the map and his phone torch to search for a way out with the dazed Poe slung over his shoulder. The worst part had been the pain in his arm; his circulation had been so poor that he'd felt close to collapsing several times. At some point Poe had woken up, meaning they could support each other for part of the way. They had had to evade the search party that had come after them and then take the lift back above ground as if nothing had happened. Luckily, Tadeus' casually draped coat had perfectly concealed his injury.

The lift stopped. They walked out of the doors and headed for the car rental office.

Tadeus hoped that no one was looking for them. They hadn't given out any personal details when they'd visited the museum in Arras. At most, someone might have noted down what they looked like, and at worst there were a few video images of the pair of them in the museum. But he doubted that word of the events had spread to Berlin yet. He patted his chest where the silent queen of hearts was hiding in his jacket and thought of Antoine. A small part of him understood the man's obsession and his desire to defend the card from everyone and everything, but he vowed never to suffer the same fate as the history student had. He wouldn't lose his mind. *I belong to the strong ones, the sane ones.*

He held the door open for Poe as she pushed their cases into the spacious office. A friendly employee smiled at them from behind the counter.

'Good afternoon,' the man welcomed them in English. 'How can I help you?'

'We booked a car online,' Poe said politely. 'Under the name Hyun-Gi-Lim.' She handed the man her old but still valid Korean passport, her credit card and driving licence. 'Do you have a nice car for us?'

'Just a moment. Let me find the booking.' He typed in her details. 'Ah, yes, here's the reservation: a brand-new Dacia Duster Blackshadow with all the extras. The car has a full tank and is ready to go, Miss Lim.' He gathered the forms and pointed to the right. 'But before you pick it up, this gentleman here would like to speak with you first.'

Tadeus recognised the man in the blue suit in his mid-thirties. He was sitting in the corner next to the drinks machine, reading a newspaper, and possessed the same talent for discretion as he did himself, which was why the pair of them hadn't noticed him. *Inspector Klim.*

The blond State Office of Criminal Investigation officer folded up his paper, stood up and walked towards them, and addressed them in English: 'Good afternoon, Miss Poe, Mr Boch.' He pointed invitingly to the chairs next to the drinks machine. 'Before you continue your journey, I have a few questions for you. And don't tell me that you're in a hurry and better be on your way. Your answers will determine whether you go anywhere at all.' His tone left no room for objection. 'Please, sit down.'

Tadeus and Poe followed his cue. The employee behind the counter focused intently on something on his computer and pretended not to listen. A newly arrived customer quickly distracted him from the impromptu interrogation.

'I'm in Berlin at the moment to discuss the Russian mafia's links to illegal gambling rounds with my colleagues. There have been some new findings, and so I thought I'd take the opportunity to ask you some questions upon your unexpected arrival in the capital.' Klim bought a round of hot drinks for everyone from the machine. 'You certainly like to travel. Would you like to tell me what you're up to?'

Tadeus knew he was guilty. 'I know you told me to stay in Baden-Baden, but I did reach out to you after our conversation.'

'Via text and email, I know. But that wasn't the arrangement, Mr Boch.' Klim glanced at Poe. 'And you've been using your old name and thought I wouldn't notice?' He pulled out his phone and read something off his screen. 'As you're one of the suspects, I've been monitoring your credit card transactions and other data. You've tried to be discreet, but the two of you have still turned up on our system a few times. Thanks to your flight from Rome to Brussels, for example, or the car that you hired there.' His eyes darted between them. 'Why are my key witness and my best suspect galivanting around Europe together days after the murders?'

'Is that illegal?' Tadeus asked politely.

'Is that a joke, Mr Boch?' Klim brushed his tie with his middle and index fingers. 'Don't tell me the two of you have fallen in love and are on some silly romantic getaway?'

'We're doing some research of our own,' Poe said. 'I already told you – I'm innocent. With Mr Boch's casino contacts, we've compiled some rumours about illegal gambling rounds. We're looking into them and trying to find the people responsible.'

Tadeus put on a straight face. At the poker table, that was called bluffing.

'The people responsible for what?' Klim interjected.

'For the murders in Baden-Baden.' Poe took a sip of her coffee without revealing what she thought of the taste. 'Mr Boch is a gambling legend and can easily get a seat at any gaming table in the world, and I play along as his arm candy at these events and use my old name as a disguise. The State Office of Criminal Investigation doesn't have such methods at its disposal, am I right, Inspector?'

If Tadeus had interpreted Klim's facial expressions correctly, he believed her. 'So you're travelling across the continent and hoping to drive away the Russian mafia. Then what?'

'Then we'll bring you the evidence,' Tadeus chimed in. 'That's always been our plan.'

'If I had committed the murders and wanted to drop off the radar, Inspector, then I'd be hiding in South Korea right now,' Poe rebuked him gently. 'But I have a great job in London waiting for me and a duty to my murdered fiancé. I want to make them pay for what they did. It's my way of taking revenge.'

'And I have similar reasons. I'm helping Miss Poe get justice,' Tadeus added.

Klim typed away on his phone. 'Even if that sounds somewhat plausible, I don't have to believe you. Where are you going next?'

'There are several gaming events happening in Berlin over the next few days.' Tadeus gestured to the counter. 'We wanted to go to a few of them and shake things up a bit.'

'Have you come to any conclusions yet?'

'None that we can be certain of,' Poe replied. 'But we're working on it.'

'You're treading on very, very thin ice,' Klim said. 'Someone has made enquiries about you two in my department. Maybe they were from the same gambling circle that you're so interested in. The only thing I can do is warn you to stop acting alone.' The inspector stood up. 'From now on, you'll report all your movements to me in advance, Mr Boch and Miss Poe. And I expect a summary of your findings so far. Names, connections, gambling venues. If you don't comply, I'll put a search warrant on you.' He pointed at them with splayed middle and index fingers. 'Whatever you're up to, don't think for one minute that I've crossed you off my list of suspects.' Then he turned around. 'Have a nice day.'

Tadeus and Poe remained in their seats and watched the inspector leave.

'Well played,' Tadeus said.

'Thank you.'

'We should get some burner phones.' Tadeus turned to look at the doctor. 'Just in case.'

Poe got up. 'Go on, up you get. We'd better get a move on.'

Then it occurred to Tadeus that modern rental cars were

equipped with GPS transmitters. Klim would know that they were travelling to Altenburg and that they had lied to him about the gambling rounds in Berlin. It was also possible that he'd linked the events in Arras to them.

Oh well. We'll just have to be quick about it. Tadeus stood up from the armchair, despite the ever-present pain, and walked up to the counter with Poe.

* * *

Leipzig, Sachsen,
the Federal Republic of Germany

Poe and Tadeus had been a hair's breadth away from making the wrong decision after the unexpected Klim interlude. On their way to the playing card museum in Altenburg, where they were hoping to find the ace of diamonds on display, they had discovered that, in actual fact, the object of their desire was in Leipzig. The card was at a special, temporary exhibition, The Devil's Playbook: Cards of Fate and the Fate of Cards, organised by the Grassi Museum of Applied Arts. This shortened their journey by a few kilometres.

'We're almost there,' Tadeus said. He steered the wheel of the Dacia Duster through Leipzig with one hand to try to avoid straining his injured arm as much as possible. 'You were brilliant in Arras,' he said, praising Poe again. 'It'll be easier this time. No dark tunnels.'

'I'll hold you to that,' she said and grabbed her tablet. She did an internet search and studied the virtual overview of the exhibition. '*The Museum of Applied Arts is hosting yet another first-class exhibition,*' she read aloud. '*Playing-card culture has been a part of European life since the 12th century. This exhibition will feature some of the most unique and beautiful pieces from museums in Echterdingen and Altenburg, as well as from various other private collections and those from associated museums. The exhibition will include hundreds of card decks with over a quarter of a million individual cards spanning seven different centuries and all five continents, card-printing presses, gaming tables and an extensive collection of writings from the Middle Ages to the present day.*' She zoomed in to the promoted exhibition previews. 'There it is: the ace of diamonds.'

'It should be easy, then.'

'Easy? To steal a card from a museum?'

He patted his side jacket pocket. 'That's what the glass cutter is for. Just a little scoring, then reach in and voilà.'

'There'll be an alarm, Boch. You do realise museums have alarms?'

'For playing cards? I doubt it. We'll have to look out for cameras and security guards, but timing will be the most important thing.' Tadeus was confident that their mission would be a success. 'You know, just like in those old Hollywood films – *Ocean's Eleven*, *The Thomas Crown Affair* or *The Italian Job*.'

Poe didn't look convinced. 'You haven't forgotten about the insane tour guide yet, I hope.'

'And the card has been on display for . . .' He looked at her and waited for her to look up the start date of the exhibition.

'A week.'

'It's been in the museum for seven days. I don't think that's enough time for any crazy lunatics like Antoine to start showing up.' Tadeus turned on to Nuremberg Street and searched for a parking spot for their compact SUV. He stopped in front of a comic-book shop. A sharp pain shot up his arm from the movement and he gritted his teeth. 'Let's go and see if we can find this lovely card then.'

What he was worried about was the GPS transmitter in their rental car. Klim could track them and would be able to see that they had been close to the museum on the day of their planned robbery; a mobile phone data analysis would confirm it. This meant that there could be no evidence against them left at the crime scene. They couldn't risk rousing even the slightest whiff of suspicion. *It'll be okay.*

'Finding the ace of diamonds shouldn't be a problem. We already know what it looks like,' Poe said as she got out of the car after him.

They walked together across the street, crossed the small park and headed for the colonnades that formed a sort of courtyard in front of the museum. The pain in Tadeus' arm slowly faded. Neither of them spoke. Poe was gathering her thoughts and Tadeus didn't feel like talking.

After Arras and Leipzig, they would only need to jump on a plane to Benin to secure the last card and make contact with Gillot. Then they could ensure he was convicted of the murders and, at the same time, free Darlan's family by sending him to prison. But they would still need a few hours first to speak with Darlan, who knew more about the man. *Perhaps we could still rope in Klim's help, too.*

Tadeus hoped to get some clues out of the Walloon about the burglars who had stolen his cards. The thieves had the nine of spades – his nine of spades – which had claimed him as its owner. He wasn't sure how he would manage that yet, but he still had time to solidify his plans.

They approached the entrance to the museum, quickly paid their admission fee and without being checked were directed to the left, where the special exhibition was located. There were usually multiple exhibitions running at the Grassi, which housed three museums under one roof.

The exhibition space was rectangular in shape, and huge; Poe and Tadeus couldn't see where it ended. The room was divided by the display walls, creating a zigzag path that left enough space for the visitors to stand in front of the exhibits, information boards and around the larger objects.

'Let's go and find the ace of diamonds,' Tadeus whispered.

He and Poe strolled through the exhibition. There was plenty to marvel at, especially the Asian playing cards: some were round, others rectangular and narrow in shape, some beautifully painted, and others worn, as if they'd been passed through hundreds of hands.

There was also a section of the exhibition that delved into the development of the card game in Europe. German, French and Italo-Spanish decks, everyday cards that had been thrown away after a while, cards that had been painted for the rich, the nobility and royalty, rough sketches of woodcuts and more detailed sketches of the copper engraving technique were all on display.

'Just like our cards,' Tadeus said to Poe, who had adopted the role of a tourist once again with her round hat and camera. There were roughly a hundred other visitors wandering around the spacious room, talking quietly and admiring the exhibits.

Tadeus and Poe walked around a card press that had once been used to print entire sheets. On the wall behind it, there was a large-scale schematic diagram of the old card-printing process.

'There it is!' the doctor said, and pulled Tadeus by the arm across the room like a girl in love. They stopped in front of the display cabinet.

'Easy, easy,' he urged, feeling the pain throb in his shoulder. He grasped her hand with his left to relieve the strain. 'Or you'll have to stitch me up again in this room.'

'Sorry, I was just so happy that—' she started to say, then stopped before uttering a horrified: 'Oh.'

Tadeus immediately spotted the issue. Ten identical aces of diamonds were displayed next to each other. They could only be visually distinguished by their slight nuances in colour and were used to explain the stamping technique, which had been used to make simple woodcut cards. These woodcuts were then used in pubs, where it wasn't the end of the world if beer was spilled over them. They cost next to nothing and often landed in the fire if they got too worn. The curators had chosen the eye-catching card to draw more attention to the process.

'Hmm,' he grumbled unhappily. 'Can you feel anything?'

'No. How am I supposed to know which card is the right one? I've lost what little I had of my mudang powers.' Poe looked horrified. 'That card in Arras! It must have drained me.'

Tadeus didn't believe her. Not yet. 'It could be from something else.' He scanned the exhibition. 'Maybe it's over there.' He pulled her to another display case on the wall, where more identical ace of diamonds cards were hanging and the structure and glued-together layers of an old card were explained. 'Anything?'

'Still nothing,' Poe said in a strained voice. She turned her head to the right and groaned in despair. 'Here we go *again*! And you said it would be easy.'

Tadeus followed her gaze and noticed a diorama that showed what happened to cards rendered unusable: they were bound into books for decoration, cut up and used in apothecaries as scrapers for salves. The ace of diamonds was consistently used as an example.

'Shit,' Tadeus muttered.

'I . . .' Poe clung to his injured arm, turning pale.

'Stay here. I'll go get you something to drink.' Tadeus sat her down on a bench and left the exhibition to fetch her a glass of water. The pain in his arm grew worse, the pulling and tugging making him feel nauseous.

The museum attendant at the information desk was concerned and sympathetic in equal measure, and promised to bring a cup of still mineral water.

While Tadeus waited, a thought occurred to him. If Poe

couldn't sense anything, then perhaps the sulking queen of hearts could help them with a shimmer, a sparkle, or something that would tell them she realised that she wasn't the only card in the room that belonged to Bastian Kirchner's deck. *Like two magnets.* He immediately decided to call Darlan to discuss the matter with her.

It took a little while for her to pick up the phone. *'Oui?'*

'This is Tadeus . . . Muller, madame,' he said quietly and held a hand over his mouth to muffle his voice. 'Can you speak right now?'

'Yes. My new guards aren't here yet. They're in Avignon, but not in the house.'

Tadeus didn't know if that was good or bad news. After all, she was hiding the three cards. 'We have a problem: there are several, identical aces of diamonds here in Leipzig, and Miss Poe is . . . struggling to use her mudang powers to identify the real one.'

'I see. Bring them all to me and I'll be able to determine which ace of diamonds is the real card.'

'That would be very hard to do. We're in a museum with pretty good security. What if something goes wrong and we lose the right card? I don't want to risk it. Do you know of any other way? Any tricks? Maybe I can use the card from Arras to encourage the ace of diamonds to give a sign?'

'Good idea!' Darlan exclaimed. 'Yes, that would work.'

'But how?'

'Bring the cards really close together.'

Tadeus looked from the entrance to one of the display cases far away where the aces of diamonds were stored. The glass was ten or fifteen centimetres in front of the cards. 'I can try, madame, but there are glass panels in front of them.'

'About a hand in front?'

'Something like that.'

'Good. Then that's close enough. As soon as the two real cards are facing each other, you'll know. Watch out for a shimmer.'

'Yes, I've seen it before, madame. Thank you,' he said, ready to hang up.

'Monsieur Muller?'

'Yes?'

'I have some good and bad news. The card from Manaus is already on its way to me, which means Gillot's card hunter will soon set off for Benin. Though he's currently stuck in Bogotá,' she explained in a calm albeit insistent tone. 'You need to travel to Benin as soon as possible. You have all the information you need about the card.'

'And the good news, Madame Darlan?'

She gave a forced laugh. 'I believe in you. In both of you. I know that I'll never be able to repay you for your efforts to protect me and my family from Gillot. *Au revoir,*' she said, ending their conversation.

Tadeus fidgeted with his phone. Benin. Africa. *Yet another mammoth task.*

He returned with the paper cup full of water which he'd been exceptionally permitted to take into the exhibition room and sat down next to Poe. He quietly explained his plan to her, pulled out a notebook from his pocket and placed the queen of hearts inside it. 'We'll see if anything happens. Or, even better, if *you* sense something.'

'I don't trust my powers right now, Boch.' Poe slowly sipped the water and leaned against the wall, massaging her temple with her hand. She was so pale that her freckles had practically disappeared. 'I've counted them. There are twenty-three cards. Twenty-three aces of diamonds. They're all identical.'

'We can ignore the cut-up and dismantled ones. That will reduce the number of possible cards,' he consoled her and himself. He picked up his vibrating phone and saw a new text flash on his screen from the casino. Management wanted to know when he could return to work. Everyone missed him, and even some of their regulars were asking after him.

Tadeus was touched.

Then another message arrived, from the German police. Klim urged Tadeus to get back to him as soon as possible. Further questions had surfaced during the course of the investigation into the events at the villa. Klim's Russian colleagues had sent some photos of known killers from the gambling mafia, which Tadeus had also been asked to take a look at.

Tadeus parried their questions and stalled both. He would prioritise the card for the next few minutes, after which he would contact the inspector. He couldn't let Klim thwart their travel plans to Benin.

At least his two ex-wives hadn't got in touch. It appeared Gillot had bigger things to worry about in hospital than threatening Tadeus' children and using them as leverage against him.

Several school groups clamoured past them. A hundred fourteen-year-olds spread out around the exhibition space, laughing and teasing. The cards received limited interest from the teenagers and the teachers callously walked past exhibit after exhibit as if the pupils were none of their concern.

And then Tadeus realised: this was the first time that he was seriously thinking about his children since his phone call with Haruka in Rome. Guilt swept over him.

He couldn't help but wonder what he'd do if Georg or Michiko were taken from him and someone demanded the cards from him in exchange. He didn't want to answer that. He was strong, he would think of something.

'Are you feeling any better?' he asked Poe.

She still looked pale around her nose, but she nodded bravely and tried to smile. 'There's no time to lose. I've counted three museum guards doing their rounds, plus the cameras on the ceiling.' She placed the paper cup on the bench. 'This is going to be a challenge.'

Tadeus filled her in on the phone call he had had with Darlan, then glanced at his notebook, which held the queen of hearts.

'I wonder if . . .' he mumbled and pulled his phone out of its case. Then he slid the queen of hearts inside and placed his phone on top of it, leaving the camera lens uncovered so he could still see what was happening under his phone when he laid it against a display case. If the card flared, he would notice immediately.

'You're going to pretend to take photos of the exhibits.' Poe grinned. 'Nice trick, Boch.'

'Thank you. Could you keep an eye on the cards behind the glass? See if you spot anything sparkle, shimmer or glow. Anything that strikes you. Just in case the queen of hearts doesn't emit a signal.'

'Sure. And if our plan works, I'll set the fire alarm off,' she said casually. 'I've memorised where the manual call point is. With this many students, they'll think it's a prank.' The short break and new plan had clearly revived her. 'Do you have everything you need?'

He did. Tadeus stuffed his injured arm into his trouser pocket to take the pressure off, which brought him some temporary relief. But as soon as he did so much as twitch a finger, his injury began to throb and ache.

They walked around the exhibition again, Tadeus pretending to snap close-range photos several times to test the guards' reactions. As soon as he turned off his flash, they paid no more attention to him beyond a quick glance. Instead, their eyes closely followed the boisterous, occasionally arrogant students. *Perfect.*

Poe and Tadeus walked up to the aces to start the test.

He carefully moved his smartphone along the glass of a free-standing display cabinet as if he were filming a video of the exhibition from all sides, and even from above. In the meantime, Poe closely studied the cards.

But even after repeating the process several times, they didn't find anything. Tadeus pretended to be having trouble with his phone so he could explain the suspicious behaviour to any museum staff who asked.

Poe, at the case detailing the structure of cards, motioned to Tadeus when he drew closer with the queen of hearts. 'There was a faint glimmer. Second from the left,' she announced, relieved. 'Only for a split second.'

'Are you sure?' he asked.

She didn't answer him, which was enough reason for him to repeat the test.

Yes, there it was – a shimmer. Tadeus bent over the display case to get a better look at the barely perceptible glow that spanned three of the cards, but he couldn't tell which of the three was the source. *Three cards? That's impossible.*

'It's the third one from the left,' Poe said suddenly.

'How do you know?'

'Because I saw it.'

'With your eyes or your mudang powers?'

Poe pursed her lips. She looked like an insulted Asian goddess. 'It's the third one.'

It's too risky to get wrong. Tadeus decided to take the entire row. Darlan would be able to use her expert knowledge to tell them for certain which card was the true ace of diamonds.

A group of nerdy and interested students approached from the left. They listened to their teacher's explanations on the making of cards by the display case next to them, while three class clowns pressed their noses against some of the other cabinets nearby. The perfect culprits for a prank.

'Let's do this,' Tadeus said. He tucked away his phone and reached into his jacket pocket, and his fingers closed around the coloured smoke grenade. There'd been a warning against doing exactly what Tadeus had planned in the enclosed building, since the smoke posed a health risk and became very, very dense. The sensors would pick up the smoke and trigger the alarm and an evacuation. While the premeditated chaos ensued, he intended to steal the row of aces. Escaping the building would be easy.

Tadeus had drawn the anarchy symbol on the shell of the smoke grenade with a sharpie beforehand, so that if it was found it would be assumed to have been a silly prank. He had hoped for some teenagers among the crowd of visitors, and the appearance of the school groups made for a huge selection of rowdy suspects.

He wiped his fingers with a handkerchief without taking out the grenade. 'Cover me,' he told Poe.

She couldn't help but laugh. 'What, because I'm almost an entire head taller than you?'

'It's the twenty-first century – women can be taller than men,' Tadeus countered. He inconspicuously took the grenade out of his pocket and bent down, ostensibly to tie his shoelace. The wound in his shoulder throbbed, but he refused to let it stop him. He dropped the grenade, pulled out the ring and pushed it away from himself.

It discreetly rolled along the wall.

He slowly got to his feet and readied himself. Five seconds and the chemical reaction would go off. The grenade hissed as it rolled down the exhibition space, and spewed out purple smoke that fogged up the back of the long room in a matter of seconds.

The alarm went off while the coloured wall of smoke rolled in. People and objects faded into silhouettes, and the lights on the ceiling and the walls were eclipsed by the concentrated purple mist. The teenagers cheered and clapped, while others cried out in shock.

Visitors were asked by staff to leave the exhibition and the building. The emergency exit signs glowed fervently against the purple.

Then the smoke reached Tadeus and Poe.

'Go!' Tadeus urged and picked up the glass cutter. He cut out a large rectangle in the display box on the wall, which fell inside. He could barely move his injured arm, so had to put the glass cutter away before reaching into the case through the hole to grab the row of aces. Suddenly, the purple smoke grew so dense that it blinded him. Tadeus could only hope that he had manage to retrieve all three. He quickly counted them with his right hand.

I'm one card short! The third ace must have fallen from its holder somehow.

'Boch? Boch, are you still there?' Poe called through the mist.

'Shhh,' he hissed and carefully felt around the bottom of the case. He didn't want to accidentally cut himself or leave any fingerprints.

He struck gold. 'I've got it,' he whispered in the fog.

'What have you got?' a man's voice demanded, coughing. 'You need to leave!'

'My daughter, I found her,' Tadeus said, improvising. 'Sweetheart?'

'I'm here, Dad,' Poe replied and took his hand. 'Let's go before we suffocate.'

'Keep to the wall and follow the light markers on the floor,' the museum guard advised them.

Tadeus and the doctor hurried through the dwindling clouds and found the exit, where the other visitors were pushing their way out. He felt a gentle pang of guilt for what he'd done, but it passed in a heartbeat. *It was worth it.*

They left before the fire brigade and the police arrived and reached Nuremberg Street, where their Dacia Duster was parked. Poe got behind the wheel and they drove off at a leisurely pace. The last thing they wanted to do was attract attention.

The discreet SUV steered through the Leipzig streets while Poe dialled Darlan on speaker phone and updated her on their successful mission. 'Mr . . . Muller's plan worked. We had to take more than one ace, madame, but we'll soon figure out which one is the original.'

'Tell her,' Tadeus chimed in, 'that we'll take the cards with us to Benin. We'd have to take quite the detour to get to Avignon, and–' He stopped himself before he could give himself away. He found the idea of Darlan guarding the cards too dangerous. The old woman would struggle to properly protect the masterpieces, and he had no idea how competent the new guards were. 'And that we have to be quick. There's a German inspector on our tail.'

Poe raised an eyebrow. She'd clearly seen through his lie, but didn't say anything. The Frenchwoman didn't protest about this new plan, and they ended their call.

'Benin . . .' Tadeus muttered as he used his one operational hand to flick through Darlan's file to look up who had the next card. 'For a long time, the ace of spades had been assumed lost,' he read.

'You've forgotten that again already?' Poe teased.

'That smoke's made me slow.'

'Well, I haven't forgotten that Mr Gondjia is a voodoo priest. He's a bokar. No, a bokor. I had to look it up online.'

'What's a bokor?'

'Someone who's an expert in evil spirits.' She flicked the indicator on and turned on to Karl-Liebknecht Street. 'Which suits the cards perfectly.'

Tadeus picked up on the unease in her voice. He could understand her worry. A duel for the eighteenth-century European playing card could transpire between Poe, an untrained mudang, and the bokor, a seasoned voodoo priest.

Tadeus found that strangely fitting. He mused on it for a moment. Then he picked up the phone to lie to Klim.

* * *

Avignon, Vaucluse,
Provence-Alpes-Côte d'Azur,
France

If there was one thing that Sebastian Ulrich had learned in the Middle East, it was that respect and lack of planning didn't get you far in a fight. He was sitting in the garden of Café et Bar Sur le Pont with a mineral water, soaking up the evening light. Through the open gate of the green oasis on Saint-Thomas d'Aquin Street, a handful of locals and tourists were chatting. Sebastian had specially selected this spot as it gave him the best view onto the street of Nicolas Lescuyer directly opposite without exposing himself like a sitting duck.

He was armed with a silenced Glock 17 pistol underneath his loose-fitting shirt, and had stuffed all the necessary equipment into a tourist backpack, which he'd plopped next to his chair – just in case he ran into trouble, as Gillot feared.

Sebastian wasn't afraid. He was confident in the deployment of his five-man mercenary troop, who were well prepared and had been contracted before by various official and unofficial employers. Guarding oil refineries, protecting people, securing buildings, transporting prisoners, raids . . . Sebastian Ulrich and his men did it all. They worked hard, were efficient and returned home alive. Too many mercenaries in the world travelled back in body bags because they'd thought for a second, even a millisecond too long before pulling the trigger, because they hadn't inspected the site properly, or had been drunk or taken drugs to give themselves a boost.

Sebastian and his men had arrived two days ago disguised as tourists and had taken up quarters in various hotels in Avignon. They had brought their equipment with them in standard suitcases. They'd wandered the streets, taken photos and made a note of every detail regarding Madame Darlan's home. They knew where the most important surveillance points were and where the best sniper spots were.

Tonight they would gain entry to Darlan's large property, and they would have to be quick about it to avoid any neighbours noticing. Sebastian took up the watchman position.

The darkening streets were emptying. The good weather attracted tourists to Avignon, which, even if you weren't particularly interested in church history, had gained a certain popularity in Europe thanks to its unfinished bridge. More people probably knew the song about the bridge, 'Sur le Pont d'Avignon', sung by Mireille Matthieu in the 1970s, than they knew about the history of the Avignon antipopes.

But in this part of the city there was hardly anything to see. People used the little streets to reach the medieval city wall, which explained why the owner of the Sur le Pont also ran a communications agency next door. The Café et Bar didn't make much money.

Sebastian finished his water and was the last guest to want something to eat. He chose a light salad with a beef fillet.

'I'm sorry, monsieur, but the kitchen is already closed.' The waiter apologised several times and offered to bring some wine as compensation.

Sebastian thanked him, ordered a coffee instead of the wine and settled the bill.

After another hour, he finished his drink and left the

courtyard, lurking in the shade of a wall. The others would bring the heavy equipment; the watchman had to be quick and agile.

The clocktower struck midnight. The streets in front of him were empty. Avignon's residents had closed their shutters and parked their cars in the bays of the one-way street where Darlan lived.

Sebastian picked up his phone, which, like all the phones used by his troop, sent encrypted messages. He dialled the number for Sergeant Crichton, a tough-as-nails SAS member who felt he earned too little in the army for what he could do. 'Major, the street is clear. You may commence entry. Just keep your distance so that I can see if there's anyone walking around or at the window.'

'Yes, General. At your signal,' came the reply.

Sebastian grabbed the thermal imaging binoculars from his backpack and checked his surroundings again. There were no outlines of people in the streets or behind the windows of the flats and cars. Cats, a rat, but nothing more. 'Force one, go,' he commanded.

It didn't take long for one of his men to silently advance with two heavy suitcases in his hands and a rucksack on his back.

The barn door swung open for him, an infrared signature briefly appeared, and the mercenary gun was already inside the house.

'Wait.' Sebastian looked around carefully once more before sending in force two, three and four.

The operation was running as seamlessly as he'd planned. One by one, the men moved into the barn and quickly reported that all was well. Then Crichton followed as the last member of the group.

'Excellent,' Sebastian said into his phone. They'd overcome the first challenge. 'Now that the team's inside, what's the sit rep?'

'The place is huge. Cluttered. There's too much junk. If some-one wanted to get in, they could easily take the roof off,' his sergeant replied. 'We'll need several security cameras, General. Otherwise someone could slip through. The lock is pathetic. My little niece could pick it.'

'Understood. I'm going in.' Sebastian put away his binocu-lars, threw his rucksack onto his back and stepped out of the little wall's shadow. He vigilantly walked along Nicolas Lescuyer Street and approached the stone building.

Gillot must be extremely fond of Darlan if he went to such lengths to protect her. For someone who'd been shot by some Mafia killers in Rome, Sebastian felt, he cared a little too much about others. But that made no difference to him. The Walloon had arranged the bank transfer in advance and payment was guaranteed, regardless of what happened in Rome.

He knew Gillot from two excavations that had taken place under his and his troops' aegis, when they had protected him from the attacks of tomb raiders. As soon as word got out about where the art dealer was digging, the vultures came after him and had tried to steal his loot. Gillot clearly had a nose for lucra-tive business, and it was obvious that he needed Darlan's help; he was safeguarding his investment.

Sebastian looked around him before stopping in front of the restorer's house and knocking on the weather-beaten barn door with a special, previously agreed-upon sequence.

The door flew open and he saw Crichton's silhouette in the darkness. His deputy hastily beckoned him inside.

It was only when he took his second step inside the building, and when it was already too late, that Sebastian realised that it hadn't been the SAS officer that had urged him inside, but some-one wearing his clothes. Crichton would never have put anything on other than his horrible aftershave, which supposedly kept the mosquitoes at bay. The man standing in front of Sebastian smelled different. His hackles rose.

The door closed behind him.

Sebastian dodged the blow to his temple. He drew his silenced pistol and aimed it at the stranger in the sergeant's uniform, who was hiding his face under a balaclava.

A voice in his mind warned him not to pull the trigger. There had to be a fair number of enemies in the house if they'd managed to overpower his men, and, whoever they were, they'd done it silently and without firing a single bullet.

'Before you fly off the handle, General, I can assure you that your people are still alive,' the masked man said. 'We've locked them in the cellar. Now, I'm going to count to two, and you're going to drop your gun.'

'And why should I believe you?' Sebastian demanded.

The enemy troops must have been in the restorer's house before the mercenaries arrived. They must have roared with laughter when they saw how much effort Sebastian had gone to with keeping lookout, sounding out the area and securing it.

The stranger flicked on a torch and its bright beam floated across the floor. 'Do you see any blood?'

Sebastian looked around. There were no red stains, no empty cartridges and no left-over smell of gunpowder or smoke. 'You could have stunned them with tasers.'

'I don't tend to play with children's toys.' He heard the masked man grin. 'Ah, yes, before I forget to count: one.'

Sebastian dropped his silenced Glock 17. He knew that there were at least two gunmen behind him who could take him out. 'I want to see my men.'

'That, General, is exactly what we had in mind.' The stranger gave a signal.

Sebastian's hands were bound behind his back with cable ties. A second cable was wrapped around his neck, making it hard to breathe. 'You'll like the cellar,' said the leader of the group. 'A few of the sheikhs' torture chambers used to look a bit like this. I'm sure you'll feel right at home.'

Someone shoved him harshly in the back with what felt like the barrel of a gun, which prompted him to start walking.

He was tormented by conflicting emotions, oscillating between frustration and surprise, anger at himself and irrepressible amusement. In all his years as a mercenary, he had never got into this kind of trouble before. But you never stopped learning. Sebastian vowed silently that he would inspect the property himself next time, even if his employer assured him that it was perfectly safe.

'Watch out for the steps.'

Sebastian stumbled and fell heavily down a long flight of stairs, rolling, tumbling and scraping against the walls. He stopped in front of a heavy, open door, his body covered in dozens of scratches.

He knew the smell that wafted towards him from under the gap in the door all too well: death, decay and fresh blood.

Play is experimenting with chance.

Novalis (1722–1801)

INTERMEDIUM

Leipzig, the Electorate of Saxony,
the Holy Roman Empire,
July 1768

Bastian hastily carried his light cargo through the sweltering city. Something was rumbling and brewing in Leipzig; the students were plotting something. They'd conspired together in Auerbach's, too, constantly putting their heads together and talking of rebellion. Someone had mentioned smashing the windows and rehearsing the uprising.

He didn't know what they were so desperate to fight against, and he preferred not to know, to avoid getting into trouble with the authorities.

Until a week ago, he had devoted all his attention to making the cards, which took longer than he'd expected. Dietrich's drawings had become increasingly difficult to engrave out of copper, and the trifles and little details had almost robbed him of all his patience. But Susanna had lovingly taken care of him and helped him with some of the complex preliminary sketches, when she wasn't bringing him tea and something sweet to keep his spirits high.

After many long months, the deck was now complete in all its splendour. Bastian had presented it to Breitkopf, who had expressed his approval for him to start working as a card-maker. Although it would still take another year or two for the matter to be settled at the printing house, Breitkopf had shaken his hand and barely been able to contain his excitement.

He stored the precious printing plates in the attic. A two-year wait wouldn't make a difference to the plates. Metal had a permanent memory.

Bastian hesitated for a moment when he had inspected the cards again. He couldn't remember having engraved and carved some of the decorative elements and symbols on the first few dozen, but, since they matched the template that he had kept, he didn't think anything of it.

He now carried the French deck, well wrapped in paper, leather and wax paper, to his client. The Devil's poodle had delivered him a message, letting him know that Dietrich wanted to meet him in an old, abandoned mill outside of the city. Since it was the delivery of an illegal deck of cards and he'd promised Breitkopf that he would destroy the samples, Dietrich's suggestion and the remoteness of the location suited him perfectly.

Bastian cursed himself for having thrown on a waistcoat over his shirt despite the summer heat. His cap was also soaked in sweat.

As much as the creation of the deck had captivated him, in the best sense of the word – even Susanna had given in despite her initial disapproval of the project – he now felt incredibly nervous carrying the cards in his pocket. He could already see himself getting stopped and checked at the city gate and then landing in prison. Card forgers were not tolerated.

'Hey, Kirchner!'

Goethe. Again. The student had a talent for catching and stalling him at the most inopportune moments, and had now managed to run into him on a bridge that he was hurrying across.

'Hello, hello. I'm afraid I've got business to attend to,' Kirchner replied.

'Why the hurry?' Goethe joined him and lifted his tricorne.

Due to the heat, he'd parted with his frock coat and only wore a shirt and trousers. 'Are you running away from the riots?'

'I'm a craftsman, what could I possibly have to fear of a student-led revolution?' Bastian returned with a grin and pointed to his strong fingers. 'Knowledge won't get you anywhere in one-on-one combat.'

'Tell that to Goliath. He was defeated by David's better judgement.'

'David cheated,' Bastian countered without slowing down. 'Well, have a good day; I'd better—'

'Stop! Wait a moment!' Goethe urged him and stepped into the shadow of a house. He retrieved a white cloth from his trouser pocket and dabbed his shiny face. 'I need to ask you something.'

'Make it quick.'

'What are you so worried about? Have you seen the Devil's poodle again?'

'No,' Bastian said, also wiping the sweat from his face and neck. 'And I haven't seen his master either.'

Goethe's face twisted into a brooding, scholarly expression. 'Me neither! It's as if the earth swallowed him whole . . . As if he's planning something. And yet, I can feel it – I know he's still in Leipzig.'

Bastian sighed. 'Why do you care about that decrepit old man?'

'He fascinates me. There's something about his manner . . . his demeanour,' the student said. 'It's as if he's a living character from a story or a play. He would make a good Faustus. Or . . . a demon. Perhaps even the Devil.'

'Faustus? Is that why you were standing gawking in front of the paintings in Auerbach's?'

Goethe nodded. 'Despite all the reading and engraving and debating literature, I can't seem to get those paintings out of my mind. Whenever I close my eyes, I always see that old man standing in front of me . . . He's the perfect insinuator and seducer. How he wrapped Frosch and the other students around his finger . . .' He scratched his head under his tricorn. 'I still don't know whether he slipped anything into their wine – a sign of a real and skilled poisoner. And Good Lord, that mutt!' He shuddered. 'My blood runs cold just thinking about it.'

'Good. Then keep looking for your Faustus, and good luck.' Bastian shook his hand. 'Oh, and don't get caught smashing the town hall windows, Goethe. That could end badly. It won't take long for the authorities to find you.'

'I'll keep that in mind.' Goethe nodded. 'And what about you?'

'What about me?'

'Where are you headed on business?'

'It's nothing special. I'm going to look at a few . . . prints that Breitkopf could use. As illustrations for books.'

'Oh, that's wonderful!' Goethe looked eager to accompany him. 'Where are these prints? In Dresden? A museum?' As an enthusiastic student of woodcut and copper engraving, he wouldn't let an opportunity like that pass him by. 'Is it a new Oeser?'

'I have to go alone, Goethe,' Bastian said, rushing off. 'I'll see you later in Auerbach's.' He had already disappeared around the corner and made several turns before the student could object. Bastian didn't need a companion or a witness who would immortalise him in some story one day.

After a long but brisk walk into the countryside along the River Parthe, Bastian passed the Abtnaundorf manor, which also belonged to Breitkopf, and found the half-destroyed water mill. He had reached their agreed-upon meeting point.

The wheel still partially hung on its axle. The house itself had rotten beams in the framework, broken walls and a roof covered in holes. A weeping willow drooped its branches over the ruins, as if protecting them from the blazing sun, casting eerie shadows over the decaying building.

Bastian wiped the sweat from his forehead with his cap and looked around cautiously. There was no one to be seen for miles, and yet he had a strange feeling that he wasn't alone.

'Must be that bloody hell hound,' he muttered as he entered the door of the abandoned mill, its crooked door hanging off its hinges.

It was cold inside. Bastian could see the faint wisps of his breath as the boards groaned and shrieked under his shoes, warning him that someone who had no business here was approaching. Light filtered in sparsely through the cracks and holes of the mill, the weeping willow's shadow only allowing for a dim glow inside the building.

He didn't dare cry out.

The crow that had suddenly appeared in the hallway had almost scared him to death. The bird looked at him, tilted its head to the right and the left, then let out two caws and fluttered past him outside.

He carefully walked through the rooms, checking the sturdiness of the floorboards before every step. An abandoned house by the water rotted quickly. Its wooden planks could break and the Parthe or the ground could swallow him up with it, not to mention the cards in his pocket.

What he laid eyes on next sent a shiver down his spine: there were bones in some of the corners, mostly those of small animals, but also several yellowed human skulls. Trembling, he inspected them; marks had been carved into the skulls, and traces of wax clung to them. They lay scattered around the rooms like forgotten debris after a successful summoning from the underworld.

'A real meat market,' he whispered, if only to hear his own voice. He wanted to hear something living in a place where only death and destruction prevailed.

The floorboards creaked ominously.

Bastian whirled around and saw Dietrich standing before him. Despite the heat, he was dressed in his coat and red beret with a long pheasant feather. The poodle sat next to him, sinister and black as ever.

'Ah, there you are,' Bastian said.

'And there *you* are, Master Kirchner,' Dietrich replied, and tipped his hat. 'I trust this place wasn't too hard to find and reach? You always kept along the cool stream, I hope?'

'Let's just say that it was tricky at first, but then I found my way.' Bastian reached into his pocket and pulled out the wrapped-up package with the deck of cards. 'But before I give you what I had the pleasure of making for you, Mr Dietrich, please accept my gratitude.'

'For silencing Voigt?'

'For letting all trace of doubt about my integrity die along with the evil man,' Bastian raised him.

'Thank you. Your praise means a great deal. Would you like me to tell you how I got the wicked Voigt to confess and hang himself?'

Bastian waved his hand dismissively. 'I didn't ask you to kill him.'

'Not explicitly, that is true. But how else could one silence the blasphemer for good and clear you of all his accusations, Master Kirchner?' Dietrich shot him a theatrically rueful look. 'Well, I did what I thought was best.' He raised his claw-like hand, his nails flashing as if they were blades. 'May I see what I'm due?'

Bastian handed him the package, pride swelling in his chest. 'No lie: they turned out beautifully. Breitkopf liked them too. It'll be the first deck of cards that the publishing house will print. They should be ready in just under a year.'

'Use the motifs and the plates as you see fit, Master Kirchner.' Dietrich sliced open the outer packaging with his nail. Layer after layer fell onto the weathered floorboards. The paper looked incongruously new compared to the ancient wooden planks.

Finally, he unveiled the final product.

He turned over each card in his hands: diamonds, hearts, spades and clubs, from deuce to ace. Dietrich inspected them seriously and tenaciously at first, and then with a cautious smile that widened into a grin. He lifted the ace of spades. 'This is the most beautiful card of the pack. And the fact that you've tied in the skull into the motif . . . It's so delicate and yet distinct.' As if focusing on the card under a magnifying glass, Dietrich spun it around so that it was under a single beam of light that fell through the roof. He placed the other three aces on top of it. 'But there is so much more to these cards than their design.'

Bastian's jaw dropped. *The cards were becoming translucent and there was an entirely new motif underneath each one!* He hadn't noticed that when he had cut them out, and the idea would never have crossed his mind, especially since the middle layer of cardboard he had used was relatively thick. The reverse side was no different. Though it was practically impossible for them to be translucent, he could clearly see the different suits and symbols from underneath.

'I'm pleased that you're happy with the final result,' Bastian breathed.

'There's no need to be so modest, Kirchner. Only you were equal to the task.' Dietrich fanned out the cards, sorted them into a pile, shuffled them and let them leap through the air as if they were made out of water. To Bastian's amazement, this also revealed new illustrations and figures on the cards that moved of their own accord. 'Aren't they simply marvellous to look at? These cards will make you famous, Master Kirchner.'

'Thanks to you,' Bastian said, reciprocating the praise.

The thin cards continued to dance between Dietrich's claw-like hands as he came closer to Bastian. The dog didn't stir from its spot on the floor. 'But there is something I must ask you before we part ways.'

'Is something not to your satisfaction?'

'I only said I had a question.' Dietrich pulled out a card from the pack as if by accident – the ace of spades. 'Do you notice anything strange about this card?'

Bastian silently looked at it. 'I don't know what you mean.'

'Did you work on the deck alone, like I asked?' His ancient eyes suddenly turned cold and unforgiving. 'The entire time? Even when you painted them?'

'I cut out the patterns, Master Dietrich. No one else.'

'That wasn't my question. We agreed that no one can know about the deck.' Two of his long nails traced the pattern on the card. 'And yet I see that my cards have been altered. All of them.'

Bastian's heart pounded and throbbed painfully. He felt a hot lump of rotten luck rise in his throat and began to sweat. If it wasn't his work, then it could only be Susanna's. Her secret alterations. She had also worked on the printing plates. That was why he couldn't remember engraving some of the decorative elements – it was his wife's work.

'I thought,' Bastian began to lie, 'that it would give the cards even more depth.'

'Ah, is that so?' Dietrich laughed devilishly. 'So you're not only a card-maker, but also knowledgeable in the arts of sorcery and witchcraft?'

'What do you mean?' Bastian was baffled. 'No, I haven't a clue about such things.'

'As I suspected. That means that the only person who could possibly have betrayed you and our agreement is your beautiful wife. Did you know that her relatives were put on trial in Leipzig just seventy years ago?'

'No.' Bastian turned pale. 'That's –'

'For practising witchcraft. And sorcery.' Dietrich stroked the cards. 'It appears your wife is well versed in the forbidden arts.'

The black poodle growled unexpectedly. The animal turned its head and bared its teeth, rose to its full height and stood protectively in front of the entrance.

'As are you, Dietrich,' a woman's voice sounded from the other side of the rickety room.

Bastian and the old man turned around.

Susanna stood at the threshold in front of the menacing dog. She held an open notebook in her hand; thin, silk ribbons served as bookmarks in several places. Her long, blonde hair loosely fell over her back and her white dress in the gloomy mill made her look like a saint or an angel that had descended from the heavens.

'Bastian, come stand by me,' she told him. 'This man is more evil than you could possibly imagine.'

Dietrich let out a loud, triumphant laugh. 'There's the little witch! Have my actions brought you to your senses? You've finally come to learn from my wisdom?'

'One of your lessons was enough,' she spat back. 'Now I'll teach you what it means to tangle with goodness!'

'I've been doing that for decades. Century after century,' Dietrich replied, rubbing his right cheek. His nails dragged across it like knives being dragged across sandpaper. 'You really think you can stand against me?' He lifted the deck. 'Because you ruined my cards? It was your work all right. I recognised the symbols – Sibylle used the same ones.'

'Ruined?' Bastian slowly backed away from the old man and Susanna.

He had never believed in the nonsense about witchcraft and sorcery, yet here he was, caught in a battle between good and evil. His own wife – a witch?

'Bastian, come here!' Susanna repeated.

'The cards . . . What were they for?' Bastian quietly asked Dietrich.

'My Devil's Playbook will bring hatred into the world!' Dietrich fanned out the cards again, shuffling them better than any talented juggler at a fair. 'Whoever plays with them will become consumed by hatred for his fellow opponents. He will seek to destroy his fellow men: with violence, cunning tricks, quickly or slowly and with relish . . . whatever suits his temperament and disposition,' he explained. 'The aftermath would range from duels to people pushing each other in front of horse-drawn carts or down the stairs, and could even lead to the outbreak of wars between nations.' Dietrich arranged the cards into a pile. 'Quarrel, strife, conflict, misery, death and endless suffering. That is what these cards will sow.'

'Not any more!' Susanna shouted proudly. 'I have put an end to it and transformed the evil into good.'

'Then . . . then it's true!' Bastian drew back even further, his eyes flitting between them. 'And . . . and the new suits and symbols?'

'They have eliminated the evil that dwelled inside the cards. Breitkopf will print a thousand copies of the deck and circulate it around the world, which means with every card that's drawn, with every trick, every victory and every defeat, ruin and destruction would have spread across the world.' Susanna lifted her notebook. 'If you don't want to come stand by my side, then stay there and don't move.'

Her lips moved quickly and silently, forming inaudible words that drove the black poodle away from her with a growl. Just as the first time Bastian and the beast had met, the dog left behind glowing paw prints on the floorboards.

Bastian looked at the skulls in the corner. He suspected that Dietrich had used this place to carry out his foul work and black magic rituals, sacrifices and other misdeeds away from the ears and eyes of the authorities.

'Who are you?' he whispered, entranced. 'The Devil incarnate? Beelzebub, Destroyer, Father of Lies?'

Dietrich laughed and flashed his white teeth. 'How about Strange Son of Chaos, to begin?'

'The Devil's child!'

'Ah, what's in a name? I've had many before and will have many more.' Susanna's magical preparations didn't appear to faze him. 'Admit it, Kirchner: 'twere better, then, were naught created. Humanity is all but one big disappointment, but it won't destroy itself. So I thought I'd try something other than floods, disease and war. With the deck.' He raised the cards. 'Yes, I worked hard. Thus, all which you as Sin have rated, destruction, aught with Evil blent, that is my proper element.'

'That all ends today,' Susanna said coldly. She bent down and drew several magic symbols on the floorboards. Her golden hair shimmered celestially. 'Hell's fugitive, witness the sign now: before which they bow, the cohorts of hell!'

Bastian had to stifle the scream rising in his throat: the marks by her feet lit up and sent glowing white sparks flying towards Dietrich at lightning speed, surrounding and enveloping him.

'With holy fire I'll scorch and sting thee!' Susanna cried. She stood up tall and stretched out a hand towards the old man. 'The threefold dazzling glow: farewell, Mephistopheles, or whatever your name may be. Servant of hell and the Devil!'

The sparks coalesced into a shooting flame that engulfed Dietrich. The fire grew brighter as if it were made of pure magnesium, burning brilliantly and blindingly, hissing and whistling. The flames pierced the crumbling roof and burned away another hole.

But it all went out as quickly as it had started

Bastian couldn't believe it: the pack of cards had absorbed the magical flames that Susanna had summoned with her incantations. No fire smoked or blazed any longer.

'Why such a noise?' Dietrich laughed. 'But the learned lady I bow before: you've made me roundly sweat, that's certain! Just like in my vault when I took you.' He looked at Bastian. 'You should know that your wife is an adulteress, Kirchner. She took pleasure in me ravishing her, filling her like you never could.'

'Don't believe a word he says!' Susanna shouted, horrified. 'He's lying!' She quickly rifled through her notebook, trying to find a stronger spell to use against her opponent.

'That's a wicked lie!' Bastian stepped forward. His fear transformed into a blind rage that overpowered his every thought and all reason. Dietrich's words prompted his imagination to conjure up vivid, hateful visions of his wife tangled up with the sorcerer.

'Oh, so it's a mere coincidence that she hasn't wanted you since I had my way with her?' Dietrich sneered. 'Think about it. *Really* think about it.'

'That's—'

'You want proof? Fine. She has a small birthmark just above her sex.' Dietrich thrust his hips back and forth. 'I saw it dance before my eyes. Then I turned her around and took her from behind. And she begged me for more, for hours and hours, that I—'

'You bastard!' Bastian lunged and threw himself at the man, pulling out his pocketknife in the process. He forgot about the terrifying dog, the witchcraft and the sorcery that he'd witnessed. The blade would cut the abominable sorcerer's throat, cut out his lies and end his life. 'How dare you accuse my wife!'

Dietrich dodged the blade and struck him with his head.

The blow to Bastian's forehead caused him to stagger sideways as he absorbed the momentum of his own vicious attack.

Susanna shouted words at him that he didn't understand. Furious, he leapt again at the old man with his knife.

Dietrich laughed mockingly and moved his upper body to the side again and again, narrowly yet unswervingly missing the blade. 'Now we'll see if the feather really is mightier than the sword.' He plucked the long pheasant feather from his beret and lifted it like a fencing foil. 'En garde!'

Bastian couldn't believe his eyes. His opponent had deflected his knife attack with the feather as if it were made of forged steel, but all he'd heard when it had collided with his blade was a soft fluttering sound. Dietrich fended off the next attack with the deck of cards; Bastian's blade broke off without leaving a scratch or cut on the glowing ace of spades.

'And now for the best part! All thanks to the spell that your wife cast to punish and destroy me,' Dietrich said. 'Everything that's happened in this mill, this was my plan all along, you fools!' He swung the feather. 'Just like I planned your death, card-maker.'

Bastian jumped back and tried to push the pheasant feather away from him with the palm of his hand, but it slashed his fingers, pierced his waistcoat and shirt, cut through his skin and drove into his stomach.

He gasped in horror and surprise that something so light and fragile could be as lethal as the toughest and sharpest of metals. Then the pain tormented him in the worst possible way. Susanna's voice mingled with his cries of pain. He still couldn't understand what she wanted him to do.

Laughing, Dietrich pulled the feather out of the wound and slashed Bastian's throat, which immediately split open and unleashed a gushing stream of crimson. 'That was planned, too!' he exclaimed and fanned out the cards. He soaked them in Bastian's splattering blood and whispered something.

Bastian sank to his knees and the light in the ramshackle

mill faded. As he died, he watched the paper inexplicably absorb his blood without becoming stained. Somewhere, ravens cawed excitedly.

Dietrich pinned the dripping, glistening, red pheasant feather back onto his beret. 'Blood is a juice of rarest quality, Master Kirchner, and yours not only seals our pact, but also completes my masterpiece. The cards will absorb your hatred for me, and for that I must thank you in advance. Your soul is now free to roam the heavens and you can rejoice: your queen of hearts will follow you in just the blink of an eye.'

Bastian collapsed to one side, wheezing, and his head hit the floorboards.

* * *

Susanna watched the man she loved die like some slaughtered animal. Her horrified scream echoed throughout the mill.

The sight of Bastian bleeding to death on the floorboards and the pools of red surrounding him made her flick past the white magic spells and resort to means she had initially dismissed. Only dark magic could help her fight Dietrich.

Susanna pointed her arm at him. She fought back tears as she read from her ancestor's notes, because she knew that, if her spell failed, she would join Bastian in the afterlife and their children would be sent to the orphanage. Dietrich would be waiting for them in his cell. He would raise them, corrupt them and do unspeakable things to them.

Her hatred for the man gave her the courage to pronounce the dangerous syllables and cruel sounds until they began to flow naturally.

Dietrich seemed unperturbed. 'What are you doing now to bring me down?' he laughed at her, and held the untarnished, bright deck of cards in his bloody hands. 'His hatred, your magic, my preparations and the symbols have made the cards indestructible. They'll take over the world.' He looked at her, gradually losing his air of superiority. 'Do you really think you can reverse my spell? Your witch symbols aren't powerful enough. Besides, I expected this anyway.'

Susanna spoke unwaveringly, her eyes fixed on her rival.

She felt the darkness take hold of her and let it consume her, harnessing its power. An irreconcilable sensation stirred up inside her, giving birth to a black diamond that entrapped everything that was bad and evil in the world, eager to unleash its power against Dietrich at once. It grew in size and gradually gnawed at her.

'You and your beloved card-maker helped me plunge the world into chaos.' Dietrich slowly approached her. The dog had gone raving mad, wanting to bite and tear the woman to pieces, but couldn't move past the markings on the floor. 'The three of us forged this curse. I could never have done it alone. Sibylle already told me as much.' He attempted to lift his foot over the obstacle and failed. 'That's right: it was your ancestor who gave me the idea, but, since she didn't become immortal like me, we brought children into the world who would support me in our endeavours when the time was right.'

Susanna didn't believe a single word that came out of his mouth. After he had defiled and robbed her of her husband, he was lying to try to escape his own doom and lure her onto his side. She would never let him live. She turned over the page. Four more lines and the death curse would strike him down.

'If you want a duel and to die in this mill, so be it,' he said, holding the glowing cards in his right hand. 'The more blood the cards drink, the better. My work here isn't finished yet.' He began to wield his own curse.

Susanna immediately felt the spell's effect – and saw it manifest. Evil collided with evil. Black and grey streaks surrounded her in a deafening pandemonium, reaching out to strangle and scourge her, but the symbol of light at her feet protected her.

Dietrich screamed in rage and doubled down on his efforts.

Arched thorns as long as daggers emerged out of the swirling mist, piercing through the protective spell and scratching Susanna's skin with poisonous needles. Without the magic to rescue her, the tendrils would have enveloped her from head to toe, stabbed and ripped her apart a dozen times. The burning sensation came first; the ice cold came second. Her arms, legs and every part of her body felt numb.

Susanna couldn't defend herself or stop her paralysed arms from dropping. She lost sight of the last and crucial line of the death curse. *No!*

Dietrich, meanwhile, suddenly looked like the old man he really was: a frail, ancient centenarian with a hunched back, scrawny body and crooked bones. The strain of the spell had taken its toll, but his eyes still blazed with the power of his mind.

He dropped his arm, panting. 'Now what are you going to do, little witch?' he croaked. 'You're going up against a master. Did you really think you stood a chance with Sibylle's little verses?'

It was over. Susanna had to admit to herself that there was nothing more she could do. Her arms hung limply by her torso. The letters from her notebook were out of reach. Dietrich would win again and corrupt mankind with his deck. She stared at the smouldering pack of cards that would drink her blood. *It was over. She had lost.*

Then, as if out of thin air, a shadow appeared by her side. It lifted her stiff arms up so that the little book hovered before her eyes, allowing her to read the last line.

'Hurry, Mrs Kirchner,' Goethe said hastily next to her. 'Or else we'll both be doomed!'

'Goethe!' Dietrich snarled. 'You'll join her in hell!' He raised his hand in the air and the tendrils tightened their grasp.

Susanna read the last line of the curse, screaming it at Dietrich with all the rancour she could muster.

The spell was a straight beam of scorching, obsidian hatred that made the air hiss and seethe as it flew from the book.

'Careful!' Goethe warned, and quickly smudged the protective markings in front of Susanna's shoes so that the conjured curse didn't bounce off it or shatter.

The poodle had been waiting for this and instantly leapt at Susanna. Goethe threw himself between them and went down with the dog behind her.

'No!' Dietrich held up the pack of cards to absorb the spell. 'I won't be defeated! Not by you!'

The entire deck gleamed bitter black. A raging storm broke out and the roar of a hundred unleashed demons erupted, making the shabby mill shake. Dust and wood splinters rained down from the ceiling.

Susanna upheld the spell and saw with malicious joy that Dietrich couldn't counteract the curse.

He fell to his knees, screaming. Smoke curled from his mouth, as if he were burning from the inside. 'I won't let my greatest work perish! Oh, Lords of Hell: I do this for our eternity!' he cried and removed the pheasant feather from his beret.

Before Susanna could intervene, he slit his throat and let his blood splatter all over the cards.

The death curse immediately evaporated.

A hissing red vapour drifted upwards. Dietrich collapsed onto his side, his eyes wide and lifeless. The cards slipped from his hand, crackling softly like hot coals.

He had sacrificed himself to save the cards from more spells and the ravages of time, which otherwise even mountains couldn't withstand. But the man, the monster and the Strange Son of Chaos was dead.

'Mrs Kirchner, help me,' she heard Goethe groan behind her.

Susanna whirled around.

The student lay next to the giant poodle whose throat and stomach he had cut open with a knife. At first she thought that Goethe had escaped the dog's teeth, but then she spotted a fine mark on his hand. It was discoloured and looked like it had just become infected.

'Poison,' Susanna murmured in horror. She had no idea how Dietrich had ever handled the beast's fangs; the slightest scratch meant certain death. Without the right herbs, she couldn't do anything to help against such a hateful, dirty trick. 'Hold on, Goethe! I'll take you to the city.'

He writhed from the agonising pain, vomiting and coughing up blood throughout the old mill. His words were drowned out by the sound of his own suffering as he spewed out his lifeblood onto the floorboards again.

'Don't you dare die on me too!' Susanna yelled at him. 'Don't you even think about it, Goethe, do you hear?' She grabbed the pack of cards and pocketed it to examine later in peace.

Goethe was trembling and drenched in cold sweat. 'I . . . can't . . . walk,' he stammered.

The young man who had bravely come to her defence urgently needed medical help. 'I'll carry you.' She helped him up and supported almost all of his weight.

Her eyes focused on her dead Bastian, whose body lay some distance from Dietrich's.

As they began to walk, her mind raced uncontrollably. How was she ever going to explain this to the council?

She wouldn't. No matter how much the thought pained her, she would report her husband as missing tomorrow. If the body was found, the council would assume that a crime had been committed. Murder out of greed. Everyone knew that Bastian Kirchner liked to have some money in his pocket to gamble with. That would be enough to attract a pack of riff-raff.

After only a few steps, Susanna was panting from exertion. Goethe could barely stand on his own two feet. She would never make it to Leipzig with such a heavy load; it would be impossible, given her own state.

So she laid the unconscious man at the entrance to the Abtnaundorf Manor, pressed the bell at the gate and hid. She didn't want to risk being seen here as she had told Mrs Stock that she was running a couple of errands in town. Besides, there was still the task of disposing of Dietrich's body.

A servant arrived at the gate, saw Goethe and ran back to the house, then returned with one of Breitkopf's sons. Together, they carried the student into the manor.

Relieved, Susanna made her way back to the mill to finish her work. She hoped that the Breitkopfs would have the presence of mind to quickly take poor Goethe to Leipzig by carriage. A doctor would know how to help him.

Once she was back at the mill again, she looked around her. *It was time to dispose of the evil man's body.* Old weighing scales and small, broken millstones lay in the far corner. *That would do the trick.*

Susanna dragged Dietrich's body into the corner, tied the weights and the pieces of stones to the dead man, stuffed his pockets and rolled him into the Parthe in the shelter of the willow. She threw in the slashed poodle after him. The fish would eat the dog and its master.

She took the time to wash out the worst of the bloodstains from her dress and rubbed wild berries over them. The fruity smell would fool any onlookers.

Then she hurried back to Leipzig furtively, did a long loop of the shops to make sure she'd been seen and bought some fruit to further explain the stains.

It was only when Susanna returned to the attic that she finally broke down and surrendered to the agony in her soul.

XIV

Cotonou, Benin,
West Africa

Hyun drank her iced coffee through a straw. It appeared people in Cotonou liked their brew extra strong and with lots of sugar. Hyperactivity and sweat episodes were inevitable for the next few hours, not to mention the brain freeze.

She was standing leaning against the window of the airport kiosk where she had bought her coffee, watching Boch negotiate with the employee of the car rental company from afar. There appeared to be some kind of issue. He held his injured arm at a slight angle by his stomach. Hyun had checked his wound several times, and the stitches and the tissue surrounding it looked as they should.

They had chosen to store their luggage in lockers this time, since they never knew how long they'd have to stay in one place while hunting down a card. That way, they wouldn't need to make a detour via a hotel should they need to rush back to the airport. Hyun had also decided not to exchange her money into the local Benin currency as she'd already exchanged her euros for US dollars at the bureau de change.

The doctor coped better than most Europeans with such humid weather. Although she had lived in London for a long time, the Korean climate had prepared her for the sweltering West African heat, where temperatures rarely dropped below thirty degrees Celsius. Even at night. And, thanks to the recent rainfall, walking around Cotonou felt like taking a hot shower.

Hyun pushed the cheap panama hat she had just bought onto her black hair, settled on one of the benches, finished her coffee and placed two ice cubes on the back of her neck. She shivered in delight as the melting, cold water ran down her light, bright-coloured blouse.

Then she whipped out her tablet and connected to the airport's Wi-Fi to read up on the latest news in Leipzig and around the world.

Her initial search revealed that the police were looking into a vandalism and theft case at the Grassi Museum. CCTV footage had been examined, but the detectives hadn't been able to pin down a concrete offender responsible for the costly prank. It was assumed to have been a dare among some teenagers from a school.

Hyun grinned. *It was just as Boch had planned.*

While searching for Cotonou, she also came across multiple hits on international news websites. Both the least and most reputable media had reported on Sowande Aristide Gondjia, the demented voodoo priest who had killed and seriously injured dozens of people in a 'demonic delirium'.

Hyun swore softly in Korean as she read the reports one by one.

In short, foreign journalists and news agencies presumed that Gondjia had been in a drug-induced haze when he committed the crimes, while some Beninese media claimed that a failed voodoo ritual had been the trigger. The statements of anonymous witnesses were cited as evidence.

But what happened to the ace of spades? Hyun meticulously searched for footage of the crime scene, found the crossroads where the killings had taken place and studied them.

One photo showed the voodoo priest stripped down to his

blood-soaked underwear, throwing himself at the shooting police officers with a bottle of rum and a machete. Then there were several blurry mobile phone videos of the raging man's execution.

Hyun paused a video where she spotted a little altar in the background that the bokor had erected at the crossroads for his summoning ritual. There was something on top of it that looked roughly the same size as a playing card, but her excitement immediately dissipated: the photos taken after Gondjia's death revealed people dancing and celebrating in the same spot along with the trampled remains of the miniature shrine.

Was the card still there? Hyun looked up. Boch was still talking to the employee. Finding the card would be tricky.

At the same time, she felt immense relief after learning about Gondjia's death. A tonne of fear left her body. Hyun had been dreading her encounter with Gondjia and had been afraid that a situation like the one in Arras – only far more violent – would repeat itself. A half mudang going up against a bokor who was worshipped in Benin and had fled Haiti thanks to his powerful voodoo capabilities . . . That would have cost her her mind. Or even her life.

And yet Hyun felt strangely regretful. However she chose to look at it, she possessed the gift for shamanism, but without her grandmother's guidance she couldn't reach her full potential and had to rely on her intuition and her instincts, which she didn't feel were strong enough to tackle their next task. The shock and the card's attacks in Arras had knocked her back once again. *Now I can't even tell the real ace of diamonds from the fake ones.*

She found herself staring at nothing, her mind spinning.

As a doctor who had worked in A&E and volunteered abroad at refugee camps, she knew that she was suffering from post-traumatic stress. She had worked in various international hospitals in developing and war-torn countries; she wasn't a stranger to operating theatres, blood, stern instructions, nasty wounds or the stench, but that had all been sterile in its own way and under controlled conditions.

It was nothing like what Hyun had experienced in the tunnels.

The journey to Benin had helped her recover a little from the bloodbath, the confinement of the tunnels and the card's malicious attacks in Arras. She'd benefited from being back above ground and some concentration exercises, as well as the tranquilisers that she didn't want to do without.

Hyun flinched as her tablet pinged: a new message.

She glanced down at the screen and saw a video message from her mother and stepfather. Acting against her better judgement, she pressed play.

'Hi, darling,' her mum began. 'We hope you're doing okay wherever you are.'

'We've spoken with the hospital board,' her stepdad added, clearly trying to be gentle with her. 'They understand how you must be feeling right now, but they're expecting you to return to work soon. You're a talented surgeon and they've put your name down for an operation.'

'Enrico wouldn't have wanted you to suffer like this,' her mother said. Her fretting had etched deep wrinkles around her features. 'We can find a therapist for you to talk to.'

'We want to be involved and help you get better,' her stepfather intervened. 'We're giving you one more month. Hide away, give in to the pain, but then . . . Come back to London. We need to talk about everything. Even Baden-Baden.'

Her mum moved closer to the camera. 'Don't forget that we love you, darling. No matter what.'

They both smiled at the camera and the video ended.

Hyun blinked and fiddled with her engagement ring. She didn't blame her parents for looking out for her and interfering, but if they knew about Baden-Baden then either Klim had side-stepped the lawyer and spoken to them, or Lazarev senior had been in touch.

Or maybe Gillot was behind this? Or someone from the press? Regardless, a month was enough time to collect the cards and destroy them.

Boch had moved away from the counter, and held a set of car keys in his hand. Judging by his body language and the expression on his face, he wasn't in the best of moods. When he was an arm's length away from Hyun, she suddenly sensed the presence of the cards again, the queen of hearts and the ace of diamonds, which he carried in a pouch around his neck. She could distinguish their individual frequencies; the cards appeared to be communicating and exchanging energies.

Hyun breathed a sigh of relief. The crippling fear of a show-down between her and Gondjia seemed to have melted away some of the mental block that had paralysed her in Leipzig. *I can do it!* Boch opened his mouth to speak, but Hyun raised her right hand to stop him.

'Give me the aces of spades. All of them,' she said.

'Here?'

'Trust me, Boch. I have a good feeling about this.'

Boch furtively handed her all of the cards as if they were some kind of contraband.

She was ready for the test.

Hyun kept her blue eyes fixed on the front of each card and slid the aces from one hand to the other. If she didn't sense any hatred emanating from a card, she simply dropped it.

The real ace of diamonds stopped shimmering as soon as Boch handed it to her. It appeared to be hiding itself from her.

The number of cards in Hyun's hand gradually decreased until there were only two left.

'Now the queen of hearts, please,' she told Boch without looking at him. She placed the ace of diamonds in her lap. Hyun picked up on the resentment radiating from the card she'd been handed and instantly remembered the profound hatred that she had felt in Arras. The queen of hearts was strong and self-assured, and it used its powers to tear down timid souls and fragile psyches.

Hyun's heart raced and she immediately began to sweat. *You can't shake me.* She held the queen of hearts over the aces, switching between them, moving the card from right to left in the same rhythm to provoke a reaction. It was exhausting to focus her entire mind on her mudang instincts.

Finally, the card on her left leg flickered and revealed itself. Hyun carelessly tossed the other card aside and placed the real one on top of the queen of hearts. She handed the pair back to Boch. 'That's the one.'

He looked at the nine duplicates on the dirty hall floor. 'I mean no offence, Miss Poe, but are you sure?'

Hyun beamed at him. 'One hundred per cent.'

She noticed that the cards were beginning to share their energies with each other again and that the hatred towards her was ebbing away. They seemed to feel calmer and more comfortable around Boch. Was it because he was more susceptible to their whispers?

'There's some news about Gondjia,' she told him, 'the voodoo priest.'

'Well, as long as he's not standing right behind me . . .'

She laughed. 'Don't worry: he's been caught.' She quickly summarised what she'd read while Boch sat next to her and looked through the photos and videos. He came to the same conclusion as her: they couldn't avoid searching the crossroads.

'It's good I got us a car.' He lifted up the keys. 'It was described as an exquisite vehicle for vintage car enthusiasts – a Land

Rover Series II Defender from 1961. It's so old it must have been in *Get Carter*.'

'You mean we've got a rusty piece of junk?'

'With dents and scratches, and a mileage of over 300,000 miles,' Boch said in a feigned salesman's voice. 'Nobody will want to rob us.' He stood up. 'Great work on the research on Gondjia, by the way. And the aces.'

'Thanks.' Hyun glanced at the discarded cards lying on the floor. She picked them up and was about to throw them in the nearest rubbish bin, but then changed her mind and slipped the nine copies into her bag.

They stocked up on drinks for their journey at the kiosk and left the airport.

Hyun and Boch instantly recognised their Land Rover in the rental car park: a sand-coloured, angular off-road vehicle, which must have survived countless knocks, collisions and crashes with both animals and other cars. You wouldn't find a scrappier model.

'Now that's what I call British quality,' Hyun said. As she still had to take care of something, she left the driving to Boch despite his injured arm.

Their drive from the airport, through the bustling trading city, and to where the voodoo priest had met his death began. The Land Rover clattered and screeched at every corner; its suspension was practically non-existent.

Hyun grabbed the laptop they had stolen from Gillot's house in Bruges and looked through its contents again, but nothing she found surprised her. None of the hidden files contained anything illuminating. It was all about Black Sara.

Only when she clicked on the recycle bin icon did she discover a document that she hadn't checked yet.

'I should have known,' she muttered impatiently.

'Found anything?' Boch asked.

'Hang on.' Hyun double-clicked on the file. 'Oh, yes, I've found something all right,' she said slowly. Her eyes scanned the document. 'And just when I was about to give up!'

'I can drive and listen at the same time.'

Hyun opened a bottle of water and took a few sips. 'Gillot most likely hired a certain Doctor Schwemer from Stuttgart to find out who hid the playing cards from the Devil's Playbook in other cards.' She kept reading and scrolling. 'Oh, wow! The historian spent a whole year researching and digging through archives.'

'Did he find anything?'

'Yes and no.' Hyun highlighted the relevant passages in a different colour so that they would be easier to find next time. 'Apparently there was a so-called Benjamin Carl Dietrich, a distant relative of Martin Dietrich from Leipzig. Benjamin Dietrich tried to find the deck of cards, but it doesn't say who he was or why he looked for them. Schwemer must have written a longer report, but it's not here.'

'Let me guess, this Benjamin looked for the cards and hid them inside others as soon as he found them?'

'That's Schwemer's theory. He bases this on some letters exchanged between Benjamin and a friend, but the friend wasn't involved in the search for the cards and dismisses their potential supernatural effects. I didn't find the names of any other people involved.'

'Why did he hide the cards?'

'It doesn't say.' Then she saw a comment. 'Wait, here it is: out of . . . malice. It seems Benjamin knew about the playbook's bad influence and secretly wanted to palm it off on players to cause conflict.' Hyun's eyes flitted back and forth. 'He then died in a pub fight in Dresden after cheating at cards,' she summarised. 'He only found two or three of the original cards.'

Boch laughed. 'Well, he certainly proved the cards' bad influence. That Benjamin Dietrich must have been a weak man!'

She didn't comment and took a long sip of water. 'Then there was someone else at the end of the 19th century, a businessman from Genoa who desperately wanted the deck. Giacomo Ludovico Santoro. He acquired over half the cards in the deck during his lifetime,' she read aloud. 'After being robbed several times, he had duplicates made and hid the originals in other cards.'

'How did he die?'

'In a carriage accident. Santoro's house was raided and his family murdered soon after the accident. There's a small list of owners of individual cards dating from 1790 and what happened to them here. None of them died of natural causes. It looks like we've solved the mystery.'

'Provided Doctor Schwemer's research is accurate.' They had reached the outskirts of Cotonou. The roads were steadily becoming worse and they eventually found themselves driving over rough terrain. He squeezed a painkiller out of a packet with one hand, chewed on it and shoved the pack of pills back into his trouser leg pocket. 'I wonder what Morgan wanted with the cards.'

'You said he told you to hide them.'

'There's probably a secret society of some sort . . . A card lodge. For all the people who know about the playbook.' Boch clearly liked this idea. 'Just like in a novel, you know?'

'A lodge that maybe Morgan had been part of,' Hyun considered, nodding. 'That could mean that Gillot's unknown rival is also part of the same circle. Schwemer would be a good person for us to talk to. He might know more.'

'Let's focus on the cards first,' Boch suggested.

'Sure.'

She turned off the laptop and stowed it under the back seat. 'It looks like we're here.'

She looked around. Tourists clearly didn't wind up in this part of Cotonou. It was clear that as soon as they stepped out of the off-roader – a tall Asian woman with a shorter white man at her side – they would attract people's attention. Their strategy of keeping a *low profile* had already failed.

Boch scanned their surroundings through the car's dusty windows. 'Can you sense where the card might be?'

He turned up the AC to the highest possible setting. The car's ventilation system was so inefficient it was almost impressive: it drew in the humid, hot air from outside and refined it with engine fumes. Hyun immediately switched it off.

Boch knew perfectly well that she had to be within an arm's length of a card to feel anything, but she could empathise with his impatience. 'I think the photos can give us a clue as to where to start looking.' She powered up her tablet and zoomed in to the pictures of the crime scene, comparing them with the footage circulating online. What she read made her feel uneasy. 'Before the police shot Gondjia, he raided the houses in the area looking for victims to satisfy his bloodlust.'

'So he might have lost the card in the process,' Boch said, inspecting the houses one by one. 'The card could be anywhere. Even in an evidence room somewhere.' He nodded to her encouragingly. 'We need your mudang powers again, whether you like it or not.'

'The ace of spades was on the little altar, remember?' Hyun held up the tablet, turned it around and compared the photos to their surroundings. 'You can stop the car now. We're in the right place. The small altar' – she pointed to the streets – 'that Gondjia used to summon his demon or spirit was at this cross-roads. The press mention a god called Kalfu.'

Boch stopped the rickety Defender on the side of the dusty track. 'Does that name mean anything to you?'

Hyun laughed. 'Did you just ask me if I know about voodoo just because I talk about Korean shamanism all the time?'

'There are more parallels between religions than people think.' Boch pulled a baseball cap over his brown hair, which was slick with sweat from the humidity. 'And you were doing research online this whole time, so who knows?'

'Voodoo is more extensive than shamanism.' Hyun got out of the car and put on her panama hat to shield herself from the sun. A pair of dark sunglasses rested over her eyes. Boch knew nothing about the invisible things she could sense. The wretched cards glowed and glimmered in his inside pocket, as if whispering to each other and trying to hide from her.

It's up to me now. Hyun suspected that the ace of spades had unleashed Gondjia's bloodlust. The card had either wanted to get rid of its old owner or had used him for a specific purpose.

They approached the crossroads.

Silhouettes appeared behind the windows and curtains. The residents followed the unusual pair's every step on the dusty street. Resentment radiated from the homes. Hyun felt like she was running the gauntlet.

Lots of empty, long bullet shells lay on the ground. Forensics hadn't bothered to collect them all. But apart from the dried blood on some of the stones, nothing was left in the dust of the crossing. Countless tyres had driven back and forth here.

Some children looked up from their game in the shadows. Curious shouts drifted in their direction.

Hyun ignored them and focused, dropping to a crouch and searching with her arms outstretched, tapping into her gift. She had shown herself in the airport that she could do it, even with a stubborn card. She moved her splayed fingers over the ground, waiting and trying to catch the faintest tingling sensation. Nothing. *The ace of spades isn't here.*

Bemused, Boch poked around the sand with a stick, uncovering little pieces of painted wood, more empty cartridges, plenty of broken glass and a fragment of a painted staff. The passing traffic had crushed everything to the ground.

Hyun glanced at the laughing and giggling African children in shorts and colourful t-shirts. They imitated Boch and the Korean doctor, making fun of their fumbling and digging around.

Children and a playing card. Hyun was suddenly struck by an idea. She stood up and walked towards the group, pulling out some US dollars from her handbag.

'Do any of you know English?' she asked, smiling, and then added in her own language: 'Or Korean?'

'Or French?' Boch cried out from a distance and continued to search the crossing. He clearly didn't want to negotiate with children.

'You're beautiful,' one of the girls with long Rasta braids said in French. She looked no older than ten.

'No, she's just different,' a boy with short-cropped hair butted in. Despite towering over the girl, he seemed younger than her.

Hyun grinned and took off her sunglasses. If only everyone saw things the way children did. The world would be a simpler place. 'Is different better or worse?'

'Different is just different.' The girl studied her Asian features. 'Pretty eyes!'

'Different eyes,' the boy corrected her, who appeared to interpret her every remark as some kind of personal challenge. The other children whispered among themselves, not taking their eyes off the stranger.

The girl remained curious and smiled. She clasped her hands behind her back. 'What are you looking for?'

'I'm Hyun,' Poe introduced herself and bowed.

'My name is Bijou. And this is Coutoucou, my brother, who always thinks he knows best. No, who always thinks *differently*.' The girl then introduced her to her ten friends, whose names Hyun immediately forgot; but she nonetheless bowed to each of them in the Korean tradition.

The children found this funny. They giggled and bowed back.

'So,' Hyun said, lowering her voice mysteriously. 'I'm sure you know about the terrible things that happened here.'

'The bokor,' Coutoucou uttered suddenly and made some sort of gesture. 'They shot him down like . . . like one of those wild dogs.' He assumed the stance of a gunman and imitated the rattling of automatic rifles. 'They fired so much.'

'They were scared. He was dangerous,' Bijou said, her eyes wide. 'Papa says he killed and injured lots of people.'

'I've been looking for the bokor for a long time,' Hyun confessed. 'And do you know why? Because he stole from me.' She reached into her bag and pulled out one of the worthless aces of diamonds. *Good thing I kept it.* 'It looks something like this. Only with a different suit.' She handed the card to Bijou. 'It's beautiful, don't you think?'

'So beautiful. Not different,' Coutoucou said, admiring it. 'Have you got another one?' He held out his hand demandingly.

'Maybe you've heard about what happened to the card that the bokor had?'

'It was on the altar.' Bijou pointed to the crossroads. 'He put it on top.'

'His Kalfu was inside it.' Coutoucou looked around importantly. 'That's what he said. I heard him say it.'

'Don't be so stupid! Kalfu was inside him,' his sister objected.

'No. The mighty Kalfu was inside the card!' Coutoucou looked at Hyun. 'That's what my maman said.'

'*That's* the card I'm looking for,' Hyun said and flashed her most charming smile.

'Can you do voodoo too?' Coutoucou marvelled. 'But how? There's no such thing as voodoo in China.'

'No, I can't. And I'm not Chinese. But the card still belongs to me.' Hyun could tell that Bijou knew more. The girl played with her braids and looked hesitant. 'What happened to the card? Did the police take it?'

'No. A woman did. She stood with us the whole time on the veranda and watched the bokor,' the girl blurted out. 'When they shot him, she went over to the crossroads, bent down and picked something up.'

'And you're absolutely sure that it was the card?'

Bijou lowered her brown eyes. She didn't want to lie, but she wanted to keep the card and earn some money off Hyun.

'Can you describe what she looked like?' Hyun asked her.

She listened to the girl's description of a black woman, which, while it was incredibly elaborate, wouldn't help her. She might as well have been told to go looking for a Korean woman in Seoul. 'Was there anything striking about her? Or could she still be nearby?'

Bijou shook her braids again.

Hyun still pressed the dollars into the girl's hand. 'Thank you.' It appeared they had a new rival, and they were losing sight of the trail. *As well as the ace of spades.*

'But I know what was painted on the card,' Coutoucou announced as if he were the mayor of Cotonou. He held out his hand longingly. 'And I know for sure that the woman took the card.'

'Aha! I can tell you want a reward.' Hyun slowly counted out the notes, passing them from one hand to the other. 'And *how* do you know that?'

'I lay under our veranda and saw everything that happened. Then I went to join the celebrations.' Coutoucou took a deep breath and described the playing card that Darlan had named as the fourth card missing: the ace of spades, surrounded by tiger lilies with golden stems, a moon in the background weeping black tears until they hit the earth, where they turned to blood. Coutoucou's description of the back of the card was also accurate. 'There was some writing at the bottom, too, but I couldn't read what it said. It wasn't in French. The woman lost her handbag and everything fell out. She had to pick everything up and then she grabbed the card and left,' he finished. 'Maman pulled me into the house when she saw me.'

Hyun paid the boy a little less than his sister because of his arrogance. 'Thank you, you two. What you've told me has helped me a little.'

Then she passed the remaining diamond duplicates from Leipzig around the group. The girls and boys snatched the cards and fanned themselves with them, laughing and snorting.

The best way to use cards.

Hyun got to her feet and walked up to Boch, who had acquired quite the collection of objects: bones, glass, wood, more glass and labels from rum bottles.

'Well, that worked,' he said. 'Your mudang was just as popular with the children as the Pied Piper.'

'It was more the foreign money and the fake aces of diamonds,' Hyun said, and told Boch what she'd learned. 'We now know that there's another rival, but we don't know anything about her.'

'And what about Gillot?'

'Don't you think he would have already sent his henchmen if that was the case?' Hyun thought about Madame Darlan's guards.

'Someone from the secret lodge, then?'

'But that's just a hunch!'

'I know. I was only joking.' Boch casually reached into his trouser pocket. He pulled out a bent and crumpled business card and held it up.

The front of it read: *Madame Spectreuse. Mambo.* There were mystical symbols drawn around the words, including a striking, laughing skull.

'Mambo. But I doubt she's a dance teacher.' Boch grinned. 'We should pay her a visit and find out exactly what mambo involves. Her business card screams voodoo to me. There's an address and a phone number. Shall we drive there?'

'Yes, we should go now.' Hyun turned and walked towards the Defender. 'Before the card possesses the madame like it did Gondjia. Good work, Boch.'

He followed her.

'And what if,' he mused as he walked behind her, 'the ace of spades possesses *you*, Miss Poe? What will we do then?'

'Then I hope you're strong enough,' Hyun replied without turning around, though she knew she would be able to resist the card's powers. Boch could think what he liked. The playbook's hatred and fear had caught her off guard once, but, now that she knew what the cards were capable of, she felt more prepared than ever. She wasn't surprised that the ace of spades' dark powers had driven Gondjia to commit endless atrocities.

On the other hand, Hyun wondered if the cards could make Boch snap and take her out. *I have to look out. For myself and for him.*

They drove back to the city centre and then to Cotonou harbour. The West African city was one of Benin's economic powerhouses – a large proportion of African trade was conducted here. Goods were loaded and unloaded at the huge wharves that Boch steered past in the rattling Defender, and there were lots of ships moored, as well as others coming and going. Huge oil and petrol tanks were guarded by watchmen armed with modern rifles and dogs. Further back in the harbour, a tangle of pipes and chimneys spewed exhaust fumes into the air.

The sat nav directed them past the warehouses, away from

the modern section with the shipping container frames and over to an area that was in desperate need of either renovation or demolition.

Soon they were driving past the smaller markets where traders sold fresh and frozen fish and towering pyramids of fruit and vegetables.

Boch turned into a small street where, as the countless sprawling washing lines with simple clothing revealed, the dock workers lived. The logos of various freight companies could be spotted on the drying laundry. Advertising signs for a bakery, a butcher's and a laundrette adorned the walls.

'There! There's *Madame Spectreuse. Mambo*,' Hyun read the words on the wall between the fluttering fabrics, which reminded her of Pride flags.

Boch stepped on the gas and swerved the Land Rover to the side. The car took a while before coming to a screeching, jolting halt. 'No brake booster whatsoever. My God! And no power steering either. I should never have been allowed to drive this thing,' he said, rubbing his injured arm.

They got out of the car. Boch went to the back of the SUV and grabbed a flat crowbar from the toolbox. Then the two of them walked towards the iron stairs that led to a rusty door under a '*Madame Spectreuse. Mambo*' banner.

'What do you call this place?'

'What do you mean?'

'Where she practises her voodoo. Is it a temple? A church?' He climbed up the first few steps. The clatter and thud of their footsteps echoed down the metal staircase.

Hyun wasn't sure either. 'Does it matter?'

'That's a little dismissive for a shaman's granddaughter.' Boch winked at her and stopped in front of the entrance. 'It says here that she's closed until further notice and to book any voodoo consultations with other available practitioners.'

Hyun stood next to him and read the handwritten notice, which had been wrapped in cling film and taped up. The message had clearly been written in a hurry. 'Do you think she left because of the card?'

'Maybe . . . Maybe she knew that someone would come after it,' Boch said contemplatively. 'What if the ace of spades eliminated Gondjia to disappear with Madame Spectreuse?'

Another shot in the dark. Hyun tried to peer though the barred windows, but some curtains obscured her view. The cards liked to keep them guessing.

Boch pounded the iron door with his crowbar. 'It's a heavy door, unfortunately.' He tapped the lock. 'But I can get it open. I've got a screwdriver and a hammer in the car. I once saw a handyman tear one off its hinges easily enough. Shall I have a go?'

Hyun glanced at the entrance. She couldn't feel a single trace of the ace of spades' presence. Hopefully there would be clues behind the door, something tangible like notes or accounting records – anything that would point them in the right direction. Otherwise their hunt for the playbook was over and they would have to face Gillot with one less card.

'Hey! Hey, monsieur et madame!' a determined voice called up to them.

They looked down. Boch hid the crowbar behind his back.

A strong young woman with light-brown skin, in a neon green shirt and matching shorts, was standing below the staircase. Her black hair was pinned up in a hairstyle that was as striking as it was tangled. 'What are you doing up there?'

'We had an appointment with Madame Spectreuse,' Hyun replied, lifting the bent business card. 'But she didn't say anything about closing.'

'Ah, yes. That all happened very quickly.' The woman gestured peremptorily for both of them to come down. 'I'm her landlady. She told me to pass on her apologies if any customers turned up.'

Hyun and Boch walked down the stairs and were immediately scrutinised from top to toe.

'Alors, you're a funny couple,' the landlady observed.

'We're so funny that we're currently working on a skit,' Boch said with a friendly smile.

'Forgive me, madame,' Hyun began, 'but when will Madame Spectreuse be back? We could come back tomorrow if—'

'That white guy *cracks me up*. He's *hilarious*,' she said, chuckling. Then her expression turned serious. 'Leila— I mean, Madame Spectreuse told me she won a trip.'

'Oh! Well we're happy for her,' Hyun replied in the same tone. Madame Spectreuse's first name wouldn't get them far. 'Where to, if you don't mind me asking?'

'Europe. To France.' The landlady paused for a moment to think. 'Or wherever the Pope used to sit. I think that was what she said,' she added. 'Slip a note with your number under her door. She'll call you when she gets back.' With that, she disappeared into the bakery.

'The Pope is in Italy, not France. In Vatican City,' Boch said, glancing at the entrance and playing with the crowbar. He clearly wanted to make sure that Madame Spectreuse hadn't left the card behind. 'What business could a voodoo priestess have with the Pope? What a poor excuse.'

Hyun was about to agree with him when another papal place sprang to mind. 'She said "where the Pope *used to sit*." Past tense.' Spectreuse hadn't lied to her landlady when she'd mentioned France, even if the reference was hundreds of years old. 'Avignon! She's gone to Avignon! That's where the antipopes once lived.' *And that's where Madame Darlan is.* Had the ace of spades chosen the mambo as its new owner because she was easier to control than the bokor?

'I'll call Madame Darlan.' Boch pulled out his phone, which almost slipped out of his hands in the mad rush. 'We have to go back now!'

* * *

Rome, Italy

Henry Pierre Gillot awoke from a nightmare to find himself grabbing his own neck. In his sleep, he'd been convinced that Saint Camillus de Lellis had climbed out of the desecrated painting to strangle him. But it wasn't Gillot's fault that a piece of the painting was missing.

The shock had shaken him awake. Gillot decided to make the most of this time before his medication caused him to doze off again.

He sat up as much as the cables and draining tubes would allow him, reached for his tablet and checked his emails. He was in desperate need of results. Nobody got to mess with him and seriously believe they had got away with it.

Gillot had spent a lot of money on his own safety, on Madame Darlan's safety, and on gathering information. He had to know who had tried to shoot him outside the basilica; he was sure that the mastermind behind it had stolen his eight of hearts from the painting and his precious cards from Bruges.

He twirled his Dalí moustache, his one shred of dignity despite the horrendous hospital gown, and felt reassured by the fact that he had reinforced his security. His bodyguards in the corridor stopped any unauthorised persons from entering his room, and his food was checked for common poisons.

Darlan was also safe again. Sebastian Ulrich and his hard-nosed men had arrived in Avignon now and had sent a brief report via email to update him on the situation. According to Ulrich, things had calmed down after a minor clash. Charles and Renard had been hacked to pieces by an enemy group, but the restorer had been freed in no time and appeared to be in good health.

That was all he'd needed to know: Darlan was irreplaceable. There were hundreds of Ulrichs and Renards, but no one quite like the elderly madame, who, despite her poor eyesight, worked miracles on the cards with her spider fingers.

Gillot heard a knock on his door. 'Come in,' he said.

The senior Doctor Spaldo, a dashing seventy-year-old with tanned skin and a thin moustache, walked into the room to check on his patient. They had an agreement that the doctor would check the most important readings and then leave if there was nothing out of the ordinary. Gillot was in no mood for conversation, but the man had annoyingly caught him wide awake and with the tablet in his hands.

'Signor Gillot!' Spaldo cried cheerfully. He wore an expensive suit under his white coat; the Italian custom of la bella figura – always dress well to make a good impression – applied to men too. 'Are you well?'

'You tell me, dottore.' Gillot smiled dismissively and put on his blue glasses. 'Scusi, but I'm actually busy right now.'

'Va bene. Then shall I tell the officer that you're fit for questioning?'

'No!' he protested, and reached into a drawer. He threw the doctor a bunch of purple euro notes that his sister had brought him. Money always helped. 'Not for another week. Grazie, dottore.'

'Naturalmente.' Spaldo pocketed the money, checked the readings and disappeared quietly outside. 'Buona notte.'

Gillot looked at the date on his tablet and tried to contain his frustration. Thanks to all the medication, he was wasting too much time sleeping. He couldn't work for longer than three or four hours a day, and spent the rest of the time dozing and lying there like a vegetable, struggling to stay focused. To top it all off, he had to wear tasteless hospital shirts that only came in ugly designs. He didn't even dare think about what his hair looked like. At least he still had his moustache.

The eagerly anticipated results came pouring in. News from various sources from the dark web and his regular network flooded his inbox.

Gillot cleaned his electric-blue glasses and read the message. It was now crystal clear. It was obvious who had sent the hit squad after him: Oprichnik, whose real name was Mikhail Aleksandrovich Lazarev. He was the father of the oligarch boy who had been shot at the Belle Époque.

Gillot swore. He had been bested by a deeply wounded, grieving father's despicable desire for revenge. Roux had killed the young Lazarev along with Solov'ëva and her mother because he had sabotaged his plan with the American in supérieur. If the evening had gone as planned, Roux would have secured the nine of spades.

Oprichnik naturally couldn't care less about that. His tsarevich had been murdered, someone had tipped him off that Gillot was somehow involved, and he had drawn his conclusions from that.

But that was where things got confusing. His sources all reported that Lazarev senior wasn't a collector, and therefore would have no interest in cutting up the Camillus painting to retrieve a card.

'Which means,' Gillot murmured and grabbed his phone 'that there was someone else in the basilica who knew what I was trying to save.' In other words, someone else knew about the eight of hearts.

It suddenly all became clear to him: there was an equally dedicated collector who had stolen the card from him in Rome, robbed him of his collection in Bruges and sent some people after Darlan to retrieve the cards she was restoring.

Gillot tried to digest this new information that complicated his life. He couldn't for the life of him think who this person trying to rob him of his victory so close to the finish line could be.

'I won't let you steal my playbook,' he muttered under his breath. He checked the position of his Dalí moustache and noticed when he touched his shaved cheeks that he'd lost a lot of weight. Gunshot wounds and hospital food didn't agree with him.

He dialled the number that Ulrich had given him for emergencies.

The phone rang.

And rang.

And rang.

'Merde!' Gillot cursed. He punched Darlan's landline number into his phone and pulled up the tracker on his tablet, which showed him the location of the restorer's ankle bracelet.

The signal was strong throughout the madame's premises.

She hadn't left the house or removed her anklet.

It rang.

And rang.

And rang.

Gillot's eyes darted between his phone and the monitor. It was possible that Darlan hadn't heard the ringing, but why wasn't Ulrich picking up?

He called Daan Mulder, who, according to his last text message, was in Frankfurt a few days later than expected due to his detour via Bogotá.

The phone rang.

And rang.

And rang.

'Merde!' he swore again and again, almost throwing the tablet and his glasses across the room. He began to panic. This had never happened to him before. Not in any situation, not during any excavation, auction, tricky business deal or even under the hail of bullets at the basilica.

He didn't know what else to do, and that was difficult for him to swallow.

He sent a message to his sister, asking her to come and see him right away. She had checked into a five-star, exceptionally comfortable and accessible hotel in Rome for *disibili* persons like herself. During the day, however, she stayed in the clinic in case he needed her. Even though their relationship as siblings couldn't be described as close or cordial, she knew that he valued his big sister's opinion on certain topics.

There was a sudden, energetic knock at his door, which could only be Samira. His sister didn't wait for an invitation to enter, just rolled into the room in her electric, ultra-modern wheelchair whose controls could be likened to a spaceship's operating panel. She was wearing a white dress paired with a black, fringed stole and countless necklaces, bracelets and rings that featured little symbols and pictures of Black Sara. He saw the deeply concerned expression on her face.

'I've almost never seen you this upset,' she said, stopping by his bed. 'Your one text was enough for me to know that something is very wrong.'

Gillot was amazed at how well she knew him. The power of sibling intuition. He could feel the blasted exhaustion catching up with him again; it would overwhelm him within minutes. 'Don't ask any questions, just listen first. Then you can tell me what you think.'

Samira nodded.

He told her everything, read out the messages and reports and presented her with his theories about the killers.

'But I have no idea,' Gillot concluded, unable to stifle his yawn, 'who this other person could be. They've only just stepped out onto the playing field.'

'Sat down at the card table, you mean,' Samira said.

'What?'

'It's a metaphor,' she explained softly. 'Like at a round of cards.' She thumbed the cross pendant that hung around her neck. 'How does Lazarev know you're involved?'

Gillot shrugged his shoulders, his eyelids as heavy as lead, drooping as if they were being pulled by invisible strings.

'. . .I'll check. Hey, Henry! Don't you fall asleep on me.'

He flinched as she shook him awake.

'Sorry. It's the drugs.' He sank back comfortably against the pillows, his mind half asleep. 'What did you say?'

'I said that I could go to Avignon to check on Ulrich with a second team as backup. We'll get Darlan out of there and leave the stranger no choice but to come after us. Set up a trap,' Samira repeated. 'You've spent too much time and energy on this collection, and I don't want someone to rob you of your triumph at the last moment. That isn't fair play.'

'No, it isn't, Samira, but that's because we're clearly not dealing with some well-mannered gentleman,' Gillot mumbled, drifting off. 'And that's exactly why you won't go.'

'Why not? Because I'm in a wheelchair?' She laughed scornfully, adjusting her fringed stole. 'You know I don't need it to get around. It's just more comfortable this way.'

'It's dangerous,' he murmured. 'Look what happened to me. And Renard. And Charles.' He exhaled deeply, succumbing to the drowsiness.

'I know. But Black Sara will watch over me,' he heard his sister say from far away. 'She will always protect me.'

* * *

Gillot tore himself from his slumber. His room was dark and he wasn't wearing his glasses. He cursed his medication. He had fallen fast asleep, and Samira must have taken off his glasses before she left.

His tablet lay on the small side table.

He fumbled around for his glasses, put them back on, grabbed the device and swiped down to check if any new emails had come in.

But what he saw gave him no peace.

Samira had left him a message on a virtual Post-it, which appeared on his display:

> *Don't be angry. I'm going to Avignon to defend your precious collection.*
> *I'll be in touch as soon as Madame Darlan and the cards are safe.*
> *Black Sara is with me. She has always been with me. You'll see.*
>
> *With sisterly love,*
> *Samira*

'That . . .!' Gillot was lost for words.

He had always presumed the stories about the Devil's Playbook cards were fiction, made up to drive up the price. He had no interest in all the superstitious rubbish. The cards were artistically unique, special, even breathtaking, but there was nothing supernatural about them.

But had he known what was coming, a part of him would have been willing to believe in the curse of the cards.

He deleted the Post-it that would have otherwise annoyed him the entire time and wrote a message to Samira. He had fallen asleep five hours ago. Assuming the weather conditions were fair and Samira had been able to secure high-speed transport, she couldn't be far from Avignon already.

As he typed, Gillot wondered who she had taken with her. Unlike him, she didn't have the right contacts in the twilight world. And Black Sara wasn't taking any bullets.

If you've gone to Avignon alone, he wrote, *then we're in for the biggest row of our lives, sister! Please—*

The door suddenly swung open and Gillot lifted his head in the hope that Samira had come back.

A man in an elegant suit and with a balaclava over his head stood on the threshold. He raised his hand, holding a muffled rapid-fire pistol. 'Greetings from Oprichnik,' the intruder said.

Gillot blinked, trying to understand what was happening. *Where were the bodyguards and the police?* He reached for the alarm button, but the smooth plastic slipped from his grasp.

'*Spokoĭnoĭ nochi!*' The Russian killer gripped the automatic pistol with both hands and pulled the trigger.

'No! Whatever Lazarev is pay—' Gillot saw a spark flicker at the very back of the thick muffler – a tiny gas flame that didn't want to ignite, a fluorescent yellow will-o'-the-wisp dancing in the gently twitching barrel.

He tried to roll away, but it was too late. The bullets struck him. They ripped open his stitched wounds and tore the cables and wires, causing wound fluids and blood to splatter all over the white wall and the bed linen.

Gillot slumped in the hospital bed, a bloody, tattered bundle. Even Dottore Spaldo was powerless against such injuries.

* * *

Avignon, Vaucluse,
Provence-Alpes-Côte d'Azur,
France

Daan Mulder parked the rented Renault in the large car park near the tourist office at the Temple Saint-Martial church and strolled along Nicolas Lescuyer Street with his heavy hiking backpack stuffed with dollar bills.

He had used the oldest and most dangerous trick in the book to get the money through customs; he liked to call it the king's messenger.

Daan had once invested a huge amount of money in a fake diplomatic passport and several diplomatic baggage labels, which he'd only used twice out of worry that he might get caught: two years ago when he'd needed a weapon on site, and now. As a member of an Arab country's diplomatic corps, he had arrived at German customs, taken the cash with him and walked out, his shirt dripping in what felt like ten litres of sweat from the thrill.

On his long journey to Avignon he had counted his new acquired wealth, which totalled just under six million US dollars. The cash weighed roughly sixty kilograms and still smelled faintly of diesel. It was his best pay cheque to date.

Nevertheless, Daan was feeling melancholy. While he was bringing back the card, he was also bringing the bad news of Fennec's death, and that would break Madame Darlan's heart.

The sacred sound of ringing church bells filled the air.

He knocked on Madame Darlan's front door and waited patiently. He saw the scene unfold in front of him: Charles most likely had a cake in the oven, and Renard would be tinkering with old tools and equipment in the barn.

The restorer opened the door, beaming at him. The familiar scent of freshly baked goods filled Daan's nostrils. 'Welcome back!' she said and brushed her patterned apron dress, visibly looking around to see if she could spot Roux. Then her smile vanished and she adjusted her thick glasses with her skinny fingers. 'Come inside, monsieur.'

'Thank you, madame,' he replied. Daan regretted being the bearer of bad news, but he had done everything in his power to try to save Roux. He would have loved to swap places with some-one right now.

He followed her into the kitchen, heaved the heavy rucksack from his back and set it down by a wall. He took a seat at the table at her invitation. The stains on the walls had disappeared.

'You made it back from Manaus,' Darlan said, pouring some coffee into a brightly decorated, gold-rimmed collector's cup as if they had something to celebrate. She sliced and dished out the cake, which smelled heavenly. It was the famous red wine and chocolate cake. 'Alone, monsieur?'

'Yes, madame.' Daan placed the card on the table. He'd wrapped it in a protective plastic cover despite its dire state. It was covered in scratches and soaked in blood, rainwater and sweat. 'This will require your utmost care.'

Madam Darlan sat down and took the card out of its cover. She held the jack of clubs up to the light, turning and twisting it around with her spider fingers.

'Is this my Fennec's blood?' she asked sadly without looking at her guest.

'It is, madame.'

'And he isn't here.'

'No, madame.'

'Is he in hospital?' Darlan tenderly ran her fingers over the ancient card as if it were in need of comfort; an unspoken promise to heal and restore it like a living, breathing patient. 'No, he isn't,' she answered for him. 'Please tell me what happened in the Amazon, monsieur.'

Daan looked at his coffee and his slice of cake. He couldn't bring himself to touch either until he'd told his story.

'I reached the crash site,' he said, then recited a detailed account. The jaguars and the panthers, the bullet wounds suffered by Roux and the woman, the poachers who had been torn to pieces, how the big cats had tried to protect the card and his escape, all spilled from his lips like a fast-flowing stream. He only missed the detail about the money he'd found. There was no harm in Darlan being none the wiser about that. 'The soldiers are dead,' he concluded. 'According to the news, the military in Manaus have launched a full-blown investigation into it. I imagine they'll blame it all on the poachers, madame.'

Darlan affectionately stroked the jack of clubs. 'My Fennec.' She swallowed. 'He sacrificed himself for the card.'

'Yes, madame. I think he waited to give it to someone he could trust before he let death take him.' Daan reached for his cup to take a sip of coffee, which was stronger than usual. Charles' hand must have slipped when measuring it out. 'Please accept my sincerest condolences, madame.'

Darlan held the card between her wrinkled, flat palms. 'This is his legacy. He treasured the cards, Monsieur Mulder. He understood them almost as well as I do.' She looked up, fixing her magnified blue-grey eyes on him through her glasses. 'He wasn't like you, monsieur. You're a man motivated by orders.' She smiled coldly. 'Forgive me, I didn't mean that as an insult.'

'I didn't take it as one, madame.' Daan placed the 30,000 euros she had given him on the table. 'I don't want it.'

'But—'

'You paid me to bring back Roux. To bring back your Fennec,' he interrupted her gently. He didn't say anything else.

'Which you failed to do, monsieur,' Darlan agreed. 'It's very honest of you to turn down the money.'

Daan opened his mouth to defend himself, but decided to hold his tongue. The restorer was in mourning and needed someone to blame in her anguish. That was fine by him, but he wouldn't berate himself. Darlan would think otherwise if she had seen Roux's wounds. It would have taken an emergency medical team, ten litres of blood and an operating theatre with all the necessary equipment to save him.

Daan finished his coffee in silence. He didn't dare touch the cake. 'Well, madame, I'll say my goodbyes,' he said softly. 'Once again, please accept my deepest sympathies.' He stood up.

'. . .weak,' he heard Darlan say.

Daan wouldn't let himself be reproached for not bringing back Roux's body with him. 'Madame, that would've been impossible. Carrying a dead man—'

Darlan lifted the jack of clubs. 'She's very weak.'

'Ah, I see.' He felt embarrassed by his faux pas. 'I'm sorry, I thought—'

She shook her grey mop of hair. 'Those wild cats feasting on Fennec is hardly a pretty picture, but I was talking about the card.' She laid it on the table as carefully as if it were made of porcelain. 'This will take a great deal of work.'

'If anyone can restore it, it's you, madame.'

'This is Fennec's legacy, you know. He sacrificed himself for the card. Ah, I've already said that, haven't I?' Darlan closed her eyes. A tear brimmed from the corner of her left eye and rolled down her wrinkled skin, running from one furrow to the next, glistening in the light. 'This will require so much strength,' she breathed.

'And I hope you're able to find it, madame.' Daan truly felt sorry for the restorer, even if she did sound a little strange. Grief and old age. 'Send Charles and Renard my regards.'

'I need you, Monsieur Mulder.'

He smiled dismissively. 'My work here is done. And I'm no restorer.'

'I need your energy, monsieur.' Without lifting her gaze, Darlan pointed her index finger to the middle of the jack of clubs. 'For the card.'

The woman's senile confusion became too much for Daan. 'Au revoir, madame. My plane leaves in two hours.' He reached for his backpack.

Suddenly, the kitchen doors swung open. Before he could even try to resist, several men in black and wearing balaclavas threw themselves at him. He could tell that they were professional killers from how they held him down and bent his arms so that his bones cracked. They wrapped cable ties around his neck and bound his wrists behind his back.

'No,' Daan croaked. He couldn't move and struggled to breathe, gasping for air. He'd walked into a trap. Someone had killed Renard and Charles and taken the restorer hostage. It was to do with the cards. Those cursed cards. 'Let me go. I won't cause any trouble or tell Gillot.' He didn't want to get caught in the crossfire between the mad collectors. 'Just let me go!'

Darlan opened her eyes, two more tears rolling down her cheek. 'I meant what I said, Monsieur Mulder. I need you. I need your energy to preserve Fennec's legacy.'

The doorbell rang shrilly.

'That's the next card, I hope.' Darlan looked at one of the masked men, her gaze hardening. 'Take him to the others in the cellar, please.'

That was when Daan Mulder realised: Odette Darlan wasn't a hostage. The squad of killers was hers.

Someone whacked him right in the back of the head with a hard object and the blinding pain flashed through his mind. The masked men dragged him into the corridor and he lost consciousness.

* * *

Odette got up from the table, cleared away Mulder's coffee cup and pushed the plate with the untouched piece of cake next to her own. Fennec was still on her mind, her dear, good Fennec who shared her passion and love for the cards.

Had shared.

She leaned back in her chair and took a long, sorrowful breath.

She didn't want to cry any more. Fennec had thought of her in his final hours. He'd gifted her the card. And she would never forget that. To honour him, she would do everything in her power to transform the jack of clubs into the most beautiful card of the deck. Her cellar was bursting with life. She could afford to be extravagant.

Odette adjusted her bun and wiped the sweat from her skin. The new guest would be here soon.

The card from Benin was still missing. The ace of spades – the most dangerous one of the lot. They needed to bring in either Boch and Poe or Madame Spectreuse, the mambo from Cotonou.

Odette felt prepared for visitors of any kind. She wasn't afraid of voodoo and she trusted in the cards.

The fact that the bokor had lost all control after summoning Kalfu didn't surprise her. The ace of spades harboured the greatest power and subsequently posed its owner and those around them the greatest danger. Gondjia had accomplished the no mean feat of containing the card and wielding its powers for his own interest for decades. He most likely had not only sacrificed rum, small gifts and animals to cast his curses and satisfy the card.

But the ace of spades hadn't wanted to be tamed any longer. It had heard its siblings' cries and fought with all its might to be reunited with them. As a result, the unwilling Gondjia had become its next victim. The ace had then looked for a willing courier to travel to Avignon.

Odette took a deep breath, smoothed her apron dress and calmly walked to the door.

One of her men followed her with a silenced, cocked Glock 17 pistol in his right hand. He stood in the corridor next to the entrance.

'There's one person, madame,' he whispered. The information

was reported to him via an earpiece. Neither he nor the rest of the mercenary group had removed their black balaclavas. 'Female. Alone. No weapons in sight. Only a carry-on suitcase.'

So the ace of spades had travelled with Madame Spectreuse. The card had left Boch and Poe in the dust. 'Black, I take it?'

'No, madame. White, around sixty.'

The lines on Odette's forehead deepened. She opened the door.

A somewhat younger woman with a careworn and disgruntled expression stood on the bottom step. While Odette was immediately struck by her resemblance to Gillot, her clothing was very plain and functional, with a touch of Romani influence.

'Bonjour! You must be Madame Darlan?' she said in a deep, powerful voice. The stranger stood at a slight angle, leaning on the doorframe with her left arm. Her other arm was in a sling, but with no cast or bandages. 'Please forgive the intrusion. We don't know each other. I'm Magdalena de Graaf, but you can call me Samira. My brother Henry Gillot sent me.'

Odette secretly signalled to the hiding mercenary in the corridor not to intervene. 'Bonjour,' she said slowly. The woman's likeness to Gillot suggested that there was some truth to her words. 'I'm sorry, but he never mentioned you. I'm . . . a little apprehensive.'

'I know. Henry told me about the attack on Charles and Renard.' De Graaf released her hand from the doorframe and swayed slightly, her leg wobbling as if it had a mind of its own. 'But I know he sent you some backup.' She pulled out an identity card and showed it to Darlan along with an old document indicating her maiden name – Gillot. 'I really am his sister.'

'Please come in, Madame de Graaf.' Odette invited her inside and covertly placed a hand on the masked man's shoulder. 'Oh, and don't be alarmed if you see my bodyguards.'

'Not at all. I'm used to it thanks to Henry.'

Odette grinned from ear to ear, stepped out onto the street, grabbed the woman's suitcase and brought it into the house. Her guest had packed light. 'There's freshly baked cake if you're hungry.'

'You can smell it from the street, Madame Darlan.' De Graaf hobbled into the hallway, limped past the armed man and greeted him warmly. The man tapped the brim of an imaginary hat and glanced at his boss. The charade had gone down well. 'Please call me Samira. That's my real name – the one Black Sara gave me.'

Odette set down the suitcase. 'Of course. The name Samira makes me think of some kind of fortune teller.'

'As far as I can remember it comes from Arabic and means the blessed one.' Samira laughed bitterly. 'But for someone like me it's rather ironic and feels like an insult.'

'Don't say that.' Odette was pleased to have come by another sacrifice for the jack of clubs. 'I presume Monsieur Gillot sent you to check that everything is in order?'

'I'll explain everything in a moment. I'd like to sit down first, if that's all right. It's ... exhausting travelling alone. I'm not used to getting around without a wheelchair or a walking aid.'

'Of course.' Odette was delighted. She hadn't had such an interesting visitor for a long time.

There are many players, but only be one winner.

Proverb

XV

Tadeus wheeled his suitcase through the arrivals hall of Charles de Gaulle airport. At first his luggage had been thought to be missing, but then he'd been called over to the check-in desk, where he'd been able to collect his suitcase. The painkillers were gradually wearing off. He felt the aches and pains all over his body.

Poe waited with her hand luggage at a tiny café, where she was enjoying a latte macchiato. On the counter in front of her lay the keys to a Volkswagen Tiguan, which she'd booked online with a car rental company. The white panama hat really suited her, and, judging by the looks of the barista and a few other men, many felt spontaneously infatuated with her. She was in plain, tourist clothes like Tadeus.

There'd be marriage proposals if she was in evening dress. Tadeus was struck by the doctor's beauty. *She looks like Michiko's older sister.*

'Coffee – good idea. I'll fall asleep otherwise,' he said.

He sat next to her without removing his baseball cap and ordered a triple espresso. With enough caffeine in his system, he'd be able to drive to Avignon without crashing the robust SUV. *Just under seven hundred kilometres to go.*

He received his order and stirred in plenty of sugar. Considering the continuous speed limit on the French motorway, he estimated that the drive would take them around six hours. Without breaks. Although the French high-speed train could cover the distance in half that time, the Tiguan gave them more flexibility.

Poe spooned up the milky froth of her coffee, the brim of her hat boldly pushed onto her forehead. Her blue eyes lit up. 'Has Darlan been in touch? Has Madame Spectreuse shown her face yet?'

Tadeus glanced at his phone. Inspector Klim would be delighted if he checked in on them: Leipzig, Benin, Paris. The man hadn't contacted them since Tadeus and Poe went through the pictures from Klim's Russian rogues' gallery via Skype. They hadn't recognised anyone. 'No. No new messages or calls.' He downed his strong espresso, which felt like hot nectar running down his throat, and then gulped down a shot of water. 'Ready to go?'

'Can I finish my drink first?' Poe looked at him sweetly and smiled. Her request was really a reprimand.

Tadeus tilted his head back in annoyance. The renewed onset of pain wasn't doing his mood any good. 'You do know that we don't have much time?'

'If Madame Spectreuse is planning on visiting Madame Darlan, we won't catch her. She had a head start on the flight over, and if she took the train then she's already in Avignon.' It appeared that Poe had already thought through the possibilities. 'Or the card possessed the mambo like it did the voodoo priest. It'll be all over the news any minute if that's the case.' She pointed to the flat TV screen with her long latte spoon. 'Up there.'

Tadeus was desperate to deliver the cards to Darlan and do whatever it took to get back his nine of spades that he so dearly missed. While he found the ace of diamonds' and the queen of spades' singing to be soothing and pleasant, it didn't match the feeling that his card had evoked in him, like a woman he loved more than anything in the world and would do anything, absolutely anything, to hold and protect.

For a card. Tadeus blinked and suddenly wondered where this desire had come from. The espresso seemed to have cleared his mind for a few seconds. *For. A. Card.* He blinked again and glanced at Poe.

She had embarked on this adventure for genuine reasons: to save people from Gillot. Her pursuit to uncover the truth about the death of her fiancé and her thirst for revenge had turned into something greater. The doctor was working towards a just cause that contributed to her self-development and linked back to her Korean roots and mudang heritage. She was helping others and wanted to do good.

But what was in it for him?

Tadeus watched the flickering news on the TV. *It's nothing more than printed paper. Old, printed paper.*

The singing in his mind swelled without warning and shrouded his thoughts in a puzzling veil. Thinking and making decisions suddenly became easier. He placed a hand on his shirt where the queen of hearts and the ace of diamonds sat in their little pouch. Of course he had to protect the nine of spades. Only he could. Alone. The card needed him.

'Shall we go?' Tadeus turned to Poe. *Hopefully she's finally finished her latte.*

The doctor was chatting away with a black woman standing next to her. They hadn't deemed it necessary to include Tadeus in the conversation, and that made him suspicious.

The stranger only had a small suitcase with her. Her clothing was exceptionally colourful, consisting of a mishmash of traditional African and European styles. Several necklaces hung around her neck, amulets dangled from her wrists and rings sparkled on her fingers.

Poe turned around to face him as if she'd just realised that he was at the same counter as her. Her cheeks were rosy with excitement. 'This is Madame Spectreuse, Boch! She's found us.'

Tadeus unconsciously turned to the side so that the cards were facing away from the woman and he could defend them from a potential attack. 'Oh. Yes, that's . . . a real surprise.'

'The spirits guided me to you.' She stretched her arm out to Tadeus. 'I'm Leila Fignolé.'

Tadeus grasped her fingers and shook her hand. 'Tadeus Boch.' His eyes darted between the two women. It made perfect sense to him that they had been talking about him. 'A mudang and a mambo.'

'The spirit world is the same, only the way we access it is different. I've pledged myself to Bondye and his good spirits.' Fignolé gestured for him to look at her. 'It's important that you listen to me, Monsieur Boch.'

'Isn't it more important that you hand over the card?' he replied. 'People's lives depend on it.'

Tadeus had an idea of where she was hiding the ace of spades. It wasn't in her suitcase, but rather somewhere close to her body. The card wanted to be found, to be rescued from the mambo. The queen of hearts and the ace of diamonds whispered in his ear, passing on the ace of spades' cries for help and pleas for freedom. 'I take it Miss Poe has told you?'

'Only briefly, but she's told me enough to understand what's happening.' Fignolé looked Tadeus in the eye, her gaze piercing and imploring. 'Monsieur, you have to stop the deck from being completed!'

'Who said anything about completing the deck? We'll deliver the cards, get Madame Darlan and her family to safety, then frame Gillot for the murders in Baden-Baden. We'll be doing good.' He felt uneasy. *Completed.* That would mean giving up the nine of spades. His nine of spades!

Unless *he* possessed the entire deck.

His card would be delighted and very grateful to him for

reuniting it with its siblings. The thought of it reassured him. 'Who wants to complete the deck?'

'The spirits told me that it won't be long before the Devil's Playbook is brought back together again.' Fignolé's steady gaze remained fixed on him. 'That can't happen. Do you hear me? Under no circumstances.'

Tadeus laughed. 'What nonsense!'

'It's not nonsense!' Poe interrupted, agitated. 'I've told you before that I sense evil in the cards.'

'So what's supposed to happen then when the cards come together? Will a demon be born? And then the world end?' He laughed at the women. 'Really?'

'Monsieur Boch, the deck was created by a desperate, hateful man,' Fignolé said coolly. 'Which gave him the power to trap the most evil forces in his work and—'

'. . .and let me guess, only true love can conquer all?' Tadeus cut in mockingly. 'Please stop talking rubbish. This is about people's lives and a triple murder for which we have to blame someone. This is about Madame Darlan's family.' *And my nine of spades.* 'This is about real life.'

'I know that. And yet sacrifices must be made to stop the cards from being united again.' It was as if the mambo was trying to hypnotise him. 'The deck was scattered across the world for a reason. To weaken its powers. I'm afraid we cannot spare anyone who has become wrapped up in the deck's charms.'

'The spirits told you that too, did they?' Tadeus had to look away. He couldn't stand to hold the woman's gaze any longer and looked at Poe instead. 'As for the scattering of the cards, we've already come to our own conclusions. Based on well-founded explanations. I'm not denying the fact that both of you can feel something, but . . . It's not exactly concrete evidence.'

The ace of spades' demand for freedom was undeniable. It joined in with the queen of hearts' and ace of diamonds' singing; he could hear it. He didn't like the idea of Fignolé keeping the third card for herself. He knew that she wouldn't treat it well. Tadeus wiped his eyes and shiny forehead. All that espresso wasn't doing him any good.

'I believe her,' Poe chimed in. 'I think that something bad is going to happen.' It appeared she had teamed up with the mambo. Two against one.

'Gillot will kidnap Madame Darlan's family and maybe even torture them. That's the bad thing!' Tadeus was suddenly struck by an idea. He would have better luck with deceiving the women than further discussion, the cards told him. 'Anyway, talking for hours isn't going to get us anywhere. Why don't we make coloured copies of the cards we have, create duplicates and see what happens?' The cards commended him for his wit. 'That'll be enough to fool Gillot or his people during a handover.'

'That's not a bad idea, Boch.' Poe slapped him on the shoulder. 'What do you think, madame?'

Fignolé nodded pensively.

Tadeus pointed to the information desk. 'I'm sure they'll be able to help us.' He held out his hand and asked the mambo for the ace of spades. 'I'll go speak to them while you two look after the luggage.'

'I'll come with you,' the mambo announced.

Poe got to her feet and paid for the drinks. 'Me too,' she said.

The three of them walked through the hall with their luggage to the information stand. There they were directed to an office centre offering a range of services, where they arrived after a few minutes of searching.

The employee didn't ask any questions as they handed him three dirty, damaged playing cards, simply proceeded to make copies of the fronts and backs with an ultra-modern photocopier.

With a little charm and a flutter of her eyelashes, Poe managed to convince the man to give them a glue stick, a thin piece of cardboard and a pair of scissors.

Tadeus collected the printouts along with the three originals as if it were a matter of course before Fignolé could grab them. She threw him a dirty look, but held her tongue in front of the employee.

'Time for some arts and crafts,' Tadeus said. He took a seat at a free table intended for laptop users and got to work.

He cut out copy after copy and passed the individual front and back pieces to the women to glue together.

'So what's your plan now, Madame Fignolé?' he asked to distract her. He had no intention of giving back the ace of spades, which sang to him joyfully in gratitude. His nine of spades would be proud of him. He missed his card more than ever.

'I'll go back to Haiti. With the card,' she said.

Tadeus had been afraid of that. 'Aren't you worried that the same thing might happen to you as the voodoo priest?'

'The spirits will protect me. Besides, you have the card right now.'

Tadeus laughed. 'Then you'd better keep an eye on me so that I don't lose my mind and start slitting people's throats and sacrificing them to Kalfu.' He twirled the scissors in his hand. The idea didn't seem so bad to him. He would have to start with the mambo – the singing cards agreed.

'We've already tried to burn one of the cards,' Poe confessed, gluing the cut-out pieces together with surgical precision. 'Wouldn't that be for the best?'

Fignolé watched Tadeus unblinkingly. 'The spirits told me that it can't be done.'

'Is even love powerless against the cards?' Tadeus quipped. 'I'm disappointed. They say that love conquers all. True, unconditional love.'

The mambo was determined not to let Tadeus provoke her. 'No power on Earth can destroy them under normal circumstances, Monsieur Boch. The cards have always found a way to survive. That's what makes this deck, and each card in it, so dangerous. As a completed deck, it'll be more powerful than ever.'

'Say, hypothetically speaking, we hand over the cards and manage to complete the deck,' Poe said as she glued together and straightened the outer edges of the duplicates. 'What would we do then?'

'I'm curious about that too,' Tadeus added. If there was a way to destroy his beloved nine of spades, he had to find out what it was and prevent it from happening. He had to shut down any possibility of it, and the three cards praised him effusively for it.

Fignolé looked displeased. She didn't have an answer to Poe's question.

'The best thing to do would be to fire the deck into space in a rocket,' she said after a while. 'It belongs somewhere no human can touch.'

'In a volcano,' Poe immediately shot back.

'The cards don't burn, though,' Tadeus said.

'But the deck would sink to the bottom.'

He grinned. 'And what if the volcano erupts?'

'Then the deck would be trapped in the solidified lava for ever.'

'Maybe, but some explorer could still find it.' Tadeus glanced at Fignolé. He liked playing devil's advocate. 'Madame, what do your spirits tell you – could the deck of cards free itself?'

'I don't know,' the woman retorted. She finished gluing the cards together and stood up, the copious pieces of jewellery on her body clicking and jangling. 'I'll be right back with some more drinks. Does anyone want anything?' Tadeus asked for water, Poe for a Diet Coke. 'I followed Gondjia from Haiti to

Benin because he did terrible things to people. Things that the card drove him to do and which made him more despicable every day. Now I have the chance to stop that from ever happening again. And I have to take it. No matter the cost.' Her gaze shifted to Tadeus again. 'No matter how, monsieur. And when I return, I'd like the ace of spades back.' She nodded to Poe, grabbed her small suitcase and walked off.

The ace of spades shrieked in Tadeus' chest pocket, insisting that the mambo was still its mortal enemy. The woman would ruin everything – the plan, its freedom and Tadeus' reunion with the nine of spades.

Tadeus agreed with the card. *That can't happen.* But he couldn't take out Fignolé at the airport, that would be too obvious. He scrutinised Poe surreptitiously and lamented the fact that she had allied herself with the mambo. Unfortunately, Poe was now his enemy too. Her vehement interest in destroying the deck meant he couldn't trust her.

The cards sang their approval and sent a pleasant shiver down his spine, encouraging him to trust nothing and no one.

A deep anger filled Tadeus. From this day forward, he would have to be more careful. But he couldn't get rid of Poe. Not yet. She was his divining rod; she could sense the presence of the nine of spades. *I have to do something.*

Tadeus casually got up. 'All that coffee has hit me. Keep an eye on our luggage.' He hurried out of the office centre and headed for the nearest toilets, which he'd seen Fignolé disappear into.

He quickly darted into the women's toilets, where two startled ladies in the anteroom shot him disgusted looks. 'Excuse me, sorry, it's an emergency. My wife . . .' He patted his trouser pocket. 'I've brought tampons for her.'

Both women left the anteroom and Tadeus entered the cubicle area. He looked under the doors and recognised which cubicle Fignolé was in by her clothing. Only two of the other toilets were engaged, the women in them chatting quietly.

Tadeus locked himself in the cubicle next to the mambo and waited anxiously.

Once the other two women had gone, he stood on the toilet seat and pulled the metal brush holder from the ring on the wall where it was attached. The cards urged him not to hold back and to mercilessly attack the enemy. Tadeus pressed the flush button with his foot to drown out any noise and looked at Fignolé over the cubicle wall. She was sitting fully clothed on the closed toilet seat, checking her emails on her phone.

Tadeus violently slammed the metal holder against her forehead.

The attack took the mambo by surprise. Her head lurched backward and smashed against the wall. Her body went limp, but she still remained seated. Fignolé lost consciousness. Blood spilled from a large gash above the bridge of her nose, dripping onto her patterned blouse and covering it in crimson polka dots. Her phone landed on the bathroom tiles.

Tadeus looked down at her like a god contemplating whether to end the mortal's life once and for all. The cards demanded it from him, especially the ace of spades, which raged and urged him to sacrifice the enemy in its honour.

Tadeus resisted and stepped down from the toilet despite the three cards' evident disappointment and rebellious screams. He and Fignolé had been seen together and there would be video footage of him following her into the toilet. But if he acted quickly, there was still a chance that when she was discovered in the cubicle it might be seen as just an unfortunate accident.

He bent down outside her cubicle and picked up her phone off the floor, then pocketed the device, left the women's toilets without bumping into anyone and stepped into the men's.

There he typed out a farewell email to Poe on Fignolé's

phone, before plucking the queen of hearts, the ace of spades and the ace of diamonds from his breast pocket and slipping them into his right shoe. He spoke to the cards, instructing them that they would have to keep quiet from now on and disguise themselves like the queen of hearts. They promised him to do so and their singing faded after a final, blissful note just for him.

Tadeus savoured it, even if it was nothing like the sensation that his nine of spades had stirred in him. This was just his appetiser to his reunion, he thought.

He then left his cubicle and returned to the office centre. Fignolé's switched-off phone landed in one of the many rubbish bins.

Poe sat with a drink in front of her that she said had been given to her by an employee.

'Let's go,' Tadeus announced and gathered the forged cards. 'Where's Madame Fignolé?'

'She left already. She sent me a message.' Poe got to her feet and read from her tablet: *'I'm flying back to Haiti with the ace of spades, the ace of diamonds and the queen of hearts. I've got to rush to catch my flight. See you soon! I'll be in touch as soon as I've found a safe place for the cards.'*

'I gave her the cards since Gillot would never expect it. He doesn't know anything about her. The real cards are safe, and now we can travel with the duplicates to Avignon.' Tadeus flashed as sincere a smile as he could muster. 'You're surprised. I can tell your mudang powers didn't predict this.'

'No.' Poe looked at him with warmth and praise, her gaze shifting for just a second to where the pouch was in his breast pocket. 'Let's end this the right way.'

Tadeus knew that there was nothing in his pocket that could give the cards away, but he still positioned his luggage in front of him to create an extra barrier between himself and her mudang powers. He didn't feel the slightest hint of the cards' presence. They had listened to him and were playing dead.

'I'm shocked,' Poe confessed. 'I would have never in a million years believed that you wouldn't insist on travelling to Avignon with the real cards.'

He laughed. 'Why? Have I been so unbearable these last few days?'

'Yes. No! Not like that.' She stuttered. 'It's—'

'Because I'm sceptical about Madame Fignolé?'

Tadeus and Poe left the airport and walked to the car park. His plan and ruse had worked; he felt as if he were walking on air. 'I still am. I know we're putting Darlan's life and her family at risk with the forged cards. If the handover fails, Miss Poe, we'll be to blame. But the alternative scenario seems far more . . . dangerous to me.'

'Thank you, Boch.'

'Like you said, let's end this the right way first.' Tadeus walked up to the Volkswagen Tiguan and unlocked the door. The boot opened of its own accord. 'And then you can thank me.'

During their drive to Avignon, he would try to find out what Poe and Fignolé had discussed. He hadn't forgotten that the mudang and the mambo had joined forces. Against him.

The cards secretly sang their praises, so softly it was barely audible, but more beautifully than ever before.

* * *

Avignon, Vaucluse,
Provence-Alpes-Côte d'Azur,
France

Odette cut a second slice for Magdalena de Graaf, who was recovering from her arduous journey from Rome with coffee and cake. 'I hope your brother is recovering well? I've received plenty of text messages and calls from him,' Odette said.

'Yes, exactly right. He's active again already.' Samira, as the woman insisted on being called, savoured the coffee with an indulgent expression on her face. 'And he was worried that no one was responding to his attempts at contact.' She pointed to the masked man standing next to the door. 'But I see that everything is well, Madame Darlan. That'll reassure Henry.'

'It is.'

'Do these poor people have to wear balaclavas the entire time? My brother told me that they really make you sweat.' Samira appeared entirely at ease with the presence of the armed man and addressed him. 'Henry often employs professionals, especially for excavations in the Middle East. I know that it's not entirely legal, with the weapons and so on.'

'We generally like to maintain our anonymity, madame. We never address each other by our real names,' the man explained pleasantly. 'It's just like the anti-terrorism forces – you don't want to be recognised on the beach. Or when grocery shopping.'

'Yes, I can understand that.' Samira faced Odette. 'You know what? Why don't you call my brother. He'll be delighted just to hear your voice.'

'I've already tried, but he's not picking up his phone right now.' Odette tasted the cake that she'd baked according to Charles' recipe. Unfortunately it didn't taste quite as good as her dead jailer's had.

'He'll be sleeping, Madame Darlan.' Samira laughed and adjusted her black, fringed stole, which she'd draped over the shoulders of her long, white dress. 'Henry sleeps more these days than he has his entire life. It's the medication. It might sound odd, but I think it's doing him good.' She turned to the guard. 'Monsieur, would you like some?' She pointed to the cake with her fork. 'It's divine.'

'Merci, but I'm watching my figure,' he replied, amused. 'If someone were to attack us, your brother wouldn't be too pleased if I were too fat to protect Madame Darlan and his cards.'

Samira laughed, relieved. 'Bon. I can understand that.'

Odette found Samira's aberration entertaining and joined in with the amusement. She wasn't sure yet whether she would let the unexpected visitor go to reassure Gillot, or if she would lock her in the cellar with the others. With a practically inexhaustible source of wealth at his disposal, the Walloon could send an even larger force to Avignon to search for his sister. She was leaning towards letting the woman go and giving her a false sense of security.

'Yes, the cards . . . Henry and his cards,' Samira said pensively and slid the bloodstained, damaged jack of clubs towards her. 'This is one of them, isn't it?'

'Yes.'

'It looks so damaged. Filthy. Can you repair it, madame?'

'*Restore* it. And yes.' Odette wanted to snatch the card away from her, but she resisted the urge. It was Fennec's legacy. 'It's from Manaus. Mr Mulder brought it to me today.'

'Who do you think stole the cards from the vault in Bruges?' Samira fiddled with the jack of clubs, which, despite her carefulness, could damage the fragile card further. 'As a restorer you must know other collectors who would be happy to a mountain of gold for these cards.'

'Of course. But nobody is as obsessed with them as your brother.'

'But there has to be someone that's *almost* as crazy about them.' Samira smelled the aged, printed and painted paper without flinching from the scent of blood. 'I wonder what it's seen and lived through.'

'Primarily death and destruction,' Odette said, worried that the woman would lick the jack of clubs too. 'Just like most of the cards from this fateful deck.' She cleared her throat. 'Forgive me, I don't mean to be rude, but would you please put the card back down on the table?'

'Oh! I'm sorry!' Samira blushed and laid the card down onto the tablecloth as carefully as if it were a raw egg. 'At least I've now held one of them in my hand.'

'You didn't know about them?'

'About the collection in my house? No.' Samira laughed bitterly. 'My brother is a funny man.'

Odette straightened the heavy glasses on the bridge of her nose and her vision improved a little. She could tell from the expression on the woman's face that she was hiding something. 'So you don't share his passion for collecting?'

'Let's just say that I'm pickier than him. Do you know of Sara the Black?'

'Of course! The Gitans' pilgrimage takes place not far from here. In Saintes-Maries-de-la-Mer in Camargue, am I right?'

Samira's hazel eyes blazed with a passionate, devout fire. 'It's wonderful! I'm her most faithful follower, Madame Darlan. Sara has alleviated my suffering many times in the past. I could hardly walk before, but I prayed to her and offered sacrifices to her during the pilgrimages and . . .' She faltered and glanced at the jack of clubs flanked by four stylised big cats. 'Did you say the card was found in Manaus?'

'That's right, Mrs Gillot.'

Samira took a breath. 'Oh.' She sipped her coffee. 'I almost managed to pinch it from my brother.'

Odette didn't believe what she was hearing. '*You* tried to get your hands on the card? But you're not a collector. Did I mishear what you said?'

'Sara the Black isn't just the patron saint of the Romani people, Madame Darlan.' Samira retrieved an amulet with the patroness' head embossed on it from under her blouse.

'Here. This is her medallion. Consecrated and blessed. You see, sometimes' – she lowered her gaze bashfully – 'I think that I'm somehow related to her. That's how strong my connection is to her.'

'And Black Sara has something to do with this deck of cards?' Odette feared that, as a result of her excessive piety, Samira was gravely mistaken. 'The deck dates back to the end of the eighteenth century. Correct me if I'm wrong, but the Romani people of the saint have been around for much longer.'

'You can't know that, Madame Darlan. Sara is a common name among the Gitans and a popular pseudonym used by card fortune tellers and palm readers,' Samira said eagerly. She clearly had few people to discuss this with in her life in Bruges.

'Ah, we're talking about cards. I see, madame.'

'Exactly! I've closely studied the stories and legends of the southern French Gitans. They mention Sara as a wise woman and the inventor of tarot.'

Odette laughed. 'That can't be true. Playing cards only arrived in Europe in the fourteenth century.'

Samira now looked insulted. 'It's true that the first *records* of playing cards date back to the fourteenth century, but what if they existed earlier?' She gestured to the card. 'I think it's possible that Black Sara brought playing cards to us when she came to us from the Orient.'

'Uh-huh.' Odette's mind was elsewhere. She was no longer listening to Samira's rambling. Whatever this woman was drivelling on about had nothing to do with historical facts or Bastian Kirchner's cards. It was the typical glorification that many devout people often fell prey to. The power of the Devil's Playbook was an irrefutable fact, irrespective of faith or locale. 'What do you plan to do with the jack of clubs, madame?'

'Take it to Saintes-Maries-de-la-Mer, to Black Sara,' Samira explained. 'It's an exceptional piece and would be very fitting to give to a fortune teller and the inventor of tarot. She would have been delighted with it and I . . .' She swallowed.

'Would be healed.' Now Odette understood. 'You thought that, if you bestowed this gift on her, then she would perform a miracle in return.'

'Yes,' Samira murmured and looked at the jack of clubs. 'My brother thought I didn't know that he was collecting the cards. But of course I knew, I just didn't know about the vault.' The expression on her face softened and became more wistful. 'I would have brought Sara all the cards. All the ones in that vault so that she healed me. So that she set me free. So that, after sixty years, I could finally start actually living my life.' Samira fumbled around in her jacket for a tissue and blew her nose, but it wasn't enough to mask her sobs.

Odette became suspicious. 'When did you almost steal the jack of clubs from your brother?

'I'm sorry?' Samira wiped the tears from her eyes.

'If you didn't know about the safe or me, when did you try to steal the card from—'

'In Manaus. I sent a female detective, disguised as a member of the rescue party. She set off to look for the Sparks couple's crashed plane.' Samira sighed. 'She called me from the road and told me she had recognised Frédéric Roux in the group. It turned out that my brother and I were in a long-distance race.'

'How did she know Fenn— Monsieur Roux?'

'From me. I sent her a photo of the man. He sometimes brought Gillot cards. The official reason for his visits was always something else, but I would eavesdrop on his and Henry's conversations from time to time.' Samira was clearly pleased with herself. Yes, well . . . Both of them were most likely killed by the poachers.' She pointed to the card. 'For that.'

Any following words became nothing but an incomprehensible murmur for Odette.

An entirely new version of the events that had led to her beloved Fennec's death unfolded in her mind: he had found the cards – for her – and then this hired detective had wanted to steal them from him. A gunfight had likely transpired that had attracted the poachers, then Fennec had been kidnapped and taken to their hut, along with the card. Then there had been the animals that had guarded Fennec and the card, Daan Mulder, and all that money that her Fennec had been entitled to for his unwavering loyalty to her and the cards.

Odette looked at Samira, who was still preaching and prattling on about Black Sara and tarot, about the saint who was supposed to be her salvation and about all the stories she had written herself. The real murderer of her Fennec, her desert fox, was sitting at her table.

The phone rang, causing Samira to fall silent.

'Just a moment, Madame de Graaf.' Odette got to her feet and answered the phone. 'Oui?'

'This is . . . Muller speaking,' she heard the German say, with the noise of a driving car in the background. 'Is everything all right, Madame Darlan?'

Odette certainly didn't feel all right. 'That depends on what you're about to tell me, Monsieur Muller.'

'We have the cards and are on our way to Avignon.'

'You mean–'

'I mean *all* the missing cards, Madame Darlan. We have all three! We'll be with you in give or take four hours. Call Gillot and invite him to meet. Now. To avoid giving him the opportunity to make any major preparations.'

'Four hours!' Odette clapped a hand over her mouth, closed her eyes and felt the silent tears of simultaneous elation and grief roll down her cheeks. Compose yourself, her father would have said. She moved her hand away and smiled. 'Thank you, Monsieur Muller. I'll have everything ready.'

'What about your new guards?'

'Don't worry about that. I already have an idea.'

'Please look after yourself! See you soon, madame. We'll discuss our battle plan when we're there.' *Click.*

Her legs buckled with joyous, bittersweet terror, but she still managed to drop into a chair. The last three cards. On their way to her.

'Madame Darlan?' Samira looked at her anxiously. She had finished two-thirds of her second slice of cake. 'Has something happened?'

Odette didn't meet her gaze. Instead, she proudly and determinedly raised her chin. 'Take Madame de Graaf down into the cellar with the others. And make sure it hurts,' she ordered.

'Oui, madame.' The masked man grabbed Samira by her hair and pulled her off her chair.

The woman screamed, flailing about with her one functioning arm. She tried to loosen the man's hand from her head, but he just dragged her behind him like a sack of potatoes – first across the floorboards, and then down the corridor.

Odette listened to her shrill cries, which ceased when Samira tumbled down the stairs. Her suffering gave her some satisfaction.

Samira – the blessed one – would be the first one to sacrifice her life. To the jack of clubs, and to Fennec's legacy.

And why wait? Odette thought, and stood up.

* * *

Hyun sat in the passenger seat of the Volkswagen Tiguan and again perused the files on the laptop that they had stolen from Gillot's house in Bruges. Finding that file in the recycle bin had inspired her to search through every byte of the hard drive one more time.

She felt on edge. The last nightmare had caught her by

surprise just two hours ago. The cards were trying to scare her off with all their might.

No matter how hard Boch tried to drop hints and make allusions to the subject, she didn't tell him what she and Leila Fignolé had discussed. They'd spoken less about the cards and more about him. The mambo had warned and urged her not to trust Boch, of all people. She'd told Hyun that her protector and companion had fallen under the influence of one or more of the cards and would find it very difficult to free himself from it. Fignolé suspected that he had some kind of former attachment to the deck and the cards, which made it easier for the evil spirits to put him under their spell.

Hyun had guessed as much from the start, but somehow her mistrust in him had faded. Her conversation with Fignolé had opened her eyes: Boch's motives for helping her were only superficially noble, and there was a dark truth lurking in the shadows that could come to light at any moment.

The doctor was torn. She still needed to use Boch to take action against Gillot, so she was forced to trust him – despite her reservations.

The Tiguan zoomed along the French motorway at a consistent, permitted speed of 130 kilometres per hour. Boch was taking no risks so close to the finish line.

Hyun's own plan solidified in her mind. She would make sure the indestructible deck was so far out of reach that it could no longer bring suffering into the world as it had done for centuries since its creation. The pack of cards had to disappear for ever.

She knew that this would make Boch her enemy, and he had surprised her when he announced at the airport that he agreed with the alternative plan. If he was able to resist the influence of the cards, his willpower was stronger than she had anticipated. But while this gave Hyun a kernel of reassurance, it wasn't enough to let her guard down.

The letters and characters on the screen swam before her eyes, her mind racing.

Despite their cultural differences and age gap, the mambo had considered Hyun her equal and had been very open during their conversation. Korean mudang or voodoo priestess, the spirit world was the spirit world.

There was a great truth to that.

Fignolé had made Hyun aware of the presence of a faint flickering around Boch, which had to do with one of the cards' effect on him. While he was surrounded by it, he could only be partially trusted. With a little practice, Hyun managed to sense this phenomenon from roughly one metre away. Like now. *I'll free him from this. The cards are far away from him now.*

Before her fiancé's death, she never would have thought that she would need her grandmother's gifts. If only she had learned everything there was to know about being a mudang, gained the practical experience, a heightened sense of compassion and the understanding of the spirits, surely some things in life would have been different.

As a mudang, I would have recognised the dangers that the card posed for Enrico. Hyun kissed her engagement ring and forced herself to focus on the laptop again.

She scrolled for what felt like the hundredth time through the files containing short stories and the beginnings of novels about Black Sara, all the way down to the Walloon's collection of findings from the early days of his hunt for the Devil's Playbook. 'How long until we're in Avignon?' she asked.

'Another two hours or so.' Boch was driving a little too fast, and spotted Hyun's reproving look. 'The French will give me a warning, but they won't kick me off the motorway,' he told her.

'What's Madame Fignolé going to do with the cards?' Hyun glanced out of the passenger seat window. The night rushed past them and yet enveloped them from all sides at the same time. 'Did she tell you anything specific? The goodbye message was very vague.'

'She said that the less we know, the better. I gave her my email address. She'll be in touch.' Boch's steady gaze was fixed on the deserted carriageway in front of them. 'I'm sure the voodoo priestess will find a way to destroy the three cards or perform some counter-curse on them.' He smiled briefly. 'Surely you know more than me, Poe.'

'My grandmother did.' Hyun leaned back as far as the seat allowed her to and stared up at the stars, which twinkled through the car's panoramic roof window.

Ever since they'd left the airport, Boch had been very cooperative. He'd made an effort to convince Hyun that he was one hundred per cent on her side, and even made little remarks about the destruction of the cards.

Perhaps the cards' negative influence had vanished and what remained of the evil energy was slowly fading.

But her renewed suspicion whispered to her all the same: *don't lose your guard until he's freed from it entirely. Until you've freed him from it.*

Boch didn't know that Hyun had also exchanged mobile numbers with Leila Fignolé. The fact that the mambo hadn't contacted her once after her short initial message concerned her. Fignolé would surely have had time to send another text before boarding her plane to Haiti. *Apparently not.*

Hyun glanced at Boch; a smile flickered across his face. *Avignon would be interesting.*

For easy won is easy gone.

from *Reynard the Fox* (1794)
by Johann Wolfgang von Goethe (1794–1832)

XVI

Avignon, Vaucluse,
Provence-Alpes-Côte d'Azur,
France

Tadeus reached a parking spot and turned off the Tiguan's engine and headlights. The narrow street was silent. Avignon was sound asleep at three in the morning, with only a few lights burning behind the windows in the modern part of the city. On Nicolas Lescuyer Street, in the old town centre surrounded by fortress walls and as if shielded from the modern world, a dead calm prevailed in the former kingdom of the antipopes.

He glanced at Poe, who snapped the laptop shut with a flourish. The blue monitor light went out. 'Did you find anything?' Tadeus asked her.

'No,' she shot back. She brushed her black hair back with one quick sweep of her hand and put her panama hat on. Then she looked at him with her blue eyes.

Tadeus didn't like the look on her face. In the semi-darkness of the car, he almost felt as if he were sitting next to his daughter, Michiko, which only made him more nervous. 'What is it? Are you having doubts?'

'*Me*? No.'

'Then why are you looking at me like that?'

Poe didn't say anything and fixed her gaze on his shirt, where he used to keep the real cards in their pouch.

He knew what she was looking for, despite the little story he had told her about Fignolé and the fake email. This was a clear indicator that they were not on the same side and never had been. Not for one second. Nevertheless, she was his divining rod, and his nine of spades hunter. And so he played along. The cards quietly approved of this.

'Ah, right! Thanks for reminding me.' Smiling, Tadeus reached under his shirt and pulled out the duplicates from the flat, rectangular leather pouch. 'Take them.'

Poe hesitantly accepted them and opened the car door without taking her eyes off him. They switched off the lights inside the Tiguan. It was pitch black. 'Are we still sticking to the same plan?' she asked him.

Tadeus felt that his Michiko was speaking to him again. 'Well, we don't have a Plan B, do we?' He got out hurriedly. He couldn't let anything distract him. 'We'll leave our luggage in the car.'

He didn't have a real plan, but the cards would soon tell him what had to be done to get his sorely missed nine of spades back. Interrogating Gillot would be a good start.

Poe picked up some dirt from the ground and rubbed it over the fake cards to make them look more damaged. On their last toilet break she'd already splashed some wine, tea and coffee over the cards and stepped on them.

Tadeus kept an eye on the street in the meantime. All the parked vehicles were empty, and neither the number plates nor the vans or hired cars struck him as odd. There were no night revellers out either. *Perfect.*

They walked the remaining few metres under the lit street-lamps to Madame Darlan's front door and rang the doorbell. Tadeus could tell that Poe was trying to make eye contact with him, but he ignored her.

After a few seconds, the grandmotherly restorer opened the door and invited them inside. 'You've made good time,' she said.

Just like last time, the house smelled of coffee and cake, but her eyes looked smaller behind the thick glasses than before. She was tired. Nevertheless, her apron dress and bun sat perfectly, no other sign of fatigue in sight. Tadeus wondered if Darlan slept fully dressed and with her hair pinned up.

'I've baked something to help you get your energy back,' she said.

'Merci, madame. It was a very long drive.' Tadeus let the women lead the way and tried his best to relax. His neck ached and his feet itched from sitting for so many hours. And his back wouldn't be forgiving him for that long drive any time soon.

Poe removed her panama hat.

They entered the kitchen, where freshly brewed coffee and a quarter of a cake were waiting for them. It would be enough to replenish his blood sugar levels and improve his concentration.

Tadeus and Poe took a seat.

'Where are your new guards, madame?' the doctor enquired.

'I've locked them in the cellar. It was easy to trick them. People underestimate old women.' Darlan poured them some coffee and sat opposite them. 'Before we start, I want to thank you for taking care of everything.' She reached into a drawer and took out a few pre-packaged bundles of US dollars. 'Here. I insist.'

Based on the revenue seals, Tadeus estimated each bundle to be worth around one million. That would halve his debts in one fell swoop. The search for his nine of spades had restored his long-lost fortune. 'That's . . . very generous.'

'It's not mine. The man from Manaus gave it to me along with the card,' Darlan said. 'And what use is the money to me? I'm an old woman.'

'What about your family, madame?' Poe remarked, surprised. She pushed the bundle back towards Darlan. 'I don't want the money. I have more than enough. Nothing good can come of it.'

Darlan shoved the money towards Tadeus. 'More for you then, Monsieur Muller.' She interlaced her bony fingers. 'Can I see the cards?' she breathed. 'Please.'

Poe set her hat down on the table, took out the duplicates and placed them around the white brim of the hat.

The queen of hearts.

The ace of diamonds.

And the ace of spades.

Tadeus was curious. This was a good test. If the restorer fell for it, Gillot could be fooled just as easily as the person responsible for the robbery in Bruges.

Darlan lowered her gaze. She inspected the cards through the polished lenses of her glasses for a moment before glancing at the doctor amusedly. 'Coloured copies with fresh traces of dirt, Mademoiselle Tanaka?'

Poe slumped slightly in her chair. 'We thought it would take you longer to notice.'

'I can even smell the glue you used, and the wine and coffee you poured over them doesn't fool me either,' Darlan said, forcing herself to stay calm. 'You're planning to trick Gillot with *these*?'

'We hoped to, yes.' Poe looked to Tadeus for support. 'We have reason to believe that . . . The deck must not be completed. A voodoo priestess from Cotonou warned us that it would have disastrous consequences.'

Tadeus didn't consider speaking up to back up Poe. He wanted to see how this conversation unfolded. The cards hummed to him softly, agreeing with him.

'Are you being serious?' Darlan's expression turned hostile. 'Do the lives of my family mean nothing to you? Is that it, mademoiselle?'

'Madame Darlan, I can feel it too! The cards are evil!' Poe protested anxiously. 'I know I'm not a trained mudang, but my grandmother ...' She was running out of words and arguments. 'I can feel it!' she repeated. 'This deck should never be completed.'

'Why?' Darlan stretched her dry, long fingers and placed them on the table.

Tadeus smiled. He had asked her the exact same question and not received a concrete answer. Poe still didn't have one.

'You told us about all the disasters and catastrophes that happened as a result of the cards,' Poe argued. 'Madame, you know they're dangerous. The notes you gave us mention voices and singing. And then there was that burst of energy in your study. The cards tried to scare me off!'

'I didn't say I *believed* in any of it,' Darlan said, squashing her objections. 'It's fascinating, yes, but you don't have the originals. Gillot will only need to take one look at the cards, like me, and my family will be in grave danger. Because you—'

'We'll try it anyway,' Poe interrupted her insolently, her voice full of exaggerated, false confidence. 'Boch and I will protect you.'

'How, mademoiselle? How do you propose to do that?' Darlan grilled her. 'Do you think he's going to turn up alone? Do you have weapons with you? Explosives? A group of mercenaries to go up against Gillot's highly trained men?' She nodded to the door. 'If you do, now's the time you invited them in.'

An awkward silence fell over the kitchen.

Poe whirled around to face Tadeus. 'Boch, say something! You came up with this plan!'

'I did. To shut you and Madame Fignolé up.' He bent down, removed his shoe and took out the three real cards. 'But I found the whole idea too dangerous. The lives of innocent people take priority,' he lied and retrieved the trio from the protective plastic cover. One by one, he placed them next to the duplicates. The cards were pleased to be out of hiding and rewarded him for his actions with a faint canon. 'Forgive us for the charade, Madame Darlan. As you've just heard, my real name is Boch, not Muller.'

'Now *those* are the real ones!' Darlan exclaimed in delight. 'Thank you, Monsieur Boch! I'm grateful to you with all my heart.'

'You bastard! What did you do to Leila Fignolé?' Poe snapped at Tadeus and tried to grab the real ace of diamonds, the queen of hearts and the ace of spades from the table.

But the restorer, striking out like a viper, snatched them away. 'It's better if I look after these treasures.'

'I suppose Madame Fignolé will be on a later flight than planned back to Haiti,' Tadeus said with a wry smile. He was pleased that the cards were now in the best of hands and would regain their former splendour. The nine of spades would soon enjoy the same treatment. 'But she'll be fine, don't worry.'

'Don't be so hard on him, mademoiselle. He knew that Gillot would never have fallen for the forgery, and that would have been very dangerous for all of us.' Darlan glared at Poe through the finger-thick lenses of her glasses. 'Gillot is ruthless. You should know that by now. But you're much younger than me and still have a lot to learn.'

Poe clenched her hands into fists. 'You fucking arsehole!' she swore at Tadeus, slowly getting to her feet. 'I trusted you!'

'No you didn't. You constantly used your mudang powers to search me for the cards.' He finished his coffee, feeling better by the second. 'Did you really think I wouldn't notice?'

'Because I knew you were under the influence of the cards!' She slammed the table angrily, causing the tableware to bounce up with a clink. 'I should have left you at the airport like I planned!'

'You know *nothing*!' His plan had worked, and soon he'd be

holding the nine of spades in his hands. He looked at Darlan. 'Did you call Gillot, madame?'

'I did. But imagine my surprise when I discovered he was dead,' Darlan replied as cheerfully as if she had just won a game of pétanque.

'What?' Poe and Tadeus exclaimed at the same time.

'There were reports on the news of a murder in a hospital in Rome. The news blackout on the case didn't hold. They announced it earlier,' Darlan said, sitting peacefully in her chair. She clearly wasn't worried about the safety of her loved ones or herself. 'Gillot and his bodyguards were shot, and an Italian policeman was injured.'

Tadeus felt like his bubble had been burst. *How am I going to get back my nine of spades if I can't interrogate Gillot any more?*

A wave of sheer panic that even the card's soft song of praise couldn't tame overwhelmed him. He needed a new plan. Now. Out of the corner of his eye, he noticed Poe's body stiffen. She was preparing to attack. Him? The restorer? Would she go as far as to steal the cards?

Darlan swept the duplicates off the table and they landed on the floor. Then, as if she were about to read the future, she carefully and slowly placed the queen of hearts, the ace of diamonds and the ace of spades in front of her. 'My poor darlings, you've suffered so much. But I've finally reunited you. Reunited you under my roof,' she said absent-mindedly. 'This will require a lot of sacrifice. Luckily, some supplies have accumulated in my cellar.'

'My God!' Poe's eyes flew wide open. '*You're* the one behind all this! You sent the thieves to Bruges. Gillot's people never threatened your family!'

Despite the rising panic, Tadeus had had the same thought. *That means the nine of spades is in this house!* His deep fear transformed into excitement. He would finally be able to hold his card. *It's got to be in the study!*

'Doesn't it make for a lovely story, how I've appealed to the heroic and the good in people?' Darlan looked at both of them in turn. 'I fooled you, I fooled Gillot and played along as the willing expert. During the restoration process, I had already swapped some of the cards for incredibly elaborate copies in order to deceive Gillot. And then I only had to get my hands on the treasures that he already had.' She smiled graciously. 'But since both of you helped me and I have grown fond of you, I'm giving you the unique opportunity to take the two million dollars and leave my house.'

'You're going to complete the deck!' Poe cried out in horror. 'What will happen then?'

'Oh, with a little skill . . . I could change the world. Thanks to you, I now have all the cards, from the two of diamonds to the ace of spades.' She sighed ruefully. 'I can see that the mademoiselle has already made her choice. She's about to jump over the table and try to steal the cards from me.' Darlan turned to Tadeus. 'And what about you, Monsieur Boch? Two million. That's a good life.'

Tadeus sat stock-still in his chair. He could taste the coffee and the fierce excitement in his mouth. All he could think about was that the restorer had his nine of spades in the house. His card! But he couldn't afford to give himself away. 'I'll take the two million, madame,' he said solemnly, 'if you would be so kind as to let me take a look at the deck before I leave.'

Darlan clapped her hands together. 'Monsieur Boch! Mademoiselle Poe, whose real name I've known for some time now, was *absolutely* right: you're under the cards' spell.' She blinked with her cruel, blue-grey eyes. 'The Devil's Playbook has got you wrapped around its little finger. I know you used to be quite the gambler – you were always going to be easy prey.'

'No. No, I just thought that, with so many people after the deck, it would be worth seeing,' he retorted, caught off guard.

'Which card?'

'I . . . I would like to see all of them.'

'You know what I mean, monsieur. One of the cards chose you as its guardian and protector.' Darlan looked highly amused and curious, like a researcher whose experiment had been successful. 'I'm sure Mademoiselle here knows. She was there when it happened, wasn't she?'

Poe prepared to pounce.

Darlan shouted an order.

'No, Poe!' Tadeus' fingers reached to grab the nimble woman's arm, and missed.

The kitchen doors flew open. Armed men in masks stormed inside.

The gunmen seized the Korean woman before she had even reached the restorer or the cards, but she suddenly performed a vigorous martial-arts kick, sending the two men flying across the kitchen before going down against their incredible strength. She was hurled against the floorboards; a gash on her chin burst open. The red blood spilled onto the wooden floor, as if trying to retrace where the old stains had been.

To Tadeus' astonishment, and before he could even think about resisting, he also landed on the floor. Their hands were rapidly tied behind their backs with cable ties, and another one was wrapped around their necks to control their breathing. The masked men shoved them back onto the chairs.

'That was rather theatrical. Hopeless. But remarkable, mademoiselle,' Darlan observed. She was on her feet, clutching the three cards in her hands. 'I'll get to work on restoring the cards, and then, monsieur et madame, to mark the occasion I'll show you what makes the Playbook so special. With a game of supérieur, I think. According to the historical rules. You can look forward to experiencing the magic for yourselves.' She left the kitchen.

The plastic around Tadeus' throat made it difficult to breathe. He looked at the silent guards and their modern, muffled machine pistols, short assault rifles, armour and balaclavas.

One of them grabbed a tea towel, bent down in front of Poe and examined the wound on her chin. He folded the fabric several times to make a thick pad and taped it over the gash to soak up the blood.

Pragmatic.

Tadeus believed Darlan. Gillot had clearly fallen victim to a second attack from Lazarev, which meant the deck now belonged to the old woman. She had taken them all for a ride.

Supérieur. At least he would hold the nine of spades again.

His nine of spades. One more time before drawing the ace of spades. *One last time!*

Nothing else mattered.

Two hours later, Tadeus was sitting at the kitchen table with six other people. Each person had a stack of dollar bills from the Belgian's reserves in front of them, and only their right hand free; to avoid any escape attempts, everyone's left wrist and ankles had been tied to the chairs with cable ties. Because they were about to play supérieur. The Russian version.

Four masked men stood in the room along the wall, holding machine pistols with loosely attached silencers. They were waiting for their cue.

Tadeus would never have expected Darlan to finish restoring the cards so quickly, especially when he thought back to her workshop, that laboratory filled with chemical substances, different brushes, colours and magnifying glasses. He had assumed that the restoration process would take days, weeks and countless steps.

Despite the strange circumstances, Tadeus could hardly wait.

The nine of spades would recognise him and come to him. It would sing for him. He was certain of it. It would be his reward for what he had done for it, for bringing the deck back together.

'Are we all clear on the rules?' Darlan asked, assuming the role of the dealer. The Devil's Playbook lay in front of her in a small, ebony box inlaid with ivory. 'You can swap your card three times. The highest card wins. If you draw the ace of spades, you draw death. The stakes and all the dead losers' money go into the pot. If anyone tries to escape or cheat, the punishment is death. And, to raise the stakes: if you run out of money to play with, you die.'

Tadeus struggled to take his eyes off the box. The original deck. Without forgeries or placeholders. With his nine of spades! He could feel its presence. 'Yes,' he said.

'The fact that *you* know the rules is hardly surprising, Monsieur Boch.' Darlan waited for people to ask questions, but the group remained silent. 'Good. The winner will be permitted to leave the house alive, along with their winnings. Alors, messieurs-dames, good luck.'

Tadeus liked this option. To live his life. With his card. Debt-free.

He made himself look around the room and size up his fellow players. No one could fool him at cards; all those poker rounds he'd played around the world had been the perfect training for this very moment.

Poe, who had put her panama hat back on as some sort of dark joke, was no match for him, and neither was the nameless young runaway. He couldn't get a read on Mulder, Gillot's former errand boy, nor the apathetic ten-year old girl. Children were often lucky, and made unpredictable moves based on intuition. If he had understood correctly, the girl was Darlan's granddaughter, Hermine. Her mother Denise was sitting next to her and weeping softly. That left Crichton, the last mercenary Gillot had sent for protection. Tadeus would be wary of him. Mercenaries were skilled gamblers and weren't afraid of taking risks.

The five players had been dragged into the kitchen by the masked men and tied to the chairs, bringing with them the stench of stone, blood and filth that clung to their hair and their ragged clothes. They must have all been stuck in a place where death – both old and new – dwelled.

Darlan had briefly introduced herself and then urged everyone to keep quiet, even during the rounds.

'Your stakes,' she said, speaking like a high priestess. She opened the little box, took out the deck of cards and shuffled them.

Tadeus pushed his bundle of cash into the centre of the table, keeping his eyes fixed on the deck.

That sound, the rustling of paper that had survived 250 years, made his skin tingle with goosebumps. Whatever Darlan had done, every single card in the deck now radiated beauty and perfection. The details, the colours and the back and the front of every card were flawless. Tadeus felt that the cards' flattering singing and beguiling murmur were more beautiful than he had ever heard before, and he could clearly single out the nine of spades from the deck's chorus. It called out to him, and eagerly anticipated their reunion. Longed for him.

Darlan dealt the cards.

He focused intently and picked up the card with his free right hand. He already knew that it wasn't his. And while he couldn't refute the beauty of the fascinating motif of the seven of spades between his fingers, he couldn't fall in love with it; it gave him nothing. The number seven glistened a gloomy black as if it were a hole in the paper, as did the seven spade-shaped symbols that spanned the card and offset the dark landscape. Seven corpses dangled from them, their faces turned in different directions.

He wondered how the tiny details that the card-maker had applied hadn't lost an ounce of their lustre over 200 years later. *The Devil must have had something to do with it.*

There was an aphorism in shimmering liquid silver the bottom of the card, which Tadeus slowly read:

> *Unwanted at birth, wanted in life,*
> *and yet a life wasted.*

Tadeus looked up at Poe, who had raised the stakes before their first card swap opportunity. He didn't think anything of it. She was rushing. *She doesn't have anything.* He matched her stake like everyone else and read people's faces: the doctor's blue eyes, pinched lips and twitching eyelids told him she was angry and nervous; Crichton appeared indifferent and calm; the young runaway was breathing frantically; Mulder was playing hardball and fidgeting with his card; the mother wept with stifling sobs, and the girl sat numbly and didn't even look at the card in front of her.

He hated them. He hated each and every single person at the table. He hated the way they moved, the way they breathed, and the very beating of their hearts. Their hearts! He wanted to stop them, wanted to wipe out his opponents and everything to do with them. Just because they existed and dared go against him. To rob him of his victory. And they all wanted his nine of spades.

But Tadeus wouldn't let it show. Only beginners did that.

No, he would win the game and leave the house alive, and, if anyone at the table apart from Darlan – *anyone* – didn't pay for their loss with their own life, he would take care of it himself.

Not right away. He'd do it properly and with a plan. Because Tadeus knew that they were after him. It was clear from the looks that they gave him and exchanged with one another. *They're joining forces to gang up against me. These assholes!*

'Would anyone like a new card?' Darlan prompted. This was their first opportunity to swap cards.

Tadeus openly discarded his seven of spades, as per the rules of supérieur. 'A new card please. From the bottom.'

Everyone except the girl exchanged their cards for new ones.

Tadeus received the ace of hearts, which featured an anatomically accurate representation of the organ, annotated as if from a medical textbook, except that the labels read *compassion*, *grief*, *sorrow*, *greed*, *love*, *desire*, *hate* and *joy*. It seemed to throb as soon as he glanced at it for longer than a second, the pounding in his head sounding in rhythm with the cards' chants, blood pumping through his veins. He could smell the card's warm, coppery scent, and the lettering on it flared with each *ba-dum*, *ba-dum*, *ba-dum* of his heart.

The aphorism read:

> *For some, the worst fear of all*
> *Is that men's hearts are made of stone and nothing more*

'Messieurs-dames, does anyone wish to raise the stakes?' Darlan asked.

Poe pressed ahead once again.

Tadeus could tell from looking at her that she didn't have anything in her hand that posed a risk to him. Her blue eyes sparkled and she looked dazed, as if she'd been drinking and had to actively think before every movement. He matched her stake. The teary-eyed mother went out and revealed the nine of diamonds. The runaway was now trembling all over and discarded a jack of spades. Crichton raised the stakes again, and Poe placed a pathetic nine of hearts on the pile.

Everyone fell silent after that, and Darlan initiated the third opportunity to swap cards. Every player held on to the ones they had.

Tadeus raised the stakes by 100,000 dollars this time. His hatred towards the players grew. He wouldn't just burn down their houses; he would hunt down their relatives and friends. He would attack the community and the city in which they lived as punishment for going against him.

Crichton folded. The apathetic girl only had the three of hearts, and Mulder lost with a king of spades.

Tadeus stroked the pot and allowed himself an arrogant, contemptuous laugh. Oh, how they stared at him, angry and envious. Their looks only confirmed for him how he planned to punish them. He had to beat them to protect his loved ones from suffering. Be more thorough. Pull up every weed that might one day grow into a real problem.

'Well played, Monsieur Boch,' Darlan noted, collected the cards and shuffled them again. 'Your stakes, messieurs-dames.'

'Merci,' he said. The shuffling of the cards mesmerised and electrified him in equal measure. He couldn't get enough, and wanted to see more of the Devil's Playbook's beauty, to finally hold the nine of spades. *His* nine of spades, which he was itching to feel again.

His hatred towards his opponents festered. His hostility would live on beyond the game. For ever. Until he'd achieved his goal.

'Hermine . . . Hermine can't play,' the girl's mother said in a faltering voice. 'Please, Grandmère. Take her out of the game. She doesn't know what she's doing.'

Tadeus was disgusted by the woman, by her weakness, her tone, her stench and her begging.

'I'm sorry, but the rules are the rules, Denise,' Darlan replied coldly. 'And who knows? Maybe the little one will outlive you.' She dealt the cards. 'I hope she does. Unlike you, she didn't betray me in the cellar.'

Tadeus listened to the cards' chanting, slid the ante into the centre of the table and picked up the card he'd been dealt. Once again, it wasn't the nine of spades, which only made him long for it all the more. The card was making him wait like a proud lover expecting to be wooed. 'I'm raising the stakes by 50,000,' he said loudly, looking forward to his opponents' aversion. Now *that* was how you played the game!

From that point, the rounds progressed very differently. Poe won, and then, twice in a row, Crichton, who Tadeus considered to be the most dangerous opponent at the table.

During the fifth round Mulder hesitated as he picked up his second card, and his bound left hand trembled noticeably.

'You have the ace of spades, Monsieur Mulder,' Darlan said, 'as I'm sure you're about to reveal to us.'

Mulder turned over the card with his fingers, and there it was: an ace featuring a skull, its jaws clenching in malicious laughter and audibly chattering in a staccato-like fashion.

Tadeus smiled, just like everyone else at the table. Apart from the child, all the players rejoiced over the Belgian's death; the little girl only stared into space.

Mulder suddenly grabbed the card with his thumb and index finger. 'I swear I'll tear it to pieces! Untie me, Darlan, then I'll take my money and disappear!'

The restorer looked at him through her glasses, which were as thick as the bottom of a glass bottle. 'I can understand your reaction, monsieur. Nobody wants to die just because they've drawn a card. But those are the rules of supérieur.'

'You sick bitch! Let me go!' Mulder roared, pulling at the cable ties in vain. 'I'll do it.' He put the card between his teeth. 'I'll tear it up!' he threatened incoherently, resembling a bad ventriloquist.

Tadeus held his breath. The Playbook would never let Mulder get away with such a thing.

Darlan smiled wearily, making her superiority plain. 'The ace of spades came to be known as the death card because it used to bear the royal tax stamp, which proved that the card-makers had paid their dues.' She looked him in the eye. 'Anyone found to have forged the stamp was executed. And anyone who tries to cheat death, Monsieur Mulder, never gets very far.' She nodded to one of the masked men.

The man raised the MP9 machine pistol, the silencer aimed at Mulder's heart from behind him.

There was an audible *bang*, louder than Tadeus had expected, and then another as the man fired a second bullet from above through the Belgian's head.

Blood spilled from his mouth and nose, and ran over the ace of spades and between his teeth. As it began to foam, it partially dissolved and absorbed into the paper, as if the card was drinking it up. The skull's jaws ground and feasted on it until the card fell from the dead man's lips onto the table.

Mulder's death and the sight of the ace of spades delighted Tadeus. As long as he didn't pick it up, he could enjoy the same sight five more times. He hadn't even noticed that the soft laughter ringing in his ears was his own.

Darlan picked up the pristine ace of spades, put it back into the pile with the remaining cards and shuffled them again. 'Monsieur Mulder's total stake, including his reserves, go into the pot. Our game of supérieur continues, messieurs-dames.'

Boch won the round with a king of clubs.

The game went on, round after round. The numb and impassive little girl's ignorance secured her another two victories as she cleaned up with a queen of spades and an ace of diamonds, causing her mother to howl in gratitude. Tadeus reckoned the woman would run out of money soon, and thus meet her death.

Then the ace of spades plucked the trembling, whimpering runaway from the table. She didn't resist when the first shot ripped through her heart and the second, from above, through her skull. The insult she hurled at Darlan was cut short by the first bullet, and her body landed on the kitchen floor. With the execution over with, it was back to the girl: she laid down the ace of clubs.

Tadeus cursed his opponents more and more. He even fervently hated the dead Mulder and the runaway, who had spilled their blood onto the floorboards.

Then Crichton risked it all while Tadeus was still waiting for his nine of spades. His desire and anticipation turned into fear. A great, terrible fear of the card passing him by and that he would draw the ace of spades.

'I'm going all in,' Crichton said and staked his entire fortune.

The girl challenged him indifferently and lost to Crichton's queen of clubs, along with ninety per cent of her giant dollar pile, without even batting an eyelid.

'Grandmère!' her mother sobbed sickeningly. 'Please. Not Hermine!'

'Denise, please, control yourself. Have you forgotten that you're the one to blame? Both you and Hermine could have avoided sitting at this table. I'm sorry, but this is what the cards demand of me.' Darlan smiled encouragingly at her. 'The game giveth, and the game taketh away.'

Tadeus nodded in agreement. 'Those are the rules.'

'Boch,' Poe said without looking at him. There was a sort of mist over her cornflower-blue eyes that he couldn't explain. 'Wake up.'

'I've never been more awake,' he told her.

Crichton won again with only a measly nine of hearts and almost robbed the mother of her last dollar. The ace of diamonds finally earned Tadeus some more cash. But the nine of spades still refused to show itself. It hid from him mischievously and feigned disinterest.

Poe wiped the perspiration from her face as Darlan dealt out the cards for the twelfth time. 'Fucking hell,' the doctor muttered incoherently. She was sweating profusely. The game had worn her out and the look in her eyes was lost and aimless.

Tadeus peeked at his card: the ace of spades.

It had found him, but he didn't let it on. His years of playing at illegal and legal gambling rounds had steeled his poker face. He was knowingly breaking the supérieur rule because he didn't want to die without holding his nine of spades one last time. Surely the Playbook had to understand that. It had to be able to hear how his card yearned for him. *Time to attack.*

'I'm raising the stakes by 100,000,' he said calmly.

No one folded.

Instead, the mother and the girl pushed what little they had left of their reserves into the centre. The last stand. Tadeus found himself wondering what their gameplan was. Was the mother trying to save her daughter by hoping to lose before her, or was this all part of a plan against him?

Poe followed suit, and so did Crichton – his worst enemy. They swapped their existing cards; low cards flew once, and then twice, across the table.

Crichton wasn't paying attention when he picked up his third card and Tadeus noticed what the mercenary had been dealt: *the nine of spades.* His nine of spades! He heard the card's singing grow louder. It coaxed and called out to him.

She belongs to me! As a test, Tadeus tugged at the restraints holding the cable ties in place, and the wood groaned softly. Unlike the plastic, it could be broken, which would give him a chance to free himself and grab the card. If he was going to die, he wanted to die holding the card in his hand.

The only thing Tadeus could now hear was the nine of spades' siren voice. He continued to mechanically place bets, like Hermine, and stared at Crichton, who he hated more than anyone in the world. He wasn't allowed to have the card. He wasn't allowed to hold or play with it.

His hatred grew into a blind rage that he could barely control. It was time for him to decide when he would strike. He had to stay alive for his nine of spades and kill Crichton for his sacrilege. The man had touched and defiled the card. He wasn't worthy of her. *Nobody was. Not even Darlan!*

'King of hearts,' Poe announced.

'Ace of clubs,' the child said flatly, her eyes empty like a puppet's.

'Ace of hearts!' the girl's mother rejoiced and leaned back in relief. 'Hermine, you've done it! You've won and got your money back.' She didn't care that she was almost out of cash herself.

'Nine of spades,' Crichton confessed sullenly.

'We have a winner,' Darlan praised. 'To complete the round, Monsieur Boch, would you kindly reveal your card?'

Everyone stared at him. The mercenary grinned and laughed loudly. He knew.

Tadeus' gaze was fixed on the nine of spades. 'May I hold it, madame?' he asked.

'Show us your card, Monsieur Boch.'

He heard two footsteps sound behind him and felt the barrel of a gun press into his back level with his heart.

'Your men will shoot me if I do.'

Darlan made an apologetic face. 'Then they might as well do it now: you cheated.'

'Please can I hold the nine of spades first?' he cried abruptly. 'I have to see it!'

Crichton picked the card up again and waved it around. 'Is this what you want? You're desperate for it, aren't you?' He laughed obnoxiously. 'You can forget it. You're about to die!' He glanced at the masked men. 'Go on. One of you blow that arsehole's brains out and then we can get on with it. Then I'll beat the Asian cunt, that filthy bitch and her fucking kid and be on my way.'

Nobody moved. The gunman pressed the barrel against the back of Tadeus' head but didn't pull the trigger. He waited for his boss to give the order.

'That's the rule!' Crichton shouted angrily. 'Get on with it!' He threw the nine of spades onto the table and slammed his palm down. 'Fuck, are you going to do it or not?'

'Monsieur Crichton! Control yourself! We're playing supérieur, not some game for savages!' Darlan barked. Her heavy glasses slid down to the tip of her nose, barely staying upright.

Tadeus' boiling rage gave him an inexplicable sense of strength. He'd experienced the same sensation in Bruges, but this time it was far more powerful. He now focused his full attention on the mercenary and acted: he dropped the ace of spades, reached for the barrel aimed at his skull and shoved it at Crichton, who ducked intuitively.

The man behind Tadeus fired the MP9, either out of shock or because his bold grip had inadvertently activated the automatic fire mode. The bullets flew out of the barrel and struck two of Darlan's stunned gunmen – one in the vest, the other in the head – and blood splattered over the kitchen cupboard behind him.

My nine of spades! In his wild fury, Tadeus broke the chair, smashing the backrest against the masked man's temple behind him. The chair legs splintered and he collapsed onto the bloody floor under the table with the MP9 in his hand.

'You motherfucker!' Tadeus yelled. He grabbed the machine pistol by its handle, pulled the trigger and fired at the mercenary he loathed.

The clever Crichton had realised that the old furniture was too weak to withstand brute force and also decided to destroy his chair, freeing himself from the cable ties and evading the bullets.

Tadeus heard a muffled bang above him as the gunmen fired

through the table at him and Crichton, sending a cloud of splinters and sawdust flying through the kitchen. Tadeus had nothing against the men. All he wanted was the nine of spades and to leave – to simply disappear.

He grabbed the runaway's body and held it above him like a shield, just like he'd seen people do in action films. The dead body's sudden twitching, a result of being hit by several gunshots, told him it had been a good idea.

Ammunition shells hailed down on the wooden floor and another two opponents fell to the ground, dead. The mercenaries must have taken them out.

The door swung open. Three more masked men stormed in, executing a combat manoeuvre. They covered themselves as they advanced, firing at Crichton, whose screams rang out above the din.

In the chaos the mother toppled to the ground in her chair, riddled with bullets. Tadeus only had to take one look at her to know that nothing could be done to save her. *Another enemy down*. But his number one enemy was Crichton.

'You bastards!' the mercenary cried from one of the corners and opened fire on the men.

The restorer crouched next to the kitchen cupboard. 'Finish him and Boch!' she ordered.

The rattling of machine pistols sounded several times. Crichton screamed angrily and retaliated with the MP9. 'I'm taking you down with me!'

No you won't. Tadeus raised the machine pistol and had just aimed it at Crichton from under a dead body when he heard something metallic clink.

Two fuse pins landed on the floor and were immediately followed by two long grenades and multiple ear-splitting explosions. The accompanying flashes left him blind and disorientated.

Panicking, he lifted the MP9 and fired at random until there was a click. The magazine was empty. He didn't anticipate the blow to his head that came next out of the glaring nothingness, knocking him senseless and causing him to slump to the ground.

'Monsieur Boch,' Darlan said reproachfully, 'that's no way to play supérieur.'

'The nine of spades,' he murmured. The kitchen was nothing but a spinning blur. It reeked of blood and faeces. 'I only wanted the nine of spades . . .'

'You cheated. You'll never see the nine of spades again and will burn with it in my house,' she explained calmly. 'I have to change the world, monsieur. Have you seen what power dwells in the Playbook? How beautiful and dangerous it is? How it seeks to take control?'

'I only wanted . . .' Tadeus protested helplessly. 'She needs me!'

'The nine of spades doesn't need you!' Poe cried out weakly. 'You need to fight against it!'

Darlan laughed. 'Miss Poe is right. The nine of spades sought you out because you're a weak man, Monsieur Boch. You're under her spell. Utterly and completely. The card has turned you into a love-struck fool, a suitor gone mad. *That's* the power of the cards. That's how they lure their followers to sow suffering into the world.'

Tadeus didn't want to listen to Darlan, but he didn't have the strength to fight her words. His bones ached, his head pounded and the room spun around him. 'That's not true,' he gasped. Then he heard a sudden dissonance in the card's singing, dulling his fascination. The nine of spades was pulling away from him – mocking him – its laughter becoming derisive.

'Oh, but it *is*, Monsieur Boch. It has been so for centuries.' Darlan was audibly enjoying shattering his illusions. 'You're not the first fool to fall for the cards and you won't be the last. You would have done anything for it, wouldn't you?'

'Anything,' Tadeus groaned, astonished at how his card reprimanded and disowned him, at how it no longer sang for him. *After everything . . . I'm replaceable?*

'You would have killed Mademoiselle Poe for it?'

'Yes.'

'And your own children, too?'

'Yes.' As the word left his lips, it struck Tadeus like a bolt of lightning. He had said it as if it were a matter of course. *Michiko! Georg!* He would kill his own children to please a card. To satisfy a thing that had just made it clear that it despised him. Would he really stoop so low?

His mind suddenly detached itself from the desire and his longing for the card faded, as if he'd finally woken up after a wild, drunken haze during which he'd done inexplicable things. Strange, unimaginable things.

The sensation swept through his mind like an icy wind, blowing away the poisonous clouds. The distorted, mocking chorales grew quieter in his mind and disgusted him. He felt sick.

Darlan laughed. 'These cards are brilliant. The more damage they cause, the more powerful they become.' Her footsteps moved away from him and he saw her silhouette, which looked like a walking broomstick. 'I can't wait to see what will happen next.'

Tadeus became aware of his own body again.

He lay on the floor and rolled around, groping for something to pull himself up with. All he saw were dark and light outlines.

Darlan was an expert on the Playbook and its effect on people, on the bizarre obsession that it induced, for which people were prepared to do anything. Her enlightening words burned in his mind. They set fire to his desire for the nine of spades and brought on an intense wave of nausea, as if he'd been poisoned.

Remorse came after the shame. His mind wrestled with this false desire that had captivated him for so long.

Tadeus suddenly thought back to Antoine, the tour guide he'd had to kill so that he and Poe could make it out of the tunnel alive. He was overcome with the abrupt realisation that he was just like Antoine, that he had *become* Antoine – a berserk madman who would not only have sacrificed Poe and Fignolé for the cards, but his own children too.

He grabbed the overturned table and tried to lift himself up, feeling like a centenarian. His stomach twisted and lurched as everything inside him fought against the nine of spades' scornful singing. An inner exhaustion overwhelmed him, a mental blow that robbed him of his strength, likely as a result of the sobering mental clarity that washed over him.

The card's mocking singing finally stopped. It had released Tadeus, leaving him with nothing other than disgust and shame . . . and a shimmering, faint trace of grief at its loss.

He gradually started to recognise more than shadows, but thick clouds obstructed his vision. Now that he was on his feet, he found himself in the middle of the smoke coming from a fire somewhere in the house. *Darlan wants to destroy the evidence and buy herself time.* Through the dense clouds he made out the hazy outlines of people lying on the floor.

Tadeus' first instinct was to take the money and flee, leaving the hateful players behind to burn, but then his reason took over and he fought against the dwindling effect of the nine of spades. *I was used.* Shame and remorse. *I was nothing but a willing instrument.*

Coughing, he staggered to the sink, turned on the tap, wet a tea towel and tied it around his mouth and nose. He ducked down and searched for survivors.

Poe lay on the floor, still tied to her chair. She was unconscious and had been shot in her thigh. The wound was bleeding quite heavily. Her limbs twitched occasionally as if she were having a vivid dream.

The little girl sat in her chair amidst the chaos, covered neither in wounds nor in bloodstains. She stared blankly into space. If he didn't take action, she would burn in the spreading flames. Just like that.

Hermine. That was her name.

Tadeus spotted the bundles of cash in the backpack, threw it over his mobile shoulder, freed Poe and Hermine from the cable ties with a knife, and dragged them out of the smoke-filled kitchen into the barn. There was a fire blazing at the main entrance to the house, making it impossible to leave that way.

But the barn was burning too. The dry wood had turned it into an inferno as hot as an oven. More flames leapt up from the cellar exit and the top floor. Chemicals fizzled out from Darlan's study and dyed the fire.

'She said she's going to change the world,' Hermine whispered absent-mindedly, staring into the flames. 'She wants to burn it.'

'What? What do you know about her plan?' Tadeus asked.

'That she wants to burn the world. That's it. In two weeks, she said.' Hermine whistled a tune. 'As a gift. A gift to the greats of the world. And then the world will burn.' She pointed to the barn. 'Burn!'

Tadeus looked around. The heat would soon make it impossible to breathe. *There must be something I can ...* He saw two large, old wine barrels. One of them was standing next to them. *That'll work.*

He quickly turned on the tap protruding from the wall less than two metres away, hastily doused himself with water from head to toe, and then did the same to the unconscious and twitching Poe and Hermine, who let the water wash over them like dolls.

Tadeus lifted them both into the barrel along with the backpack full of cash and sealed it with a lid. He poured water over the container several times and covered himself with an old horse blanket that he'd pulled off a beam and likewise drenched in water.

He was the last one left standing, and someone had to roll the barrel through the fire. Roughly fifteen metres of blazing hell stretched out between him and the exit, though it seemed more like one hundred and fifty metres to Tadeus.

I am not! A weak! Man! Tadeus buried his fear, placed his hands on the wooden barrel and began to push.

Some say that the best way to know someone is to play them at cards;
their passions reveal themselves as openly as in front of a mirror.
I have found this to be true.

Johann Wolfgang von Goethe (1794–1832)

XVII

Nîmes, Gard,
Occitania,
France

'Did you find somewhere safe to leave the girl?' Hyun asked, looking at the evening view of the brightly lit Nîmes amphitheatre.

Music from what sounded like an opera performance drifted into their room from the open hotel windows. According to one of the brochures, the Roman amphitheatre with its antique atmosphere was often used as a venue for concerts and various other events.

Hyun wore a white shirt and dark green shorts. She had woken half an hour ago from a nightmare-free slumber, exhausted from the events, the blood loss and the mental strain. She had deliberately fallen into a sort of half-trance during their game of supérieur and had relied on her mudang powers to minimise and alter the Playbook's influence.

It hadn't quite worked as she'd hoped, but who knew what would have happened without her help? *Boch wouldn't have saved me and the little girl.*

Hyun wanted her only ally back. She needed him and his expertise in this bizarre battle against time and the cursed deck, and his help in clearing her name.

'Her name is Hermine,' Boch said. Despite there being a comfortable armchair in their suite, he was sitting on a hard chair in front of the TV. The screen was split into smaller previews, various French channels reporting on the major fire in Avignon. The sound would play as soon as he selected one. 'She's safe.' He was perfectly content in his black tracksuit bottoms and a fine, ribbed vest, the silver chain and his shoulder wound making him look like a veteran rap star. 'Did you really think I'd just leave the girl outside the house?'

'It wouldn't have surprised me if you did, to be honest.' Hyun turned around and followed the broadcasts. She'd tied her black hair into a ponytail, which pulled slightly when she lay down.

The images were striking. The fire had spread from Darlan's house to the neighbouring buildings on Nicolas Lescuyer Street; the narrow road had made it easy for the flames to travel. It had taken hours for the fire brigade to extinguish the largest of the fires, and they were still fighting to bring the flaring, glowing embers under control, which meant the experts hadn't yet been able to begin investigating the cause of the events. What had happened in mediaeval Avignon was described as a tragedy. Several people were reported missing, including Odette Darlan, who was said to be a famous restorer who had been living in seclusion for some time.

Boch had found the duplicates of the Playbook that Darlan had long used to deceive Gillot within the backpack where the money had been. It appeared she liked to keep all of her valuables in the same place. The cards now lay fanned out on a white blanket on his side of the bed.

Hyun reached out her hand and held it a few millimetres above the cards. She didn't feel a single trace of an aura. It was painted, old paper, which, while breathtakingly beautiful, had no mystical or malicious influence. There was nothing to fear.

The restorer had dispatched these cards to the Walloon, who had failed to see through her ploy, and kept the originals for herself. The burglary she had organised had secured her the missing cards, and now she had completed the deck.

Hyun turned her gaze to Boch. When she first woke, she had found him finishing an emotional phone call with his daughter, Michiko, the half-Japanese girl who she reminded him of. She had watched him wipe tears from his eyes and smile in relief at the things that had been said.

His posture had changed. She could see the shame and inner torment on his aged face. He was haunted by what he had done and what he would have done for the nine of spades in his deluded state. That spoke in his favour. He hadn't lost his humanity.

The glow of the cards' wretched power still surrounded him, but it no longer controlled him – comparable to a nasty hangover after a wild night. He appeared to have freed himself of the Playbook's influence and to be fighting against its power. Hyun's work in weakening and altering the cards' whispers, however, had been the decisive first step.

She gently slid up the bed and leaned her upper body against the padded headboard. 'Why are we sitting in a hotel room, Boch?' she asked.

'Because I have a debt to repay and you had a clear goal.' He turned to look at her. 'You wanted to destroy the deck.'

'You didn't.'

'I do now.' Boch propped his elbows on his knees. 'I learned the hard way how dangerous it is. How enticing and destructive it is. This hatred, it . . .' He shuddered and ran a hand over his stubble. 'I wouldn't have spared anyone. Without your help, I would have been done for. I know you intervened.'

Hyun looked at him. She was searching for clues that told her he was telling her lies, the kind that had slipped off his tongue over the last few days, prompted by the nine of spades. But the steady, basic glow, as Leila Fignolé had called it, was gone. *He's changed.*

Boch tried to smile. 'You were able to fight the hatred that the deck planted in all of us.'

'There are advantages to being a half mudang. I remembered some simple exercises that my grandmother drilled into me. They protected me. For you . . . I would say it sort of worked. It was enough to make you realise the truth. But you're not entirely free of the cards' unfortunate influence yet.'

'I will be when the cards are destroyed.'

'That's noble of you to say, Boch, but Darlan has run off with them.'

'She'll turn up. And so will the cards.' He pointed his finger at her. 'Thanks to your mudang powers.'

'It's not that easy. Have you forgotten that I can only sense the cards at a really close distance?'

'Don't you think that the Playbook as a complete deck will have a much more powerful aura?'

'Yes, but that doesn't mean I'll able to sense it from kilometres away.'

Boch picked up the glass of water that stood on the table next to him and took a sip. He had dissolved a tablet in it; white particles floated in the liquid and clouded it. 'Hermine gave me some clues about Darlan's plan. Maybe that'll make it easier for you to find her.'

'You know where—'

'No. I only said clues.'

Hyun got up from the bed and carefully put weight on her injured leg. The flesh wound throbbed and pounded painfully and there were some pink marks on the bandage. It was bleeding slightly. 'Did you dress it?'

'Yes, but only provisionally. I knew that you'd do a better job than me as soon as you woke up.' Boch turned to look at the TV.

Hyun couldn't hide her smile. She unwrapped the bandage to inspect the wound he'd dressed while she'd been unconscious.

Boch could have killed her, left her to burn in Darlan's house or simply vanished without her. It would have been all too easy for him to drive back to Baden-Baden in the car, feed Klim some lie about the gambling mafia and go back to living his old life. He didn't have to worry about what conclusions the police came to about the murders in the villa. His career wasn't on the line. It was the officers who needed his statements.

But he had stayed and rescued her from the flames.

She examined the wound and the stiches. 'You wouldn't make a good seamstress,' she said and asked him for the military first aid kit he had bought on their way.

'I've always been fine with buttons.'

'I can see that. But it's not a button I need sewing onto my leg. Come here and help me, please.' She didn't want to be left with a nasty scar so undid the stitches. After disinfecting the thin thread again, she pulled it through the flesh with clenched teeth and a few groans, dabbing it several times as she secured the edges of the wound together. Then she washed the blood from her skin. *That's better.*

Boch was impressed. 'Bravo,' he said.

Hyun smiled. 'That hurt all right, but I've had patients who've been through much worse.'

In the meantime, a correspondent reported on a neglected girl covered in soot who had been found outside the police station in Avignon. She was in shock and didn't want to speak. So far, no missing persons report had been filed for her, and it was unclear whether she was connected with the events of the fire. A search for her parents and other relatives had been launched.

'I hope someone recognises Hermine.' Boch drank the rest of his tablet water. 'That poor girl. What has Darlan done to her own family?'

'Darlan is under the influence of the cards. Just like you,

Boch. Strictly speaking, you can't even blame her for it.' Hyun tentatively paced up and down the massive room. The stitches held. She dabbed the bright, oozing blood with a compress and then wrapped a bandage around it. 'I think Darlan's mind is far more poisoned than yours ever was. She spent years tending to the cards and serving the Playbook.'

'I'm not a weak person,' Boch whispered, his voice filled with doubt. 'I'm not, am I?'

'What do you mean?'

'Darlan. She said the nine of spades chose me because I'm a weak man.' He sighed loudly. 'I convinced myself that it was the other way around, but I'm afraid that—'

'A weak man would have left me and Hermine to die,' Hyun reasoned. He needed the reassurance. 'It was the card, Boch. Never forget that. It still influences your thinking, even now, and you'll have to fight against it for a while.'

He nodded. 'Whatever you want to do about the deck, I'm in. And then we'll take care of the Baden-Baden case. Just because Gillot is dead doesn't mean we can't still prove he was behind it. If anything, it makes it easier.' He cleared his throat and stretched out his hand to her. 'I'm Tadeus, by the way.'

'Hyun.' She shook his hand. She believed him, despite his ardour and the flickering that surrounded him. He would keep his word. The expression on his face was sincere and the card's influence had visibly waned. Still, that didn't mean that he was now immune to the nine of spades' magic. Knowledge alone wouldn't protect him from the cards' unfathomable, dark power. He might not be a weak man, but he was still a vulnerable one. 'Will you tell me what you did to Leila Fignolé?'

'I knocked her out in the ladies' toilets,' Tadeus confessed. 'I've already tried calling her Beninese number, but she's not picking up. I . . . I broke her phone.'

Hyun sighed. Fignolé had been a faint glimmer of hope for

quickly locating the Playbook. She had a far stronger sense of, and control over, the good spirits and therefore had a better chance of being able to help. 'You said that Hermine gave you some clues.'

Tadeus stood up and poured himself a cognac. It was the first time that she'd seen him have a stiff drink, especially with a tablet. 'I tried to memorise what she said. She didn't know much about Darlan's plans.' He downed the drink and topped himself up again, clearly wanting to quell his guilt and shame. 'She only said that Darlan was going to change the world and let it burn.'

'Hm,' Hyun said and settled in the armchair. She began to feel dizzy; her blood pressure was dropping. Perhaps some sparkling wine would help. She put her injured leg up and got Boch to pour her a prosecco from the minibar. Then she would treat herself to some painkillers. 'How would someone burn the world?'

'The girl said it would be easy. That it would happen in two weeks.' Tadeus repeated Hermine's ominous hints. 'She said something about a gift. A gift to the greats of the world.'

'The greats of the world . . .' Hyun ran through the potential prospects in her mind: businessmen, prime ministers and presidents, the Pope, politicians, scientists, tycoons, CEOs and poets. *Too many possibilities*. 'Did she say anything else?'

'No.' Tadeus swirled the cognac in his glass and slipped one hand into the pocket of his tracksuit bottoms. 'Hang on. Yes, there was. She hummed a melody, but . . .'

'You don't know what it is?'

'I can't figure it out!'

'Let's hear it.' Hyun sipped her prosecco and listened for a while. Then it hit her. 'That's the Russian national anthem!' She grabbed the hotel-owned tablet from the table on the side and searched the internet for *Russia* and *the greats of the world*.

'What is it?' Tadeus asked, curious.

'One second.' She skimmed the results. The prosecco had

gone to her head, driving away the merry-go-round feeling that had previously left her feeling woozy. Her circulation improved, and she scrolled through a number of promising articles – those that were left after discarding any which were about Catherine the Great, the biggest Russian churches, the largest construction projects in Russia and Russia being the fifth top gold producer in the world.

'Here it is!' she said, clearing her throat.

'Historic nuclear security summit in Moscow. Heads of state and government from over fifty countries will travel to Moscow in two weeks to discuss the fight against nuclear terrorism, the protection of nuclear materials, and the battle against the smuggling of highly enriched uranium and plutonium. Unlike in previous years, at this year's nuclear security summit countries such as Pakistan, India and North Korea will be represented by delegations who will meet with international business representatives on the sidelines of the official talks.

The Russians and the Americans are co-chairing this year's summit – a real triumph and hopefully the beginning of a new era of collaboration that could lead to a whole new wave of disarmament work.'

Hyun looked at Tadeus. 'The greats of the world. And the girl whistled the Russian national anthem.' She pointed to the report. 'Darlan wants to go to Moscow!' She dropped the tablet.

'And for the world leaders to play a round of cards there,' he added. 'That's her plan.'

'And clearly one she's been plotting for a while.' The Devil's Playbook was restored and complete. During the round of cards at the summit, it would unleash its terrible power in all its entirety, just as they'd experienced. Unless there happened to be a mudang, shaman, voodoo priestess or some other well-versed spirit-world expert in the same room, the round of cards and the summit in Moscow would come to a very different end than anticipated.

Tadeus downed his cognac and decided against a third glass.

'This summit of hope will be the meeting that leads to the out-break of wars. Wars between countries with nuclear weapons. The Americans and the Russians might still be more or less rea-sonable, but . . . North Korea and Pakistan? Or Israel or Iran? There'll be a multi-front world war.'

'The Russians and the Americans wouldn't be impervious to the cards' influence either,' Hyun disagreed. 'Remember the Play-book's boundless power, its hatred. Nobody is immune to that.'

'You are.'

'You know what I mean.'

'The world will burn.' Tadeus furrowed his brow. 'But who's going to let Darlan just walk in and present the deck to one of the presidents? And how is she going to make sure that the cards don't just get set aside and left with the other presents? She wants them to be played with.'

Hyun contemplated for a moment. 'She could disguise her-self as a delegation member and smuggle herself in, or give the deck to a delegate . . . No, you're right. Darlan wouldn't leave such a thing to a stranger or to chance.' *And the cards would never stand for it, either.*

'So we need to be in Moscow in two weeks.' Tadeus turned his head back to the TV. The reports about Avignon were pour-ing in. 'We need to have thought of something by then.'

The prosecco had made Hyun feel bold. She grabbed a note-pad and jotted down a number from memory, correcting it until she was sure she had the right combination.

'What are you doing?' Tadeus asked.

'Thinking.' Hyun quickly punched the area code in and picked up the cordless phone. 'And calling someone.' She smiled briefly at him, dialled a number that she had only needed once before and limped out onto the large balcony into the cool, evening air. She didn't want Boch listening.

The amphitheatre cast bright beams of light into the sky.

Loud opera singing and the sounds of an orchestra echoed throughout the city. Nîmes looked beautiful with its gardens and ancient Roman buildings, and she regretted not having the time to soak up its atmosphere. She decided she would return to the city for a weekend getaway. *Once the catastrophe had been averted.*

'What do you want?' a man asked on the other end of the phone, in English with a distinct Eastern European accent.

'You had Gillot shot without me giving you any evidence,' Hyun flung back.

Lazarev laughed. 'That's a funny reason to call me, Miss Poe. Or is this you wanting to hear that you're no longer in my debt?'

'*You're* in *my* debt,' she countered. 'Without me, you wouldn't have known that Gillot was responsible for your son's murder.'

'You're right about that, Miss Poe.'

'And you treated me like shit when we met. No – shit is an understatement!'

'You weren't received with the usual Russian hospitality, that's true.' Lazarev sounded willing to negotiate. 'How much do you want?'

'I don't want any money. I need . . . a favour.'

The man laughed again. 'That's a principle I'm familiar with. So, what can I do for you?'

'A summit is taking place in Moscow in two weeks.'

'That's no secret.'

'As a trusted friend of the Russian president, you'll either be part of a delegation or be conducting business surrounding the summit. Catering, taking care of the entertainment programme, etcetera,' Hyun said and inhaled the fresh evening air. She barely felt the pain in her leg.

'And?'

'And I want to get back into the modelling business,' she lied. 'I've had some enquiries from a cosmetics company that makes, let's say ... medical claims about the effectiveness of their products, and I'd like to increase my market value before I enter into any contract negotiations.'

'Ah, I see.' He laughed. 'You want me to get you in so that as many reporters and photographers as possible take your picture.'

'Exactly. Can you arrange that? Using my old name for a new label.'

'Absolutely. But behave yourself. Anything else?'

'A good hotel and details of where I need to be when to keep the cameras on my face,' she demanded. 'Some gifts to hand out would be good. I'm great at that. Oh, and it goes without saying that my bodyguard will travel with me.'

'That can be arranged.' Lazarev laughed. 'I have to admit, Miss Poe, I didn't expect this.'

'No?'

'I didn't take you for someone who'd ask for such a thing. But fine. But after that, we're even, Miss Poe. I'll send you the details via email. All the relevant documents and credentials will be waiting for you at the hotel.'

'And I'd like the room from next week,' she added.

'Done. With Crimean sparkling wine in your room – it's better than any champagne you've ever tasted, you'll see.' She heard someone call his name in the background. 'Business calls, Miss Poe. *Do svidaniia* and I hope your time in Moscow proves lucrative. If you find yourself needing a guide, call me. The city can be an all-consuming metropolis.' Lazarev hung up.

Feeling pleased with herself, Hyun returned to the room. 'We're going to Moscow with you as my bodyguard.'

Tadeus gave her a quizzical look.

Then she realised that she still had to come clean to him about spying for Lazarev and being indirectly responsible for the attack in the basilica. Though Tadeus suspected as much already, Hyun felt she owed him the truth, and hoped he would be lenient with her.

'. . .the first rescue team have recovered a second survivor under a heap of burnt bodies and corpses,' the news blared from the TV. Both of them turned to face the screen and followed the urgent report from Avignon. 'The survivor is a boy of around eleven years old. The volunteers believe that he is suffering from shock and smoke poisoning. But one thing is clear: something out of a nightmare awaits the forensics team in the cellar, and we're in for a hell of a story.'

* * *

Moscow, the Russian Federation

Tadeus had to admit it: for better or for worse, Mikhail Aleksandrovich Lazarev kept his word, and booking them a suite at the Krasnye Kholmy Hotel definitely belonged to the former. The hotel was very luxurious, with a view of the capital from their room and from the panorama bar, which seemed vaguely familiar.

The staff had also greeted him in an exceptionally friendly manner. It appeared that he had stayed at the Krasnye Kholmy in his gambling days.

Hyun and Tadeus had spent a week studying the events scheduled for the summit. They'd annotated the programme and turned one of the wall cabinets in their room into a huge whiteboard. Lazarev provided them with all the information they required. They also kept their eye out for potential opportunities such as excursions, sightseeing tours or official gift ceremonies that Darlan could use to hand over the Devil's Playbook.

Tadeus now knew where the killers who had initially attacked Gillot in Rome and then finished him off in hospital had come from. Hyun had disclosed that information to him. He refrained from making any accusations when she told him how she had secretly teamed up with Oprichnik; given his own actions, he didn't feel he had the right. He also remembered the ligature marks on her wrists.

The week before their train to Moscow, they had split their time between Nîmes and Baden-Baden, as well as taking a detour to the State Criminal Police Office in Stuttgart to discuss the murders at the villa with Inspector Klim. Hyun's lawyer had already disclosed with delight that the murder weapon had disappeared from the evidence locker, which Klim begrudgingly confirmed. His team were making no progress with the investigation, and the inspector no longer appeared to suspect either of them were involved in the murders. As a result of the disappearance of the Beretta Bobcat, he was now focused on exposing the mole in his own ranks. Klim was now also convinced that there was an unknown killer from the Russian gambling mafia, which he believed was supported by the theft of the piece of evidence. That made it fairly easy for Hyun to secure her unofficial acquittal. Klim confirmed that he would withdraw the investigation against her and urged her to drop her own enquiries.

According to the latest reports from Avignon, over two dozen complete corpses and more body parts had been found in the cellar of the restorer's winery, where the boy had taken shelter from the fire. Among the rubble on the first floor, forensics had also discovered several modern pistols, assault rifles and bullet-proof vests on some of the bodies, which complicated the investigation further. There was soon talk of a shooting that must have taken place before the fire, but the French investigators were still in the dark as to how the two events were connected. The internet and the newspapers were teeming with reports and speculation.

Tadeus stood up in front of the jumble of papers. 'If I were Darlan, I would—'

'Wait! There's been another update!' Hyun interrupted.

Lazarev was keeping them informed of any changes before the start of the summit. Due to the weather, certain formalities, illnesses and cancellations, things changed every minute, which consequently also ruined their own plans.

'*Presidential visit to the Moscow State Historical Museum. Russian President to present an art-historical object to the French President,*' Hyun read out the email from her tablet. '*A Fabergé egg.*' She fixed her eyes on the screen. '*That's it!*'

'What is?' Tadeus knew she wasn't talking about the egg.

'The French president to present a historical pack of cards to the Russian president as a state gift to Russia.' She tapped the tablet. 'At the Historical Museum.'

'A German pack of cards being gifted by the French to the Russians?' Tadeus pondered. 'That sounds very confused and diplomatically complicated.'

'Maybe it's supposed to represent an international understanding of some sort. It says here that the little box for the cards was made in Russia.' Hyun laughed mirthlessly. 'The Playbook has all the power now. It'll insist that people hold it in their hands and turn over the cards. It knows exactly how to wreak havoc.'

'Yes, it'll inject hatred into the feelings and thoughts of the summit's participants.' Tadeus looked at the illustrious group of heads of state in front of him and thought about the horror the cards would inflict upon the world. 'When is the gift ceremony taking place?'

Hyun swore in Korean. 'Today. In' – she glanced at the display on her device – 'about three hours.'

That's not much time. Tadeus pointed to the fanned-out cards on the bed. 'What if we swap them? The originals with Darlan's copies. No one will notice.'

Hyun smiled. Since they'd stopped carrying the real cards from the Playbook around with them, she no longer suffered from nightmares, and, despite the stress, was now finally recovering from the physical and mental strain of the events.

'Nobody will check. By the time they notice, the deck will be . . .' Tadeus had wanted to say *destroyed,* but then he remembered that the Playbook was indestructible. *But was that really true?* The deck had been created and brought into this world by a man named Bastian Kirchner, so surely there was a way to eliminate it from this world, or at least rob it of its power.

'Fine. Let's make sure the deck doesn't fall into the hands of the greats of the world.' Hyun threw her phone onto the bed, got up and went into the bathroom. 'I'm going to get ready. After all, it's been twelve years since I did any modelling.' She shut the door behind her. 'And I want to see you in a suit!' she shouted at him through the wood.

Tadeus glanced at the cognac. Two was enough. 'You will,' he said. He then typed out a message to his son and daughter to let them know that he loved them. They'd be surprised and think that their father had either become sentimental or turned into a permanent drunk.

Let them. Tadeus simply wanted to let them know.

His eyes fell on his backpack in the corner. It was brimming with dollar bills, around four million of them. If he managed to get out of Moscow alive, he would be free of debt. *I can always say I won it playing poker.*

And if he didn't make it out of Moscow alive, his children wouldn't have to worry about how to pay off his debts.

* * *

Odette Darlan sat in the empty, adjoining room of the Grand Café Dr Zhivago with coffee and a slice of cake and looked past the wide boulevard and the bordering square. The Historical Museum, which lay behind it, was nothing but a mighty, red block to her poor eyes.

Her coffee was lukewarm and she'd barely touched her cake; she could hardly bring herself to eat. Being away from the cards affected her like nothing ever had before. No death and no loss could ever come close to what she felt in deep in her soul.

Every thud of her heart pained her. Odette lacked strength and vigour. It seemed that the Devil's Playbook had fuelled her, provided her with momentum, but, now that that power had disappeared from her life, existence suddenly felt like a burden.

She disliked the café's classic decor, which deliberately mimicked the Viennese coffee houses of the turn of the century. The interior was primarily white, which accentuated the red upholstery of the chairs, sofas and the red chandelier. Mirrors and paintings printed onto glass hung on the walls and white statues, both big and small, served as centrepieces. Odette couldn't make out the details on the painted ceilings. The staff kept a low profile as they served customers; the women wore skirts and bonnets and the men wore light-coloured suits.

Odette forced herself to take a bite. It was bland. Everything tasted bland and meaningless to her since she had given away the cards. That was what the Playbook had wanted her to do, and that was what she had been working towards for years, but she had still hated the moment she had handed them over, only twenty-four hours ago. She would leave it to the power of the cards to let the world burn. They would become the new, secret rulers of the Earth and play with the so-called world leaders however they pleased. Odette couldn't imagine anything more beautiful, but she had underestimated how hard the sacrifice of being apart from them would hit her.

The restorer sighed and took a sip of her now cool, bitter coffee.

The journey to Moscow had been smooth sailing despite the mess in Avignon, a fact she knew she should be celebrating, but she only felt numb. Her mercenaries had accompanied her. Her and her troop's passports had been flawless forgeries, but the inspections on the train had turned out to be sloppy, and she needn't have bothered.

In Moscow, one of her people had delivered the cards in a little box to the French embassy disguised as a courier. She herself had proposed the cards as a potential gift a year ago and had pointed out their Russian, French and German history. The French government had gratefully accepted her gift and thanked her for her engagement. It was Odette Darlan's last official work. Her burnt, dead body was presumed to be lying somewhere in the wreckage of her workshop.

Odette fought back the tears. She couldn't bear the silence in her mind. The longing for the cards caused her physical pain.

A waiter approached her table. He must have applied some new aftershave in the meantime. As Odette adjusted her glasses, she realised her mistake.

The man sitting opposite her had a brazen expression in his eyes and a mullet that drew attention to his round face. His hands, which he'd clasped together, were as strong as a bricklayer's. The huge, gold signet ring on his left middle finger caught the light, and Odette thought she saw the Russian coat of arms embossed on it. The fiftysomething-year-old man was wearing an aubergine-coloured shirt underneath a pinstripe suit. He kept the top button of his shirt undone.

She looked around and spotted three other men standing by the doorway leading into the adjacent room who were shooing away staff and guests with kind remarks.

'I think you've got the wrong table,' Odette said in English. She didn't know the man and didn't feel like company. 'Find a lady of your own age to flirt with.'

'My name is Mikhail Aleksandrovich Lazarev, Madame Darlan,' the man introduced himself. 'My son died as a result of the cards that you restored.'

Odette froze. She knew the name.

'At first I thought Henry Gillot was to blame for his death, which is why I killed him in Rome,' the Russian went on. 'Then the unusual events in Europe caught my attention, and I made some enquiries. 'The deck you restored' – he grinned – 'is really quite something.'

'You're mistaken,' Odette mumbled. 'My name isn't Darlan.'

'No, of course not, your fake passport is in another name. But your mercenaries have been partying hard and drinking like fish,' Lazarev explained. 'I hear a lot of things in this city, and your men didn't take much convincing to start talking.' He massaged his broad fingers. 'They're gone now, madame, and they'll never be able to let anything else slip about the cards. You owe me for that, actually.'

Odette wrestled with her fear. If Lazarev wanted the cards for himself, her plan was in danger, and her sacrifices and hard work would have been for nothing. The world had to burn, just as the cards demanded! 'What do you want?' she croaked, her hand trembling as she reached for her cup.

'I've learned things that are hard to believe. About the cards, their curse and their power when one plays with them,' he began. 'I'm a sceptic when it comes to anything supernatural, but when I dug deeper . . . Well, imagine my surprise when I found out how wrong I'd been.' He waved one of his men over and gave some instructions in Russian. The man nodded and disappeared to the bar. 'And now here I am, sitting opposite you, madame, and I would love to know more. It seems you know more about the Devil's Playbook than anyone.'

'Why?'

Lazarev laughed. 'Why do you think?'

'You want the cards for yourself.'

'Perhaps,' he said with a gentle tilting gesture with his left hand. 'My son died because of the cards, Madame Darlan. And even more people seem to have wound up dead in Avignon. According to the media, your cellar looks like something out of a horror film.'

Odette blanched but kept her composure. 'And?'

'What did you do?'

'Me? It was Monsieur Gillot—'

Lazarev gave another laugh as a waiter brought over some fresh coffee. 'Gillot was just your stupid sponsor. You played him like a fiddle.' He added milk and sugar to his coffee. 'The cards require human sacrifices, don't they?'

'I . . .' Odette wasn't sure where this conversation was going, and that filled her with more panic and worry for the deck. The man could arrive at the museum and take the gift for himself under false pretences. She had to dissuade him. 'I can assure you that it's all nonsense,' she said resolutely. 'The material, historical and artistic value of the Playbook is considerable, but everything else is nothing but ghost stories based on coincidences. Legends. People like their scary stories.'

'Like the one about your cellar, Madame Darlan?' Lazarev bared his teeth. 'Two dozen people's bodies and remains? Unless you're a cannibal, I don't know what you did to them before they died. The only other explana—'

'I was Gillot's prisoner! He sent his people to—'

Lazarev slammed the table with his palm; china and cutlery bounced up in the air. 'Do you think I'm stupid?' he said quietly. 'Tell me, what can this deck do?'

Odette gently slipped her hand into her bag, where she kept the Mauser M712 loaded with a twenty-round magazine, plus another two spare magazines for reloading. The deck didn't belong with Lazarev, and it needed her help. She would shoot the Russian if she had to. 'It's magnificent to look at, but that's all, monsieur.'

Lazarev shook his head in reproach, his long blond hair remaining fixed to his head with hairspray like a helmet. 'I managed to get hold of a certain Arthur Patrick Morgan's belongings. He was shot in Baden-Baden after trying to steal one of these special cards.' He clapped his hands together and Odette almost drew her pistol and pulled the trigger from the shock. 'Can you guess what I found?'

'More superstitious stories?'

'The more you insist that there's nothing special about these cards, the more sure I become that I'm right.' Lazarev retrieved several folded papers from his jacket pocket and spread them out across the table. 'These are eighteenth-century fragments of records written in the Old German script, which I had to have translated. They're from a handwritten book by a certain Martin Dietrich.' The papers were covered in mystical symbols and instructions, as well as ornate sentences. 'They're instructions on how to cast spells to hurt people. Morgan's notes clearly point to this. Dietrich was a sorcerer, Madame Darlan, who was put on trial. Morgan meticulously researched his life and discovered that Dietrich lived in secret for over a hundred years. Morgan considered the man to be the one behind the cards. He tricked Bastian Kirchner, the engraver of the cards.'

Odette listened carefully. She hadn't known anything about Morgan. 'Sounds like just another person who likes a good story.'

'Morgan believed in the danger of the cards. He wanted to collect them and exorcise the evil from them.' Lazarev collected the papers into a pile again. 'His notes mention that you can breathe something into the cards with life. The word itself is illegible, but I expect it says *power* or *strength*.'

'Monsieur Lazarev, I—'

'The bodies in the cellar. They suddenly make sense. All these human sacrifices were part of your method.' He finished the rest of his coffee. 'I want to learn the cards' secret. Perhaps the deck will make me immortal if I play with it? Or grant me superpowers? Or make me the next Russian president?' Lazarev pointed to the cake in front of the restorer. 'Not a fan of the taste?'

'You want to steal the cards!'

'I won't have to. I'm a good friend of the president. All I'll really need to do is ask him for a favour. He gets so many gifts he doesn't need . . . As soon as the gift ceremony at the museum takes place, it'll be in my hands.' He glanced at his watch. 'In roughly two hours.'

No! Odette's grip tightened around the Mauser M712.

'And you, Madame Darlan, are now part of my team. On record, you're dead. You've even already sorted your own new passport. Besides, someone has to help me solve this mystery.' His feigned friendly mask disappeared. 'And that you will.'

Odette was about to pull out the Mauser when a loud conversation distracted her. The bodyguards were speaking with some guests in English who didn't want to take no for an answer.

'Gospodin Lazarev,' she heard a man's voice say as he pushed past the guards into the adjoining room. 'I'm Klim, a chief inspector from Germany. I have a few questions for you. Unfortunately, you didn't come to see me in Baden-Baden or respond to my enquiries.'

Someone shouted something after him in Russian that sounded like 'excuse me'.

Odette held her breath.

The two new arrivals approached their table. The longer Odette was separated from her beloved cards, the more her vision seemed to deteriorate. The men stopped in front of them like two blurry copies of each other.

'Inspector Mosorov, how is your family?' Lazarev greeted the Russian investigator first to make it clear who had the upper hand.

'Very well, thank you,' the policeman replied hastily. 'Forgive the intrusion. My colleague from Germany insisted on speaking with you.'

'Thank you for your precious time, Gospodin Lazarev. This is about the death of your son and the illegal gambling round organised by the Solov'ëvas,' Klim explained. 'May I ask you to step to one side so that we—'

'Go ahead and speak. My great-aunt and I don't keep secrets from each other.'

Odette flashed a forced smile.

'The latest clues have brought me to Moscow, Gospodin Lazarev,' Klim said. 'The Solov'ëvas had some contacts here. A certain Aleksandr Nikitin and a Dimitriĭ Markov, both of them from Moscow. During questioning, I discovered that—'

'I don't know these gentlemen,' Lazarev curtly interrupted him. 'Thank you and have a nice day.'

'Gospodin Nikitin claimed that his travel company—'

'I don't know either of them,' Lazarev repeated and waved his hand dismissively. 'Thank you for your efforts, Mr Klim. And Mosorov, will I see you next week at the golf tournament?'

Odette began to lose hope of getting any help from the German policeman. Her hand tightly gripped the Mauser and she secretly released the pistol's safety.

'Of course, Gospodin Lazarev.'

'I still think you should accompany us,' Klim interjected. 'Even if my Russian colleague—'

'Mr Klim, you're from Germany and are unfamiliar with Muscovite customs,' Lazarev said, cutting him off. 'I'm a very busy man. I'm meeting with the president immediately afterwards, a meeting that cannot be postponed.' He turned to Mosorov. 'Have him arrange a meeting with me, Inspector, as is proper.'

'Of course.' The policeman pulled Klim away by his shoulder. 'Have a nice day,' Klim grumbled in German, admitting defeat.

Lazarev waved to them and quickly glanced at his phone before turning back to Odette. 'Slight change of plan. I'd better go check on my future deck.' He looked at her. 'Madame, I suggest you come with me, quietly and without making a scene. I can promise to give you the best possible life for as long as you work for—'

Odette pointed the Mauser at the Russian's face. 'You're not going to do anything to my beloved cards,' she whispered. 'Because they're going to take over the world and burn it to the ground, just as I planned. Just as they demand. And you, Lazarev, are not part of that plan.'

Lazarev froze. His bodyguards didn't dare intervene. 'I knew they held some sort of great power,' he whispered back, his eyes ablaze.

'And now that knowledge can die with you.' Suddenly, just as Odette was about to pull the trigger, she found herself gasping for air. The Mauser felt so heavy that she could barely hold it any more.

A burning stab of pain shot through her upper body, causing her old heart to come to a standstill. Her arm dropped, trembling, but she still managed to squeeze the trigger twice before the recoil from the pistol knocked the weapon out of her hand. The Mauser fell onto the cake plate with a clatter.

Odette clutched her chest with both hands, as if she could stop the heart attack. Her vision dimmed.

'My men will call a doctor. I'm not letting you die,' Lazarev said, speaking hurriedly. 'One of my guards will stay with you.

The others will follow me. We have to get to the museum to secure my cards.'

With sheer force of will, Odette tried to propel her heart to beat again. She had to protect her darling cards. *He can't have them!* Then, with one hand on her chest and the other twitching for the Mauser, she collapsed onto the café table.

* * *

Tadeus had always thought of the Kremlin when he thought of Red Square, that centre of Russian power with its walls, turrets and facades behind which political strategies were contrived. The fact that there were other buildings there too had never occurred to him.

And yet here they were.

One of them was the State Historical Museum, located at the northwest end of Red Square, which he now approached with Hyun. Security guards had stopped their taxi a few metres away. While the museum was traditionally on every domestic and foreign tourist's places-to-visit list, today it was closed to the general public until the official meeting had finished.

'One more hour until the presidents arrive,' Hyun said.

'It'll be tight, but doable.'

Hyun had slipped on a crimson and black dress with such a sophisticated cut that it was sure to turn men's heads. She had covered her long black hair with a brown wig in an avant-garde curly hairstyle with Russian jewellery pinned in it. A pair of square white glasses created an accent and brought out the blue of her eyes.

'You look a bit like you raided Gillot's closet,' Tadeus told her.

'You should work on your compliments,' she said.

'I'll try.'

Tadeus regarded the building. A carpet had been rolled out

before the entrance and photographers had taken their positions, some with folding ladders to take better photos.

Dark red brick covered most of the decorated facade, which comprised several pointed turrets as a tribute to the mighty towers of the Kremlin. Sixteen different sections, with four and a half million exhibits, awaited inside to overwhelm visitors with history. Even if they hurried through all the different rooms, it would take them at least an entire day to see everything – a perfect bad-weather-day destination.

Tadeus liked places that were visibly rich in history. He glanced at his newly purchased smartphone and looked up some information about the museum. Inside, there were paintings, sculptures, archaeological finds from the Stone Age to the Middle Ages, ancient Russian paintings, coins, jewellery from different eras, weapons, written documents, glass and ceramics, fabrics, as well as a scientific archive, and plenty of other curios to marvel at.

'The handover is going to take place in the precious metals section,' he murmured. 'Huh, that's funny.'

'What's funny?'

'That you can find everything from Ivan the Terrible's wardrobe to Napoleon's field kitchen and Russian jewellery and gems in the museum.' He stowed away his phone and pinned his name badge onto his jacket so that it was visible: *Aleksandr Smolkov.*

Hyun spoiled her breathtaking look with an equally plain badge, which she wore on a ribbon around her neck: *Nadia Murasova.* The credentials made them officially part of the Russian delegation; Lazarev had secured them access as members of the Russian National Trade Association. And while this gave them neither rank nor importance, it was enough to sneak them into the museum and the ceremony. That was all they needed.

Tadeus carried the duplicates of the cards with him. They couldn't take any weapons inside, but Hyun's tae kwon do skills and high heels were enough for the both of them.

'Can you tell that I've got a limp?' Hyun wanted to know before stepping out onto the red carpet. She had dressed the wound again. The gash in her leg was healing well, but she knew that the strain from walking on her wounded leg would slow down her recovery.

'No. You're handling it like a pro.'

'What did I just say about compliments?' she replied. 'I know that I remind you of your daughter, but you're allowed to say that I look good. That would give me a little confidence boost after my years away from the catwalk.'

Tadeus laughed. 'You look gorgeous, Hyun!'

'See? Was that so hard?'

Heavily armed policemen stopped them and checked their badges and names against the list that Lazarev had added them to. Then they waved them inside.

Tadeus and Hyun exchanged a look of relief.

'Let's go to the precious metals section,' he said.

They walked through the entrance without being photographed and had to present their badges again at the opulent reception with its sky-high ceiling. The architecture gave the museum a majestic and cathedral-like feel.

'It's very . . . colourful,' Hyun said. 'Was there a colour they didn't use while painting it?'

'It was all white until 1986. The Soviets didn't like the nationalist romantic style very much.' Tadeus repeated to her what he'd just read. 'It took eleven years to restore the old colours.'

He spotted five men from the OMON forces – the most ruthless Russian special police division, which didn't hesitate to act if there was trouble. They were armoured, armed and dressed in black. Their plan was proving more ambitious than they had anticipated.

Hyun and Tadeus slowly made their way further into the building to avoid attracting any attention. The kaleidoscope of colours from the romantic period followed them through every room, where security personnel, museum guards and officials stood around, chatting with one another, going through lists and making final preparations.

Before they set foot in the precious metals section, where, among other items, the crowns of the tsars were on display, it became clear to them why the French were presenting the Devil's Playbook. A sign informed visitors that the museum organised special exhibitions several times a year that extended beyond Russian history. Gambling had once been extremely popular in Russia and had inspired the works of renowned composers and famous writers, which a current exhibition on the theme explored.

They saw some sheet music from Tchaikovsky's opera *The Queen of Spades*, original manuscripts from Dostoevsky's novel *The Gambler*, old roulette balls, an ancient revolver that was supposedly used to play the notorious game of Russian roulette, and various playing cards from different centuries with accompanying legends and explanations.

'Now it makes sense,' Tadeus said quietly.

In the next room, there were bottles of champagne and vodka in ice buckets, plenty of glasses and caviar canapés that had been piled high by a squadron of chefs. After the presentation of gifts for the exhibition, it would be time to celebrate.

Hyun tapped Tadeus' arm to get his attention. 'The box.'

Tadeus turned his head and saw the ebony and ivory case, as well as smaller gifts, just opposite the buffet. Two security guards with earpieces were guarding the gifts. The museum director, as his badge revealed, was waiting nearby surrounded by guests with name tags that read *Friends of the Museum* People chatted in English over a drink before the event, some with vodka, others with champagne.

'Let's get closer so you can check whether the cards–'

'They're glowing, Boch! Wow, they're shimmering like crazy! I don't even have to try,' Hyun said, linking arms with him. He felt her slender frame tremble slightly. 'The cards recognise and hate us. They know what we're planning to do.'

He thought of the nine of spades, but the card only evoked an echo of his former desire. 'Are you sure that they–?' Tadeus stopped himself. Of course she was sure. She was the one who had freed him from the cards' curse.

They had arrived at the museum without a real plan for how they were going to exchange the cards. Improvisation was the magic word. Tadeus knew how to make cards disappear and appear again out of thin air. Con artists would often work together at poker games without the other players realising, and their victims would lose all their assets within a few rounds. *Teamwork.*

Hyun seemed to be reading his mind. 'Admit it, I'm the best distraction you could have,' she whispered. 'Do you think we'll be able to swap the decks?'

'Oh, I'm not worried about that.' He secretly pulled the duplicates out of his pocket and slipped the deck into the right sleeve of his jacket. 'I just need an opportunity.'

'Follow me as if you're my bodyguard,' she said and moved towards the group standing around the museum director, the majority of whom were men.

Tadeus witnessed what happened when a stunningly attractive woman looking to flirt approached a group of men. This wasn't the first time that Hyun had played the game, and it had nothing to do with luck and everything to do with the merciless exploitation of the laws of biology. The ladies in the group remained friendly yet reserved towards the stranger, whereas the men went out of their way to shower her with compliments and engage in small talk under false pretences. They swanked and showed off.

Hyun smiled and lightly touched the men's arms, making every one of them think that they were her favourite. Engrossed in shallow conversation, the group moved closer and closer to the box holding the Devil's Playbook.

'Oh, is that the old deck of cards?' Hyun exclaimed enthusiastically. 'I've read so much about it! May I take a look at it before the president takes it home?'

And sure enough, after a quick glance at the security guards the director opened up the box for her and offered her the cards.

She was so good. Tadeus prepared himself for the trade, but he was also afraid of a relapse. *The nine of spades.* He would have killed for it in Darlan's house. But the infatuation never came. He neither sensed the card nor heard its malicious singing. His desire for it didn't ignite and only a twinge of nostalgia for it remained; he could control it.

'From the eighteenth century, you say?' Hyun took the Devil's Playbook into her delicate, well-manicured hands. Then she pretended to trip over a crease in the carpet and fell backward against her bodyguard.

Tadeus caught her and immediately felt the cards touch his fingertips. He was about to grab them when one of Hyun's suitors rushed over to help her up. The man pulled her by the arm and the historic deck went flying into the air. Tadeus almost lost the copies from the shock and the man's tugging movement.

'Oh that's so . . . I'm so sorry!' Poe cried.

'I'll handle it.' Tadeus was the first to bend down and instantly pick up the cards before any of the men or ladies could move. *Fuck!*

Hyun noticed and made a discreet gesture to reassure him. She closed her eyes for a moment, swaying slightly. 'I feel a little dizzy.' She drew attention to herself and was immediately and gently supported by two willing helpers in suits.

'Could one of the gentlemen fetch the lady a drink of water?' a woman asked the men standing around. One of them left the group and hurried off, waving at waiters.

In the meantime, the real Devil's Playbook found its way into the sleeve of Tadeus' jacket. His heart wanted to burst with excitement.

'Are you all right?' he asked Hyun and handed her the duplicate deck.

The helper returned with a waiter and some water.

'Yes, I'm fine.' Hyun nodded politely to the waiter and accepted the glass, gratefully greeted the relieved group and drank. The fake, slightly narrower pack of cards passed from her hand back into the little box. 'They'll be safer in here,' she said, replacing the lid and brushing her fingers against the startled museum director's.

The director expressed his understanding, insisted that something like this could have happened to anyone and said that he would find out who was responsible for the tripping hazard. 'You could have broken one of your beautiful legs,' he said charmingly.

'Let's go,' Tadeus whispered to Hyun, noticing the security guards' hostile looks.

The stolen Playbook was gathering troops to prevent the robbery. The vulnerable first, and then the rest. The fact that an OMON unit were on site didn't make for a good prospect. The nine of spades remained silent, neither singing nor screaming at him. *I could glance at them briefly and see what happens.*

'Will you excuse me for a moment? I still have to pick up the delegation's gift and use the bathroom,' Hyun addressed the group pleasantly and moved away with her bodyguard. 'I'll see you at the buffet.'

The pair of them left the exhibition without anyone calling after them.

After they had passed two more rooms and neared the reception hall, Hyun gave a stifled cheer. 'We got it!' She laughed. 'I thought I was going to die in there.'

Tadeus stopped himself from celebrating prematurely. He had the cards in his left sleeve, which he inconspicuously held with his fingers. 'The Playbook won't let us get away that easily.'

'This reminds me of Arras.' Hyun's sense of relief faded and she walked faster, trembling. 'It's not directing its hatred at us this time, it's—'

'I know. It's making allies.' He nodded imperceptibly to one of the heavily armoured special police officers as they passed. 'He alone would be a problem.'

They were nearing the exit. Suddenly, a security guard gestured for them to stop. 'The delegations from all the countries will be arriving soon,' he told them. 'You can't leave.'

'But we still need to pick up a gift,' Hyun said, batting her eyelashes.

'Please use the side exit.' The man pointed to a door next to where the OMON forces were standing.

Tadeus pressed the cards harder together – not because it would harm them in any way, but because he liked the idea of the Playbook feeling pain. No voices or singing filled his mind, but a kind of restlessness overwhelmed him, coupled with a faint desire to look at the nine of spades one more time. Only out of curiosity.

I'm falling for it again. Tadeus pulled himself together.

As they hurried past the policemen dressed in balaclavas and helmets, Tadeus couldn't help but think how much they resembled Darlan's mercenaries. The OMON unit watched them with zombie-like stares, but didn't move.

They went through the door and ended up in a corridor, at the end of which lay Red Square. The soft conversations of museum staff, who had been allowed to watch the big event on monitors, drifted out of the open doors as they passed by.

Tadeus deliberately didn't turn around. 'Good. We're almost—'

'*Stoĭ!*' came the order behind them.

Tadeus stopped and grabbed Hyun's arm. 'Let's do as they say,' he whispered. 'We can always run if something goes wrong.' They slowly turned around.

'What's the matter?' Hyun said, irritated. 'We've got to collect the gift before the event starts.'

Three museum guards had followed them, and they didn't look too friendly. 'Gospozha Murasova, may we speak with you?' The three men trotted over to them, their foreheads and cheeks glistening with sweat.

'The trade association's gift is urgently expected,' Hyun replied indignantly, just as one would expect from an important delegate. She slowly walked backward. None of the trio seemed bothered by the fact that she was speaking English to them. Perhaps they attributed that to arrogance.

'It's about the playing cards, Gospozha Murasova,' one of the men explained, panting. They must have had to run to catch up with them. 'There are some things that we'd like to clear up with you before the handover with the Russian president takes place.'

Tadeus wondered how they were going to wriggle out of this one. The museum staff would insist on searching him, too. A body search could end badly for them.

'The Playbook,' Hyun whispered. 'They're under its spell! I can clearly see it from the shimmering that surrounds them. The cards have summoned them.'

So Hyun and he were not suspected of having stolen from the museum; it was purely the power of the Playbook that had driven the three men to turn against them.

'Gentlemen, there's been some mistake,' they heard an authoritative, familiar voice say. 'Return to your posts. The president is about to roll up. I'll take care of this.'

The three guards' heads turned, and through the gap they spotted Mikhail Aleksandrovich Oprichnik Lazarev, surrounded by four bulky security guards of his own, who made no effort to hide the weapons hanging from their belts. It was clear that the man hadn't made an appearance out of the goodness of his heart.

Hyun smiled at Lazarev. 'How lovely to see you!'

The museum guards exchanged looks with one another. Everyone knew and feared Oprichnik, so much so that they greeted him in an obsequious manner and retreated one by one into the reception hall, casting eager looks at Tadeus' sleeve, at the Playbook, which raged and screamed at being abandoned.

'It appears I now owe you a favour, Mr Lazarev,' Hyun said in a voice as sweet as honey. 'Thank you for saving us from this inconvenience.'

'Is he vulnerable to the cards' influence?' Tadeus whispered, anticipating more trouble.

Hyun shook her head pointedly.

'My pleasure,' Lazarev said and glanced at his gold Rolex. It sat firmly around his wrist and was the same model as his son had worn. 'I've got to see the president very shortly, Miss Poe. Please give me back the playing cards and then you can be on your way and enjoy your millions.' As she smiled and opened her mouth to object, he made a dismissive gesture with his hand. The four bodyguards gripped their weapons with their gloved fingers at the same time. 'My men use SPS firearms, the best Russian pistols on the market. Their bullets can penetrate conventional body armour, even from a distance of a hundred metres – I'm sure you know what I mean by that. Now, please give me the cards. I know you have them.'

'What do you want with them?' Hyun asked fearlessly.

'To own them. Study them. In memory of my son, who was murdered for them.' Lazarev held out his hand and the smell of aftershave wafted towards them. 'Do you think I don't have informers in the hotel that I booked for you? The bugs and cameras in your suite kept me up to speed. I've known your plans since the moment you checked in, and I have to say: I like the Devil's Playbook very much. It's a unique piece, as I learned during a conversation with a mutual acquaintance of ours.' Oprichnik crossed himself in the Russian Orthodox way. 'Poor Darlan. It broke her heart when I told her that I would get the cards. There was nothing else the emergency doctor could do to save her.' His eyes flickered between them. 'Now, may I have it?'

Darlan was dead? That was a little justice, at least.

Tadeus stood up straight and slowly walked towards the Russians. 'I've got the deck,' he said. He wouldn't let anything happen to Hyun and he wouldn't let anyone take the cards from them. 'But you're not getting it.' He slipped the Playbook from his sleeve and fanned it out, then split the deck and fanned it out again, crossing his hands so that the cards covered him. As a former gambler, he had a few tricks up his sleeve. 'You can look at it all you like, though.'

Then he started to retreat. 'Hyun, get down!'

Lazarev's men drew their SPS pistols and fired at him.

This was the moment of truth. Tadeus saw the muzzle flash and heard the soft plop of the muffled pistols as the bullets flew past his head. *I hope it lives up to its promise.*

A few projectiles bounced off the shimmering cards and were deflected and thrown back at the men. The charged Playbook did what no steel plate or Kevlar vest could do, defending itself from destruction and hurling the bullets back at its opponents.

The ricochets hit the armed men and Lazarev. The men collapsed in the corridor, shouting and screaming, blood oozing out of numerous wounds.

Two of the bodyguards didn't realise that they'd been struck by their own bullets. They reloaded and continued to fire lying down.

Tadeus dropped to his knees, slid forward and held the cards in front of him again to cover himself. *This has to work, or else . . .*

The same thing happened again. The volley of bullets from the attackers' pistols rebounded and struck the men. The opposition was crushed; the bodyguards hit the ground, either dead or unconscious.

Only Lazarev refused to give up. He held a hand over a wound in his neck, blood gushing uncontrollably from between his fingers. He tried to say something and bent forward, fishing for a pistol on the floor.

Suddenly, the door flew open behind Oprichnik and the OMON forces advanced. Someone yelled orders in Russian, and Tadeus found himself staring down the barrels of their AK-12 assault rifles.

'The cards!' Hyun cried, horror-struck. 'The Playbook has found itself some new allies!'

The automatic rifles' rate of fire was far better than that of the SPS pistols. Tadeus had counted himself lucky before, but no luck could save him from a shelling like this. 'Into the room!' he shouted to Hyun, then pocketed the cards and threw himself into the adjoining room, which turned out to be an empty office and sitting room.

Hyun appeared in the doorway, slammed the door behind him and locked it. Her wig was gone. 'Let's climb out of the window!'

Tadeus grabbed a chair and hurled it out of the window, then jumped onto the table, and out onto the street through the splintered frame. 'Come on! I'll help you.'

Hyun removed her heels and jumped out. Tadeus caught her so that she didn't land on the glass shards.

'Your hand!' she shouted, frightened. 'You're bleeding like a stuck pig!'

Tadeus glanced at his left hand, stunned: his little and ring finger were missing, red spilling from the torn stumps. Not all the bullets had only hit the cards.

Hyun wrapped his pocket square around the wound as they walked. 'Squeeze it tight. I'll take care of it in a second.' She put her high heels back on. 'Don't faint.'

The adrenaline blocked out most of the pain, and he stuffed his hand into his jacket pocket.

They ran for several metres, until they reached the equestrian statue in front of the State Historical Museum, further along Red Square. There they slowed down in order to look like museum guests who had simply left the event early.

After a few more steps, around the corner they spotted some barriers and a handful of policemen, who were securing the building for the president's visit.

'Just keep walking,' Tadeus said. 'Until we reach the metro.'

They presented their badges and passed through the barriers. The men in uniforms didn't care about authorised visitors leaving the museum.

The entrance to the metro was less than twenty metres away from them. *Not far now.*

Hyun looked over her shoulder as they walked along the street. 'OMON are here,' she told him. 'They're behind us.'

'Shit! As long as we have the Playbook, they'll follow us like sniffer dogs,' Tadeus said. He didn't know how they would go up against five highly trained, special unit police officers who appeared just as determined as Antoine had been in Arras.

Their surroundings offered them zero protection from their pursuers: wide, open streets with hardly any walls to dive behind. The Playbook would easily be able to secure more allies from the crowds to stall them.

A bang sounded and Tadeus' calf stung. His ankle twisted.

'Keep going!' he yelled. Even though his every step felt like a hundred, giving up was not an option.

The orders behind them grew louder as the men caught up with them. 'Stop! Stay where you are! On the ground! Now!'

The people in the square ran away from the pursuers in different directions to avoid being attacked or arrested themselves.

'Hyun, you have to go on without me,' Tadeus groaned. He pulled out the deck from his pocket. 'Get rid of it. I—'

Suddenly, a dark-skinned woman in striking, colourful clothing emerged from a group of tourists. She spoke in an unintelligible language and stared at them as if she were in a trance, her eyes wide open. Jewellery and ribbons jingle-jangled around her wrists as she made sweeping movements with her arms.

It didn't take long for the effect to become apparent: the OMON men fell to their knees and covered their ears with their hands. They collapsed onto the pavement, screaming.

'Leila!' Hyun laughed, relieved. 'That's Leila Fignolé!'

'Run! I'll catch up with you!' the mambo shouted, pausing her ritual for a few seconds. 'There's a way to destroy the Playbook. We'll—'

One of the armed men rose up with a hollow, rebellious roar and resisted the voodoo priestess's influence. He aimed his AK-12 at Fignolé and fired volley after volley of bullets at her.

The gunshots covered her clothes in red dots, tearing open wound after wound in her upper body until she fell.

The muzzle of the Kalashnikov suddenly swivelled towards Hyun and Tadeus.

Click.

The gunman swore and changed the empty magazine.

'Go!' Tadeus swung into a parked Mercedes off-roader, where a terrified man had hoped to hide.

'Drive!' Tadeus yelled at him as Hyun threw herself into the back seat and crouched. 'Drive!'

With the voodoo priestess dead, the OMON troops were back on their feet, the Playbook cracking its invisible whip and forcing the men up. There was a metallic clattering as the rapid-fire rifles sprayed the Mercedes with bullets; the rear window shattered into a thousand pieces.

The man started the engine, whimpering from fear and looking hopelessly overwhelmed.

'*Davaĭ, davaĭ!*' Tadeus jerked the automatic gear stick into sports mode and forced his healthy leg under the steering wheel, slamming down onto the gas pedal with the driver's foot still on it.

The kick-down effect caused the SUV to accelerate with a jolt as the over 300-horsepower engine roared to life and sent the Mercedes screeching away from the lethal OMON troops. Bullets thudded behind them. A side window smashed and showered Hyun in shards of glass. Two holes suddenly appeared in the windscreen.

A cartridge had narrowly missed Tadeus. He grabbed the steering wheel and drifted around the bend, knocking two small cars out of the way. The shelling ended in the same second.

'Make a few turns and then stop!' he yelled, and moved his leg back into his own footwell to get out of the driver's way. He anxiously glanced into the rear-view mirror. The pursuers were still nowhere to be seen. 'We'll get half a minute, no more,' he said to Hyun in Korean. 'The city is swarming with security guards.' He groaned and looked at his bullet-riddled hand. 'Fucking hell!'

'We have the Playbook,' Hyun said, leaning over and giving

him a kiss on the cheek. 'See? You're not a weak man.' She handed him a freshly dry-cleaned bag of clothes from the back seat. 'They're our driver's. Will they fit?'

'Should do.' Tadeus gritted his teeth and fought the throbbing pain. The car's lurching and shaking tore at his wounds and made them burn with pain even more. His heart was pounding at an extraordinary speed from all the adrenaline and shelling.

The traffic whizzed past them. The driver remained silent and made several turns.

Even in Moscow, a bullet-riddled Mercedes wouldn't go unnoticed. Tadeus didn't want to drive around in it in the city for much longer, and asked the man to turn off into a backyard to escape the bustling streets. Apart from some overflowing rubbish bins, there was nothing here, and he allowed himself to breathe a cautious sigh of relief.

He looked at the driver, who switched off the engine. 'This never happened, do you hear me? Keep your mouth shut and you'll be fine,' he said to him in Russian.

The man did as he was told.

'You need a bandage before we can keep going. Otherwise you'll bleed to death,' Hyun said and dug out the first aid kit from the glove compartment of the Mercedes. She squatted down next to the open passenger door. She treated his torn-off fingers and the wound in his lower leg as best as she could, masterfully creating bandages out of the limited supplies available. 'I'll tidy it up as soon as I have better instruments,' she said. 'Sadly I don't have any painkillers on me.'

'It'll do,' Tadeus replied. He changed out of his bloody clothes into the Russian's. *It has to.*

'As for the Playbook, we'll find a way.' Hyun sounded confident for someone who would soon be put on Russia's most-wanted list.

'We'll never find out from Fignolé how to destroy it, but we have to act fast. The Playbook will keep sending its helpers after us until it gets what it wants. We need a plan,' Tadeus breathed, the world gently spinning before his eyes. His wounds were making him feel nauseous. 'I say we leave the Mercedes here and use the metro. Let's get to our hotel and then the train station.'

Hyun grabbed the adhesive tape from the Mercedes' toolkit and secured the driver to his seat so he couldn't follow. 'You'll be fine,' she said. 'Let's go.'

Tadeus was grateful for her optimism. He couldn't think straight from the incessant pain in his hand and leg.

Hyun took him by his healthy hand and began to walk. He simply followed her. The world became a blur; the noises around him grew muffled and his circulation faltered. He tried not to limp as his legs rose and fell. He was sweating as if it were summer in Moscow.

Eventually he realised that they were on the metro, and allowed himself to doze off to escape the agony. The train jerkily slid over the rails, nothing like the gentle rise and fall of the waves that he would glide through on his cutter, which was waiting for him in Stralsund in Germany. He wouldn't have to wait much longer.

Tadeus opened his eyes. 'Hyun! I've had an idea.'

* * *

The Western Pacific,
170 nautical miles north of Guam

The small trawler ploughed through the gentle waves, the sun beating down onto the deck, where a few fishing lines had been left to dry. The spinnerbaits glistened and turned in the breeze.

Tadeus sat in the shade of the helm, drinking an iced tea, in shorts and a colourful Hawaiian shirt, watching the three fishing lines that he had cast. He hadn't attached any hooks, but the crew didn't need to know that. Bags and boxes filled with fishing tackle stood next to him.

The team on board was made up of a skipper with American heritage and four Chamorro men with a mix of Indonesian, Spanish and Filipino roots. Guam had endured many colonisers who had not only been fond of its flora and fauna. The crew pottered around Tadeus, applying fresh coats of paint, removing spots of rust and scrubbing the boat. Since they didn't have to worry about taking care of the trawl nets, their captain kept them busy working on different areas of the boat.

Tadeus and 'his daughter' supposedly wanted to do some deep-sea fishing in the Pacific, or so they'd told the captain whose cutter they'd rented for a tidy sum for one week. Guam nominally belonged to the territory of the United States, meaning their smuggled dollars had come in handy. Hyun had deposited a large share of their backpacking millions into her international Swiss account. Nobody asked a doctor where so much money came from. Especially not in Switzerland.

Hyun sat next to him and offered him a beer, which he refused. 'Don't you have something to celebrate?' she asked. She wore a checked shirt that came down to her thighs and a pair of Bermuda shorts. A pair of sunglasses rested over her eyes and a panama hat sat atop her shoulder-length, black hair.

'Not yet,' he said and pointed to the fishing lines. 'The little beasts just don't want to bite.' He reached beside him for the GPS device and checked the position of the trawler.

Hyun grinned. 'It's like they know death's coming for them or something.' She cracked open her beer, toasted him and took a sip. 'Any news from the Old World?'

Tadeus pulled his tablet out of his bag. There was no reception this far out at sea, and no Wi-Fi on the boat. He showed her an article that he'd saved. 'Lazarev's death has been officially recognised as an assassination attempt carried out by his bodyguards after the ballistics team and the forensic experts confirmed that all the bullets found belonged to the bodyguards' weapons.'

Hyun took the tablet from him and read on: 'Ah, the OMON forces shot an innocent tourist from Haiti in an unfortunate accident on the sidelines of the summit. OMON claim that her behaviour led them to presume she was an assassin. Weapons had also been found,' she said ruefully. 'So that's how they're hushing it up.'

'There's not a single word about us,' Tadeus said. He wasn't sure whether to feel reassured by that or not. He hadn't the faintest idea what went on behind the scenes in Russia, but nobody had gone after them after their escape in the car in Moscow and they hadn't been prevented from leaving the country. Perhaps they were simply regarded as friends of the dead Oprichnik Lazarev and, by extension, a protected party. 'They found Darlan. An old French woman suffered from a heart attack. Her identity only became clear once she was taken to hospital. Oh . . . she's dead.'

'Are you sure?'

'Positive. I guess her escape to Russia gives the French authorities something else to wrap their heads around, but that's none of our concern.'

'The ceremony at the State Historical Museum went off without a hitch,' Hyun read aloud. 'The Russian president thanked his French counterpart for the valuable playing cards and promised to send them to Germany on a permanent loan, so that the deck could return to its native home.' She took another sip of her beer. 'Things haven't turned out so bad for us.'

'Until they take a closer look at the cards, or even just count them.' Tadeus laughed. 'Well, our trip was really something. I think the word *arduous* sums it up pretty well.'

The Devil's Playbook hadn't stopped sending animals and people after them who treated them with hostility, attacked them and hunted them down. Knowing that Hyun and Tadeus wouldn't submit to its powers, it wanted to free itself from their clutches, but they were vigilant and had managed to escape the traps and ambushes without causing any more deaths. There had only been a few injuries involving tasers or pepper spray.

Hyun sighed. 'I'm glad the deck has been making things difficult for us.'

Tadeus held up his hand with his two missing fingers by way of response. The stumps had been taken care of and his stitches had been removed, but he was suffering from phantom pains. His hand looked strange, as if it was some separate entity from his body.

'No, no of course I don't mean *that*. And hey, I've got a hole in my leg too.' Hyun patted him on the shoulder. 'What I meant to say was, the deck causing us so much trouble proves that we got the right one.'

His ears pricked up. 'Did you have doubts?'

She sucked in the Pacific air and exhaled slowly, as if she were afraid to answer. 'You never know.'

'But you've acquired quite the sense for it by now,' Tadeus said. 'You've done everything right, Miss Poe.'

'Why thank you, Mr Boch.' She tipped the brim of her hat. 'Have I told you yet that my lawyer informed me that I'm officially no longer a suspect?'

'The gambling mafia is entirely to blame. Perfect.' He was pleased to see Hyun in high spirits. He faintly remembered how he had initially only looked at her as a means to an end, how he had planned to get rid of her as soon as she had fulfilled her purpose. Shame filled him again for his past behaviour and reckless intentions. *As if it had all been from another life*. Then he glanced back at the GPS receiver. 'I'm looking forward to being back at the casino.' He smiled. 'You've freed me from my gambling addiction for good.'

'Who would've thought that the Devil's Playbook could have a positive influence?' Hyun kissed her engagement ring. 'Even if just this once,' she added quietly, and finished the rest of her beer in one go.

Tadeus suddenly felt tearful. Hyun had lost the person she loved. Two fingers seemed ridiculous in comparison.

'I've been thinking about Leila Fignolé,' he said, trying to distract her.

'Me too.'

'What's your verdict?'

'That it's a shame I'll never get to speak to her again. I could have learned a thing or two from her.'

'Oooh, a voodoo mudang?' He grinned.

'Who knows.' Hyun sighed. 'I'm wondering whether I should continue my training as a mudang, but . . .' She looked indecisive. 'Maybe I'm good as a surgeon. Should I give it up? Or find a way to combine the two?'

'Maybe you'll finally discover how to destroy the cards.' Tadeus stood up, set down his iced tea on the deck and picked up the GPS device. 'No. Forget I ever said that. I don't think it's possible.'

'It sounds like you know more than you're letting on,' Hyun pushed her sunglasses further up the bridge of her nose. In the short time they'd been at sea, her freckles had multiplied so much that the thirty-year-old doctor now looked like a young girl. 'Have you been keeping secrets from me?'

'No,' he said, unable to quite verbalise his thoughts. 'Fignolé must have got it wrong.' He shifted his gaze to the bags next to the fishing rods. 'There are evil things in this world that nothing can conquer. I have a gut feeling about this.'

One of the crew members had moved closer to the fishing

lines while painting the railing. His eyes kept flicking to the bags.

Tadeus pressed his lips together into a thin line. They had learned during their trip to pay attention to the smallest of signs.

'It's happening again,' he said, glancing at his GPS device. 'The cards are trying to turn people against us.'

'What do we have with us?' Hyun asked.

He reached into the cargo pockets of his shorts and grabbed two stun guns. He handed her one of them and kept the other. 'Pepper spray?'

'This will do.' Hyun got to her feet, rolled her shoulders back and shook her legs like she was about to run a marathon. 'In emergencies I can always rely on my tae kwon do.'

'Thank God for that. Imagine if the Korean national sport was cricket. Or football.' Tadeus grinned. They walked together to the rear of the boat and he greeted the Chamorro, well aware of the aggressive look that the man threw at them. Tadeus didn't even try to defuse the tension – the Playbook made conciliation impossible – just waited for the attack that would inevitably follow.

The Chamorro dropped the paintbrush and pulled out a knife from his belt. He shouted something loudly in a language that Tadeus didn't understand. *I guess I've never been to Guam.*

Within seconds, the three other crew members came running towards them, clutching harpoons and swinging fishing lines with long hooks on them.

'We should have taken more than stun guns with us,' Tadeus said, pulling out the pepper spray.

'Hey! Hey, what the hell's going on down there?' the skipper yelled in English through the bridge window. When none of the men responded, he left his command post and stalked down the rung ladder, holding an old, semi-automatic Smith & Wesson pistol in his hand without pointing it at anyone. 'I said, what are you doing? Are you guys crazy?'

The Chamorro with the harpoon pointed at Tadeus. 'He said that we're nothing but dumb cunts!'

The agitated captain glanced at his passengers. In the same instant, a harpoon impaled him from behind. It protruded out of his heart, blood gushing forth. He raised the arm holding the Smith & Wesson as the spade-tipped spear was ripped out of him, then collapsed onto the deck. Pools of red spread around him.

The GPS device beeped.

The Chamorro with the knife made a move towards the lost semi-automatic.

Tadeus threw himself at him, pressed the stun gun against his neck and triggered it. Twitching, the man dropped next to his skipper.

'Jump overboard with the bags!' he shouted to Hyun, dodging the bloodstained harpoon. A razor-sharp spade stabbed towards him and missed, was pulled aside again and followed his every movement. The barbed hooks caught Tadeus by his clothes at his waist and snagged at his belt loops, pulling him to the ground.

'You can't take them all on alone!' Hyun cried. There was a cracking sound as a body slumped heavily onto the deck outside of his field of vision.

The Chamorro lunged towards him again and Tadeus rolled away from the twitching tip of the harpoon, right into the taut fishing lines.

The long hooks, meant for tuna and other large fish, dug into his flesh in several places as the nylon tangled itself around his arms and body. Tadeus screamed in pain.

He spotted the skipper's pistol beneath his injured hand and quickly grabbed and cocked it. Despite the twisted metal inside his body, he forced himself to lie on his side so he could fire.

But the firing pin only made a clicking noise. The captain hadn't reloaded the gun so there was no cartridge in the barrel.

The GPS receiver beeped frantically, as if the noise was somehow going to help Tadeus.

The harpoon whizzed towards him out of thin air, swooping lower, lower and lower.

Tadeus spun around again and again, the blade clanging against the deck behind him. He roared with pain as the hooks tore deeper into his flesh, devouring him and wrapping him in nylon. He couldn't get the S&W working; he simply didn't have enough traction to pull the slide back.

The Chamorro grabbed the line, yanked it, laughing, and dragged Tadeus towards him.

You'll regret that. As he was being pulled forward, Tadeus finally managed to load the pistol. Bleeding from several small wounds, he rolled onto his side, groaning, and shot the man holding the nylon line in his fingers, who collapsed after four shots. He fired the remaining bullets at another approaching crew member with a harpoon until he fell. The lost weapon rolled harmlessly across the boat.

'Hyun?' he called and hastily cut the nylon, leaving the hooks jutting out of him. He leapt to his feet and looked around.

Hyun was engaged in close combat with the enemy, who had slumped onto the deck after a taser attack. But the Playbook drove her attacker on, demanding that he push himself beyond his physical limits. The man deftly stabbed at Hyun with the knife and received several kicks and brutal blows, leaving him staggering and tumbling. Still he wouldn't give up.

The last standing Chamorro was making his way to his friend and turned his head to face Tadeus. He raised his harpoon.

Tadeus knelt down, grabbed a stray fish spear and hurled it at his opponent. He'd never thrown a harpoon before in his life.

The sharpened dagger skewered the Chamorro's ribcage, causing him to stagger over the railing and topple into the Pacific Ocean. His fish lance lay behind on the deck.

Thank God for that.

Tadeus found Hyun. 'I'm here!'

The doctor had annihilated her enemy. The man's deformed face was no longer recognisable, blood poured from his mouth and nose, bone splinters protruded from his cheeks and one of his ears was half torn off his head.

Hyun followed up with a swift roundhouse kick and the man threw himself at her with the knife, screaming.

She instinctively blocked his wrist, which broke with a crack under the impact, but before she could use her elbow the Chamorro yanked the featherweight woman up by her hair and threw her overboard. Hyun landed in the water with a splash.

Then the man came for Tadeus. He walked and looked like a zombie. The Chamorro bent down, picked up the lost harpoon and deftly spun it around.

Tadeus glanced at the drying fishing lines and at the net hanging above his opponent. *Just you wait.*

He quickly reached over to the control panel of the boat and released the lines and the attached cords, ensnaring the Chamorro a second later. The weight of it pinned him down; the man screamed and shouted, trying to cut his way out of the tangled net with the harpoon.

Tadeus grabbed a fire extinguisher from the wall and smashed it against his opponent's head until he went still. He then stole the harpoon from the man as a precaution and ran to the railing.

Hyun bobbed up and down in the calm ocean and waved to him to let him know that she was all right.

'I'm coming!' he told her. He climbed up the rungs onto the small bridge and examined the trawler's control panel. A boat was a boat. In the process, he found a spare magazine for the Smith & Wesson pistol and took it with him. The hooks in his flesh made even the smallest movement painful, but he refused to let it distract him. He was no stranger to pain by now.

He turned the boat around, slowed the engine down and chugged towards Hyun, leaving a few metres between them and switching off the propeller so that she wouldn't get sucked in.

'Swim to the back of the boat!' he shouted and walked to the stern to throw her a rope.

'But the water's lovely,' she said sarcastically. 'So refreshing.' Then she spotted the hooks digging into his skin. 'Oh, shit.' She swam to the rope. 'Does it hurt as bad as it looks?'

'Yes. My failed attempt to fish with live bait.' Tadeus grabbed a pair of combination pliers from one of the tackle boxes and removed the first scraps of metal while she climbed onto the trawler, wiped the water from her face and wrung it out of her hair.

'Give me those,' she said and took over removing the hooks from his back. 'I'd better go get some disinfectant, too.'

'And a beer.' Tadeus picked up the beeping GPS device and turned it off. The numerous tiny wounds burned and throbbed.

Hyun returned a moment later wearing dry clothes and holding two beers – one for Tadeus and another for herself. 'I'm ready.'

He stripped down to his grey boxers and she snipped and retrieved the hooks from his flesh. 'Is that a tattoo of a black Pac-Man? Or is it a skull? God, you've got some truly awful art-work back here.'

'Don't ask.'

'Ah. More remains of your lost memories?' She sprayed disin-fectant over the areas that were oozing blood so that they wouldn't fester. 'This is a bit like working in A&E after some

THE DEVIL'S PLAYBOOK | 622

major fishing competition. It's getting me in the mood for a hospital shift.'

While she attended to his wounds, Tadeus loaded the semi-automatic with a fresh magazine.

'And we're done,' Hyun said, taking a seat next to him. 'Are we in the right place, old man?'

As if on cue, they cracked open their beers at the same time, a little foam and carbon dioxide escaping out with a hiss.

'We are.' Tadeus slipped his shorts back on and clinked his can with hers. 'Give me a second.'

He got to his feet, climbed up to the bridge and set a new course and the sailing speed to moderate. The activated auto-pilot programme did the rest. He found some more beer in the skipper's small fridge and took it with him.

As soon as he returned to the stern, he reached for their bag, which was supposedly filled with fishing equipment. 'Let's do it together.'

Hyun grabbed the bag. 'On three.'

'Three,' Tadeus said, grinning.

With a plop, the almost forty-kilogram bag dropped into the sea and sank to the bottom.

In Guam, Tadeus and Hyun had divided the deck, moulded the cards into concrete and packed them in different-sized boxes. The pair had posed as tourists wanting to do some deep-sea fishing in order to 'accidentally' drop the equipment into the ocean, precisely at the point where the GPS alarm had gone off.

'The deck may be indestructible,' Tadeus said, raising his beer.

'But it'll never be found again. The cards will not be able to hurt anyone any more. I'll drink to that! And to all the Play-book's innocent victims, especially Leila Fignolé.' Hyun struck her beer can against Tadeus'.

Suddenly, a shadow leapt between them, a furious cry escaping its throat, and swan-dived into the Pacific.

Hyun and Tadeus were too stunned to react. The last Chamorro survivor had followed the desperate Playbook's irresistible cry for help.

'It's a good thing he didn't attack us,' Tadeus said and watched the surface of the water with Hyun. He held the Smith & Wesson pistol at the ready.

There was no sign of the man.

'Eleven kilometres below sea level. He won't reach the cards. And he definitely won't make it back up.' Tadeus took three painkillers from the first aid kit and washed them down with the last of his beer. In addition to the surface pain in his back, a deep-seated ache emanated from within him; the strain of it all caused a searing pain to spread over his right knee joint.

He walked over to the bodies. 'Let's throw them overboard. They're fishermen after all. They won't mind being buried at sea.'

Hyun helped him heave the dead into the ocean while the trawler steered through the Pacific on autopilot, following a course for the Mariana Trench.

There wasn't a deeper, more inaccessible place for life on Earth. They had considered various scenarios in advance, including the fact that the Mariana Trench was sometimes a point of interest for oceanographers. But the distance of over 2,550 kilometres from the seabed to the surface, the cold and the immense pressure made it the perfect spot. Even using diving robots, marine researchers would, at most, find some pieces of concrete that would garner no attention nor any desire to recover.

Hyun doubted the cards would send their enticing signal from the trench to randomly passing boats and ships, and, apart from her and Tadeus, nobody else knew enough about the deck to go looking for it. The Devil's Playbook wouldn't wreak any more havoc.

Ever again. With his work done, Tadeus popped a sixth pain-killer and sat next to Hyun on the stern. 'Mission complete.'

The boat safely pulled them forward. As there was nothing out on the open sea that the trawler could crash into, they decided to put their feet up at the back of the boat. After each beer they emptied, they tossed one, sometimes two pieces of concrete into the sea.

'What are we going to do once we've discarded all the cards?' Hyun asked, throwing another grey block over the railing. She was slurring slightly. Her alcohol tolerance wasn't the best.

'We'll get close to the coast and sink the trawler on a reef. That way no one will ask what happened to the crew.' Tadeus looked at her. 'You're a good swimmer, aren't you?'

Hyun pointed to the lifebuoys hanging on the wall next to the rungs leading up to the bridge. 'Better safe than sorry.'

Tadeus smiled and relished his next beer with his eyes closed. 'And then, what's *your* plan? Are you going to become a mudang or stay a surgeon? Has the beer opened your eyes?'

'I am and will remain a surgeon.' Hyun spoke over the chug-ging of the engine and the lapping of the waves. 'And then, when I go on holiday, I'll consult a mudang. A skilled one. And ask her for advice. Hopefully the spirits will guide me and help me see the light. More than the beer.'

Tadeus raised his can in response and revelled in anticipa-tion for his own future, which was looking bright. Debt-free. Addiction-free. More contact with his son and daughter. Hours of relieved laughter together. He'd already arranged their first plans to see each other and could hardly wait.

'Do you think Kirchner created another deck like the Devil's Playbook?' Hyun interrupted his idyllic daydream, shifting in her chair.

'One so full of hatred for humankind?' Tadeus sighed and took a sip. 'No. He didn't.'

'Are you sure about that?'

'I am.' He didn't want to hear otherwise and washed down her question with the beer, focusing his mind back on his boat. 'One hundred per cent.'

Their journey on the trawler had made him excited to sail the Baltic Sea on his own cutter without any commotion or violence on board. The waves, the smell of the sea and the seagulls' calls promised peace and freedom in its purest form. There was so much to see without the drugs in his brain. He would discover the world a second time.

And he could hardly wait.

EPILOGUE

Leipzig, the Electorate of Saxony,
the Holy Roman Empire,
August 1768

Susanna had opened all of the windows in the attic to allow the sweltering heat to escape. The passing breeze gave the illusion of coolness.

Outside, Leipzig's cacophony of conversations, the chirps and chirrups of sparrows, the lively calls of sellers, the hoofbeats and the rattle of wheels, as well as the marching of laced-up boots and occasional military orders, could be heard. Not much time had passed since the last war, and yet the soldiers were already taking to the streets again.

Ilse and Johann were busy reading and writing. The youngest chewed on an apple slice and pulled a face when the sourness became too much, laughed, and then immediately took another bite.

Susanna sat in her late husband's work corner, where he had engraved the deck out of copper. Her ancestor's notebook lay in front of her, the one she had used to defeat Dietrich.

Widow Kirchner. The funeral had been difficult for her. She had very nearly collapsed at his grave, but her children had been her anchor. She couldn't recall who had been there to pay their last respects. All she could remember was the carpentered wooden cross with a small wreath and black ribbon that someone had donated. It was as if the day had never happened for her.

Bastian's body had been discovered by chance by the manor servants' little ones. The playing children had found him when they had snuck into the creepy mill on a dare against their parents' instructions.

The case had been plain for the authorities: a ruin, a skull, magic and a human sacrifice. Susanna had been told to keep the events a secret so as not to alarm the masses. After all, they already had enough to worry about with the student riots. But the council had assured her that they would do everything in their power to find the people responsible. According to the public, Bastian Kirchner had been abducted and murdered by highwaymen. He was considered another victim of criminal activity in the city, and there was no mention of his death having anything to do with the Devil.

Susanna then wrote an anonymous letter to the lords of the council, in which she accused Martin Dietrich of witchcraft and sorcery in his hideout in the almshouse and drew attention to his past.

But she didn't read a word about that in the *Leipzig Zeitung* either.

Susanna stood up and hid her ancestor's book in her fail-safe secret place.

'Play nicely,' she said to the children. 'And Johann, look after the others.'

She made her way downstairs into Johann Gottlob Immanuel Breitkopf's office. He had asked to speak with her.

Susanna had a feeling she knew what this would be about: the cursed playing cards.

Soon she was sitting in front of his desk, dressed in black and with her hands folded. She recognised Breitkopf's shock when he saw her careworn features. The last few weeks had drained her and the witchcraft that she'd performed had left her looking frail. Her ancestor's notebook explained that in comparison to white magic, evil demanded more than it gave in return, which was why it always got the better deal.

She tried to look happier, even if Breitkopf didn't take offence at her appearance. She was in mourning, after all.

'To quell your worries, Widow Kirchner,' Breitkopf began and pulled on his curly, white wig. 'You can stay here and work on some engravings for me. I've already seen that you have a talent for it. The new Oeser that you engraved was truly breathtaking!'

'Thank you, Mr Breitkopf.'

He reached into a drawer and pulled out a sealed letter. 'I was told to give this to you. It's from Goethe.'

Guilt swept over her. She had had to pretend that she knew nothing of what had happened until Mrs Stock had told her about the student's mysterious condition. 'Is he feeling better?'

'He's gone back to Frankfurt without a degree in his pocket.' Breitkopf rubbed his ink-stained hands, as if trying to remove the coarse dirt. 'His father won't exactly be thrilled, but I can understand it.'

'Did he tell you why?'

'He said that he wouldn't have any good memories of his time here. First his failed love affair, then the student riots, which had the king dispatching soldiers, and now the severe haemorrhage.' Breitkopf looked concerned. 'Tuberculosis.'

'Oh.' Susanna was relieved that the doctors had been able to save Goethe and that the young man had kept what had happened in the mill a secret. She glanced at the letter. It clearly contained some sort of explanation. 'When did he—?'

'Not long ago.' The publisher smiled. 'Let's just say that the military's arrival in the city and their search for the most boisterous rioters made Goethe's decision to leave very simple.' He rested his forearms on the table. 'Goethe aside, I wanted to speak to you about the cards, Widow Kirchner.'

She feigned ignorance. 'What do you mean?'

'The French deck. Your husband made something so magnificent that the Germans, the English and the French will be begging to buy it from me,' he enthused. 'I want to start printing them in less than a year, and I'll need to have everything ready by then. And I still need to convince my father – he's a tough nut to crack.' He beamed at her. 'Your husband told me that the printing plates were ready.'

'That's true, Mr Breitkopf.'

He could tell from her face that she was about to tell him something that he wouldn't like. His expression hardened. 'But?'

'But the thieves who took him and robbed him,' Susanna said, 'also stole the printing plates.'

'Good heavens!' Breitkopf clutched his head with his hands in disbelief. 'They broke in? Into the attic?'

'Yes. They must have been quiet, because neither I nor the children woke up. They were looking for more money, I think.' Susanna prayed that he believed her. 'Keep your eyes wide open, my dear Mr Breitkopf. Maybe some similar cards will shortly be printed by a competitor. Then we'll know where to find the plates.'

The publisher grumbled disgruntledly and then cursed. 'What about the original? The first deck. We could use it as a template.'

'Also stolen. My husband always carried it with him and it wasn't on him when they found his body.' Susanna thought about where it really was: together with her notebook under the floorboards. She'd scraped and scratched, hammered and smashed, battered and destroyed the Devil's Playbook's printing plates as much as humanly possible before throwing them into the river. They would remain there until the end of time. As for the preliminary drawings of the cards, she'd burned them to ashes in the oven on the day of Bastian's death.

'Oh how dreadful, how dreadful!' Breitkopf threw his hands up in the hair and then turned to look at her with hope in his eyes. He tugged his wig. 'Widow Kirchner, don't leave me stranded! Is there any chance you could—'

'I'm sorry, Mr Breitkopf, but that was my husband's master-piece.' She felt her throat tighten. 'And, if I may be frank: I won't be making any cards for you. They took my Bastian away from me, even though I warned him not to touch them.' Her voice dropped to a whisper. 'You'll need to find another pair of skilled hands for cards.'

Breitkopf sighed. 'Very well. Oh, if only I'd known . . . I'd have stored the plates in my own house.'

'I'm sorry.'

He waved a hand dismissively. 'Perish the thought! It's not your fault.' Susanna could clearly see the cogs in Breitkopf's brain turning. He was already thinking about where he'd find another card-maker. 'Well, I won't keep you any longer.' He stood up and Susanna got up from her chair. 'As I said, give Stock a hand, engrave me some beautiful pieces, and you won't find yourself short of a living. I'll pay you what I paid your husband.'

She nodded, shook his outstretched hand and left the office.

As soon as Susanna was outside, she broke the seal and unfolded the letter that Goethe had left for her.

Dear Mrs Kirchner,

The doctors said that I was seized by tuberculosis, and that it was the illness which cost me precious blood.

But I'm not so sure. I'm haunted by visions, despite at times being unable to recall entire days. The last thing I remember is following your husband. He was being very secretive about his business, and I couldn't contain my curiosity. If I'm not mistaken, he ventured out of town.

And then my mind goes blank.

The disease and the fever have robbed me of my memories.

It grieves me to hear what happened to him. Had I continued to follow him, would he still be among the living?

I talk of mysterious visions, and cobwebs haunting my mind, words and sentences that trick and convince me that you were there, in that abandoned mill where your husband's body was found. You. Dietrich. The Devil's poodle. Me. We were all there, and then . . . my hand falters as I write this . . . It sounds ludicrous, but I witnessed magic. And heard spells.

In my delirium, and until I recovered from the tuberculosis, I wrote many a line, and I must confess: it makes for a good play.

It echoes the theme of Doctor Faustus and I've been consumed with the idea ever since.

Why am I leaving for Frankfurt?

You're the only one who knows the truth: I have nothing but praise for my Leipzig, and yet, I fear the spirits that dwell there and the powers that vie for dominion.

I must reconcile myself with what I experienced or dreamt of. Who knows what I saw? But I know I must leave and reflect.

One day, my dear Mrs Kirchner, I shall return to Little Paris and you can tell me your story. Until that day, I wish you God's blessing and the strength you'll need to care for and raise the children.

J.W. Goethe

Susanna folded up the letter and breathed a sigh of relief. She wouldn't even tell Goethe what had really happened. She was the only one who could know the truth.

She smiled and fondly thought of her Bastian.

She would never remarry.

As she walked through the workshop, she wondered if the city was filled with others like Dietrich who sought to bring misery upon the world. After the events in the mill, it seemed to her that Dietrich had been one of many.

And though it seemed indestructible, Dietrich's tool of choice, the deck of cards, hadn't served its purpose. Susanna had tried to destroy it with hammers, burins, fire, acid and by other means, but evil protected the cards made out of nothing but thin paper. She had then tried working her ancestor's magic and had already waded through half of the notebook. One or two spells had given her hope. At least she could use magic to weaken the cards before attacking them with blades, knives and fire. It would take time, but she would be the one to destroy the Devil's Playbook.

As she opened the attic door, she heard her children screaming. There was an acrid, burning smell and bluish-grey clouds of smoke filled the room as if there had been a fire.

'Have you been playing with matches?' she cried out in horror and looked around. 'Johann, I told you—'

'It wasn't our fault!' he shouted and pointed to the spot under the floorboards where she'd hidden her ancestor's notebook and the cards. There was a big burn hole in the wood, which they'd poured water over to extinguish the fire. 'There was smoke. We opened it with your tools, Mama, and threw the burning thing out the window.'

'Far away,' Ilse added.

'Whee!' Armin cried.

Susanna hid her anger and stroked their heads one by one, then picked up the youngest and walked over to the hole. 'Well done,' she told them.

She looked down at the hiding spot.

Her ancestor's notebook lay inside, burned cover to cover. The leather and a narrow edge from the pages had survived, but the cards had mercilessly destroyed the rest, burning it to the ground like a festering wound.

The Devil's Playbook was missing.

I was too naive. Susanna picked up the ruined notebook, closed her eyes, and took a couple of deep breaths before turning around. 'Which window did you throw it out of?'

Johann and Ilse pointed to the large, wide-open window. Smoke poured out of it.

The cards destroyed what could harm them. Susanna poked her head out of the window and looked to the right and left over the tiles. *And I gave them that opportunity.*

She wanted nothing more than to find the deck, but all she saw were pigeon droppings and moss covering the burnt bricks.

Then she heard a consistent, frantic tapping of a beak, followed by an angry caw and a thump.

She set her little one down, stood up on her tiptoes and peered outside.

A crow sat on the roof, holding a card in its beak: the ace of spades.

'Come here,' she said, trying to lure the black bird. 'Show me what you've got there. I'll give you a reward if you give –'

The crow looked at her for a while, then spread its wings and flew off into the sunset. After a few gentle flaps of its wings, it disappeared over the rooftops, never to be seen again.

Death's messenger had flown away with the most dangerous card from the deck. How fitting. Susanna turned back to the room and sorrowfully looked at the burnt notebook.

It was no longer of any use to anyone. All that was left were unintelligible words and damaged symbols. As if to scorn her, the ace of spades had burned its intricate skull pattern into the leather as a final farewell and a wicked reminder.

She sat down, laid the remains of her ancestor's ancient knowledge to one side and kissed each of her children. 'You did the right thing,' she praised them again. 'Otherwise it would have burned down the roof of our house.' Susanna pointed to the cut-out pictures on the misprints. 'Now, why don't you make me a story?'

As Ilse and Johann rushed off, she took Armin into her arms again and gazed up at the crimson evening sky.

The mantle of responsibility for the cards had been snatched away from her. Others would discover that that the deck was a danger to humanity and ensure that the cards never found their way back to each other again. She clung on to that hope.

It was my fault. I should have expected this to happen. The Playbook had known that she would discover how to destroy the cards over the coming months and years. It had been trapped under the floorboards, afraid, and had escaped. From her. Perhaps because she was not only Sibylle's ancestor, but Dietrich's too.

And maybe it was better this way. Otherwise she would have ended up like him. *The strange daughter of chaos.*

AFTERWORD

I cannot deny my inner historian. After countless rounds of mau-
mau, skat, sheep's head, canasta, rummy and poker, after building
houses of cards, marvelling at card tricks and frequently blaring
out Motörhead's 'Ace of Spades' and Iron Maiden's 'Aces High',
I've always wondered:

Where do cards actually come from?

I was once equally curious about the subject of vampires,
and in my search for answers I made some astonishing discoveries (you can read more about it in my book, *Vampire, Vampire!*,
which was published by Piper Verlag in 2015).

As I began to dig deeper into the history of playing cards, I
quickly realised that there was more than meets the eye. And
once I learned about the clerically puritanical, pejorative term
for cards – The Devil's Playbook, The Playbook of the Devil or
even The Devil's Picturebook – no one could stop me.

It became evident that cards have fascinated people in
Europe for a very, very long time. People gambled life and limb
for them. They lost money, houses, farms, acres of land and
their lives over them, to such an extent that playing cards were
banned as early as the Middle Ages.

Cards were used by fortune tellers as a means of predicting
the future.

Cards were used as educational games.

Cards were used as a tool to scrape ointment off a pestle or to
stabilise a wobbly table.

And let us not forget the notorious death card, the ace of spades.

I needed a special deck of cards for the novel, and what could be better than creating one whose individual cards had already caused disastrous consequences? And what would happen if someone played with this entire special deck?

The interplay between Leipzig's history, the characters involved in the card-making process, Goethe's adventures, my own ideas and *Faust* have all shaped my writing with regards to how some of the scenes from the original *Faust* (1808) might have played out.

This led to the birth of *The Devil's Playbook*.

In addition, I came up with my own card game, supérieur, though I strongly advise against playing it according to the historical, Russian rules. Please don't!

Otherwise, happy playing.

As always, I couldn't have done without the feedback of my test readers, namely Marc Roseto, Sonja Rüther and Yvonne Schöneck, who got a glimpse of the novel behind the scenes and who became my very own jokers.

Hanka Jobke deserves the highest praise for her proofreading and editing expertise. She also drew my attention to Robert Louis Stevenson's short story collection, *The Suicide Club*. Watch out for the ace of spades there too. And for the deadly cream tarts!

Of course, my gratitude extends to Knaur-Verlag and my editor, Martina Wielenberg. Thank you also to Anke Koopman from Designomicon for the cover and the magic card tricks. It's spectacular!

And thank you to composer Marcus Gorstein and singer Nina de Lianin, who worked on the song 'CARDS – The Devil's Playbook' to accompany the book – a ballad fit for any Bond film.

Markus Heitz

THE (HARMLESS) RULES OF SUPÉRIEUR

With a standard poker deck (fifty-two cards), this game can be played by up to seventeen players, but the ideal number of players is between five and twelve. If you play with a standard skat deck (thirty-two cards), this game can be played by up to ten players. However, with thirty-two cards, there's a higher chance of drawing the ace of spades.

The order of the card values is in ascending order of numbers (2 to 10 or 7 to 10) to face cards (Jack, Queen, King, Ace). Ace is the highest card. The order of the suits from lowest to highest is as follows: diamonds, hearts, spades, clubs. The highest-ranking suit wins if there are two cards of the same number or face card (e.g. a 7 against a 7 or a queen against a queen).

<u>Note:</u> If a player draws the ace of spades, their round ends immediately. As soon as a player draws the ace of spades, they must reveal it to the group. The player is then out of the game, but their entire stake remains in the pot.

The ace of spades is put back into the pile, and the deck is shuffled, meaning it can be drawn again. The game continues according to the same principles.

The game can be played without a dealer if players take the role of the dealer in turn, alternating at every round in a clockwise direction.

1. The players place their initial, previously agreed-on stakes into the pot.
2. Every player draws a card (either from the top or the bottom of the deck). Unless the card drawn is the ace of spades, the card must be kept face down in front of the other players.
3. Three rounds are played.

4. In each round, the players may:

   Check: the player chooses not to do anything, and simply remains in the game.

   Raise: the player raises the stake, which is binding for all players; players can either match the stake, raise the stakes again or fold.

   Fold: the player reveals their card, discards it and leaves the game. Discarded cards are set to one side and are not shuffled back into the main deck.

   Draw a new card from either the top or the bottom of the pile: however, the player must reveal their old card first and set it aside with the other discarded cards.

5. Every player can check, raise, fold or draw a new card once per round. This applies for each of the three rounds.

6. After the third round, everyone reveals their card one by one. The player with the highest card wins all of the players' stakes.

THE HISTORICAL RULES OF SUPÉRIEUR

Whoever draws the ace of spades is killed or shoots themselves. Their stake and their assets on the table are placed into the round's pot. The ace of spades is shuffled back into the deck.

THE SUPÉRIEUR WINNERS
IN AVIGNON IN THE BOOK

Game 1: Boch, ace of hearts

Game 2: Poe, queen of clubs

Game 3: Crichton, queen of spades

Game 4: Crichton, ace of diamonds

Game 5: Mulder, ace of spades: is shot. Boch, king of clubs

Game 6: Hermine, queen of spades

Game 7: Hermine, ace of diamonds

Game 8: the runaway, ace of spades: is shot. Hermine, ace of clubs

Game 9: Crichton, queen of clubs. He now has the most money because Hermine keeps raising the stakes. Hermine is almost bust.

Game 10: Crichton, nine of hearts. Denise is almost bust.

Game 11: Boch, ace of spades, but he doesn't reveal it. The game continues.

<u>Showdown:</u>

Poe: queen of hearts

Crichton: nine of spades

Denise: ace of hearts

Hermine: ace of clubs. She's won.

APPENDIX

My historical research proved so extensive that I didn't want to include every single detail in the novel. Less information dumping; more plot.

For anyone who is interested in the history, I recommend reading this appendix.

THE HISTORICAL FIGURES IN THE NOVEL

There really was a Breitkopf family who had a publishing house in Leipzig, which made a name for itself in printing music scores before the aforementioned Johann Gottlob Immanuel Breitkopf also tried his hand at card-making.

The following was said of Breitkopf: 'His restless spirit drove him to consistently embark on new ventures. He took over a bookshop in Dresden, and for a short time also in Bautzen. In 1770 he founded a playing card factory, which he sold in 1782 while continuing to manage the affiliated coloured-paper factory. He sought to replace calico-patterned English wallpaper with plainer paper, decorated in the "good taste of Greek and Roman architecture". A prehistory to this forms the basis of his book, *Versuch, den Ursprung der Spielkarten, die Einführung des Leinenpapiers, und den Anfang der Holzschneidekunst in Europa zu erforschen*, part one of which appeared in 1784 and which was supplemented by a part two as published by Roch in 1801.'[1]

Anyway, back to cards!

During my search for something sinister for the novel, I stumbled across the witch hunts. Between 1479 and 1730, twenty-four people were tried for witchcraft in Leipzig and six were executed.

There was a man called Martin Dietrich, a sixty-year-old soldier who was accused of witchcraft and quackery in May 1730 by a Doctor Balthasar Friedrich Jacobi in Leipzig for trading 'curio boxes' and herbs. It is also known that the accused was released after being briefed by the priest and taking an oath of purgation.

Then there was a Sibylle Schöne. Old court records state the following: '1699, Sibylle, wife of Hans Georg Schöne, copperplate engraver, forty years of age, charge: sorcery, witchcraft, imprisonment, then release.'[2]

In previous centuries, people were less fortunate.

The copper engraver Johann Michael Stock was also a real person. He worked for the Breitkopfs and was renowned for his engravings, the majority of which were portraits of well-known figures and landscapes, especially those based on Adam Friedrich Oeser's originals. Stock was also active in letterpress printing. He taught the young Goethe copperplate engraving and woodcut printing while the poet was a student at Leipzig. In his autobiography, *Poetry and Truth*, Goethe wrote: '. . . The copper-plate engraver, STOCK, had moved into the attic. He was a native of Nuremberg, a very industrious man, and, in his labours, precise and methodical. He also, like Geyser, engraved, after Oeser's designs, larger and smaller plates, which came more and more into vogue for novels and poems. He etched very neatly, so that his work came out of the aqua fortis almost finished, and but little touching-up remained to be done with the graver, which he handled very well.'[3]

And, last but not least, let us not forget about Johann Wolfgang von Goethe. He was good friends with the youngest Breitkopfs, who studied with him in Leipzig, as well as the artist Stock.

'The domesticity established in the following year soon became a fine sanctuary for all artistic endeavours and refined socialising; as a young student, Goethe was received in Breitkopf's home like a close relative and found abundant inspiration for life in a friendly, relaxed atmosphere, including music and drama performances, the curation of antiques, as well as his use of the rich library.'[4]

In July 1768, Goethe suffered from a severe haemorrhage as a result of a tuberculosis infection, or so the story goes. It's also possible that he was forced to flee after getting into trouble with the authorities. In August he travelled back to Frankfurt.

Auerbach's Keller existed long before then, and the historical wine tavern is still open to visit. So, if you ever fancy a ride on a barrel . . .

A BRIEF HISTORY OF PLAYING CARDS

Humans have been hunters, gatherers and game-players for thousands of years.

Playing and games are firmly ingrained in human nature, from the complexity of chess, which is primarily based on tactics and the ability to think ahead, to simple dice games where chance tends to be the overriding factor. Card games are a mixture of chance and tactics.

Today, card games are played all over the world. A variety of different decks have developed, and, if they previously weren't prevalent in a culture, cards were sooner or later and quite literally brought into play from elsewhere.

Currently, poker is the most popular and well-known card game in the world, but where would Germany be without skat,

England without bridge, and the world without children playing mau-mau?

THE WAY OF CARDS: HOW THEY CAME TO EUROPE

First and foremost, it's important to note that the history of
how cards arrived in Europe still remains unknown. Some
claim that cards were imported from the East by the Arabs,
Egyptians or Traveller communities, while others maintain
that they were a Western invention based on observations of
games in the East.

One theory from the 18th century claims that the painter
Jacquemin Gringonneur invented playing cards in 1392 to amuse
the mentally ill King Charles VI of France (1368–1422). (Author's
note: And I think, well yes, perhaps the cards were to blame for
his condition. And maybe they triggered the 'Ball of the Burning
Men' too). The theory mentions three card decks.[5] Charles
Poupart, a treasurer to Charles VI, paid fifty-six sous to the artist.[6]
According to some, cards originated in the East along with paper
thanks to the Saracens;[7] others say that Traveller communities
are the inventors and the distributors of cards; those with wilder
imaginations talk of Atlantis and the freemason Antoine Court
de Gébelin, who believed that the mysterious paintings of ancient
Egyptian temples were preserved on playing cards over the centu-
ries(!).[8] More on that later.

Asia appears to have played a significant role, to say the least,
in the origin of cards, but there are hardly any reliable sources
on this available.

Two examples:

According to the 1678 Chinese encyclopaedia Ching-tse-tung,
the Chinese Emperor Seun-ho allegedly introduced playing
cards in his court in 1120 to provide his concubines with a little

more entertainment. In *The Invention of Printing in China* (1925), T.F. Carter writes that he discovered a 969 reference to playing cards in China, but this also remains an unsubstantiated point.[9]

One theory asserts that the earliest playing cards can be traced back to 12th-century Korea and China, when they were made in oblong strips. It is unknown what games were played with these cards, however. Early illustrations tell us that the cards were originally folded rather than fanned out, which suggests that these cards were initially only used to play games of chance and not combination games.[10]

Another controversial thesis claims that playing cards were already a familiar concept in Korea before the 12th century in the form of sticks – the 'original' cards – which were twice as long as a thumb and half as wide.[11]

Originating in China, playing cards were brought over to India, Persia and the Arab countries. They then arrived in Europe, where they first became popular in Italy and France.[12]

But there is no concrete proof of this, either.

India likely played an even more important role, even if it is better not to give any credence to Captain D. Cromline Smith's report. Smith was a British colonial officer in 1815 and claimed to have received a pack of cards from a Brahmin man who said that the pack of cards had been in his family's possession since time immemorial, or at the very least for a thousand years.[13]

One popular theory suggests that the Indian game of chess was a sort of precursor to playing cards, since the similarity between the two was obvious: sets of kings and their retinue compete against each other.

The archetype for chess, Chaturaji (meaning four rajas, i.e. four kings), was played by four players with pieces and dice on a square board. There were four kings – one green, one red, one yellow and one black – and their armies. In addition, the game was not played with pieces, but with painted little stones or tiles.[14] The pieces to be moved were determined by rolling the dice, which made for an unpredictable battle.

Before the game arrived in Europe as a two-person version via Persia, the four-player chess game's board and pieces were replaced by thin, often round sheets of parchment or paper made for travelling, as these were easier to stow in luggage. This gave rise to the four-coloured card game, which spread to the West during the rule of the Mohammedans over large parts of India.

In turn, the Mamluks introduced their own symbols. Formations were assigned numbers for their strength and the kings and marshals were labelled accordingly. For a long time, playing cards in Italy and Spain were called *naipes*, after the Arabic *naibe*. *Naibe* is the Arabic word for a military rank in the Egyptian Mamluk state, which was reinterpreted in Europe as marshall, a rank that is still used in German-speaking countries, with the sub-ranks upper and lower marshall.[15]

Albeit without any understanding of the meaning behind the warlike game, a similar template and the rules were adopted and expanded in Europe. Chance and tactics were still included and the new game was well received by nobles and peasants alike.

In Italy and Spain, the presumably Islamic suits of swords, batons, cups and gold coins were retained almost to the letter, whereas in Germany they were reinterpreted as acorns, leaves, hearts and bells. The French simplified the suits even further to clubs, spades, hearts and diamonds in order to make them easier to stencil, and opted for just two colours – red and black.[16]

While the word *naipes* for playing cards was retained in Italy and Spain, the word card, which is derived from the Latin *charta* (meaning paper sheet), became widespread in the Holy Roman Empire.[17]

PROHIBITION AND PROSECUTION

The first known outright ban on the 'Devil's Playbook' can be traced back to the city of Bern in 1367.

Playing cards must already have been around in Bern, and, most importantly, have become 'socially conspicuous' when the Bernese council banned them in 1367. This ban is the earliest mention of playing cards in Switzerland.

It is important to note that the punishment imposed for violating this ban was rather severe. Not only would the guilty party be required to pay a fine, but they would also be subject to an extended period of exile from the city. There was also a betting ban on stone-throwing and ball games. As profit-seeking activities based on chance, they didn't align with religious values of the time and often led to negative consequences: cheating, impoverishment, violent quarrels and even murder and manslaughter.

In stark contrast, since board games such as chess, nine men's morris and trictrac had more to do with tactical skill than luck and wagering money, they were explicitly excluded from the 1367 Bernese ban: '. . .but we do not include board games.' Even in subsequent bans on games in Bern, board games, and in particular chess, were repeatedly excluded.

Over time, the Bernese authorities grew more lenient towards playing cards. Around 1400, cards were finally permitted for 'modest play', i.e. without high stakes and in 'respectable company'.

These conditions were not least an attempt to prevent the playing of cards in certain public spaces, especially in pubs and taverns where strangers and dubious characters met with locals. Although the disinhibiting effect of alcohol in such environments encouraged people to indulge in vices of all kinds anyway, it was not uncommon for gambling to be the initial trigger of conflicts.

There was also the concern that innocent people were enticed and tricked into 'schedlich winckelspil' (deceitful play). It's no coincidence that the prodigal son who gambles away his inheritance in a dingy pub, and the cheat in a tavern, are popular themes in literature. This winkelspiel or deceitful play was punished with a massive monetary fine, and the cheating party also forfeited some of their worldly goods.[18]

Cards became the subject of law, and not for the last time.

What is certain is that a ban was also introduced in Germany before 1378. There is evidence dating from the same year of a ban on playing cards in Regensburg and Constance.[19]

Two mentions that supposedly came earlier have been refuted by research. The first is an entry by Sandro di Pipozzo in the Chronicle of Venice from 1299, but no one who ever cited this manuscript actually saw it with their own eyes.[20] The second mention is a reference to the year 1300 in the German book, Daz Guldin Spil (The Golden Game). Though the author claimed to have come across this reference somewhere, his book was not printed until 1472.[21]

A text passage from 1337 in Marseille and other passages and discoveries that haven't been confirmed by further documentation are also still in dispute.

Francesco Petrarch (1304–1374), Giovanni Boccaccio (1313–1375) and Geoffrey Chaucer mention games, but not card games, in their works, which is an indication that cards experienced a later breakthrough. Card games are also absent from Dante Alighieri's (1265–1321) works, although he does list a number of human vices, including board and dice games.[22]

Cards not being explicitly mentioned in these sources, however, does not mean that they were not already prevalent in society.

Cards seem to enjoy being shrouded in mystery.

What we know for certain is that the word *naipes* appeared in a Spanish book of rhymes in 1370, and that on 23 May 1376 playing the game *naibe* became a punishable offence in Florence.[23]

From 1377, playing card documents – often bans – became more common. John of Rheinfelden, a Dominican friar in Freiburg, wrote the most detailed report.[24] The most fanatical monks, including Bernardino of Siena, John of Capistrano and also Girolamo Savonarola, were often involved in the prosecution of offences and generally enjoyed having games and other reprehensible trinkets burned at the stake.

John of Capistrano, who was later canonised, led a particularly radical crusade against playing cards and had stakes erected for those who played with them between 1453 and 1456, including in Altenburg – the city of playing cards – and in other centres of card production.[25]

According to certain accounts, after Capistrano delivered a sermon in Nuremberg, the audience publicly burnt 3,640 board games, 40,000 dice and even more playing cards as a symbol of their repentance and atonement. This is a significant number given the fact that Nuremberg only had a population of 30,000 at the time.[26]

In 1423 in Bologna, one of the three birthplaces of tarot, Bernardino of Siena delivered a sermon condemning playing cards, branding them an invention of the Devil.[27]

A 1519 woodcut by Hans Leonard Schäufelein portrays the practice of burning cards along with other games.

As a result of the card burnings and the fact that the cheap cards used by common folk were discarded after repeated use, there are hardly any surviving pieces from the 15th and 16th centuries. Only a few expensive cards owned by the rich and the nobility survived. From 1500 onwards, cheap cards were usually found as waste material in between the bindings of old folios (see The Production of Cards p. 654), behind wall panelling[28] or under parquet flooring.[29]

The card game was under constant scrutiny of the law and the Church.

The Puritan John Northbrooke criticised playing cards as late as 1576 in his book, *Spiritus est Vicarius Christi*, where he condemns the 16th-century practice of identifying face cards as certain historical figures: 'The Kings and Coate Cards that we use nowe ware in olde times the ymages of Idols and false Gods; which since they that woulde seeme Christians have changed into Charlemane, Lancelot, Hector and suche like names.'[30]

A 'renewed and refined edict' against any 'existing or future' playing cards was issued by the Prussian king Frederick William in 1787. The king's edict renewed the bans of 1714, 1731, 1744, 1763 and 1774 and threatened penalties of up to 1,000 guilders, one year's imprisonment, expulsion from the country and dismissal from service for civil servants and officers.[31]

THE WAY OF CARDS: HOW THEY LEFT EUROPE

As mentioned above, cards suddenly began to make frequent appearances in documents after 1376: in St Gallen in 1379, in Brabant in 1379, in Nuremberg (as a ban) in 1380, in Flanders and Burgundy in 1382,[32] in Lille (as a ban) in 1382,[33] in Zurich in 1389,[34] in Milan and Paris,[35] in Holland in 1390, in Augsburg in 1391, in Frankfurt am Main in 1392,[36] in Strasbourg in 1394 and in Augsburg in 1400 (as bans).[37]

Rosenfeld concludes the following: 'These dates tell us that playing cards rapidly spread from Italy to the Upper Rhine by 1377, and that from 1378 they began to spread to the large trading cities of southern Germany along the Rhine and travelled down the main trade route south of the river, arriving in France via Flanders. However, playing cards only arrived in eastern Germany, Austria and Poland in the mid-15th century, and in Spain, northern Germany and Northern Europe by the end of the 15th century.'[38]

Rosenfeld's conclusion is contradicted by the fact that John I of Castile issued a ban on playing cards as early as 1387. Moreover, in 1540 a Flemish man named Eckeloo claimed that, while he was unable to obtain the bare necessities during his travels through Spain (neither bread nor wine), he could have easily purchased playing cards in any miserable village, further disputing Rosenfeld's theory.[39]

In 1492 Spanish cards travelled with the Spanish explorers to America, where they became widely popular.

In 1519, the Aztec emperor Montezuma was supposedly the first Native American to take an interest in the conquistadors' playing cards. When the cards were worn out, a certain Pedro Valenciano is said to have painted new ones onto drum skin.

From Mexico the cards spread to the north; the Apache people later painted their own playing cards onto leather.

Playing cards arrived in mainland North America with Hernando de Soto's expedition, which anchored in Espiritu Santo Bay (today's Florida) with four ships and just over 700 men. Garcilaso de la Vega stated that once, in a battle with the Native Americans, all the playing cards had been burned, and that the men immediately painted new ones onto parchment.

However, there were no other traces of the Spanish cards left behind by the Apache people; the French, English and Dutch brought over their own cards, and clubs, spades, hearts and diamonds took over the continent.[40]

And wherever there are cards, trouble seems to follow: in 1663 several people were fined for playing cards in Plymouth Colony in New England; in 1656 the fine was forty shillings for adults (children and servants were only given a warning the first time and were publicly flogged the second). As late as 1703, playing cards in public was still a punishable offence.[41]

THE PRODUCTION OF CARDS

The oldest surviving playing cards are hand-painted and made from leather, parchment and occasionally paper. They were commissioned by royalty and other rich individuals who were able to pay the artists for their miniature paintings. The so-called Stuttgart deck, which is considered to be the oldest surviving pack of cards in the world, is worthy of a mention. They were crafted in 1430 in the Upper Rhine region, possibly in Basel. The cards' opulent decoration, which is reminiscent of an illuminated manuscript, hints at the noble background of their commissioner. Another example is the Court Hunting Pack of Ambras, which was made between 1440 and 1445.[42]

Paper

Paper production was very important to the development of cards. The production of paper began in China around 100 CE using a scoop sieve, then spread to what is now Thailand, then to Korea around 600 CE and Japan in 625 CE. Paper production reached the Arab world by 750 CE at the latest and then arrived in Europe thanks to cultural contact with the Christian West in the East and the Arab conquerors in southern Spain. The first paper mill in Germany appeared in Nuremberg in either 1390[43] or 1389.[44]

Printing

Around 1398, woodcut printing became popular in Europe, which made it possible to cheaply produce cards on a mass scale.[45] Even before the 14th century, European letter painters used their knowledge of textile printing using wooden models to adopt this technique for printing on paper.

Before 1440, goldsmiths likely came up with the idea of printing on paper using engraved copper plates. Both of these printing techniques facilitated the even faster and cheaper production of cards.[46]

The Germans had an edge and were very skilled in the art of woodcutting. Card-making centres were established in Ulm, Nuremberg and Augsburg.[47] Nördlingen is also mentioned as having played an important role in card-making.[48]

With the beginning of card production, the card-making profession grew into its own trade and became separate from the craft of letter painters and iconographers; block cutting also developed as a new craft.

A document from 1577, in which the Friedberg town council addresses the Frankfurt council, highlights just how linked these crafts were at the beginning. The document mentions how the people of Friedberg had discovered that a deck of cards had been bought in Frankfurt's Jewish ghetto with a depiction of the crucifixion of Christ, an incident that those of the Christian faith found 'distressing'. It transpired, however, that a woman from Friedberg had bought six packs of cards for five hellers each from a Jewish merchant and that the small, holy picture had been accidentally packed together with the cards in the same workshop.[49]

Woodcut (for basic, cheap, everyday cards) and copper plate engraving (for intricate, special and luxury cards) with certain modifications essentially determined the technology of playing-card production well into the 19th century.[50] It was only then that relief and intaglio printing was replaced by planographic printing.

The card-making profession relied exclusively on woodcut printing until well into the 18th century. Cards engraved using the copper plate method were also supplied to wealthy customers by artists, engravers and engraving publishers during the same time period.[51]

A printed sheet was made from cuttings or copperplate engravings, which had several card motifs. If something went wrong with the print, the sheet was set aside and the valuable paper was used for book bindings. This was how many old playing-card motifs were passed down.[52]

For cheaper stamping, either brushes or stencils were used to apply colour by hand to the black and white prints.[53] The colours red, yellow, green and blue were applied using a stencil and the black and red French suits were stamped on using a stencil. The four German suits, however, required drawings, so the stencil could only be used for the colouring. Even after the colouring was complete, printing sheets were discarded.[54]

Card-makers glued several sheets of paper together to create one paperboard sheet with a printed front and then later also a printed back, as well as a supporting layer in the middle. Rubbing balls that had previously been rubbed with soap were used to make the finishing touches. Once the sheets had been prepared, they were smoothed out on both sides with a special stone on a polished slab of marble. Then they were ready to cut out.[55]

Finally, the cards were packaged, usually with the card-maker's name and their place of residence on the packaging.[56]

Between 1796 and 1798, the Prague-born Alois Senefelder invented lithography, a planographic printing technique using chemicals. This meant that a new production process for playing cards gradually began to take over. After a few years of further development, it became possible to print multicoloured decks and the subsequent application of colours was no longer necessary.

Colour lithography and chromolithography were crucial for the production of playing cards until the last decades of the

19th century; the method was used well into the 20th century. Today, the offset printing technique is widely used.

MOTIFS

Until the 15th century, cards featured images and depictions of life at court, the lives of soldiers and Traveller communities. It wasn't until the 15th century onwards that the card values that we're familiar with today in the form of numerical values from one (ace) to ten and face cards – jack (lowest), queen (higher) and king – were established.

It appears that some artists from the 15th and 16th centuries soon grew tired of the simple suits and took artistic liberties (also known as arbitrariness) by decorating the cards with the most peculiar suits, such as plants, animals or other objects. These cards were not played with as often since they were considered expensive collector's items for the rich and the nobility. Standard playing cards used by the masses, on the other hand, were simple and even crude.

In the 16th century, the local four-suit-system became widespread in Europe, replacing the animals, flowers, coats of arms, helmets and other previously commonplace suits.[58] The most popular decks gradually became the clubs, spades, hearts and diamonds French deck, the acorns, leaves, hearts and bells German deck and the clubs/batons, swords, goblets and coins Spanish and Italian deck.

Generally speaking, these are today's suit systems: the Italo-Spanish system, the German system and the French system. Playing cards still travel around the world with these constants. However, there are so many regional differences that they exceed the scope of this small appendix. Therefore, if you're interested in taking a closer look at the Franconian, Altenburg,

Bavarian and tarock deck, want to learn more about the development of the French deck and why an ace is called an ace, are curious about what the face cards represent in Hungary (Alexander the Great as the king of clubs), want to know what a sheep's head tarock deck is and what tell cards are, why the king of hearts is also known as Max, how the Altenburg deck and the Bavarian deck developed and where the Brünig-Napf-Reuss line lies, you'll have to do some independent study.

And for variety's sake, there are hundreds of other motifs and countless card decks with their own designs on the market.[57]

While there are essentially an unlimited number of design options for face cards and card numbers, the backs of cards were usually fairly innocuous.

This is because the backs of playing cards only had one job: to look identical and not be translucent, so that you couldn't see what cards the other players had in their hands.

Ensuring the backs of cards were opaque was a simple task from the beginning and was easily solved by either gluing several layers of sheets together or using a coloured middle layer or a dark-coloured paste.[59]

White backs were a bad idea since stains and marks quickly gave away who had what cards – ideal for card sharks and cheats. From the 16th century onwards, there were fewer and fewer white card backs in circulation, despite the production of coloured card backs being more complicated and raising the cost of the end product. Card backs were coloured in black and had diamond or rhombus patterns, the lines of which were once again filled with floral ornaments.

These woodcut card backs were widespread until the start of the 18th century, when the patterns became less intricate and were replaced with plain black card backs. Only then did different-coloured card backs start to appear, including red, blue and purple. From the second half of the 18th century, dot patterns became more popular, which were printed with steel and brass plates and were very fashionable until the middle of the 19th century. Card backs with a chequered pattern have been around since 1860.

With the advance of letterpress printing and newer presses, vignettes came into play. Previously, the ornaments had simply been cut off along the edges, whereas now each card had a fine border that ran around the edges with a self-contained ornamental ensemble or pictorial representation covering the playing card.[60] This is the most common layout used for the backs of cards today.

TAROCK AND TAROT

Tarock refers to a large group of trick-taking cards, which, in addition to face cards, have a series of twenty-one classic and consistent trumps, which are usually labelled using Roman or Arabic numerals.

Tarock, as well as other early European playing cards, first appeared in 1415[61] and between 1430 and 1440 in northern Italy as *tarocchi*.[62] The previously familiar deck was initially called *trionfi*, *triumph*, *ludus triumphorum* or other similar names, i.e. the Italian and Latin names for the German *triumph* or *trumpf*, which were first mentioned in February 1442 in a Ferrarese account book with reference to playing cards. The first mention of these names in France was in 1482.

Many earlier Italian documents illustrate that the tarock deck first developed in Italy and then spread to the south of France. The classic Italian suits, spade (swords), bastoni (batons), coppe (cups) and denari (coins), were added to the special *il matto* card (the fool) and the numbered *trionfi* (trumps), which had higher trick-taking power. The details of the history of the origin of tarock can no longer be pieced together, and a number of legends have transpired as a result. For example, it is said that Michelangelo invented tarock cards to teach Florentine children arithmetic and how to read.[63] (Author's note: Ah, yes, another 'legend' surrounding playing cards . . .)

The tarock deck typically consisted of twenty-two cards, twenty-one of which were labelled with Latin numerals; the twenty-second tarock card was the fool, *il matto* or *il misero*, which is thought to be the precursor of today's joker card.[64] Venetian tarock had seventy-eight cards: twenty-two tarock cards and fifty-six normal cards, with four face cards and ten number cards per suit. The Bolognese tarock deck only had sixty-two cards – twenty-two tarock cards and forty suit cards – while the Florentine tarock deck had ninety-seven cards.

Whether people really played with works of art such as the *Mantegna Tarocchi* cards (from around 1485) is debatable. Considering the fact that Duke Filippo Maria of Milan owned valuable, hand-painted tarock cards for which he paid an artist 1,500 gold pieces in 1415, it's far more likely that these decks were for admiring purposes only.[65]

Tarock cards became widespread and the tarock game cego is still played to this day in Baden-Baden, Germany.

Tarock later developed into fortune-telling cards known as tarot cards. In his 1782 book, *Le Monde Primitive*, the aforementioned Antoine Court de Gébelin claimed that an Egyptian book of wisdom had been preserved in the twenty-two tarot cards, with the hierophant as the pope, the high priestess as the popess and Typhon as the Devil.

According to these and his own findings, a wigmaker called Aliette, whose pseudonym was Etteilla, drafted these venerable cards. He called it *The Book of Thoth* and published a new book almost every year about the mysterious art of card divination and applying the wisdom of the ancient Egyptians to everyday life. His book appeared in several translations, with prints of the cards that could be cut out and glued onto cardboard.[66]

The seventy-eight cards are split into the so-called major and minor arcana, sometimes also referred to as the major and minor *arcanum* (from the Latin for mystery or secret). The three most influential and well-known decks are the Marseille Tarot, the Rider-Waite Tarot and the Crowley Thoth Tarot. If you'd like to learn more about the subject of tarot, I suggest doing some independent research.

CARD-MAKERS, BUSINESS AND TAX

Card-making was a lucrative and fiercely competitive business.

In Germany, the first reference to a card-maker, a certain Hensel von Wissenberg, dates back to 1392 in Frankfurt.[67] In Toulouse, the guild of the *naiperii* (card-makers) has existed since 1465. In Lyon, card-makers formed a corps consisting of 172 men at Henry II and Catherine de Medici's visit in 1548.

Between 1490 and 1500, travelling card-makers moved around the German lands and initially settled in, among other places, Nördlingen, Augsburg, Nuremberg and Leipzig (author's note: Aha! Leipzig!).[68]

Regional card decks were not the only popular playing cards. Foreign cards, especially Italian cards, were also in high demand. The 1474 Ulm Chronicle mentions that the city's card-makers exported playing cards '*barrelwise*' (in small casks) to Italy, Sicily and further overseas in exchange for spices and other wares.[69]

In Italy, card manufacturers conceded the speed and skill of their well-trained competitors, but they were powerless against the cheap imports. As early as 11 October 1441, Venetian card-makers submitted a petition to the city council, demanding a ban on the import of both painted and printed foreign cards. Their petition was granted.[70]

French cards were very popular thanks to their simple, dual-coloured suit system, and replaced German cards due to their pre-eminence on the market. They were even smuggled into England, both when the British imposed a ban on importing French cards and when they introduced high custom duties. The card-makers in Lyon and Paris even printed *London* on their products as the (supposed) place of manufacture to avoid getting their English customers into trouble.[71]

During the Thirty Years' War, the French colours became increasingly popular in parts of Germany and replaced the old German suits, especially in Prussia and in the Scandinavian countries. Only the southern European countries retained their original card suits.[72]

From the 16th century onwards, card games were played among social circles in gaming parlours. Many well-known card games originated in France and spread to Germany and other regions between the 17th and 18th century, including games such as basset and its successor, faro, as well as piquet and ombre. Games like skat, whist and bridge also emerged at this time, followed by canasta and rummy in the early 20th century.[73]

Over the centuries there was a steady demand for playing cards, which provided card-makers and manufacturers with a reliable source of income. It wasn't long before the playing card tax came into effect.

Tax on playing cards was first introduced in the 16th century in France and England,[74] in the 17th century (at the latest) in the German lands, and in 1681 in Saxony.[75] This meant that a certain amount had to be paid per deck of cards, depending on its make and the number of cards in it. The rate was different in different territories of the Holy Roman Empire. Once the tax duty had been paid, every deck of cards would be officially stamped on the red deuce or the ace of hearts.[76]

The same system was introduced in Prussia in 1714 and was replaced by a pure stamp duty (an official, documentary stamp issued on playing cards) in 1838. In 1867, the playing card stamp duty was reformed, when the German Customs Union agreement on 8 July the same year recognised it as a state tax. This was then taken up by the German Empire after the 3 July 1878 Imperial Act. In the Imperial Playing Card Tax Act of 10 September 1919, it was declared a consumption tax, and in 1949 it was declared a federal tax by the German government. From 1949, this playing card tax was levied and managed by the Federal Revenue Administration (the main customs office) until it was abolished for tax simplification reasons and due to its low return as a petty claims tax with the 3 July 1980 Act (BGBl. I 761) on 1 January 1981.[77] Until its abolition, the playing cards tax generated roughly five million German marks for the Federal Republic of Germany.[78]

In France, Henry III was the first king to crack down on card-makers. On 22 May 1583 he issued a tax edict, which the Lyon card-makers refused to pay. In response, they depicted the queen of hearts with a sceptre and the king of hearts with a women's fan as subtle mockery of the king. (Henry's mother Catherine de' Medici, was known for being in charge of business affairs and was traditionally believed to be behind the horiffic St Bartholomew's Day massacre.)[79]

The disagreements between the Crown and card-makers continued; the state raised the taxes, but the makers either didn't pay or paid reluctantly. In 1607 the tax was reduced. In 1671, after lengthy discussions, the tax was abolished, but was reintroduced again in 1701 due to the Crown's lack of funds after the War of the Spanish Succession. Card-makers were now also required to stick precisely to the Parisian card design.

The state had no qualms about cracking the whip. In 1746, a certain Monsieur Lacour and his wife were caught stealing two wooden printing blocks for playing cards from the tax collector. The man was made to pay ten livres, tied to the pillory, branded and sent to the galleys for three years. His wife was also branded, flogged naked with canes and banished from Paris for three years.[80]

Cards were also a popular pastime in England, though preferably only played with English products. This is why, in 1463/64, there was a ban not only on the import of frying pans, tennis balls and hairpins, but also of cards. This ban was intended to protect the interest of local card-makers.

In 1526, things took a turn for the worse for card games. Of all people, and despite being a passionate gambler himself, Henry VII imposed a ban on playing cards. Naturally, this had very little effect, and in 1541 there was an attempt to regulate the matter. Workers, farmers, servants, clerks and other ordinary citizens could now only play cards at Christmas time; but that also made little difference. Nonetheless, it did give rise to the tradition of playing cards between 25 December and 6 January.[81]

In 1628, Charles I of England introduced a tax on playing cards – parliament failed to intervene. Charles demanded a three-pence tax per pack of cards. The tax collector was permitted to keep one penny. It was also in 1628 that the London Worshipful Company of Makers of Playing Cards was founded. The company offered to willingly cover Charles I's tax costs if he banned the import of French cards. It was at this time that the import of French cards did in fact cease, but the French deck had been in circulation for long enough to make a lasting impression on English cards.[82]

What is striking about the English bridge deck is the ace of spades' rich and elaborate design. This fact stems from the playing card tax. In 1710 the tax was raised, and, in order to make it easier to levy, English card-makers were forbidden from making the ace of spades themselves in 1711. Instead, the card had to be purchased from the state and manufactured in a banknote print shop in London as official proof of tax. To make the ace of spades forgery-proof, it was specifically designed to look more like a banknote than a card, so it was difficult for card-makers to imitate. Forging the ace of spades was no trivial offence. On 21 September 1805, one Richard Harding was even sentenced to death for it and hanged in the Old Bailey in London.[83]

The playing card tax was raised in 1756, 1776, 1789 and 1804 until it amounted to half a crown per deck. It was then reduced for the first time in 1828 (when roughly 300,000 packs of cards were sold per year), then for the second time in 1862 (when roughly 750,000 packs of cards were sold per year), and ultimately abolished in 1960.

The use of one specific card as proof of tax was also standard practice in Russia (the ace of diamonds), in the Royal British-Hanoverian Provincial Government (deuce of hearts) and in France (jack of clubs). In France between 1581 and 1789, according to the regulation of the status of card-makers, it was compulsory for card-makers to print their name, surname, their sigil and distinctive mark on the jack of clubs.[84]

America only began to produce their own cards at the end of the 18th century, which was when two changes were introduced: the joker and the card index. In the late 19th century, poker became popular in the US and replaced faro; in 1920, auction bridge (the precursor to contract bridge) was played by fifteen million people around the world. By 1950, thirty million people in the US and Canada were playing canasta.[85]

Interestingly, there is an old Persian game called as-nas, which was played in a similar way to poker. Each player receives five cards, which are shuffled and dealt. The players then place bets on who has the highest card. At the beginning, the game was supposedly played exactly like poker, or at least that was how the English travelling actor Joseph Cowell described the game in his 1829 memoirs.[86]

Even with the end of the card tax, the German government continues to profit from cards; pure games of chance using playing cards, such as poker and blackjack, are still only permitted in casinos under state supervision. In addition, tax officers are still in operation behind the scenes, deducting a sizeable portion of the winnings for the state.

Incidentally, in Germany, according to the Civil Code that came into force on 1 January 1900, gambling debt is not enforceable (section 762 of the German Civil Code) unless authorised by the state and is instead regarded as a debt of honour.

KIBITZERS AND CARD SHARPS

Kibitzers are people who stand on the sidelines of a game, watch and commentate. At best, they ruin the atmosphere. At worst, they ruin the game by giving out tips and advice.

Kibitzers still exist today, just as they did back then, which the 1583 New Penal Code for Berlin Innkeepers confirms: 'Anyone who looks over a hard-working player's shoulders and causes them any distress should be chased away and called a kibitzer. Anyone who spies upon the cards of two players and succumbs to the temptation of winking or revealing something should be fined thirty pfennigs in good coin or buy a jug of March beer for the common good, then chased away. But anyone who thinks they know it all and gives a player advice or criticises them should be punched in the mouth and have their cap pulled over their ears, for they are a donkey. Then they should be beaten up and thrown out onto the street.'[87]

There have also always been card sharps since people played

for large sums of money at card duels, leading to a plethora of state decrees against risky, high-stakes games. According to the following note from Altenburg in 1537, 'Balthasar Reichhardt, who was sat in the city's prison as a result of a high-stakes game, was fined twenty groschen for sitting in the bathing area, where he had wanted to hang himself.'[88]

Another example of the despair that cards can cause.

In 1777, a card sharp was caught in Norwich, England. The merchant was thrown into prison for half a year and had to pay a twenty-pound fine. If he refused to pay, he would have been placed in the pillory and nailed to it by his ears.[89]

Joachim Bellachini explains the secrets of card cheats in his 1921 *Textbook on Magic*, including false pickups, sleight of hand and much more. Dexterity appears to be key.

ACCESSORIES

We all know that we are influenced by our environment and the things that surround us, and cards are no different.

This starts with the packaging, which for simple, cheap, standard cards almost always consisted of folding boxes or paper labelled with the manufacturer's details and the words *extra fine playing cards* printed on them.

Luxury cards, on the other hand, had beautifully designed packaging: imaginatively crafted boxes, slipcases and leather cases to accommodate buyers' differing desires.[90]

There were also more permanent storage containers, which were usually specially made, such as painted or chip-carved wooden boxes with various patterns and playing card symbols, metal cases with etched, hammered or engraved decorations, embossed or painted leather cases, as well as inlay work and slip-cases covered in straw, cases with colourful lacquer paintings from East Asia and playing card boxes made from Meissen porcelain. One curious example includes a playing card case from 1880 made from leather and pieces of fur, decorated with a brightly painted ivory devil's mask in reference to the term the Devil's Playbook.

Jetons served as an invaluable substitute for money. Some jetons could be found in the form of small cards in different colours with declarations of their value, while others were made from bone, ivory, porcelain and mother-of-pearl and were often painted.

In addition, playing card presses were required to press the cards back into shape after frequent use. They ranged from the simplest of models (suitable for pubs) to the most elaborate ones (for collectors and the wealthy). The wealthiest in society had special gaming tables, usually square-shaped and covered in fabric, with holders for glasses, ashtrays, jetons and money. There were even special notepads for recording results and card shuffler machines if you wanted to save time.[91]

DIDACTIC, COMICAL AND FORTUNE TELLING CARDS

Cards were not just used to play games with.

Some cards were used as political propaganda, others were used for teaching, moral and religious instruction, and some had satirical purposes or were linked to literature. These cards enabled artists to better express themselves in their designs, providing future generations with an artistic and historical record. Cards made from wood, metal or ivory panels and fabric, such as jewellery cards from the Baroque period (silk coverings) are unusual, and yet well known.[92]

Then there were the cards intended to amuse or provoke

reflection. These emerged in the middle of the 18th century and included thought-provoking, subtle or crude allusions, such as a depiction of two gentlemen fighting with the annotation *serious discussion* underneath.[93]

Other cards were used to impart knowledge – so-called teaching cards.

Thomas Murner was the first person to use playing cards for didactic purposes, both in his book *Logica Memorativa* (1509) and in his *Chartiludium Institute summarie* card deck and book (1518), both of which were written in Strasbourg. Murner combined statements of logic with corresponding card illustrations.[94] In the mid-17th century, card games for learning Latin were also used.[95] In 1603, Andreas Strobl published the *geistliche Teutsche Kartenspil*, a pack of thirty-two cards with eight cards per German suit (bells, leaves, acorns, hearts) with biblical scenes and a 300-page accompanying text.[96]

The eight-year-old Louis XIV allegedly received four decks of cards from Cardinal Mazarin to familiarise himself with: one on the succession of the French kings, one on the particulars of different countries of the world, one on Ovid's *Metamorphoses* and a final one on the lives of famous queens.[97] Cardinal Mazarin was a keen gambler himself and left his fortune and his penchant for gambling to his nieces. As a result, one of his nieces lost all of her inheritance at the gaming table and died penniless.[98] Louis XIV's passion for cards, on the other hand, continued well into adulthood. It is said that he played cards every evening from six to ten o'clock, and if there was urgent state business a servant would hold his cards until he returned.[99]

Teaching cards were very popular and, in the late 18th century and in the 19th century, a whole flood of them arrived on the market, especially those used for educational reading games. These covered almost every subject you could think of; there were cards with heraldic explanations, 'country cards' with geographical specifics and cards featuring depictions of warfare and historical scenes. At the end of the 18th century, Alexander von Humboldt also learned from his tutor in this way.[100]

Although teaching cards became obsolete in the 19th century, they were instrumental in the development of the common game quartets.[101]

Furthermore, cards were used as parlour games. The distinctions between regular cards and those used for certain games are sometimes blurred; question and answer cards have been found with and without suits. These kinds of cards could usually only be used for a specific game (e.g. bell and hammer, Hulda die Donaunixe, Preciosisa das Glueckskind) and the rules were included in the pack. Sometimes, these types of card games had supplementary dice.[102]

* * *

So-called divination, oracle or fortune-telling cards have always been popular. After all, who wouldn't want to know their future?

People either used cards that were specially made for this purpose, or used ordinary decks and assigned possible interpretations to different cards.

In the late 15th century, simple playing cards were used to tell the future by matching a drawn card to a certain prediction from a corresponding list. It was only a matter of time before the fortune-telling sayings were written onto the cards themselves.

Card divination or cartomancy, which can be traced back to around the 1500s, only really caught on in the 18th century when it replaced the practice of palm reading. The 17th century gypsy or chiromancy deck is a combination of fortune-telling and teaching cards: at the same time, you can get a fortune reading based on your constellation of palm lines and learn how to determine the future using palm lines.

A special set of fortune-telling cards make up a deck named after Madame Lenormand, who practised cartomancy in Paris at the beginning of the 19th century. It is unclear whether she developed the deck herself, though it was and is still common practice to link the names of famous magicians or fortune-tellers with a deck as a way of branding.[103]

At the age of seventeen, Madame Lenormand successfully predicted the early convening of the 1789 Estates General summoned by the French king; she predicted the rise and fall of Napoleon; and her last great prophecy also came true: the 1830 July Revolution and the ascension of Louis Philippe I.[104]

The Book of Thoth by the enterprising Etteilla should also be mentioned here (see Tarock and Tarot p. 659).

There were also less mystical fortune-telling cards during this period. For instance, a pack of very simple cards with an expression, a saying or a number at the bottom that was intended to provide a snippet of information about one's wellbeing, troubles and future.[105] A deck from 1806, which was likely produced in Nuremberg, featured proverbs in German and French, the meanings of which were different from each other, presumably because people thought that a German would have a different fate to a Frenchman.[106]

For example, one king of hearts card has the following written on it in German: 'It is better to marry than to burn with lust', while the French one reads: 'Garde toi de faire un mariage sans précaution' (which roughly translates to: beware of entering into a marriage without taking precautions first).

The skat deck can also be used to predict the future. For instance, the ten of hearts represents wish fulfilment, great love, happiness in marriage or a strong partnership, an invitation, a request, an offer, a marriage proposal or a wedding. The ten of hearts is considered the highest card in the emotional sphere and can indicate the beginning of a new phase in life or a positive solution to a problem. So you don't necessarily need a special deck to tell the future.

Some cards were no longer needed by their users for the usual purpose of playing games, and so people would simply write words on the cards by hand – *happiness, a letter, death*, etc. – and use them for fortune-telling.[107]

THE ACE OF SPADES AS THE DEATH CARD

While conducting my research into the history of playing cards, it proved difficult to uncover extensive details on the ace of spades' infamous reputation as the death card.

The card first appeared to have become associated with this sinister connotation around 1900, in lots of different ways:

- The ace of spades adorned the armour of the British 12th Division during the First World War.
- Giuseppe 'Joe the Boss' Masseria was the 'boss of all bosses' of the US Cosa Nostra in New York until his murder in 1931. On 15 April 1931, Masseria was shot in Scarpato's restaurant on Coney Island. The murderers had put an ace of spades in his hand, as the striking crime scene photo shows.
- In the Second World War, the ace of spades was the insignia of the German Jagdgeschwader 53, a Luftwaffe fighter wing often called the Ace of Spades Wing.
- The card was also highly utilised during the Vietnam war by US troops. The card was stuck onto helmets by ordinary soldiers or used as a unit symbol on helicopters.

- Finally, during the first Iraq War, the US Department of Defence printed a pack of cards with the faces of the most wanted Iraqi commanders. Saddam Hussein's face adorned the ace of spades.

I have three theories regarding the origin of this connection between the ace of spades and doom:

Firstly, there is the famous dead man's hand: the two-pair hand consisting of an ace of spades, an ace of clubs, two black eights and the queen of spades as the 'kicker'. Wild Bill Hickok held these cards in his hand when he was shot in the back of the head by Jack McCall in No. 10 Saloon on 2 August 1876. However, there is some doubt surrounding exactly what cards he was holding when he died.

Secondly, there is the use of the ace of spades as a tax card in England, the forgery of which was punishable by death. This strikes me as a more conclusive origin, yet the question remains as to why the ominous association with the ace of spades began so many years later and if this was fuelled by Hickok's death.

Thirdly, there is the story collection *The Suicide Club* by Robert Louis Stevenson, which was published in 1878. Without giving too much away, the collection is about a club full of people who have grown weary of life, as the name suggests. Here, too, a deck of cards plays a central role. The cards are dealt and whoever turns over the ace of spades is the next victim; whoever picks up the ace of clubs is their murderer. It's a brilliant premise, but sadly (and annoyingly) not one I came up with. I recommend you have a read if you'd like to find out how the story unfolds!

Stevenson's story could also explain the fatal significance of the ace of spades, especially given the fact that *The Suicide Club* is a popular tale and has been adapted into dozens of films since the start of the 20th century.

But then again, nothing is certain, as is so often the case in the history of cards.

TRIVIA

Magic performed using playing cards is known as a card trick. Both unprepared card decks and specially prepared card decks are used for card tricks, such as cards with two different face sides, folding cards or conically cut cards.[108]

In his 1921 *Textbook on Magic*, Joachim Bellachini explains how to perform card tricks that have nothing to do with mysticism and have a lot to do with preparation.

Today's standard playing cards likely originated in the regular, four-by-thirteen-centimetre-sized cards, which came in a deck of fifty-two cards, as described by John of Rheinfelden in 1377. One deck had ten number cards and three court cards.

The three most commonly used formats for cards in the world are upright and rectangular, and the most common size is 8.7 by 5.7 centimetres. Larger variations of cards fulfil special purposes, such as cards for people with visual impairments, for magic tricks, travelling, waterproof cards for playing in the swimming pool and so on. The smallest playing card in the world allegedly comes from Leipzig, and dates back to around 1900. It can be found on an uncut sheet and has edges of less than one centimetre long. The sheet was intended to make cards for a doll house. A doctor in New Delhi, however, claims to have a pack of cards with edges of just eight millimetres, but this is unproven.

While rectangular cards were widespread in Europe and America, round cards were the shape of choice in India.[109] Indian cards are very colourful and used to be made from painted ivory or lacquered cardboard.

Japan, the oldest isolated island power, inherited playing cards from the Portuguese, and quickly came up with their own variations, such as *hanafuda* (flower cards) and the deck of one hundred poets, which is played during the New Year period and has a quiz character.[110]

At the time of Louis XIV, card games were so en vogue that ballets, balls and plays were influenced by card motifs. For instance, the play *Le Triomphe des Dames*, which was written by Thomas Corneille and performed in Paris on 7 August 1676, included an intermezzo featuring a ballet enacting a game of piquet.[111]

In Stravinsky's ballet, *Jeu de cartes*, poker cards are the focal point of the action on stage. Tchaikovsky's opera *The Queen of Spades (Pique Dame)* is based on a hero addicted to the card game faro. Finally, Richard Strauss' favourite card game, skat, featured in his 1924 opera *Intermezzo*.[112]

The use of playing cards as a substitute for money comes from New France, or today's Canada. In 1685, when there were delays in the payment of soldiers' wages from Paris, the provisional governor at the time, Jacques de Meulles, collected all available playing cards and had them quartered and stamped with the governor's seal. The resulting playing card money was in circulation for over seventy years and is now considered a popular rarity among collectors.[113]

Political events were also recorded on cards. For example, a certain three decks of cards served as court records during the time of the French Revolution and include notes about the life-long deportation of a noble lady.[114]

Moreover, the French revolutionaries changed not only the regime, but also the cards: they swapped the kings and queens for Jacobins. Not a trace of nobility was to be left.

Occasionally a card was also a receipt, as was the case in 1767/68 when a volume of files owned by the House of

Schönburg in Glauchau was found that contained steel-engraved, stencil-coloured cards from various decks as receipts. One of the card notes, among other things, mentions the delivery of 'Jagdt-oder Fröhner Semmeln'; for a hunt, twelve pounds of bread and thirty-six bread rolls were to be delivered daily.[115]

Artist Guss, 'the small man with the iron hand', placed three complete decks on top of each other and ripped through all ninety-six cards in one go. Karl Schindler, who was born in Altenburg, raised the record in 1934 to one hundred cards – a world record at the time.[116]

Last but not least, where would the Joker (!) from the Batman comics be without his special calling cards, or the superhero Gambit without his playing cards?

Fortune tellers feature in various horror films and thrillers. In the film *Smokin' Aces*, on the other hand, everything revolves around a Las Vegas card magician who the Mafia is after. Jean-Paul Belmondo was the 'Ace of Aces', and let us not forget the band Ace of Base . . . Or perhaps the better known Motörhead and Iron Maiden and their songs 'Ace of Spades' and 'Aces High'!

The bottom line is, the Devil's Playbook is everywhere.

Now also in a novel.

As the main character.

And I'm not surprised.

REFERENCES

1 Oscar von Hase: Breitkopf
 und Härtel, in: Allgemeine
 Deutsche Biographie 3.
 Leipzig: Duncker & Humblot
 1876, pp. 298–301.
2 Manfred Wilde: Die
 Zauberei-und Hexenprozesse
 in Kursachsen, Köln/
 Weimar/Wien: Böhlau 2003,
 pp. 531–8.
3 Johann Wolfgang von Goethe:
 Aus meinem Leben. Dichtung
 und Wahrheit. Berlin:
 Hofenberg 2016, p. 270.
4 Von Hase, p. 298.
5 Detlef Hoffmann:
 Spielkarten. Inventarkatalog
 der Spielkartensammlung
 des Historischen Museums
 Frankfurt am Main.
 Frankfurt a. M. 1972, p. 4;
 Peter Weise: Rund um die
 Spielkarte. Ein Streifzug
 durch das Altenburger
 Spielkartenmuseum. Berlin:
 Tribüne Berlin 1986, p. 19.
6 Claus D. Grupp: Die
 Spielkarten und ihre

Geschichte. Historisches
 um des Teufels Gebetbuch.
 Bergisch Gladbach: ASS
 Verlag Leinfelden
 1973, p. 55.
7 Erwin Kohlmann, Hellmut
 Rosenfeld (Hrsg.): Die
 schönsten deutschen
 Spielkarten. Leipzig: Insel
 1964, p. 38.
8 Hoffmann, p. 4.
9 Grupp, p. 10.
10 Erhard Gorys Das Buch der
 Spiele. Über 500 Freizeitspiele
 für Erwachsene. Herrsching:
 Manfred Pawlak
 Verlagsgesellschaft 1975, p. 7.
11 Grupp, p. 83.
12 Gorys, p. 7.
13 Grupp, p. 12.
14 Grupp, p. 13; Kohlmann,
 Rosenfeld, p. 40.
15 Kohlmann, Rosenfeld, p. 39.
16 Kohlmann, Rosenfeld, p. 41.
17 Kohlmann, Rosenfeld, p. 39.
18 Claudia Engler: Kartenspiel
 im spätmittelalterlichen
 Bern, in: Librarium:

Zeitschrift der Schweizerischen BibliophilenGesellschaft, Band 50, Heft 1, Zürich 2007, p. 5.

19 Grupp, p. 16.

20 Grupp, p. 15.

21 Grupp, p. 16.

22 Grupp, p. 18.

23 Grupp, p. 17.

24 Grupp, p. 16; Weise, p. 18.

25 Weise, p. 20.

26 Grupp, p. 44.

27 Grupp, p. 34.

28 Hoffmann, p. 9.

29 Weise, p. 86.

30 Grupp, p. 58.

31 Grupp, p. 17.

32 Hoffmann, p. 5.

33 Weise, p. 18.

34 Hoffmann, p. 5.

35 Weise, p. 19.

36 Hoffmann, p. 9.

37 Weise, p. 18.

38 Hoffmann, p. 5.

39 Grupp, p. 36.

40 Grupp, p. 37.

41 Grupp, p. 72.

42 Hoffmann, p. 5.

43 Kohlmann, Rosenfeld, p. 38.

44 Weise, p. 21.

45 Grupp, p. 33.

46 Weise, p. 21.

47 Grupp, p. 33; Weise, p. 20.

48 Weise, p. 20.

49 Hoffmann, p. 9.

50 Weise, p. 22.

51 Weise, p. 23.

52 Hoffmann, p. 26.

53 Weise, p. 23.

54 Hoffmann, p. 26.

55 Weise, p. 24.

56 Hoffmann, p. 26.

57 Weise, p. 24.

58 Gorys, p. 7.

59 Weise, p. 24.

60 Weise, p. 25.

61 Grupp, p. 33.

62 Wolfgang Mayr, Robert Sedlaczek: Die Strategie des Tarockspiels. Wien: Edition Atelier 2008, p. 9 ff.

63 Grupp, p. 26.

64 Grupp, p. 27.

65 Grupp, p. 33.

66 Hoffmann, p. 45 f.

67 Hoffmann, p. 9.

68 Weise, p. 20.

69 Grupp, p. 41.

70 Grupp, p. 34.

71 Grupp, p. 57.

72 Grupp, p. 37.

73 Gorys, p. 7.

74 Grupp, p. 61 and 64.

75 Grupp, p. 71.

76 Weise, p. 77.

77 Spielkartensteuer, in: Gabler Wirtschaftslexikon. URL: http://wirtschaftslexikon. gabler.de/Archiv/-2046854405/ spielkartensteuer-v1.html (effective: November 2016)

78 Grupp, p. 71.

79 Grupp, p. 62.

80 Grupp, p. 16.

81 Grupp, p. 64 f.

82 Grupp, p. 67.

83 Grupp, p. 70 f.

84 Grupp, p. 71.

85 Grupp, p. 73.

86 Grupp, p. 86.

87 Weise, p. 80.

88 Weise, p. 82.

89 Grupp, p. 16.

90 Weise, p. 83.

91 Weise, p. 84 f.

92 Hoffmann, p. 27.

93 Hoffmann, p. 28.

94 Hoffmann, p. 29; Grupp, p. 79.

95 Hoffmann, p. 29.

96 Grupp, p. 80.

97 Hoffmann, p. 29; Grupp, p. 80.

98 Grupp, p. 80.

99 Grupp, p. 82.

100 Grupp, p. 82; Weise, p. 76 f.

101 Hoffmann, p. 29; Grupp. p. 82.

102 Hoffmann, p. 36.

103 Hoffmann, p. 34.

104 Grupp, p. 76.

105 Hoffmann, p. 36.

106 Grupp, p. 76.

107 Hoffmann, p. 36.

108 Weise, p. 75.

109 Weise, p. 85.

110 Grupp, p. 86.

111 Grupp, p. 82.

112 Weise, p. 79.

113 Gorys, p. 7; Grupp, p. 73.

114 Weise, p. 86.

115 Weise, p. 88.

116 Weise, p. 88.